Rachael English

The Paper Bracelet

HACHETTE
BOOKS
IRELAND

First published in Ireland in 2020 by
HACHETTE BOOKS IRELAND

1

Cataloguing in Publication Data is available from the British Library

Trade paperback ISBN 9781529380620
Ebook ISBN 9781529380637

Typeset in Garamond by redrattledesign.com

Printed and bound in Great Britain by
Clays Ltd, Elcograf, S.p.A

Hachette Books Ireland policy is to use papers that are natural, renewable and
recyclable products and made from wood grown in sustainable forests. The logging
and manufacturing processes are expected to conform to the environmental
regulations of the country of origin.

Hachette Books Ireland
8 Castlecourt Centre
Castleknock
Dublin 15, Ireland

A division of Hachette UK Ltd
Carmelite House, 50 Victoria Embankment, EC4Y 0DZ

www.hachettebooksireland.ie

Praise for Rachael English's novels

'A true storyteller who keeps you turning the pages' Cathy Kelly

'A cracking page-turner in the best tradition of Maeve Binchy'
Patricia Scanlan

I read [it] greedily, unable to put it down ... beautiful, compelling and
sincere in the way of the very best stories and the best books'
Sunday Independent

'Richly imagined and searingly empathetic ... compelling reading'
Sunday Business Post

'Rachael English paints a vivid picture of a changing Ireland in this
page-turning tale' *The Irish Times*

'[English] weaves a tale with the natural ease of a born storyteller ... I
couldn't help but be reminded of Maeve Binchy for her warm style and
distinctly Irish voice ... heart-breaking and uplifting all at once'
RTÉ Culture

'An evocative read ... powerful ... If you read authors such as Diane
Chamberlain, Sheila O'Flanagan and Maeve Binchy then you
should also check this out'
Between My Lines

'Enchanting, emotional, heartbreaking, ultimately uplifting and just
perfect ... Rachael English is a wonderful storyteller' Being Anne

'A remarkable read with a very captivating story at its core'
Swirl and Thread

'Brilliantly engaging ... this beautifully written tale kept me engrossed
from start to finish' Novel Delights

Rachael English is a bestselling novelist and presenter on Ireland's most popular radio show, *Morning Ireland*. During more than twenty years as a journalist, she has worked on most of RTÉ Radio's leading current affairs programmes, covering a huge range of national and international stories. *The Paper Bracelet* is her fifth novel.

Twitter: @EnglishRachael
Facebook: rachaelenglishwriter

Also by Rachael English
The Night of the Party
The American Girl
Going Back
Each & Every One

For Eamon

Chapter 1

Then, Patricia

They skulked in the dark like animals, the only illumination coming from the fanlight over the front door. It was safer that way, her father said. You'd never know who might be rambling about. He eased open the door and peered left and right. Stars were splashed across the sky, and a swing-boat moon hung over the street. It was cold for April.

'I hope there hasn't been an accident,' he said.

'He'll be here soon,' replied her mother. 'Ten o'clock was the time he gave us. It's only five past.' She twisted around, her long face creased with irritation. 'Stand back, Patricia. You don't want anyone catching sight of you.'

Already they were using her new name, the name she would be known by in Carrigbrack. It was for her own good, they insisted. She'd have more privacy that way. And privacy was vital. One stray word, and a young woman's life could be damaged beyond repair. She might never find a respectable husband or enjoy a proper family life. Judgement would follow her, and no good man would want to be tarnished by association.

She suspected that using a different name made the situation a little easier for them. It wasn't their daughter who'd disgraced herself, it was Patricia. Their daughter was dutiful. She sang in the choir and passed every exam. She obeyed the rules. Patricia was a messy imposter.

The secrecy didn't end there. They'd found a wig and instructed her to wear it. The hair was long and black and smelled of plastic and cigarette smoke.

'It's for fear anyone sees you in the car with Father Cusack,' her mother had explained. 'We don't want people asking questions.'

'Sooner or later someone will enquire after me. What then?'

'They'll be told you're in England.'

'What about work?'

'We'll tell them the same.'

For a time, she had denied the truth. She hadn't said anything because she hadn't been able to admit it to herself. Then she'd bargained with God or the universe or whatever was out there. *Make it go away, and I'll change. I promise.* When, finally, she'd confessed, time had speeded up. The questions, the looks zipping between her parents, her mother's weeping, her father's controlled fury; they'd all blurred together. She regretted not running away. She'd considered getting the bus and boat to London, but she knew no one there, and the few pounds she'd saved wouldn't have lasted long

'Where did we go wrong?' her mother kept asking.

'We didn't,' her father said. 'Some girls are raised to be no better than tramps, but that was never the case in this house. Her failings are her own.'

Although neither parent was given to displays of affection, Patricia had always assumed they loved her. Their love had shown itself in polished shoes and a new school coat, dinners on the table and drives to the sea. Compared to many parents, their use of the wooden spoon had been sparing. Sometimes they spoke about the sacrifices they'd made. Other girls were forced to leave school at fifteen and earn their keep. She'd been allowed to complete the Leaving Cert. They spoke too about how girls were a constant worry. She remembered fragments of conversation; her mother saying to a neighbour, 'You're always nervous with girls. You're better off with boys. Boys are straightforward.'

After a couple of hours, her father's rage had eased. He'd left, only to return thirty minutes later with the parish priest. Father Cusack's white hair was combed into an elaborate arrangement, but it wasn't thick enough to mask his pink scalp. The lines on his face were deep, like cracks in dried mud. Her parents brought him into the good room, where he sat on the brown sofa and lit a cigarette. He took a pull and exhaled a long curl of smoke. Save for a brief admonishment for the shame she was bringing on a well-respected family, there was no anger. He had the air of a man performing a familiar ritual.

Patricia focused on the strip of green and orange wallpaper that was peeling from the wall behind him. Out on the street, some girls were skipping. In giddy voices they chanted, 'Cinderella dressed in yella went upstairs to kiss her fella.'

'Remind me again,' said Father Cusack, 'how old are you? Nineteen, is it?'

'Twenty, Father.'

'And how many months, do you think?'

'Four,' she replied, her voice stronger than she felt. 'Perhaps five.'

'The baby's due in August, then. There's no chance the father would be willing to marry you, is there?'

'Oh God, no. That definitely won't be happening.'

'Hush,' said her mam. 'You're in no position to be speaking like that.'

'All I'm doing is telling the truth.'

'Very well,' said the priest. 'I think it would be best if you went out to the kitchen and made us some tea.'

She eavesdropped from the hall. Her parents' words were easy to make out. They were telling him about Mike. The priest was softly spoken, however, and she caught only snatches of what he had to say. 'A reliable institution', she heard, then 'right from wrong', followed by 'surprisingly common' and 'tomorrow'.

Outside, the girls had changed their rhyme. 'Vote, vote, vote for de Valera,' they sang. 'Here comes Annie at the door-io.'

Later, Patricia's mother accompanied Father Cusack to the parochial house. They had a telephone there. He called the home in Carrigbrack and spoke to a woman called Sister Agnes. Her mam came back with instructions.

'One small suitcase,' she said. 'Two nightdresses, a face cloth, a toothbrush. Underwear. Practical shoes. No fripperies, books or make-up.' The girls wore uniforms, so there was no need for a change of clothes. 'Not that your own clothes will fit you for much longer,' she added.

Twenty-four hours later, and they were standing in the grainy light, pretending that everything made sense. The atmosphere was septic, all their rancour and disappointment lingering in the air.

Patricia pressed her fingers against her forehead. 'What if I decide I want to keep the baby?'

The question prompted another snap of anger from her father. 'Please,' he said, 'we don't need any foolish talk.'

'But I've heard of girls holding on to their children. It happens in Dublin, apparently. No one here need know.'

'Don't mind what they're doing in Dublin. What's wrong is wrong. Do you want to kill your mother? Is that it?'

There were a thousand replies she could have given, but there seemed no point. She was flat-on-the-floor exhausted. There was a dull pain around her eyes, a heavy feeling in her chest. She worried too that if they argued, she'd start crying again. Crying would be a mistake.

Presently, they heard the putter of an old Hillman Minx. Her father opened the door just wide enough to confirm the priest's arrival.

He nodded in her direction. 'You'd better not keep the man waiting.'

She paused, wondering if they'd give her a kiss or even a hug. She hoped for a sign, no matter how slight, that they would forgive her. Neither parent moved, and eventually she picked up her suitcase.

'This is it, so,' she said.

Her mother turned away. 'Please God, we'll see you later in the year.'

Chapter 2

Now, Katie

Katie Carroll sat on the edge of the bed. Every day she sat in the same place and recited the same lines, and every day she walked away again. Was there a specific word, she wondered, for the one task you couldn't do? A special way of describing how your brain turned to sludge and your limbs refused to function? If not, she ought to invent one.

The bedroom was filled with milky sunlight. Dublin had enjoyed a rare hot summer, and while the temperatures had dipped, the days remained bright. In the near distance, a lawnmower buzzed. On Griffin Road, untidy gardens were taboo.

If there was one job Katie couldn't tackle, there were a hundred questions she couldn't answer. Two months on, and they continued to ripple through her head. What will you do now? Is the house too big for you? Would you consider selling? What about moving home?

Margo had been the first to ask about her plans. Others had followed. It was funny how she could ignore the enquiries of friends and acquaintances, yet Margo whittled away at her. There was something about her sister's tone, its blend of sympathy and condescension, that made Katie want to give an inappropriate answer. To say she was thinking of moving to Thailand or finding a young lover. Of course, she hadn't said any such thing. She'd mumbled about not being sure and needing more time.

There were moments when she forgot. She'd get irritated by the creaking board at the top of the stairs and think, I'll get Johnny to fix that. She'd roll over in bed, expecting to inhale his warm, soapy smell. Or she'd wake up, and for one happy minute her mind would be blank.

That was when the truth would find its way in.

People, well-meaning people, maintained her behaviour was normal. 'Don't be too hard on yourself,' they'd say. 'Honestly, you're bearing up well. Considering.' The last word was an acknowledgement of the suddenness of Johnny's death. From the day of his diagnosis, he'd had four months. Her time as a nurse had taught Katie that no disease was as unfair as cancer. Receive one diagnosis, and a year down the road you could be sitting in Lanzarote swapping hospital stories. Receive another, and you barely had time to say goodbye. She told herself that there was nothing exceptional about her husband's passing. He'd been seventy-four, not a grand old age, but a decent one. Old enough for his death not to be considered a tragedy.

At the funeral, she'd been restrained. She'd been brought up to be suspicious of showy demonstrations of grief. That had been the way back then. Wasn't it crazy that a sixty-nine-year-old woman could be influenced by what she'd been told as a child? But she was. Truth to tell, she'd just wanted to be alone. Oh, she knew she shouldn't be ungrateful. It was wonderful that so many people had made the effort to be there, to say 'Sorry for your troubles' and swap soft reminiscences. It had been years since she'd seen some of those who'd travelled from her home village of Danganstown. Others had come from abroad. One of Johnny's nephews had made the journey from Madrid, and Margo's daughter, Beth, had arrived from London.

For the following month, Katie had been busy. Friends had swooped in, offering meals and chats and cups of tea. She'd written thank-you notes and attempted to tackle the endless stream of paperwork. But lives moved on. Even close friends had other priorities, other concerns and demands.

Besides, Katie had never been one for relying on others. Early on, she'd learnt it tended to lead to disappointment. For most of her life, Johnny had been enough. He'd said the same about her. Through a mix of accident and design, they'd had a tight circle of friends. She'd always preferred small gatherings to the dazzle and noise of the crowd.

Now, here she was, back in the bedroom, bags at the ready. All she had to do was parcel up Johnny's best clothes and take them to the Vincent de Paul. She rose from the bed, opened the mahogany wardrobe and removed a pale blue shirt. Instead of stuffing it in a bag, she rubbed its fabric across her face. For some minutes she stood there, rocking on her heels, a familiar burn at the back of her eyes. This was stupid. The clothes were in good condition. There were men who could put them to use. But, as life had taught her, there was a wide gulf between recognising the foolishness of your behaviour and doing something about it.

She returned the shirt to the wardrobe. 'Another day,' she whispered. 'Another day, but not yet.'

Katie's grief was a slippery thing. Much of the time she was crippled by tiredness. She wanted to curl up with her loss and mourn in peace. There were other times when she felt a throbbing anger. She was angry with neighbours for coming out with platitudes about time being a great healer. She was angry with Johnny for leaving her. She'd been happy with their life together; there'd been no need for anything to change. Mostly, though, she was angry with herself. Why hadn't she spotted that something was wrong? What sort of nurse was she? Why, over the years, had she wasted energy worrying about nonsense? Why hadn't she made the most of what she'd been given? She would march around the house like a madwoman, wanting to kick and scream. Then it would hit her: maybe what she felt wasn't anger. Maybe it was guilt.

She'd fret about this until she remembered one of Beth's favourite phrases: get over yourself. Katie was doing too much thinking. She had to get over herself.

Rather than shutting the wardrobe, she reached into the back and took out a box. Once upon a time, it had contained a pair of cork-heeled sandals. As she recalled, Johnny hadn't been keen on them. He'd also had mixed feelings about the current contents of the box. 'Seriously, Kateser,' he'd said, 'you shouldn't go upsetting yourself. Anyway, most of those women are probably dead by now.'

She didn't believe this was true. Yes, the women would be old, but then again, what was old? Age, she'd discovered, was a complex business. If the news referred to a woman as being sixty-nine, Katie would picture a small lady with white hair, ill-fitting dentures and a wardrobe of Crimplene and tweed. It was an image from her childhood, when anybody over pension age was left to wither in a corner with a blanket on their knees. But that wasn't how she looked or felt. The knowledge that women of her age were expected to shrivel and fade made her doubly determined not to. Even on her worst days, she put on lipstick and mascara. Two weeks after Johnny's death, she'd had her blonde highlights refreshed. She liked to think he would have approved.

She sat down again, lifted the lid from the box and sifted through its contents. The notebook and the fragile curls of paper took her back almost fifty years. She'd been twenty-two when she'd started work in Carrigbrack. In those days, most people had said little about what happened there. If they did, they spoke in euphemisms. It was a home for girls who 'got themselves into trouble', a place where they could 'reflect on their failings' and 'get back their self-respect'.

The notebook had a mottled brown cover and its pages were crisp with age. She opened it at random. The writing, in fountain pen, was small and precise. *19 October 1971*, the entry read. *Boy, 6 lb 10 oz. Mother aged 19, from Co. Limerick. Named Goretti. Says she will call her baby Declan. Her boyfriend is in Birmingham, and she wants them both to join him there.*

No doubt some of Katie's memories had been warped by time, but she could still picture the young women and their babies. The 'fallen women', as some had insisted on labelling them, as if they were characters from the Bible or a Regency novel. She'd be going about her business when a sound or a smell would return her to another era. To a time of flared trousers and platform boots, black-and-white televisions and Vietnam. A time of calculated cruelty and unexpected kindness. She could still hear lonely sobs echoing through the building. She could smell the disinfectant and boiled dinners; see the spots of damp on the walls; sense the isolation and hopelessness.

She would also recall her own failures.

An outsider might assume that Johnny had forbidden her from doing anything with the bracelets. That wouldn't be fair. He'd been a protective man but not a controlling one. She'd been held back by her own fears. And yet, no matter how hard she tried to push her memories aside, they continued to seep in. Like her childhood in Danganstown and her marriage to Johnny, Carrigbrack was part of her story. And if that story finished now, it wouldn't have the ending she wanted.

'Carrigbrack?' said Beth with a wrinkle of her nose. 'Yeah, of course I've heard of it. It's in north Clare, up near the Burren. Wasn't it a big mother-and-baby home?'

'Mmm. Not as massive as some of the others, but pretty sizeable all the same.'

'So what were you doing there?'

'I was a nurse,' said Katie, trailing a hand along the edge of the shoebox. The two of them were in the kitchen, drinking the milky coffee that Beth had bought from a café near the college in Drumcondra.

A month after Johnny's funeral, Katie's niece had returned to Ireland for good. 'I'd forgotten how much I like Dublin,' she'd explained. She'd found a job with one of the large internet companies near the docks. Securing an affordable flat was altogether more difficult, and she was staying with old college friends in Stoneybatter. Despite the age gap, Beth and Katie had struck up a rapport. This was helped by the fact that, unlike her mother, Beth had shown no interest in rearranging Katie's life.

For years, their contact had been infrequent. Katie had rarely returned to her home village. Nevertheless, she'd always been fond of her niece. She'd been a chatty, lively child, full of questions about Katie's life in Dublin. Margo had seemed exhausted by her. But what mother of six wasn't perpetually exhausted?

'Didn't you have to be a nun to work in a place like Carrigbrack?' asked Beth.

'Most of the staff were nuns,' said Katie, 'but two or three of us weren't. We were just … well, I suppose you'd say we were helping out. I was newly qualified at the time.'

'Was nothing else available?'

'Not much. Getting a job wasn't easy. And, in the grand scheme of things, Carrigbrack was close to home. Danganstown's only thirty or forty miles away.'

'I hear what you're saying, but didn't working there make you uncomfortable?'

Katie was beginning to question the wisdom of confiding in

Beth. That was the problem with her niece's generation: everything was black or white, spectacular or unforgivable. They had a certainty about the world – and their place in it – that Katie had never acquired. They were direct, too. There was none of the let's-pretend-everything's-fine behaviour of the past. This was, she reckoned, a change for the better. Still, she wasn't always equipped for Beth's candour.

'I didn't have much choice,' she said. 'Mam and Dad heard about the job, and that was that. What I wanted was irrelevant.'

'How bad was it?'

'If you mean was there physical punishment, the answer is no. Not officially, at any rate. The regime was harsh, though. The girls were expected to work right up until they went into labour. And conditions were bleak. You couldn't have called it a happy place.'

Beth shook her head. 'What gets me is why everybody put up with this carry-on for so long. Did people really think that packing your daughter off to an institution was a good idea?'

Katie attempted to put some order on her thoughts. She didn't want to be evasive, but neither was she able to give a full answer. Before replying, she took a deep breath. 'I've thought a lot about it, and looking back, it can be hard to tell where misguided ended and cruel began. People were scared. Scared of the Church. Scared of their neighbours. Scared of being seen as less than decent.'

'But—'

'I suppose what you've got to understand is that for most ordinary people, life was far more limited than it is now. When we were growing up, there was no contraception. You were warned not to have sex before marriage. If you did, and you became pregnant, you were marched up the aisle. If that wasn't possible, you were sent away and the baby was adopted. That was how it was, and mad as it sounds, most people accepted it.'

'It sounds mad because it *was* mad. It was absolutely mental.'

Katie recoiled at the sting in Beth's voice. Five years in London had stripped most of the Danganstown from her accent, but it was still there around the edges, especially when she became emotional. 'Mad' sounded more like 'mid', and 'mental' came out as 'mintal'. Katie remembered how, in their early years, Johnny had poked fun at her own country accent. She, in turn, had laughed at his Dublinisms. At 'banjoed' and 'spanner' and 'get up the yard'. They'd both marvelled at how such a small country could have so many ways of speaking.

For a while, the two of them sat in silence. On the street, a group of children were enjoying the summer's last hurrah. Their squeals and hollers crashed through the quiet.

'I'm sorry, Katie,' said Beth. 'I was wrong to snap at you. I do appreciate you telling me this. I just find it all so grim, y'know?'

Katie leant over and tapped her niece's wrist. 'You're fine, pet. I won't put a gloss on it. Grim's the right word.'

'So what's the story with the box?'

'Ah. Well, when I was working in Carrigbrack, I decided I ought to record the births in some way.' She stopped to remove the lid and take out the notebook. 'New babies were a non-event. Celebration was forbidden, and no one was allowed to make a fuss. The mothers were told to reflect on the sin that had brought them there. "The more pain you suffer, the better," one of the nuns, Sister Sabina, used to say. Anyway, I knew what would happen. In most cases, the mother would be given a few weeks, perhaps a few months, with her baby, and then – *whoosh* – the child would be whipped away.'

'And the mother wouldn't be entitled to any information about where they'd gone?'

'That's right. In a way, the longer a baby stayed, the worse it was. Even though the girls were told not to form an attachment, many of them did.'

Katie paused, and an image drifted in. An image of a frightened young woman who'd been able to keep her boy for five months. She'd wanted to hold on to him. She'd been adamant she could cope. One dank Friday afternoon, he'd been taken away. Later, when she'd accepted that she would never get him back, she'd stretched out on the floor and howled with misery.

It was just one image. One story in an ocean of stories. But it never went away.

Katie was surprised to realise that her eyes were wet. 'Sorry, love,' she said. 'There's no call for me to get maudlin. That's not what this is about.'

'I don't blame you,' said Beth. 'I can't imagine what it must have been like. So …'

'You're wondering about the notebook? Well, I decided to keep a record of the births – a few details about the mothers and their babies. And I also kept these.' She reached into the box and plucked out two paper bracelets. 'The babies were given identity bands. As you can see, they're not like the high-tech things they have in hospitals nowadays; just bits of paper with the name of the mother and her baby and so on.' She handed over one of the bracelets.

'Boy. Eugene,' read Beth. 'Fifth of January 1972. Seven pounds two ounces. Mother: Loretta.'

'Loretta wouldn't have been her real name,' said Katie. 'They were all given different names in the home. And I can tell you, they used to get a right talking-to if they didn't use them.'

'Presumably Eugene's name was changed after he was adopted,' said Beth, running a finger over the tiny lettering.

'I'd say so. The Lord only knows where the little chap ended up.'

'But wherever he is, he'd probably love to have this. It might even help him find his birth mother.'

'If that's what he wants. Or maybe he already has. Remember, he's forty-six now. And I guess Loretta's nearly seventy.'

Beth's round blue eyes were suspiciously misty. Along with her small mouth and narrow nose, she'd inherited those eyes from her mother's side of the family. But while Katie and Margo had been cursed with flat faces, Beth had been blessed with her father's delicate cheekbones. At twenty-eight, she was a remoulded version of her mother. 'How many bracelets have you got?' she asked.

'Forty-seven. I was in Carrigbrack for a year and a bit, long enough to see the births of more than fifty children. There were three stillbirths, and three others died when they were very young. Oh, and I missed a couple of bracelets. Obviously, we weren't supposed to hold on to them. If my stash had been found, I'd have been in serious trouble.'

As she spoke about the babies who'd died, Katie noticed Beth's mouth tighten. Although the number was higher than it should have been, she'd tried to console herself with the knowledge that other homes had been worse. That being said, practices in Carrigbrack had made a mockery of her training. There had been unnecessary suffering, and she had contributed to it.

'And you've kept the bracelets all this time?' asked Beth.

'To be fair, it wasn't as though I was looking at them every day of the week. I just couldn't bring myself to get rid of them.'

Going back to her school days, Katie had always been embarrassingly organised. She'd been the child who did her homework so that others could copy it. Throughout her career, she'd valued detail, record-keeping, lists. Odd as it might have seemed to others, she could never have thrown away her box of names.

Beth handed back one bracelet and took another. 'Girl. Jacqueline. Tenth of November 1971. Six pounds four ounces. Mother: Hanora Culligan,' she read.

'I remember her. Bless her, she was only fourteen, and a young fourteen at that. Christine was her real name. She called herself Chrissie. She'd been raped by a neighbour.'

'Jesus.' Beth swiped at a tear. 'The poor girl. I hope life turned out well for her, though she must have been totally screwed up by the time she left Carrigbrack.'

'But you never know, do you? I'm amazed by what people can survive. Maybe she marched out and never looked back.'

'Do you really believe that?'

'I'm not sure. It's what I'd like to think, though.'

'It'd be great to find out.'

'It would,' said Katie, in a low voice. The more they spoke, they more convinced she became. Yes, there were risks. Some of the stories were likely to be upsetting. She might be drawn into contact with people she'd rather forget. Plus, she had only a hazy idea of how to go about this. What she did know was that if she could help someone to unlock a door, that was what she should do. She smiled at Beth. 'Like you say, the men and women born in the home might appreciate some information about where their story began.'

'Except ...' Beth hesitated.

'Go on.'

'Don't get me wrong. I think it's a brilliant idea, but I was wondering if this is the right time. Look at the two of us. We're all teary just looking at pieces of paper. I can hear Mam giving out. "Are you mad?" she'll say. "Bringing all that hassle on yourself, and Katie's husband not long in his grave."'

'We'd better not tell her, then.'

'That's cool with me, but what about my question?'

'There doesn't have to be hassle. And as far as the timing's concerned ... as much as I always hated those clichés about death, it turns out they're true. When someone close to you dies, you begin to measure your own time. If I don't do this now, there's a danger I'll regret it. Some of those involved mightn't have many years left. Besides, it's not as though I can go hunting down women and harassing them. I'll put an ad in the paper, and if anyone gets in touch, I'll talk to them.'

'The new job doesn't start for a couple of weeks,' said Beth. 'I can give you a dig-out if you like.'

'Thanks, love. I'd really like that.'

'And if people do contact you, what then?'

'I'll pass on what I have, and that'll be it. Believe me,' said Katie, 'I've no intention of getting involved in anybody's life.'

Chapter 3

Katie

According to Beth, an online adoption forum was what they needed. They could put up a post to let people know about the bracelets. At the bottom, they'd include a dedicated email address. If anyone wanted more information, they could send a message.

Katie wasn't convinced. 'Don't look at me like I'm some sort of behind-the-times old woman,' she said. 'I've a feeling the folks we want to reach are more likely to see an ad in the paper.'

'In the short term, maybe so. Only it would disappear after a day. A post on an adoption message board would be there indefinitely. I promise you more people would get to hear about it. They'd be the right people too. If you put an ad in the paper, there's a danger the rest of the family will come across it. And from what you were saying yesterday, you'd rather do this on the down-low. Am I right?'

'It's not as though I'd put my name in the paper. I'd call myself "Carrigbrack Nurse" or some such.'

'All the same, if Mam saw the dates, she'd guess it was you. There's far less chance of her spotting a message board post.'

'Hmm. Show me this forum you're talking about, so I can see whether it's suitable.'

Beth laughed. 'You're a hard woman to please.'

They were back in Katie's kitchen in Drumcondra. Apart from the occasional student house, Griffin Road was a street of tidy red-brick homes where the railings shone, the roses were pruned, and the bins were left out – and taken in – on the correct day. Katie and Johnny had bought number 89 in the mid 1970s. Now, youngsters would laugh at how small their mortgage had been. Back then, however, Katie had stalked the bare rooms saying, 'Thirty thousand pounds' in a way that someone might say 'A million euro' today. She'd been torn between the safety of owning something so solid and her fear that the loan was too big.

Johnny, being Johnny, had taken everything in his stride. Gradually, his carpentry and building skills had transformed the terraced house. Furniture and decorating had been Katie's responsibility. She'd haunted Roches Stores, Clerys and Guineys. She'd visited every wallpaper shop, auction and warehouse sale, and spent her every spare hour painting and sewing until Number 89 was just right. She remembered her husband's hand on her back and the way he'd liked kissing the top of her head. They'd had big plans back then.

Looking around now, she could see the kitchen was outdated. There was a stain in the bath, an annoying creak on the landing, and two light switches needed repairing. And, yes, a three-bedroomed house was too large for a woman on her own. Yet there was one thing Katie could say for sure: she wouldn't be moving.

She pulled her chair closer to Beth and looked at the computer screen. *Born May '67 in Cork – Hoping to Find Birth Mother*, said one heading. Another asked: *Should I Take a DNA Test?* A third was titled: *A Message for My Daughter, Born in Mayo, January 1982.*

Beth clicked on the next post. A man called Richie was seeking advice. A woman had turned up at his mother's funeral and sat at the back crying. Later, she approached the family. Their mother had also been her own birth mother, she said. The two of them had been reunited, but the elderly woman had been scared to tell her family. By way of proof, the stranger showed them her birth certificate. It contained their mother's name. *The thing is*, Richie wrote, *Mam had a very common name. How can we be certain this woman is our sister?*

'You know what, Richie?' said Beth. 'You're an almighty tool. Do you think the unfortunate woman gets a buzz from travelling the country and having a weep at the funerals of strangers?'

'Maybe you should tell him that,' said Katie. 'In slightly more diplomatic language.'

'Don't worry. Half a dozen other people already have.'

'You've spent a bit of time on here, then?'

'This and several other sites. And, honest to God, I'm raging. I'd no idea that tracking down your birth parents was so difficult. Not just difficult; in plenty of cases it's impossible. Half of the files appear to have been destroyed in mysterious fires and floods. And the official channels take forever. You can be on a waiting list for months, and even then, there's every chance you'll get nowhere. No wonder people take matters into their own hands.'

Katie watched her niece's shoulders stiffen. For the first time, Beth was seeing how the sins of the past reverberated around them. She'd realised that the story wasn't confined to black-and-white film and bleached-out Polaroids. The women weren't exhibits in a museum.

'The lack of records is amazing,' said Katie, 'because, as I remember it, everything was catalogued and recorded. Be it a baby's nappy or a bar of soap, it was on a list somewhere.'

'So,' said Beth, 'will you give the message board a try? Please?'

'All right, you've won me over. But if we find it's not working, we'll do things my way.'

Beth grinned. 'Katie, I promise you, it'll work.'

For an hour or more, as rain tip-tapped against the windows, the two played with words and phrases until both were happy.

Were you born in the Carrigbrack Mother and Baby Home in County Clare between July 1971 and December 1972, and were you adopted from there? Would you like to know more about the circumstances of your birth? If so, I may be able to help.

I worked as a nurse in Carrigbrack at that time and collected the discarded identity bracelets of many of the babies born there. I still have those bracelets. I also have a small amount of information about the young women who gave birth.

Even if you don't want to trace your birth family, you might like a memento of your earliest days.

If you think this may be of assistance to you, please contact me. My email address is CarrigbrackNurse@gmail.com.

I promise your query will be handled with strict confidence.

I regret that I can't answer any questions about births before July '71 and after December '72. Neither am I able to help with any wider queries about the operation of the home. I was an employee, not a member of the order that ran Carrigbrack.Good luck with your search. My thoughts are with you.

'There we are,' said Beth a few minutes later as she refreshed the screen and their post jumped to the top. 'The replies and emails will soon start rolling in. Then we can go sleuthing – like Miss Marple and her assistant. Except without the dead bodies, obviously.'

'Like I told you yesterday,' said Katie, swallowing a smile, 'there'll be no detective work. If someone contacts me, and I can help, I will. If I'm certain they're the right person, I'll put the bracelet in the post. Oh, and I'll have you know I'm years younger than Miss Marple.'

'Consider me told.' Beth tucked her long fair hair behind her ears. 'Can I ask you something?'

'Okay.'

'What did Mam make of your job in Carrigbrack?'

'I'm not sure. Remember, Margo's nine years younger than me, so she was only thirteen. And our parents were strict. I don't think she was allowed an opinion.'

'You can bet that wouldn't hold her back now.'

Katie said nothing. Margo had an opinion for every occasion, and a few spares in the cupboard. When her sister had been very young, Katie had been delighted with her. She'd toted her around like a doll. After the novelty had faded, however, there'd been nothing there to replace it. Unfortunately, their connection had never been strong. Katie should probably have made a greater effort to understand her sister, but she feared it was too late for that now.

At twenty-two, Margo had married Con Linnane, the eldest son of the largest landowner in Danganstown. It was decent land too, not like the marshy fields of their neighbours, where only ragwort prospered and only snipe could be assured of a decent meal. The Linnanes had renovated and decorated a mini mansion and filled it with children. Given that Beth was the lone girl, Katie had expected Margo to be thrilled by her return to Ireland. Yet, for some hard-to-pin-down reason, their relationship was uneasy. She'd been tempted to ask if there was a problem, but decided against it. Besides, what she'd said to Beth about Margo and Carrigbrack wasn't the full story. In Katie's experience, too much honesty could be as dangerous as too little.

*

For three days, nothing happened. Again and again Katie returned to her new email account, hoping that someone would get in touch. On the forum itself, some of the responses were hostile. One poster demanded to know why it had taken her so long to offer help. Another questioned why she'd worked in Carrigbrack to begin with. In capital letters, he accused her of being a collaborator and an accessory to cruelty. Poison dripped down the screen.

She wanted to explain, but Beth urged her to hold back. 'Don't feed the trolls,' she said.

Not for the first time, Katie had to ask for a translation.

With her inbox remaining empty, she pored over the forum, reading the stories of others, each one sadder than the next. After that, she turned to other message boards. If your mood was already low, she discovered, internet forums were not your friend. Although the adoption board contained plenty of empathy, there was scant sign of it elsewhere. Politicians were pathetic; television presenters were talentless; most neighbourhoods were dangerous; the country was broken and corrupt; and if you doubted any of this, you were stupid.

That night she dreamt about Carrigbrack, one of those vivid dreams where every tiny detail was magnified and every scene, no matter how implausible, seemed real. She woke up coated in sweat, her nightdress stuck to her skin.

When morning came, she was sluggish, her head filled with concrete. Every step felt as if she was walking up a down escalator. It occurred to her that in trying to dodge the 'What will you do now?' questions, she'd made a mistake. Yes, she needed a task to fill her days, but this wasn't it. Would Beth be able to take down the post? she wondered.

And then it arrived.

The email was titled *All Help Appreciated*:

Hi,

I've just come across your online message and I was hoping you might be able to help.

I'm forty-seven years old, and for reasons too complicated to go into here, I've only recently discovered I was adopted.

It turns out that my birth certificate is a fake. It gives my name as Gary Winters, but that wasn't my original name. My adoptive parents are registered as my birth parents.

According to my adoptive mother, I was born in Carrigbrack. She says she doesn't know any more than that.

My date of birth is 12 August 1971. Do you have a bracelet for a boy born on that date? And do you remember anything about my birth mother?

Yours in hope,

Gary Winters

Co. Wicklow

Katie tingled like a child with a surprise present. Even if she did ask Beth to take down the post, she would reply to Gary. No sooner had she sent her email than he came back again. He said he'd learnt to expect complications but was confident her information was important. *If I hop in the car,* he wrote, *I can be with you in less than an hour.* Katie rang Beth for advice. No answer. She texted, then rang again. Still no answer.

Twenty minutes later, Beth called back. 'I take it there's been a development,' she said. While Katie read out the email, her niece made small humming sounds. When she reached the end, Beth jumped in. 'Gary Winters? As in *the* Gary Winters?'

'Should I know him?'

'Not necessarily, but if he is who I think he is, lots of people do.'

Katie was sitting in front of her laptop. She ran the name through Google. A Wikipedia page popped up, as did several images of a dark-haired man with a sprinkling of tattoos. In most of the pictures he wasn't wearing a shirt.

'Oh,' she said.

'Is he the right guy?' asked Beth.

'He's definitely the right age for our Gary. In fact …' she opened the Wikipedia page, 'the date of birth listed here is the same as the one he gave me.'

'Wow.'

'Are you doing anything tomorrow morning, by any chance? I arranged to meet him.'

'You're not serious?'

'I'm afraid I am,' said Katie, already regretting the combination of curiosity and politeness that had made her agree to Gary's request. She'd known that in some cases a meeting might be necessary, but in this instance, she feared it was pointless. 'The snag is,' she said, 'I've been through my notes and examined all the bracelets and I'm certain there were no births in Carrigbrack on the twelfth of August 1971.'

'Right,' said Beth. 'That means …?'

'That someone's not telling the truth.'

Chapter 4

Gary

Gary couldn't remember when he'd last been this nervous. Was it the first time Black Iris had played the Hollywood Bowl, and it had felt as if every star in the universe was backstage? Or was it when they'd headlined the third night of Rock in Rio, and two hundred thousand people had spread out in front of them like ants on a highway? Or was it all the way back when he'd told his parents he was dropping out of college to go on tour with a rock band?

He picked up a teaspoon, passing it from one hand to the other. 'You see,' he said to Katie, 'I keep thinking about the times I came across those pictures on TV – the girls in convents and boys in reform schools and that place in Galway where the babies were buried in a tank – and I never had any idea I was part of the story. But now that I do, I've got to find out who my people are.'

'Your people,' said Katie, her voice soft. It wasn't a question, he decided, so much as a comment on his choice of words. Gary was aware that he sounded slightly American. People in Ireland smirked at the way he said 'garaage' and used phrases like 'touch base', 'reach out' and 'cell phone'. But he'd spent so much of his life in the States that the words of his adopted country were first on his tongue. He had to focus on being Irish.

Katie didn't tally with his expectations. She was old, sure. But not old old. He'd pictured a large woman with thick legs and steel hair. Someone forbidding. Instead, he'd been met by a small blonde lady wearing beige trousers and a navy jacket. He was taken by the way she'd described herself as a widow, like she was trying out the word. He guessed the bereavement was recent. Neither had he expected an assistant, but from the way Beth and Katie finished each other's sentences, he sensed they were close.

'We know who you are,' Katie had said as she rose from the black leather armchair to greet him. 'Well, to be honest, Beth here had to fill me in. Grunge passed me by, I'm afraid, but I gather you're very successful.'

He was touched by her use of the present tense. Black Iris had had their heyday – three *Billboard* number one albums, nine Grammys, four *Rolling Stone* covers – in the nineties. They hadn't been on stage or in a studio for three years. One or two heads had turned as he'd entered the Gresham Hotel and walked towards the bar, but even at the height of the band's fame, he'd rarely caused an out-and-out stir. After all, Anton had been the charismatic front man, Ray the famed guitarist, Liamo the crazy-as-hell drummer. Gary was the bass player. And unless you were Paul McCartney or Phil Lynott, who remembered the bass player?

Although Katie had warned him that she didn't have a bracelet for the relevant day, he hadn't been too disheartened. If his natural parents could be erased from history, it was hardly surprising that his given date of birth was wrong. He figured the details on the certificate couldn't be that far out. If he could get all her records for July, August and September 1971, he'd be able to find his birth mother.

Katie took a delicate sip of tea. 'You said in your email that you've only recently found out you were adopted. That must have been tough.'

'Yeah, at the start I refused to believe it. The thing is, I look like the rest of the family. I have two sisters, my parents' biological children, and we all have dark hair and brown eyes. And if you've been told a lie often enough, it becomes hard to accept anything else. For a while, I railed against my folks. In the end, though, I ran out of anger. You do, don't you? Anyhow, it's not like I have any complaints about my childhood. The three of us were treated the same – and we were treated well.'

The recognition that he'd been raised by kind, generous people had helped Gary to accept his situation. He'd never approve of what they did, but he'd heard enough stories about miserable childhoods to make him appreciate the Winters family. His bandmate, Ray, had suffered a horrific upbringing, with regular beatings and a mother who defended her husband no matter how cruel his behaviour. Complaining to Ray was like moaning about a paper cut when the guy beside you had a bullet wound to the chest.

'If you don't mind me asking,' said Katie, 'why did your parents wait so long to tell you?'

Gary's first impulse was to flim-flam around the question, but he had a hunch she'd see through him. 'It's kind of complicated. In my thirties, I had a relationship with a woman called Posy Fuente. You may have—'

'She's an actress,' said Beth to Katie.

'Oh, yes,' said Katie, with a deep nod, 'she won a prize at the Sundance Festival.'

Gary doubted that Katie was genuinely familiar with Posy's work. She'd done her research.

'So,' he said, 'Posy and I have a daughter. Allegra's her name. She's ten. I don't get to see her as often as I'd like, but ... we're in regular touch. And we're good now, her mother and me. A year or so back, Allegra began having seizures. They were fairly bad, and her doctors couldn't track down the precise cause. They wondered if there might be a clue in her background. Like, could she have inherited some sort of genetic disorder? When they couldn't find anything on Posy's side, they asked about me. I wasn't aware of any issues, but I thought my folks might be able to help. To begin with, they were vague. There was a lot of shilly-shallying and staring at the floor. A week or two later, Allegra was no better, and the doctors were still asking questions. By that stage, I was in LA. I called home and said, "Listen, if there's anything, anything at all, you've got to speak up." That was when they came clean. I can hear my old man's voice crackling down the line. "We can't tell you," he said, "because we don't know."'

'How's Allegra doing now?' asked Beth.

'She's a lot better, thanks. She's on medication and everything, and Posy has to keep an eye on her, but she's a great kid.'

'That's good to hear,' said Katie. 'I assume you haven't been able to find out if there's a family connection to her illness?'

Gary rearranged his legs. He felt too long for the chair. 'No. Only that's no longer such a big issue. I want to find my birth mother because I want to hear her story. I need to know why she didn't keep me. Oh, and I'd like to know if she's okay. Did she ever get married? Do I have brothers and sisters? And, if she needs anything, I'm not short. I could help.'

'I understand,' Katie said, reaching for the tea strainer and placing it over her cup. It was a while since Gary had seen proper tea with leaves. 'I know it might feel like your birth mother didn't want you, but, believe me, there's every chance she did. I'm sure she loved you very much. The way it was back then … girls weren't given a choice. And, awful as it sounds, quite a few of the mothers thought their babies would be better off elsewhere. Bless them, they were brainwashed into believing they weren't fit to raise a child.'

She faltered in a way that suggested she found this difficult to discuss. Gary figured he'd be the same if he'd worked in such a terrible place. Still, her reassurance was welcome.

'That's not all,' said Beth. 'I've been reading up on this. Apparently, there was no support for single mothers. Not a penny. Unless your birth mother's family had agreed to help, she probably wouldn't have had the money to feed you.'

'What a system, huh?' said Gary.

'Did your parents say why they'd kept your adoption a secret?' asked Katie.

'I mean,' added Beth, 'isn't it unusual for someone's birth certificate to be forged?'

Gary signalled to the black-uniformed waitress for another coffee. This was going to take a while. 'Not as unusual as you might think.' He turned to Katie. 'When you were in the home, did you ever hear about birth certs being written up without the natural mother's name?'

She paused to consider the question. 'I didn't, but I wouldn't read too much into that. Carrigbrack was a secretive place. The mothers were forced to sign a document promising they'd never attempt to find their child. A certificate of surrender, it was called. They had no rights, and there was nobody to speak up for them, so the logical next step was to remove their name from the baby's papers.'

'It was as though an adoption had never taken place,' said Beth.

Gary's Americano arrived. He took a welcome mouthful. 'And that's my problem. There are no records. The arrangements were made through a cousin of Dad's who happened to be a nun. They were told next to nothing, just that I was born in Carrigbrack, I was in excellent health, and my birth mother was from a "decent" family. Whatever that meant.'

'And ...' started Katie.

'Sorry. You wanted to know why they didn't tell me the truth when I was a kid?'

'Yes.'

'First off, they'd recently moved to a new house so they didn't have to say anything to anybody. They weren't going to face any awkward questions about the sudden arrival of a baby. Plus, they genuinely thought they were doing the right thing. They worried that if the other boys at school knew I was adopted, there'd always be some lowlife giving me grief about it.'

'I see,' said Katie. 'If this nun was related to your father, it's easy to imagine her cutting a special deal for your family.' She stopped and raised a hand to her face. 'Gary, you'll have to forgive me. I've made it sound like your parents were buying a second-hand car or a barn of hay.'

He found himself smiling. 'It's cool. I understand.'

'Could the nun give you any information?' asked Beth.

'She died more than twenty years ago.'

'Ah.' Katie played with her teacup. 'Now, don't get me wrong, I'll help if I can. But I was wondering: you're a well-known man; might it not be easier for you to go public? To talk to a newspaper or a chat show? They'd be delighted to do an interview, I'm sure.'

She was shrewd, was Katie. Gary paused to gather his thoughts. Light Muzak tinkled in the background. He didn't mind; musicians had to make a living. To explain why he didn't want to make his private world public, he would have to tell Katie and Beth the story of his life. He would have to make them see that he'd moved in circles with the potential for limitless good times. From the age of nineteen, when Black Iris had first travelled to America, every rock-and-roll cliché had been available to him, and he'd tried most of them. As the warning at the start of his favourite true-crime podcast put it, his story contained coarse language and adult themes. For two decades, he'd bounced from one city to another. He'd been to all the best parties – and many of the worst. He'd been involved in every kind of excess on every continent.

He liked to tell himself that he'd fared better than most. He'd avoided alcoholism and addiction to hard drugs. His brain hadn't been liquefied. He had no infectious diseases. What he did have was a personal life that was monumentally screwed up.

His first marriage, to a singer called Lorena Sands, had produced two sons. They were adults now, and he saw them from time to time. Thankfully, his second marriage, to the model Carly McCall, hadn't lasted long enough for them to have children. He did, though, have another son, from a flirtation with a journalist. Then there was Allegra. Even though she was six thousand miles away, he liked to think he had a good relationship with his daughter. More than twenty years after the birth of his first child, he reckoned he was getting to grips with the fatherhood thing.

While he'd never had sex with a woman who wasn't willing, he hadn't always treated women well. He'd walked out on too many and considered the feelings of too few. His story had been part of the tapestry of the times in which he'd grown up, but times had changed. Talking about his life would give others the excuse to go rooting around. In the era of #MeToo and #TimesUp, he saw how his behaviour would be framed, and the picture wouldn't be pretty. He'd be vilified as a toxic love rat, a tawdry abuser, a guy who'd taken what he wanted and damn the consequences. He'd be part of the gallery of obnoxious entitled men.

A close examination of his life might also raise questions about why Black Iris hadn't played together in three years and why the bass player and the vocalist, friends since the age of nine, spoke only through their management and lawyers.

He figured that Katie already knew some of his history. Many of the bare facts were available online. He needed her to understand that speaking to the press would be a mistake, so he blundered through an explanation, emphasising his concerns for his parents. They wouldn't enjoy the spotlight, he said. If Katie didn't appear fully convinced, she didn't argue either.

She picked up her red handbag and took out a tattered brown notebook. 'Remind me,' she said to Beth, 'to get a new cover for this. Otherwise there's a danger it'll fall apart.'

'Will do.'

Next, she took out a pair of gold-rimmed reading glasses. 'Now, Gary,' she said, 'like I told you in my email, there were no babies born in Carrigbrack on the twelfth of August 1971. Neither do I have any mention of a Gary, so your adoptive parents must have chosen your name. There were, however, three boys born during the month of July and another two in August. Either side of those dates, there's quite a gap. In fact, it was October before another boy was born. Taking that into account, the chances are that you're one of the five. Have you a piece of paper so you can take all of this down?'

'I can put the details in my phone.' Gary took it from the pocket of his leather jacket. He also put on his glasses. 'It happens to all of us eventually,' he said to Beth, hoping he didn't sound too pathetic.

'Right,' continued Katie, 'there's a chance, then, that you are one of these five boys.'

She spoke slowly and clearly, giving the women's real names rather than the ones they were forced to use in the home. Even so, Gary had trouble recording everything she said. His hands trembled. This was the closest he'd come to finding out the truth.

The names fluttered around him. His mother might have been Gráinne. She might have been Tina or Edel, Noreen or Olivia. He might have been called Paul. Or he might have been Séamus or Kevin, Martin or John.

'Thank you,' he said to Katie. 'Thank you. Thank you. Thank you.'

She smiled. 'You haven't got anywhere yet.'

'But it's a start,' said Beth.

'Can you …' he asked, 'can you remember any of the women?' He then thought better of his query. 'Sorry, that was a dumbass question. It was almost fifty years ago. I can barely remember people I met last week.'

'As it happens,' said Katie, 'I do recall two of them. I remember Olivia because she attempted to escape. The guards brought her back, though what business it was of theirs, I don't know. She was a real beauty, a gorgeous young woman.'

Gary gave a nod of encouragement.

'And Edel has stuck in my memory because she was older than most of the others. She was in her mid thirties.'

'Which means she'd now be in her eighties,' said Beth.

'That's if she's still alive,' added Gary. 'I figure I ought to begin with Edel. Edel Sheehan.' There was pleasure in just saying the name. And if Edel wasn't the right woman, it had to be Olivia Farnham. Or Tina McNulty. Or Noreen Nestor. Or Gráinne Holland. All he had to do was whittle down the list and he would find his birth mother.

'Good luck,' said Katie. 'It's not an easy task. And … well, I'm not certain how to put this, but please tread lightly. If you do find your birth mother, it may take her a while to adjust.'

Gary's head was full of possibilities. 'Thanks,' he said. 'I … um, I was hoping there was one other thing you could help me with.'

Chapter 5

Then, Patricia

'What you'll learn here in Carrigbrack,' said Sister Agnes, 'is that actions have consequences. I'm aware that nowadays some girls dismiss this as an old-fashioned concept. "Sister," they say to me, "the world has changed. We can do what we want." You may even have thought something similar yourself. But,' the nun paused and focused her gaze on Patricia, 'no doubt you're beginning to understand how misguided such notions are. We can't abandon personal morality, and we can't fill the country with illegitimate children.'

Patricia had been sitting in the wood-panelled office for ten minutes, and most of Agnes's speech had been unexpectedly low-key. From behind a heavy desk, she'd rattled through a series of petty rules with the mechanical demeanour of a woman who'd done this a thousand times before, which she probably had. Save for a Sacred Heart lamp, the walls were bare. A tall bookcase was devoted largely to stories about female saints. A dark corner of Patricia's mind imagined the nun hiding contraband copies of *The Country Girls* or *Valley of the Dolls*.

This was her first encounter with the woman who oversaw the day-to-day running of the home. She'd arrived in Carrigbrack late the previous night. While Father Cusack had been brought to the parlour for tea and cake, a pencil-thin nun in a thick black dress and veil had shown Patricia to a dormitory. There, she'd been instructed to change for bed as quietly as possible. 'The other girls won't thank you for disturbing their sleep,' the nun had said. Patricia's request for a glass of water had been met with a raised eyebrow and a slow shake of the head. In the far corner, a girl had been crying, her muffled sobs amplified by the silence.

Agnes had a comfortable look that belied her position. With her pudgy face, small glasses and rosy cheeks, she looked kindly. Soft, even. Patricia had already seen enough of Carrigbrack to know that there was nothing soft about the place.

She'd heard about the homes. Who hadn't? From the age of ten or eleven, every show of disobedience had been met with a warning: if you don't watch yourself, you'll end up in Carrigbrack. Reality appeared to be even harsher than rumour. A substantial entrance hall, its floor gleaming, gave way to a series of sombre corridors. The mothers-to-be slept in dormitories, the children in a spartan nursery. There were no photographs or personal items, and few toys. Every room was decorated with religious statues and holy pictures. The penitents, as Agnes called them, wore indigo uniforms made from stiff cloth that seemed designed to rub and scratch. They ate in a draughty refectory. The nuns, and the nurses who helped deliver and care for the babies, had a separate dining room. Mass was every morning at seven, the rosary was at six, lights-out at nine.

New mothers could hold their babies only while feeding them. For much of the day, talking was forbidden. Any attempt to escape was likely to fail. The nearest village was more than a mile away, and most of the locals were supportive of the home. Runaways were easily spotted and returned. Anyone breaking the rules could expect to be disciplined. The punishments ranged from extra work to extra prayers to having your hair cut off. Happiness was viewed with suspicion.

Patricia had learnt some of this from a whispered conversation with the girl in the next bed and some from Sister Agnes. From what she had seen of the other women, many were cowed and docile. She had the impression that even if the doors were unlocked and the gates thrown open, few would leave. After all, where would they go?

Agnes was still speaking. There was more force to her words now.

'What you'll have to do,' she said, 'is reflect on the sins that brought you here and on how you can atone for them. You've caused grave distress to your family. When I spoke to your mother earlier in the week, it was clear she was heartbroken. Remember, despite what some would claim, there's nothing wrong with deference and humility. Men can't help themselves, so the burden falls on women to keep society safe and close to God. Do you understand?'

As much as she would have liked to argue, Patricia's compliant streak came to the fore. 'I do, Sister.'

'We may not get much thanks today, but future generations will be grateful that we stood firm and protected children from lives of corruption and sin.'

When, finally, Patricia was allowed to ask a question, her words were stilted. 'I was wondering, Sister, if I could work in the nursery. I think—'

'That's out of the question. Such valued positions are given only to our most trusted girls, and from what I've heard about the circumstances of your downfall, I don't think I can include you in that category. Some time working in the fields will be of more benefit to you. We grow our own fruit and vegetables here, and there's plenty to be done.'

'But—'

'I said no.'

To her annoyance, Patricia felt tears pooling at the back of her eyes. Don't cry, she thought. You can't cry.

'There are those,' said Sister Agnes, 'including some of my own sisters, who believe your shame will be eternal. As it happens, I don't share that view. You have fallen and you can rise again. The day will come when you walk out of here and begin afresh. But I warn you, Patricia, if you behave as though you belong in the gutter, the gutter is where you'll end up.' She shuffled some papers and gave a watery smile. 'Now, before we lose any more of the day, I'm going to bring you out to the garden. Sister Sabina is in charge. She can tell you what to do.'

That night, Patricia couldn't sleep. She hadn't been able to accept that she was pregnant. Now, she couldn't grasp that she was here, in a place of strangers, forced to use a name that wasn't hers, bound by rules that made no sense. A place without colour or comfort, where she had no control and no voice. Even her body was no longer her own.

She thought of Mike and of how sweet everything had been at the beginning. She thought of how they'd kissed the hours away. Of how she'd believed what he'd said. She wondered if he would hear about what had happened to her. If so, what would he think? Would he, too, think it was for the best?

In the dark, alone with her thoughts, she allowed herself to cry.

To begin with, Patricia cried every night, mopping her tears on the starched sheets. Her brain was clogged with 'what ifs' and 'if onlys'. She was regretful and angry and a hundred other emotions besides. The chaos in her head matched the awkwardness of her body. She was the wrong shape for sleep. During the day, she was too hot; at night, her limbs became rigid from the cold. If she learnt nothing else, she learnt that complaints were futile. Worse, they might lead to punishment.

Gradually, she came to terms with her situation. It wasn't what she would have chosen, but there was a person inside her. A boy or girl who kicked and squirmed. They might go on to achieve great things. They might play football or sing in a pop group or cure cancer. Or maybe they'd have a regular life with an ordinary job and a standard family. For the first time, she saw the appeal of a straightforward existence with someone who loved you. No hiding or game-playing; just honesty and commitment. Either way, the baby was real, and it was hers. It didn't belong to Mike or her parents. It didn't belong to Sister Agnes or Mother Majella or Sister Sabina. The dreaded Sabina had an extensive line in insults and a voice that could strip paint. Under her watch, even those in the final stages of pregnancy were forced to keep on working. Patricia had looked on in horror as the nun shouted at a girl who'd got sick while picking cabbages.

'I don't care if you're here until midnight,' she'd said, 'you'll finish your work.'

When Patricia had asked her parents about keeping the baby, she hadn't been serious. She'd been trying to shock them. As time passed, however, she wondered if it might be possible.

The more she got to know the other women, the more interesting she found them. It was easy to dismiss them as all the same when, in truth, no two were alike. Some were silent and downtrodden, while others appeared to have only a hazy idea of how they'd got pregnant. More were clever and funny. In snatched moments, they'd forget about their circumstances. They'd tell stories of home or impersonate the nuns or, imaginations soaring, dream up plans for the rest of their lives.

A few of the girls were in bad shape. One was bruised and emaciated, another had ringworm on her face, while a third had a permanent barking cough. Little was done to help them. Surely, thought Patricia, the nurses could do more? She'd taken a dislike to the nurses, who strutted around as if they belonged to a superior species.

From the nuns, and from Agnes and Sabina in particular, the mothers were subjected to regular diatribes about their own failings and those of others. Mini skirts, maxi skirts, long hair, short hair, English television, American music, depraved novels, the spread of the vernacular Mass: all were blamed for the rise of godlessness and the sorry state of the nation. More than once, Patricia caught the eye of one of the other girls, and they were forced to suppress a giggle.

After a few weeks, life fell into a rhythm. Every day was the same: prayer and work and more prayer and more work. As the evenings grew brighter, Patricia and the others spent endless hours in the fields, picking cabbages and cauliflowers, lettuces and scallions. They sowed and thinned and pruned until their swollen bodies screamed for rest.

'At the start, I thought you were stuck up,' said Winnie, 'but you're all right.'

'Thanks, I think,' replied Patricia, who was planting cucumber seeds in small mounds of earth, the way Sister Sabina had shown her. Sabina had been called away, so they were free to chat.

'No offence, but you do have a stand-offish look about you. It's like you're more educated or something. Still, I reckon that behind that, you're the same as the rest of us.'

'We're all in the same position, anyway.'

'Knocked up and abandoned, you mean?' said Winnie, and they both laughed. The humour in Carrigbrack was dark.

Winnie was from County Sligo. She had bouncy black hair, a smattering of freckles and a wide, full-lipped smile. By comparison, Patricia felt washed out and drab.

'Jesus, this is uncomfortable,' said Winnie. 'Crouching's definitely not good for pregnant women. Sit down there for a minute.'

Patricia hesitated.

'Don't worry. We'll see Sabina coming.'

'Or if not, we'll definitely hear her. I'm more afraid that if I do sit down, I won't be able to get up again.'

Winnie tilted her face towards the sun. 'What's your story, then?'

'Not too different to yours, I'd say. I met the wrong man and … well, you know yourself.'

'Did he run off?'

'Yes and no.' *Oh, why not tell the truth?* 'He's married.'

'Ah. And did he used to tell you he'd leave her?'

'I never asked.'

'Weren't you the brazen hussy?'

Winnie's tone sounded amused rather than judgemental, and Patricia smiled. 'What about you?'

'Pure eejitry, to be honest. When we first met, I was cracked about him. He pestered me for sex, and I gave in. I hope he enjoyed himself, because it didn't do much for me: lots of pushing and panting and not many thrills. I remember Sabina saying, "All this for ten minutes' pleasure." And I thought, ten minutes? That'd be a miracle. Anyway, before I knew where I was, I'd missed three periods. I threw up at school, they sent me home, my parents put two and two together … and here I am.'

'What did your boyfriend say?'

'Not much. After I told him, he moved to Manchester.'

Patricia attempted to clean one fingernail with another. 'That's desperate.'

'I know. The miserable fecker. When I get free of this place, I've a mind to head that way just to haunt him. I have this fantasy where he's sticking his tongue down some young girl's throat, and I pop up behind him shouting, "Surprise! Remember me?"'

As Winnie spoke, her curls bobbed in time with her voice. Patricia felt laughter rising in her throat like a cat's purr, and before she knew it, they were both laughing hard.

'I can see you, all right. The poor lad, I almost feel sorry for him.'

'I wouldn't go that far. To be fair, he might have been worried about my father calling the guards on him. I'm sixteen now, but I was only fifteen then.'

'Oh. I thought you were older. As Sister Agnes would say, you've got your whole life ahead of you.'

Winnie ran a hand through the dirt. 'Is that what she said to you? She told me I only had myself to blame and that, chances were, I'd never amount to anything. "You messed up your own life," she said, "so we're not giving you a chance to mess up the life of an innocent child."'

Patricia decided to change the subject. 'When are you due?'

'Next month. You?'

'August.'

'That's one big baby you're carrying. Could you be having twins, do you reckon?'

'Jeekers, that's an awful thought,' said Patricia, a drop of sweat trickling down her back.

'Don't panic, I'm only messing.'

'Do you know what you want to do? Like, if it was possible, would you keep your baby?'

'Every day I change my mind. I'm not certain I'd be any good with a child. But, at the same time, I'd like to have a choice. Does that make sense?'

'It does, yeah. Will you go back and finish school?'

'You're codding me,' said Winnie. 'They wouldn't let the likes of me infect the place with my filthy ways. Believe me, I've a better chance of becoming Miss Ireland than doing the Leaving Cert.'

'By the time we leave here, you'll be an expert gardener anyway.'

'That's if I stay.'

'What do you mean?'

Winnie leant in close. 'I've spotted a gap in the hedge that runs around the back of the building. Even in this state,' she patted her stomach, 'it should be possible to squeeze out.'

Patricia was about to ask where Winnie would go when she saw a couple of the other girls scrambling to their feet. 'Damn, Sabina's on her way back.'

From then on, she kept an eye out for Winnie.

Every two weeks, Patricia received a letter from home. Mostly they were dreary, and she suspected her mother filtered out anything worth knowing. More often than not they were accompanied by an article torn from *The Sacred Heart Messenger* or the *Saint Martin Magazine*. Not being allowed to write back was a relief.

The letter that arrived in mid June was different. Her mam mentioned Mike – or Mr Langan, as she insisted on calling him. Her father had arranged to meet him, and they'd had a conversation. The thought brought bile to Patricia's mouth.

She couldn't remember when she'd first seen Mike. He was one of those people who'd always been there, a fixture of village life. When she'd been in her early teens, she'd fancied him. He had the sort of straightforward good looks that appealed to fourteen-year-olds: floppy black hair, toffee-brown eyes and skin that tanned easily. Locals maintained he had 'a touch of the Armada' about him. (This claim, of descent from one of the Spanish men whose boats had foundered off the west coast, was made about anyone who wasn't as white as a handkerchief.) Mike was seven years older than Patricia, a grown-up with a job selling insurance door-to-door. By the time he looked her way, she was nineteen. And he was married.

She recalled how it began. They'd met on the street, and she'd been surprised by his friendliness. No, it had been more than friendliness.

It had been flirtation: sparkle and flash, push and pull. She'd walked away in a glow of compliments. A couple of weeks later, they'd met again. This time in Sheehy's bar. Patricia's father hadn't approved of her spending time in pubs; they weren't for respectable girls. If he'd had his way, she'd have kept her confirmation pledge until she was fifty. Mike had suggested they go outside – 'To talk in peace,' he said.

She remembered standing in the long west-of-Ireland twilight, her back to the wall. The night was mild, with barely a breath of wind. He cupped her chin, and they kissed. One moment he kissed hard, the next he paused to nuzzle her face and neck. He smelled of cigarettes, beer and spicy aftershave. She remembered the lurches and whooshes of pleasure. She remembered thinking, so this is what proper kissing is like.

Yes, she'd known that what she was doing was wrong. Mike was another woman's husband. Just thinking about him was a mortal sin. But, in truth, hadn't that also been part of his appeal? Her life had been heavy with duty, light on thrills. Her tightly regulated world hadn't allowed for excitement. All the same, in her idle moments, guilt crept up on her and told her she deserved to be punished.

After the evening in Sheehy's, Mike and Patricia met whenever they could. The first time they had sex was in a disused barn. Afterwards, they shared a cigarette and joked about rolling in the hay. To begin with, she didn't like doing it out in the open like a farm animal. She fantasised about a more sophisticated setting. She wanted to make love in a proper double bed with music and gentle light. As time passed, she accepted that this wasn't going to happen. By then, she was in love. Or, at least, she thought she was. It was more like a sickness, really. She craved Mike's company, his touch. She wanted to be with him all the time. And when they weren't together, she fantasised about him. Despite what some might want to think, she never felt pressured or bullied. She desired him as much as he desired her. She tried not to think too far ahead. She tried not to think at all. For a brief, glorious time, she considered herself special. He told her she was special.

He didn't complain about his wife or make any claims about Vera not understanding him. If he spoke about her, it was in passing, like he was talking about a friend or a sibling.

Patricia was aware that this sounded naïve. Others would be more severe in their judgement. As her mother put it, 'What kind of imbecile messes around with a married man? Nobody will have you now.'

Before she told her parents about the baby, she'd spoken to Mike. He asked what she wanted to do, as though there was a range of options. Then he said, 'It's probably best if we avoid each other for a while. People will talk.' She shivered as the truth worked its way in: she couldn't expect support from Mike or anyone else. The baby was her burden.

Now, she stood near the entrance to the nursery and read on. According to her mother, the meeting had been useful. *Mr Langan admitted he'd made a mistake, and he apologised. He said his head had been turned and he would never be tempted again.*

Patricia's forehead was damp. In the nursery, a baby cried, its thin wail cutting through the silence.

The letter continued: *He told your father that his wife is expecting. Their baby is due shortly before your own, but you probably know that.*

Again, Patricia paused. One of the nurses passed by, sent a concerned look in her direction, but walked on.

Mr Langan pleaded with your father not to take matters any further, and he agreed. As your father pointed out, it takes two to tango, and you share the blame. We talked it all through and decided that Mrs Langan is better off not knowing about her husband's infidelity. In every other respect, they have a good marriage. Please God, he's learnt his lesson. For your sake, and for hers, it's best if this matter isn't discussed again.

Patricia stopped reading. Her parents' initial reaction had been easier to accept. Tears and spiky fury she could understand. In the circumstances, she might have behaved the same way. She could also forgive how distant they'd been on the night of her departure. They'd been in shock. But this was colder, more calculated. This was a swift punch to the stomach followed by a kick to the back of the knees. She wanted to fall to the floor, crumple up and hide.

She could see why, on leaving places like Carrigbrack, many young women went to England or America. It wasn't because they were ashamed. It was because they'd been abandoned.

In the nursery, another baby began to cry. Sister Eunice scurried by, then stopped and returned.

'Did you get bad news from home, Patricia?' she asked.

'No, I'm grand, Sister.'

Eunice, who wasn't much older than most of the girls, patted her arm. 'Well, if you need to talk, let me know. You're very pale.'

'Thanks, Sister.'

Patricia folded the letter and walked to the dormitory. Thankfully, it was empty. There, she tore the paper into narrow shreds and threw them in the bin.

Chapter 6

Katie

'Weren't you the woman who wasn't going to get involved?' said Beth as they rounded the corner from North Frederick Street onto Dorset Street. The day had turned out fine with just a scattering of thin white cloud, and they'd decided to walk back to Drumcondra.

'Strictly speaking, I don't think I've broken my word,' said Katie. 'It's not like I'm hammering on anyone's door making a nuisance of myself. And it'd be a terrible trip for him to make on his own.'

Gary's suggestion that she accompany him to Carrigbrack had caught her by surprise. Without stopping to think, she'd agreed.

'I reckon you just want a spin in a Ferrari – or whatever it is he drives,' said Beth.

She chuckled. 'I hope he brings something more sensible, because, let me tell you, a sports car wouldn't last long. When I worked there, the nearest road was no better than a dirt track, and I've no reason to believe things have improved. The place was abandoned years ago.'

What Katie didn't say was that she'd found the morning fascinating. Now that she'd started the process, she wanted to see where Gary's search would lead. Of course, this was partly because of the sprinkle of stardust surrounding him. (At one point, she'd spotted two women staring and she'd wanted to say, 'Yes, ladies. It is!') But that wasn't all. Trying to piece together Gary's background was like doing a particularly complex Sudoku.

Also, the more she engaged, the less time she had to think about herself. She'd enjoyed the previous night's research, tracing Gary's glamorous life and complicated times. She'd sat in her fluffy dressing gown and slippers, a glass of white wine at her side, and tapped and scrolled until she'd found everything worth finding. While she would never be as internet savvy as her niece, she liked to think she was improving.

Despite this, she'd struggled with some of Gary's questions and observations. She needed to be better prepared.

'When did Carrigbrack close?' asked Beth.

'Sometime in the early eighties, but the numbers began to dwindle in the mid seventies. After the nuns left, it became a centre for people with disabilities. That shut a few years later. If you see the place, you'll understand why. It's very isolated. The back of beyond – and then on another bit, as Johnny used to say.'

'Have you ever been back?'

'Gosh, no. I was so happy to get out of there, I never had any desire to return.'

Katie had made her escape from Carrigbrack – and escape was how she thought of it – in the winter of 1972. The previous summer, on a day trip to Lahinch, she'd been sitting on the low wall at the top of the beach when a wiry, wavy-haired man had sat down beside her.

'That's some day,' he'd said, before introducing himself as Johnny Carroll. Along with a group of friends, he was spending a week in Clare. Katie was with another nurse from Carrigbrack, a marble-hard Galway woman called Rita Farragher. Although they weren't especially strong friends, Rita had a car, and Katie never said no to a few hours of freedom.

Forty-six years later, she remembered the briny air and the power of the waves as they surged and fizzed towards the shore. She remembered eating salty periwinkles from a paper bag, the tinkle of pennies sliding down the coin cascade and the thump and scrape of the bumper cars. Mostly, however, she remembered Johnny's good humour and his insistence that she accompany him to the dance in the seafront ballroom.

'I've got to get back to work,' she said. 'I'm on duty first thing in the morning.'

'I'll stay off the gargle and drive you back,' he promised.

He did, too.

At the time, she'd found it hard to describe Johnny's appeal. He was an average-looking man of average height holding down a steady but unspectacular job with Dublin Corporation. Yet there was something about him, something that allowed Katie to shake off her reserve. Now, she realised that she'd fallen for his enthusiasm. Johnny saw the positive in everything. No day was dismissed as too wet, no dinner too tasteless. No neighbour was too cantankerous, no colleague too dull. Every item had its merits, every person their saving grace. In some, this near-constant sunniness would have been grating, but Johnny got away with it. It was as if he gave everyone, Katie included, permission to have a good time. He taught her that it was okay to hug people, to compliment them, to tell them you valued their friendship. Simple acts, but important ones. It seemed to her that Beth's generation possessed an easy intimacy, and she envied them that.

A year working in Carrigbrack had hardened her. So immersed was she in the home's rules and practices that she began to ignore all but the worst instances of cruelty. On more than one occasion, she snapped at a young woman over some minor issue when she should have offered comfort. True, she continued to collect the babies' bracelets; true, she jotted down the details; but she did so by rote rather than through any sense of solidarity or affection. With hindsight, she saw how she'd had to grow a shell for self-protection. Back then, she'd worried she was being brainwashed. To this day, some of her decisions gnawed at her.

The second time she met Johnny, she told him about her unhappiness. All she wanted was someone to listen. Instead he said, 'We'll have to get you out of there, Kateser.' At their third meeting, in the Imperial Hotel in Lisdoonvarna, he proposed.

Neither Oliver nor Mary Ann O'Dea was impressed by the idea of their elder daughter marrying an unknown Dubliner. In Oliver's view, the capital city was a nest of thieves and chancers where sin was rampant and women were losing the run of themselves. 'Soon enough, we'll be no better than the English,' he'd say to anyone willing to listen. He also argued that Katie was too malleable, and that Johnny was after her money. Whatever about his first claim, the second one was complete nonsense. The O'Dea family was long on respectability, short on cash. Their house was cold and rickety, with an outside toilet and mildew-infested bedrooms.

For once, Katie was determined to make her own decisions. Her parents boycotted the wedding and confined their communication to the occasional letter. No matter; she floated through those months, as light as a dandelion clock. She felt as if her life was beginning, which in a way it was. For her, Dublin was liberation. It helped that Johnny was from one of those happy families where the most serious fight was over who got to eat the skin of the rice pudding.

While her mother softened with the years, her father never fully accepted Johnny. Katie was struck by how old-fashioned this sounded. She'd effectively waited for a man to rescue her. Then, she'd been cold-shouldered by her father. Beth would be appalled. In 1972, however, it had all seemed logical.

'So, what did you make of Mr Rock 'n' Roll?' Beth was asking. They were striding along Dorset Street, past a jumble of shops: a pizza place, a bookmaker's, a Polish supermarket and a black-windowed 'adult store'.

'Do you know,' said Katie, 'I quite liked him. He's interesting. He strikes me as someone who got lucky but never quite knew how to handle his luck.'

'You're very charitable.'

'Why so?'

'When he was talking about his children, I wanted to say, "Listen, bud, if you're that careless with the family you already have, I'm not sure you deserve to find any others." There he was, talking about a son here and a daughter there. At one point, he sounded like he'd lost track of the precise numbers.'

'Did you not get the feeling that he's making more of an effort now?'

'Yeah, but only because he's knocking on a bit and the pretty ladies aren't falling at his feet.'

Katie smiled. From her vantage point, Gary was as young as the morning. She'd warmed to his low rumble of a voice and his slightly lopsided walk. Also, with his tattoos hidden beneath a shirt and jacket, he'd looked quite presentable. Still, she couldn't argue with Beth's observations. Judging by what she'd seen online, he'd lived much of his life like a bee in a field of clover. Why had his behaviour changed? she wondered.

They were approaching the Royal Canal. On one side, Croke Park rose up, more like an alien spaceship than a sports stadium. On the other, the water stretched out to Kildare and the country beyond. All these years later, Katie still got a lift from walking in her adopted city.

'I'm sorry,' she said. 'I never asked if you wanted to come to Carrigbrack. I just assumed you would.'

'Oh, you can count me in,' replied Beth. 'Now that I've heard more about the place, I'd love a look around.'

'That's great. One thing, though. Even though we won't be far from Danganstown, it's probably best if you don't mention our trip to your parents. Like I said before, I doubt your mother would understand.'

'You can relax. There's no danger I'd say anything to them.'

'I see,' said Katie, sensing this might be the time for some gentle prying. 'Is there an issue with your mam and dad?'

'Nope. Not with Dad, anyway.'

'What's my sister been up to?'

'Is it okay if we talk about it another day?'

'No bother, love. I don't want you to think I'm sticking my nose in.' This was precisely what she was doing, but an idea was beginning to take shape in Katie's head and she didn't want to fall out with Beth.

As they approached the bridge, Beth took her phone from the pocket of her denim jacket. 'I've felt several notifications,' she said as she peered at the screen, prodded it, then grinned. 'Well, what do you know? Two new enquiries, and both appear genuine.'

'Really? May I have a look?'

They turned down by the canal and found a quiet spot for Katie to examine the emails. The dark water flowed silently past.

'The first one's important,' she said. 'We'll have to tell Gary not to waste his time trying to find Edel Sheehan. She wasn't his birth mother – and she's dead. The email's from her son.'

Edel's son revealed that she'd managed to track him down. They'd become close in her final years, and he would like the wristband as a keepsake. *She was a wonderful woman,* he wrote, *who deserved much more than life gave her. I was fortunate we had some time together.*

'What about the other email?' said Beth. 'The one from the woman called Ailish?'

Katie leant back against the rough gable wall. With her free hand, she massaged her forehead. 'Do you remember the other day, when I told you about a young girl who'd been raped?'

'Uh huh.'

'I think Ailish Dwan's her daughter.'

'Oh,' said Beth. 'Oh.' She paused. 'God, that's desperate. But it's also good, if you know what I mean. What are we going to do?'

'By the looks of things, she didn't travel far. She's still in Clare. In Kilmitten. I reckon we ought to go and have a chat.'

Chapter 7

Ailish

If you asked Ailish, they did it deliberately. There was, she believed, a certain type of person who got their kicks from causing as much damage to a hotel room as a one-night stay would allow. Five-star hotel. One-star behaviour.

'Animals,' she said as she walked into Room 15. 'Out-and-out animals.'

The first thing she saw was the red-wine stain on the pale blue carpet. Then she noticed that one of the pictures had been knocked from the wall. And the smell was putrid. You'd swear someone was decomposing under the bed. She opened the windows as wide as they would go and inhaled several lungfuls of morning freshness.

A quick look at the bathroom confirmed her fears. There was a ring of scum around the bath, a layer of tan make-up on the white bath towel, and the toilet … Well, the less said about the toilet the better.

The couple who'd spent the previous night in Room 15 deserved a particularly hot corner in housekeeping hell. A special kind of hell, Ailish had invented it years earlier to house the very worst guests.

The people who tore the bed linen and spilled nail polish on the dressing table. The people who insisted on wearing muddy boots and using the wastepaper bin as an ashtray. Oh, and the people who clicked their fingers and shouted 'Maid!' in her direction.

Sometimes she wanted to say to them, 'Would you do that at home?' She knew full well, though, that the answer would be yes. Many of Rathtuskert Manor's guests could do whatever they liked at home because they had cleaners there too. Ailish divided the world in two: those who cleaned and those who let them.

And yet she enjoyed her job.

She'd had been working at the Manor for twenty years. Save for a brief period of maternity leave when her younger boy, Stevie, had been born, she'd barely taken a break. She felt as if she'd cleaned each of the forty-five rooms a million times. She was familiar with every suspect floorboard, every troublesome tap, every temperamental socket. There was nothing she didn't know about polishing smeared mirrors, unblocking sinks and removing the smell of vomit. Once, she'd been offered a promotion. The head housekeeper had left, and the general manager had suggested to Ailish that she might like to take over. She'd decided against it. Her reasoning was hard to explain. What sane person would understand why she'd prefer to push an iron cart around the Manor's uneven-floored halls and clean up the filth of others? Why would she choose to have an aching back and hands that reeked of cleaning products? Why wouldn't she want to spend her day planning and inspecting?

The truth was that she got satisfaction from her work. She took pride in her ability to transform a room. She cherished the calm of working on her own. And, daft as it sounded, she prized what the wealthier guests left behind: pricey shower gels, high-end moisturisers, American magazines, and a library's worth of books. She wouldn't be able to buy any of these luxuries for herself, and she'd be a long time waiting for anyone else to buy them for her.

Deep down, she knew that this wasn't the complete story. She just couldn't picture herself as anyone's boss. She didn't have it in her.

She was an unusual housekeeper. An outlier. She'd seen scores of others come and go. Almost all her colleagues were either under thirty or from eastern Europe, but that suited her fine. She liked the banter in the staffroom, the young ones with their stories of raucous nights out and the Polish and Lithuanian women with their tales from home.

Jodie, her daughter, maintained that cleaning had become cool.

'Honestly, Mam,' she'd said, 'there are women on Instagram and YouTube making fortunes from cleaning tips. It's all about the best way to polish your windows, or how to stop your bin from smelling.'

Ailish hadn't believed her until she'd had a look for herself. It was a mad world, and no mistake.

She hadn't told Keith about the spurned promotion. He wouldn't have understood. He was forever complaining about how little she earned. Just the other day, she'd mentioned something about saving for Christmas, and he'd got all snarky, saying there was no point in buying presents for ungrateful children or for grandchildren who'd already been given too much. Then he'd delivered a speech about her low wages. It wasn't as if he earned much himself. Ailish resisted the temptation to say so. That would be asking for trouble.

Neither would she tell her husband about the message she'd spotted that morning on the adoption noticeboard. Before caution could take over, she'd fired off a reply.

Twenty years earlier, before the nuns had handed their files over to the authorities, Ailish had attempted to track down her birth mother. She'd told them everything she knew, including her belief that she'd been born in the mother-and-baby home in Carrigbrack. No, they said, we have no record of you, and even if we had, you probably wouldn't like what you found. It was best to leave well enough alone, they claimed.

She tried again a couple of years later. Once more, she was given the run-around. Keith, voice stained with disapproval, maintained she was deluding herself. 'Listen,' he said, 'children were given away for a reason. If you turned up on your birth mother's doorstep, she'd probably die a thousand deaths.'

Ailish abandoned her search.

She knew that not everyone wanted to find their biological mother. That was grand. That was their choice. But she did. The older she got, the more she wondered about the woman who'd given her away.

Who are you? she'd think.

What happened to you?

How has life been for you?

Do you ever think about me?

She suspected that if her experience of adoption had been happier, she might not feel so haunted. While her parents had been upstanding, they'd had no warmth about them. 'You're lucky we rescued you,' her mother used to say. 'Imagine the squalor you'd have grown up in if we hadn't taken you in.' As a child, she'd twisted herself into shapes to try and earn their approval. When her behaviour had fallen short of their standards, her mother had said, 'You didn't get that from us.' Later, Ailish had rebelled. She'd left school at the first opportunity and got married at nineteen.

Bed made and carpet scrubbed, she set about cleaning the sink. The woman in the mirror wasn't the woman she wanted to see. She'd read that, after forty, you got the face you deserved. If so, she must have been a right cow. There were grooves between her nose and her mouth and smudges as black as bruises beneath her grey eyes. Her hair was too thin, her eyebrows too wayward.

Occasionally, while buffing a table or pulling hair from a plughole, she tried on other lives. She imagined she owned the hotel and cleaned rooms for the fun of it. She ran a café beside the sea. She lived on a farm in the Australian outback and rode horses every day. She was Melanie Griffith in *Working Girl* or Madonna in *Desperately Seeking Susan*. They'd been her favourite films as a teenager and remained so today. Her taste in music was the same: if she'd liked it when she was a youngster, she liked it now. Not that long ago, 'Into the Groove' had come on the radio, and Ailish had strutted around the room like a sixteen-year-old. It was only when the song had ended that she realised the bedroom door had swung open and a guest had been watching. She'd been mortified.

Truth to tell, one of the reasons she'd shied away from trying to find her birth mother was her fear of not being good enough. She was a forty-six-year-old mother of four and grandmother of two who lived in a tiny house with a husband who would cross the road to be offended. She had a mediocre Inter Cert education, a low-paying job and a fifteen-year-old Nissan Micra. It wasn't that she was complaining. She had lots of joy in her life. She just figured her biological mother would have hoped for more.

She was bracing herself for the scummy bath, when she heard her phone make a silly *bing-bong* sound. The notification alert had been chosen by Stevie – he was an awful messer – and Ailish didn't know how to change it.

Already behind time, she told herself to ignore the message. She would finish the bathroom before taking a look. But what if the *bing-bong* meant there'd been a reply from the woman who'd posted the message on the adoption website?

Ailish had to find out.

Please, she thought. Please be good news.

As she read, a flapping sensation rose in her chest, as if birds were nesting there.

The woman's name was Katie, and she had information about Ailish's birth mother. As chance would have it, she would be in Clare the following day. Would it be possible for them to meet?

Ailish considered the question for at least ten seconds. Keith wouldn't approve, but Keith would be at work. He didn't have to know.

Yes, she replied. *That would be great. What would suit?*

Chapter 8

Katie

They left early for Carrigbrack, far earlier, Katie suspected, than Gary would have liked. For a long time, he spoke only to complain about the failings of other drivers.

Beth, on the other hand, was a morning person. She chatted away in the back of the car – a disappointingly boring Volvo – about her friends in Stoneybatter and what she was expecting from her new job. She threw the occasional question in Gary's direction, but got little in return.

'You live near Enniskerry? That must be beautiful?'

'It is.'

'And are your family nearby?'

'Stepaside,' he said, his voice gruff.

Katie felt compelled to fill the vacuum. As they passed the exit for Naas, she updated them on the responses to the forum. The night before, Carrigbrack Nurse had received another email, this time from a woman who'd already traced her birth mother. While the reunion hadn't gone well, she wanted her identity band. *Don't mind the online whingers*, she wrote. *You are doing a GOOD THING.* Katie promised that the bracelet would be with her soon. As for her critics, she found herself drawn towards their posts. Not that she'd say this to Beth. Her niece had little patience for the forum's more caustic members.

'Some folks shouldn't be allowed to have paper and crayons let alone access to the internet,' she'd said.

Katie would admit that there was something disturbing about her compulsion to read the judgements of people she'd never met.

You took part in this barbarity and now you're hoping for absolution? wrote one.

Where's your remorse? asked another.

You supported a vile regime. What did you do to stop it? added a third.

Even as her heartbeat accelerated, she continued reading.

Gary was unruffled by the news that Edel Sheehan couldn't have been his birth mother. 'It's cool that I've found out now rather than a few months down the line,' he said. 'I'll just move on to the next name on the list.'

'And will you be doing the work yourself?' asked Katie.

'I don't see why not.'

'I hope I'm not being presumptuous here, but I expect you have a few euro in the bank. Would it not be easier to hire a genealogist … or even a private detective?'

'Maybe. For the time being, though, I'll do my own thing. I've got plenty of time.'

'Won't you have to go back to the band? I mean, I know you've been having a bit of a break and …' Katie realised that she had wandered into sensitive territory, and she allowed her voice to trail off.

'No,' replied Gary. 'That won't be happening.'

He offered no further information, the conversation stalled, and for a while they travelled in silence. Katie watched the signs flash by. Monasterevin. Portlaoise. Mountrath. She remembered making the journey west with Johnny. Back then, they'd had to travel through a succession of towns and villages. These days, every last one was bypassed. It was almost as if they no longer existed. Although the morning was bright, it was the sort of bright that said, 'Don't be fooled, I could change at any minute.' Autumn was moving in.

At Katie's suggestion, they left the motorway at Birdhill and drove to Killaloe for coffee. Afterwards, they went for a walk beside the Shannon, the water clear as glass, the trees a deep green.

'County Clare,' said Gary, like a man visiting a foreign country.

'Has it been a while since you were over this way?' asked Katie.

'It's my first time.'

'Really?'

'Yeah. I joined the band when I was fourteen, and most of the gigs we played were in Dublin and Cork. I was nineteen when we went to America. There was never any reason to visit this part of the world. Well, that's not entirely true. I've been to Connemara. I was in Kerry once too … with my first wife. But, apart from an emergency stop at Shannon Airport, this is my first time in Clare.'

'Except it's not,' pointed out Beth. 'You were born here.'

Gary came to an abrupt halt. He ran a hand through his hair and smiled his slow smile. 'I guess you're right. I guess I'm a Clare man.'

Beth laughed. 'On behalf of the natives, may I say we're happy to claim you. By the way, Katie and I are from up that way.' She gestured past the marina and upriver.

Katie felt a ridiculous pride at the simple beauty of the landscape. No matter that she'd left nearly fifty years before, she wanted outsiders to admire her home. She also had a fresh appreciation of how much Gary's world was shifting. 'There's not much in Danganstown.' she said. 'We'll spare you the tour.'

'The girls … women, I mean … in Carrigbrack, were they mostly local?'

'When I was there, some were from as far away as Cork and Dublin. There was a handful of mothers from Limerick and Galway, a couple from Sligo and Tipperary. But, yes, they were mostly local. If I recall correctly, two of the women on your own list were from Clare.'

Gary looked out over the river. 'So it's possible my birth mother came from around here?'

'I suppose it is.'

'She might be in this area now?'

'Yes.'

Afterwards, Gary opened up, and as they motored towards Carrigbrack, he offered small pieces of information. Before retirement, his father had been a teacher, his mother a school secretary. He hadn't told them about today's trip because he wasn't sure how they'd react. Neither had he spoken to his sisters.

Beth told him about growing up as the only girl in a large family, and about her tricky relationship with her home village. 'I'm fond of the place,' she said, 'but I don't think I could live there. If that makes sense.'

'It does,' he said, his tone that of a man who'd run away from home at nineteen and kept on running. His escape Katie could understand. What she found harder to fathom was his return. If Gary wanted a strong relationship with Allegra, why wasn't he in Los Angeles?

'The problem with being from a small place,' said Beth, 'is that you're expected to have an opinion about everybody. And I could never be bothered.'

'What about your own kids?' Gary asked Katie. 'Do they live in Dublin?'

'Johnny and I didn't have children.'

'Oh, I'm sorry. I just assumed … Nah, scratch that, it's none of my business.'

Katie wasn't surprised by Gary's assumption or by his ham-fisted attempt at recovery. In her experience, strangers often asked the questions that friends couldn't. More than ever, she wished they'd had a son or daughter, if only because it would mean some part of her husband had been left behind.

'We're not far away,' she said. 'You'd want to keep an eye out for the sign.'

Gradually, the landscape was changing, the fields turning to stone. The former mother-and-baby home was a mile or so from the village of Carrigbrack, on the edge of the Burren. Beth began a commentary on the area. She spoke about the limestone, the rare plants, the dolmens, the high crosses and ring forts.

'Sorry for sounding like the sixth-class geography book,' she said to Gary. 'I can't help myself. Dad used to bring us here as kids, and every time he'd give the same lecture about the wonders of the place. We'd all be wriggling in the back, asking when we were stopping for ice cream. He never mentioned that this was also a convenient spot for hiding a pregnant daughter.'

By now, they were on one of those narrow west-of-Ireland roads with a stripe of grass along the centre and unruly hedges on either side. Even to call it a road was to exaggerate its status. The hedges were laden with blackberries and rosehips. When the lane snaked to the left, they abandoned the car and walked the last short stretch. Gary strode on ahead with Beth a step or two behind and Katie at the rear. She couldn't quite believe that she was back.

What struck her most was the absence of noise. The breeze was too light to make a sound, the birds unusually subdued. The only sign of life came from a large hare that bounded onto the lane, took one look at them and scampered off again.

The tall iron gate, once so forbidding, hung open. The padlock and chain were smashed and scabbed with rust.

'This is it, then,' said Gary. 'The infamous Carrigbrack.'

Katie nodded.

The former home consisted of a series of grey buildings, some long and narrow, others small and squat. All were crumbling. The main house sagged. Branches and weeds poked through the roof. The windows were boarded up, and white paint peeled from the warped front door. An abandoned car was slowly disintegrating outside what had once been the nursery. Black rubbish sacks were heaped beside the main dormitory. Clumps of nettles had sprung up everywhere. The smell of decay, while faint, was unmistakable.

Beth touched Katie's shoulder. 'What's it like to be here again?'

'Odd,' was all she could say in reply. 'Odd.'

If she tried to say anything more, it would be incoherent. She'd been pitched back to a different time. A different century. And, in that moment, she was frozen. Girls milled around; some cleaning, others in the kitchen, more in the walled garden. A fortunate few were in the nursery, the unluckiest ones in the laundry. All wore the same drab blue uniform, its cloth chafing against their skin. There were determined faces, stoic faces, mischievous faces, but many of the women appeared beaten down and wary. The light had been turned off in their eyes. Sister Agnes patrolled the halls, her face round and pink-cheeked, her voice as thin and sharp as a razor. There too was Sister Sabina, permanently on the lookout for breaches of the rules. Sabina, who had the doleful eyes and emaciated face of a character from an El Greco painting, divided the girls into two groups: those she regarded as capable of reform and those dismissed as beyond redemption. In every case, she told them their shame would follow them forever. Beside her was Sister Faustina, who always looked like she'd rather be somewhere – anywhere – else. Faustina was obsessive about the rules. A couple of the other nuns were kinder, more flexible.

Katie wondered, as she had all those years ago, if kindness could cut you open more effectively than cruelty. The girls, of course, said nothing. Talking was forbidden.

Her mind lurched forward again. There were few nuns left now. Those that remained tended to do good work. Others, the ones who'd had power, hid behind public relations companies.

Gary's voice broke through her thoughts. 'I was just asking,' he said, 'if there was a doctor here.'

'No. There was a midwife, an older woman who'd been in the home for years. And then there was me and another nurse.'

'What happened if a child was ill?'

'You did your best, and they either recovered …' she faltered, 'or they didn't.'

Gary looked away.

'Is it what you were expecting?' she asked.

'Yes and no. Knowing that once upon a time this place was full of life feels strange.'

The wind was getting up now, the sky filling in.

'Come on,' said Beth, 'let's go and look around the back before it starts to rain.'

At first glance, the back of the site looked like derelict ground. Katie knew otherwise. This was the part of their trip she'd been dreading.

A dilapidated wall was dotted at irregular intervals with rusty nails. Some were clearly visible. Others were obscured by brambles. A single headstone stood nearby. *In Memory of the Little Angels*, it said.

'I was reading about this,' said Beth. 'This is where the babies were buried. The nails give a rough indication of where the graves are.'

'But how can you tell which grave is which?' asked Gary.

'You can't,' said Katie. 'That was the point.' A heaviness came over her; a sense that, like the buildings, she could crumble into the ground. 'The nuns didn't want anyone making a fuss.'

'What I'll never get,' said Beth, her face shining with the zeal of the recently converted, 'is how women could be so hard on other women.'

Katie felt a snap of pain across her forehead, as if she'd been struck. 'I know I should have complained. If nothing else, I should have done something to make sure the children were given a proper burial. When I think—'

'I wasn't having a go at you, Katie. That's not what I meant.'

They stood in silence, Katie blinking back tears. Beth placed an arm around her. Gary stared at the ground.

'I think this is the saddest place I've ever been,' said Beth. 'I can't imagine how difficult it must be for you. Please forgive me for putting my foot in it. You did your job, and I'm sure you did it well.'

'You're fine, lovey,' said Katie. 'There's nothing to forgive. Unless you were here in those days, it's hard to understand what it was like – and why everyone behaved the way they did. To try and answer the question you asked: in some cases, the nuns were blinded by religious belief. In others, well … we all like to have someone to look down on, don't we?' She turned towards Gary. 'Has coming here helped you at all? I mean, it doesn't really bring you any closer to finding your birth mother, does it?'

'No, but I'm glad we made the journey. It makes her, whoever she was, feel more real.' He paused. 'And thanks for coming with me. It's obviously not easy for you.'

When they got back to the car, the first drops of rain were landing on the windows. Gary reached into the glove box, took out a bag and passed it to Katie. 'I meant to give you this earlier. It's about the right size, I think.'

The bag contained a cover for her old notebook. Made of emerald-green leather, it was perfect.

'I wouldn't want the notebook to fall apart,' he said, 'not while you still have work to do.'

'Thank you,' replied Katie. 'That's ... that's very kind.'

'Aw, it's nothing,' replied Gary, apparently embarrassed by his own thoughtfulness.

As they left Carrigbrack, Katie turned towards the passenger window, rested her forehead against the glass and closed her eyes.

The door was answered by a small, spare-framed woman in a maroon top and trousers; so small and spare-framed that Katie, who was handy-sized at best, felt like a giant.

'Katie?' said the woman.

'That's me. You must be Ailish.'

'The very woman. Come in before you get soaked. You'll have to forgive the gear. I'm just home from work and I haven't had the chance to get changed.'

The rain, which had fallen intermittently on their journey to Kilmitten, had suddenly intensified. Before stepping into the hall, Katie turned and waved to Gary and Beth, who'd spotted a café a short way down the street. The downpour hit her face like a fistful of gravel. Gary, who'd stopped to pull on a black woolly hat, waved back.

'Is that ...?' started Ailish. 'No, obviously not.'

Katie shrugged off her anorak. Even in a leather jacket and jeans, with wild hair and several days of stubble, Gary stood out. He looked like someone who ought to be famous.

'What were you going to ask?' she said, finding it hard to keep the insider knowledge from her voice.

'Ah, nothing. I just thought I recognised the man you were with. Come in and I'll put the kettle on.'

'You probably did.'

Ailish's delicate face was split by a huge grin. There was a gap between her front teeth. 'You mean that genuinely was Gary Winters?'

'I do.'

'Nooo.' She clapped her hands with joy. 'I can't believe you know him. When I was young, I was a massive fan of Black Iris. Massive. I remember leaving the children with Keith – that's my husband – so myself and my friend could go and see them in Slane. The bus didn't get back until seven the next morning. I thought Keith would go insane.' She clapped again. 'But it was worth it. Totally worth it.'

'If I'd any idea you were a fan, I'd have asked him to come over and say hello.' Katie wasn't sure that this was true. Neither was she sure that Gary would have agreed. In her limited experience, he could be warm and chatty one minute, withdrawn bordering on sullen the next. Ailish might be disappointed by her hero.

By this point, they were in the next room. The house was in the middle of a pale pebble-dashed terrace, and its kitchen was small and functional. The cupboards were a yellowish cream, the table chipped brown Formica, and the fridge hummed in a manner that suggested its best days were behind it. The room was saved by little touches of life: a photo of a group of women all glossed up for a night out, a child's multicoloured painting, and, pinned to the fridge, a local newspaper clipping about a victorious football team.

Katie sat down while Ailish filled the kettle. She was still smiling. 'Forgive my nosiness, but what's Gary Winters doing in Kilmitten? Are you related? And who's the young woman? Is she his wife or girlfriend or something?'

'No, that's Beth. She's my niece. Gary's …' Katie hesitated. While she shouldn't break a confidence, she reckoned Ailish deserved an exemption from the rule. 'We've been visiting Carrigbrack. Gary's trying to learn more about his background too.' She gave a carefully edited version of the story.

Ailish put down the mugs she'd taken from the cupboard and turned around. 'You're saying I was born in the same place as Gary Winters?'

'Yes.'

'And I may have been there at the same time?'

'There's only three months between you, so it's almost certain that you were. The difference is, I remember you. Unfortunately, I don't remember him.'

'So what you're saying is, Gary and me – we're part of the same gang?'

'I suppose I am.'

'That's amazing. I swear to God, if I learn nothing else, I'm happy knowing that.' She took a white box from a bag and placed its contents – four dainty cakes – onto a plate. The cakes were elaborately iced, like the ones served with afternoon tea in pricey hotels. 'I knew I wouldn't have the chance to get to the shop,' she explained, 'so I took these from work. Anyway, they owe me. I had to clean three extra rooms today, and two of them looked like a pack of hounds had been let loose.'

Katie knew that Ailish was a chambermaid and that she was married with four children. Her knowledge ended there. Unlike Gary, Ailish Dwan had left no imprint on the World Wide Web.

For a few minutes, the two women drank tea and traded titbits of information. Ailish revealed that, in the past, she'd made fruitless attempts to track down her birth mother and that Keith hadn't approved. This time, she hadn't told him. Thankfully, he wasn't due back from work for a couple of hours. Three of their children were in their twenties and had left home. Their youngest, Stevie, was at a friend's house. Not, Ailish added, that he'd have any difficulty with what she was doing.

'But just say he let something slip to his father,' she said, 'where would we be then?'

'Will it not be hard for you to make progress without telling your husband?' asked Katie.

Ailish's large grey eyes were troubled. 'For years, I tried not to think about it. I told myself there was nothing more I could do, and that maybe my birth mother wouldn't want to meet me anyway. The problem is, I can't stop wondering. I hear other people's stories and, even when they don't work out, I find myself thinking, at least they did their best. Every day, I follow the stuff in the papers and online. I read the forums and whatnot. And I've never been more certain about anything. I've got to do this.'

'What if Keith finds out?'

'We've been married for twenty-seven years, and I don't want to fall out with him, so I've decided I'll do as much as possible without telling him. But, in the end, he'll have to accept my decision.'

There was a slight wobble in Ailish's voice, enough for Katie to gather that this was hard for her. 'Are your adoptive parents still alive?' she asked.

'No.'

She waited while Ailish picked the icing from one of the cakes.

'Mam and Dad were "good" people.' Ailish didn't make the air quotes; she didn't need to. 'I was their only child, and I think the nuns chose them for their devotion to the Church rather than any fondness for children. No matter what I did, they were unimpressed. I was never smart enough or polite enough. I never looked right. They'd hoped for an obedient girl, someone they'd be able to shape. Instead, they got scrappy old me.'

'I'm sorry it didn't work out.'

Ailish nibbled the cake before responding. 'They did their best. I did too. We kept in contact after I left home, but we were never close.'

Although she said no more, there were worlds of information in her silence.

'So, then,' said Katie, 'you'll be wanting this.' She handed over a padded brown envelope. 'It contains some information, and I'll do my best to answer your questions.'

Ailish opened the envelope and took out the paper bracelet. She passed it from one hand to the other and back again. 'So tiny,' she said. Then she read the details, the same details that a few days earlier had moved Beth to tears. 'I was Jacqueline. Jacqueline Culligan.' She took a deep breath. Then another. When she spoke, her voice was flecked with pain. 'My mother picked a lovely name for me. Was Hanora her real name?'

'No. Her name was Chrissie.'

'Do you have any idea where she was from?'

'She was from somewhere in County Clare, but I'm afraid I can't remember the exact spot.'

Although her voice remained low, Ailish's smile returned. 'She's local, though. Isn't that brilliant? She might be down the road. Do you know anything else about her?'

Katie wasn't sure how much was hers to tell. She'd run it all past Beth, and they'd agreed that one fact would emerge anyway. The rest was up to Chrissie.

'There's something you should be aware of,' she said. 'Your mother was young.'

'I see. Like seventeen or eighteen? I was only twenty when my eldest was born, and, believe it or not, she got pregnant at the same age. I was ripping with her. Jodie's not like me. She's clever. I remember shouting at her, "You could have done anything with your life, and now you'll be stuck here like the rest of us."'

'Where is she now?'

'She's three hundred yards away, in the new houses beside the church. And you know what? I was wrong. Her partner's a great fellow, and everything's worked out okay for them. They have two kids, and Jodie's in college, studying business, no less. I wish I knew where she got her brains from.'

'That's great to hear.' Katie swallowed. While she prepared herself for the next part of the story, Ailish placed the bracelet back in the envelope and put it in her bag.

'I don't want anything to happen to it,' she said, 'not after you've minded it so well.'

'The thing is …' Katie paused, 'when I said Chrissie was young, I meant very young. She was fourteen.'

The words floated between them.

Ailish raised a hand to her mouth. It was older than her face, the hand of someone who'd done decades of cleaning. 'Oh, bless her. Imagine being sent to that place when she was only a baby herself. She must have been petrified. Was she all right? Were people nice to her?'

'From what I can recall, she was fine. Or as fine as she could be. When I left Carrigbrack, she was still there. You know the way it worked: she had to spend another while in the kitchen or the laundry to meet the cost of her stay.'

'Pfft. I've read about that carry-on. The fucking pettiness of it, if you'll excuse my language.'

'No apologies needed. It was a terrible practice.'

'Do you know what happened? Like, did she have a boyfriend?'

'I don't know,' said Katie, hoping her lie wasn't obvious.

Ailish's eyes filled with tears. 'Don't mind me. I swore I wouldn't get emotional, but it's hard, isn't it? Do you recall what she looked like?'

'Petite. Red hair. Big eyes. A lot like you.'

Ailish's mouth twisted and she began to sob, spasms passing through her thin body. Her shoulders rose and fell, rose and fell. 'The poor thing. All these years, I thought she'd given me away because I wasn't good enough. You'll probably say that's stupid, but it's how I felt. And there she was, only a little girl. I doubt anybody asked what she wanted.'

Katie reached over and rubbed Ailish's hand. 'She wouldn't have been able to care for you. You see that, don't you?'

'But her family would. They could have looked after us.'

'You can't say that. You don't know their circumstances.'

'I suppose.'

'They may have been given no choice.' Katie took a packet of tissues from her bag and handed them across the table. 'No doubt you've heard what it was like: the whispers and the nasty looks and all the local busybodies gathering around until the priest knocked on the door. Many ordinary families were given no say in their daughter's fate.'

Ailish blew her nose and dabbed at her face. 'Trust me, it wasn't much better when I was a teenager. There were people around here who got their entertainment from looking down on the rest of us. Anyway, that settles it. I need to find her.'

Earlier, in Carrigbrack, Katie's doubts had returned. She'd questioned whether she was robust enough for the task. Dedicated enough. Those misgivings had evaporated. She was helping Gary and she would help Ailish.

Something else occurred to her. 'I'd better get going,' she said, 'but before I do, I'll give Gary and Beth a ring. I'd say he'd like to meet you. You've got a lot in common.'

Panic flashed across Ailish's face. 'Oh no, I couldn't. Not here. The state of the place. And the state of me! In my manky uniform with my face all blotchy and my eyes red.'

'Don't worry about any of that. You look grand. And Gary will understand that this is an emotional day for you.'

'I'm pleading with you, Katie. I know you mean well, but Gary Winters wouldn't want to meet the likes of me. Please.'

'If you're sure …'

'I'm sure.'

They heard the front door open, then close again with a sharp click.

'Oh hell,' whispered Ailish. 'I hadn't expected him for hours yet. How are we going to explain—?'

'Ailish!' came a roar. 'Who owns the coat in the hall?'

A man entered the kitchen. A solid slab of a fellow with shaggy eyebrows and skin like corned beef, Keith was as tall as his wife was tiny. 'What's the story?' he asked.

'Well ...' said Ailish.

Katie stood and put out her hand. 'Mr Dwan, how nice to meet you. Katie Carroll's my name. My niece and I have been staying in Rathtuskert Manor. Ailish looked after us so well that when we were leaving we went to say goodbye. Well, we were devastated to learn that she'd already finished for the day. Thankfully, the manager was kind enough to pass on her number, and I invited myself in for a cup of tea.' She smiled what she hoped was her sweetest smile. 'My niece is having a look around the village. I was just about to leave.'

Reluctantly, he shook her hand. 'You do know there are laws against that class of thing. A worker is entitled to privacy.'

'Mrs Carroll's been very good,' said Ailish, her tone suggesting that cash had changed hands.

It was enough to placate Keith. 'That's decent of you. Plenty of rich folks have stayed in that hotel, some of them rotten with money, and they haven't left as much as two euro for Ailish.'

'That's shocking,' said Katie. 'I find manners aren't what they used to be.'

'How right you are,' he said. 'Mind you, Ailish can be her own worst enemy. I'm worn out from telling her she's too timid.'

Katie guessed that this wasn't all he told her. Keith struck her as a man who valued his own opinion. No wonder his wife was so nervous. She picked up her bag. 'I'd better make a move. It was a pleasure to meet you, Mr Dwan. Your wife's a fantastic woman. And Ailish, promise me you'll stay in touch.'

'Don't worry,' she said, 'you haven't heard the last of me.'

Chapter 9

Then, Patricia

It started with the rat.

They were in the walled garden, picking strawberries, when it ran across Jacinta's foot. Jacinta was a tall, snippy girl from the Ennis Road in Limerick. Patricia knew where she was from because she mentioned it – a lot. Although the Ennis Road meant nothing to most of them, they guessed it was a well-to-do area and that Jacinta wanted everyone to understand that she wasn't a lower-class scrubber. She also moaned – a lot – about getting fat.

'I wonder,' said Winnie, 'if she's noticed that she's single, nine months pregnant and living in a prison full of women. She might have more serious problems than putting on a few pounds.'

The rat – a greasy, long-tailed creature – scurried over Jacinta's foot before veering left into the blackcurrant bushes. Many girls would have shuddered. A hardy few would have taken it in their stride. Jacinta began squealing. In a blink, she was bawling like a banshee.

Sister Sabina, who was a short distance away, shouted at her to stop. When her instruction was ignored, she tried again.

'Quieten down, will you,' she said, her voice twanging with irritation. 'It was only a mouse.'

'It was a rat,' said Jacinta. 'A dirty, disgusting rat. He could have bitten me. My baby could have died.'

'Whatever it was, it's gone, so put an end to your snivelling and get back to work.'

Jacinta resumed her keening.

The June day was warm, the sun prickling their skin. If you asked Patricia, Jacinta shouldn't have been at work. She should have been inside with her feet up, waiting for her big day. Her baby was due within the next couple of weeks. Patricia herself was hot and uncomfortable, and her baby wasn't due for two months.

Jacinta was a messy crier, her face scrunched up with misery, her body shaking. Eventually, Sabina walked over and slapped her – *thwack* – across the cheek. For half a moment, Jacinta stopped, only to start up again even louder than before. Sabina administered another slap and received the same response. Jacinta had worked herself into a frenzy.

Patricia was disturbed by the scene. Although they were treated like errant schoolgirls, most of them – Jacinta included – were grown women. No matter that the regime was strict; the nuns weren't supposed to engage in physical punishment.

Winnie stood up. 'Ah, Sister,' she said, 'will you look at the cut of her … and her about to give birth at any minute. She's in a bad way.'

'Winnie, this is none of your concern. You've a job to do. Those strawberries won't pick themselves.'

'She has a point, though,' said Patricia, getting to her feet too. 'Imagine if Jacinta was so upset that something happened to her or the baby. I gather her parents are well connected.'

Jacinta gave a loud sniffle of acknowledgement.

Patricia raised an eyebrow at Sabina, her way of saying *I have the measure of you*. The letter from her parents, in which they'd essentially said that Mike's happiness and well-being were more important than hers, had knocked something loose in her. She was less deferential than before. Less respectful. She also dwelled on what they'd said about Mike's wife. Patricia hadn't known that Vera was pregnant. The information made her feel dirty.

Winnie looked at her and nodded. 'As I understand it, Sister, Jacinta's people have a fair bit of money.'

As often as the Carrigbrack women were told that they were all the same, they knew this was untrue. Some sinners were more equal than others.

For at least a minute they stood there, staring at each other. Six girls who'd been working nearby also got to their feet. One of them, a tiny little thing who said she was fourteen but might be younger, looked terrified.

Finally Sabina sighed and said, 'This pathetic behaviour is distracting us from our task. Come on, Jacinta, you'd better go indoors for a while so you can regain control of yourself. The rest of you can return to the strawberries. I'll be back shortly, and have no doubt, if I hear any chatter, there will be consequences.' She glanced at Jacinta. 'Like I always say, empty vessels make the most sound.'

In Sabina's absence, they worked slowly. As Winnie put it, 'One strawberry for the bucket, one for the mouth.' Patricia and the others followed her example. It wasn't as though they were stealing from their own table. Most of the soft fruit was either sold or turned into jam. The girls rarely got jam, and, on such a hot day, the strawberries were delicious.

The food in Carrigbrack was meagre and poorly cooked. Their diet consisted of porridge, soup, bread and fatty bacon. Everything was either too watery or too lumpy, too cold or guaranteed to scald your mouth. They suspected the nun who ran the kitchen went out of her way to ensure the meals were borderline inedible. Otherwise, they might get pleasure from their food, and pleasure was forbidden.

They ate because they were hungry and because their babies deserved the nutrition.

'All we need is a jug of cream,' said Patricia, wiping the juice from her chin.

Winnie grinned. 'Aren't you the fancy one with your cream?'

'My father used to say, "I don't know where you get your notions from."'

'Are you sure he's not related to my old man? He says exactly the same thing.'

When she wasn't chewing, or teasing Patricia, Winnie was singing to herself. After Sabina returned, she continued. While her friend wasn't especially tuneful, Patricia thought she recognised 'The Mountains of Mourne'.

'How many times do you have to be told to work in silence?' asked the nun.

'We're not allowed to talk. Nobody told us not to sing.'

'I'm telling you.'

'Grand, so,' said Winnie, who hummed instead.

Sabina walked towards her. 'You're determined to cause trouble, aren't you?'

'Not really.'

'We've had some cheap straps in here, but you're among the worst of them. I've always thought that some girls are led astray and others, God help them, are abused. But the likes of you? You're pure bad. If I had my way, you'd be kept in here indefinitely.'

Patricia wondered if Sabina genuinely believed this. If so, what had happened to sour her view of human nature and strip her of empathy? Yes, Winnie could be cheeky. But she was also as kind as the day was long. She'd been the first to support Jacinta, a girl she didn't particularly like.

Winnie stood up. 'Hold on a—'

Sabina was warming to her theme. 'You're a disgrace to your

family. No wonder they threw you out. Mind you, they've questions to answer themselves. If they'd made any attempt to teach you right from wrong, you'd still be above in Sligo studying your books. Now do as you're told.'

Again, Winnie looked like she wanted to say something. Instead, she paused, stuck out her chin and began to sing.

'*I believe that when writing, a wish you expressed …*'

She faltered, and for what felt like an agonisingly long time, there was silence. Patricia looked at her friend. There were tears in her eyes, a reminder that, for all her bravado, she was only sixteen. Patricia stood and finished the line: '*As to how the fine ladies in London are dressed.*'

From the other side of the garden, a third girl joined them: '*Well, if you'll believe me, when asked to a ball …*'

And then a fourth: '*They don't wear no tops to their dresses at all.*'

By the time they'd reached the final line, all eight workers were singing.

'That's enough,' said Sabina, with a brisk clap of her hands. 'In fact, that's more than enough. I want you to get back to work. Except you, Winnie – you're coming inside with me.'

Patricia didn't know many songs, and most of those she did know were religious. But the warmth of the day and the nastiness of Sabina's words had combined to create a restive atmosphere. This was no time to give up. She cleared her throat and began:

'*When boyhood's fire was in my blood,*
I read of ancient freemen,
For Greece and Rome who bravely stood,
Three hundred men and three men.'

Once more, Winnie and the others joined in. That only a couple of them had strong voices didn't matter. When they all came together, they sounded formidable.

Sabina hadn't bargained for mass insubordination. 'You'll stop that racket,' she said, 'and you'll stop it immediately. Do you hear?'

Emboldened, they sang on. Their repertoire was short but varied. After 'A Nation Once Again', they tried 'Daydream Believer'. This segued into 'Hey Jude' which somehow led to 'An Poc Ar Buile'. Here they were, cut off from the rest of the world, with no audience but themselves, their voices lifting and soaring. They sang with spirit and exuberance, and occasionally they even sang in tune. When they forgot the words, they *la la la*-ed. When a girl paused for breath, another took over. At one point, Patricia's baby delivered an almighty kick, but still she sang.

They were a ragtag bunch, their stomachs swelling against their ugly uniforms, their hair tied up in topknots, their faces pink from heat and exertion. They'd been assaulted, abandoned, discarded, left in the lurch. They'd been branded, insulted and punished. They were sluts, tramps, whores, fallen women. Their babies would be taken from them without consideration or permission.

And still they sang.

At first, Sabina shouted at them. When this didn't deliver, she poured scorn upon them, their families and their pregnancies. She spoke in an assortment of monosyllables and grunts. At one stage, she mentioned the devil. She was no fool, however, and after a while she went in search of reinforcements. Presumably, she also hoped her absence would bring their singing to a halt.

Briefly, they did stop. The sun was scorching through the cloth of their uniforms and beating down on their bare heads. They needed a rest. The arrival of Sister Agnes rekindled their enthusiasm. Oh, and there was something else. Something remarkable. The respite was long enough for them to hear the faint but unmistakable sound of 'Black Velvet Band' drifting from the main house. Their protest had spread.

Agnes was white with anger. Two deep pleats formed at the top of her nose. She made no attempt to silence the women, however. She told them to leave the buckets of strawberries behind and return to the house. Two by two, they linked arms and, like refugees from a musical Noah's Ark, did as she asked. On their way, they sang 'The West's Awake'.

Inside, they were met by more singing. From the kitchen, they could hear 'All You Need Is Love'. The girls in the laundry sang 'The Raggle Taggle Gypsy', while in the nursery a lone voice performed 'Oklahoma'. Several babies did their best to follow the soloist's lead. Sister Agnes and some of the other nuns ushered all the women into the refectory and closed the doors. They would be corralled there until thirst, exhaustion or the need to go to the lavatory forced them to stop.

Patricia saw Sister Eunice standing beside a dresser. The nun smiled before quickly turning away.

For an hour or more the women continued, pausing only to listen to Bernadette, a shy slip of a girl from Tipperary. It was unusual to hear her speak, let alone sing. She stood at the top of the room, closed her eyes and sang 'We Shall Overcome'. Her voice was powerful and pure. None of them would have guessed at her talent.

Even as Bernadette's voice floated over the room, and even as Patricia hummed along, she knew it was a lie. She doubted that all of them would overcome. She also knew that this harmless revolt would be punished. In that moment, though, they were united against a common opposition: not just the nuns, but every damn thing that had caused them to be trapped in Carrigbrack.

What Patricia felt then was as close to joy as she had experienced in a long time.

Chapter 10

Gary

It was odd that such a bleak experience could be so energising, but after his visit to Carrigbrack, Gary was doubly determined to find his birth mother. At the start, he'd been irritated by Katie's plans for a detour. He hadn't wanted to drive to some throwback of a village so she could hand over a bracelet to a woman lucky enough to know her own mother's identity. Now, he regretted not calling in to Ailish's house to say hello. It wasn't so much the news that she was a Black Iris fan that had changed his mind, as something Beth had said while they waited in the café.

'This could have been your life,' she'd said, as rain pecked the window. 'You could have been brought up in Kilmitten. Maybe you'd still be here, working nine to five and looking forward to a quiet pint in some kip of a bar.'

She had a no-nonsense way of speaking that made her pronouncements difficult to challenge. That didn't stop him from trying.

'I suppose. But who's to say I wouldn't have ended up in a band anyway? I might have had the same experience only with a different bunch of guys.'

Beth blew across the top of her cappuccino. 'That's true. I'm not saying you wouldn't have had the talent. I'm just suggesting there would have been more obstacles in your way.'

'So I should thank the stars I was born two months before Ailish and got my parents rather than hers?'

'That's about the size of it, yeah. It's unbelievable to think the two of you were in that awful place at the same time. You're part of the same tribe, if you get my drift.'

He did, and it was.

She was an attractive woman, Beth. Gary liked how animated she was. Physically, she was right too. He'd always preferred his women on the chiselled side. He'd considered making a move, but had a feeling he might not be her type.

The following morning, he sat at his desk, making lists, jotting down possibilities, adding and subtracting. According to Katie, his birth mother was likely to be one of four women. Two had been from Clare, one from Galway and one from Kerry. Of these, he reckoned Olivia Farnham was the leading candidate. Admittedly, he had no hard evidence to support his theory. He just liked the fact that she'd tried to run away. The idea of his birth mother being a bit of a badass appealed to him. He pictured her, dark and gangly, setting out from Carrigbrack, giving hell to the nuns and whoever else got in her way.

He already knew that officialdom was unlikely to be of much assistance. Officially, the boy born in Carrigbrack in the summer of '71, the bass player, father and sometime husband, didn't exist. Olivia Farnham hadn't given birth to a son; Lillian Winters had. All the authorities could do was confirm this.

There must, though, be a record of Olivia. According to Katie's notebook, she'd been twenty in August 1971, which meant she'd been born in 1951 or in the last five months of 1950. The notes also said she was from Clare. It was a substantial county but an underpopulated one, and Farnham wasn't a common name.

'I'm going to find you,' he said aloud.

That was the trouble with being on your own in a large house in the countryside. You ended up talking to people who weren't there: to ghosts and former friends and women who might be your mother.

After he'd abandoned LA, Gary had spent a few months in the apartment he owned in Dalkey. For twenty-five years, most of his visits home had been brief. He'd returned for concerts or big family events. Actually living in Dublin was strange. He'd left in 1990, when the city had felt suffocatingly small. Everyone you met had been to school with someone you knew or had slept with your cousin or played a gig with your neighbour. The place had teemed with bands, all of them sharing the same teenage dream, all of them wanting to be the next U2 while insisting that wasn't the case. A&R men had trawled the city for youngsters who sounded and looked like they might be famous. They'd all competed to be the wildest and the hottest, and Black Iris had won.

In 1990, kids had still got unreasonably excited about a trip to McDonald's, and the opening of a British high street store had been regarded as a national event. Girls in bikinis had made a living from photo shoots at the top of Grafton Street, the dole had been less than fifty pounds a week, and everything had been faded and broken. Dublin had been parochial, homogeneous, more of a town than a city. By the time Gary returned, many of his reference points were gone. Unknown people lived in unknown suburbs. Teenage girls spoke like they were from Calabasas and dressed like junior Kardashians. There were fewer bands, but everyone had a YouTube channel, a blog or a podcast. The city wasn't uniformly white. Women wore Repealed sweatshirts, and guys held hands in the street.

There were troubles, too, troubles from which Gary was insulated.

News bulletins warned of the growing scourge of homelessness. The papers reported that qualified people with responsible jobs were living four to a room while families with children were spending months in tiny hotel rooms.

Still, in almost every other way, this Dublin was better than the one he'd left behind. It had thrived without him. The problem was, it no longer felt like home. Then again, he wasn't sure that anywhere else did either.

That wasn't all. Gary had spent twenty-five years behind a velvet rope. Life in Ireland was less sheltered. To show that success had changed you was to invite mockery. To begin with, his family was delighted to see more of him. After a while, his novelty value dimmed, and his parents became suspicious. Why had he returned on his own? Was he sick or in trouble? What would he do with his house in America? Where were the rest of the band?

He dodged and deflected until they gave up.

It didn't take long for him to grow tired of the apartment. When you were accustomed to thousands of square feet, a two-bedroom flat was never going to be more than a bolthole. Eventually, he found a modern five-bedroom house down a winding road in north Wicklow. Rowanbrook – not Gary's choice of name, but he couldn't be bothered changing it – had been the dream home of a businessman who'd lost everything in the crash and was starting over in Dubai. It was all light and space with heated floors and an indoor pool. The kitchen contained more marble than the average cemetery, and the view was stunning. Even on the murkiest of days, it looked like the entire county was on display before him.

Gary wasn't a hermit. He met up with old friends, he saw his family, he'd had a couple of short-lived relationships (these aside, he'd have to admit his sex life had been unusually fallow). In so far as he was isolated, he'd imposed the isolation on himself. He wouldn't claim he was happy, but he'd needed to escape the noise, the mayhem and, frankly, the rank seediness of his final years in America. He'd also had to get away from Anton Toland, his collaborator and best friend.

In his innocence, Gary had expected to find Olivia online. A general search yielded plenty of Olivia Farnhams, but they were either too young or too far away. He'd assumed the birth records for 1950 and '51 would be digitised and easy to find. Again, he was wrong. He emailed Katie, who advised him to go to the General Register Office, where he could inspect the index books for the relevant years.

He did so with trepidation. His origins must have been obscured for a reason. Perhaps his birth mother had wanted to make sure she would never be found. After a few minutes, he dismissed this thought. The women in Carrigbrack had been given no say in either their own fate or that of their children. They'd had no voice. Literally. He couldn't forget what Katie had said about the enforced silence in the home. For someone who'd spent most of his life revelling in being heard, that felt like the most poisonous of punishments.

The Register Office was not what he'd expected. He had imagined that the records – decade after decade of births, deaths and marriages – would be housed in grand style. Instead they were kept in an ugly grey building surrounded by high walls and prison-style gates. The registers themselves looked to have passed through hundreds of anxious hands. It was impossible not to think of all the people who had pored over the pages. For two, three hours, Gary scoured every line. The writing was looped and sometimes indistinct. His back grew sore, his eyes tired. And then … there she was: Olivia Mary Farnham, born Coolerra, County Clare, on 27 February 1951. Her father was Timothy Farnham, a tradesman. Her mother was Geraldine Farnham, formerly Clancy.

Gary was surprised to find that his hands were shaking. He was giddy with a mixture of pleasure and relief. Okay, he had another distance to travel, but having found a record of Olivia's birth, he was confident he'd be able to find more. Track down a marriage certificate, and he'd be almost there. He felt a surge of what his bandmate Ray called 'famous person confidence': the belief that if you wanted something badly enough, it would be yours.

He decided to order the full version of Olivia's birth certificate. First, though, he needed a walk and a coffee. Outside, he switched on his phone to find a message from Katie. 'Gary,' she said, her voice even more precise in recorded form, 'I'd appreciate it if you'd give me a ring. I have news.'

Convinced that whatever she had to say would be positive, he called back. After a minute of bland chatter, Katie revealed that through a friend of a friend, Olivia Farnham – *the* Olivia Farnham – had heard about the message board.

'And?' he said.

'Well, I know you had a notion that she was your birth mother …'

Keep going, thought Gary, his free hand clenched into a fist. Keep going.

'… but she was reunited with her son quite a while ago. Back in the late nineties, I think. And then – oh, you won't believe this – wasn't he killed in a car crash?'

'I see.'

'She'd put her number on the email, so I rang, and we had a nice long talk. I feel desperately sorry for her. Imagine finding your child, only to lose him again.'

'I see.'

'She asked if I'd send on the baby bracelet. She'd like it as a keepsake. She sounds like a lovely woman.'

'That's good.'

'Now, Gary, I get the impression you're disappointed, but you shouldn't be.'

'But I'd thought she was the right woman.'

'I understand, only you've got to see this for what it is: a positive development. This time yesterday, you were looking for four women. Today, the list is down to three. You're getting closer to finding your birth mother. You do see that, don't you?'

Gary thanked her and returned to his car. The first setback had hardly registered. This was different. He told himself to consider Olivia and the tragedies she'd suffered. She'd lost her son. Twice. In contrast, the chances were that his birth mother was still out there. He was lucky. He needed to believe that.

Allegra was in high good humour, brimming with chat about school and friends and the competition she'd won with her track team. Ten was a perfect age: old enough to have lots to say, young enough to say it. Even at six thousand miles' remove, Gary got a buzz from watching his daughter. He loved the way she paused before answering a question, how she could be thoughtful one moment and bubbling with life the next. She had Posy's wide green eyes and sleek brown hair, but she was tall and narrow like him. He wondered if their Skype conversations were all the sweeter because her childhood was nearly over. Soon, she'd be more guarded, less given to sudden enthusiasms and wild inventions. Rather than being the smart, funny guy, he'd be that old fool who used to have a thing with her mother.

It was late afternoon in Los Angeles, after midnight in Wicklow. In all the time he'd been doing this, Gary had never got used to watching his daughter in glowing sunlight while his skies were dark.

'Are you coming to see us soon?' she asked.

'I hope so, but remember how I told you about trying to find my original mom?'

'Uh huh.'

'Well, I'm fairly busy with that at the moment. I'll definitely see you before Christmas, though.'

'Okay.' Allegra frowned, and Gary assumed he'd given the wrong answer. 'Mom wants to talk to you,' she said.

Gary's conversations with his former partner tended to be short. They spoke about their daughter and occasionally about mutual friends. While no one would describe her career as stellar, Posy earned a decent living. She'd managed to make the role transition from quirky girlfriend in cut-off jeans to anxious wife in flannel shirt with less difficulty than many. Still, in as much as Gary prayed for anything, he prayed that Allegra would steer clear of show business. He knew how pretty girls could get mangled and crushed.

For a talented actress, Posy had a transparent face. Gary could tell that something was up. His immediate fear was that, despite appearances, Allegra was ill. Then he guessed she wanted to talk about herself. She'd been seeing a guy. Maybe she was pregnant, or they were getting married.

It was his day for being wrong.

'So,' she said. 'I met Anton last night. At a party.'

'Oh?'

'He was asking after you. I told him about how you'd discovered you were adopted and were looking for your birth mother. He said to wish you all the best.'

'Did you have to tell him?'

'Aw, Gary. He was being friendly. He seemed genuine. The two of you can't go on punishing each other. At some stage, you'll have to talk it through. Either that or announce that you've left the band.'

'Now's not the right time.'

'There's never going to be a right time, though, is there?'

'I can't say.'

'Do you not miss making music? You should be doing something with your life rather than talking to the frigging trees or whatever it is that fills your days.'

'I do stuff.'

'You mess around. It's not the same.'

Gary was about to defend his production and soundtrack work, but Posy gave an impatient flap of the hand before continuing.

'Okay, so here's the other thing.' He should have known there'd be another thing. 'Anton mentioned that next year it'll be twenty-five years since *Overboard* was released.'

'I'm well aware of that.' *Overboard* was the band's biggest album, the record that had bounced them to a different level. From arenas to stadiums. From tour buses to private jets. From being four Dublin lads having a laugh to the cover of *Time*.

'Anyhow,' Posy continued, 'the record company wants to do an anniversary reissue.'

'Good luck to them. Nobody buys CDs any more.'

'Your audience does.'

'Old people, you mean?'

She laughed. 'You said it. Seriously, though, from what I can gather, they're talking about packaging it in different ways, including vinyl and downloads. They also plan on releasing out-takes and old footage. They hope the band will record a few new tracks too. And, well … they want you to go on tour to support it all. Not a huge tour, just a few dates in the US and Europe. Oh, and you'd get the full Rock and Roll Hall of Fame treatment.'

'Nobody told me about this.'

'I'm telling you, and Frank's likely to get in touch later in the week.'

Frank O'Toole was the band's manager. He'd spotted them early on when they'd been churning out lousy cover versions in McGonagles. He'd assured them that their own material couldn't be any worse. Frank was a seminary dropout with the professional and personal morals of a jailhouse snitch. He was also the best in the business.

'I don't want to be a heritage act,' said Gary.

At the best of times, Skype tended to make people sound hollow and shouty. Posy's voice might only have risen by half a notch, but it filled the room. 'Yeah, that's right,' she said. 'You stay over there and wallow in your misery. You don't think Anton regrets what happened?'

'No doubt he does. Only a monster wouldn't.'

'Short of crucifying himself, what more can the guy do? It's not as though you're entirely blameless. Besides, from what I hear, he's been leading a clean life.'

'He can't have changed that much, because he obviously worked his charm on you.'

No sooner had the words left Gary's mouth than he wanted to reel them back in. This was how it always was with Posy. They became enmeshed in an argument, and all subtlety disappeared. They were two kids in a schoolyard. Two drunks at closing time.

'Screw you,' she said.

'Aw, please,' he said, 'you don't want Allegra to hear.'

She'd already cut the connection.

Gary considered calling back, but there was no point. She wasn't going to change her mind, and they'd fall out all over again. He poured a large measure of Canadian Club and stepped outside to the deck. The high black sky was filled with stars, the fields bathed with silvery light. He sat and savoured the slow burn as the whiskey washed down his throat.

'This is a mess, isn't it?' he said to the sky, half expecting it to offer an opinion.

He had screwed up his life, and somehow he'd convinced himself that finding his birth mother would give him a chance to begin again. Roll up, roll up for the new improved Gary Winters. The problem was, no matter how far he ran, his regrets came with him. He'd wanted to press delete and start over, but everything was on a loop in his head, as real as the day it had happened.

Chapter 11

Ailish

Ailish hid the bracelet at the back of her underwear drawer. This was also where she put the few euro she had managed to save. Stevie, her youngest and smartest child, was in his final year of school, and she wanted him to do the course of his choice, even if that was in Dublin. Everybody knew that Dublin was ruinously expensive, so each fortnight she tried to put a little aside. Ailish regretted her own lack of education, not because she would like more money – who wouldn't? – but because she was frustrated by her ignorance. People would mention places or books or historical events, and she'd have to nod as though she knew what they were talking about. How she wished she had something to contribute.

As well as the money and the bracelet, she stored a handful of other mementos in the drawer. It was where she kept a lock of each of her children's hair and a thin silver chain given to her by Keith when they'd started going out. Oh, she knew it was sentimental, but she liked a reminder of the days when everything had felt simple.

These days, all her thoughts led back to Chrissie. She wondered if, having had a baby at fourteen, her birth mother had been able to return to school. Probably not. She guessed the Culligans had been poor. Those had been poor times. Had Chrissie been able to recover from the stigma of being an unmarried mother? Or had she become one of those sad, withdrawn women who spent a lifetime drifting from one institution to another, hair matted, eyes empty?

If Chrissie had stayed in County Clare, there was a chance they'd seen each other. They could have stood side by side in the supermarket or the pub. They could have walked the same lanes, travelled on the same bus, breathed the same air.

Ailish had to stop herself from becoming obsessed with the bracelet; from taking it out and staring at the tiny writing. The narrow strip of adhesive that had fastened the slip of paper no longer worked. Otherwise the bracelet was as perfect as it had been five decades before. She was amazed that Katie had kept it safe for so long.

Optimism crept over her. She was meant to find Chrissie.

An internet search gave her a shock. The first entry on the page was a recent death notice. She cried out in disappointment before realising that she was reading about the wrong woman. Christine Culligan had been the deceased's married name. Next, she looked at several Facebook pages. Katie had said there was a strong resemblance between the two women, and Ailish kept hoping she was one click away from seeing a mirror image of herself. Unfortunately, none of the Christines or Chrissies sounded right. Most didn't appear old enough, while one looked about twenty years too old. Aware that a considerable number of the women had gone to the United States, she decided to try some American sites. A search unearthed fourteen Christine Culligans in New York, New Jersey, California, Florida, Texas and Wisconsin. While it was possible that one was her birth mother, contacting them would be sensitive work. Plus, there was every chance that Chrissie had married and changed her name. She could be Chrissie Aaron or Chrissie Zysman or anything in between.

This was, Ailish concluded, a needle-and-haystack task.

She could try a DNA test and see if there were any matches out there, but it was a long shot, and taking the test would cost more than she could afford to lose. That left her with one obvious option. Although the rest of the family had always made fun of her for following the rules, Ailish decided to try the official route. If the authorities couldn't provide her with more information, she'd think again. Not that she looked forward to any of this. Officialdom made her nervous. Even when asking for what was rightfully hers, her hands became clammy and her throat tightened. Confrontation made her unwell.

She soon discovered that pass-the-parcel had been played with her files. The information once held by the nuns and St Saviour's Adoption Agency had been transferred to the old health board, which had become the new health executive, which, in turn, had given its files to the newer Child and Family Agency. She pictured sheaves of paper being stuffed into filing cabinets, and cabinets being wheeled between offices. Thousands of lives being hawked from place to place. No wonder so much paperwork was missing.

Giving the hotel as her return address, Ailish wrote to the relevant office and to the Adoption Authority and filled out all the necessary forms. Then she prepared for a long wait. She contemplated talking to one of her daughters. She was sure they'd encourage her. On the flip side, they might reveal something to Keith. That wasn't a risk she was willing to take. And, honestly, just thinking about Chrissie, just having the information and running it around her head, was enough.

It could never mean as much to anyone else.

The weeks passed, one fading into another with no word from the authorities. Despite telling herself not to visualise an ideal outcome, that was exactly what Ailish did. She pictured herself receiving a letter saying that Chrissie had been searching for her and would like to make contact. Her old daydreams were replaced by a new set in which the two became firm friends. The desire to find her birth mother pulsed through her. That she might not be everything Chrissie had wished for no longer mattered.

This fantasy life shielded her from the worst of Keith's crabby humour. The factory where he worked as a forklift operator had been sold, and the new management weren't to his liking. They insisted on changing the rosters and shaking up work practices. He dismissed them as 'kids who know feck-all about feck-all'. She pretended to listen. Meanwhile, Stevie continued to hum and haw about his university choices. Sometimes, Ailish suspected his vagueness was a ploy to annoy Keith. If so, it was effective.

One morning, after she'd cleaned her first three rooms, she sat down on the bed in Number 24 and made a phone call.

'Hello, stranger,' said Katie. 'I've been thinking about you. How are you getting on?'

Ailish explained her predicament. 'I didn't call you before because I didn't want to make a nuisance of myself. I'm trying to do the right thing, but I don't know if I have the patience.'

'It's funny you should say that. Beth and I are learning such a lot about how to work around the system. Of course, she doesn't have as much time now that she's started work. Did I tell you that she's a data analyst with Google?'

'That sounds impressive.'

'Doesn't it? To tell you the truth, I haven't a notion what it means.'

Ailish laughed. 'That reminds me of Stevie and his college plans. "What do you think?" he says to me, and I have to say, "Stevie, I don't understand the title of the course, not to mind what you'd actually be studying."'

'So,' said Katie, 'let's talk about your search. What you've got to do is find your birth certificate – which should be fairly straightforward.

Then you need Chrissie's birth cert. Oh, and if you could find a marriage cert for her, you'd be well on your way.'

'That sounds great, only …'

'… only the records are in Dublin, and you're in Kilmitten?'

'That's the snag. I'll have to find a way of escaping for the day without Keith getting wind of what I'm at.'

'Why don't I have a look for you?'

'Seriously?' Although this was precisely what Ailish had hoped for, she'd been too nervous to ask. 'I'd be very grateful. I mean, I'll pay you for your time or—'

'You will not,' said Katie. 'I'd be delighted to give you a dig-out. I'd love to find out what happened to Chrissie.'

Ailish was amazed by Katie's efforts on behalf of people she barely knew.

Two days later, when she was scrubbing the bath in Room 11, her phone rang. In her haste to answer it, she tripped over a mound of linen and went flying into the dressing table.

'Hello?'

'There you are,' said Katie, 'Jacqueline Ann Culligan, daughter of Christine Marie Culligan of Hackett's Cross.'

'You found us!'

'Didn't I tell you I would?'

Ailish stopped to consider the information. The words danced in front of her.

Katie was still talking. 'There's no mention of your birth father. That was often the case, though, so I wouldn't read too much into it. While I was there, I had a look through the marriage records. I didn't come across anything. Then again, we knew that'd be a tougher task. I'll have to get Beth to give me a hand. She's very sharp-eyed. Mind you, so was I when I was twenty-eight.'

Ailish felt dizzy, as though the room had tilted and nothing was quite where it belonged. She perched on the edge of the bed. 'I think I know Hackett's Cross. Isn't it over in the west of the county?'

'That's right, not far from Kilkee. Chrissie must have grown up beside the sea.'

'If memory serves, it's only a little place.'

'So little it's hardly a place at all.'

Ailish could hear the smile in Katie's voice. She tried to steady her thoughts, which were swerving in every direction. 'That means the Culligans should be easier to find.'

'It does. You need to think carefully about what you want to do next. I know you're impatient, but there's a reason why social workers get involved in reunions. They can be delicate matters.'

'I ... I can't thank you enough. Sorry if I'm a bit stuck for words. This is all brilliant. Just brilliant. How do I go about getting copies of the certificates?'

'They're already in the post.'

Ailish inhaled with surprise – and panic. Before she could say anything, Katie intervened.

'Don't worry. I sent them to the hotel. With any luck, they'll be with you in the morning. But ...' She hesitated.

'Go on.'

'I wish you didn't have to do everything in secret. If you're going to continue, you'll have to talk to Keith at some stage.'

The truth of this was dawning on Ailish. She knew, however, that not only would her husband's reaction be hostile, he would probably stymie her attempts to trace Chrissie. 'I will tell him,' she said. 'I promise I will. Just not yet.'

'I understand,' said Katie. 'Believe you me, I know what it's like when a job feels too big.'

*

The certificates arrived on schedule the following morning. Thankfully, Ailish's first room was a nice handy one: a couple on the second of five nights, no need to change the sheets, no excessive wear and tear. She settled onto the bed and opened the large brown envelope. The first certificate confirmed what she already knew. The second belonged to her natural mother. Christine Marie Culligan had been born on 12 June 1957. Ailish couldn't stop herself from doing the maths. Chrissie had been only thirteen when she'd got pregnant. Far, far too young to consent to anything. Her parents were named as Patrick and Bridget Culligan. Patrick was described as a labourer.

For a short while, Ailish sat and thought through everything she'd learnt. Afterwards, she went about her work without comment or hesitation. All the while, her brain crackled and whirred.

Stevie had texted to say he was going to a friend's house, so when Ailish got home, she decided to go for a walk. She needed to think everything through. She put on her red anorak and set off towards Toomey's Hill. Kilmitten, like many of the neighbouring villages, was small and ramshackle. Despite the best efforts of the Tidy Towns committee, it had a bruised, dishevelled look. The supermarket was forever running out of stock, and the most popular bar was like an outpost of the 1980s. Outsiders might question how anyone could be fond of such a place, but Ailish was. Briefly, she wondered what Gary Winters had made of it. The thought made her smile.

Whatever the village's shortcomings, the surrounding countryside was gorgeous. After a hard October rain, the sky was clear, and as she climbed, Ailish could see for miles. The lanes surrounding the hill were carpeted in brown leaves, with the occasional shot of yellow or red. While Chrissie was at the forefront of her thoughts, memories of her adoptive parents, Deirdre and Jarlath, were there too. How often had she walked these fields with her mam? At this time of year, they'd collected blackberries. In December, they'd searched for holly. In the spring, they'd picked cowslips and primroses while in the nearby woods they'd gathered bluebells. Those had been some of the best days of Ailish's childhood.

Often, on their way home, Deirdre had stopped at the church to say a prayer. She'd been old-style devout, given to First Fridays and novenas. The family had eaten fish on Fridays and recited the rosary every evening. When they'd left Kilmitten, it had been for trips to Knock or Croagh Patrick. Late in life, Deirdre had travelled on the diocesan pilgrimage to Lourdes. She'd regarded it like a round-the-world cruise, a once-in-a-lifetime treat rather than five days saying prayers and tending to those frailer than herself. Ailish had never heard either of her parents complain about their drab lives. Indeed, she suspected that even a lottery win wouldn't have changed them. Martyrdom came in many forms.

For her, religion was a conundrum with too many sorrowful mysteries and not enough joyful ones. She reflected on what had been done to Chrissie: wrenched from home, sent to a place that was no better than a prison and forcibly separated from her child. No doubt she'd also been branded a sinner and made to endure endless mumbo-jumbo about hell and shame. Religion had treated her like a criminal when in reality she'd been a victim. Ailish's parents had adopted her through a sense of Catholic duty rather than any affection for children. So no, she wouldn't call herself religious. And yet, neither could she sever all ties with the Church. Once a month or so, she went to Mass. She usually sat at the back on her own and allowed the prayers to wash over her. She found it restful.

By the time she began her walk back to the village, the last light was seeping from the sky. Someone was burning turf, its distinctive smell lingering in the chill air. On Main Street, she called into the shop for a few groceries. June Mangan, a woman with crow's feet so deep it looked like she was she wearing winged eyeliner, was at the till.

'Aren't we blessed to have such a grand evening?' she said.

'Indeed we are,' agreed Ailish.

As soon as she entered the house, she sensed that something was wrong. Keith was there ahead of her, his face slightly off kilter.

'I went for a walk and lost track of time,' she said, as she removed her anorak and threw it over the banister. 'I'll put the dinner on in a minute. I bought sausages below in Mangan's.'

'Where's Stevie?' asked Keith.

'Round in Declan's house. He'll have his dinner there.'

'It's well for him. I thought he was supposed to be studying.'

'He is. They're doing their homework together.'

'A likely story. The pair of them are probably smoking at the back of the church. Or hanging out with young ones. You're far too soft on him. I'm tired of telling you that.'

Ailish noticed a twitch in Keith's left cheek. There must have been more hassle at work. She bent to scoop up her handbag. The birth certificates were tucked inside, and she needed to put them in her hiding place.

'I'm popping upstairs,' she said. 'I'll be back in a tick.'

She opened the drawer and, without thinking, sought out the envelope containing her baby bracelet. It had been moved. She looked inside. The bracelet was gone.

Before she had the chance to absorb what had happened, she heard Keith's footsteps, slow and heavy, on the stairs. Quickly, she shut the drawer and slid the certificates under a pillow. She turned and stood in front of the dressing table.

Keith took several steps into the room. He opened his mouth, then paused. 'It's about time we changed this,' he said, scuffing the toe of his boot against the pink and green carpet. 'I'm sure you'd prefer something more modern. What have they got in the hotel at the minute?'

'Powder blue. It's nice.' She stared straight at him, at the moss-coloured eyes she'd once found irresistible.

'Any chance of an offcut?' He was toying with her.

'I can ask.'

He stepped forward again. The air felt taut. 'Why do I get the feeling you're looking for something?'

If he wanted to be cagey, she could be cagey too. 'I don't know. Like I say, I'm about to go down and cook the dinner.' She attempted a 'nothing to see here' smile, but her mouth was too stiff.

'You were keeping money from me.'

She edged away until she couldn't go any further. 'I wasn't keeping anything from you. I've been trying to save for Stevie's college fund, that's all.' There was an irritating crack in her voice. Stay composed, she thought. He's taken what belongs to you, and you've got to get it back.

'Isn't Stevie the lucky fellow? I hope he appreciates you. Anyway, there I was, getting ready to go out … I'd arranged to meet the lads for a quick pint in Pilkington's … when I realised I needed a few euro. "Not to worry," says I. "Can't I borrow from Ailish? Haven't I seen her slipping money into the drawer?"'

Silently, she cursed her stupidity. She should have been more careful. 'You could have asked me,' she said. 'I'd have given it to you.'

'You weren't here.' His tone became harder. 'I don't hide anything from you. Every cent I earn goes towards keeping this family.'

This wasn't true, but Ailish was scared to argue. 'I'm here now.'

She was frightened that he would hurt her. That he would twist her arm behind her back or pull her hair or punch her in the stomach. He was always careful to avoid her face, and she was skilled at hiding her bruises.

Instead, he reached into his jeans and pulled out the bracelet.

Already it was folded over. Damaged. 'What's this?' he asked, waving it in front of her.

Her stomach lurched. 'You know what it is.'

'Why are you keeping secrets from me?'

'I'm not. It's just a scrap of paper. I figured it wouldn't mean anything to you, so I didn't mention it. It means a lot to me, though. Can I have it back, please?'

'Where did you get it?'

'Does it matter?'

'If my wife has been lying to me, of course it matters.'

'You can take all the money you want, but give me back the bracelet. Please.'

Blotches of colour had risen in Keith's face. 'It was that old woman, wasn't it? The one I found here a few weeks ago sitting in the kitchen like Lady Muck. Where did she get it?' He passed the bracelet to his other hand. 'Here, she's not your real mother, is she?'

'No. She's ... she's someone who worked in the home where I was born.'

He laughed, a brittle sort of laugh. 'She's a good liar, I'll give her that. A crafty one. I wasn't convinced she was giving me the full picture, but I didn't see this coming.' He held the bracelet up again. 'When you think about it, though, what class of sad old biddy holds on to the likes of this?'

'If you'll just hand it back to me, I'll put the dinner on. You'll want a bite to eat before you go out.'

The blotches deepened. 'Forget the fucking dinner, would you? What I want is the truth. Why did you lie to me? I was reasonable about this adoption bullshit before, but you got nowhere. And do you know why that was? Your mother doesn't want to be found. She didn't want you then, and she doesn't want you now.' He leant in and, with his free hand, tapped Ailish's head. 'Why can't you get that into your little skull, huh?'

Ailish flinched, and her eyes began to water. 'You don't know that. You don't know anything about her.'

'And neither do you. You can be certain that whatever airy-fairy crap you've got in your head is wrong. I'll bet any money there's nothing special about her. Chances are she was like all the rest: some dizzy young one who got herself knocked up because she was too stupid to know any better.'

'Don't say that.'

'Listen to me, Ailish. You've lost all perspective here. You probably think I'm being unkind, when I'm doing you a favour. If you get all worked up about this nonsense, you'll end up hurt. Again. The last time, there was no talking to you. You went around with a face as long as Lent until you made everybody in the house as miserable as yourself. You've got to realise how selfish you're being. And there's no call for the whimpering. You know how thin the walls are. If you don't shut up, we'll be the talk of the village.'

Keith looked at her with the bottomless distaste in which he specialised, a look that made her feel like the detritus in the sink after the washing-up water had drained away. It hadn't always been like this. It wasn't always like this now. Back in June, they'd had a week in Spain, their first genuine break in years. Along with Stevie, they'd spent the days laughing and messing, playing in the pool and coating themselves in factor 30. They'd got burnt all the same. But it had been great. A proper family holiday.

Still, this was no time for getting wistful. Ailish had to focus on the bracelet. She considered making a lunge for it, then decided against. Keith was far stronger, and there was a danger the fragile paper would rip in two. Or he might hit her. She wiped her eyes with the cuff of her cardigan.

'Okay,' she said, 'I hear you, and I'm sorry I didn't tell you about the identity band. That was wrong of me. I would like to keep it, though … as a reminder of my roots. I won't go looking for my birth mother, if that's what you're concerned about. I swear I won't.'

'So you say.' He stepped back, turned away and walked over to his side of the bed. 'Except I don't believe you. You know what your problem is, Ailish? You're a fucking liar.'

'I'm telling you the God's honest truth, Keith. The bracelet … well, it's a sentimental thing, no more than that.'

He placed the bracelet beside the glass of water on top of his bedside locker and took a purple lighter from his pocket. One click, and a long orange flame appeared. With his other hand, he picked up the bracelet and held it to the flame. Before Ailish could move, the edge was alight. It curled towards him, glowing slightly at first. Then the paper truly caught fire.

For a moment, she froze. Then she hurled herself in her husband's direction, shrieking, 'Stop it! Stop it!' She was too late. He dropped the ashy remains into the glass and returned the lighter to his pocket. The smell of smoke hung between them. Katie had kept the bracelet for almost forty-seven years. Ailish had managed less than two months. She went to speak, but no words came. Instead, she collapsed onto the bed, buried her face in the pillow and balled her hands into fists.

A thick silence fell over the room.

After a minute or two, Keith left. A short while later, she heard the front door closing and the sound of his feet on the street below.

Chapter 12

Katie

Katie and Beth had established a ritual. On Saturday mornings, they sat at Katie's kitchen table and reviewed progress. In the two months since they'd placed the notice on the adoption forum, sixteen bracelets had been returned to their original owners. Katie had bought a special notebook to keep track of developments. She'd also printed the emails and placed them in a new blue folder. Beth made fun of her, but there was something pleasing about having all the details on file. She kept the shoebox in her wardrobe, bringing it out only when she was certain a bracelet should be passed on.

She'd spoken to several of the recipients. It was fascinating to hear how life had turned out for them. Although they used different words and displayed different emotions, they shared a yearning to reconnect with the woman who had brought them into the world. They didn't want to interfere, they insisted; they just wanted to know that she was all right. Most said this desire had intensified as they'd got older. One man, a lovely fellow from Tipperary called Larry, told Katie that every time he heard something on the news about mother-and-baby homes, it ripped him apart. 'I had no idea how badly the women were treated,' he said. 'To my shame, it never occurred to me.'

Even before her feet hit the ground in the morning, Katie was thinking about the bracelets and their original owners. There were days when she found the task almost unbearably difficult; days when fear and darkness tugged at her, and she felt as if she'd returned to a place and time she wanted to forget. On those days, she muddled on, hoping that no one, especially Beth, noticed her struggle.

This had been one of those weeks when she'd felt Johnny's absence as keenly as if he'd just left her. Every song on the radio, every picture on the wall, every story on the news had rekindled her sorrow. The previous evening, she'd been flicking through the television channels, looking for something other than a cookery programme or a soap, when she'd chanced upon the channel with all the quiz shows. Johnny had been addicted to *The Chase*. She could hear him shouting out answers: 'fear of butterflies', 'the Bee Gees', 'Saturn'. A wave of tenderness had come over her, and she'd realised she could no longer watch. Even though it was only seven o'clock, she'd swallowed two sleeping tablets and climbed into bed.

These Saturday-morning sessions with Beth made the weekends feel a little less lonely. For many years, Katie and Johnny had gone walking on Saturdays. Sometimes they'd travelled to Wicklow; occasionally they'd spent a couple of days in Mayo or Galway, but the Cooley peninsula in County Louth had been her favourite destination. She'd loved the gentle slopes, the coconut scent of the furze bushes and the view over Carlingford Lough. She could, of course, make the journey on her own. But she knew she wouldn't.

Now, as Beth tapped at her laptop, Katie reviewed her to-do list. Some of their correspondents, like Larry, were content to take the official route. He trusted he'd eventually trace his natural mother. Others were less sanguine, and Katie found herself offering advice –

and cautioning against moving too quickly. She remembered suggesting that Gary hire a private detective, and it occurred to her that she'd become a detective of sorts. Gary was in her thoughts that morning, as was Ailish. Above everyone else, Katie wanted to help Ailish. This was partly explained by the sad circumstances of her birth, but there was more to it than that. She had known too many Ailishes: people who spent their lives facilitating others and getting little in return. In particular, she'd worked with nurses who'd given everything to everybody only to find themselves burnt out and alone.

Having found Chrissie's birth certificate, she'd made several unsuccessful attempts to unearth her marriage records. Ailish's birth mother appeared to have vanished, and in her gloomier moments, Katie suspected she might be dead.

'Ailish has gone quiet on me,' she said to Beth, who was reading an email from a Carlow man. While he thought he'd been born in Carrigbrack, he was vague about the details, and they weren't sure how to handle his case.

'Have you rung her?'

'I don't want to make a nuisance of myself. I might give her a shout next week. I have to be careful in case her husband's around.'

'From the way you described him, it sounds as though Keith Dwan's a man who needs to get over himself.'

'Ah, no. That's far too generous. As they'd say in Danganstown, he's a ferocious gobshite altogether.'

Beth looked up from the computer and winked. 'I'd say you were great crack in your youth.'

'I thought I was great crack now,' Katie said, and they both laughed.

To be honest, Katie didn't think she had been much fun as a teenager. It wasn't that she'd been especially earnest or dour. More that she'd been too needy. Thirsty, she believed was the modern-day term. She'd maundered around the village, grateful for any scrap of attention that came her way. If that attention was male, so much the better. It would be easy to blame her insecurity on Margo, but her sister had been a small child at the time. Plus, while the lack of affection at home hadn't helped, it was hardly unusual. Katie had grown up in austere times, when showy displays of endearment were frowned upon, and 'spare the rod, spoil the child' was viewed as sound parenting advice. She'd been fifteen the last time her father had slapped her. She'd skipped Mass in favour of sharing a cigarette with a buck-toothed charmer named Billy Tuite. Unfortunately, they'd been spotted by a local gossip-merchant. She wondered where Billy was now. Buck teeth seemed to have gone the way of hand-me-down clothes, corned beef sandwiches and the measles: not extinct, but no longer commonplace either.

Had Katie ever been as outspoken as Beth? Probably not. She liked to think she'd had a certain spirit about her, but spirited girls had been viewed with suspicion back then. Time and experience had dulled her edges. It seemed to her that nowadays, young women were allowed to make a splash. Older ones were still expected to colour inside the lines.

Beth took a deep breath. 'I hope you don't mind me asking, but was there a reason you didn't dust down that old shoebox and start looking for people while Johnny was alive?'

'You mean would he have disapproved?'

'Seeing as you've put it like that, yes.'

'It's not that simple. It's not like he agreed with what went on in Carrigbrack, far from it. If I'd been keen to return the bracelets to their original owners, he'd have supported me. But, at the same time, he'd have been wary. He used to say that if you went around turning over logs, you mightn't like what crawled out.'

'Fair enough,' said Beth, but her tone suggested the answer was less than satisfactory.

'Besides, if I'd done it any sooner, I wouldn't have had you to help me.'

'I'd say you'd have been just fine. Oh, you know what I meant to tell you. I saw a piece online this morning about Black Iris. They're re-releasing one of their old albums. Rumour has it they're going back on the road too – but without Gary.'

'That's odd,' said Katie. 'Why wouldn't he go with them?'

'I haven't a clue. Have you heard from him lately?'

'We spoke the other day. I get the feeling he's struggling. He thinks he's found another one of the contenders, if we can call them that. A woman named Gráinne Holland. He wrote to her but hasn't heard anything back. So far, he's got nowhere with the others.'

'He's a funny fish.'

Katie lifted her reading glasses. 'He speaks highly of you.'

'Yeah, right.'

'No, seriously, he's got great time for you. He says you're very clever.'

'In Gary's lexicon, I'm not sure that's positive. I reckon I'd need to be called a "foxy chick" or a "hot piece of ass" for it to be considered a compliment.'

'Now, Beth Linnane, even I know those phrases are old hat. I doubt Gary speaks that way any more.'

'Okay, then I'd need to be a "total honey" or a "lush babe", or whatever this week's term is.'

'I get the idea that something else is on his mind. I tried asking, subtly of course, but he didn't give a proper answer. He's an enigmatic sort of character.' Katie pushed her glasses down again. 'Mind you, he does have quite a complicated life.'

'Understatement of the century, right there,' said Beth, before returning to her laptop.

Katie closed her notebook and rose to fill the kettle. The tree in the back garden was beginning to take on its spindly winter form.

The sky was quilted with pale grey. She watched next door's cat streak past. He was always in a hurry, was Grover.

'Time for a break,' she said, spooning coffee into two striped mugs.

Beth leant back in her chair. 'Great stuff. Is there cake?'

'There's a cupboard full of cake. I got a bit fidgety during the week, so I did some baking.'

While Katie cut thick slices of apple cake, Beth spoke about work and about her unsuccessful attempts to find a flat of her own.

'Would you consider …' said Katie, 'and I promise I won't be offended if you don't want to, and take as much time as you need to think it through … would you consider moving in here with me?'

For a moment, the kitchen was quiet, so quiet they could have heard a piece of dust drop. (Not that this was likely. Along with the baking binge, Katie had indulged in a manic clean. It really had been a challenging week.)

Then a smile spread across Beth's face. 'I thought you'd never ask.'

'Honestly?'

'I'd be delighted to be your tenant.'

'Gosh, pet, you wouldn't be a tenant. You're family. I couldn't take money from you.'

'Katie, I'm paying rent, and that's that.'

'Something small, then. Anything more, and your mother would never forgive me.'

'Don't mind Mam, I'm paying my way.'

'We'll see. I would have asked sooner, only I didn't want you thinking I was meddling, or, worse, that I wanted someone to look after me. You've always been the independent type.'

Beth looked over the rim of her mug. 'Sit down there and stop your old guff. You're the last person who needs looking after.'

Katie joined her at the table. 'Well, this is great. Have you any questions? You know the house as well as I do. You can have either of the spare rooms.'

'I have three requests,' said Beth, selecting a slice of cake.

'Oh?'

'First off, we need to get Netflix … and a coffee machine. Don't worry, I'll sort both of those.'

'Fair enough, though what's wrong with instant coffee, I don't know. You young people and your fancy ideas. What's the third request?'

'That you keep making apple cake.'

'We have a deal. Apple cake was Johnny's favourite, too.' Katie slapped herself on the cheek. 'Listen to me, getting all nostalgic. You needn't fret that I'll rattle on about Johnny all the time, because I won't.'

'You're fine,' said Beth. 'You can talk about him as much as you like.'

'That's something else I meant to say. Don't hesitate to bring friends – or boyfriends – home. I promise not to interfere or ask about their intentions.'

Another silence, this one longer. Katie realised she must have said something out of turn, but for the life of her, she couldn't see what.

Finally, Beth spoke. 'This is kind of awkward, but I don't want you getting the wrong end of the toothbrush. The truth is, I'm unlikely to bring men home, because I'm not interested in them. Admittedly, I had a couple of teenage boyfriends; nobody wants to be different when they're sixteen, or at least I didn't. Since then, all of my relationships have been with women. I'm not seeing anyone at the minute. But if I ever do bring someone back, it'll be a woman.' She looked down. 'Please tell me you're cool with that.'

Katie had a sensation of missing jigsaw pieces slotting into place. She needed to choose her words carefully. 'Oh, Beth, love, of course I am. I just … well, it never occurred to me. I feel like a bit of an eejit.'

'Katie, there's no reason for you to feel foolish. It's not as though I go around with a sign over my head – warning: lesbian in the room. Although to listen to my mother, you'd think I should.'

'Ah, I see. Has she known for long?'

'Only since last year, which was ridiculously late, I know. For ages, I figured the less Mam and Dad knew about my life, the better. But, honestly, pretending to be someone you're not becomes exhausting.'

'Do I take it they didn't react well?'

'Dad was brilliant.'

'That doesn't surprise me. He's a decent man. Don't get me wrong, I'm not suggesting my sister isn't. It's just – how do I put this? – she's very fixed in her views.'

'You can say that again.'

That Margo had snared Con Linnane had always been a source of fascination to Katie. She thought of Con as the definition of fair-minded. His wife, on the other hand, had a gift for highlighting the shortcomings of others. However buoyant you felt at the start of a conversation with Margo, by the end you'd be flat as roadkill. In Katie's charitable moments, she didn't believe her sister intended to offend. She was so single-minded, so determined that everything match her idea of perfection, that she didn't notice the harm she was doing.

Beth cradled her mug. 'Dad's one of those people who spent a long time believing what had been drummed into him at school. All the usual rot about sin and suchlike. Then, at some point, he realised that you can't live other people's lives for them; that, basically, there's nothing wrong with being nice to folks and accepting them as they are. He wants me to be happy, simple as that. With Mam, nothing's straightforward. It's not like she's an out-and-out bigot. She's friendly with Paddy McElligott who runs the newsagent's in Danganstown, and he's as camp as Christmas. She even voted yes in the marriage referendum. Yet she behaves like I've let her down. Like I'm not quite what she ordered.'

'I'm sorry to hear that.'

'The problem with Mam is, she wants everyone to conform to her version of the ideal life. According to her, we should all live in a bee-you-tiful detached house with a Lexus in the driveway, a hairdresser on speed-dial and a clatter of photogenic kids in the back garden. Anyone who doesn't want that is somehow lacking.'

'I fail on all counts, I'm afraid.'

'You're not alone. Most of all, though, she's annoyed that I won't supply her with grandchildren. Or, should I say, the right kind of grandchildren.'

'But don't four of your brothers have children?'

'She has nine grandkids … and another on the way.'

'Is that not enough for any woman?'

'Apparently not.'

'Correct me if I'm wrong,' said Katie, 'but could you not have a child all the same? If that's what you wanted, I mean.'

'I could, and I may well do. Who can say what's in the future? Except in Mam's view, that wouldn't be quite right.' Beth rolled her eyes. 'Ideally, I should have forgotten about college, stayed within a ten-kilometre radius of home, married some local yokel and started reproducing in my early twenties. Actually, better still, what's that thing they teach you about in biology? The thing that keeps splitting in two?'

'An amoeba?'

'That's the one. If I could be an amoeba, she'd be beside herself with happiness.'

Katie tried, and failed, to hold back a smile. 'That's quite an image.'

'You've no idea how crazy she is. The last time I was talking to her, she started yammering on about this young one down the road – Sophie Fitzgerald – who's expecting. I had to listen to a monologue about how fabulous Sophie looked and how heartening it was to see young people settling down close to home. The thing is, not only is Sophie unmarried, she's been going out with the baby's father for about five minutes. And, let me tell you, he's not the brightest bulb in the chandelier either.'

'It's amazing how the world changes, isn't it?' Katie tipped her head towards her notebooks, old and new. 'All of the women in there were banished for something similar.'

The heresy of one generation becomes the orthodoxy of the next: Katie had read that somewhere. How true it was. She considered the situation. Not for a moment did she think that Margo didn't love Beth. Nor did she believe her love was conditional on Beth being a certain type of person. And yet she could see how Margo, one of life's planners, would react badly when those plans went awry. Tact had never been her strong suit. Reluctant as she was to draw her sister upon herself, Katie reckoned she should say something to try and heal the rift. After all, she would have to mention that Beth was living with her.

'Should I have a quiet word with your mother, do you think?'

'Lord, no,' said Beth. 'She'd take offence. Big-time offence.'

'I'd be very subtle.'

'I appreciate the offer, but I'd prefer it if you let matters rest. When it comes to what she sees as family business, Mam can be very sensitive. You might only make matters worse.'

'Okay, then. But I hope you sort out your differences. Take it from me, when these situations fester, they can get out of control.'

Later, Katie decided to go for a short lie-down. No sooner had she made herself comfortable than Beth bounded into the room, cheeks so flushed they matched her coral jumper.

'I'd wondered if this would happen,' she said, waving her phone like a semaphore flag.

'Sorry, love,' said Katie, scrambling to sit up. 'You'll have to explain.'

Beth folded herself into the brocade armchair beside the bed. 'It's an email from a woman called Robyn Bennett. She's writing on behalf of her husband, Brandon. He was born in Carrigbrack in August 1972.'

'What date in August, does it say?'

'Um, the fourteenth. Does it matter?'

'It does, as it happens,' said Katie. 'Go on.'

'The fascinating part is this: Brandon's in Boston. That's where he was raised. He's an American.' Beth said 'American' as though describing a particularly rare and beautiful beast. 'I knew lots of babies were adopted, or let's be honest, *sold* in the States. What I didn't know was that Carrigbrack was involved. You never mentioned it.'

Katie scratched her neck. She was genuinely taken aback. 'I didn't know myself. No one told us where the children went. Does Robyn say whether Brandon is up to speed with what she's doing?'

'She doesn't. Why don't you read the email and see what you think?'

'Pass me the phone, there. Oh, and my glasses too, if you wouldn't mind. They're on the dressing table.'

'No bother,' replied Beth, practically pirouetting across the room.

The window was slightly ajar. Outside, magpies and crows were cawing and rattling and clicking.

Katie scanned the email. Then she read it more slowly. She didn't remember every birth in Carrigbrack. Some memories were muddled, others clear as spring water. She hadn't been there on the day Brandon was born, but she knew what had happened and she knew that a crucial detail was missing from Robyn's account. No matter how they handled this, it would be tricky.

'Well?' said Beth, who was back in the armchair, arms wrapped around her knees.

'I don't think Robyn has the full story,' said Katie. 'Then again, perhaps Brandon doesn't either.'

Chapter 13

Brandon

They were walking on Summit Avenue, the November air biting at their cheekbones, when Robyn told Brandon about the email. By now, he was accustomed to her passions and foibles, but this was different.

'Can you run through that again?' he said, steps accelerating as they passed the red-brick colonial that reminded him of his parents' house. (Important as it was to reach their daily target, Brandon would prefer to do so without freezing to death.)

'I emailed a woman in Ireland who worked as a nurse in Carrigbrack in the early seventies. Apparently she held on to the babies' identity bracelets. She replied this morning saying she wants to help. She asked for our address so she can send us what she knows.'

'She didn't ask for our bank details too? A credit card number maybe?'

Robyn squeezed his arm. 'Don't be silly.'

'I'll bet it's a scam.'

'And I'll bet it's not. She's called Katie Carroll, and she sounds lovely.'

'So lovely she worked in a baby factory, churning out nice white Catholic kids for the export market.'

'Aw, Brandon, don't get all political on me,' said Robyn, her breath forming plumes in the air, her cheeks glowing from a combination of exercise, enthusiasm and youthful good health.

'I'm only kidding. What I don't get is why this Katie lady kept the ID bracelets. Isn't that kind of odd?'

Robyn chose not to answer. 'I've a feeling this could be the breakthrough we've been looking for.'

A sudden gust picked up some dry leaves, sending them hurtling in a circle. Brandon shivered. He didn't point out that he wasn't looking for anything.

Not that long ago, a guy at work had called him a 'status-quo warrior'. The guy had been baffled when Brandon had taken it as a compliment. But why would he agitate for change? He lived in Brookline, one of the most beautiful neighbourhoods in one of the most beautiful cities in America. He had a high-paying job with a prestigious investment firm and a dazzling – if slightly eccentric – wife. From time to time, he measured his life against those of friends and acquaintances. He usually came out on top. Yes, this sounded superficial. That was why he would never say it out loud. But he'd thought about it many times, tested himself from every angle, and he was satisfied there was nothing missing. Well, nothing that wouldn't in due course, and with the grace of God, be provided. No nagging questions. No gaping void. Even if a void did appear, it wouldn't be filled by learning the name of the woman who'd given him up for adoption.

Brandon had made sacrifices to achieve his position in life. When others had been partying, he'd been working. When others had been settling down and having kids, he'd still been working. But that was okay. He was content with the choices he'd made. He bore his biological parents no ill will and hoped his birth mother had gone on to have other children in better circumstances. In the unlikely event she ever came looking for him, he'd be happy to meet her, but he couldn't imagine they'd have much in common.

Also, to be blunt about it, wasn't there a danger that complications would trail in her wake? What if she wanted to involve herself in his life? What if she had other children, his half-brothers and sisters, who decided to seek him out? He had a vision of convoys of raucous Irish people invading his house.

Here was the problem: Robyn saw things differently. She was *fascinated* by Brandon's backstory. How can you not want to know? she'd say. How can you not be curious!? (When Robyn got worked up, she tended to speak in exclamation points and italics.) Too many episodes of *Who Do You Think You Are?* combined with countless internet articles about family trees had fuelled her interest in amateur genealogy. Unfortunately, her own background was as bland as oatmeal. For generations, the Archers had enjoyed lives of uneventful middle-class rectitude. By contrast, Brandon's origins were as intriguing as they were obscure.

She was constantly urging him to sign up to one of the main genealogy websites. So far, he'd resisted.

In recent months, Robyn had become an expert on Irish adoptions and mother-and-baby homes, seizing upon every article for nuggets of information. Given the secrecy surrounding foreign adoptions, most of her findings had been general in nature. She'd been angered by statistics or saddened by individual stories. Brandon had been touched by her interest.

He had also underestimated her tenacity.

Although careful in their choice of words, Brandon's friends had been sceptical about his marriage. He'd been forty-four on their wedding day, and he'd got to that age without so much as a starter marriage. Robyn had been twenty-nine. The mistake outsiders made was to judge the book by its cover, or to be more precise, the woman by her Lululemon leggings. With her honey-coloured ponytail, large brown eyes and pert body, Robyn was the ideal advertisement for her job as a personal trainer. What most people didn't know was that she also had a communications degree from Northeastern. She took pleasure in soaking up patronising comments before flooring her tormentor with an astute observation or well-honed put-down. (Brandon applauded her career change. While the traditional media were dying, wellness was a booming industry.)

Following the email from Ireland, Robyn obsessed about Carrigbrack and the bracelet. If she wasn't talking about them, she was poring over online message boards or Dublin news sites. He did his best to divert the conversation with anecdotes about the office or mutual friends, but she invariably worked her way back to Katie Carroll.

Every morning, she waited for the mail like a child waiting for Santa Claus.

'A letter from Ireland's bound to take at least a week,' he said. 'Why doesn't she email you the details?'

'Well, *duh*. Because she's going to send us your ID bracelet, that's why. I wonder if she remembers you and your birth mother, or if she's relying on the date I gave her.'

Brandon had always known he was adopted. When he'd been six or seven, his mother and father, Art and Ellen Bennett, had given him the basics. He'd been born in an institution called Carrigbrack, they'd said, and almost a year later he'd arrived in Boston. 'We were specially chosen,' his mother had added, 'so you could have a wonderful life in America.' Fanciful as that sounded, they hadn't let him down. While both of his parents were from Irish families, they'd never shown any strong attachment to the place.

Once, his mom had asked if he'd like to learn more about the country of his birth. He'd replied, truthfully, that he'd heard enough. In sixth grade, his friend Davy McGann had spent two weeks with cousins in County Mayo. His report had been alarming. 'Straight up,' he'd said, 'it's the Third World over there. You know how many television channels they have? Two. And the food? Yee-uch. It's like having every meal at your grandma's house.'

Being adopted hadn't always been easy. At school, a kid called Scott Miller had revelled in giving him a hard time. While Miller's taunts had varied, his theme had been constant: Brandon was in America because nobody in Ireland had wanted him. He'd been too ugly or too slow or his mother had already had too many children. Sometimes, the bullying had taken on an extra dimension. Not only was Brandon personally inadequate, the country of his birth was a backwards dump where people took pleasure in killing each other. That no one else had behaved like Miller hadn't mattered; every jibe had left a mark. Brandon hadn't complained – who wanted a reputation as a snitch? – and after a while, Miller had moved on to fresh targets. But neither had he forgotten. His experience had taught him that standing out from the crowd was for other, braver souls. He wanted to belong.

Back then, he'd been called Brendan. At eighteen, with the approval of his parents, he'd filed a petition and changed his name. He'd prefer to sound more American, he explained. In truth, he'd been ambitious and hadn't believed there was much to be gained by sounding like a bartender from Southie with ginger hair, cornflake-sized freckles and an accent thick as chowder. In those years, he too had viewed the Irish as less than appealing. Several of his friends, including those of Irish ancestry, had agreed. Their people were either rough as a cat's tongue or overly sentimental about the land that had rejected them. Oh, and they were ugly. In the contest for the world's least attractive race, the Irish – with their small mouths, big noses and blue-white skin – would be finalists. Obviously, Brandon would never cast such a slur on any other race, but he was entitled to think what he liked about his countrymen. He thought of his own face as a composite sketch: all the features were solid, but nothing quite matched.

Religion didn't play much part in his life. He'd made his confirmation at St Mary of the Assumption, but, save for the occasional wedding or christening, he wasn't a guy for going to church.

In more recent times, his attitude towards Ireland and the Irish had mellowed. He knew the country had changed. Most places had. But if he didn't have any animosity towards it, he didn't have any great enthusiasm either.

The parcel arrived two days before Thanksgiving.

Brandon was late home from the office. He was working for a particularly lucrative client and couldn't afford to skimp on his hours. Robyn was in the kitchen chopping vegetables. He could tell from her preoccupied face, and the fact that she'd already chopped enough peppers to feed the five thousand, that she was on autopilot.

'It came,' she said.

'And?'

'I decided to wait until you were here.' She put down her knife and shrugged. 'I'm kind of nervous.'

'No kidding,' he said, nodding towards the vegetable mountain.

Outside, a storm was gathering, the wind picking up then dying down again.

Inside Katie's parcel, there were two smaller envelopes. One, he presumed, held the bracelet. The other contained a letter.

They read the letter first.

Dear Robyn and Brandon,
My apologies that this has taken a few days longer than expected.
It's an unusual situation, and I wasn't sure what to do for the best.

Rest assured, I have given it a lot of thought. I have also discussed everything with my niece, Beth, who's of great assistance to me.

When you open the accompanying envelope – if you haven't already done so! – you will find two identity bracelets. One for Edward Markham, the other for Brendan Markham, both born on 14 August 1972.

Brandon, from what Robyn told me in her emails, I have the feeling you grew up without knowing that you have a twin. I believe that you were originally named Brendan and your brother was Edward, or Eddie as he was known in the home.

Even though I worked as a nurse in Carrigbrack, I wasn't informed about what happened to the babies after they had left. I can't say for certain, but given the secrecy of those times, it's unlikely your parents in the United States were aware you had a brother.

Your birth mother is named Linda and is from County Galway. I remember her well. She was a beautiful young woman with long light-brown hair and blue eyes. She was twenty years old when you were born. Please know that she loved you very much, but in those times very few unmarried women were allowed to keep their children. The consequences of those decisions are still being felt today.

I understand that your parents in Boston are good people who gave you a fantastic upbringing. Robyn spoke highly of them in her emails. May I say, you also have a lovely caring wife!

Brandon, I could be wrong, but I sense that this search has been instigated by Robyn. No doubt the information in my letter is hard to take on board. I have sent both bracelets in the hope that one day, if you so choose, you will be able to meet your twin and pass it on.

Whatever you decide, I would urge you to call me so we can talk this through. I'm sure you'll have questions and I'll do my best to answer them. My number is at the bottom of the page

With all best wishes from Dublin,
Katie Carroll

Robyn and Brandon exchanged a look, her eyes suggesting she was as bewildered as him.

'Oh my God,' she said finally. 'Oh. My. God.'

Brandon's hands were shaking so hard he had difficulty opening the second envelope. As Katie had promised, it contained two narrow curls of paper, for Brendan and Edward Markham. Brendan had been the heavier of the pair, weighing a shade under five pounds.

How can this be happening? he thought. How can it be real?

'Are you all right?' said Robyn. 'We should sit down.'

Still without speaking, he followed her to the living room. They sat side by side on the sofa. Robyn clasped his hand.

'I had no idea,' she said. 'No clue. How could I?'

'Why is she so confident that I'm Brendan?' was the first thing he said.

'Guesswork, I'd say. I told her that Brendan was your name as a kid. Most adoptive parents change their child's first name, but some don't. Or so I've read.'

'It's wild,' he said. 'I assumed I had half-brothers or sisters. It stood to reason. But this? This never occurred to me. Never in a million years would I have thought it possible.'

'From what I've read, when it came to those homes, anything was possible.'

'I suppose. Did you notice that she didn't say whether we're identical?'

'No, I hadn't thought of that. Perhaps it means you're not, but—' Robyn came to a sudden halt. 'What about your mom and dad?'

'They can't have known. They wouldn't have lied to me.'

Or would they? Brandon needed to think, but his mind had seized up, and his surroundings appeared to have taken life. The white walls and denim-blue chairs, the 1950s coffee table and vintage rugs, all chosen to create an atmosphere of serenity, had become a messy blur.

'I'll fix us a drink,' said Robyn. 'What would you like?'

'I'm not sure there's a liquor strong enough for how I'm feeling. I'll settle for a whiskey, though. Just ice.'

When she returned, Robyn asked the obvious question, the one he'd been avoiding.

'Do you want to find him?'

'If you'd asked an hour ago, I'd have said no. But the guy's my twin. We're two halves. So … I don't know.'

A quick internet search failed to supply any suitable Eddie or Edward Markhams. Brandon hadn't expected otherwise. Chances were his brother had a different name. Chances were the guy was living an uncomplicated life in Ireland, ignorant of the fact that he had a twin. Then again, he might also have been sent to America. He might be in LA or New York or Boise, Idaho. He might be elsewhere in Boston.

'Will you call Katie?' asked Robyn. 'She's obviously keen to hear from you.'

'Sorry to be repetitive, but I don't know. I probably will, if only to get the complete story.'

Brandon put down his glass and pulled Robyn close. He buried his face in her hair. Until an hour earlier, his life been perfectly ordered. As with the decor, he'd put considerable effort into ensuring that everything was harmonious. Now, he'd been tipped into the universe of the unexpected, a place of sharp edges and dangerous bends, and it wasn't where he wanted to be.

He woke at 3.13, his brain busy busy busy. Beside him, Robyn slept, her breathing shallow and steady. Outside, the wind had strengthened. Something – nothing important, he hoped – creaked.

Almost immediately, he was gripped by irritation. Why couldn't she have left well enough alone? Why did she have to meddle? There'd been no need to go poking and prodding and looking under stones.

He thought of his childhood enemy, Scott Miller. How Miller would have enjoyed this. 'There you go, Bennett,' he'd have said, 'your mom must've held on to the better twin and rejected you.'

Stop, he thought, you're being stupid.

If he was angry – and he was – Robyn was the wrong target. He'd been born in a country where children had been sold, at a time when not telling someone they were a twin had been considered acceptable. The knowledge caught in his throat until he felt he would choke.

He wondered if some part of him had always known, and if this explained why he'd been reluctant to explore his origins. Had his instincts told him it could all get complicated? Or were these the deluded three-in-the-morning thoughts of someone who'd received a shock?

One minute, he would decide to call Katie. Hell, he'd think, I'll do it straight away; it's already past eight in Ireland. The next, he'd consider throwing the letter in the trash and trying to forget. He switched the pillow over to the cool side and closed his eyes. He turned one way and then the other. But sleep wouldn't come.

Chapter 14

Then, Patricia

'Do you think I'm bad?' asked Winnie, examining her shorn hair in the bathroom mirror. 'I mean, is there a chance that Sabina's right, and I'm going to spend the rest of my days causing trouble?'

'Ah, here,' said Patricia, who was standing behind her, 'you've more sense than to listen to that old witch. Of course you're not bad. If there's anyone who ought to have a look at themselves, it's her. You're to forget her nonsense.'

'That's easy for you to say,' said Winnie, her tone surprisingly humorous. 'You've got all your hair.' She ran a hand over what remained of her own curls. 'The state of me. There's no danger of a fella looking in my direction any time soon. Mind you, given that I'm likely to be working here until I'm twenty-five, I'll probably never meet a fella again.'

'You don't think your family will pay to have you released?'

'Do you know how much it costs? A hundred pounds! Short of winning the Sweepstakes, they'd never be able to afford that. What about you?'

'I don't expect my family'd have the money either.'

Winnie sighed. 'Maybe I'll end up running away after all.'

When she'd first arrived in Carrigbrack, Patricia had overheard a conversation between Agnes and one of the other nuns. From it, she'd gathered that the government also contributed to the cost of running the home. She suspected that making women stay after their babies had been adopted was as unnecessary as it was unkind.

Three days after the singing protest, its repercussions rippled on. Sister Agnes, a cunning operator, had waited until they were worn out and parched for want of food and drink. Gradually, their shoulders had slumped, their voices had weakened and their solidarity had leaked away. Some had felt sick. Others had needed to feed their babies. By nine o'clock that night, they'd had to surrender.

It wasn't as though the protest had been in pursuit of any particular aim or agenda; more that, for a short time, it had made them feel like they had some control over their lives. They'd sung because it had felt good.

The retribution had started the following morning with a rare appearance by Mother Majella, who'd delivered a lengthy sermon about the evils of self-indulgence. So severe was the talking-to that Patricia had been transported back to her school days. She'd half expected a few slaps from a size 15 knitting needle or the metal edge of a ruler, both favoured punishments in St Joseph's National School. Instead, along with Winnie, she'd been transferred to the laundry. The work there was hard, the temperature unbearable. Patricia's baby had taken to dancing jigs, and she regularly had to pause and wait for him, or her, to stop. On the plus side, she no longer had to put up with Sister Sabina.

Winnie was brought to Sister Agnes's office, where her hair was cut back to her scalp. Agnes went out of her way to do a bad job. There was no hint of Twiggy or Mia Farrow about Winnie's crop. Nothing gamine or sophisticated. She looked like a boy who'd fallen foul of a short-sighted barber. Or like a convict. Patricia steeled herself for something similar, but the summons never came. She felt guilty. Did she not deserve the same fate as her co-conspirator? Winnie told her not to be silly. 'Don't draw attention to yourself for the next few days,' she advised. 'One of us looking like we belong in a horror picture is bad enough.'

To begin with, Winnie reacted with stoicism. She said nothing as she swept up her beautiful hair and threw it into the bin. Afterwards, she went about her work without complaint. Spool forward a couple of days, however, and the punishment was wearing her down.

The bathroom beside their dormitory had cracked black lino, walls the colour of cooking fat and a stench of disinfectant. The mirror was marked with brown dots. It was also one of a handful of places where it was possible to talk without facing the wrath of Agnes or Sabina.

After Winnie had inspected her hair, the two girls sat on the floor. They needed to take the weight off their swollen feet.

'Why did she have to do this to me? I mean, I was already the size of a house. Now I'm pig-ugly too,' said Winnie, before adding, 'Jesus, I sound like Jacinta.' She steepled her hands and looked skywards. 'Please, God, don't let me turn into Jacinta.'

Patricia grinned. 'I don't think there's much fear of that.'

Winnie patted her bump. 'Sorry, in there, by the way. I didn't mean to be nasty about you. I hope everything's going okay.'

'Speaking of Jacinta, I hear she had a tough time.'

Jacinta's baby had arrived the previous day. A giant of a boy, his delivery had been long and agonising. Word had it that she'd suffered a bad tear. The nurse had argued that she needed stitches, but Sister Agnes wouldn't hear of it. 'Let her mend in her own good time,' she'd said.

Winnie grimaced. 'Her story put the frighteners on me, all right.'

'Anyway,' said Patricia, running a hand through the pale brown hair that had become increasingly streelish during her time in Carrigbrack, 'don't worry about your curls. When they grow back, they'll be lovely again. Some of us are stuck with wishy-washy hair.'

'Would you ever go blonde?'

'My father would have a conniption. He says that dyed hair is cheap.'

'I hate to break it to you, but if he survived the news that his daughter was in the family way and the baby's father already had a wife, he'll probably survive anything.'

'Blonde it is, so,' said Patricia.

'Feck. Did you hear footsteps?'

'Can we pretend we're saying a prayer?'

Winnie giggled.

'Shush,' said Patricia, but she was laughing too.

'Hello,' said a young voice. 'What's going on in there?' It was Sister Eunice. 'What are you doing on the floor?'

'We were dying for a rest, Sister,' said Winnie. 'We were melting below in the laundry. You won't tell anyone, will you?'

'No, I think you've had more than enough bother for one week.' With that, Sister Eunice hitched up her skirt and eased herself to the ground. 'Move over there, if you wouldn't mind. I could do with a rest myself.'

Although Eunice was the friendliest of the nuns, Patricia was taken aback to see her joining them on the floor, especially given their reputation as troublemakers.

If Winnie was similarly surprised, she didn't let it show. 'You must be roasting in that gear,' she said, glancing at the nun's heavy black dress and tights as thick as bandages.

'I'm used to it, but yes, at the minute, something lighter would be nice.' Eunice removed her clumpy grey shoes. 'I was sorry to hear about your hair, Winnie, but it'll be back to normal in no time.'

'Thanks.'

'Don't tell any of the others I said that. Obviously.'

'You're grand. Do you mind if I ask: how old are you?'

'I'm twenty-three.'

Patricia was wary. She assumed Eunice would give them a lecture, however gently worded, about their wayward behaviour. Still, there was nothing to be gained by being rude. 'That's only three years older than me,' she said.

'Did you always want to be a nun?' asked Winnie.

Eunice smiled. 'Now, there's a question. Not always, no. But I was happy to take on the challenge. I'm fortunate that my faith is strong.'

Patricia was tempted to ask how she felt about imprisoning women who'd committed no crime, but she didn't want to make Eunice uncomfortable. 'Do you ever miss the outside world?' she asked.

'She means, would you like to go out with men,' said Winnie. 'She's got a terrible dirty mind, that one.'

'I do not.'

Eunice gave a nervous tinkle of laughter and sidestepped the question. 'This is the life I've chosen, and I've got to make the most of it.'

'If I had a few hours' freedom, do you know what I'd like?' said Winnie. 'I've a fierce longing for chips from the chip shop, steaming hot, with a good shake of salt and plenty of vinegar. What about you, Patricia? What would you do?'

'I wouldn't mind a proper sleep in my own bed.'

'Ah, stop, you can do better than that.'

'Okay, then. I'd go to the pictures.'

'What would you see?'

'I'm not sure. Something with Paul Newman ... or Omar Sharif.'

'Aren't you the wild one? You see, Eunice, there you are thinking we're right bold hussies, when all we want to do is eat chips and watch soppy films. Oof.' Winnie placed a hand on her stomach. 'Whoever's in there is doing a fair amount of dancing today. I reckon they're learning the hucklebuck.'

'You haven't long to go,' said Eunice.

'Three weeks or so, I think.'

The nun arched her feet. 'If I had to pick a small pleasure, I'd choose nicer shoes. And I wouldn't mind wearing lipstick occasionally. A nice pale pink, perhaps.' She blushed. 'I probably shouldn't have said that.'

'Your secret's safe with us,' said Patricia.

'If all else failed,' said Winnie, 'I'd settle for a day without any sin-and-misery talk.'

'Amen to that.'

Eunice closed her eyes. 'Don't worry,' she said. 'I promise you, it won't always be like this.'

The hot weather continued into July, and the laundry became ever more hellish. Every day, they washed sheets, towels, baby clothes, nappies, uniforms and habits. The sheets had to be passed through an enormous metal machine called a calender. Its roller was red hot, and many of the girls suffered nasty burns. Without exception, their hands were raw and blistered. Some had developed a rash as far as their elbows, but if you scratched and drew blood you were in serious trouble. As well as the steaming heat and dust-filled air, they had to endure constant noise: the roar of the boiler and the whine of the machines.

What made the laundry bearable was the camaraderie of the workers. Despite being forced to carry out their tasks in silence, they supported each other through smiles and shrugs. Patricia marvelled at their ability to communicate without making a sound.

One day, when the nun in charge, Sister Faustina, had left the room, they had a chance to talk.

Winnie asked a familiar question. 'Suppose,' she said, 'you could have anything you wanted, what would it be?

Without hesitation, one of them replied, 'Cream for my rash.' She displayed her hands, which were a mess of weals and sores.

The others voiced their agreement.

The following day, Winnie told them that if they went to the toilet beside the refectory, they'd find a treat. 'Don't all go at once,' she said. 'I can't risk Faustina or any of the others finding out. I've no more hair to give.'

Somehow, she'd managed to steal a tub of Sudocrem from the nursery and hide it in the cistern. One by one, the women went to the bathroom and applied the cream to their sore hands. They had to rub it in well for fear Faustina noticed. Thankfully, she wasn't overly observant. When the theft was discovered, there was an inquiry, but no one told tales, and the fuss died down again.

As her time drew closer, Winnie became more skittish. When they were able to talk, she mused about how awful giving birth might be. 'I'm sure it's rough no matter where you are,' she'd say. 'The difference is that here they actually want you to suffer.' Patricia would try to change the conversation, but her successes were rare. In a way, she envied Winnie's ability to speak about what frightened her. All her friend's emotions were on the surface. In contrast, Patricia could barely acknowledge her fears, not to mind articulate them.

They were in the laundry when Winnie started to complain that she was in pain. Without looking up from her prayer book, Sister Faustina told her to wait a while. It became increasingly apparent, however, that Winnie's baby was in a hurry. At least, that was how it looked to Patricia. One of the others, who'd already given birth, agreed.

'Patricia, this is no concern of yours,' said Faustina. 'It's a well-known fact that first labours are slow. Just because the contractions have begun, it doesn't mean the birth is imminent. Some of the penitents have taken a couple of days to deliver their baby.'

Winnie, who was as white as one of the sheets she was supposed to be ironing, squealed. 'I can't put up with this for another two days.'

'Nobody's suggesting you'll have to stay here for that long. Whisht a moment, will you? You're distracting the rest of us from our work.'

'Please, Sister,' said Patricia, 'I think she needs to go to the delivery room.'

The others murmured their agreement.

'Aaaargh,' called Winnie, gripping the side of the sorting table.

'You do know,' said Faustina, 'that Sister Agnes frowns upon too much noise during labour. You're expected to offer up your pain for the poor souls in purgatory.'

'Fuck the souls in purgatory. They can take care of themselves.'

Faustina shook her head and blessed herself. 'That's a desperate thing to say, Winnie. Desperate entirely. One of these days that mouth is going to get you into serious trouble.'

'She's in trouble right now, Sister,' said Patricia, wiping the sweat from the back of her neck.

'I've already told you to stay out of this. Winnie, describe the pain for me.'

For a while, Winnie said nothing. Or, rather, she said nothing intelligible. Eventually, the terror lifted from her face, and she spoke. 'Everybody told me it was like very bad period pain. But it's not like that at all. It's really intense ... as though ... as though everything in my back is twisting. And I feel like all my insides are going to pop out – not just the baby. Please, Sister, I can't take any more.'

'Sit down over there. We'll wait until the next contraction comes and monitor the situation then.'

Ordinarily, Sister Faustina wasn't the worst of the nuns. Tall, and thin as string, she had a face that appeared to have been carved from the limestone that surrounded them. Patricia thought of her as someone who'd had the religious life foisted upon her. She'd encountered a few similar figures. Often the youngest girl in a large family, they'd taken their vows either because it was expected of them or because it was the only way to get an education. Faustina wasn't as prone to mentioning God or the devil as Sabina. Nor did she have Agnes's predilection for delivering speeches about the failings of modern society. Instead, she chivvied the women along with mild exhortations to do their duty. Mostly she spoke in a low monotone. If anything, Patricia felt sorry for her. On this occasion, however, she believed the nun was making a mistake.

It didn't take long for Winnie's next contraction to arrive. A sheen of sweat covered her face as she moaned and roared. Patricia walked over and held her hand. Winnie attempted a smile, but couldn't quite manage it.

At last, Faustina told her to go to the delivery room.

'May I go with her, Sister?' asked Patricia.

Faustina tilted her head. 'Why would you do that?'

'She needs a friend.'

'Indeed and she does not. If ever a girl could look after herself, it's Winnie.'

'But she's only sixteen, and she's scared.'

Winnie, who was trembling, looked at the nun with pleading eyes.

'No,' said Faustina, with a lethargic wave of her hand, 'and that's my final word on the subject. The rest of you, including Patricia, are to get back to work. We've had enough disruption for one day, and if we don't finish the laundry by our designated time, you'll have to put the hours in this evening.'

'Good luck, Winnie,' shouted several of the women, but she seemed too dazed to acknowledge their support.

The time trickled by. Patricia's head felt as if it was filled with molasses. Unable to concentrate, she burnt her hand on the roller.

Sister Faustina instructed her to hold it under the cold tap. 'If it gets infected, you won't be of any use to anyone,' she said.

Patricia took the opportunity to enquire after Winnie. 'Perhaps I could drop over and see how she's getting on. The baby might have arrived.'

'How many times do you have to be told?' replied Faustina, eyebrows drawing together. 'Winnie's child is none of your business.'

'Yerra, go on, Sister,' said one of the girls. 'We're desperate to know.'

The rest joined in until the chorus became too much for the nun. 'Very well, I'll go and find out. In the meantime, you're to continue *in silence*.' She slapped the table to emphasise her words. 'Any more of your shenanigans, and I'll inform Sister Agnes.'

Patricia found that she could barely move. Winnie's baby had become as important to her as her own. That the child was destined to be raised by someone else was irrelevant. She was filled with anticipation. They'd already decided that Winnie was having a lively girl and Patricia a great lump of a boy.

Not for the first time, she wondered why the babies and their mothers couldn't be treated with more dignity. Maybe even some kindness. Surely someone like Sister Eunice would understand that? She remembered hearing a discussion on the wireless. A woman had proposed that unmarried mothers be allowed to stay with families rather than in a home. Their parents would be saved from embarrassment, she'd said, but the atmosphere would be less judgemental. They could do housework, or help on the farm, to pay for their keep. Afterwards, the babies would be adopted. In a limited number of cases, the mother would be allowed to bring up her own child. This appealed to Patricia.

She touched her bump. 'Today's a big day,' she whispered.

When Sister Faustina returned, her announcement was terse. 'Winnie had a girl,' she said before giving a short, tight smile.

'How big was she, Sister?'

'How is she?'

'How's Winnie?'

'Did Winnie's roaring drive Sister Agnes demented?'

The questions overlapped until Faustina raised one hand. 'That's none of your concern. Settle down, and we'll all return to our jobs.'

Patricia's skin turned cold. 'Is Winnie all right?' she said.

'I've told you to get back to work.'

'Please say she's all right.'

Faustina folded her arms across her chest. 'I won't tell you again, Patricia. The rules apply to everyone here, and there's a job to be done.'

A babble rose up around them. Patricia wasn't alone in thinking there was something disturbing about the nun's behaviour. 'Sister, I asked you a question.'

'And I told you to follow the rules and finish your work.'

The others stopped talking.

'I don't give two hoots about the rules,' said Patricia. 'I want to know about Winnie and her little girl.'

'If I have to tell Sister Agnes about your behaviour, I will. You were moved here because you couldn't be trusted in the garden, and I'm starting to see why.'

Had she been asked, Patricia would have said that, at eight months pregnant, she wasn't capable of running. She would have said there was no way she would break the rules and court further punishment. Before she fully appreciated what she was doing, however, she'd barged out of the laundry and was darting helter-skelter down the corridor towards the delivery room. She careened around two girls carrying pails of water before flying past a nun. The nun yelled at her to come back. She ran on.

Lungs burning, legs aching, she arrived at the delivery room. Sister Eunice was standing outside, telltale stains on her cheeks.

Patricia, who'd been clinging to the slim hope that everything was okay, pushed open the door. Winnie was sitting up in bed, her eyes red-rimmed and wild.

'They've taken my baby from me,' she said. 'Why won't they let me see her?'

Chapter 15

Ailish

In more than twenty years, Ailish had never taken a dubious sick day. This was a first. She left home at the usual time, but rather than setting off for Rathtuskert Manor, she turned left and headed towards the coast.

After Keith had burnt the bracelet, she'd felt as low as it was possible to feel. A cold sore had popped up on her top lip, while her eyes had been raspberry red. He'd behaved as if nothing had happened, roaming the house while complaining about work, the weather and anything else that crossed his mind. Yes, she should have tackled him, but she didn't want to make the situation worse. Stevie, who'd always been adept at spotting trouble, spent most evenings with friends or at Jodie's house. Several times, he asked if something was wrong, but she fobbed him off. She didn't think she could talk without getting emotional. Her son needed to focus on his exams, not some pointless parental stand-off about an old strip of paper.

A malaise came over her, a form of paralysis. She ate dinners she couldn't remember cooking. She did her job by rote. The problem with Keith was that he resented anything he considered to be hers and hers alone. She wished she could convince him that finding her birth mother would be positive for them both.

She'd considered leaving. No doubt that was what the experts would advise. But where would she go? Where would Stevie go? She couldn't disrupt her son's life. Not now.

If she couldn't talk to her husband, she also feared contacting Katie. She'd let her down. For decades, Katie had kept the bracelet safe. Ailish had allowed herself to get caught up in a fantasy world where all she could think of was meeting Chrissie. She'd been careless and she'd paid the price.

Not being in contact with Katie meant she hadn't been able to find out more about Gary Winters's search. She'd told Stevie about his visit to Kilmitten, and while Black Iris weren't his sort of music (he'd referred to them as 'old white dudes with guitars'), he'd been impressed.

For more than a month, Ailish had tried to find the strength to push on. During that time, she'd received a letter from the Adoption Authority, confirming that her request was on file. In due course, the letter said, her case would be considered. It also warned of a lengthy wait. She decided she'd waited long enough. If she was going to find Chrissie, she would have to do it herself.

Hackett's Cross was set back slightly from the ocean. In early December, the Atlantic was greenish-grey; white-tipped waves crashed to the rocky shore. Wind and salt water had combined to give the few buildings a battered appearance. The trees were buckled and bent. Although Ailish didn't expect to find Chrissie in her home village, she hoped someone would remember her.

In the shop, a woman in an electric-blue tabard sat behind the counter watching *Judge Judy* on a small grey television. She looked

Ailish up and down, then up again. At this time of year, it was unlikely she encountered many strangers. Ailish explained that she was trying to track down the Culligan family.

'Years ago, they were friendly with my parents,' she said. 'They lost touch, and as I was in the area, I thought I'd see if I could find them again.'

'Christine Culligan?' said the woman, whose eyelash extensions crossed the line between glamorous and Daisy the cow. 'The name means nothing to me. I've only been here since 2005, mind. You'd want to ask in the Cross Tavern. One of the regulars might be able to help.'

Ailish glanced at her watch. 'Will it be open at this time of the morning?'

A smile passed across the shopkeeper's doughy face. 'What else would people be doing on a day like this? Take it from me, you'll find one or two in there.'

Ailish didn't argue. Hackett's Cross was so quiet, it made Kilmitten look like Beijing.

The Cross Tavern was two doors down from the shop. No matter that smoking in pubs had been illegal for the past fifteen years, the place managed to smell of cigarettes and stale beer. The purple carpet had a spongy quality, and the housekeeper in Ailish recoiled. In the one concession to Christmas, a lacklustre strip of silver tinsel hung over the bottles of spirits.

As predicted, there was a handful of customers. In a far corner, a man and woman were drinking tea and having a low-level argument. One man sat at the bar with a pint of stout, while three more occupied the seats closest to the television. A cookery show played silently on an old-style set. Ailish was glad to note that all the patrons appeared to be over seventy. The older they were, the greater the chance they'd recall something about Chrissie.

The barman, a fellow with a beak of a nose and a thatch of red hair, was guarded bordering on hostile.

'Why would you want to know that, now?' he asked.

Ailish repeated her line about the Culligans being old family friends.

'Patsy and Biddy Culligan?' said the man at the bar. 'Low-sized people? Quiet?'

A chill ran down her back. On Chrissie's birth certificate, her parents had been named as Patrick and Bridget. 'That's right.'

'I'm afraid they're a long time dead, pet. The Lord have mercy on Patsy, he must be gone thirty years or more. And Biddy didn't last long after him.'

'Did they—?'

'They'd a son, Collie; he's dead too.'

'Oh. Wasn't there also a daughter? That's who my parents knew. She'd be in her sixties now. Christine … or Chrissie, maybe?'

'A daughter? No, I don't think so. I only remember Collie. A harmless lad, if ever there was one.' The man tipped his head towards his pint. 'A bit of a martyr for this stuff, if you get my drift.' His face was opaque, and it was impossible to say how truthful he was being.

The barman, who was polishing pint glasses on a stained tea towel, decided to make himself useful. 'Lads,' he called to the three men near the television, 'do any of ye remember the Culligans? Patsy and Biddy? Had a son called Collie? May have had a daughter called Christine?'

'The only place you'll find them is above in the graveyard,' replied the eldest of the three, a squat man in a loud sports jacket. 'God love them, they made no age.'

His friends murmured in agreement.

The bar became silent, and Ailish was aware that her presence wasn't welcome.

'Sorry not to have been more use to you,' said the barman. 'Can I get you anything?'

'No, thanks,' she replied, her disappointment tempered a little by the knowledge that she could visit the family grave. She'd noticed the church and graveyard on her way into the village. 'And thanks for your help.' She smiled at the man with the pint and pulled out a fiver from the pocket of her jeans.

'No bother, sweetheart.' He accepted the money without demur. 'Oh, if you want to see their house, it's up the lane there,' he pointed towards the back of the bar, 'and on a little bit. There's not much of it left, mind.'

She followed his directions, such as they were. As she walked the lane, a thin wind whipped around her. She dug her hands deep into the pockets of her navy winter coat. For some reason, she was hit by a childhood memory. Her mother, Deirdre, had attached her gloves to either end of a long piece of wool and threaded it through the sleeves of her anorak. 'You've a head on you like a sieve,' she had said. 'I can't trust you to mind those gloves.' At school, they'd laughed at Ailish. But she'd never lost her gloves.

After about five hundred metres, she arrived at an abandoned cottage. While not quite a ruin – all the walls were standing – it was ravaged beyond redemption. The once white facade was pockmarked with brown and grey. The windows were boarded up, while the faded green door was warped and peeling. Slates were poised to slide from the roof. Grass grew to waist height. Ivy and brambles wrapped themselves around every available surface. In the undergrowth, something scurried and rustled. The house where her birth mother had grown up was being reclaimed by nature.

Ailish stamped her foot with frustration. Once again, she'd thought that if she wanted something badly enough, it would be hers. Once again, she'd been wrong. She felt like she was trying to crack a walnut with her teeth. While technically possible, the task was slow and painful. She stood there letting everything sink in, tears stinging her eyes.

The men in the bar had claimed not to remember Chrissie, but Ailish didn't believe them. Rumour and innuendo lived long in a small village. How plausible was it that they could recall three of the Culligan family but not the one member about whom there must have been gossip? How absurd was it, how twisted, that half a century later, those men were still governed by a code of silence? A lot might have changed, but Hackett's Cross remained a village of blind eyes and deaf ears.

She removed a tissue from her coat pocket and blotted her tears. Then she took several photos of the crumbling cottage. Finally she bent down and picked up a tiny black stone. She wanted a token from the place where Chrissie had spent her childhood. It wasn't an adequate replacement for the bracelet, but it was something.

As she reached the graveyard, drizzle began to fall from the grout-grey sky. Two huge seagulls swooped in and perched on the wall. A third hovered, squawking all the while. St Aidan's church was mottled with lichen and moss, but its door was freshly varnished. The Culligans' house had spoken of poverty, and Ailish wondered if the family had a gravestone. To her relief, they did. To her surprise, it was shiny and well kept. Although there were no flowers, the grass around it had been cut.

The stone told her that Patrick Culligan had died in November 1984. His wife, Bridget, had died in March 1985; their son, Colm, ten years later. Her grandfather, her grandmother, her uncle. All had been tragically young. Ailish said a prayer, a few hurried lines, hoping that if there was a heaven, that was where they were. For the first time, a sliver of hope rose within her. At the very least, Chrissie must have returned for her family's funerals. Who else could have paid for the headstone? Again, Ailish got out her phone, crouched down and took some photos.

As she did so, she noticed a man crunching along the path towards her. A sludge-coloured woolly hat was pulled low over his face, and it took her a few seconds to recognise him as one of the three fellows who'd been sitting near the television.

'That wind would skin you,' he said, in a quiet rasp of a voice.

''Twould.'

He shuffled from one foot to the other. 'I was hoping you'd still be here.'

'Oh?'

'A word to the wise. The girl of the Culligans? She went to England. As far as I know, she's in London.'

'You don't happen to know whereabouts?'

'I don't.' He peered at the ground. 'I do recall that she was married, so she's no longer Culligan.'

'Thanks a million,' said Ailish. 'Would any of the folks around here be likely to have her married name, do you think?'

'I doubt you'll find anyone willing to tell you more than I can.'

'I see. I really appreciate your help.'

The man looked up. He was older than she'd thought. His cheeks were a criss-cross of deep lines, and his blue eyes were so pale they were practically colourless. His face was damp from the rain. 'I wish you good luck,' he said. 'She was a lovely young girl, and, bless her, she was treated very badly.' He hesitated. 'You're the living image of her.'

He didn't say any more. He didn't have to.

'Thank you,' she said again, but he was already on his way.

In the car, she tried to compose her thoughts. London. It wasn't a lot, but it was more than she'd had this morning. The haystack was ever so slightly smaller. She examined the images of the Culligans' cottage and their gravestone. Then she made a call.

'Hello,' answered a friendly voice.

'Katie?' said Ailish. 'I've got to tell you something.'

Chapter 16

Katie

If Katie had mixed feelings about her conversation with Ailish, it was because she was appalled by Keith's behaviour. Even as Ailish told her about the progress she'd made in Hackett's Cross, all Katie could think of was the burnt bracelet. In the grand scheme of things, it didn't matter. It was just a slip of paper. What disturbed her was Keith's malice – and how Ailish kept apologising for it. Katie didn't want contrition. She wanted anger. That wasn't all. More than once, Ailish made excuses for her husband. 'He's under pressure at work,' she said, 'and, to be fair, I could have done a better job of handling things.'

Katie tutted and clucked but managed to avoid raising her voice. Altogether more pleasing was the news about Chrissie. Okay, they still had a distance to go, but Ailish's birth mother being in London rang true. Many women had left the country. Katie had heard them on the radio, talking about their teenage experiences in one institution or another, their accents shot through with Liverpool or New York.

She'd assumed that this would be a quiet time of year for Ailish. Not so, apparently. Between dinner dances and Christmas parties, Rathtuskert Manor was constantly busy, and a lot of the partygoers stayed overnight.

'All one-night stays,' said Ailish, 'which is a complete pain. But now that I'm on Chrissie's trail again, I'm determined to make enquiries whenever I can.'

Katie convinced her that she too should make some calls. 'I've plenty of time,' she said, 'and I've got a willing assistant.'

Ailish asked about Gary's progress. Katie told the truth: there hadn't been any. Neither had she had much contact with him lately. They'd both seen pieces in the paper about Black Iris playing concerts the following year. The speculation still had it that Gary wouldn't be there. Katie wished she knew why but was scared to ask. She didn't want to appear meddlesome. She'd watched several Black Iris videos on YouTube, as well as a documentary about one of their most popular songs. 'Overboard', it was called. The music was more melodic than she'd expected, joyous and sad in equal measure. How cruel was it that Gary's biological parents didn't know what he'd achieved?

The priest in Hackett's Cross was taken aback to receive an enquiry about long-dead parishioners. Although he might have guessed at the story behind Katie's query, neither of them acknowledged it. In a hesitant voice, he explained that he was new to the parish and couldn't say what had happened back in the eighties or nineties. Katie asked if his predecessor might know.

'Ah,' came the answer. 'That'd be a bit tricky. His health isn't the best, and he's wandering a little.'

Recognising this as west-of-Ireland-speak for 'That's out of the question because he's seriously ill and has advanced dementia', she moved on.

The funeral director was brusque. His father would have known who'd arranged the Culligans' funerals, he said, but the old man had died ten years earlier. The records didn't go back that far, and he wasn't aware of anyone else who would know.

Katie decided she'd have to try a different angle. In the meantime, she had other work to do. There was momentum to the process: one person would see the online noticeboard and contact someone else, who would mention it to a third person, who would talk to a fourth. In quite a few cases, she hadn't been able to help. The person didn't have enough information, or they'd been misled, or they hadn't been born during her time in Carrigbrack. Nevertheless, she was now on friendly terms with the staff of the post office in Drumcondra, who were amused by the woman with the padded envelopes.

So far, twenty-two bracelets had found their way home, and she was at the kitchen table parcelling up number twenty-three. It belonged to a woman called Maeve, whom Katie remembered because she'd been such a sickly baby. How brilliant was it that she'd grown up to become a marathon-running orthopaedic surgeon? Even better, her birth parents had reunited. Maeve had two sisters and a brother to add to the two brothers from her adoptive family. Hers was one of those sweet, sweet cases – and they did exist – where everything was out in the open and everybody got along. It lifted Katie's heart.

Other stories continued to gnaw at her. Every day she thought of Brandon. She'd received an email from Robyn, who said he was finding the news hard to process. Robyn promised to stay in touch, but, three weeks on, Katie was less optimistic. She feared that sending both bracelets had been a mistake.

Beth was unimpressed. 'That fellow has no manners' and 'What sort of loo-la wouldn't want to know about their *twin*?' were two of her milder observations. Katie was slower to judge. His world had been upended. He needed time to adjust.

The longer she spent at her task, the more she treasured contact with the Carrigbrack children. She was fascinated by how their unorthodox beginnings had moulded their lives. Since the first contact from Robyn, the Carrigbrack Nurse account had received another query from the United States. Sadly, that adoption had taken place five years before Katie's stint in the home, so she wasn't able to help. She replied to the man, a plumber from Philadelphia, offering advice about the best way to proceed.

'What are you like?' said Beth, who was patrolling the kitchen, waving her freshly painted nails in the air in preparation for a Christmas party. 'Could you not give it a rest for one evening?'

'It's good for the older person to have an interest. Isn't that what the magazines advise?'

Beth smiled. 'I think they mean golf or yoga or something.'

'Can you see me playing golf? Anyway, as you might say, I've got to look after my posse.'

There was another job on Katie's to-do list, one she was dreading. For the first time in her adult life, her Christmas cards would have only one signature at the bottom. Her mind skipped back to how Johnny had scrutinised their lists. 'Why are we wasting a stamp on that old killjoy, Kateser?' he used to say, or 'Are you certain she's still in the land of the living?' But he'd only been messing; he'd loved sending and receiving Christmas cards. Beth's generation weren't so enthusiastic. She'd assured Katie that no one would blame her for giving the cards a miss this year. She didn't understand the importance of ritual.

'So,' she said now, 'will you be coming home with me for Christmas?'

'I'm not sure you need me around the place.'

'Sorry, I made that sound like a question. It's an order. Mam said no sister of hers would be spending Christmas on her own.'

'You're determined to make me suffer, aren't you?'

Margo remained in the dark about the bracelets. When they

spoke, Katie reeled off a list of make-believe activities she claimed were occupying her time. 'I'm unbelievably busy,' she'd say.

Beth laughed, then sat down beside her. She was wearing a cornflower-blue leopard-print dress. On many, it would have looked garish, but Beth was pretty enough to carry it off. 'You'd be doing me an enormous favour. Relations are still a bit on the strained side, and it'd be great to have another ally about the place. Besides, I'd feel like an almighty cow if I left you here on your own.'

No matter what Katie did or where she went, this was going to be a difficult Christmas. She and Johnny had created a lifetime of traditions – Midnight Mass, chicken rather than turkey, a walk in Howth on St Stephen's Day – and they'd been stolen from her. She'd had no opportunity to prepare. Twelve months earlier, she hadn't even known he was ill. She didn't want to go to Danganstown, wear a paper hat and eat an overly fussy dinner. Deep down, Margo probably didn't want her there either. She was fulfilling what she saw as her obligation, and Katie didn't want to be anyone's obligation. She'd prefer to stay in Dublin and mark the day in private. Alas, she didn't have a choice.

'Go on, then,' she said to Beth. 'I'm not staying past the twenty-seventh, mind. I'm a busy woman.'

Three days later, the email arrived. Brandon was ready to talk.

Beth fixed up her phone so they could use FaceTime. Call her old-fashioned, but Katie could never adjust to watching people on the telephone. It was too science fiction for her. This was what Brandon had suggested, however, and she was keen to accede to his wishes. She took a moment to reflect on the strangeness of it all. Here she was on Griffin Road in Dublin, talking to a man in Boston, Massachusetts; a man she'd known as a baby but could never have expected to see again.

She'd already seen him online. The first picture she'd found was on the website of a company called Longwalk Investments, where he was a senior fund manager. With his neat hair, navy blazer and cautious smile, he looked like he'd stepped out of a back-to-school catalogue. The images on Robyn's Instagram were more interesting. He was pictured at a barbecue, on a beach, in a bar. There was something wooden about him. Although she told herself not to judge a person's character from a handful of photos, Katie suspected that Brandon was one of those people whose eyes scoped the room at parties. Not because he wanted to hook up with a different woman (he would have to be completely mad), but because he was permanently on the lookout for someone important or successful.

Robyn, on the other hand, was born to have her picture taken. Like many young people, she knew how to pose without appearing gormless or drunk or double-chinned. When she looked at the lens, she was fully engaged. Oh, and she was beautiful, with the glossy hair and dewy skin of the wealthy and the blessed.

The Brandon who called was a little less manicured, a little more baggy-eyed than his photos had suggested. His shoulders were in a tense line, his hair in need of a trim. For a minute or two, they swapped nervous chit-chat. Katie had expected him to have a strong accent, but it was disappointingly neutral. He sounded only slightly more American than Gary. He told her that, while he'd been to London and Paris, he'd never returned to Ireland.

A flock of butterflies had set up home in her stomach. As a nurse, she'd often had to face challenging questions, and she feared that in many cases, she'd flubbed the answer. She'd told patients less – or more – than they'd needed to know. Still, her uniform had been her chain mail. It had helped her feel like a woman in control. This was different.

'So then,' she said, after they'd tiptoed through the initial pleasantries. 'I'm sure you're anxious to hear what I remember about your birth, your brother and your mother.'

'Yes. A little nervous, too.'

That makes two of us, thought Katie. 'I should say that I wasn't there for your delivery, so any knowledge I have is second-hand. But I'll do my very best to answer your questions.'

'Okay.'

'Like I mentioned in the letter, your birth mother's real name was Linda. She was a bright spark, a fine young woman. While her bump might have been bigger than average, no one, including Linda herself, suspected she was having twins. Afterwards, lots of people said, "I should have spotted this", or "You should have noticed that." Folks wondered why she hadn't guessed herself. But it was her first pregnancy, and while she did report a lot of kicking and thrashing, that was dismissed as a good sign. "A fine healthy baby," everyone said.'

Brandon blinked. 'That sounds kind of odd. Was there genuinely no way of knowing she was carrying twins? Shouldn't you or one of your colleagues have had suspicions?'

'You've got to understand that we're talking about almost fifty years ago … and we're talking about an isolated home in the west of Ireland. We had no tests, no ultrasound, nothing. That's not to say we shouldn't have considered the possibility.'

'All right.'

'As is often the case with twins, Linda went into labour early. Even before the first baby was delivered, the midwife suspected there were two of you in there. You were wrapped around each other, so, as you can imagine, it was a challenging birth. Your mother suffered a lot, and afterwards there were fears for her well-being. Some of the nuns wouldn't have been particularly sympathetic, and they usually expected a new mother to return to work a week or so after the birth. In Linda's case, it was three weeks before she had the strength to go back to her job in the laundry.'

'Three weeks?' said Brandon. 'Is that normal? I'm no expert, but would she not have needed more recovery time?'

Katie stopped herself from telling him that, by Carrigbrack standards, a three-week break was an eternity – and an indication that Linda had been seriously ill. 'Yes. Your mother was badly treated, Brandon, and I wouldn't try to defend it. She should, of course, have been given more time.'

'So tell me about us. My brother and I. Were we identical?'

'You were. You were small and delicate, but you were fine. There were no immediate signs that either of you had a problem. After a short while, the other young mothers were lining up to admire you.' Katie remembered everyone cooing over Linda's twins. She also remembered Sabina shooing them away as though there was something sinful about wanting to cuddle a baby.

Brandon looked to the side. There was a delay before he spoke again. 'When you say "no immediate signs", do I take it a problem emerged?'

Katie swallowed. 'Yes. No doubt you've asked yourself how I could be certain that you were the twin called Brendan. It wasn't just the name that answered that question for me. Within a couple of months, it became apparent that there was something different about Edward, or Eddie, as we called him. Sometimes he was too floppy. At other times, too rigid. There were no issues with your development. Right from the beginning, you were sharp and alert.'

A hint of understanding ran across Brandon's face, but he said nothing.

'Because she'd had a hard time of it, Linda had trouble feeding you both, and one of the nuns – Sister Sabina – accused her of not looking after you properly. She said that if there was something amiss with Eddie, it was his mother's fault.'

'That was a crock of BS anyway,' said Brandon. 'I can't believe they were allowed to speak to her like that.'

'They were, and unfortunately some of them did. Now, obviously, whatever was wrong with Eddie wasn't Linda's fault. But

I do remember she was distraught. Bless her, she was so upset, the nuns threatened her with the psychiatric hospital.' Katie paused to collect herself. This was proving to be harder than anticipated. 'They sometimes made those threats, but in reality, few girls were sent there.'

'But some were?'

'I'm afraid so.'

'So, correct me if I've got this wrong: a pregnant young woman was abandoned by the father of her child, or, as it turned out, children. Then she was banished from home and sent to a brutal institution. After she'd endured a terrible birth, she realised that one of her babies wasn't well. Sick, and no doubt exhausted, she found it hard to cope. Despite this, she received no help. Worse, she was forced to do manual labour. Oh, and she was told that everything was her own lousy fault. When that upset her, she was threatened with an even harsher institution, one where she might be locked up for the rest of her days.'

'Yes. I … I can't argue with any of what you've said.'

Brandon was becoming increasingly agitated. Katie might not know much about him, but she could tell he was someone who didn't like the unexpected. Momentarily, she thought of Johnny. He'd been skilled at soothing the anger of others. It wasn't so much that he'd said the right words; more that he'd known how to sound reassuring. Stop it, she thought. This isn't the time to get wistful.

She was also conscious that Brandon could see *her* expressions. This amplified her awkwardness. Did her face look too stiff? Too unfeeling? Oh, why couldn't they have spoken on the phone in the old-fashioned way?

'Allow me to be blunt here,' he said, 'but how could you work in a place like that? How did you get up day after day and watch what was happening?'

Beth, who was sitting nearby, attempted to interrupt, but Katie waved her away. She repeated her well-rehearsed lines about not being given a choice and trying to do her best. She didn't make a good job of it. Brandon's face barely moved. Like many others, he didn't accept her explanation.

'I left Carrigbrack in December 1972,' she said, 'when you were four months old. You were both still there, as was your mam. After my departure, I tried to cut all contact with the place. From time to time, I did talk to another nurse. I always asked after Eddie. I don't want to sound patronising, but he was a very likeable baby. And, by all accounts, he grew into a lovely child. By the time he was eight or nine months old, it was clear he had a disability of some sort. He couldn't move his hands or sit up properly. Eventually, the staff realised he had cerebral palsy.'

'Is that because our delivery was screwed up?'

'The simple answer is, I don't know. I promise you, I'm no defender of what happened in Carrigbrack, but, as far as I'm aware, it's just as likely he was starved of blood or had a stroke in the womb. If you want to read up about it, you'll find that twins are at greater risk of being born with cerebral palsy. It'd be wrong to describe it as common, but it's not unusual.'

Brandon frowned. 'Are you saying it was my fault? That I deprived the guy of blood and oxygen?'

Once again, she'd got it wrong. 'Of course I'm not. That never crossed my mind. I'm so sorry. Please don't think I was ...' She instructed herself to remain calm. To try and describe everything in a logical way. As she did so, she noticed Robyn's hand rubbing Brandon's arm. 'Like I told you, it happens. Not enough was known about cerebral palsy back then, but that's all changed.'

The conversation faltered. After what felt like a very long time, but was probably five seconds, he spoke again. 'Can I ask you,' he said, 'about Linda's folks? Given the trauma she must have been through, did they not come to take her home? Did they not intervene?'

'No. That wasn't … that wasn't how things were done.'

'What a fucked-up way to behave. Those people should be ashamed of themselves. Frankly, I'm ashamed to be related to them.'

Katie should have foreseen Brandon's reaction. Wading into a situation in which she had no expertise had been a mistake. Technology might advance and mutate; emotions were more constant. What had happened to Linda, and to many, many others, had been outrageous.

Fearing she was losing control of the conversation, she started afresh. 'I've given this a fair amount of thought down the years, and the best word I have for those times is "mean". There was a meanness about, a lack of generosity. We all liked to see ourselves as generous. We had our collections and our sponsored fasts, and we were always going on about how much we gave to the Missions, but …'

'… generosity was for faraway children, not your own family,' said Brandon.

Faraway children, she thought, and the dead. Usually, back then, the dead had been well treated. In Carrigbrack, however, even that hadn't been true.

'And after I was sent to America,' he said, 'what happened to Eddie?'

'I'm sorry. I don't know.'

'And our mother?'

'Again, I'm afraid I don't know.'

'Should you not have found out before you contacted me?'

'Oh, Brandon, I wish it was that simple. Robyn asked me to pass on the information I had, and that's what I'm doing. The fact that you're only finding out about Eddie now shows you how everything was wrapped in secrecy. If you want to find out more, there's a process you can follow. Who knows, you might discover that Linda and Eddie have been looking for you.'

'If you don't mind me saying so, Mrs Carroll—'

'Katie, please.'

'If you don't mind me saying so, I feel I'm being manipulated. That's why you sent both bracelets to me. Eddie's probably not in any position to ask for his.'

'I know this isn't easy,' she said, 'but I promise I'm not being cagey or playing games with you. I simply don't have all the information. Like I said a moment ago, facts can be hard to come by.'

Katie heard Robyn say, 'That's right.'

There was another pause. Brandon ran a hand through his hair. 'What you've got to appreciate,' he said, 'is that I didn't ask for this. I was completely taken aback by your letter, so I thought about it, and in the end, I said, "A twin, yeah. I should meet my twin. We can have a few beers, compare our lives." And then I thought a bit more, and I said, "Well, maybe it'd be good to get in touch with my birth mother too." From what you're telling me, though, she was put through ten kinds of hell. It'd be a miracle if she held onto her sanity. Oh, and the brother I was looking forward to meeting? He mightn't even know who I am.' He shook his head. 'I'm sorry, this is all too much for me right now.'

'I'm not sure you're reading Eddie's situation correctly,' said Katie, failing to keep the irritation from her voice. 'He has a mild disability, that's all.'

Immediately, she chastised herself. Her memory was of a contented baby. But what if Eddie's disability was more severe than she remembered? While no expert, she was aware that in some cases, cerebral palsy could be extreme. It would be wrong to mislead Brandon.

'The truth,' she said, 'is that I don't have much information about your brother. But, honestly, wherever he is, there's every chance he's perfectly happy.'

'You don't know that.'

'And you don't know otherwise. Either way, if we can find him, I'd say he'd be absolutely delighted to meet you. Please don't be blinded by the fact that he's disabled.'

On the screen, Brandon's eyes narrowed.

As soon as the words left Katie's mouth, she regretted them. 'Sorry,' she said. 'Sorry. I didn't mean that. As I say, I'm conscious that this is a lot to take on board. I shouldn't have sounded judgemental. Please forgive me.'

'No, I'm sorry,' said Brandon. 'We're wasting each other's time here. It's a bleak story, and I feel desperately sad for Linda, but there's nothing either of us can do to change what happened.'

'What are you saying?'

'I'm saying that my first instinct was right, and we should leave the past where it belongs.'

Katie thought she noticed Robyn attempting to say something, but before she could intervene, the line went dead.

Chapter 17

Then, Patricia

Winnie named her daughter Diane. She was buried at the back of the main building, in the same small plot as the other children. The grave had been dug by two girls who'd already had their babies. Later, they would replace the dry stony soil and flatten it out again. Save for a nail knocked into the adjacent wall, Diane's grave would go unmarked. No one would know that an infant girl was buried there. It was better that way, Sister Agnes said.

Four people attended the ceremony: Winnie, Patricia, Agnes and Eunice. Because Diane had died before she could be baptised, there was no priest or funeral Mass. Instead, they said two decades of the rosary at the side of the grave.

According to Agnes, the baby was in heaven. 'Diane left the world in the same hour she entered it,' she'd said. 'She did no harm.' Sister Sabina had loudly disagreed. She'd insisted that, while the child hadn't committed any sins of her own, she'd been tainted by original sin and was trapped in limbo. Winnie hadn't been allowed to hold her daughter. The first time she saw her, she was wrapped in white cloth and ready for burial.

The sky was an uninterrupted blue, the breeze like a warm breath. Patricia felt as if the beauty of the day was mocking them. She imagined how the scene would appear from above. There they were, a tight huddle surrounded by pale grey rocks and bright patches of grass. A hundred yards away, women went about their work: planting and harvesting, chopping and boiling, washing and ironing. Babies gurgled and cried.

Despite the heat, there were goose pimples on Patricia's arms.

Throughout, Winnie was uncharacteristically quiet. Her uniform, which had always been too large, looked absurd, as did her cropped hair. She joined her hands together and kept her gaze on the tiny body. Not once did she cry. Patricia couldn't comprehend her friend's composure. How could she be so strong? She tried to force back her own tears, but they spilled out. At one point, she made an involuntary sound. 'Glug,' she went, prompting a glare from Agnes. Warmth rushed up her neck. If the girl who'd lost her baby was able to maintain her dignity, she should be capable of it too.

In the hours leading up to Diane's burial, Winnie had barely spoken. Patricia believed that one of the few things she did say would stay with her forever:

'Just because I couldn't keep her, it doesn't mean I didn't want the best for her. I wanted her to be brilliant. She deserved to be brilliant.'

Patricia hadn't known how to respond. Every line that entered her mouth sounded like a platitude, like something you'd say on the death of an aged aunt. She simply squeezed Winnie's cold hand.

News of the tragedy had spread through the home, fast as fire. Although a baby had died the previous month, he'd been several weeks old and had already been baptised. There was sympathy for Winnie, but unease too. Those yet to give birth became more anxious. Those with babies in the nursery wanted to spend more time there, something disapproved of by Sister Agnes.

Patricia hadn't expected to attend the burial. Agnes had summoned her to the office, where she'd been scolded for running out of the laundry and for asking questions about Diane's death.

'It may be difficult for us to understand,' she'd said, 'but the Lord works in mysterious ways. You must pray for the grace to accept that.'

Patricia wasn't satisfied. 'But suppose Winnie had been able to go to the delivery room when she'd first raised her concerns? And suppose ...'

Her voice had trailed off. What she'd wanted to say was 'Suppose the nurse in charge had taken more care? Suppose her mind had been on her job rather than on a dance or the pictures or whatever she does when she's not here?' Even in her unsettled state, she realised this would be an accusation too far.

As it was, Agnes's tone was icy. 'I don't ever again want to hear an uncharitable suggestion about Sister Faustina. She could have done many things with her life but she followed her vocation and devoted herself to the service of penitents such as yourself. She deserves your gratitude. Do you follow me?'

'I do, Sister, only—'

'No, Patricia. You've said enough.' Agnes removed her glasses. 'You asked if you could accompany Winnie to the burial. My initial instinct was to say no. However, Sister Eunice tells me you've been a good friend to Winnie. So, given her young age, I've decided to bend the rules. Let me warn you, though, any further disobedience will be punished. Severely.'

Patricia's burnt hand throbbed. 'Thank you, Sister. Have Winnie's parents been told?'

'I don't know why you have to ask so many questions. Meddling is not an appealing trait. Can you not accept that we're dealing with the situation?'

'I was only—'

'Her parish priest has been contacted. In due course, he will inform her father and mother. Now listen to me, Patricia. You're not a stupid young woman, yet you persist in acting like one. I only wish you could see that everything we do here, we do for the right reasons. If it wasn't for Carrigbrack, and other institutions like it, the country would be in chaos. We do our best to help people and to keep Ireland safe. Only the very selfish would think otherwise.'

It probably wasn't the right time for her next question. She thought she'd try anyway. 'Sister, do you ever allow women to keep their babies? Like, say if you knew a mother would be able to take care of her child? That she'd love them and mind them and be able to earn a living? What then?'

'That's a dangerous notion,' said Agnes, a flare of anger in her voice, 'and one you'd do well to forget. We can't allow silly young girls to harm innocent children. As for earning a living: what respectable employer would give work to the mother of an illegitimate child? And what about the good Catholic couples who can't have children of their own? Have you thought about them? Should they be made to suffer?' She gave a brisk shake of her round head. 'Tell me, where does a girl from a decent family hear such ludicrous ideas?'

'I didn't hear the idea so much as think about it myself. I mean, with the way the world is changing and …' The rest of the sentence vanished. There was no point in having this argument now. She would have to make her move at an appropriate time.

After Diane was laid to rest, Winnie was told to spend the rest of the day in silent prayer and contemplation. Patricia returned to the laundry. The atmosphere was sombre. The others glanced at her, then quickly looked away again. She felt as if the connection between her brain and hands had been severed. She knew what to do, but the actions were impossible. Sister Faustina instructed her to sit in the corner.

'Strictly speaking,' she said, 'I should force you to carry out your duties. At the moment, though, you're more hindrance than help.'

'I'm sorry.'

'Sorry isn't of any use. Considering the circumstances, you can sit there for the afternoon, but tomorrow you'll need to be back at full strength. If one person is allowed to shirk, it's not fair to the others. Do we understand each other?'

'Yes, Sister.'

In her heart, Patricia would always blame Faustina for what had happened. She blamed herself too. She should have been more insistent. She should have taken Winnie's arm and marched her out of the laundry. It was what a proper friend would have done. She dwelled on what Sister Agnes had told her at their first meeting. 'Actions have consequences,' she'd said. How, then, could the death of a baby be glossed over and described as God's will? Maybe negligence hadn't been responsible for Diane's death. Maybe Patricia was being unfair. What was clear, though, was that consequences were for little people.

If the burial was handled in a perfunctory manner, Winnie's treatment was devoid of feeling. Three days after her baby's death, she was ordered to return to work. The one concession was that she'd be employed in the kitchen rather than the laundry. The work there wasn't quite as onerous. Patricia suspected the change had more to do with Faustina's guilt than any consideration of Winnie's grief.

Physically, she was in a poor state. She was sore, and her breasts continued to produce milk. It was her mental condition that worried Patricia most. Her speech was staccato, her eyes blank. The real Winnie didn't smother her emotions. She sparkled and fizzed. But that Winnie had disappeared, to be replaced by a hollowed-out person who seemed unaware of what was happening around her.

The following week, she received a letter from home. She showed it to Patricia, who was shocked. Written in pale blue ink on a thin sheet of paper, its contents read as though dictated by Sister Agnes.

The baby's death is sad, wrote her mother, *but it wasn't as if you could have held onto her anyway. You're young, and your chance will come again. Hopefully, next time you'll find a husband first.*

'Daddy would have been more sympathetic,' said Winnie, 'but writing isn't his strong point.'

The letter also revealed that Winnie's eldest sister, to whom she was close, had moved to London.

Patricia did everything she could to make Winnie feel better. She made fun of the nuns and the other girls. She fantasised about what they both might do with the rest of their lives. They could go to London themselves, get good jobs and a flat. They could meet men who cared about them, exotic men with grand English accents who drove sports cars and hung about with pop stars. While Winnie gave a weak smile, it was obvious her mind was elsewhere.

Eventually, she snapped. Two weeks after the burial, she sought out Sister Agnes to ask when she could leave. 'I've no baby to mind,' she explained. 'I've nothing to contribute. May I go home?'

Agnes told her that this wasn't how Carrigbrack operated. She had to pay for the cost of her stay. 'You'll need to work here for another six months,' she said. 'Possibly longer.'

Winnie left the office. Rather than returning to the kitchen, she turned in the opposite direction and went to the nursery. Patricia, who was in the laundry, didn't witness what happened at the start. She had to rely on rumours and second-hand stories. What she did know was this:

Since Diane's death, many of the women in Carrigbrack had been kind to Winnie. Take the young girl with whom they'd worked in the fields. At considerable risk, she'd stolen several strawberries, wrapped them in a handkerchief and given them to Winnie. 'I remember how you liked them,' she'd said, with a nervous smile.

Others, though, were less supportive, and some effectively shunned her. In their superstitious minds, she was damaged. She was bad luck, and bad luck was contagious. They might as well have rung a bell and shouted, 'Unclean, unclean.'

In the nursery, Winnie asked two of the new mothers if she could hold their babies. Both turned their backs. The one person to step forward was Jacinta, who'd been feeding her son, Lorcan, a calm boy with solemn grey eyes and a full head of deep brown hair.

'Here,' she said. 'He wants to say hello to the girl who stood up for his mam.'

Winnie cradled Lorcan with tears running down her cheeks. 'Sorry,' she kept saying. 'Sorry, I don't want to make a show of myself.'

Jacinta told her it was all right and that she understood. 'You won't upset him,' she said. 'He's very good.'

'You smell great,' Winnie said to Lorcan. 'I had a baby girl. She was as gorgeous as you, only they killed her.'

'Hush now,' said Jacinta. 'Don't go upsetting yourself, Winnie.'

'They wouldn't let me see her, either. Not until she was bundled up like a mummy and ready for the grave. They didn't want me to see how lovely she was.'

Lorcan remained quiet.

'They kill babies, you know. Just for spite.'

Jacinta sent a look of alarm to the nun in charge, who went to find Sister Agnes. She arrived five minutes later in a lather of indignation. By then, word was travelling around Carrigbrack. 'I hear Winnie's gone mad,' one of the girls in the laundry said. Patricia put down what she was doing and walked out. Faustina called after her, but she was wasting her breath.

When Patricia reached the nursery, Winnie was sitting beside the window with Lorcan in her arms. Sister Agnes was ordering her to hand him back to his mother.

'You're not the first girl to lose a baby and you won't be the last,' she said. 'I don't want to hear any more lies about anyone killing your daughter. Give that child back to his mother and go to your dormitory.'

Patricia watched as Winnie followed the nun's orders. Jacinta took Lorcan and kissed him on his placid head. Instead of going to the dormitory, however, Winnie walked to the corner of the room, faced the wall and slumped to the floor, where she rocked back and forth, sobbing and moaning. Her misery was all-pervading. It filled the room and seeped into every one of them. Sister Eunice, who'd also heard about the commotion in the nursery, tried to comfort her, as did one of the young nurses. Patricia joined them. They attempted to defuse the situation with soothing words and gestures. Agnes scowled, but didn't intervene. Winnie swayed to and fro. She was inconsolable, her speech little more than gibberish.

'Wanted to see her,' she said. 'Kiss her and smell her. Tell her I loved her.'

After ten minutes of coaxing, they convinced her to leave. Patricia wanted to bring her friend to the dormitory, but Agnes stepped in and ordered her back to work.

'It's okay,' whispered Eunice. 'Don't get yourself into trouble. I'll look after Winnie.'

It was as Patricia was returning to the laundry that she spotted Sister Sabina. Their old adversary was standing beside the door, drinking everything in as if it was a scene from a John B. Keane play.

Don't say anything, Patricia told herself. She's not worth it.

'Winnie's lost all of her backchat and cheek, I see,' said Sabina.

Don't say anything.

'Ah, and you've lost your voice too. It was about time you were both taught a lesson.'

Patricia couldn't stop herself. 'You're bitter because you were cruel to her, and she had the gumption to stand up for herself. A sixteen-year-old girl got the better of you, and your pride was hurt.'

'Well, she certainly paid for her insubordination.' Sabina stabbed a thin finger at Patricia. 'You, on the other hand, were let off far too lightly. You're indulged by Sister Agnes because you're better educated than some of the others. In my book, that makes your sin even more heinous.'

A black anger rose within Patricia. She wanted to strike out at the woman standing in front of her. That wasn't a realistic option, however. She was eight months pregnant, as wide as she was tall, and her right hand was stinging with pain. 'How is it that you have no charity or mercy?' she said 'Winnie is devastated by her loss, and you're here smirking at her and making snide remarks. What sort of Christian are you? Then again, I could ask the same of most of the nuns here. For the past two weeks, you've watched that poor girl fall apart and done nothing to support her.'

'Is that right? If you ask me, she has no one to blame but herself. I heard she refused to pray for the tortured souls in purgatory. She got what was coming to her.'

Carrigbrack could be a callous place, yet Patricia didn't think she'd heard anything as stony-hearted as this. 'If you really believe what you've just said, I pity you. If there is a God, I'm sure he can see that Winnie's worth ten of you. No, a hundred of you. You're an evil bitch, and no mistake.'

Sabina smirked again. Patricia knew she had to walk away. When she turned, she saw Sister Agnes standing behind her. She'd been listening to every word.

'You can't say you weren't warned,' said Agnes as she brought the scissors close to Patricia's scalp. 'You were given chance after chance.

I gave you permission to attend the burial, and you repaid me with a foul-mouthed attack on Sister Sabina.'

'I couldn't listen to her being mean about Winnie,' said Patricia, as she watched a hank of light brown hair tumble to the floor. 'She went too far, Sister.'

'It's not your place to tell Sister Sabina, a woman who's been a devoted servant to Carrigbrack, what she can or can't say. Imagine calling her evil! Everything she does is designed to help girls like you. Girls whose failures have got them into trouble. At this advanced stage in your pregnancy, I'm reluctant to discipline you further. But if necessary, I will. Now, close your mouth and take your punishment.'

Agnes continued until the floor was covered with hair. Finally, she declared her job done. 'Get a brush and sweep up that mess,' she said. Patricia put a hand to her head to feel the damage. She'd been left with an inch all round.

She found Winnie in their old hiding place: the bathroom beside the dormitory. Her friend's reaction was as unexpected as it was wonderful. She lifted a hand to her mouth and said, 'Jeepers, she's made a shocking job of you.' Then she giggled.

'To tell the truth,' said Patricia, examining herself in the spotty mirror, 'it was never great-quality hair. With any luck, it'll grow back a bit thicker.'

'Or blonde.'

'Even Agnes can't work miracles.'

Winnie laughed again, a proper throaty laugh. 'St Agnes of Carrigbrack, patron saint of hairdressers.'

'Did I ever tell you,' said Patricia, 'that when the priest was driving me here, my mam and dad made me wear a wig? They were terrified for fear the neighbours caught sight of us. Perhaps I should dust it down and put it on.'

'A wig?' said Winnie, with another snort of laughter.

'Hmm. It's an awful-looking yoke, like something you'd see on a mannequin in a shop window.'

'I thought I'd heard it all, but that's something else.'

It was so wonderful to hear Winnie's laughter and to see the haunted look lift from her eyes that Patricia decided her haircut had been worth it.

'This is probably a stupid question,' she said as she lowered herself to the floor, 'but how are you? I was really worried earlier. We all were.'

Winnie slipped down beside her. 'Honestly? I don't know if I'm strong enough for Carrigbrack. Here I am surrounded by pregnant women and babies, knowing there was only one thing I had to do – deliver a healthy child – and I couldn't even get that right.'

'You can't think like that.'

'I keep asking myself, did I do something wrong? Did I kill her?'

'No, you didn't, Winnie. Those are bad thoughts. You've got to push them out of your head.'

Winnie played with the frayed hem of her skirt. 'When I was down in the nursery, I blamed the nuns, but I was only lashing out. I just wanted to point the finger at someone else. I'm rotten with anger and bitterness, and for as long as I'm here, that's not going to change.'

Patricia didn't feel equipped to deal with Winnie's fragility. Every single thing about Carrigbrack was designed to cut her open and rub bleach in her wounds; to tell her that she'd failed. Patricia's own baby moved, yet she was reluctant to say so. It would sound cruel.

After the evening rosary, she sought out Sister Eunice.

'I heard about the hair,' said Eunice. 'You didn't deserve it. I usually try to defend Sabina, but this time she went too far. I wish I knew why she's so hard. Maybe that's what a long time in an institution does to you.'

'I'll be grand,' said Patricia. 'Sure who's looking at me anyway?

I'm very worried about Winnie, though. I'll miss her, but they've got to let her go. If she's forced to stay, she'll never recover. It'll only be a matter of time before she returns to the nursery, and the next mother mightn't be as reasonable as Jacinta.'

'I don't know what to do either. I asked Sister Agnes if there could be a dispensation for her. She said no. She claimed that ignoring the rules would send the wrong message to everyone else.'

'There's no way, is there, that Winnie's parents would be able to pay for her release?'

'As I understand it, they're in very bad circumstances. Winnie's the third eldest of ten, and the house doesn't have running water or an indoor toilet. A hundred pounds or a million pounds: it makes no difference to them. I doubt they could even afford her bus fare home.'

For the most part, Patricia viewed the nuns not as individuals but as enforcers of a regime. They recited the rules and warned about sinful behaviour. Eunice was the exception. In different circumstances, the two of them might have been friends. She wondered why Eunice had chosen religion. Or had she been given a choice? Although she allowed occasional glimpses into her life, she didn't reveal much. Patricia knew she had a sister and that she liked reading, but that was about all.

She said good night to Eunice and made her way to the dormitory. As she did so, her anger returned. She wanted to roar and howl. What sort of rancid system could treat a distressed girl like Winnie in such a shoddy way? How warped was their religion if someone like Sabina could come out with such poison and get away with it? The only positive Patricia could find was this: so consumed was she with the injustices of Carrigbrack that in more than a week, she'd barely given a thought to Mike or her parents.

*

Patricia was in the laundry, passing sheets through the calender and cursing her blistered hand, when an out-of-puff Sister Agnes pushed open the door.

'Has anyone here seen Winnie?' she asked.

The honest answer was no. A murmur to that effect travelled around the room.

'What about you, Patricia? When did you last see her?'

'This morning at breakfast, Sister. Is she not in the kitchen?'

Agnes looked at her like she was half-witted. 'If she was in the kitchen, I wouldn't be looking for her here, would I?'

'I suppose not.'

'Have you tried her baby's grave, Sister?' one of the others asked. 'She might have needed a few minutes with her little one.'

'We've already looked,' replied Agnes, glasses fogging up. 'Patricia, you're to come with me. The rest of you are to continue with your work.' She nodded at Faustina and ushered Patricia into the corridor.

'If you have any idea where Winnie has gone, I'm ordering you to tell me. Covering up for her would be a mistake. A serious mistake. If she's left the grounds, she'll be found and she'll be brought back. Do you hear me?' Such was her fury that she spat as she spoke. Patricia didn't dare wipe her face.

'I promise you, Sister, the last time I saw her was this morning. I haven't a clue where she is. In fact, I'm concerned about her. She's been finding life very difficult. Don't take this the wrong way, but I don't think you appreciate how vulnerable she is.'

Clearly, the possibility that Winnie might harm herself hadn't occurred to Agnes. She pursed her mouth before replying. 'What are you suggesting?'

'I ... I'm not sure. All I know is that she hasn't been herself. How could she be?'

'I see,' said Agnes, whose face had lost its colour.

'May I help you look for her?'

'That wouldn't be advisable.'

A dark feeling wrapped itself around Patricia. 'If Winnie's hiding somewhere, she might come out for me. She trusts me.' She scratched her hand. 'Please?'

'Very well, but you're not to go anywhere on your own. And before you do anything, you're to get a bandage for that hand. You shouldn't have allowed it to get into such a sorry state.'

For two hours, they looked everywhere. Then they looked again. They scoured the fields and outbuildings. The combed every hedge and thicket. They tried all the rooms and all the cupboards, every nook and crevice. They searched the church and the attic. Sister Agnes made enquiries in the nearby village.

Patricia did everything with a rising sense of panic. Winnie wasn't in the right frame of mind to escape. Even if she didn't intend to hurt herself, she wouldn't be able to cope on her own. She was a child grieving the loss of a child. Oh, and she was wearing that terrible uniform. Any sensible person would ask about her clothes and wonder where she'd come from. Plus, she was penniless. She couldn't afford to pay for a bus, not to mind spend a night in a bed and breakfast. The weather might be fine, but that wouldn't last, and she was in no condition to sleep in fields and barns.

Patricia realised she was trembling. Oh Winnie, she thought, where are you?

At ten o'clock, with the light fading, they gave up.

'She can't just have vanished,' everyone said. But it looked as if she had.

Agnes called the guards, who said that while they'd keep an eye out for Winnie, there'd been a bad car accident near Kilfenora and a robbery in Ennistymon. They were up to their tonsils, the officer explained, and a young girl who'd committed no crime wasn't their top priority.

'Girls go missing,' he said. 'That's what they do.'

Agnes was raging. She told him that Carrigbrack runaways had always taken precedence over minor incidents and that he'd regret his lack of respect. The policeman wasn't for turning. Or at least, that was how it sounded when Eunice relayed the news. Despite everything, Patricia smiled.

That night, she lay in her narrow bed, running through the possibilities, almost all of them troubling. Every inch of her body ached. After an hour or so, she turned over the thin pillow. There was an envelope underneath. It could only be from one person.

While the women weren't supposed to use the lavatory at night, a blind eye was turned to those in the final stages of pregnancy. Patricia tucked the envelope into the top of her knickers. Then, quiet as a shadow, she tiptoed to the bathroom. All the while, her mind was spinning. The letter hadn't been there earlier in the day; she was sure of it.

She didn't open the envelope until she was safely inside the cubicle. The note was short.

Dearest Patricia,

Hopefully by the time you read this, I'll be far away. I'm sorry I didn't say goodbye, but I decided it was safest this way. Had I been capable of staying, that's what I would have done. But the past few weeks have torn me in two, and I wasn't able to take any more.

Please don't worry about me. Just take care of yourself and your baby. Oh, and wish me well. Please wish me well.

I was very lucky that we became friends. Thank you! I hope we meet again one day. Even if we don't, I promise I'll never forget you.

With love,

Winnie

Patricia sat in the bathroom for as long as she dared. She was part relieved, part scared, part thrilled. Oh, and if she was being honest, she was disappointed. As much as she knew that Winnie had needed to flee, she couldn't imagine getting through the days in Carrigbrack without her. There were questions too: how had she escaped in the middle of the day without being spotted? She couldn't have left through the hole in the hedge. Anyone trying to get out that way would have been located within ten minutes. And where had she found writing paper and an envelope?

'Travel safely, my brave, brave friend,' whispered Patricia, as she unlocked the door and returned to her dormitory.

Chapter 18

Gary

Frank was there before him, in the corner of the bar, phone clamped to one ear, lolling with intent. Gary had chosen the Palace because he wanted a neutral venue where Dubliners enjoyed an afternoon pint and tourists took each other's pictures. In such a public place, they'd be forced to keep their tempers in check.

The search for his birth mother was at a standstill. Worried that too direct an approach would scare her, he'd written what he hoped was a cleverly worded letter to Gráinne Holland. In it, he described himself as an 'old friend' from 1971. *We last saw each other in north Clare*, he wrote. He wondered how life had been for her and expressed an interest in renewing contact. If she was the right woman, and he suspected she was, she would understand the letter's significance. If she wasn't, there was no harm done. She had yet to reply.

The other names on Katie's list were even harder to trace. Her original message board post had become a lengthy thread in which people spoke about Carrigbrack and traded tips. Some of the messages related to 1971 and '72. Others referred to earlier or later years.

Every day, Gary checked the discussion. He'd also provided DNA samples to two ancestry websites. Spitting into the tube reminded him of the time an Ohio woman had claimed he was the father of her four-year-old son. Gary had been – almost – certain he'd never met the woman. On that occasion, he'd been glad to draw a blank. This time, he wanted a different outcome, but he wasn't getting his hopes up.

The more he learnt about Carrigbrack and the heartbreak behind its walls, the more he thought about his birth mother. Had she meekly accepted her lot, or had she stood up for herself? Had she been relieved to see her baby go, or had she fought to hold onto him? Was she musical? Was that where his talent had come from?

And what was she doing now? Had her life been blighted by what had happened to her? Or had she shucked off her early misfortune?

Frank bought him a pint and told a string of entertaining stories. One, involving a racehorse, a famous guitarist and a cheap flight to Thailand, was especially brilliant. Stories had always been his forte. Back when he'd first managed Black Iris, when they'd been four skinny young bucks without a penny to their names, he'd made them laugh until they'd keeled over. He'd made them believe in themselves too.

Frank's trip to Dublin was a fleeting one. He'd been in Los Angeles just two days earlier. The following morning, he would fly to New York, where he spent most of his time. He was still scouting bands, cutting deals, adding to his fortune. Nobody would ever have accused him of being handsome, but he looked well. Gary reckoned he'd had something done to his eyes. They both wore a uniform of sorts: factory-faded jeans and pricey suit jackets. They looked out of place.

Outside, the pre-Christmas mania was at full tilt, the streets crammed with shoppers and drinkers. Women wore cocktail dresses at two in the afternoon while young guys put on plastic antlers and pretended to drink a beer in twelve different bars. Stalls were laden with wrapping paper and tinsel, Conor McGregor posters and cheap make-up. People had more money; they were better groomed and better travelled. Yet in lots of ways, Dublin at Christmas was the city of Gary's childhood. It was glittering and tawdry, beautiful and dark. And he loved it for that.

Frank was there to soften him up. That was okay; he could handle it. He wouldn't be coerced or cajoled into something he didn't want. They'd already had several phone conversations. Ray and Liamo had been in touch too. Anton continued to do his talking through intermediaries. The reunion plans had been stepped up, and the guys were keen to go back into the studio. They'd been working on new tracks. They had ideas.

'So, then,' said Frank. 'What's the story? Are you in?'

Gary ran a finger down the side of his glass. 'It's not the right time for me.'

'So you say. I'm not sure I understand why, though.'

'Like I explained on the phone, I'm busy.'

'Nah you're not. You're messing around.'

'You're wide of the mark there, Frank. In case you weren't listening before, I'm committed to finding my birth mother. I've been putting in the work and I've narrowed the list down to three.'

Frank took a mouthful of Guinness. 'Did I ever tell you about where my ma grew up? Until she was ten, she lived in a tenement in the north inner city. Rotten kip of a place. Four sisters in one bed, and six families sharing a toilet. Vermin galore.'

'I'm sorry to hear that, but I don't know what it's got to do with me.'

'Yes, you do.'

Gary lifted one shoulder, as if to say, *Tell me, so.*

'What I'm saying, Gar, is that life in those days was tough and unfair. Everybody had it hard. No sooner had we got rid of the Brits than we handed the keys to the Vatican. But you can't let that control you. Your fixation isn't … healthy.' He gestured towards the door. 'Look at this city. There's building going on everywhere. All the cranes are back, like the bust never happened. There are thousands of tourists out there in Temple Bar, spending all their lovely dollars and pounds and yen and whatever you're having yourself. This is no time to hide away and become a recluse.'

'I want to find her, Frank. It's a need I have. I want to talk to her.'

'And then what?'

Gary stared at his pint. 'What do you mean?'

'What do you do after you've found her? That's *if* you find her. Are you allowed to restart your life? I mean, Jesus, man, you already have a family. Your folks are fine people. Compared to many kids, you had a peach of a childhood. Have you told them about this obsession of yours?'

Gary had mentioned the search to his parents but only in the most general of terms. They didn't know about Katie or Beth or the bracelets. Nor did they know that he'd been to Carrigbrack. It was hard to argue with Frank. His upbringing had been privileged. His father had taught at a private school, which had made it possible for Gary to attend on reduced fees. Alone among his friends, he'd been taken on foreign holidays. He'd never had to wear cheap chain-store jeans. His crooked teeth had been fixed.

'Yeah,' he said, 'we talk.'

'You see, what gets me is this: a couple of years back, you didn't know you were adopted, and your life was none the poorer. The people who raised you, Shay and Lillian, they're your parents. What can a stranger give you that you don't already have, huh?'

'I can't unknow what I've learnt, man. Simple as that.'

Frank slapped his knees. 'I reckon we need two more pints.'

Gary drained his glass. Beside him, two middle-aged men were discussing their cholesterol. Three Englishwomen, Christmas shopping pooled at their feet, were planning the hours ahead. He caught a whiff of perfume, and although it reminded him of someone, he couldn't remember who.

A recluse. Was that how people thought of him? A month back, he'd dipped a toe into the dating pool. He'd spent a few nights with a model he'd met through a friend of a friend. She'd been all right, if a little Instagram-obsessed. Did people really need to know what she wore to the cinema, aka her 'off-duty look'? Finally, she'd thrown a tantrum over his reluctance to pose for her page, and he'd realised that she was just a reheated version of his second wife, Carly McCall. Carly had been hot hot hot. She'd also been as mad as a bag of spiders.

On his return from the bar, Frank employed a familiar tactic. He began talking as if the previous twenty minutes hadn't happened. He restarted the conversation from a different angle.

'I met up with Anton,' he said.

Gary replied in his flattest voice. 'That's good.'

'He's keeping well. I don't know how the guy does it, but he looks like he's just walked out of 1992. Did you hear he's totally clean and sober? Twelve-step programme, the whole lot. He's raring to go.'

Gary's eyes roamed the ceiling. 'There's nothing stopping him.'

'That's not true.'

'Well, that's how it looks to me.'

'You said you were going to LA for the holidays? You might come across him yourself.'

'It's Los Angeles, Frank, not Stepaside. We're unlikely to bump into each other at Midnight Mass.'

'We want to do this reissue of *Overboard* in style.'

'I've already explained that now's not good for me.'

Frank rested a hand on Gary's arm. 'I'm not saying I don't know what your issue is … because I do. What I'm saying is, the time has come to sort it out. Obviously, we can do the reunion without you – and, believe me, if we have to, we will – but we'd prefer not to.'

Overboard was Gary's finest achievement. The bassline for the title song was his 'Under Pressure', his 'Dancing in the Moonlight', his 'Lust for Life'. The thought of some other guy, some glorified session-head, playing it on stage brought him actual physical pain.

And yet …

'Listen to me, Gar,' Frank was saying, 'music is your life. And, yeah, that sounds corny, but it's true. You and Anton are the core of the band. You can't stay away forever.'

Gary couldn't argue with the first part of that statement. Music had been his life. From the time he'd learnt 'Twinkle, Twinkle, Little Star' on the tin whistle, he'd known he was a musician. Yeah, he'd put in a lot of effort, but he'd been rewarded tenfold. He thought of it all: the exhilaration of a track coming together, every beat and every note; the buzz of the stage; the thunder of guitars; the roar as they played the opening notes of a favourite song. Black Iris had been everything he'd ever wanted. He recalled hearing a line about another musician: the thing that made him different had never made him happy. Gary had been convinced that didn't apply to him.

And yet …

The cholesterol men had abandoned their chat and were listening in. He didn't care. He wriggled his arm free of Frank's hand.

'Do you remember,' he said, 'back when we were starting out and shit used to go wrong? When the van broke down or an amp blew or a record company said "thanks but no thanks". You'd always say the same thing. "Nobody's dead, lads," you'd say. "Nobody's dead."'

Frank spoke slowly. 'I hear you.'

'I can't brush it all aside and pretend it didn't happen.'

'It's not like everyone else is cool with how things turned out.'

'Sometimes I wonder.'

'That's not fair.' Frank leant in. 'And remember, you were complicit, whether you choose to admit it or not.'

'I never said I wasn't,' replied Gary, before taking a deep drink of stout. 'She had a name, by the way. In case you've forgotten, her name was Shanna Ellis.'

It had been a long time since he'd said it out loud. It left a metallic taste in his mouth.

'I haven't forgotten her,' said Frank. 'None of us ever will.'

'Really? If you ask me, everyone wants to sail on like nothing happened.'

Whatever Frank said, however he protested, Shanna's death couldn't have affected him in the same way. He'd been a bystander, a cleaner-upper. Gary had been part of the story, and he carried the guilt like a sackful of rocks.

'You know what you need?' said Frank. 'You need to go back to therapy. You sit here talking about your mother and about stuff that went on fifty years ago and how everyone's got to be brave and face up to that. But when it comes to your own life, you want to run away and hide.'

'Whoa there. You accuse me of being unfair? What do you think you're doing?'

'I'm being straight with you, that's all. You've got to move on.'

Gary got to his feet, prompting worried looks from cholesterol men and shopping ladies.

'Thanks for the pints,' he said, 'but I could do without the amateur psychology. Oh, and you've made up my mind for me. You'd better find a new bass player.'

Half an hour later, and he'd have missed it. The letter arrived as Gary was zipping up his case and preparing to leave for LA. Guessing it was from Gráinne, he paused and told himself that, either way, everything was good. If she wasn't his natural mother, he would redouble his efforts with the remaining names on Katie's list. He would work on and he would find her. It was all good.

Oh, who was he kidding?

He had a hundred reasons for wanting the news to be positive, not all of them pure. Over the coming days, he'd be spending time with his four children, his ex-partner and his first ex-wife. He'd have to tell them that he was quitting Black Iris. 'You know that thing that keeps us all in high style?' he'd say. 'Well, it's no more. Or, rather, it carries on, but without me.' Breaking the news would be much easier if he had a distraction, a shiny bauble to display. He pictured his *ta-dah* moment where he told them all about his birth mother and his new life.

Four days had passed since his falling-out with Frank. He hadn't heard from Ray, Liamo or anyone else connected to the band. The fact that nothing had appeared in the press or online made him suspect that, so far, the manager had kept the news to himself.

He opened the envelope slowly and unfolded two sheets of lined paper. Gráinne wrote in small, round letters.

Please forgive the delay. Had I replied sooner, I might have written in anger, and that wouldn't have been fair. Despite its cryptic wording, I understood the meaning of your letter. I don't know how you found me, but you obviously have reason to believe that I'm your birth mother. It's a shame you didn't give more thought to the likely impact of your query.

To answer the question you appear to be asking: yes, I did give birth to a boy in Carrigbrack in August 1971. I was young and naïve, and my baby's father refused to accept his responsibility. I had no choice but to give my son up for adoption. Although it wasn't easy, I'm satisfied it was the best course of action. I had neither the money nor the support to raise a child.

Gradually, I got back on my feet and put what had happened behind me. I met a better man, we married and had three children. None of them knows about my fourth child, and I'd like to keep it that way.

Gary stopped and cursed his hubris. Why hadn't he given more thought to the possibility that she wouldn't want to reconnect? The letter continued:

My children are in their late thirties and early forties. They're fine people, but I can't say how they'd react if I told them the truth. One thing's for sure, my marriage would be over. Think about it: how would you feel if your wife told you she'd been lying for more than forty years?

Gary felt a pain in his chest. This wasn't how it was supposed to be. The script called for an emotional yet joy-filled reunion. For tears and shared photos and unquestioning love. He read on.

For the avoidance of doubt, let me assure you: you're not my son. I can say this with certainty because my real son found me, through the adoption authorities, a number of years ago. We met once, I explained my situation, and he agreed not to contact me again. While this might sound hard, I don't think I'm a bad person. Rather, I'm a woman who's had to deal, in the best way she can, with what life gave her. I made my choice and I'm content with it. I have great respect for my first child, but my relationship with him could never match the love I have for my other children. Once ties are severed, they can't always be joined together again.

There are many of us out here living delicately balanced lives, fearing that a stray word could blow the house down. Not everyone can revisit the past.

Gary put the letter down. The pain in his chest had eased and was replaced by a dull sadness. Gráinne said she was content with her choice, but what a shadowy existence. Her life was built on lies. Did she really believe that telling the truth would drive her family away? His head was a mishmash of thoughts. He should be positive: her reply had brought him closer to solving the mystery. The list of names had been cut to two. Why, then, did he feel so low? There was, he realised, another possibility. Perhaps she was the right woman after all, and this was her way of giving him the brush-off.

Outside, a scattering of snow lay on the fields like desiccated coconut. The sky was marbled with grey. He ought to get moving. A sunnier place was waiting. First, though, he needed to talk.

While Katie didn't sound down, neither did she sound like her normal self. Her questions and answers lacked their usual precision.

'Ah well,' she said, 'that's one bracelet that's likely to remain in the box. I'm sorry things didn't work out the way you'd hoped, but you don't need me to tell you ...'

'... that there are only a couple of women left. Yeah, I just wish I felt more upbeat.'

'Tell me you're not judging Gráinne for what she's done.'

'I didn't say—'

'You've got to understand, Gary, that when we were growing up, everyone was more guarded. Nowadays, we're all expected to chat about every last element of our lives. And if we don't, we're labelled secretive or repressed. I heard Beth say that about someone the other day. "No, lovey," I said, "our generation are more reserved. And, whether you like it or not, that's our right. When we were young, we were told to keep our mouths closed because no one cared what we thought. And that's hard to shake off."'

'The silent generation,' said Gary.

'That's us.'

'How did Beth react?'

'She harrumphed a bit, but she's got a sound head on her, has Beth. My heart goes out to Gráinne. You can be sure that writing the letter wasn't easy.'

'I hope that if I do find my birth mother, she doesn't feel the same.'

'If she does,' said Katie, 'you'll have to accept her wishes.'

'I suppose.' He'd expected a more understanding response. And, yes, he was judging Gráinne. He didn't like the sound of her at all.

'Is everything else okay with you?' Katie said.

'Why do you ask?'

'Because you sound defeated. And you shouldn't. We've been through this before; you're making progress.'

'I know. I know.'

'There's something else, isn't there?'

Gary figured that Katie and Beth had spotted the media speculation about Black Iris. They were quite a pair.

'Aw,' he said, 'it's a band thing. It'll get sorted.' That wasn't true, but this wasn't the day for full disclosure. 'It's a long story. Maybe I'll tell you some time.'

'I'd like to think I'm a decent listener. Mind you, a few days ago, I made a right mess of a situation. A total hames.'

'Was it connected to one of the bracelets?'

'Yes. I'm afraid I wasn't gentle enough with someone. I should have known that he needed more time.'

Her weary tone made more sense now. Gary tried to come up with some reassuring words, but reassuring wasn't part of his repertoire.

Katie continued. 'I'm convinced that in the new year you'll find the woman you're looking for.'

'Fingers crossed you're right. I've got to get over Christmas first, mind.'

'That makes two of us,' she said.

Chapter 19

Katie

They drove west on Christmas Eve. Beth insisted on a meandering route.

'Come on,' said Katie. 'We've got to make an effort. Surely you're looking forward to seeing everybody?'

'The problem with this country,' replied Beth, 'is that Christmas is never-ending. It's a form of penance. Why can't we be more like the Americans? One day of family and overindulgence, and then you're back to work with no harm done.'

'That's what it was like when we were growing up. Well, without the overindulgence … and with a lot more religion.'

'You sound like Mam when she does her routine about how children were content with an orange and a new pair of socks.' Beth adopted Margo's clipped voice. 'Ask for more, and you'd get a good hiding.'

'Don't pay any heed to your mother. Mam and Dad never said boo to her. Although what the pair of them would've made of Christmas nowadays, I don't know.'

Katie was trying to push her misgivings aside. She reminded herself that she was fortunate to have family who wanted to share their Christmas. The country was full of people who'd love to spend a few days in a large house of plenty. She did her best to think generous thoughts about her sister. It was too easy to dismiss Margo as a Central Casting social climber. True, her need to be seen as living a life of endless success was tedious, as was her mania for organising the lives of others. To be fair, though, she'd achieved a lot. Her six children were educated, productive members of society. She'd nurtured and loved them. Her house was spotless, her garden well tended. She was never over- or underdressed, and whoever tweaked her face was skilled at their craft. She was elegant and entertaining and tough as saddle leather.

She also lived in a world of post-recession excess, where Christmas trees were dressed according to a colour theme, spa weekends were a necessity, and weddings lasted for three days. But she had the money, and those were her choices. She'd grown up in a make-do-and-mend house where shop-bought cake was considered extravagant and the purchase of a new towel was viewed as a major event. Who was Katie to judge her?

They should have been close. In an era when families of six or more had been the norm, they'd had no other siblings. Yet Margo remained an enigma. Rarely combative, the sisters weren't affectionate either. Like a pair of parallel lines, they could carry on forever without connecting.

Christmas in the Linnane house was an elaborate affair. The rooms of the farmhouse were decorated in red, green and silver, while white lights twinkled on every tree. In the sitting room, there was a real Christmas tree, its pine scent prompting burst upon burst of nostalgia. The cupboards were full, the drink flowed, and the heating was cranked up to tropical levels. Even Ranzo the dog – part collie, part who-knew-what – wore a special velvet collar.

On Christmas Day, they all maintained a determined politeness. They went to ten o'clock Mass, the one ceremony of the year when a capacity crowd was guaranteed. Everyone wore their new Christmas scarf and mumbled along to 'Silent Night'. There was a kerfuffle over whether to put the family name on the envelope for the priest's collection. Margo claimed that to do so was vulgar. She also complained about the men who made a swift exit after communion and the altar girls who wore jeans and runners under their surplices. Whatever else had changed, Mass etiquette in Danganstown was still a delicate business. Afterwards, the parish priest waved at his flock but didn't stop to speak.

'We have to share him with Clonbreen and Lacken's Mills,' said Margo. 'The man barely has time to bless himself.'

During the afternoon, various brothers, wives and children came and went until Katie lost track of who was who. There were presents galore. She was touched by her gifts from Beth. They included a voucher for a manicure (she had shocked her niece by announcing that she'd never had one) and a scarlet storage box.

'That old shoebox is in danger of falling apart,' said Beth, prompting a quizzical look from her mother.

Katie gave Beth an antique silver and enamel bracelet.

'What an inspired choice,' said Beth.

There were eleven of them for dinner: Margo, Con, Beth and Katie, plus two of Beth's brothers, Barra and Eoin, along with their wives and children. True to form, Margo insisted on doing almost everything herself. Even though Katie had never had much of a taste for turkey ('a horrible dry old bird', according to Johnny) or sprouts ('the filthy things smell like a fungal infection'), she had to admit the food was a triumph. It was a wonder the table didn't collapse under the weight of dishes. Along with the turkey, there was a Limerick ham, carrots, sprouts, peas, parsnips, three types of potatoes, stuffing, gravy and cranberry sauce. Afterwards, there was a choice of Christmas pudding or trifle. Margo had found the trifle recipe in the latest book by a popular TV chef. Con made the mistake of saying that his mother had made a lovely trifle. For the next five minutes, his wife sent withering looks in his direction. Eventually, he qualified his statement by saying that his mam's plum pudding had never been great, and her gravy had been too thin. Harmony was restored.

Only a careful listener would have caught the imbalance in the dinner table conversation. While the minutiae of the boys' domestic lives were discussed, Beth's personal life was ignored. She could talk about her job or the state of the nation, but anything else was taboo. While she wasn't subdued, she wasn't her usual witty, outspoken self either. Katie became irritated on her behalf. Not that she said anything. For the most part, she was quiet. If the loneliest sound was a couple having sex in the next room, the loneliest experience was Christmas in a full house when the person you most wanted was gone. Six months on from Johnny's death, Katie craved intimacy. By that, she didn't necessarily mean sex – though sex would be welcome – but the loaded glances, conspiratorial smiles and shared memories that made up a relationship; the countless subtle signs that said the two of you were together. The knowledge that all of this was gone, and wouldn't be back, filled her head.

If Johnny was still alive, she wouldn't be here. It wasn't that he hadn't liked Margo; more that they were very different people who'd struggled to find common ground. While her husband had made an effort to get on with most people, he'd rarely bothered with Katie's sister. 'That's just it, Kateser,' he'd said. 'She's family. I shouldn't have to spend every blessed minute on my best behaviour. It shouldn't feel like hard work.'

A couple of days earlier, Katie had left flowers at his grave.

Although people still offered their sympathies and asked how she was getting on, she suspected they didn't want an honest answer. Other people's grief was tedious.

More than once, she'd wondered if her memories of Johnny were too golden-hued. It wasn't as if they'd never fallen out. There'd been times when she'd felt smothered by his overly protective behaviour. 'Be careful in town,' he'd say. 'There are fellows who'd steal the fillings from your teeth.' Or, 'I can't believe you walked home on your own. That was asking for trouble.' Then there'd been the way he'd insisted on talking to casual acquaintances whether they'd wanted to engage or not. He'd been particularly zealous on holiday, when it had felt as if every other couple in the hotel had been quizzed about where they were from and how their summer was going. Oh, and there'd been his mania for talking to the radio. 'What would you know, sonny boy?' he'd ask a presenter. Or, 'That's a lie if ever I heard one,' he'd tell a politician.

But these were petty complaints. Johnny and Katie could have annoyed each other fifty times a day, and it wouldn't have mattered. What mattered was the love they'd shared.

The bracelets were also ever-present in her thoughts. She remained annoyed with herself for falling out with Brandon. She'd toyed with the idea of contacting him, then decided to wait. As a fictional Irish American had famously said, tomorrow was another day.

The following morning, the dam broke. They were at the kitchen table eating breakfast. In the background, country music played on the local radio station.

'I'll get the news,' said Con, as he turned up the transistor, the oldest item in the room by a good two decades.

Katie smiled. She said the same thing, and it usually prompted a teasing reminder from Beth that the world had moved on. 'You can get the news on your phone any time you like,' she'd say, 'twenty-four hours a day, as much or as little as you want.' Katie would try to explain that, while she knew what was possible, a fifty-year habit was hard to break.

The muddy boots beside the door revealed that Con had already been at work. He farmed close on one hundred and fifty acres, and even at Christmas, there were jobs to tackle. Like his wife, he crammed a lot into the day.

The main story on the local news bulletin was about a three-car pile-up outside Kilmitten. One man had been killed, and two women were in hospital, both in a critical condition.

Beth put down her spoon. 'I hope no one belonging to Ailish was involved.'

'Who's Ailish?' asked Margo.

They could have ignored her. They could have lied. But Katie didn't want to. She'd had enough of ducking and dodging. She decided that, while this wasn't the time for full transparency, it was wrong to hide everything from Margo. Plus, if she was going to talk, it was safest to do so in the presence of Beth and Con. She steadied herself for the backlash.

'Ailish is a woman who's looking for her birth mother,' she said.

'What?'

'She was born in Carrigbrack,' added Beth, 'when Katie worked there.'

They told Con and Margo about the box of bracelets and about the work they'd been doing to reunite birth mothers and their children. After their outbreak of honesty, both tried to be diplomatic.

'We didn't tell you before,' said Beth, 'because we didn't want you thinking we were mad.' She looked at Katie. 'Because, let's face it, it is a bit of a mad scheme. But it's a great one too. You wouldn't believe the people we've met ... like Gary Winters.'

Margo pressed her lips into a thin line before speaking. 'Should I be familiar with him?'

Con appeared more impressed. 'He's in that band, Black Iris. Tall fellow. Plays the guitar, is it?'

'Bass,' said Beth.

Margo fiddled with the sleeve of her green cashmere cardigan. As usual, she was immaculately turned out. In the way that expensive clothes often were, her cream silk T-shirt and black jeans were understated. Her ash-blonde hair was blow-dried to lightly tousled perfection. Katie sensed that she was casting around for objections.

Finally, she spoke. 'You're both grown women, and it's not my place to tell you what to do. But it doesn't sound like a particularly sensible plan. If a reunion goes wrong, you can be certain you'll get the blame.'

'You know, Mam,' said Beth, 'I reckon we'll jump that fence when we get to it.'

'What about you, Katie? Are you sure this is the wisest way to use your time?'

Katie, who'd been buttering a slice of soda bread, stopped and reflected on how much they'd achieved: the emails they'd received, the conversations they'd had, the tips passed on, the bracelets returned. It had taken over her life in a way she hadn't expected. Sometimes, the collision between past and present threatened to overwhelm her. At other times, it felt like she was trying to break through a wall of granite, one chip at a time. But what was the alternative? Sitting at home smelling Johnny's old shirts and allowing her loneliness to fester? She'd been given an opportunity to meet different people and to see life in different ways. She thought of the men and women who'd written to her as part of a mosaic: it was only when you brought their stories together that you had the full picture.

'I'm sure,' she said.

*

Later, when Con was outside and Beth upstairs, Margo was more vocal.

'For the life of me,' she said, 'I can't fathom what you're doing. I mean, I can see why Beth would view it as an interesting historical project. But you? You ought to have more sense.'

Katie examined the kitchen. There was something intimidating about its glass, steel, stone and wood. Although Margo's home was only five miles from the house in which they'd grown up, it felt like another world. It was a world created by Margo, and she was its ruler. Katie twisted the gold band she still wore and reminded herself of her extra nine years. She was the senior party here.

'Please don't talk down to me,' she said. 'I've already told you that I'm satisfied we're doing the right thing.'

'And I don't believe you've thought it through. Is this bracelet business … is it some sort of delayed reaction to Johnny's death? Is it that you now feel free to … talk about those times?'

'I understand your concerns. Of course I do. But this isn't about you. We've made a lot of progress, and we're determined to continue. And Beth has been fantastic. She's really supportive and understanding.'

Their eyes locked. Margo went to say something, then drew back. She'd never enjoyed discussing the past. Despite being the one who'd stayed close to home, she rarely spoke about their parents. When she did, it was in the jokey way that Beth had mentioned in the car. She would ramp up her childhood poverty to *Angela's Ashes* levels and scold her sons and daughter for failing to appreciate their own good fortune.

Was this, Katie wondered, a genuine reflection on her childhood and teenage years? Did she recall her youth as unrelentingly bleak, or did she also have happier memories? It seemed to Katie that, when it came to families, memory was especially unreliable. Even among Johnny's contented clan, there had been disagreements. One family member would tell a story about their childhood only for another to say, 'That's not how it happened at all.'

'You've nothing to worry about,' she said, in what she hoped was a confident voice. 'You'll have to trust me on that.'

Margo played with her hair. 'Please don't belittle my concerns. Are you certain that Johnny's passing hasn't affected your judgement?'

'That's not fair.'

'It's a legitimate question.'

'I'm doing it,' said Katie, 'because I believe we can help people.'

'And what if I don't agree?'

Katie told herself to stay calm. While there was never a good day for an all-out row with Margo, this was definitely the worst possible time. If they raised their voices any further, Beth would hear. The atmosphere at the previous day's dinner still on her mind, she decided to change tack.

'I meant what I said about Beth. She's been brilliant. I couldn't have done anything without her. I know she's her own woman, but she's a credit to you.'

'She's her own woman all right.' The reply was heavy with meaning.

'Ah, Margo.'

'Don't "Ah, Margo" me. You don't know anything about our relationship.'

'I know she's upset about the way you're treating her.'

Margo put up a hand, as if to bat her away. 'I can't imagine what Beth has told you, but no doubt she's put her own slant on it.'

'I don't think that's fair. I'm telling you how it looks to me.'

'Listen, I'm not going to be the cartoon bigot here. If you had a daughter of your own, you'd understand.'

The words hit Katie like a slap from a wet towel. 'Let's not fall out,' she said. 'I wanted to tell you that you're a lucky woman to have such a fantastic daughter, that's all.'

Margo was still floundering when the kitchen door swung open and Beth came in. Katie worried that her niece had been listening. Thankfully, the jauntiness of her walk suggested she was unaware of their argument.

'Has someone new been in touch about Carrigbrack?' Katie asked.

'Nope. There's a sheepish email from Robyn, though, wishing you a happy Christmas. Funnily enough, she didn't mention Brandon.'

'Ah. I'd say we can assume that, as far as Eddie's concerned, they're not on the same page.'

'Poor Brandon.'

'You've changed your tune. I didn't expect you to have sympathy for him.'

Beth sat down. 'I wouldn't go that far, but there's something a bit sad about him. He's very uptight. When you were telling him about Eddie, he was so stiff he looked ready to be embalmed. Anyway, that wasn't what I wanted to say. I've got good news.'

Margo's words continued to sting. Katie told herself to focus on Beth. 'Go on,' she said.

'After we were talking, I messaged Ailish. Everything's grand. None of her family was involved in the crash. While I was thinking about her, I decided to do another trawl for Chrissie. The old man in Hackett's Cross said she'd gone to London, so I thought I'd see if there was any mention of her in the British records. I assumed that, like here, it'd be hard to get much information online. And in some ways, it is. There's an official site you can email, or there are several others where you have to sign up and become a member. But I also found a separate site where volunteers have posted images of original birth, death and marriage records. Just a line or two ... nothing overly revealing.'

'And?' Katie glanced at Margo. Despite what she'd said about the bracelets, her sister was following Beth's story. Who wasn't fascinated by other people's family secrets?

'I entered Chrissie's name, and I discovered that a Christine M. Culligan got married in west London in 1978.'

Katie did the sums. 'Our Chrissie would have been twenty or twenty-one then, so, yes, that's possible. And the middle initial is right too. Did it give you a name for her husband?'

Beth moved closer. 'Yes and no. Just a last name, Mulcahy. I was excited, but I thought, ah, no, it's too much to hope for. Either there'll be no other reference to her, or it'll become clear she's not the woman we're looking for. So I typed Chrissie Mulcahy into Google … and up she popped.'

'Is she the right Chrissie?' asked Katie, who already knew the answer. Nothing else could explain the beam of satisfaction on Beth's face.

'Uh huh. And wait until you see her.' Beth tapped her phone and showed the screen to Katie. 'She's absolutely one hundred per cent the right Chrissie. And she's amazing.'

Chapter 20

Ailish

When the text arrived, Ailish was pulling the last of the turkey meat from the carcass. She'd torn a recipe from a magazine she'd found in the hotel and planned on making a casserole. Keith was in the sitting room watching television. Stevie was out with his friends. Although it wasn't yet four o'clock, the dark was closing in. She'd lit the fire several hours before, and the afternoon had a sleepy post-Christmas feel. Tired from the previous day's festivities, she was looking forward to a rest.

Because Beth had already contacted her about the car crash, she was surprised to see a text message from Katie.

Can you talk? it said.

Not really. Ailish lowered the sound on her phone. If Keith heard the *bing-bong* of her message notifications, he'd ask questions.

Beth's about to send you an email. It's very important!!

Please tell me it's good news.

Yes!!

She'd never known Katie to use even one exclamation mark, not to mind four in the space of two lines.

Another text arrived: When you've read the article, call me (if you can).

Article? Did this mean that Katie and Beth were sending her a newspaper cutting about Carrigbrack? Was Chrissie mentioned? From the sitting room, Ailish heard a familiar snort. Keith was asleep.

Will do, she replied.

She washed the grease from her hands, put on her coat and climbed into her boots. Her heart thumped so loudly she worried her husband would hear. Slowly, stealthily, she opened the front door and closed it behind her. She slunk down the road like a fugitive and turned the corner onto Kennedy Crescent before risking a look at her email.

The article, from a London newspaper called *The Irish Herald*, was five years old. It was headlined 'The Woman Who Listens'.

She tapped to enlarge the image. She didn't have to see a caption or read a word. With one finger, she lightly traced the outline of Chrissie's face. The solemn eyes, the thin lips, even the gap between her front teeth: Ailish knew them all. They stared back at her from every mirror.

'It's you,' she said.

She sat down. That the footpath was wet didn't matter. She could have been sitting in the middle of a rushing river and she wouldn't have noticed. The article was far longer than expected. And it was entirely about Chrissie:

When Chrissie Mulcahy arrived in London at the age of sixteen, she'd already been through more than many people experience in a lifetime. Chrissie, who's originally from County Clare, was just thirteen when she became pregnant. She'd been raped by an elderly neighbour.

It was, she says, 'a different and distant world. We didn't use the word rape back then. Nor did we know words like paedophile or abuse. "Interfered with" was about as far as people would go.'

It was made clear to young Chrissie that she was a source of shame, not just for her family, but for the whole village. 'I don't think my parents fully understood what had been done to me,' she says.

'I was sent to a mother-and-baby home, a place called Carrigbrack, and I was terrified. Most of the girls were older than me, and at that age, even a year or two can feel like a generation. For the first month, all I could do was cry. I prayed that God would take me during the night.'

Sitting in her cosy kitchen in Shepherd's Bush, it's hard to reconcile the confident, accomplished woman Chrissie has become with the frightened teenager who wanted to die. Most of her memories of Carrigbrack are grim.

'It wouldn't be right to describe all the nuns as cruel,' she says. 'One was very kind to me. To this day, though, I believe that one or two of them were evil. And they were supported by a system that gave free rein to bad people. There was a poison in that system. A wickedness.'

At fourteen, Chrissie gave birth to a baby daughter. When the little girl was six months old, Chrissie was instructed to wash and dress her for a photograph. The photo was never taken. Instead, without her knowledge, the baby was driven away and adopted. That was the last time she saw her.

For the next two years, she toiled in the fields in Carrigbrack. 'It was back-breaking work,' she says with a rueful smile. 'All the same, I found it hard to leave. I didn't want to go home, and I feared what would happen to me in the outside world.'

Eventually, Chrissie agreed to accompany another young mother to London. By then, it was early 1974. For a girl who'd never even been to Dublin, London was quite a shock.

'I grew up in a parish of scarcely three hundred people,' she laughs, 'so you can imagine what I made of my new home. I remember arriving into Victoria coach station and thinking I wouldn't last a week. I saw more people that first morning than I'd seen in my entire life.'

Chrissie found work as a cleaner. Then, having attended night classes in shorthand and typing, she got a job in an insurance office. It was there that she met Iggy Mulcahy, who's originally from Listowel in County Kerry. They married in 1978 and have three children: Donna, Kirsty and Diarmuid. The Mulcahys' kitchen is filled with photos of their grandchildren.

In those days, it wasn't unusual for women to hide the fact that they'd already had a baby. Chrissie chose to tell the truth. 'It wasn't an easy thing to do. I hoped Iggy would understand. If he didn't, then he wasn't the right man for me.'

Not only did he understand, he pledged to help Chrissie should she ever decide to track down her daughter. In the 1990s, she did try to find her, but wherever she turned, there were obstacles.

'I was told there was no record of us. It was like we never existed,' she says. 'At one stage, I was asked if I'd imagined giving birth.'

The memory brings a tear to her large grey eyes. 'I can only trust that my girl found a loving home, and that life has been good to her,' she says.

This failure to find her daughter prompted Chrissie to set up a support group for other Irish women who'd spent time in mother-and-baby homes or Magdalene laundries.

'Our children have had lives big and small,' she explains. 'They've had choices. The women I meet had no choice. They were treated shamefully. And there were boyfriends too who were given no say in what happened to their babies.'

Chrissie remembers someone giving her a statistic: in 1967, 97% of children born outside marriage in Ireland were placed for adoption. To begin with, she didn't believe the figure. It sounded too extreme. It turned out to be true.

As she talks about the survivors of the homes, Chrissie becomes more animated, and her west Clare origins come out in her voice. 'It's not every town that has a story,' she says. 'It's every village. Every street. It's the cousin who disappeared, the neighbour who was supposed to be helping an aunt, the friend who suddenly moved to Dublin. They were banished, and their lives were altered forever.

'When I was younger, I couldn't have articulated any of this. For years, I buried my anger, then it came bursting out. I had to do something, and that was how the support group came about.'

For almost twenty years, Chrissie Mulcahy has been a familiar face in London Irish circles. She campaigns for, and offers advice to, survivors of the homes.

'I've been very lucky,' she says, with characteristic modesty. 'Many others have had difficult, fractured lives. Some have felt the need to suffer in silence. Forty or fifty years on, they're still trying to cope with a stigma they never deserved.'

She talks of one woman whose baby died in a home and who never received an explanation. 'We live in a time when motherhood, in all its forms, is celebrated. Only the other day, this lady was in a shop. She picked up a magazine, and there was a celebrity on the cover saying that since she'd had a baby "the world shone with a different light". The poor woman ran out of the shop in tears. All these years later, the pain is still there.'

Through the support group, many of the women have become friends. Chrissie says they can talk more openly and honestly than with others. 'There's a bond there,' she says. 'It's like we went through a war together.'

This weekend, she will receive the Lifetime Achievement Award at the London Irish Centre. It's in recognition of the time she has spent lobbying and campaigning. But above everything else, it's for her willingness to listen to the stories of others.

'When I was a young girl, no one would listen to me,' she says. 'I know how much damage that can cause.'

As for her own story, Chrissie hopes that one day she'll be reunited with the daughter who was taken from her. In the meantime, she keeps a candle in the window for the girl she never got to know.

When she'd finished reading, Ailish sat and allowed the tears to run down her face. Her teeth chattered, not from cold but from shock and exhilaration and a hundred sensations she couldn't explain. She'd had this skewed notion that her birth mother would be a feeble God-help-us character, worn down by abuse. Instead, she was a heroine.

After a few minutes, she called Katie. Her fingers felt thick and awkward, as if they belonged to someone else.

'Well?' said Katie.

'Thank you,' replied Ailish. It was all she could say. 'Thank you.'

'It was Beth who did the work. All this time, Chrissie was … what's that phrase? Hiding in plain sight, that's it. And she's been looking for you.'

'I can't believe I never came across the article. As soon as I saw the picture, I knew it was her.'

'She's the spitting image of you, right enough. To be fair, you only recently discovered the London connection, and you didn't know her married name. What do you make of her?'

'I'm … I'm stunned. She's incredible, isn't she?'

'She surely is. Imagine having that much strength. And she's so articulate, too. She said everything I would have liked to say. What a fantastic person.'

'I know,' said Ailish, half laughing, half crying. 'I've gone back to feeling inadequate.'

'Now, Ailish Dwan, you're not to get silly on me. Do you hear?'

'Sorry. I'm not sure it's fully registered with me yet. Also, God love her, I'd guessed she might have been abused, but seeing it in black and white is awful.'

'It's a shocking tale. No wonder people in Hackett's Cross were reluctant to talk.'

Ailish was taken aback by how emotional Katie sounded. 'The one thing that concerns me is …'

'… the fact that the article's five years old? There's no need to fret. Beth's been doing some more sleuthing. She found a London Irish Community Facebook page. There's a photo of Chrissie from earlier this year. You've got to remember she's only sixty-one. She's still a youngster.'

'Tell Beth I said thanks.'

'I will. She's practically gone into orbit, she's so happy. Oh, and she found a few other mentions of Chrissie too. There's a printer here, for the farm paperwork, and we're going to print everything out. We'll send it to you at the hotel. When are you back?'

'Tomorrow, unfortunately.'

'Ah, I see. Would it be possible for us to call in, do you think?'

'I don't see why not.'

After they'd hung up, Ailish remained on the kerb, allowing what she'd learnt about Chrissie to circle her brain. Night was falling fast, and the half-moon had been joined by a sprinkling of stars

She was jolted from her reverie by a neighbour and his daughter. The young girl was on a pink bicycle.

'How are you going on, Ailish?' said her neighbour. 'Are you all right down there?'

'Do you know, Lar, I'm the grandest,' Ailish said. 'Hello there, Saoirse. I see Santa Claus brought you a lovely new bike.'

'Yes,' said Saoirse, in her practical seven-year-old tones. 'It's been a very good Christmas.' She gave a smile as wide as a piano, albeit one with a few missing keys.

'It has indeed,' replied Ailish as she got to her feet.

All the while, happiness swelled inside her. Tomorrow she would try and find a phone number for Chrissie. In the meantime, she'd have to go home, make turkey casserole, iron her uniform and act as if everything was normal.

The three of them sat in Beth's car. Short of commandeering a hotel bedroom, it was the only place they could speak in private. Nearby, a bird sang: *twiss, twiss, twiss.*

'We've got some more news,' said Katie. 'Well, Beth does.'

'The centre where Chrissie's support group hold their meetings has a website. I had a poke around and I found a contact number. I'm pretty sure it's for Chrissie herself.'

Ailish clapped. 'No way!'

'Ordinarily,' added Katie, 'I wouldn't recommend calling out of the blue like this, but we know she's anxious to find you.'

'I've put the cuttings in here,' said Beth, handing over a large brown envelope, 'and written the number on the back. There's an email address too, so you can try that first if you'd prefer.' She smiled. 'I never thought I'd be handing over brown envelopes in hotel car parks. This is what spending time with Katie Carroll has done to me.'

Ailish laughed, then stared at the envelope. 'I'm overwhelmed. I'll never be able to thank you enough.'

'In a way,' said Katie, 'you already have.'

'I don't follow you.'

'What's happened this week proves that trying to return the bracelets and pass on what I know is worthwhile.'

'Please don't ever doubt that,' said Ailish.

For a short while, they chatted about Christmas. Ailish talked about her grandchildren and showed them some photos. Katie spoke about her sister, Beth's mam. They'd told her about the bracelets. It sounded as though she didn't approve. This puzzled Ailish. Then again, who was she to talk about difficult families? She hadn't said a word to Keith about finding her birth mother. Neither Beth nor Katie mentioned him.

'We'll have to get going,' said Beth. 'When you've spoken to Chrissie, do get in touch.'

'I promise,' said Ailish, 'you'll be the first to know.'

She went straight to Room 215, the Dolmen Suite. Such an important call deserved the best room in the hotel. Ailish had spent most of her life preparing for this moment. She must have visualised it ten thousand times. That didn't make it any easier. She sat in one of the enormous red and white armchairs, counted to ten and prodded out the number.

After three rings, a man answered the phone. 'Hello?'

'Hello, is that Mr Mulcahy?'

'Yes, Iggy Mulcahy here. Can I help you?' He had an English-Irish accent, like the singer with the V-neck jumpers who'd been on the television when Ailish was a child.

'Hi, um, gosh. My … Sorry, I'm going to start that again. My name is Ailish Dwan, but my original name, back when I was born, was Jacqueline Culligan.'

A pause followed. 'I see … Oh … Really?'

'I've been trying to find my birth mother and … well, you obviously know who I am. I'm sorry to ring you at home, only I got the number and—'

'There's no cause to apologise. I'm shocked to hear from you, that's all. Where do you live, Ailish?'

'I'm in Clare. In Kilmitten. I didn't get very far.'

'There's no harm in that,' said Iggy, his voice warm. 'I have a million questions, and I know a woman who probably has a million more. She's not going to believe this.'

'If me making contact is too much of a shock for her, I can give you my number, and she can call me back. Oh, and I can send you a photo, so you know I'm not an imposter. We look alike.'

'Don't worry. You can talk to Chrissie about that.'

The background noise suggested Iggy was walking up the stairs. Then the sound became more muffled, like he'd placed a hand over the receiver. Finally, he returned.

'I'm going to hand you over to the woman herself,' he said.

A moment later, a hesitant voice came on the line. 'Hello. Is that Ailish?'

A tingling sensation took hold of Ailish. 'Hello, Chrissie,' she replied

There was a pause, as if Chrissie was collecting herself. Then she said, 'I've been waiting nearly fifty years to talk to you, but I still can't think what to say. Could you speak so I can listen to you? I'd love to hear you.'

Chrissie's voice was melodic. Although only a whisper of her Clare accent remained, she was unmistakably Irish.

'I'm the same as yourself,' said Ailish. 'I've been preparing for this for as long as I can remember, and now the moment is here, my mind's gone blank.'

'Tell me about yourself, my love. About where you are and what you do. Do you have a family? Where did you grow up? And how did you find me? I'd almost given up hope of us meeting again.'

Ailish surprised herself and spoke for a long time. Rathtuskert Manor could have dissolved into dust around her, and she wouldn't have noticed. She talked about her children and grandchildren, about Keith and her adoptive parents, about Kilmitten and her job. If nothing she said was untrue, neither did she give a completely accurate picture of her life. She hoped there would be other conversations where she could be more candid. She was conscious too that this was a once-in-a-lifetime moment. It was a little bit strange, a little bit awkward.

It was entirely wonderful.

The Chrissie she spoke to wasn't as talkative as the woman in the article. Her words came in fits and starts. Occasionally she fell into silence, then they'd both speak together. There was something slightly off about her voice, like she was lying down. It was the middle of the afternoon, though, so that didn't make sense.

Ailish told Chrissie about how she'd found her. About how a blend of chance and determination had guided her in the right direction.

'If it wasn't for Katie and Beth,' she said, 'I'd still be looking for you.'

She explained about Katie's notebook and the box of bracelets. Needless to say, she omitted the part about her own bracelet being reduced to ashes in a bedside glass. Chrissie had only vague memories of Katie, which was understandable. The two hadn't met in almost fifty years. Even then, Katie had been a professional woman, Chrissie a timid teenager.

While they spoke, the light began to dim. The phone in the hotel room rang twice. There was a danger the head housekeeper would come looking for her soon. For once, Ailish didn't care. No one, not even Keith, could spoil this day.

Chrissie spoke about her other children and grandchildren. She was amused to discover she was a great-grandmother. 'That's terrible,' she said with a chuckle. 'I'm far too young and glamorous to be anyone's great-grandmother.'

'I have so many photos of them all,' said Ailish. 'You wouldn't believe how many photos I have.'

'I'm sure I would. Hasn't the world gone crazy for taking pictures? My grandchildren think I'm lying when I tell them I've only got one photo of myself from before I came to London.' She paused. 'And I've never seen a photo of you.'

'If you give me your mobile number, I'll send you some as soon as we've finished speaking.'

'And would you be able to send a few of your lovely young men and women? I'm desperate to see them all.'

For the first time, Ailish realised that Chrissie was crying. 'I didn't mean to upset you,' she said.

'Oh, my love, how could I not cry? This is one of the best days of my life.'

'Mine too. And would you send me some pictures? I'm dying to see everyone.'

'That'll be no trouble. Wait until they hear you've turned up. They'll be very excited.' Another pause, this time a lengthy one. 'Will it be possible for you to come and see me, do you think?'

Ailish had been hoping to hear this question. At the same time, she'd been dreading it. Chrissie's husband appeared to be in every way supportive, whereas Ailish was on her own. Once upon a time, she'd fooled herself that if she could only locate her birth mother, Keith would come around. A successful reunion would pacify him, she'd thought. The past couple of months had taught her that this probably wasn't true.

She longed to meet Chrissie. She needed to kiss her and hold her hand and tell her how proud she was to have such an amazing woman as her birth mother. They would have to meet in secret, though, and the only way this could happen would be for Chrissie to travel to Ireland.

'I was hoping,' she said, 'that you might be able to come over this way.'

'If money's an issue …?'

'No,' replied Ailish, a touch too quickly. 'No, not at all.' While she didn't have much spare cash, she could raid Stevie's college fund.

A sigh fluttered over the line. When Chrissie spoke again, there was a tremor in her voice. 'I didn't mention this because I didn't want to ruin such a fantastic day. What it is … I'm afraid I've been unwell over the past while.'

Ailish closed her eyes. She should have guessed. The clues had been there.

'There's no cause for alarm,' continued Chrissie. 'There's plenty of fight in me yet. I was diagnosed with breast cancer earlier in the year. I had a mastectomy, and then I needed chemo. Thankfully, that finished before Christmas. Now I'm due to have radiotherapy, so unfortunately I've got to stick around.'

'I'm sorry,' said Ailish. 'I had no idea.'

'Of course you didn't. It's just … like I say, at the minute, I can't travel. To be straight with you, I've been a bit depressed. Well, the chemo does that to you, doesn't it? But getting your call … it's like I'm being compensated for the past few months. Oh, and for fear you're worried, my cancer isn't the hereditary kind. I made sure to ask.'

Ailish's mind shifted in all directions. She would have to go to London, but even if she managed to fly there and back in one day, Keith would find out. You would have to be stupid not to, and whatever his failings, stupidity wasn't among them. The thought of telling him, of admitting she'd gone back on her promise to abandon the search, brought bile to her throat. She feared what the consequences might be. Since the day he'd destroyed her bracelet, she'd been preparing herself for his next eruption.

She realised Chrissie was waiting for an answer. 'I'd love to come and see you,' she said. 'When would be best?'

Chapter 21

Then, Patricia

For a week or more, they all believed Winnie would be found. Disappearing wasn't possible. As Sister Agnes was fond of saying, no one escaped from Carrigbrack, and on the rare occasion they did, they were hauled back and disciplined.

Every day, Patricia expected to see her friend. More than once, she imagined she had. She thought she spotted her at Mass or in the refectory. Wasn't that her shorn head? Wasn't that her striding walk? It was always someone else.

Everyone had a theory about Winnie, some plausible, some outlandish. One woman claimed she'd escaped through the hole in the hedge and joined up with a group of Travellers. Another maintained she hadn't left at all but was hiding in the attic. A third was adamant she was dead. Sister Sabina had killed her, she insisted, and buried her in the potato field. That this was accepted by several others said a lot about the general perception of Sabina.

Mother Majella gave a speech about aiding and abetting sinful behaviour, while Sister Agnes summoned everyone who'd been friendly with Winnie to her office. All insisted they knew nothing.

Patricia stayed quiet about the letter, which she'd hidden in the lining of her suitcase. While doing so, she'd got a surprise. The wig was missing. Wherever Winnie was, it was likely she'd gone there with black plastic hair. Patricia was grateful she'd never have to wear the cursed thing again.

Gradually, a possible explanation took hold. One of the nurses, a clodhopper of a Galway woman named Rita Farragher, had a car. On the day of Winnie's disappearance, she'd driven into Ennis to buy new sandals. No one, not even Agnes or Sabina, suspected that Rita would willingly have helped. She was an enthusiastic rule-follower. What was more likely was that Winnie had somehow stowed away in the boot of her old Ford Anglia. How she'd been able to get out, and where she went next, no one knew.

As the days turned into weeks and July faded into August, it became clear that Winnie wasn't coming back. Patricia wasn't sure she believed in God. If He did exist, what did He think of the cruelty inflicted in His name? She was forced to spend a lot of time on her knees, however, so she might as well pray for something. She prayed that Winnie was safe, that her own baby was born healthy and that Sister Sabina got a vicious dose of something painful. She found it hard to be civil to the people who annoyed her, not just Faustina and Sabina but also the nurse who'd been there when Winnie's baby had died.

At some point, the weather changed. While the heat continued, the blue skies were replaced by heavy cloud. It felt as if a thousand miles of sky were pressing down on them. At night, lightning crackled and thunder roared.

More and more, Patricia thought about her baby; about who they were and what they'd look like. She decided that if the baby was a girl, she'd call her after her friend. Not Winnie, but Gretta. That was her real name.

She also thought about Mike. She wondered if his other baby had arrived. How bizarre was it that her boy or girl would have a sibling who was almost the same age? While she didn't want to be with Mike, this didn't stop her from resenting his decision to stay with Vera. It would be easier if she could belittle his wife, if she could dismiss her as grasping or ugly or dumb, but, hand on heart, Patricia had never heard an unsympathetic word about the woman.

Her mother continued to send drab letters in which the only people mentioned were ill or dead. There was considerable detail about the funerals, all of which had attracted big crowds. At the rate people were dying, there'd be no one left in the village. Patricia felt bad about letting her parents down, but not so bad that she wanted to live under their roof again. When she left Carrigbrack, she would have to create her own life. She would like to live in a city where no one knew who she was. She didn't want to be followed by the swish of gossip. She couldn't bear the thought of her behaviour being monitored, either by her parents or by the local rumour-mongers.

Sleep was hard to come by, and when she did drop off, she had long, violent dreams, populated by unfamiliar people. She was always running or falling and sometimes she called out in panic. This usually prompted an ill-tempered *shh* from the woman in the next bed. Patricia would wake up feeling as if her mind and nerve endings were on fire. At other times, she forgot where she was. For a moment, she'd be back at home. She saw herself with more detachment now. She hadn't had a lot of freedom, certainly not as much as the women in books and films, but she'd had some. She worried that she'd never be free again.

What would Mike make of what she'd become? Here she was, without lipstick or perfume. Without hair. She had no conversation to offer. No insights or quips. Being discarded was hard. Every day, it chipped away at her. Mike was the only man she had slept with.

What if there were no others? What if her parents were right and no one else was interested in her?

One morning, she peeled away from the band of women going to the laundry and went to Diane's grave. Briefly, she considered the risk she was taking. Her baby was due within the next couple of weeks, however, and the range of available punishments was limited. It was unlikely that Winnie would ever return to her daughter's resting place. It was even more unlikely that anyone else would visit. Soon, the grass would grow over the earth, and no one would know that a little girl was buried there.

No sooner had she reached the right spot than the rain started. Great drops the size of rose petals fell, slowly at first, then gathering pace until the water was running in rivulets down Patricia's face, and what was left of her hair was glued to her scalp. The ground gave off the beautiful earthy smell of rain falling on dry soil. By the time she thought of moving, it was too late. She was drenched to the core, her uniform sodden and plastered to her body.

Agnes found her. 'I despair of you,' she said.

'I'm doing no harm, Sister.'

'Let me be the judge of that,' said the nun, before ordering her back inside.

That evening, after the rosary, Agnes announced that all discussion of Winnie was banned.

The following day, Jacinta's baby was taken for adoption. Only six weeks old, Lorcan was a premium child, born to a healthy young woman from a prosperous family. That explained why he was snapped up like a bargain in the January sales when the children of poorer women were left behind. Some were two or three years old before they were adopted. There was, thought Patricia, a contradiction in how their babies were treated. In one way, they were seen as lesser. They weren't as important as the sons and daughters of married women. Or as worthy of love. But in another way, they were valuable commodities. When Lorcan left, Jacinta whimpered like a puppy. One of the others tried to comfort her, and got a swift rebuke from Agnes. Jacinta left two days later. Her parents had the money to pay for her release. A group gathered to say goodbye, but were ordered back to work by Sabina.

Another baby was adopted that week. Her mother, seventeen and skinny as a drainpipe, was glad to see her go.

'Her father's an awful dose,' she said. 'I'm lucky not to get tied to him. I hope her new family have pots of money and give her all the things I didn't have.'

Every morning, Patricia wondered if this was the day her own little boy or girl would arrive. Work in the laundry was a hard grind. She was too big to be cooped up in a hot room. Her burnt hand healed slowly. She resolved that when she had a life of her own, she'd get the best washing machine money could buy. She'd rather go hungry than endure any more drudgery.

In the main, Agnes's diktat about Winnie was obeyed. It was as if she'd never existed. Patricia said as much one night when she met Sister Eunice in the corridor.

'It's probably for the best,' said Eunice. 'The speculation was getting out of hand.'

'You mean Sister Sabina didn't kill her and bury her among the spuds?'

Eunice laughed, then put a hand over her mouth. 'That's a desperate thing to say.' She winked. 'There's no way Sabina would endanger the potatoes. I'd say the cabbage field is a far better bet.'

'Oh, listen to us,' said Patricia. 'Here we are laughing and joking about Winnie when she could be sleeping by the side of the road – or somewhere worse.'

'Do you worry about her?'

'I do.'

Eunice gave a quick look around. 'You really don't need to,' she said, her voice scarcely louder than a whisper.

'What do you mean?'

'That's all I can say, but trust me, you shouldn't fret about her.'

With that, Eunice smiled and continued her walk down the corridor towards the nursery.

Chapter 22

Brandon

Christmas was frosty. When they weren't arguing, they were recovering from the last row or preparing for the next. Long silences were punctuated by tart remarks. Brandon had hoped that, given time, Robyn would accept his decision. Instead, she became more entrenched in her views. She never missed an opportunity to let him know he'd mishandled the conversation with Katie Carroll.

He conceded that some of the blame was his. He'd become too prickly too quickly. But he'd been ambushed. Who wouldn't recoil from such misery? And why did both Robyn and Katie keep telling him how he should react? It was as though there was a spectrum of appropriate responses and he'd fallen off the edge.

The Carrigbrack described by Katie was even worse than he'd anticipated. Who needed dystopian novels and TV shows when, in the recent past, those homes had existed? What baffled him was why Katie had stayed working there. One thing was for sure: he'd been lucky to escape a country where that kind of behaviour was the norm. How many people had ended up spending years in therapy because of what had been done to them? Brandon guessed psychiatry must be a lucrative business in Ireland.

Over and again he told himself that his real and lasting bond was with his parents, Art and Ellen. They were the people who'd chosen, raised and cared for him. He'd also worked hard at shaping his own life. As far as he was concerned, that was what mattered. To use a modern phrase, that was his identity.

In the immediate aftermath of the conversation with Katie, he'd again been tempted to throw the bracelets away. Their presence dragged him down. The only thing that stopped him was fear of Robyn's reaction.

Ordinarily, Brandon avoided arguments. They were corrosive and pointless. He'd long been skilled at finding the right emollient words, at reaching an appropriate level of compromise. Nobody could change the subject more smoothly or walk away more calmly. Until now, he hadn't thought that Robyn was given to confrontation either. How wrong he'd been. She took to pacing the house like a caged animal, listing all the reasons why he should trace Eddie and Linda.

'You're assuming they can be found,' he said. 'If there was one thing Katie made clear, it was that tracking people down is difficult.'

'Difficult, but not impossible.'

'What I can't understand is why it matters so much to you.'

'What *I* can't understand,' she replied, 'is why it doesn't matter more to *you.*'

'That's unfair. I'm not saying I'll never look for them. I'm just saying not right now.'

Around and around they went, having the same circular argument until one of them – usually him – found a way to defuse it. Every day, he felt as if he was carrying explosives over cobblestones; one misstep and – *boom!* – everything he valued would be gone. All his certainties were cracking and shifting.

*

In early January, on a day when Boston was shivering under the sideswipe of a storm, he came home from work to find Robyn in the bedroom. Her black case sat in the middle of the bed surrounded by neatly folded T-shirts. He'd always admired her packing skills.

'I'm going to see Zinzi,' she said. 'I need a break.'

Zinzi was an old college friend who worked as a TV news anchor in Miami.

'Why didn't you tell me? Were you going to leave without saying anything?' The unspoken question: are you leaving for good?

She placed a fuchsia-pink top into the case. 'I only made my mind up this morning, so they agreed to rearrange some stuff at work. And no, of course I wouldn't have gone without saying goodbye.'

Brandon wondered what she'd said at work. January was the busiest time of year for personal trainers. There were fortunes to be earned from the 'new year, new you' crowd. He trusted she hadn't told the truth.

'If you'd given me some notice,' he said, 'I could've come too. I've got vacation time left from last year, and while it wouldn't be easy, I could probably have—'

'That wouldn't have been a smart idea. I'm going to Florida for fun, not to argue.'

'I wouldn't have argued. You're the one who insists on falling out. I just want a quiet life. I mean, come on, Robyn, we're *married*. You can't go on vacation on your own.' Brandon was babbling, like a child who wanted to play with the big boys and girls.

She folded a blue gingham dress, his favourite, and put it in the case. It was followed by a pair of white pants, a red sweater and a pink scarf. She was taking a lot of clothes. How long was she planning on spending in Florida? Not for the first time, he was hit by the feeling that Robyn belonged elsewhere with someone who was more like her.

Two years into their marriage, there were still times when he found it difficult to believe that she was his wife. Everything else in his life had entailed hard work and sacrifice. Meeting Robyn at a client's party had been sheer luck. That she had fallen for him had been little short of miraculous. Prior to her, there had, of course, been other women, but no lasting commitments, no one to ruffle his orderly existence.

'Maybe,' she said, 'you've put your finger on the problem. I don't want a quiet life.'

'I'm older than you. My priorities are different. I thought you were cool with that.'

She placed two pairs of sandals on top of her clothes and began zipping up the case. 'It's nothing to do with being older, so don't use that excuse. I've tried to see everything from your point of view. Believe me, I have. But I can't process the fact that you have a twin brother out there, not to mention a birth mother who went through a horrendous time, and you don't want to find them. It's just not …'

'It's not what?'

'Nah, forget it.'

'No. What were you going to say?'

'I was going to say it's not human.'

His stomach twisted. 'Jesus, that's a cruel thing to say.'

'I'm sorry, Brandon. It's how I feel. I've done my best to see where you're coming from, but I can't. Even at the most basic level, your lack of curiosity bugs me.'

'Are you saying you don't love me any more?'

Robyn pinched the bridge of her nose. Her perfect nose in her perfect face. 'No. I … I'm saying that perhaps I got you wrong. I thought I'd married this big-hearted guy who valued family and hard work and loyalty and all the good stuff. Compared to other men, you seemed so solid, so generous. So kind. But, faced with a challenge, you've chosen to run away and turn your back on your family. On people who might need you.'

Brandon had always said that he'd walk barefoot to New York for Robyn. And he would. That would be different, though. That would be his choice. Trailing around a foreign country looking for people who might no longer exist *wasn't* his choice. If he gave in … Well, that was it, he would be giving in. He'd be getting involved in a messy situation that wasn't of his choosing. He had to make her see that he was doing the right thing.

'They're not my family. Mom and Dad are. And you are. Or at least I thought you were.'

'Don't bring Art and Ellen into this. They've no issue with you looking for Linda and Eddie. They said as much over the holidays. If you ask me, Ellen *wants* you to try and find them.'

There was more than a splinter of truth in what she said. Taken aback to discover that Brandon was a twin, both parents had urged him to trace Eddie and Linda. Again, he'd felt like he was being railroaded. He hadn't spoken to them in four days, which for the Bennetts was a lifetime.

Robyn went to lift her suitcase from the bed. Brandon tried to help, but she batted him away.

'I'm going to raise something I've shied away from,' she said. 'Do you have an issue with Eddie's disability?'

'Aw, Robyn. What do you think I am?'

He'd tried to inform himself about cerebral palsy. It turned out that much of what he thought he knew wasn't true. Katie had been right: usually, the causes were related to the woman's pregnancy rather than the birth. Some people with CP lived regular adult lives. Others had trouble not just with movement but with speaking, eating and sleeping. They suffered pain and became depressed. There was one fact that nagged at him. Early intervention was vital. Without it, children were in danger of becoming passive and uncommunicative.

Their lives were diminished far more than they should be. It was impossible to imagine that Eddie, stranded in Carrigbrack, had received much intervention or support.

Robyn's voice cut through his thoughts. 'Okay,' she was saying, 'let me phrase it another way. Does Eddie's level of disability matter to you? Like, if you found out he was only mildly disabled, and that you could go for a beer with him after all, would that change your view?'

'I don't follow you.'

'It strikes me that if you were sure your brother could bring something to your life, you might want to meet him. The same goes for Linda. Only you're worried she never recovered from what was done to her.'

'Please,' he said, 'you can't see it like that. You can't see *me* like that.' Brandon was annoyed by how congested he sounded. Getting emotional wouldn't help. He touched Robyn's wrist. Even her wrists were perfect.

She pulled away. 'I need to get going. My flight's at eight.'

'I'll take you to the airport.'

'I've booked a cab. It'll be here in a minute.'

'Christ, Robyn,' he said, 'you can't go like this.'

'I'm sorry.' She shifted her gaze so she was looking anywhere but at him. 'It's what I need to do.'

After she'd gone, Brandon leant back against the bedroom wall and slid down until he slumped onto the floor. She hadn't said when she'd be back, or even *if* she'd be back. She was young. She could get a job anywhere. If she didn't want to be with him, there was nothing to keep her in Boston. Everything he'd worked for was unravelling. His luck was running dry.

Once, he'd been content on his own. He'd read that, contrary to popular belief, most bees didn't live in hives. Many were solitary creatures. He remembered finding solace in that. But those days were behind him, and he'd mapped out a future with Robyn: a baby, ideally two; a bigger house, or a place near the coast. There wasn't space for a dark backstory or damaged family members.

As much as he hated to admit it, some of his wife's accusations had been accurate. He was turning his back on people who might need him. But there was more to it than that. He was the man who'd walked away from the plane crash, the man who'd jumped clear of the burning building. His survival, once a source of comfort, now filled him with guilt. Why couldn't Robyn see that? To him, it was as plain as a rash.

Chapter 23

Ailish

'Would I like to come to London with you?' said Katie, her voice brimming with happiness. 'Of course I would. I'd swim the Irish Sea if I had to.'

Beth was equally enthusiastic. 'We won't make a nuisance of ourselves. We'll hide in the corner and pretend we're not there. Unless you need us ... which you won't.' Then she laughed. 'Sorry, Ailish, I'm rambling. But it's all so exciting.'

Ailish assured her that rambling was entirely acceptable. Her own head was in fifty different places at once. The previous day, she'd tried to shine a mirror with toothpaste and clean a bath with bleach.

The three would leave Dublin on an early flight and return that evening. Ailish would stay in Drumcondra the night before. She booked two days off work and confirmed her plans with Chrissie. Despite her birth mother's illness, she felt a pleasure she hadn't experienced in years. Everything was in place. Everything was great.

Except it wasn't.

She'd had several conversations with Chrissie. They'd swapped snippets of information about their lives and families. She'd learnt more about her half-sisters and brother and about her birth mother's life after she'd left Carrigbrack. In return, she'd told stories about her own children and grandchildren. She'd done her best to talk warmly about her adoptive parents. Negativity wouldn't be fair, either to them or to Chrissie. The problem was Keith. When it came to her husband, Ailish had lied. He was delighted for her, she'd said. He wouldn't be travelling to London, but only because he was busy at work. Mostly, she guided the conversation in another direction.

In truth, she still hadn't said anything to Keith about Chrissie or London. She knew she'd have to tell him. She couldn't disappear, then reappear two days later with stories of her travels. The trouble was, even thinking about it brought a tightness to her chest and a tremor to her hands. She'd rehearsed several options, but the right words escaped her. The thought of Chrissie, and the gutsy way she'd risen above her rape and incarceration, made her feel worse. She was letting her birth mother down.

For a while, she didn't say anything to the children. She was scared that, however unwittingly, one of them would let something slip. Eventually, she had a coffee with Jodie. Then she called Lee in Kerry and Lorraine in Limerick. They bombarded her with questions.

'What does Dad make of your news?' they all asked.

'I wanted to tell you first,' she replied. 'After all, Chrissie is your grandmother. Do me a favour and keep it to yourself until I get a chance to talk to him.'

Although they must have been sceptical, none of the three challenged her. Jodie, always the plain speaker, came closest.

'Holy moly, Mam,' she said. 'If it was me, I wouldn't have been able to stop talking about her. I can't believe you've kept it all to yourself.'

'I'll tell him tonight,' promised Ailish.

She meant it. Sort of. Her hopes, such as they were, hinged on getting Keith into a good mood, then convincing him that Katie had done the legwork. 'Everything was arranged before I knew where I was,' she would claim. His attitude had been coloured by the belief that Chrissie would be impossible to find. Now that those fears had proven groundless, his objections would wither away. Wouldn't they?

Then she told herself to stop being stupid. Obviously Keith wouldn't agree to her meeting Chrissie. She would have to work her way around his disapproval.

First, she needed to speak to Stevie. Even though she still referred to him as her baby, Ailish was the smaller of the two by almost a foot. There were times when she questioned whether she'd really given birth to this broad-shouldered, curly-haired giant. Her first three children had grown up gradually. Stevie was different. In a finger click, he'd morphed from a rosy-cheeked kid to an adult who looked at her with benign confusion. At seventeen, he had a pink-haired girlfriend, a passion for something called grime and a habit of smoking Marlboros out of his bedroom window.

She would never admit it, but he'd always been her favourite. Right from the start, he'd been easy to love. Not only was he clever, he was sunny-natured. Ailish recognised her double standards. Behaviour for which she'd scolded the others – traipsing through the house in muddy shoes, drinking milk from the carton, spending half of Saturday in bed – now went over her head. She was relieved that he'd finally chosen a college course. He wanted to study data science. She pretended to understand.

When Stevie got back from school, Ailish was in the kitchen peeling potatoes. Her kitchen was weighed down with the accumulation of almost three decades of family life. There were saucepans and bowls, outdated utensils and recipe books. In among the books were bills and letters and pieces of paper she'd never got around to filing away. The kitchen was her place, and she liked it there. She especially liked the days when her son joined her before starting his homework.

'There's something I've been meaning to tell you,' she said.

He responded to the news with enthusiasm, giving her a bone-crushing hug then demanding to see every photo Chrissie had sent.

'This is amazing,' he said as he swiped through the pictures on Ailish's phone. 'She can't deny you, anyway. You're the absolute spit of each other.'

'It's great, isn't it? As you can see, her other children all take after their father.'

Stevie read the newspaper article too.

'That's crazy,' he kept saying. 'I assume the old guy who raped her got away with it?'

'No doubt.'

'Does Dad know about this?'

'I was hoping to tell him this evening.'

Stevie handed back her phone. 'But you probably won't.'

'What do you mean?'

'Don't take this the wrong way, but we both know what'll happen. He'll come home in bad form, and you'll say to yourself, "Nah, I can't risk it tonight. I'll leave him be."'

How well you know us, thought Ailish. 'I have to tell him. I'm going to London on Monday.'

'Like, four days from now?'

'Yep.'

'I can't understand his problem with you finding your birth mother.' He held up a hand, as if making a stop sign. 'And don't say he doesn't, because I've heard him banging on about it. Is that what the row before Christmas was about?'

'Yes. I'm sorry about that.'

'Ah, Mam. Don't you be saying sorry when you've nothing to apologise for.'

'Okay, okay. You go and do your homework. I'll give you a shout when dinner's ready.'

Ailish hadn't expected Stevie to be so outspoken, and as the three of them sat down for their evening meal, she was more uptight than ever. She chewed slowly. Without the help of a mouthful of water, swallowing was impossible. Even mashed potato was tricky. Her grip was unsteady, and she worried the knife and fork would fall from her hands. Stevie was no better. He examined his fish fillet like he'd never seen food before and wasn't sure what to do with it.

Keith complained about work. Stevie told an anecdote about an eccentric teacher. Ailish spoke about a well-known couple who'd stayed in the hotel and left the room looking like a tornado had passed through. When the conversation stalled, she knew she had to speak. Still she hesitated. Stevie fixed her with a questioning look, which was noticed by Keith.

'What's the story?' he said.

Neither of them replied.

He turned to Stevie. 'What have you done?'

'Nothing.'

'Is anybody going to put me in the picture here? Ailish?'

Maybe, she decided, it wasn't too late to back out of the London visit. She could come up with an excuse and go another time when she'd found the strength to talk to Keith. Katie would be annoyed, but she'd forgiven her for the bracelet, so she'd probably forgive this.

'Ailish?' he repeated.

'If you're not going to tell him,' said Stevie, 'I am.'

'I …' she started.

Keith put down his cutlery with a clang. 'Sweet suffering Jesus, will one of you talk to me?'

Ailish had dreaded this moment, but now that it was here, she had to get on with it. 'It's my biological mother,' she said. 'I've found her.'

'Hold on a minute. I thought we'd agreed you were going to let that business rest.'

She did her best to explain what Katie and Beth had done.

'Aren't they the right pair of busybodies? Have you approached this woman?'

'Yes. Her name's Chrissie. She's lovely. She wants to meet.'

'And where is she, this Chrissie?'

Ailish couldn't look at her husband. Instead, she focused on a stain on the wall, created years before when Lorraine and Stevie had gone through a phase of flicking cornflakes at each other. 'She's in London.'

'I see. Whereabouts in London?'

'Shepherd's Bush.'

'That's a fine spot, isn't it?'

'I think so, yes.'

'She must be fierce disappointed in you. Living in a poky house in Kilmitten, your days devoted to clearing up other people's filth.'

Stevie tipped forward. 'Don't speak to her like that.'

'I can't remember asking for your view,' said Keith. 'Eat your dinner or go upstairs and do your homework. When you're old enough to have an opinion, I might listen to it.'

Ailish started telling Chrissie's story. If he knew what a heroine she was, it might soften his attitude. She took her phone from her bag and showed him the photos. He held the phone in front of him and raced through the pictures in a way that suggested he wasn't particularly impressed.

'Why didn't you tell me before?' he said.

'I was nervous. We haven't always seen eye to eye on this, and I didn't know how you'd react.'

Keith tilted his head to one side. 'At least you admit you've behaved badly. What kind of marriage is it where you promise not to do something then lash ahead and do it anyway, huh?'

Stevie, who'd been slumped in front of his dinner, straightened his back. 'Why can't you be happy for her?'

'I told you to mind your own business. This is between me and your mother. Go upstairs, would you? You see, Ailish, this is what happens when you spoil a child. They get all mouthy.'

'I'm not going anywhere.'

'You'll do as you're told. When I was your age, I was out earning a living, not dossing around in a classroom learning Shakespeare and French and other crap that's of no use to any man. Mind you, if I'd spoken to my father like you speak to me, I'd have felt the back of his hand.'

'I'm staying here while you listen to what Mam's got to say.'

'Oh, there's more, is there?'

Ailish clasped her hands together. Her mouth was dry, as if she'd been gargling vinegar. 'I'm going to London to see her.'

Hardly had the words cleared her lips than Keith snapped back, 'Like fuck you are.'

'She's not well. She's got breast cancer, and I'm going to see her.'

'Where's the money coming from?'

'You know I've a little bit put by.'

Keith laughed. 'There you are, Stevie boy. For all her talk about your college fund, she's quick enough to spend the money on herself.'

'Don't worry about me,' said Stevie, his voice low. 'I want Mam to go to London.'

'What's that? Speak up there.'

'I said I want Mam to go to London. What sort of person wouldn't want her to meet her mother?'

Keith switched the phone from one hand to the other and back again. Save for the tick of the kitchen clock, the room was quiet. 'She lied to me. She lied and kept on lying. That's the reason she's not going. And while I pay the bills, my word is more important than yours. Isn't that right, Ailish?'

She didn't answer.

'I said, isn't that right, Ailish?'

There was a cold anger to his words. She ought to back down. Backing down was what she knew best, but she'd spent long enough with her nose pressed against the window, gazing on while others did what they wanted. She looked from her husband to her son and back again. They had the same eyes, but Stevie's were keener, more alert. If Stevie was drawn with a sharp pencil, Keith was more of a charcoal smudge.

'I'm going to London,' she said. 'My mother's unwell, and you can't stop me from seeing her.'

'Come again?'

'You heard me. I'm going to London.'

Keith tightened his grip on the phone and hurled it hard against the far wall. It fell asunder and the parts clattered across the floor. 'And I said you're not.'

Although Ailish's left eyelid twitched, she was unusually clear-headed. Before she could reply, Stevie intervened.

'What's wrong with you?' he said to Keith. 'Why do you have to behave like this?'

'For the final time, go to your room and study your precious fucking books.'

Ailish could hear Stevie's breath shaking.

'No,' he said. 'You've pushed everybody around for long enough. Did you ever wonder why the other three left as soon as they could? Why they practically ran out of the house? It was because of you and your roaring and your bullying. Lee says he'd rather sleep rough than come back here. Did you know that?'

Ailish gasped. It was a feeble sound and she hoped the others hadn't heard. Lee had often clashed with his father. She'd had no idea, though, that he'd been so badly affected. She should have done more to protect him. And the girls: her sweet, funny girls. Had they too had miserable childhoods? They'd never said as much. Oh, she'd known that life with Keith was far from ideal, but she'd done everything she could to shield the children. When he'd been in bad humour, she'd shooed them out of the house. They'd never seen her cry. She'd tried to be upbeat. Why hadn't they told her that she'd got it all wrong?

Keith rose from his chair and grasped the shoulder of Stevie's hoodie. 'You little bastard. Go. Up. Stairs.'

Stevie stood and shook off his father's hand. 'No. We spend all our time in this house pretending that everything's okay. That we're normal. I've had enough of it.'

'Please, love …' started Ailish.

Stevie looked at her. 'And you're the worst. You pretend he doesn't hit you when we all know he does.'

A long beat of silence followed. Ailish felt something inside her shrivel. She'd been careful to camouflage her injuries. And some of what Keith had done to her had barely left a mark. The pinches, the pokes, the pulled hair: how could Stevie know about those?

Keith's eyes narrowed. 'I've never touched your mother.'

'You mightn't have given her a black eye or a swollen lip, but you've done everything else. I've heard her squeal. And I've seen the bruises on her arms.'

'Ailish, tell him he's wrong.'

Stevie glanced at her. 'Don't lie for him.'

Ailish stayed quiet. For the first time, she noticed that Stevie was the taller of the two. Keith attempted to shove his son. 'I've had more than enough of your lip. You reckon you're better than me, don't you? With your loud music and your slut of a girlfriend and your college notions. Now, if you don't move, you're going to be very, very sorry.'

Stevie stood, still as stone.

'Please,' said Ailish. 'Please can we take a step back? There's no need for any of this.' Everything felt fragile, as if she was surrounded by tripwires and there was no safe way to escape.

'I won't be ordered around,' said Keith. 'Not by you, and definitely not by him.'

Stevie's face had turned egg-carton grey. He shrugged. 'I'm staying right here.'

Keith's shoulders dropped slightly, almost as if he was giving in. Ailish knew better. She recognised it as a preparatory move. Before she could shout a warning, before she could even open her mouth, she heard the crunch of his fist against Stevie's jaw. Stevie stumbled back. His head cracked against the jamb of the door and he hit the ground.

'I warned you,' said Keith. 'Now get up off the floor.'

Stevie was motionless.

It took Ailish a second to realise that the piercing sound was her own scream.

Chapter 24

Katie

The new year brought a flurry of enquiries. The Carrigbrack Nurse inbox was inundated with queries from people who'd resolved that this would be the year they found their birth parents. In the first ten days of January, Katie sent out three bracelets. She was waiting for further information before posting another three. Replying to those she couldn't help was tough. Their emails usually started with an apology for asking about a birth outside her time frame. Always polite, sometimes intense, they filled her with tenderness. She told herself not to get involved. The people who'd been born while she worked in the home were her priority.

As usual, Saturday saw them reviewing the week's correspondence. Sunlight was falling through the kitchen window. It was one of those crisp January days that caught you off guard with their beauty.

Beth leant forward on her elbows. 'We're good at this,' she said, 'and we're learning all the while. Ailish is proof of that.'

Katie put down her pen and removed her glasses. 'You know

she's vanished again? I've been ringing, but her phone's permanently switched off. She's a terrible woman for disappearing.'

'Don't worry about her. I mean, everything's far from ideal, but she always struggles through in the end. Anyway, what I was saying was that if you look at the emails we're getting, and at the posts on the message board, it's extraordinary. I'm stunned by how many people are talking about Carrigbrack.'

'There were worse places, you know.'

'That's the point. What we're doing – no, what you're doing – is opening up the discussion about one of the homes. Others are bound to follow.'

Three weeks had passed since Katie had last read the message board. She couldn't do it any more. The debate had taken off in too many directions, and in some cases the anguish was overwhelming. There was too much honesty, and it scared her. She didn't want this complication. As much as she admired Chrissie and other campaigners, it wasn't a path she wished to follow. She'd set out to complete a task and, day by day, she was getting there.

'What are you suggesting?' she said.

'I suppose what I'm asking is whether we can do more to help people who were born before or after your time in Carrigbrack. Plus, there must be women in a similar situation to yourself; women who worked in homes and have information that could nudge someone in the right direction.'

Reluctant to discuss her reservations, Katie tried a conciliatory approach. 'I hear what you're saying, lovey, but I want to concentrate on the people in here.' She patted the lid of her new red box. 'That's enough work for me.'

'You wouldn't be on your own.'

'You're already doing more than your fair share. You have a job … and a life to live.'

'Work's fine, but I get more of a buzz from this. There are some heartbreaking stories on the forum, most of them from before your time. Like, there's this one message from a guy who reckons his birth mother was from Limerick. His health is poor, and it sounds as though he'd like to find her before he dies. Wouldn't it be brilliant if we could help him?'

'But we can't. We don't know anything about him or his birth mother.'

'Are there not ways of finding out?'

Katie touched Beth's arm. 'You've very good, really you are. And I'm not saying we should never look at these other cases, but for the moment, why don't we focus on the people we know we can help?'

'Okay,' said Beth, finally, her tone suggesting she'd be revisiting the subject. 'I meant what I said about Ailish, by the way. You shouldn't worry. By now, she must have told Keith about finding Chrissie.'

'That's exactly what worries me.'

'If there was a serious problem, she'd have been in touch. We're going to London in two days' time. She can't just disappear.'

'I hope you're right.'

Katie assumed that if there was bother, Keith was the cause of it. The man was as slippery as black ice and twice as dangerous. The only other possibility was that Chrissie was in poorer health than Ailish had indicated. The nurse in her knew that these days most breast cancers were highly treatable, but it was only six months since stomach cancer had claimed her husband, and the word put her on edge.

'Oh, I forgot to tell you,' said Beth. 'Mam says hello.'

'Does she indeed?'

Beth grinned. 'It was a very cordial conversation, actually. You'd swear we were best buds. She asked about Ailish, and I told her we were off to London. I can tell she's still iffy about the bracelets, but at least she wasn't hostile.'

Since their Christmas skirmish, Katie hadn't spoken to her sister. While she didn't regret what she'd said about Beth or the bracelets, she'd no desire to get into a protracted row. By the sounds of things, Margo was keeping tabs on her through Beth.

Earlier, she'd received an email from Gary, who'd returned from Los Angeles. He'd attached some photos. One was of his three sons, each as dark and gangly as their father. Another was of Allegra and her mother. What beauties they were, and what a shame he didn't see more of them. The big news was that he believed he'd found Noreen Nestor, one of the two women who remained on his list. Her married name was O'Callaghan, and she lived in Galway.

To Katie's surprise, she'd also received an email from Brandon. The snag was, it didn't say anything of any significance. He wished her a happy new year and thanked her for her help. He didn't apologise for his crabby behaviour on the day of their phone call. Neither did he mention Robyn. Brandon, Linda and Eddie continued to nibble at Katie's brain. She suspected Eddie might be easier to locate than some of the other Carrigbrack babies. All the same, she was wary. Would it be right to try and trace him without Brandon's approval? Would she be crossing an ethical line? Her queasiness didn't end there. To find him, she'd have to reach out to others who'd been in the home, and she wasn't sure she wanted to do that.

At least Brandon was safe, with a thoughtful, supportive spouse. Others weren't so fortunate. Throughout the day, she fretted about Ailish. By eight o'clock, she was in a lather of nerves. Finally, a text arrived:

> Sorry for not being in touch. Stevie hasn't been well and my phone was broken. Have a new phone now. Looking forward to seeing you tomorrow night and jetting off to London on Monday xxx

Yes, phones broke and teenagers got sick. Yes, Ailish was a busy woman with a full-time job and a demanding husband. Yet something about the message troubled Katie. She prodded out a reply:

> Beth and I are excited about the trip. Hopefully you'll be able to get here at a reasonable hour, so we can go out for a bite to eat. Is Stevie okay? Are you okay?

Several minutes passed before she heard another ping:

> All okay. Sometimes things get complicated, but you know that. Don't worry about me. And for fear I've never said this properly, I'm grateful for everything you've done. I feel very lucky.

Katie wasn't reassured. She'd have consulted Beth, only her niece had gone out.

Her thoughts returned to Chrissie in Carrigbrack. How clearly she remembered her pinched face and air of confusion. She was fascinated by everything Chrissie had done yet nervous about meeting her again. She thought of others, too, especially Linda. The bright, spirited women had suffered terribly. Sister Agnes had seen herself as a custodian of the old ways, and any woman who protested had received a robust response. Linda had known she was being mistreated yet had been powerless to do anything about it.

There was a prickling at the back of Katie's eyes, an anger in her chest. If Linda was still out there, she deserved to know that one of her twins had been sent to America and that he'd made a success of his life.

She went upstairs and after some rummaging found an old black-covered address book. A few weeks before, Beth had informed her that people no longer carried address books. Everything was 'in the cloud', apparently. Although it didn't take Katie long to find what she was looking for, she wasn't optimistic. Landlines were on the same road to extinction as address books. When she tapped out the number, her doubts were confirmed. All she got in return was a hurried series of beeps. Then it hit her: she was missing a digit. Even in rural areas, numbers now had an extra digit. But which one, and where to place it?

An internet search told her that she needed to put a 3 before the old number. She tried again, and – hey presto! – it connected. It rang five, six, seven times. She was about to hang up when a woman's voice said, 'Hello?'

'Er, hello. I'm not sure if I've got the right person or the right place. If I have, I hope you can help. This is Katie Carroll. You might remember me from Carrigbrack. Well, I was Katie O'Dea in those days.'

She heard a quick breath.

'Oh yes,' said the woman. 'I remember you.'

Chapter 25

Then, Patricia

She would never admit it, but Sister Faustina had been chastened by the death of Winnie's baby. Afterwards, girls with burns were given more time to dunk their hands in cold water, and pains were taken seriously.

There was no sign of the others softening. If anything, they became more authoritarian. As far as Sister Agnes was concerned, one girl's escape meant they were all in need of a hell-and-damnation tutorial. She gave several sermons about the sixth and ninth commandments, the gist being that while you could probably get away with breaking some of the others, six and nine were mortal-sin territory. Sister Sabina told a simple young girl from County Galway that she was ruined and would be lucky to get work cleaning lavatories. An older girl protested and had her hair chopped off. Sister Eunice said no more about Winnie, and when Patricia asked, she just smiled like a ruddy-cheeked Mona Lisa.

On the day her baby started to push its way into the world, Patricia was in the laundry, ironing a mountain of pillowcases. It was one of the less arduous jobs, but even so, it was difficult. She was too big, too ungainly. She remembered how Winnie had joked about her having twins, and felt a flutter of panic. For a while, she said nothing. When, at last, she couldn't continue, she approached Faustina and asked to be excused. Her calm appearance belied her fear. She was scared of all the usual things: pain and infection and her own inadequacies. Most of all, she was scared that what had happened to Diane would happen to her baby. Winnie had claimed that women were better off being stupid because that way they didn't know what could go wrong. Patricia could see the wisdom in her words.

Over the following hours, time became distorted. There were stretches when she thought pain would defeat her. Then a respite would come, and she'd tell herself she could cope. As soon as she began to accept this, the agony would return. She'd sworn she wouldn't shout, not out of any deference to the rules, but because she wanted to be strong and dignified. It turned out this was impossible. She shrieked and roared until the nurse warned that if she didn't quieten down, she'd be punished. She'd been relieved to see Rita Farragher in the delivery room. The midwife was too aloof, and however irrational it might be, Patricia still believed the other nurse could have done more to save Winnie's daughter.

Twenty-two hours later, when she reckoned she couldn't take another minute of torture, her baby arrived. He had soft dark hair and a nose so small it was practically transparent. He was red and noisy – and huge.

I have a baby, she thought, a gorgeous, living, breathing person.

'Ten pounds four ounces,' said the nurse, in a tone that suggested she was weighing potatoes.

Nobody congratulated Patricia on her son's safe delivery. There were no smiles or celebrations. The nurse wrote down his particulars, then asked what she wanted to call him.

'Graham,' she replied.

'I don't think that's allowed. It sounds very Protestant. Is there a St Graham?'

Sister Sabina stalked over. 'No. We can't allow that. Pick something else. Paul or John, maybe.'

That summer, there was a glut of Johns and Pauls in Carrigbrack. There was a George, too. Unfortunately, until the Pope canonised a Ringo, the band would be incomplete.

'I think Graham's a lovely name,' said Patricia, 'and that's what I'm calling him.'

'Put down Paul,' said Sabina to the nurse. 'His parents will probably give him a different name anyway.'

Rita added Paul to her notes before transcribing the details onto a thin strip of paper. 'I'll put this on his wrist,' she said.

'May I hold him?' asked Patricia.

Sabina shook her head. 'You most certainly may not. You'll be shown how to feed and wash him, and that'll be enough for you. If you'd wanted to moon over a baby, you should have got married first.'

'What's wrong with holding him? Doesn't he deserve to be welcomed into the world the same as any other baby?'

'There'll be time for that when he's with people who are fit to look after him.'

Patricia decided not to argue further. She was sore and weak. What was important was that Paul was alive and healthy. She didn't care what Sabina said: he was her child, and he was entitled to know that she loved him.

After the first frantic days, life took on a pattern. She was forced back to work in the laundry, something she found exhausting and frustrating. As Sabina had warned, her contact with Paul was limited to feeding, bathing and the occasional nappy change. Some days, it felt like he was made of right angles. At other times, he wriggled and thrashed. He wasn't a fretful baby, though. Right from the start, he seemed satisfied with life and keen to find out more. When no one was looking, Patricia would kiss his feathery hair and tell him how handsome he was.

On several occasions, when she should have been asleep, she crept out of the dormitory and went to see him. No matter that she was shattered from her day's work, ten minutes in the nursery brought solace.

The babies slept in steel cots, lined up in military-style rows. At night, two young mothers took care of them. One, Imelda, was a chatterbox. Her own baby, a girl, had already been taken for adoption, and she must have found her job difficult. Nevertheless, she did it with grace and generosity.

'I'll be free to go in a couple of months,' she whispered to Patricia, 'which is great. Only to be honest with you, I'll miss these little ones. I used to think that all babies were the same, but even the tiniest tots in here have their own personality.'

'You're very good with them. Did you ever consider becoming a nurse?'

'I can't see anyone giving me a chance. Sister Sabina says I'm damaged goods, and that you'd only have to look at me to know that.'

'That's pure rubbish,' said Patricia. 'I'd say any hospital would be lucky to have you.' Although the light was dim, she could see Imelda was blushing.

A fortnight after Paul's birth, Patricia received a letter from home. Her parents told her that a girl down the street had done well in the Leaving Cert, a man out the road had been injured in a farming accident, and one of Father Cusack's sisters had died. There was no acknowledgement of the birth of their grandson. There was no reference to her pregnancy at all. Patricia's parents were not bad people. When she was a child, her mother had given her the cream from the top of the milk and gently brushed the tangles from her hair. Her father had held her hand as she'd crossed the road and taught her how to tie her laces. What was more, her mam had doted on the babies of others, tickling their chins and admiring their minuscule nails and asking who they took after. What was it, then, that caused them to be so hard-hearted now? They must have known that Paul had been born. How could they have no interest in him?

As she became more attuned to the ways of the nursery, Patricia realised that a handful of women felt no connection to their children. The saddest case was a woman in her mid twenties called Nancy. Nancy's arms and legs weren't much thicker than the bones beneath, and her hair was so thin her scalp shone through. She held her son in an awkward, detached way, as though there was something distasteful about him. When he was at her breast, she cried, not from physical pain but from unhappiness. The baby, too, appeared stringy and malnourished. Echoing the way Winnie had been regarded, some of the others saw Nancy as a latter-day Typhoid Mary. They swerved around her and turned their backs. Patricia wanted to find out what was wrong, but every time she attempted to have a chat, a nun zoomed in and ordered her to stop.

Finally, Imelda filled her in. According to rumour, she said, Nancy's own father was also the father of her baby. 'I didn't think such a thing was possible,' she added. 'There was a lot I didn't know until I came here, mind.'

'That makes two of us,' said Patricia. From pregnant children to the unexplained deaths of infants, Carrigbrack had introduced her to a catalogue of horrors.

The next morning, she asked Eunice if anything could be done to help Nancy.

'The problem,' said Eunice, 'is that she's better off here than at home. The moment she goes back, her father will interfere with her again. Apparently her mother pretends it isn't happening. And you've seen the state of the girl; she wouldn't survive in the outside world.'

Grim as this sounded, it was probably true. Afterwards, Patricia tried to be kind to Nancy. She made a point of sitting beside her and offering to share her food. She tried to engage her in conversation about the habits of small babies and the foibles of elderly nuns. She was wasting her time. Nancy was barely conscious of her surroundings. Having a proper chat was beyond her.

The weeks whipped past. New girls arrived. Others were allowed to leave. Babies were born. Others disappeared. There was no logic to how their departures were handled. Some mothers were given a chance to say goodbye, while more were only informed when their child was already gone.

The longer she spent with Paul, the more certain Patricia was that she wanted to keep him. If she didn't fool herself that this would be easy, neither could she believe it was impossible. Remembering what Agnes had said about silly young girls not being able to take care of children, she set out to prove her maturity. She increased her work rate in the laundry and ignored Sabina's goading. She never asked for more food or moaned about getting up for early Mass. Although her hair was growing back in uneven hanks and whorls and her burnt hand still throbbed, she didn't complain. She was a model penitent. When she had time to think about it, she was uncomfortable at collaborating with the Carrigbrack regime. She didn't like pretending that everything was normal. But she was desperate, and if she had to play Agnes's game, so be it.

Despite everything, there were days when her head hummed with contentment. Insofar as it was possible for a prisoner to be happy, Patricia was.

Her new-found obedience didn't prevent her from sneaking in to see Paul. She did, however, ration her visits. She tried to convince herself that in the long run her sacrifice would be worthwhile.

One late October night, with a full moon throwing pale yellow light into the dormitory, she padded out to the nursery. First, she apologised to Imelda, who was on her own. It was unfair to wake a sleeping baby. The glorious thing about Paul was that he never grizzled. He nuzzled into her and clamped his fat fist around her index finger. Then he gurgled, as if to say, *Ah, it's you.* This was followed by a muted whimper, which she took to mean, *If there was a feed available, I wouldn't say no.* Bless him, he was a hungry child. He was also Patricia's confidant. Winnie's departure had left her without a close friend, and while Paul didn't have much to contribute to the conversation, he was a good listener. He would look at her with his bright eyes, and she'd be convinced he understood every word.

No sooner had she sat down to feed him than she heard a grunting sound from one of the cots. This was followed by a prolonged wheeze, then another grunt. Patricia returned Paul to his own bed.

'I'll be back in a sec,' she said.

He let out a howl of impatience, which was repeated by another baby. She ignored them. The wheezing sound was being made by Nancy's son.

'Has he been unwell for long?' she asked Imelda.

Because Nancy never spoke, Patricia couldn't remember her baby's name. Something with a J, she thought. Was he one of the Johns, perhaps? Or was he a Jerry?

Imelda nodded. 'He had a temperature earlier. I thought he was fierce hot, but Sister Agnes was doing her rounds and she told me not to be making a fuss over nothing. It was only a sniffle, she said. Is there something wrong with him, do you think?'

Nancy's baby wheezed again. This time, the sound was more disturbing, like he was fighting for breath.

Patricia bent and picked him up. Even in the half-light, she could see that his lips and hands were tinged with blue. His face felt clammy. Once more, he tried to breathe, but the air wasn't making it as far as his lungs.

'Is he all right?' asked Imelda.

Instead of replying, Patricia urged the baby to breathe. 'Come on, little chap,' she said. 'Come on.'

The muscles in his neck appeared to move and his chest sank. He gasped. The baby in the adjacent cot began singing, 'Ba, ba, ba,' as though it was all great fun. Another joined in, chirruping away for all she was worth.

Patricia turned to Imelda. 'You should go and get one of the nurses.'

'But if they find you here, they'll—'

'Go. Please go.'

The sudden rise in the pitch of her voice disturbed another baby, who squealed. Imelda didn't move. All the while, the child in Patricia's arms struggled to breathe.

'If you don't go,' she said, 'I will. Then we'll both be in serious trouble. If he doesn't breathe soon, he might die, and I don't know what to do. Please, Imelda, I'm not making this up.'

Imelda hesitated for another second, and then, at last, she took off like one of the young hares that loped along the nearby lane.

Sister Agnes peered over the top of her glasses.

'So here you are,' she said, 'in trouble again.'

Patricia, standing at the other side of the mahogany desk, fiddled with the sleeve of her uniform. 'I did my best for the baby, Sister.'

'That's not in dispute. I hope that any good Christian would have done the same. The fact remains: you shouldn't have been in the nursery. Do you think that your baby is more important than the others, is that it?'

'No, Sister.'

In that moment, Patricia felt an intense dislike for Agnes. She couldn't let it get the better of her, though. She had to try and use the situation to her advantage. 'How's Nancy's baby this morning, do you know?'

'I gather the child, James, is doing well. According to Nurse Farragher, his respiratory distress has passed, and his temperature has eased.'

'That's good. I was very concerned. He's a delicate boy, and his mother ... well, his mother isn't as sturdy as the rest of us either.'

During the night, she had mulled over her intervention. Had she made the right decision? The signs were that, far from loving him, Nancy could barely tolerate her son's presence. He was a sickly child, listless and prone to infection. That wasn't all: Patricia had heard that the children of incest victims had all sorts of mental challenges. There was a danger that no couple would want him. Maybe she should have ignored his distress. Maybe she should have pretended she didn't understand what was happening. Immediately, she rounded on herself. Of course she couldn't have let a baby die. All the same, she couldn't help but wonder: what if she'd spent years here and had been ground down and hardened by suffering? Would she have made a different choice? She'd lain awake for hours, fretting about the ways in which her mind had already been distorted by the misery around her.

Sister Agnes had fallen silent, and Patricia feared she was choosing her punishment. When she spoke again, her tone was brusque. 'Apart from reporting on the baby's condition, Nurse Farragher also said that, if it hadn't been for your intervention, James mightn't have survived. I'm not condoning your misbehaviour. Indeed, any repeat will be regarded most seriously. However, it seems your responsible attitude was important last night.'

Patricia had to stop herself from smiling. She liked the sound of the word 'responsible'.

'Thank you, Sister,' she said.

Chapter 26

Ailish

In the air, Ailish attempted to relax. Below, Dublin's houses and factories were giving way to a patchwork of fields. She was on her way to see the woman she'd spent most of her life thinking about. She told herself to focus on the day. To savour every second.

If only it was that simple.

At the airport, she'd tried not to see herself in the bathroom mirror. Even though she was wearing her favourite blue jacket and a month's worth of make-up, she looked wrung out. Her cheeks were hollow, her skin yellow-grey.

So far, she'd managed to avoid an honest conversation with Beth and Katie. Not that fooling them was easy. Beth was smart and quick-witted, and Katie was experienced. She had an old-fashioned intuition that Ailish respected. They'd peppered her with questions about Keith's attitude to their visit, and she'd done her best to slip-slide around the answers.

She was grateful that Katie was preoccupied. Uptight, almost.

She supposed this shouldn't be a surprise. Katie was also revisiting a difficult part of her life.

There'd been a funny moment in the taxi. The driver had been listening to a classic rock station, and as they reached the airport turn-off, 'Overboard' had come on.

Beth had said, 'There's Gary earning another five cents.'

Ailish had laughed. 'How's his search going?'

'He's making progress,' Katie had replied. 'As I keep telling him, he's getting closer every day.'

Ailish had been pleased to hear this, if not for his sake, then for his natural mother's. She deserved to know what he'd achieved.

'Overboard' was her favourite Black Iris song. She knew it wasn't poetic or profound, but the lyrics and melody lingered in her head, exciting her and soothing her. Like all the best music, it enhanced the good times and made the bad times more bearable:

> *I thought I was safe, I stayed close to shore,*
> *But the dangers were there,*
> *Unheeded, ignored.*
> *You ripped up the sail and burnt both our oars,*
> *I'm a long way from safety,*
> *I'm lost overboard.*

As they glided over the petrol blue of the Irish Sea, Ailish ordered a coffee and flicked through the in-flight magazine. She looked at pictures of Toulouse and Connemara, rugby players and chefs, but couldn't get any purchase on the words. Her thoughts kept skittering back to Kilmitten. For the ten thousandth time, she asked herself if she should be here at all. Should she not be at home, safeguarding Stevie and tackling Keith? The day after the fight, she'd resolved to cancel the trip. Oh, listen to her, calling it a fight. It had been an assault. Her husband had assaulted her son, and she'd done nothing to stop him. It had been Stevie who'd insisted she stick with her plans. 'If you don't go,' he'd said, 'you'll only be giving him what he wants. For everyone's sake, you need to get on that plane and meet Chrissie.'

She'd left Kilmitten the previous evening without saying anything to Keith. He hadn't tried to stop her. Neither had he made any attempt to wish her well.

She would never forget Thursday night. For a long two minutes, she'd thought her son was dead. She'd screamed, and then when Keith had bent down and touched him, she'd screamed again. She'd heard about similar incidents. They'd been on the news. People thought that one punch couldn't kill you, but fall the wrong way and it could. Gradually, Stevie came round. He was groggy and his head was bleeding. She wanted to call an ambulance. Failing that, she'd drive him to hospital in Limerick. He needed tests. He might be seriously hurt. She spoke too about calling the guards and having Keith removed from the house. Throughout, her voice quivered with hysteria.

She didn't know which was more unsettling: Keith's attack on his son or the way he attempted to deflect responsibility. He moved smoothly from shock to mild contrition to blaming everyone else. 'I'm under pressure,' he said. 'I was provoked.'

Irritated as she was by his excuses, she needed to focus on Stevie, who was adamant that he'd be fine. She fussed and nagged until he snapped. He was off to bed, he said, and would think about everything in the morning. Keith stayed put. Ailish didn't call the police. She spent the night in the girls' old room, shivering and staring at dog-eared posters of Katy Perry and the Kings of Leon.

In the morning, Keith left early for work. Although Stevie maintained his head wasn't troubling him, he didn't look well. Eventually, he gave in and went to the doctor, who cleaned his wound, asked a string of questions and told Ailish to take him to hospital. He also had a quiet word with her.

'There are people you can talk to,' he said. 'They can give you advice.'

'Honestly,' she replied, 'it was an accident. Sure you know how clumsy teenage lads are.'

After a six-hour wait in the regional hospital, Stevie was examined. The doctor decided his injuries weren't serious. It was then that he told her he wouldn't be coming home. He'd called Jodie and, for the time being, would be staying with her.

'You can't expect me to sleep in the same house as that man,' he said. 'I'm amazed you've let him stay.'

Pummelled by the force of her son's words, Ailish went to hug him. He squirmed away, not because he was embarrassed, but because she'd betrayed him. She'd betrayed all four children. She hadn't been malicious or neglectful, but she'd been wilfully blind, and the result was the same. The greatest gift you could give someone was a happy childhood. She'd had the chance – and she'd failed.

As they made their descent through gauzy cloud and landed at Heathrow, as they bought their train tickets and threaded their way to the platform, her failures were all she could think about.

Number 32 Annaville Street was a red-brick terraced house with a turquoise door and a deep green creeper. Katie and Beth had offered to wait in a nearby coffee shop, but Ailish was nervous and wanted them to accompany her.

'Just drop in and say hello,' she said. 'Please? I'll find it a lot easier if you're there.'

'We've been amateur detectives for a while,' said Beth with an encouraging smile. 'We might as well be amateur social workers too.'

Ailish hadn't known what to expect. She'd fretted that Chrissie would be too weak for anything other than a short chat. Her fears were misplaced. The woman who greeted them was thin, her hair sparse, but she hugged with such ferocity that Ailish worried they'd squeeze the life out of each other. It was a good job Beth was holding the flowers they'd brought as a gift.

'My beautiful girl,' said Chrissie. 'My beautiful girl.'

As often as Ailish had imagined this moment, she wasn't prepared. The woman embracing her was a ghost made flesh. Sensible words wouldn't come, and all she could say was 'Thank you.'

She wanted to hold this moment in her hand. To make sure she would remember every second and every detail. Even if they never met again, this was perfect.

Chrissie was wearing a navy dress, a crimson scarf and silver earrings in the shape of stars. Despite her physical frailty, she twinkled with joy. Her perfume smelt like freshly cut grass.

When they disentangled, Iggy stepped forward. He was a trim man with an intelligent face and corrugated grey hair. He hugged Ailish, then ushered them all into the front room. Despite more than forty years in London, he walked like he was herding cattle.

The room they entered was pale green, cream and brown; the fireplace a shiny black. The walls were dotted with prints, some old-fashioned, others more contemporary, as if they'd been chosen by a child or grandchild. Her years in Rathtuskert Manor had taught Ailish well, and she appreciated the quality of Chrissie's furniture. She was happy to see that her birth mother was surrounded by nice things, though, truth to tell, they could have been sitting on upturned crates with old fertiliser bags for curtains and it wouldn't have mattered. Her eye was drawn towards the family photos on top of the bookcase, some of which she hadn't seen before. These were her children's aunts, uncles and cousins. This was her family.

Her thoughts swung back to Stevie. Jodie was great, but she was a student with a husband and two small children. She had no space in her life for a seventeen-year-old. And what about Stevie's exams? How could he study in such a noisy house?

For a minute or so, the five of them sat in silence, grinning at each other. Strangely, Ailish felt no compulsion to speak. She had a thousand questions, but if they went unasked, so be it. Although she'd seen many photos of Chrissie, meeting her was mesmerising. She kept spotting small similarities: the point of her chin, her unexpectedly broad wrists, her child-sized feet.

'You have a lovely house,' she said.

'Thank you,' replied Chrissie. 'We were lucky. Back in the early eighties it was possible for regular people to buy on a street like this. I can tell you, it wouldn't happen today.'

'It's the same in Dublin,' said Katie. 'I don't know how Beth's generation are supposed to live at all.'

'We rely on kindly aunts,' said Beth.

Chrissie told them that her treatment was going well, and fingers crossed her prospects were good.

'At least my hair's still red,' she added. 'I was worried that when it grew back it'd be grey. But it's strong stuff, red hair. None of your children are redheads, are they, Ailish?'

'No, they all take after Keith.' As the words left her mouth, she found herself hoping they weren't true. She didn't like to think of her children inheriting any part of their father.

Chrissie touched her scalp. 'I've always been glad of it. Of course, the English insist on saying "ginger". "Ginger's for cats and cake," I tell them. "My hair is red."'

Iggy was on catering duty and, having confirmed that they'd all prefer coffee to tea, he went out to the kitchen. Slowly, the conversation moved to more personal matters. Katie and Beth offered to leave, but Chrissie insisted they stay.

'It's funny,' she said, 'how even well-meaning people expected me to forget about my daughter – and about Carrigbrack. I've tried to be open, but I couldn't tell you how many times I've heard things like "You were only a child yourself. At least you were able to move on." And in some ways, I did, but I could no more have forgotten my girl than I could have forgotten an arm or a leg.' She bent her head towards Ailish. 'I wish there'd been some way of knowing how you were getting on. Even brief updates would have helped. No matter what else was happening, I thought about you every day.'

'It was the same for me, except because I had no memories of you, I had to invent you. I called you my other mammy, and I'd walk down the street thinking, could that woman be my other mammy … or what about that woman? Then I'd get it into my head that you were in Dublin and I'd find you there.'

'Why Dublin?'

'Because it was about as exotic a place as I could imagine.'

'Bless you. For me, the worst day of the year was the tenth of November.'

Ailish smiled, and a tear dribbled down her cheek. 'My birthday.'

'I'd do nothing but think about you. I'd be wondering where you were and what you were doing and if you were having a party.' She looked at Katie and Beth. 'I'm so grateful, more grateful than you can imagine.'

Katie's eyes were also damp. 'I should have done this years ago. I regret that I didn't. It's not too late for the two of you, but I'm afraid it might be for others.'

'What matters is that you're doing it now.'

Katie took a handkerchief from her pocket. 'Sorry, I feel like a right eejit.'

'Well, you shouldn't,' said Chrissie, her voice firm. 'I've often cried at other people's reunions. I just never thought I'd get to experience it myself. I remember you more clearly now, by the way. Didn't you leave Carrigbrack while I was there?'

'Yes, in late '72. There were two other nurses there at the time.'

'That's right. There was an older woman, and then there was another nurse who also seemed ancient to me. Looking back, though, she can't have been more than twenty-five or six. Rita, was it? She was still there when I left.'

'Rita Farragher's her name. You won't believe this, but I was talking to her only the other day. I had a feeling she might know what happened to one of the babies. Do you remember the twins?'

'Yes,' said Chrissie, 'I do. They were little dotes. One of them was ... we said handicapped back then, but I'm sure there's a better word.'

'Eddie had cerebral palsy.'

Iggy came in with a clanking tray of mugs. The smell of coffee filled the room. 'I don't know,' he said. 'I turn my back for five minutes, and you're all crying.'

Chrissie handed round the mugs. 'Forgive my husband,' she said. 'He's a terrible messer.'

'Yes, but I'm the messer with the cake. I'll be back in a moment.'

Beth leant forward. 'Do you mind me asking, Chrissie: have you come across other Carrigbrack women? Through the support group, I mean?'

'That's a good question. I know a couple of ladies who were there in earlier years, and there are three or four from after I'd left. There's only one woman from my time, though. Tina Dennison's her name. Let me see, she would have been ... Tina McNulty back then.'

Katie and Beth exchanged a glance.

'Was she originally from County Kerry, by any chance?' asked Beth.

'Yes, I always remember the Kerry women, on account of them being Iggy's county folk.'

'And did she have a son?' said Katie.

'She did. He tracked her down too, only the reunion didn't go well. Tina's a bit ... scattered, shall we say ... and her son's wife didn't take to her. It's a shame when that happens.'

Ailish thought of her own family troubles and closed her eyes.

'Why are you interested in Tina?' asked Chrissie.

When Katie answered, her voice was so bright it practically bounced off the magnolia walls. 'We've been trying to help a man called Gary, only he doesn't have a correct date of birth. He's narrowed the list of likely birth mothers down to two.'

'And Tina McNulty is one of them,' continued Beth. 'So if Tina has already found her son, then fingers crossed, the other woman on his list – Noreen, is it?' Katie nodded. 'Noreen must be the right one.'

'Isn't that fantastic news?' said Chrissie, her smile as wide as the Shannon. 'Fantastic news altogether.'

When Iggy returned with a plate of sandwiches and the promised cake, she filled him in.

'That's a gas one,' he said. 'Dig in there, ladies. You must be hungry after your early flight.'

Ailish noticed that the longer he spent with them, the more Irish his accent became. By the time they left, he'd probably sound more Irish than her own children. She couldn't stop thinking about them – and about Stevie in particular. She shouldn't have come here today. What if, safe in the knowledge that she was out of the country, Keith decided to have another go at him?

While they ate, Chrissie spoke about Carrigbrack.

'Say what you like about Sister Sabina,' she said, 'but at least she was a straightforward bitch. With Agnes, you were never quite sure. Sometimes, she'd turn on the "I care about you" charm, and you wouldn't know what to think. She used to give these homilies where she'd brainwash us into thinking we were worse than useless. "I gather," she'd say, "some of you think you're capable of rearing your child. Well, let me put you straight about that: you're not." She used to make it sound like we'd all be out in the town, and our children would spend their lives in pubs and dance halls.'

'Were any women allowed to keep their babies?' asked Ailish.

'I've heard of one or two,' said Chrissie, 'but no more than that.' She sipped her coffee. 'I remember the day I left. I was sixteen by then and I'd paid my dues. They couldn't force me to stay. The bold Agnes called me into her office, and you know what she said? "You've made a lot of progress while you've been here, Hanora." She insisted on using my home name. "I trust you can keep that up."'

'The miserable cow,' said Beth.

Chrissie's eyes rose to the heavens. 'Wasn't she something else? You'd swear I had sins to atone for.'

'Were the nuns not able to think for themselves? They can't have believed everything they came out with.'

'No doubt Agnes thought she was fulfilling her duty,' said Katie. 'She was big on duty.'

'I had the last laugh,' said Chrissie. 'She put me on the bus, but instead of getting off at Hackett's Cross, I went as far as Limerick. Then I got another bus to Dublin and the ferry to Holyhead.'

'You did go back, though,' said Ailish. 'Didn't you? I saw the gravestone. And I ... I assumed you must have paid for it.'

Iggy touched his wife's hand.

'Yes, I returned for Mam's funeral and for my brother's. Perhaps I should have made more of an effort to see them before they died, but going back was difficult. A lot of people in the village knew the real story, only no one would admit it. Some of them were cool towards me. I held my head high, but it was hard.' With her free hand, Chrissie dabbed at her eyes.

'You don't have to talk about it. I don't want to upset you.'

'No, love. You deserve to know. It's important that these things are spoken about. If I've learnt nothing else, I've learnt that.' She paused. 'Mammy died in the spring of 1985, and I got it into my head that I had to attend the funeral. I don't know why I felt that way when I hadn't gone back for Daddy. I suppose I hadn't wanted to face either of them while they were alive. They'd given me no support. No understanding. I can see now that they weren't evil people. They were products of their time. Simple as that.'

'When your parents found out you were pregnant,' said Beth, 'did they not consider calling the guards?'

'If they did, they didn't mention it to me. Mind you, nobody said much of anything to me. And say they had contacted the police? You can be certain the man who abused me would have denied all knowledge. Either that or he'd have claimed I led him on.'

'You were *thirteen*.'

'I hear what you're saying, only who do you think the guards would have believed? A scrappy girl with holes in her pinafore or a big landowner ... because that's what he was? The other thing is, and this might sound mad, I wasn't certain what he'd done to me. In my innocence, I wondered if this was the sex that people talked about – or was it something else. He raped me four or five times before I found the courage to run away from him.'

'I'm so angry for little you.'

'Thanks, Beth. These days, a child would be taken seriously. Or, at least, I hope they would. Now, where was I?'

'You were talking about the funeral,' said Ailish.

'Yes. Iggy came with me, of course. We'd been married for several years by then. We had the two girls, and Diarmuid was on the way. So there we were, at the top of the church, and who turned up but him.' Chrissie breathed out heavily. 'I hate to refer to him as your father, Ailish, but biologically speaking, that's what he was. His name was Manus Sheedy. Like I say, he was a farmer. Not only did he have a big farm of land, he had a wife and a tribe of kids. He's dead, but to the best of my knowledge some of his family are still there.

'He stood in front of me and offered his hand. I was so shocked I nearly took it too. Thankfully, I pulled myself together in time and declined the offer. "Sorry for your trouble, ma'am," he said, as though he'd never seen me before. "It's fifteen years too late for that,"

I said, "and if you don't make yourself scarce, I'll start talking about how you raped me when I was a child." Well, you've never seen a man scuttle out of a church so quickly. You'd have thought the place was on fire.'

'Fair play to you,' said Ailish. 'You were very young to take control of the situation like that. And at your mother's funeral too.'

'With everything that had gone on, I was an adult by the age of fifteen. I'd had no choice.'

'My late husband, Johnny, used to say that once you've grown up, you can't grow back down again,' said Katie. 'That seems to be true for all the girls who were sent to Carrigbrack.'

The pride with which she spoke about Johnny, and the love between Iggy and Chrissie, brought a rush of sadness to Ailish. It didn't feel appropriate, and she tried to will it away. 'This is an awkward question,' she said, 'but am I not a reminder of what Sheedy did to you?'

'Oh, Ailish, love, you can't talk like that.'

'I promise you,' said Iggy, 'for as long as I've known Chrissie, she's wanted to find you. You're not to blame for that man's crimes.'

'Do you know,' said Chrissie, 'I often think of Hackett's Cross, and not in a melancholy way. It's spectacular around there, especially in the summer. I only wish I'd been allowed a proper childhood to enjoy it.'

Katie looked at her watch. 'Come on, missus,' she said to Beth, 'we ought to leave these people in peace for a couple of hours.'

'And we'd better ring Gary so we can pass on the news.'

Before they left, Beth took some photos. Ailish tried to mask her face with her hand, like the accused going into court. Why, on this day of all days, did she have to feel so awful? Afterwards, Iggy drifted away. He had calls to make, he said. Chrissie rose from her armchair and moved to the sofa beside Ailish. 'I want to show you around the house, and I have a million pictures you might like to see. But before I do …'

Ailish took her hand. 'Is everything all right?'

'Everything's great with me. I'm on the mend, and my long-lost daughter is here.' She hesitated. 'I don't want to be a nuisance, but over the years I've developed a nose for unhappiness. Iggy says it's my greatest talent. There's something wrong, isn't there?'

Chapter 27

Gary

'Come in, come in,' said Katie. 'We're only just back ourselves. It's great you could drop over.'

Gary stepped into the warm hall and removed his overcoat. It was a typical January night, blustery with flecks of rain in the wind.

Katie had called from London. 'Gary, you are not going to believe this,' she'd said before outlining the information they'd received, and just like that, his search was almost complete. 'I'd better give you the bracelet belonging to Noreen's baby,' she'd added. 'You must have been Paul.' In a moment of giddy relief, he'd agreed to drive to her house and collect it. She'd explained that Ailish would be there, and he was cool with that. The idea of meeting someone who'd spent the first months of her life in the same place as him was appealing. He was excited, too; although she hadn't replied to his letter, he was almost certain he'd located the right Noreen.

To be honest, there was another reason for accepting the invitation. Embarrassing as it sounded, he could do with an hour of regular company. Straightforward, undemanding company. He'd taken one piece of advice from Frank and returned to therapy. He was seeing a counselling psychologist, a young guy who spoke a lot about tools and techniques and appropriate responses. Actually, he was pretty helpful, but when the only person you'd talked to in three days was charging by the hour, you'd got to wonder about your life.

That Gary didn't spend more time with his family wasn't a reflection on them. He was avoiding them because he wasn't sure how much to say. From the start, he'd worried they would consider him disloyal. He swore that when he met Noreen, they'd be first to know. Well, second. He'd have to tell Katie and Beth first. In the meantime, there was no point in stirring up unnecessary trouble. He'd had enough of that.

If there was one thing he had learnt from Black Iris, it was this: early fame meant you spent the rest of your days checking behind you. You worried constantly about being supplanted by the next generation. You fretted that the younger, hotter, more relevant guys were biting at your heels. Eventually, the day came when you saw that your fears had been premature, but by then you really were past it. Gary Winters, a man who'd once believed that every night needed nudity and epic drunkenness, was looking forward to a cup of tea with three women: one in her late sixties, another a grandmother and the third a lesbian. Hail! Hail! Rock 'n' Roll!

The women were drinking wine.

'I'd better not,' he said, refusing Katie's offer, 'what with the DUI laws being the way they are.'

She gave him an enquiring look.

'He means drink-driving laws,' explained Beth.

'You're back in Ireland, Gary,' said Katie, in the voice that always made him feel like a ten-year-old whose football had shattered the kitchen window. 'Will you have a cup of tea?'

Her house was like his parents' place: old-fashioned but not excessively so. There was a dusky-pink three-piece suite, a pine coffee table, an ageing television, a CD player, a standard lamp with a low-watt bulb and plants galore. Oh, and there were several photos of her late husband, including one of those early seventies wedding pictures where everyone looked pale and surprised. While he acknowledged that rating people on their physical appearance was wrong, any fair observer would say that Johnny Carroll had done well for himself.

Katie bustled about supplying snacks and drinks and offering snippets of conversation. Beth chatted away, droll one minute, earnest the next. Ailish was quiet. Knowing she was a Black Iris fan, Gary initially assumed she was tongue-tied by his presence. He quickly realised that he was kidding himself. She'd been through an extraordinary day. Her mind was elsewhere.

'I liked your message board post,' he said.

'How did you …' she started before tapping herself on the side of the head. 'Of course you guessed it was me. Thanks.'

'It's good to give people hope, y'know.'

'What's this about?' said Katie, as she sat down and placed a red box on the floor beside her.

'Last night,' said Ailish, 'I wrote a few lines on the message board to say I was about to meet my birth mother, and that it wouldn't have happened without your help. I didn't give my real name, but …'

'As soon as I saw it, I guessed,' said Gary, 'and then when Katie called from London, my hunch was confirmed.'

'That's lovely,' said Katie. 'Thank you, Ailish. With one thing and another, I haven't had much time for the message board lately.'

'I thought I'd let people know what was happening, because sometimes it feels like no one's making progress.' A smile danced across Ailish's face. 'And the truth is that some of us are.'

'Speaking of which,' said Katie, picking up the red box, 'I have baby Paul's bracelet in here.' For some seconds, she was quiet. Then she removed the lid from the box. 'Chrissie remembered Noreen and Paul a lot more clearly than I did. Her recollections jogged my memory.'

'Really?' said Gary.

'Yes. I can see her now. She wasn't particularly tall or dark, so you must have got your looks from your biological father. She got into a couple of scrapes in Carrigbrack, but then again, quite a few girls did.'

Katie took her notebook from the box. Gary was pleased to see she was using the cover he'd given her. Then she produced a thin piece of paper. She peered at it as though seeing it for the first time.

'She guards that box very carefully,' said Beth. 'She's got nuclear codes and all sorts in there.'

'Here we are,' said Katie. 'According to this, you were born on the seventh of August 1971.'

She passed the bracelet to him. Even though Gary had done nothing, he felt a sense of achievement. He was part of the inner circle; one of the people who had either found their birth mother or were just a step away. He couldn't remember his own children ever being small enough to wear such a tiny band. Chances were he hadn't paid sufficient attention. He'd been on the road when Clark and Sam were born. Angus's mother hadn't wanted him there ('You're only a glorified sperm donor' had been her exact phrase). And while physically he'd been present for Allegra's birth, mentally he'd been in the studio with the rest of the band.

His daughter was growing so quickly that Gary had been tempted to extend his stay in Los Angeles. The day before he'd left, she'd said, 'It's more fun when you're here.' He'd almost cartwheeled with delight. Then the truth had hit: it was a criticism not a compliment. He needed to spend more time with her.

During his three weeks in LA, he'd stumbled around giving vague answers about the band and what he was up to in Ireland. Although he'd managed to avoid Anton, he'd met up with Ray. He missed Ray and Liamo. 'We're firing ahead with our plans,' his old buddy had said. 'It's not too late to change your mind.' They'd talked about Shanna, they'd talked about Anton, but ... Gary realised that Katie had asked him a question. Beth had said something too.

'Sorry,' he said. 'What was that?'

'We were wondering what you're going to do now,' said Beth.

'Step up my efforts with Noreen, I suppose.'

There was a lull in the conversation. Katie's thoughts appeared to be elsewhere, while for once, Beth didn't have much to say. He guessed they were tired.

It was Ailish who spoke. 'This morning, when we were in the taxi, "Overboard" came on the radio. It was funny. Well, not funny exactly, but you know ...'

'Yeah, I do.' Gary was still holding the bracelet. He needed to find somewhere safe for it.

'I probably shouldn't ask, but is it true you're not going on tour with the band? I mean, that's what it said in the paper, only ... it wouldn't be the same without you.'

'That's my plan at the minute all right.'

'Is everything okay?' said Katie who appeared to have returned to the present. 'Beth and I had the feeling that something was bothering you.'

'Not that we want to pry,' added Beth, 'only we read about the tour, and we thought it was a shame you wouldn't be there.'

'But, like Beth says, we wouldn't want to be nosy.'

He could choose to say nothing. He could allow the story to emerge, drip by corrosive drip. Or he could go ahead and tell the truth. Talking wasn't the easiest option. It probably wasn't the wisest, either. But if he didn't tell them, they'd keep on wondering. They'd keep on asking. They were looking at him, faces upturned like birds waiting for a worm. Besides, learning about Noreen had put him in a reflective mood. And he owed Katie more than a cheap piece of leather.

First things first, though. He held up the bracelet. 'Would you have a bag I could put this in? Oh, and I've changed my mind. I'll have a glass of wine after all.'

Two minutes later, with the bracelet in a plastic bag and a glass of white in hand, Gary began a rarely told tale. There was no good way of telling it, and he'd have to edit along the way, but so be it.

'I need to go back almost four years,' he said. 'We were touring the US on the back of a mediocre album.'

'*Sands of Time*,' said Katie.

Jesus, she was something else. She must have memorised their entire back catalogue. She probably knew how the album had been rated, too: three stars from *Rolling Stone* and *NME*; a pathetic 4.2 out of ten from *Pitchfork*. Not that he could complain. For several years, they'd been trying to pass stones off as diamonds. They'd finally been found out.

'Yeah,' he said, 'even the title was crap. It made us sound like a metal band from 1985. The tour wasn't happy, either. Too many egos, too little energy. And most of the time, Anton was off his head. Up until then, wasted or not, he'd put on a show. It's that special front-man thing: even when we were in the world's dreariest city, he'd make the audience believe we were having the wildest time ever. Nobody could do intense like Anton. On that tour, he lost it. Sometimes, he forgot half the lyrics.'

'What was he taking?' asked Beth.

'Heroin.'

'Shit.'

'You said it. As you can imagine, it led to a hell of a lot of friction. Whatever else I've done, I've had the sense to avoid smack. You come from this city, you know its power to screw you up. For years, Anton had been the same. He was convinced it was a mistake he'd never make – and then he did.'

'What about the others?' said Katie.

'Liamo had fought his own battles with drink. By that stage, though, he was sober. Ray had always been a clean-living guy. He'd had a rough childhood, and out of the four of us, he probably had the greatest appreciation of what we'd achieved. What you've got to bear in mind is that we were surrounded by enablers. When you reach a certain level of success, there are lots of people there to tell you you're right – and that you can have whatever you want. It's a power thing. And, yeah, it's a money thing too.'

Gary stopped and took a long drink. Although in some ways his story was about wealth and fame, it was also pretty basic. That was something else he'd learnt: how basic most people were. And how a handful of decisions could shape your life

'Anyhow,' he said, 'at some point, a woman drifted into our orbit. Shanna was her name. Shanna Ellis. She was a friend of one of the crew. And she was just … there. I'm probably making her sound like a groupie. Y'know, a girl who—'

'We know what a groupie is,' said Katie. 'I'm fairly sure they originated with my generation.'

Beth and Ailish smiled.

'Right,' he said. 'Anyway, Shanna wasn't like that. She wanted an adventure. She came from a well-to-do family in LA. Her father was – still is – a scriptwriter, and her mother's one of those underfed, overdressed types you meet everywhere. I won't pretend Shanna wasn't beautiful, because she was. She was a blonde, blue-eyed California girl. So far, so generic. But there was more to her. You get accustomed to everybody being jaded and blasé. Shanna was the opposite. She was an enthusiast.'

Beth swooped in. 'Did she do anything? Like, did she have a job?'

'No, not really. She was seeing America.'

Before Beth could say anything else, Katie gave her a gentle look that said, *Let the man tell his story, will you?*

Gary took another drink and continued. 'I'd split up with Posy,

Allegra's mother, and I was on my own. And, well, it wasn't long before Shanna and I were together. I would've been happy for us to be properly together, but she was more laid-back about the relationship. Some nights she disappeared, which, of course, made her all the more appealing.'

He paused and drank the last of his wine. He was waltzing around the truth. When it came to Shanna, he always had.

'How old was she?' asked Beth.

'Twenty-three,' he replied, wishing the answer sounded less sleazy. 'So, yeah, she was a bit younger than me.' To be precise, twenty-one years younger, only slightly older than his eldest son. When Shanna had been born, Black Iris had already made the move to America. They'd already been adults. 'It was cool to see everything through the eyes of someone who hadn't seen it all before. The tour was a long one, filled with cities like Tulsa and Glendale and Newark; places I'd been to fifty times but still wouldn't recognise. She gave everything a different perspective. She was a reminder that I'd once loved being in the band. That every day had been a thrill. After I hooked up with Shanna, the tour became bearable, and, foolish as it sounds, I loved her for that.'

'Hold that thought,' said Katie. 'We need more wine.'

'I'll get it,' said Beth.

She returned a minute later with another bottle of Sauvignon Blanc and another question. 'You mentioned that Shanna sometimes disappeared. Where did she go?'

Gary put down his glass and pressed his fingers against his temples. 'Part of her appeal was her edge, if you know what I mean. She alluded to stuff in her background, like how at university she'd been part of a hard-core scene with a lot of drugs. Her stories were entertaining, though, and I didn't read much into them. I suppose I should have seen what was happening, but I didn't.'

'You haven't—'

'She was with Anton,' he said, picking up his glass. 'I wasn't enough for her. The problem was, Anton wasn't capable of having a proper relationship. The other problem was that his wife, who was back home in LA, was pregnant.'

Beth rolled her eyes. 'The poor woman.'

'How did you find out?' asked Katie.

'In the old-fashioned way. I walked in on them. After I got over the immediate shock, I called her all the names I could think of, which was quite a few. We were in Orlando – Mickey Mouse country – and that night on stage, the atmosphere was toxic. Nah, toxic doesn't do it justice. I'd happily have killed him. And yeah, I know that's a phrase everyone uses, only in this case it was true.'

'Was she … was Shanna taking drugs with Anton?'

'I assumed so. Later, it turned out I was wrong. In an odd way, it might have been better if she had been shooting up.'

Both Katie and Ailish frowned.

'Bear with me and you'll understand. I couldn't find her that night, but the following morning she found me. I'm not certain what I expected; some kind of apology maybe. What I knew was that I still wanted her and that I didn't think she should be fooling around with a married smackhead. She got all high and mighty, saying we'd had fun, but she was young and couldn't handle being tied down. Now, I can see what an idiot I was. I was trying to recapture my twenties, but in the safest possible way. An actual twenty-something was going to hanker after a different life. She wanted all the euphoria and the angst and the craziness. I'd had that, and I couldn't go back. I wanted a sanitised middle-aged version.'

He stopped and swallowed some wine. He could still see Shanna. She'd been wearing a bright green floral dress, a tiny thing that had barely covered the tops of her thighs. Her hair had been braided on top of her head, like an untidy milkmaid. The morning was sunny –

they were in Florida, after all – and she'd appeared to shimmer in and out of the room.

He saw Anton too. Anton in his heyday, light brown hair flopping into his clear blue eyes. Anton with his disdain for mediocrity and his knack of turning humdrum days into adventures. Anton with the voice that soared over every venue and the strut that belied his suburban insecurities.

'I'll always regret what happened next,' said Gary. 'Always. But I felt as if I'd been taken for a fool, when in reality, she was the one being conned. I asked her if she knew Anton was married. "Yeah," she said, "except I'm not looking to become his wife. I'm looking for fun. Anyway, they have an open relationship." I couldn't believe she'd fallen for the corniest line in rock. So I told her. "That'll be news to Aimee," I said. "Especially as she's due to go into labour at any time." I could tell Shanna was surprised, but she pretended she was okay. "And the twins," I said, "poor mites. Only two years old. What kind of childhood are they going to have, huh? Not only is their father whacked out of his skull, he's spent the last six months screwing anything with a pulse." She asked what I meant, and I told her there'd been at least three or four others like her on the tour.'

'Was that bit true?' asked Beth.

'Not as far as I'm aware. But I loved her, and she was never going to love me. I felt the need to punish her. It was clear she was grappling with what I'd said about Anton, so I could have left it there. I was angry and humiliated, though, and I kept on turning the knife.'

He went to take another drink, then noticed his glass was empty. Katie refilled it.

'Thanks,' he said. 'So, I told Shanna she wasn't wanted on the tour. She said I couldn't force her out if Anton liked having her around. I pointed out that Anton had far more reasons to be loyal to me than to her, and that all I had to do was click my fingers and she'd be gone. By that stage, she was fairly chastened, but I didn't stop. I told her that if she had any heart or humanity, she'd run back home to Mommy and Daddy in Beverly Hills.'

The more Gary spoke, the clearer his memories became. He saw Shanna in sharp detail: the short green dress, the messy blonde hair, the tears carving tracks through her make-up. He'd wanted her to feel as low as he did. The difference was, he'd been a twice-married father of four, with decades of living behind him. She'd been a naïve kid. A gorgeous, funny kid who should have gone on to have a great life. She should have been allowed to make mistakes.

'After that,' he said, 'I left. I had a tour bus to catch. We were moving on to Tampa. That was the last time I saw her. Well, no, that's not quite true.' He hesitated. 'Sorry, I need a minute.'

The silence was broken by Katie. 'You don't have to say anything else.'

'Nah, you should know the rest.' Gary's knee was jiggling. He tried to make it stop, but it had a mind of its own. 'We played the next couple of dates. Anton and I weren't speaking. There was no sign of Shanna. She was on my conscience, so I called her. When I didn't get an answer, I kept on calling. Don't ask me how, but I knew.'

Gary's right hand shook. This was hard.

'The last time I called, a cop answered. They'd found her body in a motel, one of the scummiest places in Orlando. She'd OD'd. The works were beside her. She'd been a user in the past, apparently, only she'd been clean for some time. She took a large dose, and when your body's no longer accustomed to the drug, that's what happens. It kills you.'

He wanted to add, *But the heroin didn't kill her, I did.*

All this time later, he could still feel the sweltering heat of the Florida morning, smell the bougainvillea, hear the hum of city traffic. He remembered how the initial flash of panic had morphed into a deeper sense of fear. Almost immediately, he'd realised that this wasn't something Frank or one of his flunkeys could magic away. There was no safe harbour. They might smooth over the cracks, but they couldn't bring someone back from the dead.

'Jesus, that's awful,' said Beth. 'What did you do?'

'The police asked if I'd identify her body. I agreed. Somehow, we got through it all without attracting any media attention. There were a few coded items online, some nudges and whispers, but nothing significant. Shanna's parents were devastated. Thankfully, they weren't aware of what I'd said to her. I planned on going to the funeral. They told me to stay away. They worried it'd become a circus.

'We blundered on to the end of the tour. It was only afterwards that it really, truly hit me, and I thought, I'm out. I can't do this any more. I never made it official. I didn't have to; we all knew we needed a break. I wondered if over time I'd be able to forgive Anton – not just for sleeping with Shanna but for souring everything by allowing his life to become such a mess. I also wondered if I'd be able to forgive myself. The answer, it seems, is no. I haven't spoken to him in more than three years. If anything, it's become harder to make peace. Cheesy as it sounds, I look at Allegra and I'm scared guys will treat her the same way.'

Katie crossed her legs. 'How's Anton these days?'

'As far as I know, he's good. It took him another couple of years, but everyone says he's clean and keen to begin working again.'

'And you're not?'

'It doesn't feel right. I can't pretend that Shanna never existed. I loved someone and I killed her.'

For most of the night, Ailish had said little. To begin with, Gary suspected she wasn't listening. Later, he noticed this wasn't true. She was drinking in every word but choosing not to interrupt. It was a rare gift, not speaking unless you had something to say.

Now she leant forward. 'You didn't.'

'Sorry?' he replied.

'You didn't kill her. Anton didn't either. Just because you treated her badly, it doesn't mean you were responsible for her death. I mean, you both abused your position and you're right to regret that. But she made bad decisions too. You didn't fill the syringe and stick it in her arm.'

'That's how it feels.'

'Well, if you don't mind me saying so, you're being a bit self-indulgent.' Ailish pushed her hair back from her face. She had a small face and large eyes, like a rare marsupial. Despite the wine, those eyes were focused. 'Sorry, that might have sounded harsh. I don't want to be harsh. But it seems to me that you've got into a bad way of thinking. We all do it. I'm worse than anyone.'

'I don't—' began Gary, part irritated, part fascinated.

'Answer me this: do you hate Anton?'

'No. I could never hate him. I had some of the best days of my life with the guy. We met when we were kids, and no matter what happened later, I'll always be glad we were friends.'

'Then you need to make your peace with him. I know it's easier to sort out other people's lives. I mean, you probably think I haven't a clue what I'm talking about. That I'm just a nobody from the back end of nowhere who can't understand how you feel. I do, though. Believe me, I know all about the stupid things we do to each other – and to ourselves. You're really talented, and you've brought a huge amount of joy to people's lives. You can't walk away because of one bad decision.'

Perhaps it was the alcohol, perhaps it was the release of telling his story, but Gary was touched by the force of her words. 'I hear you,' he said.

She nodded. 'You want to know what happened in my house the other day? And, Katie and Beth, please forgive me for not telling you before, but I was ashamed. My husband hit my son, Stevie, so hard he knocked him out.'

'Oh, Ailish, love,' said Katie, 'please don't be ashamed.'

'Well, I am. Today should have been brilliant. It should have been about Chrissie, this fantastic woman who's been through so much but managed to rise above it all. Instead, I spent an hour sobbing on her shoulder and telling her what a mess I've made of everything. Afterwards, I realised something: I hate Keith. I don't think I can ever stop hating him. But I'm too much of a coward to do anything about it.'

Chapter 28

Katie

Katie paced the kitchen, willing Beth to get up. She was pleased her niece had decided to take another day off work. They had a lot to talk about. Unfortunately, Beth slept like an elderly cat, and even though it was almost midday, she remained in bed. Ailish and Gary had left a couple of hours earlier. Ailish had spent the night in the spare room, and he'd slept on the sofa. 'I've bunked down in far worse places,' he'd said. She didn't doubt him.

What a night.

Katie couldn't stop thinking about what both of them had said. She couldn't decide which had shocked her more. Despite knowing what Keith was capable of, she was taken aback by the fact that he'd knocked his son to the ground yet wanted to carry on as if nothing had changed. The man must have the hardest neck in Ireland. She worried about Ailish's safety. She'd said as much, but Ailish had shrugged off her concerns. No matter that she'd stopped making excuses for him, she was still living under the same roof, while Stevie had moved out.

In the end, Katie had asked her directly. 'Does Keith hit you?'

'Yes,' she'd replied, 'but never in the way he assaulted Stevie. He's never broken a bone or punched my face.'

Oh, Ailish.

Then there was Gary. It occurred to Katie that somewhere along the line, she'd stopped seeing him as a rock star and had been lulled into thinking of him as a regular person. Now, she was forced to re-evaluate. In reality, he had very little in common with her or anyone she knew. And yet Ailish had spoken to him as if he was a friend in need of robust advice. What was more, he'd listened.

While Katie waited for Beth, there were things she could do. Well, one thing in particular. Her hand hovered over her phone. It was early in Boston. She would catch Brandon before he started work. Then she decided she'd do it later. The snag was, she'd been saying that for days.

She turned on the radio. People were complaining about bad driving, poor internet access and the price of beef. She turned it off and did another loop of the kitchen.

She was looking forward to Beth's take on Gary and Ailish. They hadn't had the chance to speak the night before. Not only had they both been mangled with tiredness, they'd been scared their words would be overheard. All they'd managed were a few furtive whispers, like schoolgirls after lights-out.

She wanted to talk about Chrissie, too. Seeing her again had brought back more memories of Carrigbrack. She recalled how the place had stripped beautiful young women of their lustre, making them grey and crumpled before their time. Despite everything, including her illness, Chrissie still shone. How had she done it? Katie could no more answer that question than she could explain why Ailish stayed with her violent oaf of a husband or why Gary was determined to abandon what he loved. Why should she understand others when half of the time she couldn't understand herself?

When this was all over, and they'd distributed as many bracelets as possible, Katie wondered if she would remain close to Beth. Margo's jibe about not having children had lodged in her mind. Over the months, Beth had become a surrogate daughter. Katie had grown accustomed to her clutter, her obsessions and complaints. To unfamiliar music on the radio, Netflix on the TV and a fridge full of exotic juices. She'd begun to like Thai food, horror films and strong coffee. She still missed Johnny, but her grief was less of a stabbing pain, more of a blunt ache.

She reminded herself that the arrangement with Beth was temporary. Her niece would move on, and she had to be prepared for that.

It didn't end there. Gary, Ailish, Brandon and the rest wouldn't be part of her life indefinitely. They would drift away, and she would miss them. Already, the bracelet box was looking depleted. Briefly, she'd considered caving in and broadening the list of those they were trying to help. But no, that would be a mistake.

Although she should have spoken to her friends about the task, something kept stopping her. The easy explanation was that she'd been too busy. The truth, as always, was more complex: the bracelets were her secret, and she'd never been one for sharing secrets.

When Beth finally surfaced, still in her navy dressing gown, hair straggling in every direction, Katie was peeling the potatoes for dinner. There was no harm in being organised.

'You're a terrible woman,' said Beth. 'Could you not have had a lie-in?'

Katie filled the saucepan with water and threw the peelings into the brown bin. 'I had to say goodbye to our guests. To tell you the truth, though, I couldn't sleep anyway. There was too much going on in my head.'

'That I can understand. Sit down there, and I'll make us a coffee.'

'So,' said Katie.

'So …'

'So, where do you want to start?'

'I don't know,' said Beth, as she put two slices of bread into the toaster. 'I was thinking of Ailish. What a mad day. There she was, finally meeting Chrissie, all the while knowing that Keith was back home resenting her happiness. Imagine hitting your own son so hard he ended up in hospital? I hope she's safe,'

'Me too. What did you make of Gary?'

'No wonder he's a bit strange. That's one bleak story.'

'Yes,' said Katie, 'only if you ask me, Ailish was right. He's doing himself no favours by staying over here and brooding about what he and Anton should have done differently.'

'Wasn't Ailish something else? She said far more than I was prepared to. And you know what? Fair play to her.'

Katie poured milk into her coffee. 'I don't think she'd have told us about Keith if Gary hadn't opened up first.'

'Yeah, how bizarre for her. She meets one of her heroes and practically the first thing he says is, "Actually, I killed a woman." It'd be like if you met – who did you idolise growing up? Perry Como? Frank Sinatra? – and that was how the conversation started.'

Katie snorted. 'Beth Linnane! How old do you think I am?'

'Sorry,' said Beth as she buttered her toast. 'I obviously got the wrong era. But you know what I mean.'

'I do.'

'Besides, I know how old you are. You're seventy in March.'

'How …?'

'Mam asked if you'd like a party.'

'Lord Almighty, no.'

Beth laughed. 'I guessed that'd be the answer. You'd want to be careful, or you'll end up with a monster of a cake and a marquee in the back garden.'

'What brought that on?' asked Katie. There were several

possibilities. Margo might be feeling guilty about what she'd said at Christmas. If so, the offer could be an attempt to salve her conscience. Or she might be looking for an excuse to show off her lovely house and cute grandchildren. Or she might be genuine in her desire to mark her sister's birthday. It was possible the latter was true. Possible but unlikely. Stop it, Katie thought. You're being mean-spirited. Why can't you see the offer as a kind one?

'I haven't a notion why she wants a big do,' said Beth. 'You can relax, though. I'll tell her you don't want any fuss.'

'Thanks. If it helps, you can say I think it would be too soon after Johnny's death.' Katie had never been one for parties. She preferred to keep everything low-key. It was one of the reasons she'd taken to Dublin. After Danganstown, where everybody knew everything about you, and had an opinion on where you were going wrong, she treasured the anonymity of the city.

Beth sipped her coffee. 'Are you all right?' she asked. 'You're very thoughtful.'

'There's plenty to think about.'

'Including Linda and Eddie?'

'Yes.'

'Why don't you ring Brandon?'

Katie looked at her watch. 'It's too late. He'll be at work.'

'He's not a teenager in a minimum-wage job. I'm sure he's allowed personal calls. If he's not interested, that's his lookout. He's had lots of time to think it all through. And you've put in a huge amount of work.'

Although it hurt Katie to think that Brandon might not want to meet his twin, the choice was his to make. He had a supportive wife and loving parents, and maybe they were enough. Still, Beth was right. He was entitled to know what she'd learnt. She counted to ten, then dialled his number. He answered almost immediately.

For a minute, they exchanged stilted greetings. Then, steeling herself for rejection, Katie began. 'We didn't get off to the best of starts, and I blame myself for that. But I've found out a little more about your brother, and while it's up to you ... obviously it's up to you ... I think it might be possible to track him down.'

There was a delay before Brandon replied, not a transatlantic phone line delay, but one that suggested he was weighing up his response. She feared he'd get angry. After all, she'd gone ahead and made enquiries about his family without seeking permission. She'd interfered when she should have let matters rest.

To her surprise, he sounded conciliatory. Conciliatory and hesitant. 'You're okay,' he said. 'I shouldn't have got annoyed with you. It's just that ... well, this has all become more complicated than I wanted or expected. But ...'

His words came to a halt, leaving Katie to fill the silence.

'If you'd like to discuss it with Robyn,' she said, 'you can call me back. Or you can take a few days. I don't want to put any pressure on you. Take as much time as you like.'

'No. You've gone to the trouble of finding out more about Eddie and Linda. The least I can do is listen. Robyn ...'

Again, his sentence ran dry, and Katie wondered what he'd been about to say.

'If you're sure,' she said.

'I'm sure.'

Relief washed over her. She gave a thumbs-up to Beth. 'It's a long story,' she said, 'but when I was working in Carrigbrack, there was a young nun called Sister Eunice ...'

Chapter 29

Then, Patricia

At five months old, Paul was a solid little fellow, fascinated by the world around him. Although the nuns insisted that 'ma-ma-ma' was meaningless babble, Patricia was convinced he was talking to her. What did they know? Not that she challenged them. As part of the campaign to keep her son, she continued to obey the rules and behave like a responsible person. She'd even broken up a fight between two girls who'd been kicking and hair-pulling after one had claimed the other's baby had a plain head. Winnie would have laughed at how compliant she'd become. It was six months since Winnie's disappearance, and Patricia still missed her. The grass had grown over Diane's grave. It was unmarked and uncared for.

Not only had Patricia become more dutiful, she took every opportunity to emphasise Paul's superiority. Surely, having the brightest, healthiest baby must count for something? And yes, she was biased, but even Sister Agnes admitted he was a well-behaved child. Sabina had no such generosity. More than once, she'd remarked on his dark hair and asked if his father might be foreign. She said the word with studied distaste.

Often, Patricia would lapse into a daydream where, freed from Carrigbrack, she went to work while Paul stayed with a friendly – yet affordable – childminder. They lived in a lovely bright flat, and in the evenings, they played and read stories. After a while, she met a man who was unfazed by her already being a mother. He loved Paul as much as she did, and they became a proper family. Then she'd snap out of her trance. She had to be sensible. If she was going to hold on to her boy, she needed more than a romantic fantasy. She needed a practical plan. And that was what she was trying to put together.

One dank evening in late January, she made her way to the nursery. At this time of year, the laundry was a prized workplace. Unlike most of Carrigbrack's other residents, the women there enjoyed a few hours of warmth. The main building was a draughty old place, with more holes than a colander. At night, you could see your breath, and in the mornings, there were slivers of ice on the insides of the windows.

That Paul wasn't in his cot didn't worry her. She was late, and one of the women who worked in the nursery was probably giving him his bath. Patricia would find them and take over. Bathtime was her favourite part of the day.

She walked to the far side of the room, where the babies, some keener than others, were having their evening wash. Each was in a neat tin tub. One of the girls looked up then quickly glanced away.

'Do you know where Paul is?' asked Patricia. 'I can't see him.'

The girl didn't reply. Nor did any of the others. They stood in line, each as mute as the next. A baby squealed. Another splashed with pleasure. Paul liked splashing.

'Has anyone seen Paul?' she asked again.

The silence continued.

She spotted Sister Eunice walking towards her, head bowed, hands clasped as if at prayer.

Eunice raised her face. 'Sister Agnes will be along in a minute.'

'What's wrong?' asked Patricia, heart pumping like a steam engine. 'Has something happened to him?'

'Sister Agnes will explain.'

A realisation crept over her. 'Is he gone?'

Eunice's cheek twitched. Otherwise, she was impassive. 'Yes.'

'That can't be right. I didn't give my permission. You've got to bring him back. You've got to tell whoever took him that there's been a mistake.'

'I'm afraid—'

Patricia grabbed Eunice by the shoulders. 'I don't want to hear any gobbledygook about the rules. Paul is my son, and I didn't agree to give him away.' By now, her voice had risen to its highest pitch. A baby began to cry. 'How could you let this happen? I thought you were my friend.'

The young nun said nothing.

Patricia was about to speak again when Agnes came pounding in, skirt rustling, face the colour of smashed plums.

'What's all this commotion about?' she said. 'Patricia, let go of Sister Eunice this minute.'

Patricia didn't move.

'I'm ordering you to let go of Sister Eunice. Do you understand me?'

She removed her hands from Eunice's shoulders then took a step towards Agnes. 'Did you steal my baby?'

'Of course not. If you'll accompany me to the office, we can talk about this without an audience.'

'If you didn't steal him, where is he?'

'Nobody stole anything. The child has gone to his permanent home.'

Patricia felt as if the ground had given way beneath her and she was falling. Down, down, down she went, through the floor, through the basement and on to the centre of the earth.

'Why my son?' she said. 'There are children here whose mothers would be happy to see them go. And, let's be straight, there are women here who couldn't be trusted with a cat, not to mind a child. Why not take one of their babies?'

'That's a lie,' shouted one of the girls.

'Take that back, you snobby cow,' said another.

Patricia ignored them. 'You haven't answered my question.'

Agnes grabbed her arm and shoved her towards the door. 'Because I won't entertain such nonsense. You're coming with me. We can discuss the child's adoption in my office.'

'Don't call him "the child". He has a name. His name is Paul.'

'Very well. We'll discuss Paul's adoption in the office.'

As they left the nursery, a grumble of voices behind them, Patricia noticed that Eunice was crying. Good. Despite her honeyed words, she was no better than the rest. She could cry for the next six months for all Patricia cared. She was finding it hard to think. She'd played Agnes's game. She'd followed all the rules. This wasn't supposed to happen. They couldn't just take Paul, could they?

In the office, Agnes made the unusual move of allowing her to sit down. Almost immediately, she began speaking. Her words were careful yet fluent, and Patricia suspected she had rehearsed them.

'Paul went to his new home this afternoon. Let me assure you that it's a very fine home with a lovely Catholic couple. Not only are they people of good character, they're comfortably off and can give him the best possible start in life. They have two other children, who are looking forward to meeting their brother.'

'He's not their brother. He belongs to me.'

'That's where you're wrong. He was conceived in unfortunate

circumstances, and we rescued him. He'll have the same advantages as any legitimate child.'

Patricia attempted to speak, but her throat was paper dry, and the words wouldn't come.

Agnes continued. 'When will you realise that this isn't about you? It's the baby who matters. He deserves better than a woman who committed adultery. When your time comes, you can leave here and begin again. You're only twenty years old. If you can stay quiet about your past shame, there's every chance you'll find a husband. Then, God willing, you can have other children. Paul will be just a distant memory.'

Patricia found her voice. 'No, he won't. I want him back. I was supposed to sign a form giving my permission for his adoption. I never saw a form and I certainly didn't sign one.'

'You'd become too close to him. That's never a positive development. I consulted your parents. They said to do whatever I felt was best.'

'We're not living in the Middle Ages. I have rights. I agreed to nothing and I want my son back.'

'Please don't give me any fraudulent modern ideas about rights. What are you proposing to do: call the guards and tell them your illegitimate child has been taken in by a loving family?'

'But—'

Agnes fluttered her hands. 'But nothing. Your mother and father sent you here after you'd disgraced yourself. I asked for their guidance on Paul's care, and they made a wise decision.'

With every second that passed, Patricia grew more scared. She might as well have no voice. What she valued most had been taken, and she had no power to change that. There was nobody on her side. 'Please, Sister Agnes, I could give him everything he needs. I promise you, nobody else will love him as much as I do.'

'What does a girl like you know about love? Now, I've said all I intend to say. Get up and go to your dormitory. Mind you, I can't imagine the penitents you so grievously insulted will have much of a welcome for you.'

'I didn't mean what I said. I was upset, that's all.'

'Well, you'd better apologise to them. Pride is a terrible sin and it's one of your deepest failings. Tomorrow, you'll be excused from your duties in the laundry. I want you to spend the day in silent prayer and reflection. You've got a lot to learn about humility.'

'Why didn't you allow me to say goodbye? What would have been wrong with letting me give him one more kiss?'

Agnes rose from her chair. 'You're too immature to understand now, but with the grace of God, you'll come to your senses. Believe me, one day you'll be grateful for the guidance and support you've received here.'

As the weeks went by, everything became more difficult. Sometimes, Patricia missed Paul so much she found it hard to breathe. She worried that he missed her. She worried that the new people wouldn't know what he liked. How would they know that he enjoyed lying on his tummy? How would they know what made him giggle and what made him cross?

She could have told them, if only she'd been asked.

He was constantly on her mind. She would think she was coping, then out of nowhere she'd be ambushed by longing for him, for his gorgeous smell and his small, squishy body. It was as if part of her had been amputated. She'd still been breastfeeding, and for a while the milk continued to build up in her breasts. The pain was raw, like a physical manifestation of the torment in her head.

She was a disaster at work, scorching holes in sheets and putting a red towel in a white wash. She refused to go to the nursery. Even the thought of the other babies was upsetting. Sister Faustina yelled at her, but what did she care? For months, she'd obeyed every rule, and it hadn't made a whit of difference.

Food tasted peculiar. She would chew and chew, but nothing cleared her throat. Her legs were heavy, her brain filled with ragged, incomplete thoughts. She wished she could slip into a deep, dreamless sleep, but sleep eluded her. On the worst days, she prayed her heart would stop.

The others hadn't forgiven her outburst in the nursery. The one person who wasn't cool towards her was poor Nancy, who still credited her with saving her baby's life. Although her parents wrote, Patricia threw away the letters without reading them. She had no interest in their catalogue of the ill and the dying, still less in their 'whatever you say, say nothing' approach to Paul.

Frequently, she thought about escaping. One afternoon, she stood near a window at the front of the building. An aeroplane ploughed a furrow through the sky. Assuming it was bound for America, she imagined being on board. Then reality hit. Even if she managed to get beyond Carrigbrack's walls, she had nowhere to go and no one to support her. Her friends must have wondered about her disappearance, but it had been almost a year since she'd seen them. She doubted any of them would be able to help.

She didn't hear Eunice sidle up behind her. They hadn't spoken since the day Paul was taken. They went to the bathroom where once they'd hidden with Winnie. As before, they sat on the floor.

'I don't want your excuses,' said Patricia. 'You could have warned me they were about to take him, only you decided not to.'

Eunice's brow crinkled. 'Sister Agnes instructed me to remain quiet, and I've got to try and be obedient. I'm not sure if you can understand that.'

'What I understand is that you could have behaved like a human being, and you chose not to.'

'I'm very sorry. I wish I'd told you.'

'Well, that's no good to me or to Paul.' Patricia attempted to stand up. Her legs felt like they were encased in concrete. 'There's no point in having this discussion. What's done is done.'

'Please stay,' said Eunice, 'just for a moment. I'm concerned about you. You don't speak to anybody.'

'What's there to say?'

'You can talk about Paul.'

'It's best if I don't.'

'Why?'

'Because I'll only start to cry. You don't get it, do you? He loved me but he won't remember me. He'll love other people and he'll never know about me. He won't know how much I cared about him.'

'You don't know that.'

'Yes, I do. He'll have a new name and a new life. Maybe the people who took him won't tell him he was adopted.'

'That would be wrong,' said Eunice, her voice low.

'That doesn't make any difference. It's what happens.' At last, Patricia got to her feet. 'I'm sorry. Like I say, I'm not able to talk about it. I've got work to do. I think you're a good person, Eunice. If you want my advice, though, you'll leave this place before it hardens you any further.'

As she left, the truth slammed into her. Paul wasn't coming back. It was unlikely she would ever see him again. She dropped to her knees, lay down on the floor of the dormitory and howled with pain.

Chapter 30

Gary

Gary hesitated before leaving the car. It was three weeks since he'd received the bracelet, more than a month since he'd sent his letter, and he'd yet to hear from Noreen. He'd considered writing again, then decided that visiting would be smarter. If he turned up, she'd have to talk to him, wouldn't she?

So here he was, parked outside a suburban Galway house, chest tight, head filled with questions. He hadn't told anyone about his journey. Katie wouldn't approve, that was for sure.

He spoke to her all the time. He'd also stayed in touch with Ailish. Well, it was just the occasional text message really. Initially, he'd been stunned by the way she'd confronted him, but the more time passed, the more he admired how candid she'd been. He also gleaned hope from her reunion with Chrissie. What he couldn't understand was why she stayed with a man who assaulted and bullied her. The guy deserved to be shown the door. As she said herself, though, other people's lives were always easier to fix.

The morning after his confession, Gary had regretted how

much he'd said. While Katie's immediate reaction had been mild, sympathetic even, he was convinced that would change. She would consider the seedy circumstances in which a young life had ended, and relations would cool. What actually happened was that she badgered him to call Anton. 'Even if you don't stay with the band, you ought to talk,' she'd said. 'You can't bring Shanna back, but you can resurrect your friendship.' Then she'd pledged that if he did tour with Black Iris, she'd go and see them. 'Don't tell me I'm too old, either. I've looked it up: I'm the same age as Bruce Springsteen and six years younger than Mick Jagger. And if you'll forgive me for saying so, I'm in much better shape than Mick.'

She cracked him up, that woman.

He could never have imagined that talking to Katie, Beth and Ailish would assist him, but somehow their conversation had cleared his mind. Or maybe it had helped to crystallise the ragtag thoughts already there. One thing was certain: he couldn't spend the rest of his life hiding away in Wicklow, compiling lists of the mistakes he'd made.

He'd considered attempting to join another band, but figured he was too old. What else was there? Writing? Production? He'd played around with both, but when it came to music, he was a collaborative sort of guy; he wasn't equipped to work on his own or be the boss. He had no other skills, and one year of a UCD arts degree hardly counted as a qualification.

Number 19 Collins Drive was coated in tired pebble-dash. Its garden was bare, its door in need of a coat of paint. The woman who answered that door had shoulder-length brown hair threaded with white. There were dark half-moons beneath her eyes and drawstring lines around her mouth. She was an old sixty-seven.

Although Gary had prepared a speech, his words were garbled. Her face said little, but she didn't turn him away. She confirmed that she was Noreen O'Callaghan, formerly Nestor, and that she'd received his letter. There was no sense that she was greeting a long-lost son – or that she was aware of his fame.

Confused, he made another attempt at his introduction. 'So I suppose,' he said finally, 'I've been wondering if you're my birth mother.'

'You'd better come in,' she replied. There was a croak in her voice, as if it had been a while since she'd spoken.

'I don't want to interrupt. I can come back, if you'd prefer.'

'No, not at all. You're here now.'

Gary followed her into the hall. He carried the bracelet in a paper bag.

The house was neat but faded. There were few personal touches and no photographs. He sat on a sagging brown sofa while she rummaged through a sideboard. In the 1980s, his parents had owned a similar model. What was she searching for? An old document that proved the link between them? A black-and-white photo? Eventually, she located a slim beige folder and sat down.

'I should have replied to you,' she said. 'I was taken aback by your letter and I didn't know what to say.' She removed a newspaper cutting from the folder and passed it to him. He put on his glasses. From the sports pages of a local freesheet, the article told him that a man called Fergus Keating had become captain of a golf club. The article was accompanied by a picture of a beaming Fergus. His pink V-neck sweater matched his round face. Beside him was a starched blonde in a white jacket and heavy gold jewellery. Gary looked from the photo to Noreen and back to the photo. Her blue-veined hands were shaking.

'That's my son,' she said. 'I called him Paul, but he's Fergus now. He lives about twenty miles away.'

'I see.' Gary handed back the cutting.

'He contacted me ten years ago. I haven't seen him in seven – no, eight – years. I've rung a few times, but he doesn't reply. If he doesn't want to see me again, that's all right. But I'd like to meet his children. No doubt he grew up dreaming that his biological mother was exciting or glamorous. And as you can see, I'm neither.' She glanced down at her grey polyester skirt and matted brown slippers. 'I'm sorry you've had a wasted journey. You seem like a nice man, and I wish I was your birth mother. But you've got the wrong woman.'

This was no artful stonewalling. Noreen was telling the truth. Gary's disappointment was joined by a sense that he was intruding on her grief.

'No, I'm sorry for making a nuisance of myself,' he said. 'And I'm sorry things didn't work out with your son. I gather it's not uncommon. Sometimes, people just need to get the answers to their questions, and then they disappear again.'

'It's hard, though, when you've built up your hopes, and your child decides you're not enough.' She handed him a blurred picture of a young woman with large eyes and a shy smile. 'That was me, a couple of years after I'd left Carrigbrack.'

'It's a lovely photo.' He took the baby bracelet from the bag and explained the story behind it. 'It's yours if you want it.'

'Thank you. I'd like that. I don't have many mementos. When my time comes, I'll leave no trace at all.' She patted her cheeks. 'Oh, what am I like? Please pay no heed.' She put the bracelet on a small table beside her. 'I remember Katie, the nurse you're talking about. She was a similar age to many of the mothers, so it must have been hard for her. She always looked like she was under a lot of pressure.'

Gary steered the conversation around to the question that had been bothering him. 'And your husband? Is he still alive?'

'As far as I know, he's in England. We haven't seen each other in more than forty years. We never divorced, mind. It wasn't possible in those days.'

He moved slightly, prompting a loud creak from the sofa. 'My apologies, Noreen. I'm asking questions that aren't mine to ask. I should learn to keep my nose out of what doesn't concern me.'

'You're grand. I didn't tell him about Paul or Carrigbrack, you see. And then, well … I wasn't easy to live with. I don't think any of us ever left that home behind. I used to dream about it all the time. In the end, I decided to confide in him and … he didn't take the news well. He said he'd never be able to trust me again, that I was a fraud and he was entitled to an annulment. After that, he disappeared. It's hard to fathom today, but that was how things were. Most folks would have said it was my own fault, that I should have confessed before we got married. Thankfully, we didn't have any children of our own.'

Her words were all the more powerful because she spoke in such a quiet, matter-of-fact way. Not that long ago, Gary had read something about the secrets of one generation becoming the traumas of the next. In truth, the pain was still being borne by the women whose children had been taken. The women who hadn't been allowed to speak. As a youngster, he'd been scornful of people like Noreen. They were quiet, unassuming, anxious not to take up too much space. They moved lightly through life, wearing dowdy clothes and becoming old before their time. Their default position was apologetic. He'd never paused to think about the forces that had made them that way.

He asked what she knew about the other young mothers. Perhaps she might have information that could point him in the right direction. She said her memories weren't reliable. Besides, in most cases she'd only known the women by their pseudonyms.

She took back the photo and smiled. Her face lifted, and the young woman in the picture came to life again.

'Please stay for a cup of tea,' she said. 'I don't have cake or anything fancy, but I have a few biscuits.'

Gary agreed. She didn't, he suspected, get many visitors. There was something gentle, almost other-worldly, about her. His mother, Lillian, would have called her a lady.

He accompanied her to the kitchen, which looked as though it hadn't been updated since the 1970s.

'I like your tattoos,' she said, as she poured milk into a china jug. 'Did they hurt?'

'Yes, to be honest. I was young, though. I'm not sure I'd be able to handle the pain these days.'

'You don't strike me as a man who plays golf.'

Gary smiled. 'You're spot on. It wouldn't exactly be my thing.'

'And I'd say you'd spent a while in America, would I be right?'

'You would.'

'What do you do in Wicklow, if you don't mind me asking?'

'That,' he said, 'is a good question.'

It was only after he'd left that Gary was able to digest the implications of their conversation. He parked near the harbour and walked along the riverbank. Beside him, the water surged and roared. He'd been convinced that Noreen was the one. He'd thought the same about Tina, Gráinne, Olivia and Edel. In every case, he'd been wrong. 'I wish I was your birth mother,' she'd said. He wished he was her son. He should have told her that.

Fuck you, Fergus, he thought. May your next round be fifty over par.

Then again, he wasn't best placed to throw stones. How many times had his parents met Allegra? Nine or ten, at most. The figures for his sons weren't much better.

He paused to assess his options. On the opposite bank, a haughty black bird, a cormorant perhaps, took up position on the roof of a stone building. Beside him, he noticed a yellow lifebuoy and a contact number for the Samaritans. Such was the power of the river, he could see why the desperate would come here. A step too close, and – *whoosh* – even the strongest swimmer would be swept away.

He had reached a dead end and he didn't know what to do. He could go back to Katie and see if there were other possibilities. If he hadn't been born in July or August '71, when had he arrived? He remembered her saying there'd been no male births in September, so maybe he should try October. Or June. These were long shots, though, and he didn't want to spend another year scouring records and writing speculative letters. Part of him clung to the belief that Gráinne had been the right woman after all. She'd rejected his approach, however, and he was powerless to do anything about it.

He was missing something – but what? All the old questions returned: why had there been an extra layer of secrecy about his birth? Why had his parents been reluctant to tell the truth?

And if he wasn't Paul, who was he?

Chapter 31

Ailish

When Gary called, Ailish was cleaning the Dolmen Suite. Her new phone had a more sober ringtone, and Stevie wasn't around to change it. She tried not to sound flustered. She imagined the conversation with her colleagues: 'Mmm, it was a regular day. The towels in Number 25 were streaked with fake tan. The hoover went on the blink. Oh, and the bass player in Black Iris rang for a chat.'

It turned out that Noreen wasn't his birth mother, and his background remained a mystery.

'Anyhow,' he said, 'the reason I'm calling is to let you know that I took your advice. I had a word with our manager, Frank. And he told me that while they'd approached a different bass player, the arrangement's a loose one.'

'The door's still open for you, then?'

'Uh huh.'

'So you're going on tour after all?'

'If they'll have me, I guess I am.' There was a lightness in his voice that suggested he'd surprised himself.

Ailish fell back on the newly made bed. 'I'll have to go and see you.'

He laughed. 'I'd say I'll be able to find a spare ticket. I haven't spoken to Anton yet, mind. But I will.'

He didn't add, *If I can make a difficult call, so can you*. He was too clever for that. It was what he meant, though. Three weeks on from that strange night in Katie's house, and Ailish still cringed at how open she'd been. The one thing that tempered her embarrassment was the knowledge that Gary had said far more.

She asked what he was going to do about his birth mother. He said he wasn't sure and that he might have to put his search on hold. She wished him luck. He told her to take care.

That was what everyone said: 'Take care of yourself.' Despite everything, Ailish remained in the house with Keith, while Stevie stayed with his sister. If she said little, her husband said less. Apart from the occasional cranky comment about work, he was silent. She continued to sleep in the girls' room. Both knew the situation couldn't continue. Neither was willing to make the first move.

Every day was a struggle. In books and films, people made decisions, then followed through. Her life wasn't like that. A step forward was immediately followed by two steps back. It wasn't just that she was scared. Ending her marriage would feel like discarding a large part of her life. She thought about the advice she'd always given others. Persevere, she'd said. Play the hand you've been dealt. Wasn't that what she should do? Then her thoughts would flip, and she'd be disgusted by her cowardice.

She was going to London again soon to meet her half-sisters and brother. Despite her protestations, Chrissie and Iggy had bought the ticket. When Chrissie was feeling stronger, she planned on coming to Ireland to see her grandchildren. Although she hadn't said, 'I trust Keith will be gone by then,' this was what she wanted.

Oh, Ailish knew what everyone thought of her. She was too

accommodating. Too timid. She was convinced that Beth considered her a hopeless case. Beth was gutsy. All the girls were these days.

No sooner had she said goodbye to Gary than her phone rang again. The number was local but not familiar.

'Mrs Dwan?' said a careful voice. 'It's Sorcha Hession here, the principal at St Ursula's. Have you got a few minutes?'

Every part of Ailish's body tightened. She rose from the bed. 'Is everything okay? Is Stevie okay?'

'The honest answer is yes and no. There's no cause for alarm, but we'd noticed that Stevie had been out of sorts in recent weeks. A couple of his teachers had mentioned it to me. And then this afternoon there was an incident with another boy. Some name-calling got out of hand and … well, there was an altercation and—'

Oh Jesus. 'Was he hurt?'

'No, he's fine. The fight was broken up before any damage was done.'

'What was it about?'

'As far as I'm aware, the other boy was giving Stevie a hard time about the fact that he's not living at home.'

Oh hell. 'I see.'

'I took the opportunity to have a chat with Stevie. I try not to pry; however, if there's a sudden deterioration in a student's performance or behaviour, we need to know what's behind it. He told me about the, er, situation.'

Ailish pictured Mrs – or was it Ms? – Hession. They were completely different, these modern teachers. The grey conformity of Ailish's youth had been replaced by beads and bangles and uplifting speeches. 'What did he say to you?' she asked.

The principal ran through what Stevie had told her, which was almost everything, including the fact that Keith had knocked him out. Hearing it from the mouth of another made Ailish want to crawl under the bed.

'Obviously,' continued Mrs Hession, 'I don't want to make a sensitive situation worse, but I do have a duty of care to my students. The days when we could look the other way while young people suffered are gone.'

'I appreciate that.'

There was a slight pause before the teacher spoke again. 'This is awkward, Mrs Dwan. What you've got to understand is that I'm not talking simply about a change in attitudes. There are child protection laws, and we have to follow them. If I suspect one of our students is in danger, I must intervene. Child welfare is paramount.'

Ailish, who'd been walking around the room, came to an abrupt halt. Was the woman suggesting she wasn't fit to take care of Stevie? 'Do you mean you might tell the guards?' she said. 'I never thought ... Please don't do that. I promise I'll sort it out. I promise.'

'I know you have a full-time job. I was wondering, however, if you and I could have a proper chat. Stevie is one of our brightest students, and I'm worried that if his circumstances don't improve, his results won't match his capabilities. You don't need me to tell you that this is an extremely important year. I don't want to see his opportunities drifting away.'

Ailish wasn't certain the words were intended as a reprimand, but for a moment, they hung there, a reminder of her failures. 'I'm not a bad mother,' she said.

'I'm not saying you are. I'm not blaming you at all. Frankly, I'm concerned for your welfare too.'

'I can be with you in half an hour, if that's all right.'

'That would be good.'

'And Stevie?'

'He's in the staffroom. I didn't think he should return to class; however, there wasn't anywhere else for him to go.'

Ailish couldn't think clearly. Her limbs moved, but only because they knew what to do. With her free hand, she picked up her cloth and polish and placed them back on the trolley. Somebody else would have to finish the room.

After she'd met the principal and learnt to call her Sorcha, after she'd rebuffed an offer of professional help and pledged to stay in touch, Ailish collected Stevie from the staffroom. Whatever else had changed, the smell of St Ursula's was constant. How well she knew the blend of socks and sweat and stale milk, hormones and spot cream and fear. She thought of all the parent–teacher meetings she'd attended. With Lorraine, Jodie and Lee, she'd never been sure what she'd hear. With Stevie, everything had been straightforward. In fact, she'd often felt a smug sympathy for other parents. She'd looked at their despondent faces and been grateful for her youngest child.

'I'm sorry,' she said.

Stevie shrugged. 'I shouldn't have given him a dig. Evan O'Gara, I mean. But I'd heard enough.'

'It's not your fault. What did he say to you?'

'Do you really want to know?'

Ailish gripped the steering wheel. 'I do.'

'He was slagging me off for living with Jodie. He claimed you'd thrown me out. Then he started going on about college and that. He said the only hope I had was an access programme.'

'What's an access programme?'

'It's like a special scheme for people whose folks don't have any money.'

'Did you—?'

'It's all rubbish, Mam. Don't pay any attention to the likes of him.' He pulled at the sleeve of his jacket. 'Are you mad at me for being a snitch?'

Suddenly, he wasn't a handsome six-footer. He wasn't smart, capable, funny Stevie, with a university application list she couldn't understand. Nor was he the young adult who'd taken control of his life because his mother wasn't strong enough to look after him. He was a child, hunched over in the passenger seat of her car, too many troubles bearing down on him. She had to stop letting him down. He deserved better. They all did.

'You did the right thing,' said Ailish. 'Will you come home?'

'I can't.'

'If I get your father to leave?'

'But will you? You've had plenty of opportunities and you've done nothing. Why should this time be any different?'

His scepticism tore at her, the pain all the sharper because his doubts were justified. 'I promise,' she said.

'You know the deal. I'll come back when he's gone.'

Keith was home before her, sitting at the kitchen table with a mug of tea. Outside, night was closing in, bringing with it a stinging frost.

'There you are,' he said. 'You'd want to get moving on the dinner.'

She put down her bag and leant against the counter for support. She needed to silence the voice that told her she wasn't good enough. Then she needed to put one word after another until Keith accepted he had to go.

'I want you to leave,' she said.

He didn't bother to look up. 'What's brought this on?'

'A million things, including what you did to Stevie.'

'That was almost a month ago. Why get into a flap about it now?'

'Because it's affecting his schoolwork, and he won't come home while you're here.'

'Great, so a child gets to decide where I live.'

Ailish dug her nails into the fleshy part of her palms. Keith's act was well practised. He planned on wearing her down by acting as though her complaints were unreasonable. 'I want you to go,' she said. 'Not just for Stevie's sake, but for mine too. What we're doing is ridiculous. We're both miserable.'

At last, he looked at her. 'I'm confused here, so you'll have to help me out. Do you want a divorce or do you want me to lie low for a couple of months so the boy wonder can do his homework?'

'In the longer term, I want a divorce. In the short term, as in tomorrow, I want you to leave the house. I want Stevie to come home where he belongs, and I want to live my life in peace.'

Ailish watched Keith's face harden.

'And where am I supposed to go?' he said.

'I don't know. Your mother's place? One of your sisters? That's not my concern.'

'"That's not my concern",' he said, mocking her voice. 'They're messing with your head, aren't they? Your new friends in Dublin and London? I can hear them urging you to throw me out. I'll bet they think I'm not good enough.'

'You weren't always like this,' she said.

That wasn't true. Keith's capacity for cruelty wasn't new, but she'd chosen to ignore it. She'd been the champion of looking the other way, the queen of self-delusion.

'No, Ailish, that's where you're wrong. I'm the same old, same old. You're the one who's changed.'

He was right. Finding Chrissie had changed her, but in ways he could never understand. Trying to explain was pointless. It was only now, when challenged, that she realised it herself.

'You've got to leave,' she said

Keith stood up. 'And what if I don't? What'll you do then?'

'You've got to leave.'

'If you're so keen for us to split up, why don't you go? I'm all right here.'

For five minutes, they tossed arguments back and forth. Lobbing and volleying. Then he pounced, throwing in something she hadn't expected. It was a skill of his, the ability to reveal information if and when needed.

'Who's Gary W?' he asked.

'I'm not with you.'

'Don't lie. The pair of you have been texting each other. At least that's the name on your phone. Who is he?'

For a moment, she froze. It hadn't occurred to her that Keith would go through her phone. She tried to recall what the messages said. 'Why were you snooping on me?'

'Because I suspected you were about to go flitting off to London again – and I was right. Anyway, you haven't answered my question. Who's Gary W?'

She explained that he'd also been born in Carrigbrack and that he was searching for his biological parents.

'There's more to it than that,' said Keith, taking a step towards her. As he moved, she felt as if air was leaching from the room.

'I swear to you there's not.'

'Well, surprise, surprise, I don't believe you. If all you were doing was comparing adoption notes, what was the other stuff about? Why was he telling you to "be brave" and "do the right thing"? Were you talking to him about us?'

'No,' said Ailish, her voice splintering.

'Is there something going on between you and this Gary W character?'

The temptation to say, 'Yeah, in a parallel universe' was strong. She managed to resist. 'You've got it wrong. It's not like that.'

Another step. 'I've told you before, Ailish, your trouble is that you're a liar, and a lousy one at that. Not only was your friend Gary texting you, Katie and Chrissie were too. What sort of tales have you been spinning to them?'

Bluffing was futile. If she didn't own up, they'd be stuck in this pattern for hours. 'Okay,' she said, 'I told them what you'd done to

Stevie. And to me. Oh, and you're right, I also spoke to Gary. They were worried about me. They still are.'

Keith took a further step. He was an arm's length away. She could see the curl of his mouth, the veins in his eyes, the pores on his nose.

'You're some bitch.'

'Chrissie's my mother. For some warped reason, you don't want to accept that, but she is. I'll tell her whatever I want.'

Before she could say anything else, Keith's right fist flew through the air. The move was too quick for her, and the punch hit hard under her eye. As his knuckles connected with the bone, pain exploded across her face, and for a second or two the world turned crimson.

'There's only so much I can put up with,' he said. 'No normal wife would behave like you, running off behind my back, telling your miserable little story to anyone who'll listen. You're pathetic. I always said you needed psychiatric help.'

Ailish found herself unable to speak. Her breath was ragged. Her skin burnt. She brushed her fingertips against her cheekbone, releasing a flare of pain. Her first impulse was to run. What if he hit her again? He'd never struck her across the face before, but what if he lost control?

Then Stevie entered her thoughts. If she wanted him home, she had to persevere. Although Sorcha Hession had outlined the law, Ailish had been in such a state that most of it had slid past her ears. What she lacked in detail, she'd have to make up for in attitude.

Eventually, she spoke. 'You ought to know that I met the principal of St Ursula's this afternoon. We discussed what you'd done to your son. She said that if Stevie was in danger, social services would have to get involved.'

'For fuck's sake, is there anyone you haven't blabbed to? Why not go on local radio or take out an ad in the paper?'

Keith's words might have been dismissive, but for the first time,

Ailish noticed a flicker of anxiety. 'I didn't contact Mrs Hession. She rang me because she was worried about Stevie.'

'If either of you accuse me of anything, I'll deny it.'

'That won't work. The day after you hit him, we went to the doctor. There's a record of his injuries.'

'Aren't you the sneaky one?'

'At the time, being sneaky was the last thing on my mind. I was terrified he was seriously hurt.' Pain radiated from her cheek, and her eye was watering. Although every word required enormous effort, she had to continue. Just breathe, she thought. Just breathe and talk. 'We've come to the end of the road, Keith. You know that; you just don't want to admit it.'

'What I know is, you're fooling yourself if you reckon I want to stay married to you.'

'Good. I want you to go. Now. If you don't, I'll call the guards. They'll see what you've done to me. And be assured that everyone in the village will hear about it too.'

For an agonising moment, Ailish worried he would strike her again.

Instead, he took a step back.

'If you think I'm going to make this easy for you,' he said, 'you're wrong. But it's been years since I had any interest in you. I should have moved on a long time ago. That's what most men would have done.' His voice cracked through the room like a whip.

And then, before Ailish could absorb what was happening, he was gone.

Chapter 32

Katie

Katie should have been working her way down her to-do list. Tomorrow was an important day. Instead, she was sitting on her bed sorting through the box. The number of queries had slowed, and more than a week had passed since their last significant email. Unusually, it had been from a woman who'd given birth in Carrigbrack. She was going through the official process and hoped to be reunited with her daughter.

Having avoided the board for several weeks, Katie risked a peek. Her post about the bracelets had been the catalyst for dozens of others to open up about their experience in Carrigbrack or their search for long-lost family. Some posts pulsed with anger. More were filled with disappointment and longing. Others were reassuring. *Please don't despair*, one woman wrote. *It took fifteen years of asking questions, but I found my natural mother in the end.*

Ailish's post about Chrissie was there, as were a number of others from people who'd received bracelets. After five minutes, Katie put down her phone. There was only so much she could read without getting emotional, and this wasn't the time for tears. If Beth was home, they could talk about it, but she was out with Iona, her new girlfriend.

The day before, Margo had called. 'Are you sure you don't want a birthday party?' she'd said. 'My offer still stands, you know.'

'You're very good,' Katie had replied, 'but I'm one hundred per cent certain. Seventy's not a big deal for me.'

Her sister had segued into a question about the bracelets, and soon they were bickering about the wisdom of the exercise. The row had only been brought to a close by Katie pretending that Beth had entered the room.

When she protested that turning seventy was of no significance, she was lying. She remembered how Johnny had seen 'three score years and ten' as a landmark birthday. 'After that, you're trespassing, Kateser,' he'd claimed. She told herself that this was no longer the case. These days, seventy was nothing. There was every chance Beth would live to be a hundred.

Sometimes, she felt that age was catching up with her. Take what had happened earlier in the day. She'd gone into town for a few bits and pieces, and while she'd expected her first destination, Penneys, to be busy, it had been frantic. Girls had swished past with armfuls of clothes and cosmetics. Katie had made the mistake of standing still for a moment and had been rewarded with a bony elbow into the side. Elsewhere, she'd found fault with everything. She'd tut-tutted over a handbag described as 'vegan'. 'Why can't they be honest and call it plastic?' she said to the slack-mouthed shop assistant. That was one of the problems with getting older: no one took you seriously. Complain, and you were dismissed as either cranky or confused. The best you could hope for was to be labelled 'feisty'. Katie hated that word.

Afterwards, she went for lunch. In a café, she ordered a cheese sandwich, only to be told this wasn't possible. 'What about hummus, pesto and beetroot?' suggested the shiny-faced young man behind the counter. 'Or bacon, coriander and Brie?' She settled for a scone and a strong cup of tea. As she was finishing her tea, a nearby mobile phone sprang to life. Johnny had used the same ringtone, and for one haunting moment, she was convinced the phone was his. She couldn't stop thinking about what had been and wouldn't be again. Exhausted and empty-handed, she got the bus back to Griffin Road.

Now, she counted the bracelets. There were twelve left. At least two, those belonging to the sons of Tina McNulty and Gráinne Holland, seemed destined to stay in the box. She was disappointed for Gary. He was back in LA, writing new music. Relations with Anton would never be quite the same, he said, but they'd shaken hands and were trying to write together. She could tell he was happy to have returned to the life he'd once loved. He pledged to keep in touch, but she feared that he wouldn't.

Lately, she'd been thinking a lot about forgiveness. It was funny how forgiving yourself could be more difficult than forgiving others. It certainly had been for Gary.

She continued to receive regular messages from Ailish. Keith might be gone from the house, but she remained uneasy. *What'll I do when Stevie leaves for college?* she asked. *I can't live here on my own.* If you asked Katie, she needed to go to the guards and apply for a barring order. Beth agreed. The decision wasn't theirs to make, however, and Ailish was under enough pressure without them adding to it. They did their best to reassure her that she'd done the right thing and that life would get better.

For a short while, Katie stayed where she was, reading and rereading the names on the bracelets. She knew every name, every date of birth. Finally, she placed the lid back on the box and returned it to the wardrobe. It really was time she got down to work. In less than twenty-four hours, their American visitors were due to arrive.

Chapter 33

Then, Patricia

Patricia thought she'd let out all the pain on the day she'd lain on the floor and cried. She was wrong. There was always more. Her grief didn't go away; it just changed shape. She would think she was coping without Paul. Then something simple – a baby's squeal or the smell of fresh linen – would spark a memory, and she'd have to fight for breath. She wished there was a way of communicating with her son. She wanted to be the voice in his head. Sometimes, she imagined she was.

What are you doing now?

Have you started to crawl?

Are you happy?

Do your new parents love you enough?

That she would never hear the answers to her questions didn't stop them from coming.

Spring arrived early, and Patricia visualised taking Paul for a walk. He'd have a smart pram, the best she could afford. Not a smelly old hand-me-down like many babies. Women would stop to admire him. 'Isn't he the fine fellow,' they'd say. 'Who does he take after?'

Her mother would get out the knitting needles and make him a matinee jacket. Maybe Patricia would take up knitting herself.

Then she'd return to the real world. Sister Faustina would whine at her over some minor mistake ('For an educated young woman, you're very slow'), or Sabina would chastise her for not eating ('When half the world is starving, it's a sin to refuse nutritious food'), or one of the other mothers would lose patience with her ('The face on you. You'd swear you were the only one who's been badly treated').

Patricia had come to hate Carrigbrack. She hated the walls, the statues, the sounds and smells. She hated every rancid thing about the place. She disliked the nurses, with their subtle ways of reminding her of their superiority, and she loathed the nuns, especially Sabina. She no longer spoke to Eunice. Why should she? Eunice had let her down. She'd also colluded in Winnie's escape, yet refused to reveal anything about where she was or how she was getting on.

Patricia tried to block memories of her early months in the home. Unbidden, unwanted, they returned. She remembered the singing protest, and how they'd all stood together. She remembered how they'd fantasised about what they'd do when they were released. She'd been a different person then. A better one. Lurking within, though, had been a seam of inadequacy, a latent flaw that prevented her from handling adversity. She was surrounded by women who'd suffered more, yet they struggled on, squeezing moments of joy from their regimented days. Even Nancy, poor abused Nancy, had become more open.

By comparison, Patricia felt suffocated by sadness. For no reason, tears would collect at the back of her eyes. Usually, but not always, she was able to hold them back. Sister Agnes had told her that she knew nothing about love, but she loved Paul. She couldn't imagine that his loss would ever become easier.

In early April, she decided she couldn't stay. She talked to Sister Agnes, who quickly put her right.

'You know the rules,' she said. 'You'll have to work here until you've paid off your debt.'

Patricia recalled something her mother had said on the night Father Cusack had taken her away. 'Please God, we'll see you later in the year.' What if her mam had never intended her to stay this long? What if her parents could be convinced to hand over the one hundred pounds that would secure her release? Actually, given that she'd already contributed several months of work, the debt was likely to be less than that. Because Patricia wasn't allowed to write to her family, she asked Sister Agnes to intercede on her behalf.

Their answer came the following week. *No,* her father wrote, in neat, narrow letters, *we don't have that sort of money, and even if we did, it wouldn't be appropriate for us to spend it. You need to pay for your mistakes.*

Patricia could picture him writing the letter, his face as pinched as his penmanship. She should have foreseen his response. After all, one of his favourite sayings was 'Neither a borrower nor a lender be.' Frugality was a virtue in Patricia's house. Her mother collected Green Shield stamps, made soup from leftovers and darned socks until the toes were a hotchpotch of stitches. Her father travelled everywhere on a battered High Nelly bicycle and still wore his wedding suit. None of this was unusual. Patricia must have known fifty families whose lives were no better than basic. Far less common was the house where money was spent freely.

The anger she'd once felt towards her mam and dad was gone. In its place was shame. Theirs was a hard life. Both came from large families where most of the children had emigrated. They didn't deserve the stigma she'd brought to their door. Regret flowed through her body like poison.

That month, her period was extremely painful. The usual dull weight was accompanied by a drawerful of hot knives. They stabbed and twisted until she thought she would faint. Although pain relief was hard to come by, the nurses had a range of pills in their office, and sometimes they could be persuaded to dispense one or two. Pretending she needed to go to the lavatory, Patricia slipped away from dinner. By then, she felt as if all her internal organs were in revolt.

The younger nurse, the one who'd been there when Diane died, answered the door. She listened to Patricia's request, then shook her head.

'I can't,' she said. 'It's against the rules.'

Patricia could tell from the nurse's narrow vowels that she was local. There was a jumpiness about her too. Patricia supposed she should try wheedling and cajoling, but she didn't have it in her. Besides, she was practically crumpled over with pain.

'I'm begging you to help me,' she said. 'It's never been this bad before.'

The nurse looked like she was going to repeat her mantra about the rules. Then she hesitated and pressed her lips together. Finally, she spoke. 'I can't give you anything. But I'm about to go and check on a baby, and if, by any chance, one tablet from the top shelf was to go missing,' she looked at the shelf behind her, 'there's a chance I might be too busy to notice.'

'Ah, I see.'

'That's *one* tablet,' repeated the nurse. 'If any more were unaccounted for, Sister Agnes would have to be told.'

'I understand.'

After the nurse had left, Patricia filled a glass of water from the sink in the corner. Then she took down the brown glass bottle. It was full. Figuring that one tablet was hardly worth her while, she shook out three and swallowed them. The label warned of drowsiness. That was exactly what she wanted: drowsiness followed by a deep, dreamless sleep. She swallowed a further two tablets. Then another handful. She would be in trouble when her theft was discovered, but so what? The worst had already happened; what more could they do to her? There was something pleasing about swallowing the pills. Something liberating. She took four – no, five – more before returning the bottle to the shelf.

The dormitory was empty. Everybody was in the refectory or the nursery. Outside, the blue-grey of dusk was closing in. Patricia lifted her mattress by an inch or so and took out her one tangible connection to Paul, his paper identity band. It was all she had left of him. She lay on her back, the bracelet in one hand, and allowed the tears to run down her cheeks. Within a few minutes, the pain started to lift, and she felt more peaceful.

Gradually, she was overcome by tiredness. She tried to focus, but no sooner had an idea entered her head than it galloped away again. Her thoughts were wild, freewheeling. Was it her imagination or was the room running out of air? What went through her mind in those moments? A tangle of memories, of Mike and her parents and Paul; of the whitewashed building where she'd attended national school and the boys and girls in her class; of the day Diane was buried and the day Paul disappeared. They danced in front of her closed eyes, blending together and forming patterns like the images in a kaleidoscope. Bit by bit, the pictures fractured and faded until everything was black.

Patricia was being tugged towards sleep, a long, dark sleep without memories, troubles or sadness. It was what she had longed for, and she was ready.

Chapter 34

Brandon

From above, Ireland was untidy. The fields were divided into irregular shapes, like a jigsaw made entirely of different shades of green. As the plane approached Dublin, the grass was replaced by a sprawl of roads, factories and houses. Forty-six years after he'd been bundled up and sent to America, Brandon was back. He didn't know what to call this country. It wasn't home, but it was where his mother had lived and where his twin still lived.

Beside him, Robyn was waking. She'd slept all the way across the Atlantic. Brandon's rest had been more fitful. He'd started watching three different films, but couldn't concentrate.

'Here we are,' she whispered, as the plane bumped onto the runway. 'Your other home.'

He decided he could go with that. His other home.

He kept expecting things to go wrong, for the weather to be foul or their luggage to have been left behind in Boston. The morning was fine, and their bags were first on the carousel. He worried that Katie wouldn't be there. Then he decided it might be easier if she left them to their own devices. He recognised Katie and Beth immediately, the younger woman a taller, more sculpted version of her aunt. By now, he'd had several conversations with both. Relations with Katie were friendly, although he sensed she still had doubts about him.

When Robyn had returned from Miami, she'd issued an ultimatum. She wouldn't have called it that. 'Setting out my thinking' had been the phrase she'd used. Echoing one of Donald Trump's campaign slogans, she'd repeatedly asked, 'What have you got to lose?' It had worked for Trump and it had worked for Robyn. Sort of. What had helped to clinch the deal was Katie coming on board with more details about Eddie. Say what you like about the woman, she was a skilled detective. Her enquiries had begun with another nurse who'd worked in Carrigbrack. One contact had spawned another until she'd found the information she wanted. In what sounded like an unorthodox arrangement – was everything in Ireland slightly sketchy? – Eddie had been fostered, and subsequently adopted, by a woman named Joyce. They both lived in a town called Ballinlish in County Longford. The internet told Brandon that Longford was flat, rural and approximately seventy miles from Dublin.

He hadn't wanted to travel to Ireland straight away. 'I'm busy at work,' he'd explained to Robyn. 'This isn't the right time for a vacation.'

'You're looking for excuses,' she'd replied. 'You figure that if you put the trip off for long enough, it'll all blow over. Am I right?'

His wife's week in Florida had taught Brandon that he couldn't be without her. That this sounded pathetic didn't make it untrue. He'd missed her enthusiasm and intelligence. He'd missed her touch, her kisses, her physical presence. He'd thought of the years he'd wasted by believing he was better on his own; the years when he'd grown so accustomed to loneliness that he'd no longer recognised its frosty grip. He'd been reading about twins. One line was repeated over and over again: *When you have a twin, you're never alone.* Every time, that line filled him with sadness.

The morning after Robyn's return, he'd called Katie and booked two tickets to Dublin.

Brandon worried that their marriage had been damaged by months of disagreement. He spoke to Robyn about his guilt, not all at once but in instalments. It was, he feared, impossible for her to understand. Her background was too conventional. She did her best but sounded perplexed. 'You were a *baby*,' she said. 'It wasn't your fault the dice rolled in your favour.' Beth probably had the best read of his emotions. 'Nothing about that system was fair,' she said. 'Everybody's trying to make amends for problems they didn't cause. But Eddie and Joyce are intrigued by you, and I think all three of you will feel better after you've met.'

Step by step, the journey back to Ireland had begun to feel less like an obligation and more like a choice. As Robyn liked to remind him, he was fortunate that his brother had been relatively easy to trace. 'Some people spend their entire lives looking down blind alleys,' she pointed out. Brandon couldn't say he felt an overpowering connection to Eddie, but he was curious, and for now that would have to be enough.

The news wasn't all good: it turned out that their birth mother, Linda Markham, was dead. In the early 1980s, she'd emigrated to Australia. Joyce and Eddie had tried to find her, only to discover they were too late. She'd died in a drowning accident in 1993. She'd been married but had no other children. Her husband knew she'd had twin boys in Ireland and that they'd been forcibly removed from her. She'd kept a photo of them, lying side by side in their crib. She'd said little about their biological father and had taken his identity to the grave. Brandon was stung by the cruelty of her early death. After everything she'd endured, Linda had deserved a long, comfortable life. But, as all of this had shown, not everyone got what they deserved.

Beth drove, with Katie beside her. From the back, Robyn and Brandon offered chit-chat about the flight and the scenery. Robyn did most of the work. Brandon's thoughts were flitting every which way. One minute, he was looking forward to the reunion. The next, he was rigid with nerves. We don't have to stay, he thought. If it's too awkward, we can leave.

'I'm glad you've spoken to Eddie,' said Katie. 'At least you know a bit about each other now.'

'Yeah, it was good to talk to him.'

'Would I be right in saying he wasn't what you'd expected?'

'I don't know that anything's been quite what I expected.'

'That seems to be the way with most of the people we've come across,' said Beth.

Their phone conversation had been brief. Eddie had told Brandon that not only had he been aware of his existence, he'd made every effort to find him. 'The files said nothing about where you'd gone,' he explained, 'so after a couple of years, I gave up.' During the call, he referred to his disability but didn't dwell on it. Like Brandon, he'd married late. His wife's name was Yvette, and they had a three-year-old daughter called Zoe. He was an administrator with the local council, while Yvette worked in a crèche.

Eddie's friendliness, and the fact that he lived a full life, had shattered Brandon's preconceptions. Was it wrong that he'd been relieved to discover his brother's disability was mild? Yes. Did this mean he was hopelessly shallow? Probably. Would others have reacted in the same way? Robyn wouldn't have. It was funny: Brandon remembered thinking that Ireland must be filled with people who needed professional help. Until now, he hadn't placed himself among them.

When he zoned back in, his wife was talking. 'Is this very strange for you, Katie?' she asked. 'Reconnecting with people after all this time?'

There was a delay, and when, finally, she replied, she skirted around the question. 'Robyn,' she said, 'you've no idea how much it means to me that you've made this journey. When I sent both bracelets to Boston, I hoped that Brandon and Eddie would meet again. It's a delight when a story ends well.'

'Isn't it just,' said Beth. 'So, Brandon, what do you make of the place so far?'

'It's … um … green?' he replied, prompting laughter from Beth and smiles from Katie and Robyn.

'You're probably wondering where all the thatched cottages are gone, aren't you?'

'Now that you mention it, I am. And where are the donkeys? I expected donkeys. Oh, and leprechauns. We need leprechauns.'

'Stop messing, the pair of you,' said Katie, amusement in her voice. 'When I was growing up, there were quite a few thatched cottages left. My own grandmother – Beth's great-grandmother – lived in one. She'd no electricity and her water came from a well. And after we'd visited, our clothes smelt of smoke for a week.'

'Ah, the good old days,' said Beth.

Brandon was relieved when they fell back into silence. He needed to focus on the hours ahead.

To begin with, his other home was disappointing, just highways and fields, swathes of grey and green, grey and green. Slowly it changed – and kept changing. Lakes, rivers, marsh, bog, pasture, villages with quirky names and peculiar signs – what was the GAA Lotto? A 45 drive? A solemn novena? – blurred past. The picture was green, blue, navy, brown, red, yellow then green once more.

'It's lovely,' he said, conscious of the word's inadequacy.

'For a small country, there's a lot of landscape,' agreed Katie.

Brandon kept looking. He might never be back this way again, and he wanted to remember it.

Ballinlish wasn't an attractive town. In the early spring light, it appeared down at heel, vacant shops scarring the main street like missing teeth. On their journey, Brandon had noticed references to something called a 'Tidy Towns committee'. The Ballinlish branch needed to up its game.

Joyce's one-storey house was two miles further along, down a narrow strip of road. She'd lived there with her husband, Cathal, until his death five years earlier. Eddie lived in a new housing development on the other side of town.

Joyce had wings of white hair and small dark eyes. She was, thought Brandon, the sort of woman who could read every uncharitable thought that passed through your head. She wore a red sweater, a jade scarf and blue earrings. He wondered if the gaudy outfit was a backlash against the years when she'd been forced to wear black.

Katie embraced her, and for a time, they clung together. They were less like former colleagues, more like women who'd been side by side in the trenches.

'How long has it been?' asked Joyce.

'More than forty-six years,' replied Katie. 'And despite everything, I'd have known you.'

'Even without the veil?'

'Even without the veil. Though I haven't quite adjusted to using your real name.'

'If the occasional "Eunice" slips through, I won't mind. Please don't call me "Sister", though. That would be too weird.'

Katie blotted a tear while Joyce showed them into the sitting room. There to greet them was a man of medium height with mid-brown hair. His smile was cautious, his eyes blue, his nose a shade too long. Save for his thin legs and the fact that he rose with the help of a stick, he was Brandon's double.

Eddie spoke first. Like Joyce, his voice was soft. 'I saw your picture, but ... This is crazy. I never thought we'd be this much alike. It's great to meet you again.'

Words came slowly to Brandon. 'When you say again, does that mean you remember when we were together?'

'No, but because I've always known about you, I liked to think you were in my memory somewhere. I used to have this image of the pair of us crawling around the nursery floor in Carrigbrack, terrorising the other kids.' Another shake of the head. 'I guess that never happened.' He extended one arm. 'Come here. My limbs don't always obey orders, but I promise I won't fall on top of you.'

'I never—'

'You're grand. I'm used to people's concerns.'

They stepped forward and folded into a hug. Brandon couldn't remember the last time he'd shared a sober embrace with a man. He'd never been a tactile person, nor an emotional one. When they pulled apart and sat down, he saw that Robyn was crying.

Like her outfit, Joyce's sitting room was a riot of colour. Ordinarily, Brandon would have cringed at the patterned carpet, the lemon walls and pink drapes. He would have removed several of the paintings and questioned the need for so many photos. But, as he drank the worst cup of coffee he'd ever tasted, he decided the garishness worked.

'What I still can't grasp,' said Eddie, 'is that you never knew you had a twin. You wouldn't believe how much time I spent making up stories about you, wondering where you were and what you were like. It never occurred to me that you might have been sent to the States.'

Brandon explained how his parents had been kept in the dark.

'They applied for one baby,' he said. 'If they'd known about you, I'm convinced they'd have wanted you as well.'

Eddie shrugged, as if to say, *I'm not so sure about that.* Then he and Joyce explained how they'd come to be mother and son.

'I left the convent in 1980,' she said. 'By then, the regime in Carrigbrack was a little gentler. The mothers wore their own clothes. They were allowed to have visitors and make phone calls. They didn't have to earn their way out either.'

'Agnes allowed all that?' asked Katie.

'She was gone. As was Sabina. Did you know Sabina's still alive? She's in her nineties and living in a home in County Mayo. Imagine: when we thought she was as old as civilisation, she was only in her forties.'

'From the tales we've heard about her,' said Beth, 'she's enjoyed a far longer life than she deserved.'

Katie and Joyce swapped a look, but neither responded.

'When you left the convent,' said Robyn, 'was it to get married?'

'No. I met Cathal, the Lord have mercy on him, several years later.' Joyce sighed. 'I left because I didn't have a vocation. To be honest, I'd struggled for years. Somehow, I'd managed to convince myself that I could do good work in Carrigbrack.' She raised her palms to the ceiling. 'I know, I know. Given everything you've heard about the place, you probably consider that odd. Troubling, even. But I reckoned that if families were going to send their daughters there anyway, the least I could do was offer the girls some support. I'd like to think that, occasionally, I lived up to that aim.' She looked down at the technicoloured carpet. 'I fear there were other times when I failed – and failed badly.'

'You were always kind,' said Katie. 'Don't doubt that.'

'By 1980, the numbers in the home were dwindling, and other similar places had already closed their doors. I was increasingly disillusioned. I spent every day questioning whether I was living the right life. Oh, and there was another consideration. By then, both my parents were dead. They'd set such store by my life as a nun, I'd never been brave enough to tell them I wanted to leave. Finally, I felt I had to make a move.'

'What did you do afterwards?' asked Beth.

'I went to university and studied social work.' Joyce chuckled. 'They didn't get many thirty-something former nuns, but the other students – mostly young women – were very kind.'

'I was devastated,' said Eddie. 'I couldn't believe she'd abandoned me.'

'*Tuh*, I'd done no such thing, as well you know. It took a while to sort out the paperwork, that's all.'

'The best part of forty years later, and I can still get a rise out of her.' Eddie winked before sending an affectionate look in Joyce's direction.

'I'd no intention of leaving him behind. We were great buddies by then. He was a lovely fellow. Mind you, he could be a cranky devil when the mood took him. In those days, single people weren't allowed to adopt. At the same time, everybody agreed that Carrigbrack was no place for an eight-year-old and that I was best placed to look after him.'

Robyn tilted her head. 'Why hadn't somebody else adopted him?'

'A good question,' said Eddie. 'From what I've been able to gather, Agnes decided no one would want me.'

'That's appalling, and I'm sure it wasn't true, either.'

'I'd like to think you're right. For quite a while, I had a strange existence. The next eldest child was three years younger than me, and she was profoundly disabled. To be fair, the mothers were very good.'

'How did you learn to read and write?' asked Brandon.

'Joyce taught me. Once I'd picked up the basics, I read all the time. It wasn't as though there was much else to do. There wasn't even a television. To this day, friends and colleagues refer to childhood TV programmes, and I've only a sketchy idea what they're talking about.'

'I don't remember there being many books in Carrigbrack,' said Katie. 'What did you read?'

Eddie laughed. 'You've a good memory. The choice wasn't that extensive. Let's just say I know a lot about the lives of the saints, especially the female ones. Anyway, to go back to Robyn's original question, being left behind worked to my advantage. It meant I got to live with Joyce.'

'I became Eddie's guardian in 1981,' she said. 'And, before you ask, I'm aware there was something ridiculous about me being allowed to raise him when his birth mother hadn't been. Linda was treated shamefully.'

Brandon put down his coffee. 'This might be a lame question, and I don't want to offend anyone, but … were you trying to make amends? For everything that had happened in the home, I mean?'

While Katie shifted in her armchair, and Robyn examined her hands, Joyce appeared unperturbed. 'I couldn't tell you how many times I've been asked that, and I'll give you the answer I always give. To me the question makes no sense. It implies that Eddie was some sort of burden. A penance. We'd spent eight years together in Carrigbrack and we were friends. I wanted him with me because I loved him.'

Brandon's cheeks burnt. 'I didn't mean—'

'Don't worry,' said Eddie. 'We know you didn't mean any harm. And listen, I probably did add a few white hairs to Joyce's head. When I was small, a doctor told the nuns I'd never be able to walk and I'd never talk properly. He said I'd probably have to spend the rest of my days in an institution. We were both determined to prove him wrong. Like she says, we were a team.'

'We were an unusual pair in Ireland in the 1980s,' said Joyce, 'but I had a job – I was working in inner-city Dublin at the time – and Eddie found a good school. And, of course, we realised that the doctor brought in by Agnes had been far too pessimistic. It turned out there were lots of therapies that could help. And then, in the middle of everything, I met Cathal.'

'Or Father Cathal, as some folks called him,' added Eddie.

Beth leant in, eyes bright. 'Don't stop there. This is quite a story.'

Joyce's face creased into a smile 'Yes, he had been a priest. But, like me, he'd left the religious life several years earlier. He was a national school teacher.' She looked at Robyn and Brandon. 'I think you call it grade school in the US. He applied for the principal's job here in Ballinlish ... and that's when we got married and adopted Eddie.'

'So there I was,' said Eddie, 'a disabled child living out in the wilds with an ex-nun and a former priest. I swear there isn't a joke I haven't heard. Some of the kids were as subtle as an ice cream van, and the word cripple was still in everyday use. But here I am.' He glanced at Joyce. 'Here we both are.'

The focus shifted to Brandon. By contrast, his story felt run-of-the-mill. His life sterile. He had achieved what someone of his upbringing was expected to achieve. No more, no less. Oh, he tried to make his job sound more exciting, his interests less banal, but for someone hurtling towards fifty, he had few anecdotes. He was relieved when the conversation flipped back to his brother.

Eddie revealed that Zoe's second name was Linda, in honour of the grandmother she would never meet. He also talked about his job. He was working on a plan to revitalise the town. It had been ravaged by the recession, he said, and recovery was slow.

'Make Ballinlish great again,' said Beth with a nod towards Brandon, and they all laughed.

No matter who was speaking, Brandon's eyes were drawn towards his twin. One part of him was relaxed. Why did I resist this? he thought. This is everything. Another part was overwhelmed. He wanted to run away and think. To measure their similarities and differences. That was why, when Joyce asked if he and Robyn would stay for a couple of days, Brandon changed the subject. He didn't know if he was ready. Returning to Dublin with Katie and Beth would be safer. There would be more room to breathe there. Robyn sent him a look of disapproval.

Katie was quiet. Perhaps she, too, was struggling to take it all in. She'd once worked side by side with Joyce, but that had been almost half a century ago.

Beth was more animated, outlining everything that she and Katie had been doing to reunite people with their birth families. Joyce was enthralled, oohing and aahing at several of the names. 'I remember him,' she'd say. 'He was an absolute dote.' Or, 'That's shocking. Completely shocking. She should never have been lied to like that.'

'We've encountered some amazing folks,' said Beth. 'A few difficult ones as well, but you get them everywhere.'

'What about my brother here?' asked Eddie, a teasing tone to his voice. 'Which category would you put him in?'

'Hmm. To begin with, he was a bit tricky, and we did have our differences. However, as the old saying goes, there was nothing wrong with Brandon that couldn't be cured by a good kick up the backside.'

'Beth!' said Katie, but Brandon found himself laughing, albeit nervously.

'And I think it's fair to say we've warmed to each other.'

'That's a relief,' said Joyce, mirth in her voice. 'Do you know, Beth, you remind me of someone I once knew, a young woman who spent time in Carrigbrack. In fact, I helped her to escape. Winnie was her name. She was younger than you, but she said the same type of thing. How she used to make me laugh. I often think of her.'

'Do you know what happened to her?'

'Unfortunately, we lost touch back in the late seventies. I hope the years have been good to her.' She hesitated. 'There were a lot of casualties back then. Far too many casualties.'

The words obviously resonated with Katie, who closed her eyes and bowed her head. Before anyone could say anything else, however, they heard a car pulling into the drive. Within seconds, a little girl came skipping in. She had large golden-brown eyes and a cap of blonde curls. She was swaddled in a bright yellow raincoat and wore cerise wellingtons. Clearly, clashing colours were popular in Ballinlish. Her mother, a neat woman with angular cheekbones, was several steps behind.

'How's my best girl?' said Joyce.

'I'm good, thank you, Nana,' replied Zoe as she assessed the room. Her gaze halted briefly at Eddie. 'Daddy!' she said. Next, she plodded towards Brandon. 'Other Daddy?' she asked cautiously.

Eddie grinned and scooped her up. 'That's Daddy's American brother. Uncle Brandon. Remember how I told you he was coming to see us?'

'Oh, yes.' She risked another shy glance in Brandon's direction. 'Are you nice like my daddy?'

'I hope so,' replied Brandon.

Eddie kissed the top of his daughter's head. 'Sure how could he be anything else when he's related to us, huh? Now, what do you say to our guests?'

Zoe smiled, revealing tiny white teeth. 'Nice to meet you and welcome to Ballinlish.'

'Thank you, Zoe,' said Brandon. 'We're delighted to be here. I'm only sorry it took so long.'

Yvette took off her coat and sat down. 'It's no wonder the child's confused. You're the spitting image of each other. You could be the same man.' She had a pleasant, slightly husky, voice.

'We could,' said Eddie.

It was raw, this connection. It was complex, but in some ways, simple too. Once again, Brandon found himself thinking about the wasted years. About the years they'd had stolen from them – and the ones he'd chosen to fritter away.

He reached into his backpack, took out an envelope, removed a tiny paper bracelet and handed it to Eddie.

'This is yours,' he said. 'And I hope Robyn doesn't mind if I accept your kind invitation. We'd be honoured to spend the next few days in Ballinlish.'

Chapter 35

Katie

'Are you sure about this?' asked Beth.

'I am.'

'Because we don't have to do it today. I mean, we don't have to do it at all.'

Katie picked a piece of fluff from the duvet cover. 'I can't put it off forever, pet. The poor man's been dead for nine months. Someone will be glad of those clothes.'

'If you're certain,' said Beth, folding a suit jacket and placing it in a large paper bag.

'Well, maybe I'll keep one shirt. That would be okay, wouldn't it? Perhaps the pale blue one. That always smells so nice.'

'Oh, Katie. What are you like?'

'Hopeless, I know.'

Katie swung her legs onto the bed. She'd promised herself that this would be the week she cleared away Johnny's clothes. Beth had offered to help. In the end, she'd decided it would be easier if her niece did the physical work while she supervised. Otherwise, she'd spend the rest of the day sniffing and reminiscing. She'd get teary over some obscure event that meant nothing to anyone else.

That morning, they'd had their weekly meeting about the bracelets. Their task was petering out. Since their visit to Ballinlish three weeks before, they'd had only four queries. Two had fallen outside their time frame, while another had been from a man who'd just wanted to vent about the way his family had been treated in the 1960s. The final email was from a woman who'd been born in Carrigbrack but was reluctant to trace her birth mother. That some bracelets were likely to stay in the box was no surprise. Short of making a televised address, they'd never reach everyone on the list. Even then, there would be those who didn't want a reminder of their earliest days. And that was fine.

Katie worried that Beth would resurrect her proposal to help other adoptees. In many ways, it would make sense. There was something addictive about success. It wasn't, however, what Katie wanted. When she'd done everything she could to help the men and women whose bracelets she had kept, her task would be over.

Brandon and Robyn had spent four days in Longford. While Katie wouldn't claim that Brandon was a man transformed, he was definitely more at ease. Beth had taken to tormenting him about his Irishness. 'The next thing we know,' she'd said, 'you'll be saying goodbye ten times before hanging up the phone and buying a newspaper solely for the death notices.' Although he'd smiled, Katie suspected he hadn't understood a word she'd said.

With her, he remained slightly edgy. This was a shame, because she'd grown fond of him. She reckoned her affection was all the stronger because of how he'd struggled to accept his background. She also worried that he was too in awe of Robyn. She's your wife, she wanted to say, not some saintly reincarnation.

Earlier that week, she'd marked her seventieth birthday in low-key fashion. Friends had called and messaged while Margo and Con had sent an enormous bouquet of flowers. Beth had bought her a sky-blue cashmere jumper, the loveliest thing she'd ever owned.

Spring was in full bloom. There were shoots of life on the trees and daffodils were making way for bluebells. Soon, that brief period would arrive when Irish people switched from complaining about living on a damp rock in the North Atlantic to claiming there was nowhere else in the world they'd rather be. Pale skin would be scorched to a flamingo pink, and the smell of burnt meat would hang over the suburbs.

'Is that your phone?' asked Beth, lifting a white shirt from the wardrobe and placing it in the bag.

Katie gave what she hoped was an airy wave. 'Whoever it is can leave a message, and I'll get back to them later.'

She could guess the caller's identity. Since their reunion, Eunice – or Joyce, as she must learn to call her – had rung every few days. Katie had answered none of the calls. Nor had she responded to any of the messages. She would have to talk to her soon. Indeed, she feared the consequences of not doing so. But not today.

Later, she would bring Johnny's clothes to the nearest charity shop, and the job she hadn't been able to do would be behind her. The problem was, she'd replaced it with the conversation she didn't want to have.

Chapter 36

Gary

Gary continued to check the message board; not every day, but often enough to monitor developments; often enough that if something significant appeared, he'd see it. The conversation about Carrigbrack had slowed, the focus moving to other institutions. St Bridget's, Long Abbey, Rossallen House, Glenarra: the names might change, but the stories had a grim similarity.

Given what Katie had been able to tell him, his task should have been straightforward. Instead, after six months of searching, he felt like he was trying to isolate a single blade of grass in a football field. After he'd scratched Noreen from his list, he'd decided to approach the Adoption Authority. While he doubted they could shed any light on his case, he had to give them a try. If they failed, he'd seek the help of a private investigator.

In early April, he returned to Ireland for a few days. On his first day back, he noticed a fresh message on the forum. The query didn't affect him, so he spooled on. Then he stopped, thought and returned.

He read it, then read it again. The post was from a man named Luke. Was it a hoax? Or was Gary's mind playing tricks on him?

By rights, he should have brought it to Katie's attention. He decided to consult Ailish first. She messaged to say she was in London with Chrissie and would have a look later in the day. He called Beth, and when she didn't answer, he left a voicemail.

In LA, everything was moving quickly. The tour to promote the reissue of *Overboard* would be short, major venues only. A more substantial tour and a new album would follow. They'd spent time in the studio, and Gary and Anton were attempting to write together. He wouldn't claim it was easy. After almost four years of silence, their relationship had altered. Some days, they tried too hard to recapture what they'd once had. At other times, they were ill at ease, desperate not to offend, their conversation reduced to trite statements of the obvious. Then there were days when it all clicked. When they remembered why they couldn't have done anything else with their lives.

Once or twice, they spoke about Shanna. They did so with trepidation, as though rubbing the scar would reopen the wound.

In his downtime, Gary was working on a couple of his own songs. He was excited about one, a ballad called 'Big Sky'. He didn't usually write ballads. He'd always dismissed them as too syrupy. This was different. A bit more work, and he'd play it for Anton.

During the band's hiatus, a lot had changed. There were new Irish bands, guys who sang and spoke like they owed nothing to no one. Guys with a splash of talent and lashings of attitude. In short, guys exactly like Black Iris had been back in 1990. Meanwhile, the industry had become even more clinical, more cynical. More industrial. It was all about data and algorithms now. To bemoan this was to risk being labelled a dinosaur, so Gary told himself to focus on his music and his families, the one he knew and the one he'd yet to find.

Buoyed by their return, Frank was telling everyone that Black Iris were going to be bigger than ever. 'Authenticity is on the way back,' he'd say, 'and my guys are as authentic as they come.' Gary, Anton, Ray and Liamo rolled their eyes and pretended to be irritated.

In the main, Frank ignored the tragedy that had torn the band apart. One day, though, while they were getting a coffee, he turned to Gary and asked why he'd changed his mind.

'Three women changed it for me,' he replied.

The manager smiled. 'Aha,' he boomed. 'The old Gary Winters lives and breathes.'

Gary chose not to put him right.

The Winters family lived in a modest house on Dublin's southern fringes. Lilac Road was middle class, but not extravagantly so. As a teenager, Gary had chafed against its dull respectability. He'd been convinced that the real him belonged somewhere else. Now, in classic middle-aged style, he was mawkishly sentimental about the place. He had offered to buy his parents a bigger, plusher house, but they insisted on staying put.

In the mid 1990s, when Black Iris mania had been at its peak, obsessive fans had taken the 44 or 47 bus and scoured the neighbourhood for the band's childhood homes. Mostly, they'd focused on Anton's house, or Ray's, but occasionally someone had pressed the Winters's doorbell and asked for Gary. Bemused by such devotion, his parents, Shay and Lillian, had posed for photos. More than once, they'd provided tea and sandwiches. They'd answered questions, too: 'We bought him an acoustic guitar for his twelfth birthday,' they'd said, and, 'No, we could never have imagined they'd become so big,' and, 'Yes, we've known Anton since he was in third class. He hasn't changed a bit.'

As Gary parked his car, the message on the adoption forum

played on his mind. He'd stay long enough to have a chat and drink the obligatory cup of tea: a quick 'God bless all here', as his old man would say. Then he'd give Beth another shout.

Walking up the path reminded him of something else: no matter what he achieved or how far he travelled, a visit home meant reverting to the age at which he'd last lived here. In 10 Lilac Road, he was permanently nineteen.

His parents were in the kitchen, his mother ironing sheets, his father polishing shoes. Although they'd both retired, it was impossible to imagine them at rest. They were in perpetual motion, as if a minute's idleness would cause the house to collapse around them.

As much as he valued their relationship, he wasn't always open with them. It wasn't fear of shocking them that held him back so much as the desire to avoid hassle. 'Don't ask, don't tell' was his motto. Then again, they'd spent well over forty years pretending he was their biological son, so the balance sheet was even. They were dishonest in equal measure. While he'd told them about his falling-out with Anton, he'd never said how serious it was – or what it was about. Neither had he revealed much about the hunt for his birth mother. He thought he'd said enough. As he told them about his encounter with Noreen, he realised how wrong he'd been. It was clear they'd had no idea how extensive his search had been.

'So,' said his dad, voice cautious, 'for the past few months, when we were wondering what you were up to, you were actually pretty busy?'

'Not all the time, but I put in a lot of hours all right. The shame is I haven't got anywhere. Yet.'

'Why didn't you speak to us about your search?'

'I was nervous, I guess. It's obviously a difficult subject for you.'

His mother put down the iron. 'If we'd had any idea, we might have …' She tapered off.

'I was going to fill you in when I'd solid progress to report,' said

Gary, starting to feel queasy about their reaction.

His father rubbed the heel of his palm against his forehead. 'You see, we mightn't have been …'

'… entirely straight with you,' finished his mother.

The smell of singed cloth hit Gary's nose. 'You'd better unplug that iron,' he said, 'and what do you mean by "entirely straight"?'

'I think we ought to sit down and talk about it,' said his dad.

And that was how the truth came spilling out. Over the next hour, Gary's parents told the full story of how he'd come to live with them. It was a very different tale to the one they'd spun eighteen months before.

'First things first,' said his father, 'you weren't born in Carrigbrack.'

'Then why did you tell me I was?'

'When Allegra was ill, we panicked,' said his mother. 'We never thought we'd have to answer questions about your background, and we didn't know what to say. If you remember, around that time there was lots of media coverage of mother-and-baby homes. All sorts of horror stories emerged. I read a newspaper article about a woman who'd been born in Carrigbrack and hadn't been able to find her birth parents. And …'

'… it felt like the easiest, most straightforward explanation,' continued his father. 'Easier than the truth, at any rate.'

'Hold on a minute,' said Gary. 'You said a cousin of yours was involved, and it was all arranged through her.'

'We may have embellished a little too much. But, like your mother says, we were in a flap and we didn't know what to do for the best. We were terrified that Allegra might die or be left with lasting damage. Suddenly, you were asking big questions, and we didn't have adequate answers.'

'Let me see if I've got this right: all this time, while I've been trying to trace women who gave birth in Carrigbrack, I've been on a wild goose chase?'

'Yes,' said his mother, tears in her soft brown eyes.

'What was so awful about the truth?'

'It wasn't so much that it was awful, although in a way it was. It was just unorthodox.'

'And illegal,' said his father, his voice barely audible.

'You'd better explain,' said Gary.

His mother took a deep breath. 'We'd wanted a decent-sized family. Not nine or ten like some people had in those days, but three or four certainly. Unfortunately, I'd been very sick when I was pregnant with both of your sisters. I'd also had several miscarriages, and the doctors warned me not to risk another pregnancy.'

His father took up the story. 'We wanted a boy and we were confident we could give another child a good home. Originally, we planned on going down the official route, but fate – or rather, a neighbour – intervened. The neighbour put us in touch with a local priest. He knew of a young girl who'd recently given birth. Her parents hadn't wanted to send her to one of the big mother-and-baby homes, so they'd packed her off to an aunt, and the baby had been born in a private nursing home. It's no exaggeration to say they were obsessed with secrecy. And, to be blunt about it, they just wanted to get rid of the baby so the girl could continue her studies.'

'We were the solution to their problems,' said his mother, 'and they were the solution to ours. Somehow, a birth certificate materialised containing our names and the name we'd chosen for you. It claimed you were born on the twelfth of August. Your actual birth was a couple of weeks earlier.'

Gary was having trouble grasping their revelations. Having accepted the initial story about Carrigbrack, he was no longer sure what to believe. Although he was angry at their deceit, he was hit by several other feelings too. Mostly, he was deflated. He'd squandered months searching for the wrong woman in the wrong place. Not only had he been wasting his own time, he'd led Katie and Beth astray. The energy they'd devoted to his case should have been spent elsewhere.

From his coat pocket, he heard the jingle-jangle of his phone. Whoever it was would have to wait.

'Okay,' he said. 'Let's go back. Who were this family?'

'We don't know,' said his father.

'Ah, come on. You must have some idea.'

'I promise you, Gary, all we know is what we've told you.'

'But why would they simply hand over a baby? You could have been a pack of gangsters, for all they knew. Or alcoholics or drug addicts. And why didn't they give me to the authorities or to an adoption society? I would've thought those folks were secretive enough for anybody. They wrote the book on secrecy.'

Gary's father straightened his back. 'Apparently, the family wanted it all handled quickly, with no comeback and no paper trail. We were told they were quite prosperous and were anxious to avoid a scandal. And, as far as our suitability was concerned, the priest and our old neighbour – Mrs Gallogly – vouched for us.'

'Right. So she knows my birth mother's identity?'

His mother sniffled. 'I'm afraid Rena Gallogly's a long time dead.'

'There's a surprise,' Gary said, the words like stones in his mouth. 'I take it the priest has also gone to his eternal reward?'

'Yes. Father Gleeson was his name. Finbar Gleeson. We saw his death notice in the paper about ten years ago.'

'And did my birth mother approve of her baby being adopted illegally?'

'We were assured that she did,' said his father. 'According to Father Gleeson, she'd no interest in being a mother at that point.'

'And her boyfriend? Did he have a say in the arrangement?'

'He didn't know about you.'

'She didn't tell him?'

'No.'

'What was wrong with him? Was he not respectable enough? Not rich enough? Not Catholic enough?'

'I think,' replied his mother, crying hard now, 'the opposite was true. Your birth mother's parents told his parents about the pregnancy, and they decided it would be better if he didn't know. It wasn't a serious relationship, and they worried his college work would be affected. Father Gleeson said he was very bright and had a wonderful career ahead of him.'

Gary stood and began pacing the kitchen. There wasn't much room for pacing. 'This shit is from the Dark Ages. You're telling me that, on the off chance I might have threatened this fellow's career prospects, he was never told I existed?'

'If you put it like that, it sounds very hard. I'm not saying what they did was right. We're just telling you what happened.'

'What a dreadful set-up.'

'It's not as though bad things don't happen to children now,' said his father, his voice becoming more prickly. 'Take a ramble into the city centre any day of the week, and you'll see youngsters who've been neglected. And what about all those lovely boys and girls being brought up in hotel rooms because their parents have nowhere to live? I'm not claiming the old ways were right. They weren't. But, let's face it, we don't have all the answers these days either.'

His mother cleared her throat and placed a hand on his father's arm. She'd always been the more conciliatory of the two, the one who'd prevented arguments from spiralling out of control or getting stuck in a swamp of whataboutery. 'We were lucky to get you,' she said. 'We've had so much joy from you. And I'm not talking about your success. Right from the start, we were delighted to have you as part of the family.'

Gary's thoughts swung back and forth. As much as he wanted to rail at his mam and dad, they'd been fantastic parents, far better than he'd ever been. If they chose to, they could point this out. But he knew they wouldn't. They were too kind. Too decent. It was then that he noticed a look pass between them. He wouldn't go so far as to call it furtive, but it suggested there was more to tell. He stopped his pacing and sat down. 'There's something else, isn't there?'

'I don't want you thinking we asked for it,' said his father, 'because we didn't.'

'That's right,' added his mother. 'We were thrilled just to get you.'

'You've lost me,' said Gary.

'When you arrived, a tiny scrap in a carrycot, we discovered a sum of money under the blanket.'

'How much money?'

'Two thousand pounds.'

'Nowadays, that would be a tidy sum,' said his father. 'In 1971, it was more cash than we could imagine.'

'Correct me if I'm wrong,' said Gary, 'but when babies were adopted illegally, was it not usually the adoptive family that handed over money?'

'Yes, but … we took it as further proof that they wanted the best for you. It also backed up Father Gleeson's statement that these were people of substantial means.'

'What were they? Bank robbers?'

His mother, whose crying had eased, gave a tepid smile. 'We also found a letter, saying the money was for your upkeep and for any little extras you needed along the way.'

'What did you do?'

'What the letter asked, of course. We spent it on you – and your sisters. Not all at once, obviously. It was wonderful to be able to give you the best of everything.'

'Such as?'

'Where do we begin?' replied his dad. 'Clothes and shoes; proper holidays, usually abroad; a great bicycle; music lessons and a quality guitar. And when you switched to playing bass, that was no problem either.'

A piercing pain had developed over Gary's eyes. 'I'd always assumed that we did okay because you both worked.'

'Take it from me,' said his mother, 'a part-time job as a school secretary doesn't pay for many luxuries. We were blessed to have that extra cash, and I'd like to think we made the most of it.'

'I'm ... I don't know what I am. Stunned, I guess.'

'We should have been honest with you when Allegra was sick. It was ... well, it all felt too ...'

'Shady?'

'Yes.'

'Have you ever wondered about my birth mother? From what you've told me today, everything happened quickly. Did she really have enough time to consider what she was doing? She gave away her baby with little chance of finding him again.'

'I think about her all the time. If she was at college then, she must be nearing seventy now.' His mother hesitated. 'I'm sorry that you've found out like this. We tried to do the right thing, but we didn't always succeed. I only wish we'd opened up about this a long time ago.'

Gary felt the remaining energy drain from his body. He attempted to drink his tea, but it had long since gone cold. His parents appeared far frailer than an hour before. His mother's cheeks had collapsed, and there was a grey sheen on his father's bald head. They asked if he'd stay for dinner, but he declined. He needed time on his own. That they'd had good intentions didn't matter. They'd lied to him — and lied again.

In the car, he tipped his head back against the headrest and closed his eyes. He'd wanted to be able to say, *Stop playing around. That type of thing didn't happen.* But it did. Over the past few months, he'd learnt that no story was too bizarre. No secret too dark. No cover-up too extreme. Children had been wiped from the record, and the practice hadn't been confined to institutions like Carrigbrack. Young women had given birth in nursing homes, and their babies had been spirited away.

Another thought hit him: the Adoption Authority was no longer an option. After all, what could he say to them? *Well, hello there. A wealthy family gave me away. They also placed a bribe in my carrycot and put my adoptive parents' names on the birth certificate. Obviously, all of this was completely illegal. Did they file any paperwork?*

It was unlikely he would ever find his birth mother. He would never know where the music had come from. Or whether Allegra's illness was hereditary.

His therapist wouldn't approve of the way he was framing what had happened. 'Is this the most appropriate response?' he would ask. 'Or is it overly negative?' Right now, however, it was the only response Gary had.

He decided to call Katie. She was entitled to know that their hunt had been futile.

It was only as he took out his phone that he remembered the message he'd spotted on the adoption forum. He squinted at the screen. There were eight missed calls: one from Frank, one from Allegra – and six from Beth.

Chapter 37

Ailish

In London that Saturday afternoon, Ailish was drinking tea with Chrissie and one of the women from the support group. Later, she was due to meet the rest of her family. She was dizzy with anticipation, examining photos of her half-sisters and brother, their partners and children until confident she could tell one from another.

She'd left Stevie at home in Kilmitten with instructions to spend the weekend studying. 'I'll be back on Sunday,' she'd said.

'Righto,' he'd replied. 'That gives me loads of time to clean up after the party.'

She wasn't fully sure he'd been joking and had to suppress images of the guards arriving while the house reeked of cannabis, drunken youngsters cavorted in the garden and the entire village was forced to listen to Stormzy.

Her deeper fear was that Keith would use her absence to get at Stevie. Although she had changed the locks, she worried he would worm his way in. That this was unlikely, and that Stevie was far more skilled at handling Keith than she had ever been, didn't make the fear go away. She'd consulted a solicitor about getting a legal separation and was determined not to backtrack.

Since her husband's departure (at what point, she wondered, could she call him her ex-husband?), she'd been able to think more clearly. With the crystal clarity of hindsight, she saw how Keith hadn't needed to assault her to ruin her life, or the lives of their children. Punching her in the face had been just another step in his campaign of intimidation. He'd controlled and humiliated her until she'd stopped recognising the harm he was doing. His malice had contaminated the house. Ailish had long dismissed talk about self-esteem as the preserve of the young and the self-absorbed. An indulgence for privileged girls who'd nothing to do and all day to do it. 'I'm busy putting food on the table,' she used to say. 'That's all I've time for.' How wrong she'd been.

She also saw now that Keith enjoyed arguing. It was how he came alive, and it was unlikely he would ever change. He had revelled in belittling her and preventing her from being herself. She couldn't imagine that he'd disappear and allow her to get on with her life. She discussed this with Katie and Chrissie. They encouraged her, urging her not to fret about things that might never happen.

All the same, there were times when Ailish felt adrift, as if all her moorings had been cut and her reference points erased.

The assault had left a dark bruise under one eye. While she'd tried to mask it with make-up, she'd only succeeded in making it more obvious. Her boss had called her in for a toe-curling meeting.

'I could make up a story,' Ailish had said, 'but I reckon you'd see through it. The truth is, my husband hit me. He's no longer in the house, so you needn't worry that it'll happen again.'

The boss, an officious young woman called Celia, had explained that while she had every sympathy for her employee's plight, a prestigious establishment like Rathtuskert Manor couldn't allow guests to encounter a housekeeper with a black eye.

'It's not the image we wish to convey,' she'd added.

'Make-up didn't work, and I can't clean the rooms in sunglasses,' said Ailish, fighting the urge to inform Celia that her empathy bypass had been a complete success.

'That's not what I'm suggesting. I'm asking you to take a few days away from work.' Celia paused. 'We will, of course, pay you during your absence.'

Ailish left the office feeling as if she'd done something wrong.

Since they'd last met, Chrissie's radiotherapy had finished, and she was getting stronger all the time. She was back doing work with the support group. 'The day I stop taking an interest is the day I'm in trouble,' she said.

She'd also invited one of the women, Gretta, to drop in while Ailish was there. 'I want to show you off,' she said. 'I hope you don't mind.'

Ailish didn't think anyone had ever said this to her before. 'Honestly,' she replied, 'you could invite every Irishwoman in London, and I'd be happy to meet them.'

Just as Gretta arrived, Ailish received a text from Gary. There was a strange post on the adoption forum, he said, and he'd be interested to know what she made of it. Her first impulse was to look it up and reply. Then she decided to wait. It would be rude to get distracted while Gretta was there. She could talk to Gary later. She still found it remarkable, and not a little odd, that he was interested in her point of view.

The previous week, she'd received a letter from the authorities to say they were working on her case. She'd written back to let them know they were too late. Chrissie had been found, she said, and all was well.

Gretta had also been in Carrigbrack, but not at the same time as Chrissie. Her life after the mother-and-baby home hadn't been easy. By the time she was twenty-five, she'd been married and divorced twice. In her thirties, she'd married again, but her husband, an alcoholic, had died from a sudden brain haemorrhage. Then she'd gone through what she called her 'sterile phase', shutting herself off from the world. It was only now, in her mid sixties, that she could call herself happy. She had friends like Chrissie, and she was in love with a quiet Welshman called Alun.

'I do enough talking for both of us,' she said.

Ailish could well believe it.

In advance of Gretta's visit, Chrissie had outlined her background. 'Her baby died shortly after birth,' she'd explained, 'and from time to time, she still gets emotional. She wasn't allowed to grieve, and it took her a long while to get to grips with that. She has two sons, but the daughter she lost is never far from her thoughts.'

Ailish figured Gretta must be the woman about whom Chrissie had spoken in the newspaper interview. The woman who'd been upset by one of those witless 'celebrity gushes about baby' interviews. One of the other notable things about her was that, shortly after her daughter's death, she'd run away. Very few women had managed to escape from the home, and in Carrigbrack circles she was a legend.

'I couldn't have returned to my parents' house,' she told Ailish as they drank their tea. 'They'd have marched me straight back to the home. Luckily, there was this one nun who was kind to me. She wrote to my sister, who was already over here, and between them they arranged my escape.'

Ailish picked up her teacup. 'It can't have been easy.'

'One of the nurses used to make a regular trip into Ennis, so I hid in the boot of her car. God love the woman, she hadn't a breeze. We'd fixed it so I'd be able to climb out when the car came to a stop. For fear someone might recognise me, I'd changed out of my uniform into the clothes I'd been wearing on the day I arrived. Oh, and I wore a wig belonging to one of the other girls. I can still smell the damn thing. From there, I got the bus to Dublin and the ferry to Holyhead. The whole time, I was petrified. I kept expecting to feel a hand on my shoulder, and to hear Agnes's cold voice saying, "Where do you think you're going?"'

'And your baby had died only a short while earlier?'

'Yes.' Gretta paused, rested her face in her palms then looked directly at Ailish. 'I can't say I've ever learnt to live with what happened. But I cope, and that's enough. I know what people think. They think it was only a short chapter in my life and I should've moved on. If only it was that straightforward.'

'People who speak like that haven't a clue,' said Chrissie.

Gretta took a mouthful of tea. 'In those days, moving to London was like moving to Mars. Once you arrived here, you didn't think you'd ever see home again. The way I looked at it, I could either hit the town or sit in the flat moping. So I went wild. Believe it or not, I was a pretty young thing back then.'

'Don't pay any heed to her,' said Chrissie with a grin. 'She's only looking for compliments.'

'As if,' said Gretta, with the rasping laugh of a long-time smoker.

If you asked Ailish, Gretta was beautiful, albeit in an offbeat way. The late afternoon sun cast a gentle glow over her face, highlighting her freckles rather than her wrinkles. She had shoulder-length silver hair and a wristful of bangles.

Despite the trauma she had suffered, she was spirited, entertaining, wise. She told other stories about her time in Carrigbrack, including an anecdote about the day the mothers had protested by refusing to stop singing. Her tales made Ailish stop and think. Although she should have known better, she'd tended to think of the women as one sad homogeneous group. That wasn't fair. Some had been gifted, some dull-witted, some hilarious, some kind. They'd been as gorgeous and glorious, as complex and difficult as any collection of young people.

Chrissie poured more tea. 'The nun who helped Gretta was the same woman who was good to me. Sister Eunice was her name.'

'No!' said Ailish. '*The* Sister Eunice? Did you know Katie and Beth met her only a few weeks ago?'

She explained that Eunice had left the religious life. She also told them about Brandon, the starchy American whose much younger wife had strong-armed him into meeting his twin.

'Isn't that a gas one?' said Gretta, whose speech was peppered with Irish words and phrases. 'Mighty', she'd said, 'grand, so' and 'get away out of that'. The fact that her accent no longer contained any trace of Ireland made the words strangely endearing.

Ailish took out her phone. 'I have a photo. Beth sent it to me. She's great at recording their successes. Do you want to see it?'

'I'd love to,' replied Gretta. 'We lost touch years ago. I've never forgotten her, though.'

'Bear with me a moment, and I'll get it for you.' Ailish scrolled through her photos before handing over the phone. 'Look, there she is with the twins, Brandon and Eddie. And there's Katie, too.'

Gretta studied the screen. She wrinkled her nose. 'Can I enlarge the picture?'

'Uh huh. Just tap it. Has Eunice – or Joyce, to use her real name – changed a lot?'

When she spoke again, Gretta's voice was thin. 'It's not Eunice I'm looking at.' She touched the screen. 'The other woman? You said her name was Katie?'

'That's right. It was through her that Chrissie and I were reunited. Well, through her and her niece. They're great women entirely. She was the one who kept the babies' bracelets. Why do you ask?'

'Was she originally from County Clare?'

'That's right. From Danganstown.' Ailish was confused. 'Have you come across her?'

'Yes, in Carrigbrack. She's someone else I've never forgotten.'

'I'm almost certain she only started work as a nurse after you'd left,' said Chrissie.

Gretta continued to stare at the photo. 'You're not following me. She wasn't a nurse. Not when I knew her. She was my friend.'

Chapter 38

Then, Patricia

Patricia had lost count of the number of times she'd been in Sister Agnes's office. She probably held some sort of record. By now, she could recite the title of every holy book on the shelves. She knew the scent of furniture polish and the slight creak of the heavy door. She also knew that, on the other side of Carrigbrack's high walls, the flowers were coming into bloom, the gentians and orchids popping up in gaps between the rocks. What she wouldn't give for a short walk through the Burren; for half an hour of birdsong, the perfumed breeze wrapping around her, the sun tickling her face. She promised herself that one day, when she was free, that was what she would do.

This meeting, she sensed, was different. The punishment wouldn't be short term. From the meagre amount she'd been able to gather, she was likely to be transferred to the mental hospital. That was often the fate of women considered to be untrustworthy or unpredictable. Once committed, it might be years before she saw the real world again.

With a wave of one pudgy hand, Agnes told her to sit down.

'Thank you, Sister.'

'You're very peaky. And thin as a scarecrow. Have you been eating? It's been two weeks since the unfortunate incident. There's no excuse for not eating.'

'I do my best, Sister.'

In truth, she felt a constant low-level nausea. Even fillet steak would have tasted like ash.

'The unfortunate incident' was Carrigbrack doublespeak for the night she'd almost died. Although she didn't know for sure that the others had been forbidden from mentioning it, she had her suspicions. If before that night she'd been unpopular, afterwards she was ostracised. She didn't mind; other people overwhelmed her. If she never used her voice again, it wouldn't bother her.

'Clearly, you need to try harder,' said Agnes. 'Have you been praying for guidance?'

'I have, Sister.'

'And has any wisdom been granted to you?'

'I think so.'

'Go on, then.'

Patricia raised her chin. The air around her appeared to quiver, like it would on the hottest day of summer. 'The boy to whom I gave birth has been accepted by a proper, loving family. It's right that he stays there and grows up with all the advantages of a legitimate child. I'm neither mentally nor morally capable of bringing him up. When I claimed otherwise, I was being selfish and immature.'

Agnes gave a single nod. 'I can see you've made progress.'

'Thank you, Sister.'

How much of her speech did Patricia believe? It didn't matter. She'd come to appreciate that people didn't want the truth. They wanted to be told they were right. Compliance worked. Deference was even more effective. All she had to do was tell them what they wanted to hear. Whether the words had any meaning for her was neither here nor there. Besides, even the smallest act of defiance would require more energy than she possessed.

She had loved Paul, but it hadn't been the right kind of love. It had been too intense. Too destructive. A line from her Leaving Cert English class came to mind: she had loved not wisely, but too well. She didn't, of course, share these thoughts with anyone. There was no point in confirming their suspicions that she was soft in the head.

No matter how often she told herself that yearning for her son was wrong, he pushed his way into her dreams. Every night, she woke to find herself whispering, 'Please go away.' She wished she could be scoured clean of her memories.

Agnes opened one of her desk drawers and took out a sheet of paper. 'One other matter: in the past, you expressed misguided notions about seeing the baby again. Do I take it you now accept that this would be wrong?'

'I do, Sister.'

'Very well. I have a form here. It may have been overlooked when he was adopted. I would appreciate it if you would sign it today.'

The form was headed *Certificate of Surrender*. Briefly, Patricia considered refusing to sign. But all that would do was create unnecessary rancour. Rancour she didn't have the strength for. She had been defeated.

'Thank you,' said Sister Agnes. 'Now, I have no wish to dwell on the unfortunate events except to say that they were extremely distressing for the community here in Carrigbrack.'

'I'm sorry.'

'As I understand it, this is what happened: you went to the nurses' office seeking pain relief. The nurse was called away. While this was unavoidable, she should have ensured that you had left the room. She should also have locked the door behind her. By that time, you were in agony. Not appreciating the consequences of your actions, you accidentally swallowed more tablets than your body could handle. At no point did you intend to do lasting harm to yourself. Had this been your intention, you would have committed one of the gravest sins possible, and I refuse to accept that any young woman who has received instruction here would be capable of such a sin.' She paused. 'Is that an accurate summary?'

Patricia looked down at the polished wooden floor. She wondered at the mental gymnastics that made it possible for Agnes to concoct – and believe – this version of events. 'It is, Sister,' she said.

Had she intended to die? Again, the answer wasn't straightforward. While her actions hadn't been premeditated, she would have been content to let go. She wouldn't have put up a fight. Also, if the circumstances arose again, she would probably do the same thing.

Her memories of the evening were jagged, half formed. She remembered lying on her bed, Paul's identity bracelet in her hand. Everything afterwards was a jumble of colours and sounds, of frantic voices and searing pain. Prominent among those voices was the woman who had found her: Sister Sabina.

Sabina, forever alert to breaches of the rules, had noticed that Patricia was missing. She'd tried several places before looking in the dormitory. Finding Patricia fully clothed and unconscious, she'd immediately raised the alarm. The nurse who'd left the office unattended had panicked, but her more senior colleague had known what to do. Somehow, she'd managed to force a tube up Patricia's nose and down her throat. Over the following hours, Patricia had retched and retched until there was nothing left inside her.

Even in her disorientated state, she'd been aware of arguments blazing around her. She'd heard a door slam. Then she'd heard sobbing. The nurse, she'd assumed.

When she was fully conscious, Agnes appeared. A deluge of questions followed. Patricia remained mute, and Agnes rounded on her. She was ungrateful, stupid, deranged, wicked. Did she know that Sister Sabina, a woman she had insulted and tormented, had saved her life? Did she understand how much distress she'd caused? Patricia, who still felt as if she was hovering between life and death, said, 'Sorry.' Her vocabulary was reduced to one word, and she said it repeatedly. She was genuinely sorry for creating a fuss and for getting the nurse into trouble. Otherwise, she couldn't claim to feel much of anything.

Later, she did as she was told and thanked Sister Sabina for coming to her aid.

'I did my duty, no more, no less,' Sabina replied. 'Hate the sin but not the sinner, that's what I say.'

Patricia regretted that it wasn't possible to choose the person who brought you back from the brink.

Only once in the following days did she cry. She was in the prayer room, where she'd been sent to beg for forgiveness, when Nancy found her.

'I saved this for you,' Nancy said.

It was Paul's wristband.

Patricia doubled over as if she'd been hit and wept until she had nothing left.

To her surprise, her parents were allowed to visit. True to form, there was no direct acknowledgement of what she'd done or how it might have ended. Her father told her that learning to endure was the mark of becoming an adult. If there was no softness in his speech, neither was there any scorn. Her mother, never robust, looked as if all the air had been let out of her. So determined was she not to mention the reason for their visit that she barely spoke at all. She spent more time lamenting the condition of her daughter's hair, which had grown back in a haphazard fashion, than she did talking about Paul. In her heart, Patricia knew her mother wasn't as shallow or unfeeling as she sounded. Rather, she was scared that a misplaced word would trigger a dramatic response. To avoid saying anything she would later regret, Patricia literally bit her tongue. She pushed her teeth in hard until her mouth filled with blood. Its coppery taste was oddly comforting.

Her parents did wish her a belated happy birthday. She'd been twenty-one the previous month. Like everything else in Carrigbrack, her birthday had not been celebrated.

Almost a year had passed since she'd entered the home. It felt more like ten years. A hundred years. She felt as though every part of her had atrophied. She could waste away. She could disappear.

Agnes drummed her fingers on the desk. 'So then, Patricia, your case presents a number of challenges. You have become a distraction to the other penitents, and it is, I fear, impossible for you to stay. However, neither can I permit you to return home as if nothing untoward has happened. You need further monitoring and guidance. Also, allowing you to leave with no consequences would send the wrong message to other girls.'

Patricia could guess the next part. She was being sent to the psychiatric hospital. Where once this prospect would have terrified her, now all she felt was a weary resignation. Shouldn't she feel more?

When she tuned back in, Sister Agnes's monologue had veered from its expected course.

'While life in Carrigbrack isn't easy,' she said, 'and nor should it be, there is scope for compassion. Having discussed your failings with my fellow sisters, we concluded that hard work would aid your spiritual rehabilitation. Like so many modern girls, you spend far too much time dwelling on your supposed rights and not enough on your responsibilities. To this end, Sister Eunice, a most enlightened young woman, has put forward a suggestion. Before your downfall, you were training to be a nurse, is that correct?'

'Yes, Sister, only I'm not certain …' Patricia came to a halt. She couldn't see where this was leading.

'Thankfully, the hospital authorities are unaware of the true reason for your sudden departure. Your parents, saints both, have made a number of enquiries, and it appears you can return to complete your training.'

For half a moment, Patricia wondered if she was being set free after all.

'Following that, you will come back to Carrigbrack and you will work here as a nurse for as long as I see fit. In that way, you can discharge your debt to the home.'

Patricia's mind was lumbering and slow, and she'd have liked time to consider the implications of Agnes's announcement. She wanted to feel something, yet, still, there was nothing there. 'When am I to leave?'

'This afternoon.'

'Thank you, Sister. Just one thought, though: won't it be strange for the other mothers if I come back as a nurse?'

'I don't envisage you returning before next summer, and 1970 seems to be rushing by at such speed that I'm sure the summer of 1971 will be here before we know it. I'm hopeful that by then all our current penitents will have moved on. Unless someone breaks a confidence, there's no reason why any of the new mothers should know your history.'

'I understand.'

'I should have stated that, as you'll be here in a professional capacity, you'll be known by your original name. It's Kathleen, isn't it?'

For the first time, she looked Agnes in the eye. 'People call me Katie,' she said.

Chapter 39

Now, Katie

Why?

The same word over and over again.

Why bother with other people when you should have been looking for your own son? Why wasn't he your top priority? Why live a life of secrecy? And most of all: why didn't you tell us?

Katie had known that something was up when Beth disappeared without saying where she was going. Two hours later, she'd returned with Gary. They'd been gentle at first, reticent even. Their queries centred on a message board post. Gradually, the questions acquired more edge. Beth, in particular, used words like 'deception' and 'devastated'. One moment, she crackled with anger. The next, she was downcast, barely able to articulate her thoughts. Her reaction was understandable. Katie had let her down.

'Strangely enough,' Katie heard herself say, 'it's fifty years this week since I first arrived in Carrigbrack: April 1969. If you'd told me then that all these years later it would still be part of my life, I'd have …'

Her voice trailed away. When she was twenty, she wouldn't have cared about what might happen when she was seventy. Seventy had been beyond her imagination. That was the blessing, and curse, of being young: you could only see short term.

They were in the sitting room, Beth and Gary on the sofa, Katie in the armchair beside the fireplace. They'd been here for more than an hour. She'd done most of the talking. She could have claimed ignorance. She could have said, 'Nope, means nothing to me.' But that would have been a lie too far. Besides, one look at the post, and her entire body had trembled. She'd known exactly what it meant. And Beth and Gary weren't stupid. She was cornered.

Slowly, methodically, she'd brought them through her time in Carrigbrack. Her first time, that was. They'd already known about her second spell in the home. She'd told them all about Paul, the day he arrived and the day he disappeared. She hadn't stopped there. Perhaps they hadn't needed to hear about her job in the laundry, or the day she'd had her hair cut off, or Diane's burial. Perhaps they hadn't needed to hear about Sabina or Winnie. Or Mike, for that matter. Once she had started, however, she'd been compelled to continue. Memories she'd thought were buried kept rising up in front of her.

Now, she wanted the two of them to leave. She wanted to be alone so she could mull over the forum in peace. She wanted space to consider her response. But neither showed any sign of going, and she could hardly blame them. In the same circumstances, she would have had a million questions.

Beth hugged a cushion to her chest. 'What I can't get my head around is why your parents agreed to send you back to Carrigbrack. You'd obviously had a breakdown. You'd attempted to kill yourself, for God's sake. Why didn't they say, "No, she's been through enough. Let her go."'

'They were dutiful people,' replied Katie, knowing how inadequate this must sound. 'I presume they didn't see an alternative. I remember my father telling me that when it got difficult, I'd have to offer up my suffering for the souls in purgatory.'

She didn't add that her parents' house had quickly become her personal purgatory. She hadn't been allowed to leave a room without one of them asking where she was going and what she intended to do there. By contrast, the nurses' home was pure heaven. Always hanging over her, though, was the knowledge that when her training finished, she would have to return to Carrigbrack.

'Why didn't you refuse Agnes's rotten deal?' asked Beth. 'Or, if you weren't brave enough to stand up to your mam and dad, why didn't you simply run away?'

That word again. Why? Why? Why?

'Beth, love, it was far from simple. For starters, I'd hurt them enough. Plus, I was completely flattened by the experience. Even a year later, I'd no more energy than the day I left Carrigbrack. Eventually, that changed. By the time Johnny arrived, I was ready to make my move.'

Gary scratched his stubble. He looked as worn out as Katie felt. 'I haven't met Eunice, or Joyce as I suppose I should call her, but according to everything you've said, she's a good woman. Why would she come up with a plan that forced you back to that godawful home? That was inhuman.'

'Not if you consider the alternative. She thought I was about to be sent to the psychiatric hospital. She was trying to make sure that didn't happen. She was taken aback when I returned. She'd been convinced that, given the chance, I'd run off and renege on the deal.'

'What about my mother?' asked Beth. 'How much did she know about what was going on?'

'It's not my place to—'

Beth shot up as though spring-loaded. 'For God's sake, Katie, did she know or didn't she?'

'I doubt she was fully in the picture at that stage. She was only a child. But later? Yes, she knew where I'd been and why I'd been sent there.'

'No wonder she flew into a tizzy when we told her about the bracelets.'

Katie didn't reply. The situation was difficult enough without whipping up further friction between Beth and Margo.

Back in 1969, when Katie had broken the news of her pregnancy, Margo had been eleven years old. Their parents had dispatched her to a relative so they could deal with the situation in secret. She must, though, have asked questions. Five years later, she'd told Katie that while she knew the truth, she would never say anything. 'The scandal would kill Mam and Dad,' she'd explained. To the best of Katie's knowledge, the only person she'd ever confided in was Con. Until last Christmas, the name 'Carrigbrack' had rarely been spoken.

Outside, the sky was an ugly pewter grey. A steady drizzle was falling. You could always rely on the rain. Some people thought of it as beautiful. Katie wasn't among them. She'd seen too much of it.

The silence stretched and grew uneasy until it was broken by Gary. 'Where does Johnny fit into this?' he asked. 'Did he know?'

'Everything I've said about him is true. We first met in Lahinch in the summer of 1972. When we met again, I'd been through a bad few days. Agnes was being extra pernickety with me, and I was taking out my frustration on the mothers. I felt wretched about it. I couldn't stop myself from telling Johnny. He gave the obvious response: "Why don't you leave?" I flimmed and flammed until, finally, I told him the full story. I remember thinking, he's going to walk away. Even so, it was a relief to have unburdened myself to someone. To my great surprise, he was sympathetic. More than that, he was angry on my behalf. "We've got to get you out of there, Kateser," he said. I'll never forget those words. The third time we met, he proposed.'

'And did you go to Sister Agnes and hand in your notice?'

'It wasn't that straightforward. When I asked, she told me I couldn't leave. The nurse who'd been there the night I took the overdose was gone. The midwife was due to retire. And, as you can imagine, young women weren't exactly queuing up to work in Carrigbrack. Johnny went to see her. He explained that we were engaged to be married, and still she said no. She claimed I hadn't yet paid my debt to the home. Johnny, bless him, guessed that Agnes wouldn't fancy being on the wrong side of the law. So a couple of weeks later, he put on a plummy accent and called her pretending to be a solicitor. He invented all manner of legal mumbo-jumbo about my continued presence in Carrigbrack breaking some law or other. I didn't think she'd fall for it, but she did. I left just before Christmas, and we got married shortly afterwards.'

'How did your parents react?' asked Gary.

'Mam was the more sympathetic of the two. Left to her own devices, she'd probably have come to the wedding. There was no reasoning with Dad, though. As time went by, Mam thawed further towards Johnny. It was hard not to. But Dad? I don't think he ever accepted the way I left Carrigbrack. And that meant he never accepted Johnny.'

'Far be it from me to side with your father,' said Beth, 'but was marrying someone you hardly knew not a bit risky?'

'I knew enough. I knew he was kind.'

'Is kindness sufficient reason to marry someone?'

'There are far flimsier ones.'

'I don't remember Grandad very clearly,' said Beth. 'I was only six when he died, and Mam doesn't say much about him.'

'He was … of his time.'

To say that Katie's parents had lived limited lives sounded unkind. That didn't make it untrue. Their existence had been stunted by poverty and blind deference to authority. Oh, she knew that others had challenged those constraints. Not everyone had tugged the forelock. But the O'Deas had possessed neither the gumption nor the imagination to defy Sister Agnes. They'd been waiting for the meek to inherit the earth.

Beth punched the top of her head, as though the bizarre nature of the conversation – and the scale of Katie's duplicity – had only just struck her. 'This is insane,' she said. 'Beyond insane. And we're still none the wiser as to why you decided to forget about Paul.'

Katie did her best to sound calm. 'I never forgot about him. You can say anything else about me, but that's not fair.'

'But can you not see, Katie, that none of this makes sense? We've spent six months trying to unite mothers with their children. And despite having scores of opportunities, you never mentioned Paul. You never said, "This is why it matters to me." Surely you can understand why I'm upset?'

Before she could answer, Gary intervened. 'Listen,' he said, 'I've had a rough day. I can appreciate your feelings, Beth, but for my sake can we step back from the family argument? We still don't have the full story. Katie, why don't you tell us what happened after you and Johnny got married?'

Although Beth pulled a face, she stayed quiet.

'No matter that Paul was always in my thoughts,' Katie said, 'I'd come to accept that he was no longer mine.' She hesitated before continuing. She doubted that either Beth or Gary would understand her reasoning. 'Johnny's family were in many ways more outgoing … more generous … than mine, but they were traditional too. Hearing that I'd already had a child would have coloured their view of me – and not in a good way. The rules were explicit in Carrigbrack. Outside, they may have been less clearly stated, but they were there all the same. Johnny and I agreed that we'd move on and have a family of our own. And I thought, yes, let's put the past behind us.'

'Did you really think that would be possible?' asked Beth.

'I don't know. In my defence, I was only twenty-three. And I wanted it to be possible.'

In the beginning, Katie had hated claiming not to have children. Denying Paul had felt wrong. After a while, it had become easier. There were times when she forgot she was lying. She consoled herself with the knowledge that nobody showed their true self to the world. Who chose to parade their wounds? Even today, when honesty was supposed to be prized, how many women devoted a large part of their lives to constructing an idealised version of themselves?

'I remember telling you about Gráinne Holland,' said Gary, 'and the way she'd cut her son out of her life. At the time, I thought you were too charitable towards her. Now, I understand why you said what you did.'

His tone was flat, and Katie realised that his view of her would never be the same. Fleetingly, she recalled the last time he'd been in this room, when he'd spoken about Shanna Ellis's death. She wished she could rewind to that night. Back then, she'd still had the chance to tell her own story in her own way.

'I didn't cut my son out of my life,' she said. 'He was taken from me, and I had to deal with that. As I said to Beth, I never stopped thinking about him.'

And that's what I want to do now, she thought. Please go, so I can have the space I need. Please.

She bent down and picked up the red box. She'd been looking through it when they arrived. There were only nine identity bands left. Well, nine plus one. She removed the plus-one and handed it to Gary.

'Boy,' he read, 'Paul. Eighteenth of August 1969. Ten pounds four ounces. Mother: Patricia.' He sighed and passed the bracelet to Beth. 'Another Paul.'

'My cousin,' she said, as she examined the tiny letters.

'I hadn't thought of him like that,' said Katie.

'There's a lot you haven't thought of, though I can understand why you guarded the box so carefully. If I'd seen its contents, I'd have asked why one of the bracelets was different. God, I feel like such a mug.'

Katie took back Paul's identity band and returned it to the red box. She knew what it was like when everyone pretended your baby didn't exist. She knew what it was like to collude in a lie. That was why she'd kept the bracelets. They told the truth.

Beth had another question. 'Are you sure you weren't coerced by Johnny? Like, if it was up to you – and you alone – would you have looked for Paul?'

'The decisions we took, we took together. If anything, I was the one who was more anxious to push on. You've got to understand, I … I'd had to try and rebuild myself. To start again as though I'd never had a baby. I also felt that, whatever I'd chosen to do, someone would have found fault. To this day, there are plenty of people who judge women mainly by the number of children they have. That number is always either too many or too few. And some of the sharpest, smuggest critics are other women. You know that better than anyone.' She looked at her niece, hoping to find common ground while fearing it was too late.

Beth bit her lip. 'When you and Johnny didn't have children, did you not reconsider?'

It had taken Katie several years to accept that what had happened by accident with Mike wasn't going to happen with the man she loved. In those days, medical attitudes to infertility had been less sympathetic. In some cases, a lot less sympathetic. One doctor had sat in front of Katie, picked a crumb from his moustache and announced that the fault must be hers. She hadn't been able to stop herself from revealing that, out there somewhere, she had a seven-year-old son. You'd swear the devil had popped up in front of him. 'Well,' he'd said, in his south Dublin drawl, 'you'll know all about adoption, then.'

Bruised by that experience, Katie and Johnny had left it a while before seeking help again. They saw a specialist who decided there was no obvious problem with either of them. They were just unlucky. 'It happens,' he said. Nowadays, in the same circumstances, they would have been able to try IVF. But in the early 1980s, IVF wasn't available in Ireland. Over the years, they tried everything: every tip, remedy and old wife's tale. They tried being clinical, they tried being lackadaisical. Finally, when Katie was forty, she discovered she was pregnant. Thrilled – and scared – they kept the news to themselves. After almost five months, she suffered a miscarriage.

Her baby would have been twenty-nine now, the same age as Beth. She remembered going to Beth's christening and forcing herself to pretend that everything was great.

Katie had learnt then that there were myriad ways in which life could be cruel. Twice, a much-wanted child had been wrenched from her. Later, she decided that if life had punished her, it had also been kind. It had given her Johnny. And, when she'd needed a friend, it had given her Beth. She considered explaining all of this, then decided that some of it was too personal.

'Did I have a change of heart about looking for Paul?' she said. 'By then, he felt more distant. I'd already missed too much. I'd missed his first tooth and his first steps. I hadn't been there when he started school and made friends and learnt to read. I hadn't been there when he needed me. Also, and I don't have to explain this to either of you, I doubted I'd be able to find him. The nuns still had all the files, and there was no chance of them giving me any details. When I was working in Carrigbrack, I considered attempting to find my file. But I was terrified what would happen if Agnes caught me.'

Beth gave a look Katie had seen many times before. In the past, it had been reserved for those who'd written to the Carrigbrack Nurse account with half-baked theories about the women who'd given birth there or the nuns who'd been in charge. It was a look of impatience mixed with bewilderment.

'I still can't understand why you didn't come clean to any of us,' she said. 'Seriously, aside from Mam, who was going to be upset with you for telling your own story? You've spent six months listening to other people talking about their lives. How could you not want to talk about what happened to you?'

Four days before he died, Johnny had asked if she regretted not searching for Paul. At the time, he'd been propped up on a bank of pillows, his eyes sticky, his face the colour of a wizened Golden Delicious. She'd looked at him, noble and good-natured despite his suffering, and squeezed his papery hand. 'No,' she'd lied. She'd hoped he would urge her to find her son, but the conversation had meandered on to another subject.

'I couldn't say anything after Johnny died. It would have felt disloyal. We'd made a decision together. If I'd wanted to change my mind, I should have done it while he was alive. And, like I've told you, he wouldn't have had any difficulty with that. At the same time, I kept looking at the bracelets and I knew I had to do something. Then you came on board, and the whole exercise took off in a way I hadn't expected. Everyone we met was so interesting, and I felt so useful.' She folded her hands neatly, one over the other. 'I'm sorry that you haven't had any success yet, Gary. You will, though.'

'I probably won't,' he said, 'only that's another story.'

Katie wanted to ask how he could be so sure, but this wasn't the time. She'd concluded that his bracelet must be one of those she hadn't been able to collect.

'Nothing you've said explains why you didn't prioritise Paul,' said Beth. 'I can sort of understand why you were reluctant before. I get that you'd been damaged. But now? When you'd seen the joy of other reunions? When you'd witnessed how Ailish's life had been transformed? Why couldn't you cast aside the secrecy and go for it?'

And there it was, the thorniest *why* of all. There was no logical answer, nothing she could say that would satisfy her niece. If she had to pick an explanation, it was this: she hadn't been brave enough. She'd been scared that Paul wouldn't be interested in her. Scared that she'd be a disappointment to him. Scared that he'd be a disappointment to her. What if the real Paul bore no resemblance to the man in her imagination? What if he was unkind? Arrogant? Mean? What if they met once and didn't like each other? What if she couldn't find him? What if he was dead?

In there too was something she didn't like acknowledging: a deep ingrained shame. The logical part of her knew this was wrong. How many times had she told others they had nothing to be ashamed of? And yet she couldn't lose the feeling that, all those years ago, she'd messed up and let people down. She hadn't been a fit mother.

'It felt safer like this,' was all she said.

'What about when you began contacting others, like Rita Farragher – and Joyce? They knew you as both Patricia and Katie. Surely you must have worried the truth would come out?'

'I asked Joyce not to mention Paul. Robyn and Brandon didn't know anything about him, I said, and it would be awkward if they were ambushed by the news. I told her that I'd been trying to trace him. When it became apparent that you didn't know about him either, she was … I won't say angry, but concerned. That's why she's been calling me.'

Katie hadn't returned Joyce's calls. That was something else she needed to rectify.

'I used to wonder,' said Beth, 'why there were times when you struggled to cope with what was happening around us. Like, I remember how quiet you were on the day Brandon and Eddie met. I assumed it was because you felt guilty about working in Carrigbrack. Or because you'd never had children of your own. Or even because you were missing Johnny. If only I'd known the truth.'

Gary peered at his phone, which had been buzzing insistently for most of the evening. Was it still evening? There was no clock in the room, and Katie hadn't dared look at her watch. It was black outside now, and rain was throwing itself at the sitting room window. Cars made a skeetering sound as they sped along Griffin Road. It could be any time between eight o'clock and two in the morning.

'Ailish is looking for me,' he said. 'I'm going out to the hall to talk to her. I asked her to run an eye over the message board. She deserves to know what's going on.'

Katie hadn't realised that he'd remained in touch with Ailish. 'Did you speak to anyone else?' she asked.

'No,' he replied, his voice suggesting that the question offended him.

Announcing that she wanted a drink, Beth disappeared into the kitchen.

Katie drew the curtains before taking the opportunity to pull out her phone and re-examine the message. Not that she needed to see it again. It was him. It had to be.

Hi. My name is Luke. I was born in Carrigbrack in August 1969 and adopted through the St Saviour's agency. I grew up in Dublin and still live here. My adoptive mother and father have been brilliant, and until recently I didn't feel the need to track down my birth parents. But you know the way it is, you get older, your own kids start asking questions, and you decide the time has come to find out more. As many of you will know, the Carrigbrack files are a disaster. Mine are even more puzzling than usual. The records show that my original name was Paul. The problem is, my birth mother's name was scratched out. There is, though, a later note to say that she returned to Carrigbrack – to work – in the summer of 1971. Luckily, I was able to find my birth cert in the register office. It told me that she was from a village in east Clare. It also gave her full name. Obviously, I won't include it here, but her initials are KOD. My dilemma is this: somebody went to the trouble of trying to conceal her identity. So should I leave her alone? Or should I try to contact her?

Katie considered his name: Luke, one of the four Evangelists. Did it mean his adoptive parents were religious? Or had they simply liked the name? She was comforted by the fact that he described them as brilliant. She would hate to think that, like Ailish, he'd grown up in a cold house. Almost fifty years later, he was still wrapped around her heart.

Re-reading the post cemented a feeling she'd had earlier. Luke had guessed she was 'Carrigbrack Nurse'. He was attempting to smoke her out. Otherwise, why make her identity clear? This prompted another question: was he upset by what she'd done? Did he, too, wonder why he hadn't been top of her list?

From the kitchen, she heard Beth stamping and sloshing. If it was possible to pour wine aggressively, that was what her niece was doing. Katie thought of all the work they'd done together. All the emails. All the conversations and journeys. She couldn't blame Beth for lashing out.

She tried to eavesdrop on Gary, but picked up only the occasional word. It sounded as though Ailish was doing most of the talking.

Beth returned and handed her a glass of wine. Katie hoped this was a positive sign, an indication that they could talk this through.

'I was at school with Mike Langan's granddaughter,' said Beth. 'Her name's Bronagh. Mam never had a good word to say about the family. She claimed they were trashy. Of course, I thought she was being a snob. Little did I know what was actually going on.'

Katie took a sip of her drink. It tasted like turpentine. 'I spotted him at the back of the church on Christmas Day. It's odd to think he's almost eighty. Vera's a long time dead. A stroke, I think.'

'Do you ever speak to him?'

'No. What would we say?'

'You could talk about what happened between you. You could talk about your son.'

'It's far too late for that. I met him shortly after I left the home. He asked how I was, like I'd had the flu or something. I … I couldn't bring myself to talk. I can see now that I was too depressed to handle the situation. We never spoke again. I gather there were other women along the way.'

At the time, Katie had been trying to focus on her nursing training, hoping that something might prevent her return to Carrigbrack. Every day had been a struggle.

Beth ran a finger around the rim of her wine glass. 'Did anyone else in the village know?'

'A few may have had their suspicions, but only one person knew for sure. Mam confided in one of her sisters, your great-aunt Esther. You wouldn't remember her. She provided the wig.'

'I see.'

'And I suppose it's possible that Mike told Vera.'

'Possible but unlikely. Now that I think about it, Mam may have muttered something about him being a womaniser.'

'I haven't always been fair to Margo. Growing up, she can't have had an easy time of it. At least she was a daughter Mam and Dad could be proud of.'

'Was she really?' said Beth.

'They don't come much more respectable than your mother. She was everything they wanted.'

'I don't think of her like that at all. The more I hear about your parents, the more I reckon they would have disapproved of her life.

They sound like simple, frugal people whereas Mam has a mania for material perfection. In a way, spending has been her rebellion.'

Katie had never looked at it that way. With hindsight, however, she could see how Carrigbrack had also helped to shape Margo's life. If nothing else, it had given her a heightened fear of the judgement of others. She was about to say as much when Gary returned. He sat down, placed his elbows on his knees and rested his face in his hands. For a minute, maybe more, he said nothing.

'Is something wrong?' asked Beth, before quickly revising her question. 'Well, obviously, everything's wrong, but is Ailish okay?'

'Uh huh. She spent most of the day with another woman who'd been in Carrigbrack. A woman called Gretta.' He looked at Katie with questioning eyebrows.

'Winnie?' she whispered, scarcely believing what he'd said.

'Uh huh.'

'How is she?'

'Good. Shocked to find you like this, but good.'

Gary passed on what Ailish had told him. Beth offered no opinion on Gretta. While Gary and Katie spoke, she drank her wine and stared at her hands. In opening the box, Katie had always known that the truth might emerge. And, in the deepest crevices of her brain, hadn't that been what she'd wanted? Hadn't she hoped that, one way or another, the bracelets would lead her back to her son? Along the way, she'd been surprised that no one had guessed her history. Some days her injuries had felt so visible she might as well have been covered in scars. What she hadn't foreseen was that she'd grow to love Beth like a daughter.

'Can I ask you about something else?' said Beth. 'Your reluctance to extend the search – was that because you were scared someone might recognise you from your first stint in Carrigbrack?'

Katie had dreaded this question. 'Yes.'

'Right, so some of those on the message board – and I'm thinking in particular of the people born in 1969 and 1970 – you might have been able to provide them with information?'

'Yes.'

'Did any of the stories sound familiar?'

'The man who believed his birth mother was from Limerick? I have a feeling his original name was Lorcan. In the home, his mother was called Jacinta. Her real name was Marian Purcell and she was from the Ennis Road.'

Apart from the tap of rain against the window, the room was silent. When, finally, Beth spoke again, her tone was firm. 'He's the guy who was sick. He was frantic, and you didn't help him.'

'I should have done.' Katie wanted to cry but knew she had no right. 'I'll contact him tomorrow.'

'What if it's too late?'

Gary, who appeared increasingly uncomfortable, went to say something.

Beth stopped him. 'Were there any others?' she asked.

'There's a message from a woman who lives in South Africa. From the details she provided, I'm nearly certain that, in Carrigbrack, her mother was called Imelda. She looked after the babies at night. She was very kind.'

Katie shut her eyes. She was determined the tears wouldn't escape. When she opened them, her niece was rocking back and forth, her face rigid with distress.

'A great wrong was done to you, Katie,' she said. 'You should have been allowed to keep Paul. You would have been a wonderful mother. But—'

'Maybe we should leave this for tonight,' said Gary. 'Maybe we should talk about it tomorrow after we've had time to consider everything.'

'No,' said Beth, her voice vibrating. 'Katie, I feel sorry for you, you've got to believe that. But what happened back then doesn't excuse the way you've behaved over the past few months. I mean, I thought you were a heroine. There you were, a woman doing a good thing when you didn't have to. I watched how you connected with people and how you seemed to care about them. But you lied to me. And to them. And then there were the folks you could have helped, people who were desperate, and you did nothing. It's all such a mess. Do you not see that?'

Katie felt as if a canyon was opening between them. 'Please, pet, don't judge me too harshly. You can't—'

Beth raised a hand as though directing traffic. 'I'm trying not to judge, but I can't help how I feel. I understand what it's like not to get on with your family. I understand what it's like to feel different and to be on the outside. I was honest with you. I told you all about myself. You could have been honest with me. You had chance after chance, and yet I had to find out the truth from an internet forum.'

Katie recoiled at the strength of her words. 'Please …' she started.

Beth got to her feet. 'Listen, I need some time to think about this. Everything we did together feels so different now.'

'I'm very sorry, Beth. I was entirely in the wrong. I admit that. Please don't leave.'

Gary also urged her not to go. 'This is a shock,' he said, 'but don't walk out like this. If you don't want to spend the night here, you can stay with me.'

She was at the door. 'I'll collect my belongings and give you back your key in the morning.'

Katie realised that the more she pleaded, the more she was likely to irritate her niece. Instead, she tried to focus on practicalities. 'It's lashing rain, and you've been drinking. You can't drive and you can't walk anywhere in this. You—'

Beth was already gone.

Chapter 40

Katie

His full name was Luke Patrick Flannery. He was six-foot-ish with toffee-brown eyes and dark hair stippled with grey. He was married to Jen and they had two daughters, Róisín and Sadie. They owned a dog called Ben. Luke worked as a probation officer, and when he spoke, he tended to lean in as if explaining the merits of a crime-free life to a freshly released prisoner. He'd played Gaelic football (but not very well) and would like to write crime novels ('Believe me, I have lots of stories').

He'd been seven when his parents told him about his original mother and father. The other mam and dad had loved him, they said, but hadn't been able to keep him.

'Like Tatters?' he'd asked, and they'd agreed.

Tatters was the Flannerys' black-and-white cat. The previous spring she'd had five gorgeous squirmy kittens. Luke and his sisters had wanted to keep them, but, one by one, their eyes still blue and their miaow barely audible, they'd found new homes. For a day or two, Tatters had looked everywhere for her brood. She'd unleashed a tirade of mewls at Luke's mother, as if to say, *Where have you put them?* His mam had gone to Quinnsworth for a tin of rabbit-flavoured Whiskas (the cat's favourite). Two hours later, the kittens had been forgotten.

While Luke's amnesia hadn't been quite as severe as Tatters', neither had he obsessed about the people who'd given him away. His parents had been great and, apart from one secondary school knuckle-dragger, no one had given him a hard time about being adopted. He'd tried to live most of his life in the moment, allowing the past and the future to take care of themselves. 'I was practising mindfulness before it became popular or profitable,' he liked to say.

Then he got older.

People started talking about mother-and-baby homes. His wife and daughters asked questions. He read and he listened. He saw that the past wasn't a foreign country; its repercussions were all around. Well, he'd already known that. How many prisoners had fathers and grandfathers who'd also served time? What began as mild curiosity grew into a burning need to find out where he'd come from.

He decided to trace his birth mother.

There was one other fact about Luke, a fact that turned Katie upside down and inside out: he'd spent most of his life within a couple of miles of Griffin Road. For the past decade, he'd been closer still. The Flannery family lived only a handful of streets away. They shopped in the same supermarket as Katie, used the same post office, caught the same bus. There was every chance that Luke and Katie had stood side by side in a queue or passed in the street. They might well have greeted each other with a generic comment about the weather. She might have admired his dog.

Should I have recognised him? she thought. But she hadn't been looking. She'd expected him to be in the west of Ireland or America or Australia, not within touching distance. She wished there'd been a tracking device, a GPS of the heart, something that could have alerted her to his presence. But even science fiction hadn't allowed for such an invention.

The day after the confrontation with Beth and Gary, Katie had replied to Luke's message, asking him to contact her via the Carrigbrack Nurse email. Her hunch had been correct: he was on her trail. One of the others on the message board had revealed that the woman sending out identity bracelets was called Katie. The dates she'd worked in Carrigbrack tallied with the information he'd received about his birth mother.

'I was putting two and two together and getting who-knew-what,' he said, 'but I thought it was worth a shot.'

'You could have emailed me directly and asked if I was the right Katie O'Dea.'

'I considered it. What if I'd been wrong, though? Putting the request out there was easier. I was giving you some leeway. If you were the right woman, and you wanted to contact me, so be it. If I hadn't heard from you, I would have tried something else.'

Of course, he'd been flummoxed by the fact that she'd helped others yet hadn't attempted to trace her own son. She'd done her best to explain. What she'd said hardly deviated from what she'd told Beth and Gary, yet it had felt different. Context was all, she supposed. It probably helped that Luke spent his working life dealing with people whose behaviour made little sense. Whatever the reason, he accepted her explanation.

Everything she knew about Luke she had garnered from two emails and two long phone calls. Despite their proximity, they had held back from meeting in person. Katie didn't know how he felt, but she was nervous. Part of her longed to see him. Another part felt as if she was trespassing. At the end of the second call, they arranged to go for tea in the Gresham Hotel, the place where she'd first met Gary. It was where her mission had begun and where it was likely to end. Several weeks had passed since the Carrigbrack Nurse account had received a genuine query. Should one arrive, Katie would have to help, but she wasn't sure she possessed either the heart or the drive. It had been a job for two people, and the other half of the team was gone.

She'd contacted Rory, the man she believed to be Jacinta's son, and Lynette, the woman she believed to be Imelda's daughter. Thankfully, Rory's health had improved a little. While both had been grateful for the information, neither had yet found their birth mother.

She spotted Luke as soon as he entered the lobby. True, she was helped by the photos he'd sent, but there was more to it than that. There was a familiar bounce to his walk, a familiar cowlick at his left temple. He was Mike Langan's son all right. As he got closer, she saw that she was there too, in his round eyes and thin nose. For a moment, she felt as if every sound was amplified, as if she was breathing different air. Her heart took off: *rat-tat-tat-tat-tat*. She wanted to examine every hair on his head, every line she hadn't been able to watch develop. How absurd was it that she'd never seen his childhood face, his teenage face, his face on the day he'd got married? She didn't know how he'd done at school, whether he'd ever been ill, how he liked his coffee, how he voted.

Two arms enveloped her, the embrace tighter than she'd expected. Tighter, perhaps, than she deserved.

'My boy,' she said, 'my boy.'

In an instant, every promise she'd made to herself flew away. She'd pledged not to get emotional, not to make him uncomfortable. But as soon as she touched him, those pledges evaporated. He was there and he was real. No longer just a memory, no longer just a sliver of paper in a box.

As they drank their tea, they exchanged pieces of personal information. Katie told herself to savour every moment. He might not want to maintain contact. There might not be room for her in his life. All the same, her mind kept flashing back to the last time she'd seen him. He'd been completely dependent on her then. Or so she'd thought.

'The girls are dying to meet you,' he said.

'Really?' It was the first time he'd mentioned meeting the rest of the family. She felt a burst of pure, uncut joy. Then, a tiny voice at the back of her head warned against getting carried away. She'd urged other people to move slowly, and that was what she ought to do too.

'Yes,' he said. 'Sadie in particular. She's fourteen and feels very strongly about everything.'

'Didn't we all at that age?'

'True, only because of what happened to you, well … she views you as a heroine.'

'Oh, dear. I hope I don't disappoint her. I don't think anyone could call me a heroine.' Beth had used the same word, and Beth had been wrong.

Oh, Beth.

'That's not how Sadie sees it. She has a list of questions for you. But don't let that put you off. Jen was wondering if you'd like to visit next weekend. Or if that would be too soon, that's fine. I mean, you don't—'

'Next weekend would be wonderful.'

Luke smiled. Katie was pleased that his smile belonged neither to her nor to Mike Langan. It was entirely his own.

'I thought you might like to see these,' he said, reaching into his jacket and removing a wallet of photographs. 'I know I emailed you some photos, but they're much better like this, aren't they?'

Katie shuffled through the pictures, shaking her head and exclaiming as she went. There he was: with an uncertain smile on his communion day; with a terrible haircut as a teenager; goofing about on a caravan holiday in Wexford; laughing during a snowstorm. And there was the rest of the family: his parents with their generation's trademark diffidence; his sisters, their hair as blonde as his was dark. And there were his daughters, her granddaughters: pretty little things with the waterfall hair and caterpillar eyebrows that all the girls favoured nowadays.

'I'm overwhelmed,' she said. 'Thank you for showing me these.'

Luke ran his hands along his thighs. 'I meant to say that Beth is welcome to come with you next weekend, if she wants to. I know she helped you with the bracelets and I'd love to meet her. We all would.'

'Ah. That mightn't be possible. She lived with me for a while. She's moved on, though. I don't know if she's around. I could check …'

She couldn't check because she didn't know where to find Beth. Her niece had left without saying where she was going. She didn't return Katie's calls or reply to her emails. Katie had written to express her regret and to let Beth know she loved her and was desperate to rekindle their friendship. *Of all the mistakes I've made, not being honest with you was the greatest*, she wrote. She'd sent the letter to Beth's work address. The following week, it had returned unopened.

Margo's reaction had been unexpectedly restrained. Even her 'I told you so's had lacked their usual bite. 'I did warn you,' she said, her speech punctuated by tuts and sighs, 'but you didn't listen. As soon as you started delving into other people's stories, it was likely that yours would be revealed. Still, I've thought about this, and it doesn't really matter now, does it? The world has changed. To be blunt, nobody cares about these things any more.'

It did matter. It mattered to Beth – and to Katie. She couldn't bear the silence. She couldn't bear knowing that Beth was out there, hurt and angry. She hadn't expected the high of finding her son to be offset by the low of losing her friend. She also found herself becoming irritated by Margo's laissez-faire attitude. *Nobody cares about these things any more.* What was Katie supposed to do? What were all the women supposed to do? Shrug their shoulders and say,

'Everything's fine now because society has decided we weren't filthy harlots after all?'

'It matters,' she'd found herself shouting at the kitchen sink.

Who would dare to tell Gretta it didn't matter? Gretta, who'd been forced back to work three days after her baby's death. Gretta, who'd fled to London at the age of sixteen because her own family would have returned her to Carrigbrack.

'I owe you a wig,' had been the first thing she'd said when Katie had called, immediately dispelling fears that they'd struggle to find common ground. Fifty years ago, they'd known each other for three months, but their friendship had been forged in such intense circumstances that the bond was still there.

'I can't believe we found each other again,' Katie had said, tears rolling down her face, 'and that you've survived so much.'

'That's me,' Gretta had replied. 'Cracked but not broken.'

And who would tell Gary that it didn't matter? Gary, who'd been handed over like an unwanted puppy, his birth mother hidden away, his birth father oblivious to his existence. It was unlikely he would ever find out where he'd come from. He could try, he said, but he feared he'd be entering another maze with no guarantee of finding his way out. Despite this, or perhaps because of it, he'd been conciliatory towards Katie.

So had Ailish. 'It's a lot to take on board,' she'd said. 'An awful lot. You've got to give Beth time.'

Katie didn't agree. She worried that all time would do was allow Beth's hostility to harden and that their estrangement would become permanent.

She chided herself for thinking about this now. She couldn't allow the day to be soured by her separation from Beth.

Johnny was also in her thoughts. It was a shame he'd never met her son. They would have got on; she was sure of it. If only she'd been courageous enough to do this sooner. If only, if only …

'Will you tell your parents I said thanks for taking such good care of you?' she said to Luke. 'I often fretted for fear you'd been given to people who didn't love you enough.'

'They said to say hello to you.' He paused. 'Would you like to meet them?'

'Yes, I think I would.'

He pulled at his ear lobe. Her father's ears, she thought. 'I was very nervous coming here today. I couldn't sleep last night.'

'That makes two of us,' she said. 'But why?'

'You sounded great on the phone, but I worried that in real life you might be strange or damaged, and I wasn't sure how good I'd be at handling the situation. I can see now what an idiot I was. I mean, you're so … so normal.' He immediately thought better of what he'd said. 'Jesus, that sounded terrible, but you know what I mean, don't you?'

Katie remembered a line from Chrissie's newspaper interview: *It's not every town that has a story. It's every village. Every street.*

We're your neighbour, she thought, your friend, your aunt, your mother. We're the women who left and the ones who stayed. Some of us have been able to talk. Others may yet get the chance.

She didn't say any of this. Instead, she smiled and squeezed Luke's knee. 'I know exactly what you mean. Can you stay for another cup of tea?'

Chapter 41

Katie

Ailish had been nervous about the idea.

'You might think it's a terrible suggestion,' she'd said. 'If you do, that's fine. But it came into my head, and I thought I'd ask.'

None of them had considered it a bad idea, including Gretta. And it was her opinion that mattered most.

That was how they found themselves on a shimmering September morning walking towards Carrigbrack, the grass still in its summer green, the hedgerows ablaze with hawthorn berries. In the near distance, a fox went slinking by. A kestrel hovered overhead. It was that time of year when every fine day felt precious because you knew that winter was lurking. It was a time of endings and beginnings.

This was Gretta's first trip to Carrigbrack since the morning she'd climbed into the boot of Rita Farragher's car. It was also the first time Chrissie had returned. Chrissie's husband, Iggy, was with them, as was Gretta's husband, Alun. Ailish was accompanied by Stevie. Despite his volatile home life, he'd secured a great Leaving Cert and was due to start university later in the month. At eighteen, towering over his mother, he radiated a confidence that had always eluded her.

'If I didn't remember the day I squeezed him out,' she said, 'I wouldn't believe he was mine either.'

'Ah, Mam,' said Stevie, 'you're forever embarrassing me.' His tone, not to mention his presence, made it clear he was joking.

Ailish didn't mention Keith, and Katie followed her example. There were days to talk about him, but this wasn't one of them.

Gretta was carrying a bunch of red roses to place at the spot where Diane was buried. Not the precise spot, obviously. That had been obscured by time. Chrissie would say a few words because, as they all agreed, she was best with words.

Gretta was quiet. She was wearing a russet jacket, a cream skirt and bronze sandals. When Katie complimented her outfit, she said she'd wanted to make an effort for Diane. To tell whoever or whatever was out there that her daughter had been worthy of respect. Katie's mind flashed back to the morning the baby girl had been wrapped in white cloth and placed in the ground. She recalled what Gretta had said then: *Just because I couldn't keep her, it doesn't mean I didn't want the best for her. I wanted her to be brilliant. She deserved to be brilliant.*

They'd been reunited during the summer, when Katie had gone to London for a long weekend. She'd stayed with Chrissie, and the three of them had laughed and cried over a roast chicken and two bottles of Sauvignon Blanc.

'If only Agnes could see us,' Chrissie had said.

'She'd definitely cut off all our hair,' Gretta had replied.

Luke was with Katie today, as was her younger granddaughter, Sadie. Katie had wondered if this was a wise idea. Sadie was at that age where everything mattered and every injustice tore at your heart. Wasn't there a danger she would find Carrigbrack too upsetting? She had a word with Luke, who told her that if he didn't bring his daughter, she'd probably stow away like Gretta and pitch up anyway.

Although they both laughed, it was unsettling to think that, at the same age, Chrissie had been imprisoned here, her name taken, her life changed forever.

They were midway along the lane, almost at the place where Carrigbrack's boundary wall began, when Katie heard an engine. She turned to see two … no, three cars, their windscreens glinting in the sun. As the occupants emerged, she recognised Gary's loose-limbed walk. The woman beside him – seventy-ish, with the complexion of someone who rarely saw sunlight – was unfamiliar.

Next came Joyce, Eddie, Yvette and little Zoe. At the rear were Brandon and Robyn.

'I hadn't expected everyone to come,' said Ailish, her fox-like face aglow with pleasure. 'But when I told them what we were doing, they all said they would.'

Gary introduced them to Noreen, one of the women who hadn't been his birth mother.

'After he came to see me, we kept in touch,' she explained. 'He told me what was happening today and asked if I'd like to come. I hope I'm not intruding.'

'Of course you're not,' said Chrissie. 'I remember you. The nuns called you Gloria.'

'That's right,' said Noreen, her eyes misty. 'And I remember you. You were the little girl, the one they called Hanora.' She smiled. It was a wonderful smile.

If Katie was taken aback by Brandon and Robyn's presence, she was even more surprised to see Gary. The tour was due to begin the following week.

'Yeah, this time next week we'll be back on stage,' he said. 'As chance would have it, the opening night's in Boston.'

'I hadn't realised that,' said Katie, glancing towards Brandon and Robyn. She was an awful liar. She knew most of the dates, including when Black Iris would be in Dublin (17 and 18 December). She knew their next album would be called *Catching Fire* and that it would include a song written by Gary about the women whose children had been taken. She'd signed up to the Black Iris website, which as far as she could gather was the twenty-first-century equivalent of joining a fan club.

'And we're going to the Garden to see them,' said Robyn. 'Isn't that great? We met earlier for coffee – Ailish put us all in touch – and Gary invited us. I'm so excited.' She linked arms with Brandon, who looked scared.

'Mam's going too,' said Stevie.

Katie felt her mouth forming an O. Ailish studied her feet. The rest of the group resumed walking.

Gary laughed. 'It's compensation for the night she spent nine hours getting home from Slane.' He turned to Katie. 'By the way, I have news,' he nodded his head towards the others, 'but we'd better get moving. I'll tell you later.'

They snaked towards the home, seventeen of them in all. A collection of mothers, sons, daughters, partners and grandchildren.

One person was missing. Katie had written again, this time sending the letter to the Linnane family home in Danganstown. It had returned, unopened, in a large brown envelope. An accompanying note from Margo advised her to leave Beth alone. *She's still upset. If anything changes, I'll let you know.* For all Katie's delight at finding Luke, she felt her niece's absence more keenly than she could have imagined. Where once she'd spent her days wondering what Johnny would have said about something, now she did the same for Beth. At least Johnny's death hadn't been her fault. With Beth, the wound was self-inflicted.

She kept telling herself that she had to walk on, that she couldn't become overwhelmed by her mistakes. But the house was too quiet. She missed their banter, their in-jokes and rituals. She'd taken to sitting in Beth's old room, thinking of new ways to try and make amends.

One of the many surprising developments was that she'd become closer to Margo. They'd never be best friends, but they were more at peace with each other. Shortly after Katie's first meeting with Luke, the sisters had had a long conversation about Carrigbrack. For the first time, Katie had spoken about how her treatment there, and the loss of her son, had scarred her for life.

'I did everything I could to recover,' she'd said, 'but I was never the same afterwards. How could I be?' She'd spoken too quickly, the words tumbling out, but she'd been waiting most of a lifetime to voice them.

In response, Margo had become emotional. 'I wish we'd talked about this before. I wish you'd been honest with me.'

Increasingly, Katie found herself thinking about the way her ordeal had affected her sister. In some ways, Margo too had been forced to live in Carrigbrack's long shadow. Katie had been wrong when she'd said it was too late to try and understand her. It was never too late.

As they approached the gate, Joyce squeezed her hand. 'Any word?'

'I'm afraid not.'

When, finally, Katie had confessed, Joyce had been sympathetic. She'd even offered to intercede with Beth. Katie had declined. After she'd told Luke, he'd made the same offer, and she'd given the same response. If she knew Beth, and she liked to think she did, an outside intervention would only push her further away.

Carrigbrack was even more dilapidated than the last time Katie had visited. Time and the elements were chipping away at it. Nature was taking over, wrapping its tendrils around the stone and slate, jutting through what remained of the roof.

Compared to a year earlier, when she'd found every step difficult, she was calm. She wouldn't describe the visit as cathartic. That would be going too far. But she was fascinated by the reactions of others. When they reached the plot and its single headstone – *In Memory of the Little Angels* – she looked around. There was Joyce, deep in thought. There were Brandon and Eddie, exchanging stories. There was Zoe, clutching a drooping toy rabbit, taking ballerina steps around them. There was Sadie, crouching to take photographs. And there was Gretta, as dignified as the day fifty years ago when her daughter had been buried.

The previous weekend, Ailish, Stevie and two of his friends had removed the worst of the brambles and weeds. While the site remained bedraggled, at least there was a clearing where they could stand and remember.

Chrissie spoke briefly about Gretta and about other women she knew. Gretta placed the flowers beside the wall, then turned around.

'I wasn't going to speak,' she said, 'and I haven't prepared anything. I just want to say thank you. I haven't met most of you before, but I know Carrigbrack is part of your story too. I hope today brings as much comfort to you as it has done to me.'

Afterwards, they split into small groups, shuffling from one foot to the other, swapping reminiscences. They were due to go for lunch at a nearby pub. It was like a proper funeral, thought Katie. She noticed Noreen talking to Joyce and Yvette. Robyn and Brandon were playing with Zoe. Ailish, permanently on duty, was clearing away more weeds. Stevie was helping. As was Sadie.

Katie was with Luke, his presence still such a novelty that she had to stop herself from staring. Every time they spoke, she discovered something new. She'd learnt that he'd once been in a bad car accident, that he'd spent a year travelling in South America and that before marrying Jen, he'd lived with a woman called Heidi. Sometimes, she overanalysed their conversations. She read too much into throwaway comments. She worried that she said too much. She worried that she said too little. She was, she supposed, scared of losing him again.

Gary tapped her lightly on the arm. Katie felt for him today, the only one among them with no connection to Carrigbrack.

'So,' he said, removing his sunglasses, 'do you remember late last year when I signed up to a couple of those DNA databases?'

'I do.' Katie had been sceptical. She'd read about long-lost family finding each other through the wonders of science, but the success stories were always far away. In America, usually.

'I didn't think anything would come of it. And to begin with, it didn't. To be honest, I'd so much else going on, I forgot about the DNA sites. And then, last month, I received a notification to say there'd been a match.'

'Go on.'

'I assumed I was going to find a sixth cousin three times removed or something. But, and I still can't quite believe this, the match was with my biological father.'

'No!'

'The guy who didn't know you existed?' said Luke.

'The very man ... only eventually he had found out. Someone in the family had let something slip, and he'd badgered his folks until they told the truth. By that stage, he'd lost touch with my biological mother. When he tracked her down, she confirmed it all. I get the feeling the scenes weren't good.'

'And did he try to find you then?'

'We're talking about twenty years ago. Like me, he didn't think it'd be possible. He'd been given hardly any information, and everyone he asked was vague as hell. Oh, and he was thousands of miles away. He was a doctor in the Mayo Clinic in Minnesota, an expert in the endocrine system or some such. His name's Peadar, by the way. Peadar Gilligan.'

'At least his career wasn't affected by your untimely birth,' said Katie.

Gary smiled. 'Yeah, that was one of the first things to occur to me too. Anyhow, recently, he decided to try again. He sent away his saliva, and up I popped.'

'That's amazing,' she said. 'Come here, I've got to hug you. I'm actually … I'm at a loss for words.' The others had found their families through hard work, perseverance and a sprinkling of luck. This was different. This felt like a miracle.

'Thanks, Katie,' he said, as they pulled apart. 'It's not all straightforward. I gather my birth mother's life hasn't been easy, and I'm not sure if she wants to meet me. I'll have to play it by ear. But at least part of the puzzle has been solved.'

'And are you going to Minnesota to meet Peadar?' said Luke.

'Ah, there's the thing. He retired a couple of years back and returned to Ireland. His wife was originally from Galway, and that's where they're living. As chance would have it, that's also where Noreen's from. So I'm going to drop her home, and then I'll go and see the Gilligans. And tomorrow I'll go back to the States.'

'You're a quick mover,' said Katie.

'Yeah, I know you'd probably advise me to take it more slowly. But if I don't go to see them today, it's probably going to be a few months before I get another chance.'

'Don't mind me. I'm the woman who told you all to be honest but didn't take her own advice. Was Peadar surprised at who you turned out to be?'

'Totally. Apparently, I have two half-brothers and a half-sister, and one of the guys is a fan of the band.'

Around them, the huddles were starting to disperse. People were drifting back towards the lane. 'I'm so pleased,' said Katie, still tingling from the news. 'So pleased. Does … does Beth know?'

'I emailed her a couple of days ago, but I haven't heard back. I'm surprised, because she was so enthusiastic about my search.'

'Maybe she's away.'

'Maybe,' said Gary, his tone revealing that he didn't believe this either. 'Listen, you can't let Beth's absence ruin the day.'

'That's what I told her,' said Luke.

Katie took her phone from her bag. She didn't plan on returning to Carrigbrack. It had swallowed enough of her life. She decided, however, that she'd like a photograph. Not as a reminder, for how could she ever forget? Rather, she wanted it as an acknowledgement of what had happened. She wanted to look at it and know that this place no longer had power over her.

She handed the bag to Luke. 'I'm going to take one photo, then we can head on our way.'

'Grand. Do you want me to take a picture of you standing in front of the building?'

'Yes. Why not?'

She gave him the phone and turned to face the lane. As she did so, she saw a fair-haired woman with large sunglasses striding through the gate. The woman stopped to embrace Gary, then walked over to Katie.

She spoke the way she always did, as if there was a tremendous amount to say and not enough time to say it. 'I'm sorry I'm late,' she said. 'It took me forever to get out of Dublin. The traffic was terrible. Isn't Gary's news fantastic?'

Katie ran a finger along the back of her son's hand. 'Luke,' she said, 'this is your cousin Beth.'

Acknowledgements

Many, many thanks to all the people who helped bring *The Paper Bracelet* to the page.

In particular, I'm grateful to my editors, Ciara Considine at Hachette Books Ireland and Sherise Hobbs at Headline. Thanks also to Jane Selley for the copy-edit.

As always, thanks to Joanna Smyth, Ruth Shern, Breda Purdue and Jim Binchy at Hachette Ireland. Thanks also to Elaine Egan and Susie Cronin.

Much gratitude to my agent, Robert Kirby, and to Kate Walsh and Amy Mitchell at United Agents.

In writing the book, I was helped by a number of newspaper articles, especially those written by Conall O'Fatharta and Alison O'Reilly. The websites of the Adoption Rights Alliance and the Clann Project were invaluable.

I'm grateful to my RTÉ newsroom colleagues, especially all the gang on *Morning Ireland*.

A big thank you to the readers, bloggers and booksellers who have been so supportive.

Massive thanks to my parents, Tony and Ruth English.

And, finally, more thanks than I can say to my husband, Eamon Quinn.

Author's Note

For the first time, Beth was seeing how the sins of the past reverberated around them. She'd realised that the story wasn't confined to black-and-white film and bleached-out Polaroids. The women weren't exhibits in a museum.

More than twenty years ago, as a young reporter, I interviewed several women who'd been born in a mother and baby home in Cork city. All were trying to trace their birth parents, and none was making progress. Even basic details about their backgrounds had been denied to them. No matter that they had been adopted by loving families, they felt as though a vital part of their identity was missing. I've never forgotten those women, and not just because of the power of their words. For the first time, I was forced to think about the sheer number of people whose lives were spent wondering about their earliest days and whose attempts to find out more were stymied.

Meanwhile, thousands of women were continuing to live with a bitter legacy, and many were doing so in secret. These were the women who had been treated like criminals when some were the victims of crime. Their children had been taken from them and they'd been warned that any attempt to find their son or daughter was illegal.

Of course, Ireland wasn't the only country where single, pregnant women were ostracised. Unwarranted shame and stigma can be found everywhere. Neither was the country alone in sending women to institutions. Nor was it a uniquely Catholic practice. Where Ireland did differ was in the scale of this practice. A report carried out by a group called the Clann Project details the experiences of women and children who spent time in the homes. Apart from the personal testimonies, one statistic stands out: In 1967, 97 percent of children born to unmarried mothers in Ireland were the subject of adoption orders. It's such an astonishing figure that I decided to include it in Chrissie's newspaper interview.

Something else made clear by the Clann Project report is that most of the women were effectively incarcerated. They had little or no control over what happened to them and their children. Those who ran away were apprehended and returned by the Gardaí. Many mothers say their babies were taken without consent. They were also discouraged from having contact with their families.

So, while Carrigbrack is fictional, the details are based on real homes. Women were stripped of their names (officially this was to protect their identity); pain relief during labour was frowned upon; children disappeared without warning; graves weren't properly marked. It's also true that women, some heavily pregnant, were forced to carry out hard manual work. There are relatively few accounts of day-to-day life in these institutions. One of the exceptions, a book called *The Light in the Window* by June Goulding, details her time as a nurse in Cork's Bessborough home (the place where the women I interviewed in the 1990s had been born). She witnessed mothers plucking the grass from a lawn by hand. Others were forced to tar a driveway.

To this day, it can be hard for women to talk about the secretive system that treated them so harshly. I spoke recently to the head of the Adoption Authority in Ireland who lamented the fact that their contact register contains the names of relatively few birth mothers. Also, while many women went on to rebuild their lives, others found it more difficult. A considerable number, like Chrissie, left the country.

Tracing a birth parent isn't easy. Most of the references to this in *The Paper Bracelet* – from the missing files spoken about by Beth to Gary's bogus birth certificate to the way Ailish was given the runaround – are based on real life examples. There's still considerable controversy about the way adopted people are treated by the state. Compared to their counterparts elsewhere, they have few rights, and legislation to change this has been a long time coming.

In recent years, the story of Ireland's mother and baby homes has become better known. There has been considerable international news coverage of the Tuam home where, following the work of local historian Catherine Corless, the remains of hundreds of children's bodies were discovered. There has also been worldwide interest in the stories of babies, like Brandon, who were sent to the United States. In these less deferential times, it can be particularly difficult for younger people to understand why families behaved the way they did and why these practices continued for so long.

I grew up in the 1980s when, too often, the women who appeared in the news were there for tragic reasons. I remember fifteen-year-old Ann Lovett who died while giving birth on open ground; Joanne Hayes, a single mother wrongly accused of killing her baby; and Eileen Flynn who lost her job as a teacher because she was living with a separated man. A few mother and baby homes, including Bessborough, were still open. I'm conscious that to younger readers such events might seem like ancient history. But, like the stories of the women whose children were taken from them, the consequences continue to reverberate. It's only in the past few years that some of those who knew Ann Lovett have felt free to talk about her. It's just two years since the State apologised to Joanne Hayes.

My background as a journalist tends to seep into my writing, and it's easy to become ensnared by too much research. While writing The Paper Bracelet, I read histories, listened to old radio programmes and scoured message boards. Eventually, it occurred to me that I was like an interviewer who's overly keen to display their knowledge. I had to remind myself that I wasn't writing about an issue, but about characters. I had to keep asking myself: What must that experience have been like? And what is it like to live with the consequences?

I also wanted to try and bring the mothers and the women who ran the homes to life. It's too easy to portray the nuns as caricatures of evil and the mothers as devoid of wit and personality. As Ailish says when she meets Gretta:

Although she should have known better, she'd tended to think of the women as one sad homogeneous group. That wasn't fair. Some had been gifted, some dull-witted, some hilarious, some kind. They'd been as gorgeous and glorious, as complex and difficult as any collection of young people.

I hope I've done them justice.

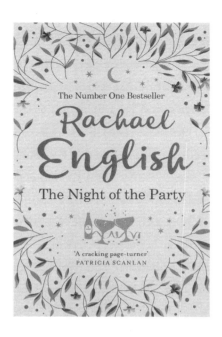

The Number One Bestseller

Rachael English

The Night of the Party

'A cracking page-turner'
PATRICIA SCANLAN

January 1982: In the rural village of Kilmitten, the Crossan family is holding its annual party during the biggest snowstorm Ireland has seen in decades. By the end of the night, the parish priest has been found dead, in suspicious circumstances.

For Tom, Conor, Tess and Nina, four teenage friends who were there, life will never be the same. One of them carries a secret and, as the years pass and their lives diverge, a bond that won't be broken silently holds.

As the thirty-fifth anniversary of the priest's death approaches, Conor, now a senior police officer, has reason to believe that Tom – a prominent politician – can help identify the killer. As his dilemma draws the four friends back together, all are forced to question their lives and to confront their differences.

The Night of the Party is a page-turning novel that combines warmth, drama and an unforgettable twist.

John Varley is a multiple winner of the Hugo and Nebula awards for excellence in science fiction, and has also received France's Prix Apollo. He is the author of *Titan*, *Wizard*, and *Demon*, which make up the Gaia trilogy, and more recently of *Millennium*. He lives in Portland, Oregon.

Also By

JOHN VARLEY

TITAN

WIZARD

DEMON

MILLENNIUM

THE OPHIUCHI HOTLINE

THE PERSISTENCE OF VISION
(stories)

THE BARBIE MURDERS
(stories)
also published as
PICNIC ON NEARSIDE

BLUE CHAMPAGNE
(stories)

JOHN VARLEY

STEEL BEACH

HarperCollins*Publishers*

This book is dedicated to the
First-Saturday-at-Herb's Literary,
Debating, and Pyrotechnics Gang.
You know who you are.
Thanks for everything, my friends.

HarperCollins*Publishers*,
77–85 Fulham Palace Road,
Hammersmith, London W6 8JB

Published by HarperCollins*Publishers* 1993
9 8 7 6 5 4 3 2 1

First published by
G.P.Putnam's Sons 1992

A catalogue record for this book is
available from the British Library

ISBN 0 586 21735 3

Printed in Great Britain by
Hartnolls Ltd, Bodmin, Cornwall

PART 1

HEADLINES!

EXCITING NEW CONTEST!

WIN FREE SEX!

"In five years, the penis will be obsolete," said the salesman.

He paused to let this planet-shattering information sink into our amazed brains. Personally, I didn't know how many more wonders I could absorb before lunch.

"With the right promotional campaign," he went on, breathlessly, "it might take as little as *two* years."

He might even have been right. Stranger things have happened in my lifetime. But I decided to hold off on calling my broker with frantic orders to sell all my jockstrap stock.

The press conference was being held in a large auditorium belonging to United Bioengineers. It could seat about a thousand; it presently held a fifth that number, most of us huddled together in the front rows.

The UniBio salesman was nondescript as a game-show host. He had one of those voices, too. A Generic person. One of these days they'll standardize every profession by face and body type. Like uniforms.

He went on:

"Sex as we know it is awkward, inflexible, unimaginative. By the time you're forty, you've done everything you possibly could with our present, 'natural' sexual system. In fact, if you're even moderately active, you've done everything a dozen times. It's become boring. And if it's boring at forty, what will it be like at eighty, or a hundred and forty? Have you ever thought about that? About what you'll be doing for a sex life when you're eighty? Do you really want to be repeating the same old acts?"

"Whatever I'm doing, it won't be with him," Cricket whispered in my ear.

"How about with me?" I whispered back. "Right after the show."

"How about after I'm eighty?" She gave me a sharp little jab in the ribs, but she was smiling. Which is more than I could say for the hulk sitting in front of us. He worked for *Perfect Body,* weighed about two hundred kilos—none of it fat—and was glaring over the slope of one massive trapezius, flexing the muscles in his eyebrows. I wouldn't have believed he could even turn his head, much less look over his shoulder. You could hear the gristle popping.

We took the hint and shut up.

"At United Bioengineers," the pitch went on, "we have no doubt that, given twenty or thirty million years, Mother Nature would have remedied some of these drawbacks. In fact," and here he gave a smile that managed to be sly and aw-shucks at the same time, "we wonder if the grand old lady might have settled on *this very system . . .* that's how good we think it is.

"And how good is that? I hear you saying. There have been a lot of improvements since the days of Christine Jorgensen. What makes this one so special?"

"Christine who?" Cricket whispered, typing rapidly with the fingers of her right hand on her left forearm.

"Jorgensen. First male-to-female sex change, not counting opera singers. What are they teaching you in journalism school these days?"

"Get the spin right, and the factoids will follow. Hell, Hildy, I didn't realize you *dated* the lady."

"I've done worse since. If she hadn't kept trying to lead on the dance floor . . ."

This time an arm—it had to be an arm, it grew out of his shoulder, though I could have put both my legs into one of his sleeves—hooked itself over the back of the chair in front of me, and I was treated to the whole elephantine display, from the crew-cut yellow hair to the jaw you could have used to plow the south forty, to the neck wider than Cricket's hips. I held up my hands placatingly, pantomimed locking up my lips and throwing away the key. His brow beetled even more—god help me if he thought I was making fun of him—then he turned back around. I was left wondering where he got the tiny barbells he must have used to get those forehead muscles properly pumped up.

In a word, I was bored.

I'd seen the Sexual Millennium announced before. As recently as the previous March, in fact, and quite regularly before that. It was like end-of-the-world stories, or perpetual motion machines. A journalist figured to encounter them every few weeks as long as his career lasted. I suspect it was the same when headlines were chiseled into stone tablets and the

Sunday Edition was tossed from the back of a woolly mammoth. I had lost track of how many times I'd sat in audiences just like this, listening to a glib young man/woman with more teeth than God intended proclaim the Breakthrough of the Age. It was the price a feature reporter had to pay.

It could have been worse. I could have had the political beat.

". . . tested on over two thousand volunteer subjects . . . random sampling error of plus or minus one percent . . ."

I was having a bad feeling. That the story would not be one hundredth as revolutionary as the guy was promising was a given. The only question was, would there be enough substance to hack out a story I could sell to Walter?

". . . registered a sixty-three-percent increase in orgasmic sensation, a two to one rise in the satisfaction index, and a complete lack of postcoital depression."

And as my old uncle J. Walter Thompson used to say, makes your wash fifty percent whiter, cleans your teeth, and leaves your breath alone.

I reached down to the floor and recovered the faxpad each of us had been given as we came through the door. I called up the survey questions and scanned through them quickly. My bullshit detector started beeping so loudly I was afraid Mister Dynamic Tension would turn around again.

The questions were garbage. There are firms whose purpose is to work with pollsters and guard against the so-called "brownnose effect," that entirely human tendency to tell people what they want to hear. Ask folks if they like your new soda pop, they'll tend to say yes, then spit it out when your back is turned. UniBio had not hired one of these firms. Sometimes that in itself indicates a lack of confidence in the product.

"And now, the moment you've been waiting for." There was a flourish of trumpets. The lights dimmed. Spotlights swirled over the blue velvet drapes behind the podium, which began to crawl toward the wings with the salesman aboard.

"United Bioengineers presents—"

"Drum roll," Cricket whispered, a fraction of a second early. I hit her with my elbow.

"—the future of sex . . . *ULTRA-Tingle!*"

There was polite applause and the curtains parted to reveal a nude couple standing, embracing, beneath a violet spot. Both were hairless. They turned to face us, heads high, shoulders back. Neither seemed to be male or female. The only real distinction between them was the hint of breasts and a touch of eye shadow on the smaller one. There was flat, smooth skin between each pair of legs.

"Another touchie-feelie," Cricket said. "I thought this was going to be all new. Didn't they introduce the Tingle system three years ago?"

"They sure did. Paid a fortune to get half a dozen celebs to convert, and they *still* didn't get more than ten, twenty thousand subscribers. I doubt there's a hundred of them left."

What can you do? They hold a press conference, we have to send somebody. They throw chum in the water, we start to feed.

Five minutes into the ULTRA-Tingle presentations (that's how they insisted it be spelled, with caps), I could see this turkey would be of interest only to the trades. I'm sure my beefy buddy up front was tickled down to the tips of his muscle-bound toes.

There were a dozen nude, genderless dancers on stage now, caressing each others' bodies and posing artistically. Blue sparks flew from their fingertips.

"That's it for me," I said to Cricket. "You sticking around?"

"There's a drawing later. Three free conversions—"

"—to the fabulous ULTRA-Tingle System," the salesman said, finishing her sentence for her.

"Win free sex," I said.

"What's that?"

"Walter says it's the ultimate padloid headline."

"Shouldn't it have something about UFOs in it?"

"Okay. 'Win Free Sex Aboard a UFO to Old Earth.' "

"I'd better stick around for the drawing. My boss would kill me if I won and wasn't around to collect."

"If I win, they can bring it around to the office." I got up, put my hand on a massive shoulder, leaned down.

"Those pecs could use some more work," I told the gorilla hybrid, and got out in a hurry.

The foyer had been transformed since my arrival. Huge blue holos of ULTRA-Tingle convertees entwined erotically in the corners, and long banquet tables had been wheeled in. Men in traditional English butler uniforms stood behind the tables polishing silver and glassware.

It's known as perks. I seldom turn down a free trip in the course of my profession, and I never turn down free food.

I went to the nearest table and stuck a knife into a pâté sculpture of Sigmund Freud and spread the thick brown goo over a slice of black bread. One of the butlers looked worried and started toward me, but I glared him back into his place. I put two thick slices of smoked ham on top of the pâté, spread a layer of cream cheese, a few sheets of lox sliced so thin you could read newsprint through it, and topped it all off with three spoonfuls of black Beluga caviar. The butler watched the whole operation in increasing disbelief.

It was one of the all-time great Hildy sandwiches.

I was about to bite into it when Cricket appeared at my elbow and offered me a tulip glass of blue champagne. The crystal made an icy clear musical note when I touched it to the rim of her glass.

"Freedom of the press," I suggested.

"The fourth estate," Cricket agreed.

The UniBio labs were at the far end of a new suburb nearly seventy kilometers from the middle of King City. Most of the slides and escalators were not working yet. There was only one functioning tube terminal and it was two kilometers away. We'd come in a fleet of twenty hoverlimos. They were still there, lined up outside the entrance to the corporate offices, ready to take us back to the tube station. Or so I thought. Cricket and I climbed aboard.

"It distresses me greatly to tell you this," the hoverlimo said, "but I am unable to depart until the demonstration inside is over, or until I have a passenger load of seven individuals."

"Make an exception," I told it. "We have deadlines to meet."

"Are you perhaps declaring an emergency situation?"

I started to do just that, then bit my tongue. I'd get back to the office, all right, then have a lot of explaining to do and a big fine to pay.

"When I write this story," I said, trying another tack, "and when I mention this foolish delay, portraying UniBio in an unfavorable light, your bosses will be extremely upset."

"This information disturbs and alarms me," said the hoverlimo. "I, being only a subprogram of an incompletely-activated routine of the UniBio building computer, wish only to please my human passengers. Be assured I would go to the greatest lengths to satisfy your desires, as my only purpose is to provide satisfaction and speedy transportation. However," it added, after a short pause, "I can't move."

"Come on," Cricket said. "You ought to know better than to argue with a machine." She was already getting out. I knew she was right, but there is a part of me that has never been able to resist it, even if they *don't* talk to me.

"Your mother was a garbage truck," I said, and kicked it in the rubber skirt.

"Undoubtedly, sir. Thank you, sir. Please come back soon, sir."

"Who programmed that toadying thing?" I wondered, later.

"Somebody with a lot of lipstick on his ass," Cricket said. "What are you so sour about? It's just a short walk. Take in the scenery."

It was a rather pleasant place, I had to admit. There were very few people around. You grow up with the odor of people all around you, all the time, and you really notice it when the scent is gone. I took a deep breath and smelled freshly-poured concrete. I drank the sights and sounds and scents of a newborn world: the sharp primary colors of wire bundles sprouting from unfinished walls like the first buds on a bare bough, the untarnished gleam of copper, silver, gold, aluminum, titanium; the whistle of air through virgin ducts, undeflected, unmuffled, bringing with it the crisp sharpness of the light machine oil that for centuries has coated new machinery, fresh from the factory . . . all these things had an effect on me. They meant warmth, security, safety from the eternal vacuum, the victory of humanity over the hostile forces that never slept. In a word, progress.

I began to relax a little. We picked our way through jumbles of stainless steel and aluminum and plastic and glass building components and I felt a peace as profound as I suspect a Kansas farmer of yesteryear might have felt, looking out over his rippling fields of wheat.

"Says here they've got an option where you can have sex over the telephone."

Cricket had gotten a few paces ahead of me, and she was reading from the UniBio faxpad handout.

"That's nothing new. People started having sex over the telephone about ten minutes after Alexander Graham Bell invented it."

"You're pulling my leg. Nobody invented sex."

I liked Cricket, though we were rivals. She works for *The Straight Shit,* Luna's second-largest padloid, and has already made a name for herself even though she's not quite thirty years old. We cover many of the same stories so we see a lot of each other, professionally.

She'd been female all the time I'd known her, but she'd never shown any interest in the tentative offers I had made. No accounting for taste. I'd about decided it was a matter of sexual orientation—one doesn't ask. It had to be that. If not, it meant she just wasn't interested in me. Altogether unlikely.

Which was a shame, either way, because I'd harbored a low-grade lust for her for three years.

" 'Simply attach the Tinglemodem (sold separately) to the primary sensory cluster,' " she read, " 'and it's as if your lover were in the room with you.' I'll bet Mr. Bell didn't figure on *that.*"

Cricket had a childlike face with an upturned nose and a brow that tended to wrinkle appealingly when she was thinking—all carefully calculated, I have no doubt, but no less exciting because of that. She had a short upper lip and a long lower one. I guess that doesn't sound so great, but Cricket made it work. She had one green, normal eye, and the other one was red, without a pupil. My eyes were the same except the normal one was brown. The red-eyed holocams of the press never sleep.

She was wearing a frilly red blouse that went well with her silver-blonde hair, and the second badge of our profession: a battered gray fedora with a card reading PRESS stuck into the brim. She had recently had herself heeled. It was coming back into fashion. Personally, I tried it and didn't like it much. It's a simple operation. The tendons in the soles of the feet are shortened, forcing your heels up in the air and shifting the weight to the balls of the feet. In extreme cases it put you right up on your toes, like a ballerina. Like I said, a rather silly fad, but I had to admit it produced attractive lines in the calf, thigh, and buttock muscles.

It could have been worse. Women used to cram their feet into pointed horrors with ten-centimeter heels and hobble around in a one-gee field to get more or less the same effect. It must have been crippling.

"Says there's a security interlock available, to ensure fidelity."

"What? Where's that?"

She gave me the faxpad reference. I couldn't believe what I was reading.

"Is that legal?" I asked her.

"Sure. It's a contract between two people, isn't it? Nobody's forced to use it."

"It's an electronic chastity belt, that's what it is."

"Worn by both husband and wife. Not like the brave knight off to the Crusades, getting laid every night while his wife looks for a good locksmith. Good for the goose, good for the gander."

"Good for nobody, if you ask me."

Frankly, I was shocked, and not much shocks me. To each his or her own, that's basic to our society. But ULTRA-Tingle was offering a coded security system whereby each partner had a password, unknown to the other, to lock or unlock his or her partner's sexual response. Without the password, the sexual center of the brain would not be activated, and sex would be about as exciting as long division.

To use it would require giving someone veto power over my own mind. I can't imagine trusting anyone that much. But people are crazy. That's what my job's all about.

"How about over there?" Cricket said.

"Over where? I mean, what about it?" She was headed toward a patch of green, an area that, when completed, would be a pocket park. Trees stood around in pots. There were great rolls of turf stacked against one wall, like a carpet shop.

"It's probably the best spot we'll find."

"For what?"

"Have you forgotten your offer already?" she asked.

To tell the truth, I had. After this many years, it had been made more in jest than anything else. She took my hand and led me onto an unrolled section of turf. It was soft and springy and cool. She reclined and looked up at me.

"Maybe I shouldn't say it, but I'm surprised."

"Well, Hildy, you never really asked, you know?"

I felt sure I had, but maybe she was right. My style is more to kid around, make what used to be known as a pass. Some women don't like that. They'd rather have a direct question.

I stretched out on top of her and we kissed.

We disarranged some of my clothes. She wasn't wearing enough to worry about. Soon we were moving to rhythms it had taken Mother Nature well over a billion years to compose. It was awkward, messy, it lacked flexibility and probably didn't show much imagination. It sure wasn't ULTRA-Tingle. That didn't prevent it from being wonderful.

"Wow," she whispered, as I rolled off her and we lay side by side on the grass. "That was really . . . obsolete."

"Not nearly as obsolete as it was for me."

We looked at each other and burst out laughing.

After a while, she sat up and glanced at the figures displayed on her wrist.

"Deadline in three hours," she said.

"Me, too." We heard a low hum, looked up, and saw our old friend the hoverlimo headed in our direction. We ran to catch it, leaped over the rubber skirt and landed with seven others, who grumbled and groused and eventually made room for us.

"I am overjoyed to transport you," said the hoverlimo.

"I take that back about the garbage truck," I said.

"Thank you, sir."

02 TOP PSYCHIC SAYS:
UFOS SHATTER TIME BARRIER!

The tube capsule back to King City was a quarter full. I used the time to try to salvage something from the wasted afternoon. Looking around me, I saw that all my colleagues were busy at the same task. Eyes were rolled up, mouths hung open, here and there a finger twitched. It had to be either a day trip from the Catatonic Academy, or the modern press at work.

Call me old-fashioned. I'm the only reporter I know who still uses his handwriter except to take notes. Cricket was young enough I doubted she'd ever had one installed. As for the rest of them, over the last twenty years I'd watched as one after the other surrendered to the seductions of Direct Interface, until only I was left, plodding along with antique technology that happened to suit me just fine.

Okay, so I lied about the open mouths. Not all D.I. users look like retarded zombies when they interface. But they look asleep, and I've never been comfortable sleeping in public places.

I snapped the fingers of my left hand. I had to do it twice more before the handwriter came on. That worried me; it was getting harder to find people who still knew how to work on handwriters.

Three rows of four colored dots appeared on the heel of my left hand.

By pressing the dots in different combinations with my fingertips I was able to write the story in shorthand, and watch the loops and lines scrawl themselves on a strip of readout skin on my wrist, just where a suicide would slash himself.

There couldn't be that many of us left who knew Gregg. I wondered if I ought to apply for a grant under the Preservation of Vanishing Skills Act. Shorthand was certainly useless enough to qualify. It was at least as obsolete as yodeling, and I'd once covered a meeting of the Yodeling Society. While I was at it, maybe I could drum up some interest in the Preservation of the Penis.

(File #Hildy*next avail.*)(code Unitingle)
(headline to come)

How far do you trust your spouse? Or better yet, how much does your spouse trust you!

That's the question you'll be asking yourself if you subscribe to United Bioengineers' new sex system known as ULTRA-Tingle.

ULTRA-Tingle is the new, improved, updated version of UniBio's megaflop of a few years back, known simply as Tingle. Remember Tingle? Well, don't feel bad. Nobody else does, either. Somewhere, in some remote cavern in this great dusty globe we feel sure there *must* be someone who converted and stayed that way. Maybe even two of them. Maybe tonight they're Tingling each other. Or maybe one of them has a tingle-ache.

If you are a bona fide Tingler, call this padloid immediately, because you've won a prize! Ten percent off on the cost of your conversion to ULTRA-Tingle. Second prize: a discount on *two* conversions!

What does ULTRA-Tingle offer the dedicated sexual adventurer? In a word: *Security!*

Maybe you thought sex was between your legs. It's not. It's in your head, like everything. And that is the miracle of ULTRA-Tingle. Merely by saying the word you can have the great thrill of caponizing your mate. You, too, can be a grinning gelding. Imagine the joys of cerebral castration! Be the first in your sector to rediscover the art of psychic infibulation! Who but UniBio could raise impotence into the realm of integrated circuits, elevate frigidity from aberration to abnegation?

You don't believe me? Here's how it works:

(to come: *insert UniBio faxpad #4985 ref. 6-13.*)

You may ask yourself: Whatever happened to old-fashioned trust? Well, folks, it's obsolete. Just like the penis, which UniBio assures us will soon go the way of the dodo bird. So those of you who still own and operate a trouser-snake, better start thinking of a place to put it.

No, not *there,* you fool! That's obsolete, too!

(no thirty)

* * *

The vocabulary warning light was blinking wildly on the nail of my index finger. It turned on around paragraph seven, as I had known it would. But it's fun to write that sort of thing, even if you know it'll never make it into print. When I first started this job I would have gone back and worked on it, but now I know it's better to leave something obvious for Walter to mess with, in the hope he'll leave the rest alone.

Okay, so the Pulitzer Prize was safe for another year.

King City grew the way many of the older Lunar settlements had: one bang at a time.

The original enclave had been in a large volcanic bubble several hundred meters below the surface. An artificial sun had been hung near the top, and engineers drilled tunnels in all directions, heaping the rubble on the floor, pulverizing it into soil, turning the bubble into a city park with residential corridors radiating away from it.

Eventually there were too many people for that park, so they drilled a hole and dropped in a medium-sized nuclear bomb. When it cooled, the resulting bubble became Mall Two.

The city fathers were up to Mall Seventeen before new construction methods and changing public tastes halted the string. The first ten malls had been blasted in a line, which meant a long commute from the Old Mall to Mall Ten. They started curving the line, aiming to complete a big oval. Now a King City map had seventeen circles tracing out the letter J, woven together by a thousand tunnels.

My office was in Mall Twelve, level thirty-six, 120 degrees. It's in the editorial offices of *The News Nipple,* the padloid with the largest circulation in Luna. The door at 120 opens on what is barely more than an elevator lobby wedged between a travel agency and a florist. There's a receptionist, a small waiting room, and a security desk. Behind that are four elevators that go to actual offices, on the Lunar surface.

Location, location, and location, says my cousin Arnie, the real estate broker. The way I figure it, time plays a part in land values, too. The *Nipple* offices were topside because, when the rag was founded, topside meant cheap. Walter had had money even way back then, but he'd been a cheap son of a bitch since the dawn of time. He got a deal on the seven-story surface structure, and who cared if it leaked? He liked the view.

Now everybody likes views, and the fine old homes in Bedrock are the worst slums in King City. But I suspect one big blowout could turn the whole city topsy-turvy again.

I had a corner office on the sixth floor. I hadn't done much with it other than to put in a cot and a coffee maker. I tossed my hat on the cot, slapped the desk terminal until it lighted up, and pressed my palm against a readout plate. My story was downloaded into the main computer in just under a second. In another second, the printer started to chatter. Walter prefers hard copy. He likes to make big blue marks on it. While I waited I looked out over the city. My hometown.

The *News Nipple* Tower is near the bottom of the J of King City. From it you can see the clusters of other buildings that mark the sub-surface Malls. The sun was still three days from rising. The lights of the city dwindled in the distance and blended in with the hard, unblinking stars overhead.

Almost on the horizon are the huge, pearly domes of King City farms.

It's pretty by night, not so lovely by day. When the sun came up it would bathe every exposed pipe and trash pile and abandoned rover in unsympathetic light; night pulled a curtain over the shameful clutter.

Even the parts that aren't junk aren't all that attractive. Vacuum is useful in many manufacturing processes and walls are of no use for most of them. If something needed to be sheltered from sunlight, a roof was enough.

Loonies don't *care* about the surface. There's no ecology to preserve, no reason at all to treat it as other than a huge and handy dumping ground. In some places the garbage was heaped to the third story of the exterior buildings. Give us another thousand years and we'll pile the garbage a hundred meters deep from pole to pole.

There was very little movement. King City, on the surface, looked bombed out, abandoned.

The printer finished its job and I handed the copy to a passing messenger. Walter would call me about it when it suited him. I thought of several things I could do in the meantime, failed to find any enthusiasm for any of them. So I just sat there and stared out over the surface, and presently I was called into the master's presence.

Walter Editor is what is known as a natural.

Not that he's a fanatic about it. He doesn't subscribe to one of those cults that refuse all medical treatment developed since 1860, or 1945, or 2020. He's not impressed with faith healing. He's not a member of Lifespan, those folks who believe it's a sin to live beyond the biblical threescore and ten, or the Centenarians, who set the number at one hundred. He's just like most of the rest of us, prepared to live forever if medical science can maintain a quality life for him. He'll accept any treatment that will keep him healthy despite his dissolute lifestyle.

He just doesn't care how he looks.

All the fads in body styling and facial arrangement pass him by. In the twenty years I have known him he has never changed so much as his hairstyle. He had been born male—or so he once told me—one hundred and twenty-six years ago, and had never Changed.

His somatic development had been frozen in his mid-forties, a time he often described to all who would listen as "the prime of life." As a result, he was paunchy and balding. This suited Walter fine. He felt the editor of a major planetary newspaper *ought* to be paunchy and balding.

An earlier age would have called Walter Editor a voluptuary. He was a sensualist, a glutton, monstrously self-indulgent. He went through stomachs in two or three years, used up a pair of lungs every decade or so, and needed a new heart more frequently than most people change gaskets on a pressure suit. Every time he exceeded what he called his "fighting weight" by fifty kilos, he'd have seventy kilos removed. Other than that, with Walter what you saw was what he was.

I found him in his usual position, leaning back in his huge chair, big feet propped up on the antique mahogany desk whose surface displayed not one item made after 1880. His face was hidden behind my story. Puffs of lavender smoke rose from behind the pages.

"Sit down, Hildy, sit down," he muttered, turning a page. I sat, and looked out his windows, which had exactly the same view I'd seen from my windows but five meters higher and three hundred degrees wider. I knew there would be three or four minutes while he kept me waiting. It was one of his managerial techniques. He'd read in a book somewhere that an effective boss should keep underlings waiting whenever possible. He spoiled the effect by constantly glancing up at the clock on the wall.

The clock had been made in 1860 and had once graced the wall of a railway station somewhere in Iowa. The office could be described as Dickensian. The furnishings were worth more than I was likely to make in my lifetime. Very few genuine antiquities had ever been brought to Luna. Most of those were in museums. Walter owned much of the rest.

"Junk," he said. "Worthless." He scowled and tossed the flimsy sheets across the room. Or he tried to. Flimsy sheets resist attaining any great speed unless you wad them up first. These fluttered to the floor at his feet.

"Sorry, Walter, but there just wasn't any other—"

"You want to know why I can't use it?"

"No sex."

"There's no sex in it! I send you out to cover a new sex system, and it turns out there's no *sex* in it. How can that be?"

"Well, there's sex *in* it, naturally. Just not the right kind. I mean, I could write a story about earthworm sex, or jellyfish sex, but it wouldn't turn anybody on but earthworms and jellyfish."

"Exactly. Why is that, Hildy? Why do they want to turn us into jellyfish?"

I knew all about this particular hobbyhorse, but there was nothing to do but ride it.

"It's like the search for the Holy Grail, or the Philosopher's Stone," I said.

"What's the Philosopher's Stone?"

The question had not come from Walter, but from behind me. I was pretty sure I knew who it was. I turned, and saw Brenda, cub reporter, who for the past two weeks had been my journalistic assistant—pronounced "copy girl."

"Sit down, Brenda," Walter said. "I'll get to you in a minute."

I watched her dither around pulling up a chair, folding herself into it like a collapsible ruler with bony joints sticking out in all directions, surely too many joints for one human being. She was very tall and very thin, like so many of the younger generation. I had been told she was seventeen, out on her first vocational education tryout. She was eager as a puppy and not half as graceful.

She irritated the hell out of me. I'm not sure why. There's the generational thing. You wonder how things can get worse, you think that *these* kids have to be the rock bottom, then they have children and you see how wrong you were.

At least she could read and write, I'll give her that. But she was so damnably earnest, so horribly eager to please. She made me tired just looking at her. She was a *tabula rasa* waiting for someone to draw animated cartoons on. Her ignorance of everything outside her particular upper-middle-class social stratum and of everything that had happened more than five years ago was still unplumbed.

She opened the huge purse she always carried around with her and produced a cheroot identical to the one Walter was smoking. She lit up and exhaled a cloud of lavender smoke. Her smoking dated to the day after she met Walter Editor. Her name dated to the day after she met me. Maybe it should have amused or flattered me that she was so obviously trying to emulate her elders; it just made me angry. Adopting the name of a famous fictional reporter had been *my* idea.

Walter gestured for me to go on. I sighed, and did so.

"I really don't know when it started, or why. But the basic idea was, since sex and reproduction no longer have much to do with each other, why should we have sex with our reproductive organs? The same organs we use for urination, too, for that matter."

" 'If it ain't broke, don't fix it,' " Walter said. "That's my philosophy. The old-fashioned system worked for millions of years. Why tamper with it?"

"Actually, Walter, we've already tampered with it quite a bit."

"Not everybody."

"True. But well over eighty percent of females prefer clitoral reloca-tion. The natural arrangement didn't provide enough stimulation during the regular sex act. And just about that many men have had a testicle tuck. They were too damn vulnerable hanging out there where nature put them."

"I haven't had one," he said. I made note of that, in case I ever got into a fight with him.

"Then there's the question of stamina in males," I went on. "Back on Earth, it was the rare male over thirty who could consistently get an erection more than three or four times a day. And it usually didn't last very long. And men didn't have multiple orgasms. They just weren't as sexually capable as women."

"That's horrible," Brenda said. I looked at her; she was genuinely shocked.

"That's an improvement, I'll have to admit," Walter said.

"And there's the entire phenomenon of menstruation," I added.

"What's menstruation?"

We both looked at her. She wasn't joking. Walter and I looked at each other and I could read his thoughts.

"Anyway," I said, "you just pointed out the challenge. Lots of people get altered in one way or another. Some, like you, stay almost natural. Some of the alterations aren't compatible with others. Not all of them involve penetration of one person by another, for instance. What these newsex people are saying is, if we're going to tamper, why not come up with a system that is so much better than the others that everyone will want to be that way? Why should the sensations we associate with 'sexual pleasure' be always and forever the result of friction between mucous membranes? It's the same sort of urge people had about languages back on Earth, back when there were hundreds of languages, or about weights and measures. The metric system caught on, but Esperanto didn't. Today we have a few dozen languages still in use, and more types of sexual orientation than that."

I settled back in my chair, feeling foolish. But I'd done my part. Now Walter could get on with whatever he had in mind. I glanced at Brenda, and she was staring at me with the wide-eyed look of an acolyte to a guru.

Walter took another drag on his cheroot, exhaled, and leaned back in his chair, fingers laced behind his head.

"You know what today is?" he asked.

"Thursday," Brenda supplied. Walter glanced at her, but didn't bother to reply. He took another drag.

"It's the one hundred and ninety-ninth anniversary of the Invasion and Occupation of the Planet Earth."

"Remind me to light a candle and say a novena."

"You think it's funny."

"Nothing funny about it," I said. "I just wonder what it has to do with me."

Walter nodded, and put his feet down on the floor.

"How many stories have you seen on the Invasion in the last week? The week leading up to this anniversary?"

I was willing to play along.

"Let's see. Counting the stuff in *The Straight Shit,* the items in the *Lunarian* and the *K.C. News,* that incisive series in *Lunatime,* and of course our own voluminous coverage . . . none. Not a single story."

"That's right. I think it's time somebody did something about that."

"While we're at it, let's do a big spread on the Battle of Agincourt, and the first manned landing on Mars."

"You do think it's funny."

"I'm merely applying a lesson somebody taught me when I started here. If it happened yesterday, it ain't news. And *The News Nipple* reports the news."

"This isn't strictly for the *Nipple,*" Walter admitted.

"Uh-oh."

He ignored my expression, which I hoped was sufficiently sour, and plowed ahead.

"We'll use cuts from your stories in the *Nipple.* Most of 'em, anyway. You'll have Brenda to do most of the legwork."

"What are you talking about?" Brenda asked Walter. When that didn't work, she turned to me. "What's he talking about?"

"I'm talking about the supplement."

"He's talking about the old reporters' graveyard."

"Just one story a week. Will you let me explain?"

I settled back in my chair and tried to turn off my brain. Oh, I'd fight it hard enough, but I knew I didn't have much choice when Walter got that look in his eye.

The *News Nipple* Corporation publishes three pads. The first is the *Nipple* itself, updated hourly, full of what Walter Editor liked to think of as "lively" stories: the celebrity scandal, the pseudo-scientific breakthrough, psychic predictions, lovingly bloody coverage of disasters. We covered the rougher and more proletarian sports, and a certain amount of politics, if the proposition involved could be expressed in a short sentence. The *Nipple* had so many pictures you hardly needed to read the words. Like the other padloids, it would not have bothered with *any* copy but for the government literacy grants that often provided the financial margin between success and failure. A daily quota of words was needed to qualify for the grants. That exact number of words appeared in each of our issues, including "a," "an," "and," and "the."

The *Daily Cream* was the intellectual appendix to the swollen intestine of the *Nipple*. It came free to every subscriber of the pad—those government grants again—and was read by about one in ten, according to our more optimistic surveys. It published thousands of times more words per hour, and included most of our political coverage.

Somewhere between those two was the electronic equivalent of the Sunday supplement, published weekly, called *Sundae*.

"Here's what I want," Walter went on. "You'll go out and cover your regular beats. But I want you to be thinking *Sundae* while you do that. Whatever you're covering, think about how it would have been different two hundred years ago, back on Earth. It can be anything at all. Like today, sex. *There's* a topic for you. Write about what sex was like back on Earth, and contrast it to what it's like now. You could even throw in stuff about what people think it's gonna be like in another twenty years, or a century."

"Walter, I don't deserve this."

"Hildy, you're the only man for it. I want one article per week for the entire year leading up to the bicentennial. I'm giving you a free hand as to what they're about. You can editorialize. You can personalize, make it like a column. You've always wanted a column; here's your chance at a byline. You want expensive consultants, advisers, research? You name it, you got it. You need to travel? I'm good for the money. I want only the best for this series."

I didn't know what to say to that. It was a good offer. Nothing in life is ever exactly what you asked for, but I *had* wanted a column, and this seemed like a reasonable shot at it.

"Hildy, during the twentieth century there was a time like no other time humans have seen before or since. My grandfather's great-grandfather was born in the year the Wright brothers made the first powered flight. By the time he died, there was a permanent base on Luna. My grandfather was ten when the old man died, and he's told me many times how he used to talk about the old days. It was amazing just how much change that old man had seen in his lifetime.

"In that century they started talking about a 'generation gap.' So much happened, so many things changed so fast, how was a seventy-year-old supposed to talk to a fifteen-year-old in terms they both could understand?

"Well, things don't change quite that fast anymore. I wonder if they ever will again? But we've got something in common with those people. We've got kids like Brenda here who hardly remember anything beyond last year, and they're living side by side with people who were born and grew up on the Earth. People who remember what a one-gee gravity field was like, what it was to walk around outside and breathe free, unmetered air. Who were raised when people were born, grew up, and died in the same sex. People who fought in wars. Our oldest citizens are almost three hundred now. Surely there's fifty-two stories in that.

"This is a story that's been waiting two hundred years to be told. We've had our heads in the sand. We've been beaten, humiliated, suffered a racial setback that I'm afraid . . ."

It was as if he suddenly had heard what he was saying. He sputtered to a stop, not looking me in the eye.

I was not used to speeches from Walter. It made me uneasy. The assignment made me uneasy. I don't think about the Invasion much— which was precisely his point, of course—and I think that's just as well. But I could see his passion, and knew I'd better not fight it. I was used to rage, to being chewed out for this or that. Being appealed to was something brand new. I felt it was time to lighten the atmosphere a little.

"So how big a raise are we talking about here?" I asked.

He settled back in his chair and smiled, back on familiar ground.

"You know I never discuss that. It'll be in your next paycheck. If you don't like it, gripe to me then."

"And I have to use the kid on all this stuff?"

"Hey! I'm right here," Brenda protested.

"The kid is vital to the whole thing. She's your sounding board. If a fact from the old days sounds weird to her, you know you're onto something. She's contemporary as your last breath, she's eager to learn and fairly bright, and she knows *nothing*. You'll be the middleman. You're about the right age for it, and history's your hobby. You know more about Old Earth than any man your age I've ever met."

"If I'm in the middle . . ."

"You might want to interview my grandfather," Walter suggested. "But there'll be a third member of your team. Somebody Earth-born. I haven't decided yet who that'll be.

"Now get out of here, both of you."

I could see Brenda had a thousand questions she still wanted to ask. I warned her off with my eyes, and followed her to the door.

"And Hildy," Walter said. I looked back.

"If you put words like abnegation and infibulation in these stories, I'll personally caponize you."

03 AMAZING!
MIRACLE MOONBEAM CURES ALL!

I pulled the tarp off my pile of precious lumber and watched the scorpions scuttle away in the sunlight. Say what you want about the sanctity of life; I like to crush 'em.

Deeper in the pile I'd disturbed a rattlesnake. I didn't see him, but could hear him warning me away. Handling the lumber from the ends, I selected a plank and pulled it out. I shouldered it and carried it to my half-finished cabin. It was evening, the best time to work in West Texas. The temperature had dropped to ninety-five in the old-style scale they used there. During the day it had been well over a hundred.

I positioned the plank on two sawhorses near what would be the front porch when I was finished. I squatted and looked down its length. This was a one-by-ten—inches, not centimeters—which meant it actually measured about nine by seven-eighths, for reasons no one had ever explained to me. Thinking in inches was difficult enough, without dealing in those odd ratios called fractions. What was wrong with decimals, and what was wrong with a one-by-ten actually being one inch by ten inches? Why twelve inches in a foot? Maybe there was a story in it for the bicentennial series.

The plank had been advertised as ten feet long, and *that* measurement was accurate. It was also supposed to be straight, but if it was they had used a noodle for a straightedge.

Texas was the second of what was to be three Disneylands devoted to the nineteenth century. Out here west of the Pecos we reckoned it to be 1845, the last year of the Texas Republic, though you could use technology as recent as 1899 without running afoul of the anachronism regulations. Pennsylvania had been the first of the triad, and my plank, complete with two big bulges in the width and a depressing sag when held by one end, had been milled there by "Amish" sawyers using the old methods. A little oval stamp in a corner guaranteed this: "Approved, Lunar Antiquities Reproduction Board." Either the methods of the 1800s couldn't reliably produce straight and true lumber, or those damn Dutchmen were still learning their craft.

So I did what the carpenters of the Texas Republic had done. I got out my plane (also certified by the L.A.R.B.), removed the primitive blade, sharpened it against a homemade whetstone, reattached the blade, and began shaving away the irregularities.

I'm not complaining. I was lucky to get the lumber. Most of the cabin was made of rough-hewn logs notched together at the ends, chinked with adobe.

The board had turned gray in the heat and sun, but after a few strokes I was down to the yellow pine interior. The wood curled up around the blade and the chips dropped around my bare feet. It smelled fresh and new and I found myself smiling as the sweat dripped off my nose. It would be good to be a carpenter, I thought. Maybe I'd quit the newspaper business.

Then the blade broke and jammed into the wood. My palm slipped off the knob in front and tried to skate across the fresh-planed surface, driving long splinters into my skin. The plane clattered off the board and went for my toe with the hellish accuracy of a pain-guided missile.

I shouted a few words rarely heard in 1845, and some uncommon even in the twenty-third century. I hopped around on one foot. Another lost art, hopping.

"It could have been worse," a voice said in my ear. It was either incipient schizophrenia, or the Central Computer. I bet on the CC.

"How? By hitting *both* feet?"

"Gravity. Consider the momentum such a massive object could have attained, had this really been West Texas, which lies at the bottom of a space-time depression twenty-five thousand miles per hour deep."

Definitely the CC.

I examined my hand. Blood was oozing from it, running down my forearm and dripping from the elbow. But there was no arterial pumping. The foot, though it still hurt like fire, was not damaged.

"You see now why laborers in 1845 wore work boots."

"Is that why you called, CC? To give me a lecture about safety in the workplace?"

"No. I was going to announce a visitor. The colorful language lesson was an unexpected bonus of my tuning in on—"

"Shut up, will you?"

The Central Computer did so.

The end of a splinter protruded from my palm, so I pulled on it. I got some, but a lot was still buried in there. Others had broken off below skin level. All in all, a wonderful day's work.

A visitor? I looked around and saw no one, though a whole tribe of Apaches could have been hiding in the clumps of mesquite. I had not expected to see any sign of the CC. It uses the circuitry in my own head to produce its voice.

And it wasn't supposed to manifest itself in Texas. As is often the case, there was more to the CC than it was telling.

"CC, on-line, please."

"I hear and obey."

"Who's the visitor?"

"Tall, young, ignorant of tampons, with a certain puppy-like charm—"

"Oh, Jesus."

"I know I'm not supposed to intrude on these antique environments, but she was quite insistent on learning your location, and I thought it better for you to have some forewarning than to—"

"Okay. Now shut up."

I sat in the rickety chair which had been my first carpentry project. Being careful of the injured hand, I pulled on the work boots I should have been wearing all along. The reason I hadn't was simple: I hated them.

There was another story for Walter. Shoes. If Lunarians wear them, they tend to be the soft kind, like moccasins, or socks. Reason: in a crowded urban environment of perfectly smooth floors and carpets and a majority of barefoot people, hard shoes are anti-social. You could break someone else's toes.

Once I had my feet jammed into the smelly things I had to search for the buttonhook. Buttons, on shoes! It was outrageous. How had people ever tolerated such things? To add insult to inutility, the damn things had cost me a fortune.

I stood and was about to head into town when the CC spoke again.

"If you leave those tools out and it rains, they will combine with the oxygen in the air in a slow combustion reaction."

"Rust is too poor a word for you, right? It rains out here . . . what? Once every hundred days?"

But my heart wasn't in it. The CC was right. If button-up torture devices were expensive, period tools were worth a king's ransom. My plane, saw, hammer and chisel had cost a year's salary. The good news was I could resell them for more than I paid . . . if they weren't rusted.

I wrapped them in an oiled cloth and stowed them carefully in my toolbox, then headed down the trail toward town.

I was in sight of New Austin before I spied Brenda, looking like an albino flamingo. She was standing on one leg while the other was turned around so the foot was at waist level, sole upward. To do it she had twisted at hip and knee in ways I hadn't thought humanly possible. She was nude, her skin a uniform creamy white. She had no pubic hair.

"Hi, there, seven foot two, eyes of blue."

She glanced at me, then pointed at her foot, indignantly.

"They don't keep these paths very tidy. Look what it did to my foot. There was a stone, with a sharp *point* on it."

"They specialize in sharp points around here," I said. "It's a natural environment. You've probably never seen one before."

"My class went to Amazon three years ago."

"Sure, on the moving walkway. While I'm at it, I'd better tell you the plants have sharp points, too. That big thing there is a prickly pear. Don't walk through it. That thing behind you is a cactus, too. Don't step on it. This bush has thorns. Over there is cenizo. It blooms after a rain; real pretty."

She looked around, possibly realizing for the first time that there was more than one kind of plant, and that they all had names.

"You know what they're all called?"

"Not all. I know the big ones. Those spiky ones are yucca. The tall ones, like whips, those are ocotillo. Most of those short bushes are creosote. That tree is mesquite."

"Not much of a tree."

"It's not much of an environment. Things here have to struggle to stay alive. Not like Amazon, where the plants fight each other. Here they work too hard conserving water."

She looked around again, wincing as her injured foot touched the ground.

"No animals?"

"They're all around you. Insects, reptiles, mostly. Some antelope. Buffalo further east. I could show you a cougar lair." I doubted she had any idea what a cougar was, or antelope and buffalo, for that matter. This was a city girl through and through. About like me before I moved to Texas, three years ago. I relented and went down on one knee.

"Let me see that foot."

There was a ragged gash on the heel, painful but not serious.

"Hey, your hand is hurt," she said. "What happened?"

"Just a stupid accident." I noticed as I said it that she not only lacked pubic hair, she had no genitals. That used to be popular sixty or seventy years ago, for children, as part of a theory of the time concerning something called "delayed adolescence." I hadn't seen it in at least twenty years, though I'd heard there were religious sects that still practiced it. I wondered if her family belonged to one, but it was much too personal to ask about.

"I don't like this place," she said. "It's *dangerous.*" She made it sound like an obscenity. The whole idea offended her, as well it should, coming as she did from the most benign environment ever created by humans.

"It's not so bad. Can you walk on that?"

"Oh, sure." She put her foot down and walked along beside me, on her toes. As if she weren't tall enough already. "What was that remark about seven feet? I've got two feet, just like everyone else."

"Actually, you're closer to seven-four, I'd guess." I had to give her a brief explanation of the English system of weights and measures as used in the West Texas Disneyland. I'm not sure she understood it, but I didn't hold it against her, because I didn't, either.

We had arrived in the middle of New Austin. This was no great feat of walking; the middle is about a hundred yards from the edge. New Austin consists of two streets: Old Spanish Trail and Congress Street. The intersection is defined by four buildings: The Travis Hotel, the Alamo Saloon, a general store, and a livery stable. The hotel and saloon each have a second story. At the far end of Congress is a white clapboard Baptist church. That, and a few dozen other ramshackle buildings strung out between the church and Four Corners, is New Austin.

"They took all my clothes," she said.

"Naturally."

"They were perfectly good clothes."

"I'm sure they were. But only contemporary things are allowed in here."

"What for?"

"Think of it as a living museum."

I'd been headed for the doctor's office. Considering the time of day, I thought better of it and mounted the steps to the saloon. We entered through the swinging doors.

It was dark inside, and a little cooler. Behind me, Brenda had to duck to get through the doorway. A player piano tinkled in the background, just like an old western movie. I spotted the doctor sitting at the far end of the bar.

"Say, young lady," the bartender shouted. "You can't come in here dressed like that." I looked around, saw her looking down at herself in complete confusion.

"What's the *matter* with you people?" she shouted. "The lady outside made me leave all my clothes with her."

"Amanda," the bartender said, "you have anything she could wear?" He turned to Brenda again. "I don't care what you wear out in the bush. You come into my establishment, you'll be decently dressed. What they told you outside is no concern of mine."

One of the bar girls approached Brenda, holding a pink robe. I turned away. Let them sort it out.

Ever since moving to Texas, I'd played their games of authenticity. I didn't have an accent, but I'd picked up a smattering of words. Now I groped for one, a particularly colorful one, and came up with it.

"I hear tell you're the sawbones around these parts," I said.

The doctor chuckled and extended his hand.

"Ned Pepper," he said, "at your service, sir."

When I didn't shake his hand he frowned, and noticed the dirty bandage wrapped around it.

"Looks like you threw a shoe, son. Let me take a look at that."

He carefully unwrapped the bandage, and winced when he saw the splinters. I could smell the sourness of his breath, and his clothes. Doc was one of the permanent residents, like the bartender and the rest of the hotel staff. He was an alcoholic who had found a perfect niche for himself. In Texas he had status and could spend most of the day swilling whiskey at the Alamo. The drunken physician was a cliché from a thousand horse operas of the twentieth century, but so what? All we have in reconstructing these past environments is books and movies. The movies are much more helpful, one picture being equal to a kilo-word.

"Can you do anything with it?" I asked.

He looked up in surprise, and swallowed queasily.

"I guess I could dig 'em out. Couple quarts of rye—maybe one for you, too—though I freely admit the idea makes me want to puke." He squinted at my hand again, and shook his head. "You really want me to do it?"

"I don't see why not. You're a doctor, aren't you?"

"Sure, by 1845 standards. The Board trained me. Took about a week. I got a bag full of steel tools and a cabinet full of patent elixirs. What I don't have is an anaesthetic. I suppose those splinters hurt going in."

"They *still* hurt."

"It's nothing to how it'd hurt if I took the case. Let me . . . Hildy? Is that your name? That's right, I remember now. Newspaperman. Last time I talked to you you seemed to know a few things about Texas. More than most weekenders."

"I'm not a weekender," I protested. "I've been building a cabin."

"No offense meant, son, but it started out as an investment, didn't it?"

I admitted it. The most valuable real estate in Luna is in the less-developed Disneylands. I'd quadrupled my money so far and there were no signs the boom was slowing.

"It's funny how much people will pay for hardship," he said. "They warn you up front but they don't spend a lot of time talking about medical care. People come here to live, and they tell themselves they'll live authentic. Then they get a taste of my medicine and run to the real world. Pain ain't funny, Hildy. Mostly I deliver babies, and any reasonably competent woman could do that herself."

"Then what are you good for?" I regretted it as soon as I said it, but he didn't seem to take offense.

"I'm mostly window dressing," he admitted. "I don't mind it. There's worse ways of earning your daily oxygen."

Brenda had drifted over to catch the last of our conversation. She was wrapped in a ridiculous pink robe, still favoring one foot.

"You fixed up yet?" she asked me.

"I think I'll wait," I said.

"Another lame mare?" the doctor asked. "Toss that hoof up here, little lady, and let me take a look at it." When he had examined the cut he grinned and rubbed his hands together. "Here's an injury within my realm of expertise," he said. "You want me to treat it?"

"Sure, why not?"

The doctor opened his black bag and Brenda watched him innocently. He removed several bottles, cotton swabs, bandages, laid it all out carefully on the bar.

"A little tincture of iodine to cleanse the wound," he muttered, and touched a purplish wad of cotton to Brenda's foot. She howled, and jumped four feet straight up, using only the uninjured foot. If I hadn't grabbed her ankle she would have hit the ceiling.

"What the hell is he doing?" she yelled at me.

"Hush, now," I soothed her.

"But it *hurts.*"

I gave her my best determined-reporter look, grabbing her hand to intensify the effect.

"There's a story in here, Brenda. Medicine then and now. Think how pleased Walter will be."

"Well, why doesn't he work on you, too?" she pouted.

"It would have involved amputation," I said. And it would have, too; I'd have cut off his hand if he laid it on me.

"I don't know if I want to——"

"Just hold still and I'll be through in a minute."

She howled, she cried, but she held still enough for him to finish cleaning the wound. She'd make a hell of a reporter one day.

The doctor took out a needle and thread.

"What's that for?" she asked, suspiciously.

"I have to suture the wound now," he said.

"If suture means sew up, you can suture your*self,* you bastard."

He glared at her, but saw the determination in her eyes. He put the needle and thread away and prepared a bandage.

"Yes sir, it was hard times, 1845," he said. "You know what caused people the most trouble? Teeth. If a tooth goes bad here, what you do is you go to the barber down the street, or the one over in Lonesome Dove, who's said to be quicker. Barbers used to handle it all: teeth, surgery, and haircutting. But the thing about teeth, usually you could *do* something. Yank it right out. Most things that happened to people, you couldn't do *anything.* A little cut like this, it could get infected and kill you. There was a million ways to die and mostly the doctors just tried to keep you warm."

Brenda was listening with such fascination she almost forgot to protest when he put the bandage over the wound. Then she frowned and touched his hand as he was about to knot it around her ankle.

"Wait a minute," she said. "You're not finished."

"I sure as hell am."

"You mean that's *it?*"

"What else do you suggest?"

"I still have a *hole* in me, you idiot. It's not *fixed.*"

"It'll heal in about a week. All by itself."

It was clear from her look that she thought this was a very dangerous man. She started to say something, changed her mind, and glared at the bartender.

"Give me some of that brown stuff," she said, pointing. He filled a shot glass with whiskey and set it in front of her. She sipped it, made a face, and sipped again.

"That's the idea, little lady," the doctor said. "Take two of those every morning if symptoms persist."

"What do we owe you, Doc?" I asked.

"Oh, I don't think I could rightly charge you . . ." His eyes strayed to the bottles behind the bar.

"A drink for the doctor, landlord," I said. I looked around, and smiled at myself. What the hell. "A drink for the house. On me." People started drifting toward the bar.

"What'll it be, Doc?" the bartender asked. "Grain alcohol?"

"Some of that clear stuff," the doctor agreed.

* * *

We were a quarter mile out of town before Brenda spoke to me again.

"This business about covering up," she ventured. "That's a cultural thing, right? Something they did in this place?"

"Not the place so much as the time. Out here in the country no one cares whether you cover up or not. But in town, they try to stick to the old rules. They stretched a point for you, actually. You really should have been wearing a dress that reached your ankles, your wrists, and covered most of your neck, too. Hell, a young lady really shouldn't have been allowed in a saloon at all."

"Those other girls weren't wearing all that much."

"Different rule. They're 'fallen flowers.' " She was giving me a blank look again. "Whores."

"Oh, sure," she said. "I read an article that said it used to be illegal. How could they make that illegal?"

"Brenda, they can make anything illegal. Prostitution has been illegal more often than not. Don't ask me to explain it; I don't understand, either."

"So they make a law in here, and then they let you break it?"

"Why not? Most of those girls don't sell sex, anyway. They're here for the tourists. Get your picture taken with the B-girls in the Alamo Saloon. The idea of Texas is to duplicate what it was really *like* in 1845, as near as we can determine. Prostitution was illegal but tolerated in a place like New Austin. Hell, the sheriff would most likely be one of the regular customers. Or take the bar. They shouldn't have served you, because this culture didn't approve of giving alcoholic drinks to people as young as you. But on the frontier, there was the feeling that if you were big enough to reach up and take the drink off the bar, you were big enough to drink it." I looked at her frowning intently down at the ground, and knew most of this was not getting through to her. "I don't suppose you can ever really understand a culture unless you grew up in it," I said.

"These people were sure screwed up."

"Probably so."

We were climbing the trail that led toward my apartment. Brenda kept her eyes firmly on the ground, her mind obviously elsewhere, no doubt chewing over the half-dozen crazy things I'd told her in the past hour. By not looking around she was missing a sunset spectacular even by the lavish standards of West Texas. The air had turned salmon pink when the sun dipped below the horizon, streaked by wispy curls of gold. Somehow the waning light made the surrounding rocky hills a pale purple. I wondered if that was authentic. A quarter of a million miles from where I stood, the real sun was setting on the real Texas. Were the colors as spectacular there?

Here, of course, the "sun" was sitting in its track just below the forced-perspective "hills." A fusion tech was seeing to the shut-down process, after which the sun would be trucked through a tunnel and attached to the eastern end of the track, ready to be lit again in a few hours. Somewhere behind the hills another technician was manipulating colored mirrors and lenses to diffuse the light over the dome of the sky. Call him an artist; I won't argue with you. They've been charging admission to see the sunsets in Pennsylvania and Amazon for several years now. There's talk of doing that here, too.

It seemed unlikely to me that nature, acting at random, could produce the incredible complexity and subtlety of a Disneyland sunset.

It was almost dark by the time we reached the Rio Grande.

The entrance to my condo was on the south, "Mexican" side of the river. West Texas is compressed, to display as wide a range of terrain and biome as possible. The variety of geographical features that, on Earth, spread over five hundred miles and included parts of New Mexico and Old Mexico here had been made to fit within a sub-lunar bubble fifty miles in diameter. One edge duplicated the rolling hills and grassland around the real Austin, while the far edge had the barren rocky plateaus to be found around El Paso.

The part of the Rio Grande we had reached mimicked the land east of the Big Bend in the real river, an area of steep gorges where the water ran deep and swift. Or at least it did in the brief rainy season. Now, in the middle of summer, it was no trick to wade across. Brenda followed me down the forty-foot cliff on the Texas side, then watched me splash through the river. She had said nothing for the last few miles, and she said nothing now, though it was clear she thought someone should have stopped this massive water leak, or at least provided a bridge, boat, or helicopter. But she sloshed her way over to me and stood waiting as I located the length of rope that would take us to the top.

"Aren't you curious about why I'm here?" she asked.

"No. I know why you're here." I tugged on the rope. It was dark enough now that I couldn't see the ledge, fifty feet up, where I had secured it. "Wait till I call down to you," I told her. I set one booted foot on the cliff face.

"Walter's been pretty angry," she said. "The deadline is just—"

"I know when the deadline is." I started up the rope, hand over hand, feet on the dark rocks.

"What are we going to write about?" she called up at me.

"I told you. Medicine."

I had knocked out the introductory article on the Invasion Bicentennial the night after Brenda and I got the assignment. I thought it had been some of my best work, and Walter had agreed. He'd given us a big spread, the cover, personality profiles of both of us that were—in my case, at least—irresistibly flattering. Brenda and I had then sat down and generated a list of twenty topics just off the tops of our heads. We didn't anticipate any trouble finding more when the time came.

But since that first day, every time I tried to write one of Walter's damnable articles . . . nothing happened.

Result: the cabin was coming along nicely, ahead of schedule. Another few weeks like the past one and I'd have it finished. And be out of a job.

I crested the top of the cliff and looked down. I could just see the white blob that was Brenda. I called down to her and she swarmed up like a monkey.

"Nicely done," I said, as I coiled the rope. "Did you ever think what that would have been like if you weighed six times what you weigh now?"

"Oddly enough, I have," she said. "I keep trying to tell you, I'm not completely ignorant."

"Sorry."

"I'm willing to learn. I've been reading a lot. But there's just so *much,* and so much of it is so *foreign* . . ." She ran a hand through her hair. "Anyway, I know how hard it must have been to live on the Earth. My arms wouldn't be strong enough to support my weight down there." She looked down at herself, and I thought I could see a smile. "Hell, I'm so lunified I wonder if my *legs* could support my weight."

"Probably not, at first."

"I got five friends together and we took turns trying to walk with all the others on our shoulders. I managed three steps before I collapsed."

"You're really getting into this, aren't you?" I was leading the way down the narrow ledge to the cave entrance.

"Of course I am. I take this very seriously. But I'm beginning to wonder if you do."

I didn't have an answer to that. We had reached the cave, and I started to lead her in when she pulled back violently on my hand.

"What is *that?*"

She didn't need to elaborate; I came through the cave twice a day, and I still wasn't used to the smell. Not that it seemed as bad now as it had at first. It was a combination of rotting meat, feces, ammonia, and something else much more disturbing that I had taken to calling "predator smell."

"Be quiet," I whispered. "This is a cougar den. She's not really dangerous, but she had a litter of cubs last week and she's gotten touchy since then. Don't let go of my hand; there's no light till we get to the door."

I didn't give her a chance to argue. I just pulled on her hand, and we were inside.

The smell was even stronger in the cave. The mother cougar was fairly fastidious, for an animal. She cleaned up her cubs' messes, and she made her own outside the cave. But she wasn't so careful about disposing of the remains of her prey before they started to get ripe. I think she had a different definition of "ripe." Her own fur had a rank mustiness that was probably sweet perfume to a male cougar, but was enough to stun the unprepared human.

I couldn't see her, but I sensed her in a way beyond sight or hearing. I knew she wouldn't attack. Like all the large predators in Disneylands, she had been conditioned to leave humans alone. But the conditioning set up a certain amount of mental conflict. She didn't *like* us, and wasn't shy about letting us know. When I was halfway through the cave, she let fly with a sound I can only describe as hellish. It started as a low growl, and quickly rose to a snarling screech. Every hair on my body stood at attention. It's sort of a bracing feeling, once you get used to it; your skin feels thick and tough as leather. My scrotum grew very small and hard as it tried its best to get certain treasures out of harm's way.

As for Brenda . . . she tried to run straight up the backs of my legs and over the top of my head. Without some fancy footwork on my part we both would have gone sprawling. But I'd been ready for that reaction, and hurried along until the inner door got out of our way with a blast of light from the far side. Brenda didn't stop running for another twenty meters. Then she stopped, a sheepish grin on her face, breathing shallowly. We were in the long, utilitarian hallway that led to the back door of my condo.

"I don't know what got into me," she said.

"Don't worry," I said. "Apparently that's one of the sounds that is part of the human brain's hard wiring. It's a reflex, like when you stick your finger in a flame, you don't think about it, you instantly draw it back."

"And you hear that sound, your bowels turn to oatmeal."

"Close enough."

"I'd like to go back and see the thing that made that sound."

"It's worth seeing," I agreed. "But you'll have to wait for daylight. The cubs are cute. It's hard to believe they'll turn into monsters like their mother."

I hesitated at the door. In my day, and up until fairly recently, you just didn't let someone enter your home lightly. Luna is a crowded society. There are people wherever you turn, tripping over your feet, elbowing you, millions of intrusive, sweaty bodies. You have to have a small place of privacy. After you'd known someone five or ten years you might, if you really liked the person, invite her over for drinks or sex in your own bed. But most socializing took place on neutral ground.

The younger generation wasn't like that. They thought nothing of dropping by just to say hello. I could make a big thing of it, driving yet another wedge between the two of us, or I could let it go.

What the hell. We'd have to learn to work together sooner or later. I opened the door with my palm print and stepped aside to let her enter.

She hurried to the washroom, saying something about having to take a mick. I assumed that meant urinate, though I'd never heard the term. I wondered briefly how she'd accomplish that, given her lack of obvious outlet. I could have found out—she left the door open. The young ones were no longer seeking privacy even for that.

I looked around at the apartment. What would Brenda see here? What would a pre-Invasion man see?

What they wouldn't see was dirt and clutter. A dozen cleaning robots worked tirelessly whenever I was away. No speck of dust was too small for their eternal vigilance, and no item could ever be out of its assigned place longer than it took me to walk to the tube station.

Could someone read anything about my character from looking at this room? There were no books or paintings to give a clue. I had all the libraries of the world a few keystrokes away, but no books of my own. Any of the walls could project artwork or films or environments, as desired, but they seldom did.

There was something interesting. Unlimited computer capacity had brought manufacturing full circle. Primitive cultures produced articles by hand, and no two were identical. The industrial revolution had standardized production, poured out endless streams of items for the "consumer culture." Finally, it became possible to have each and every manufactured item individually ordered and designed. All my furniture was unique. Nowhere in Luna would you find another sofa like that . . . like that hideous monstrosity over there. And what a blessing *that* was, I mused. Two of them might have mated. *Damn,* but it was ugly.

I had selected almost nothing in this room. The possibilities of taste had become so endless I had simply thrown up my hands and taken what came with the apartment.

Maybe *that* was what I'd been reluctant to let Brenda see. I supposed you could read as much into what a man had not done to his environment as what he *had* done.

While I was still pondering that—and not feeling too happy about it—Brenda came out of the washroom. She had a bloody piece of gauze in her hand, which she tossed on the floor. A low-slung robot darted out from under the couch and ate it, then scuttled away. Her skin looked greased, and the pinkish color was fading as I watched. She had visited the doc.

"I had radiation burns," she said. "I ought to take the Disneyland management to court, get them to pay the medical bill." She lifted her foot and examined the bottom. There was a pink area of new skin where the cut had been. In a few more minutes it would be gone. There would be no scar. She looked up, hastily. "I'll pay, of course. Just send me the bill."

"Forget it," I said. "I just got your lead. How long were you in Texas?"

"Three hours? Four at the most."

"I was there for five hours, today. Except for the gravity, it's a pretty good simulation of the natural Earthly environment. And what happened to us?" I ticked the points off on my fingers. "You got sunburned. Consequences, in 1845: you would have been in for a very bad night. No sleep. Pain for several days. Then the outer layer of your skin would slough off. Probably some more dermatological effects. I think it might even have caused skin cancer. That would have been *fatal*. Research that one, see if I'm right.

"You injured the sole of your foot. Consequence, not too bad, but you would have limped for a few days or a week. And always the danger of infection to an area of the body difficult to keep clean.

"I got a very nasty injury to my hand. Bad enough to require minor surgery, with the possibility of deep infection, loss of the limb, perhaps death. There's a word for it, when one of your limbs starts to mortify. Look it up.

"So," I summed up. "Three injuries. Two possibly fatal, over time. All in five hours. Consequences today: an almost negligible bill from the automatic doc."

She waited for me to go on. I was prepared to let her wait a lot longer, but she finally gave in.

"That's it? That's my story?"

"The *lead*, goddamit. *Personalize* it. You went for a walk in the park, and this is what happened. It shows how perilous life was back then. It shows how lightly we've come to regard injury to our bodies, how completely we expect total, instant, painless repairs to them. Remember what you said? 'It's not *fixed!*' You'd never had anything happen to you that couldn't be fixed, right now, with no pain."

She looked thoughtful, then smiled.

"That could work, I guess."

"Damn right it'll work. You take it from there, work in more detail. Don't get into optional medical things; we'll keep that for later. Make this one a pure horror story. Show how fragile life has always been. Show how it's only in the last century or so that we've been able to stop worrying about our health."

"We can do that," she said.

"We, hell. I told you, this is your story. Now get out of here and get to it. Deadline's in twenty-four hours."

I expected more argument, but I'd ignited her youthful enthusiasm. I hustled her out the door, then leaned against it and heaved a sigh of relief. I'd been afraid she'd call me on it.

Not long after she left I went to the doc and had my own hand healed. Then I ran a big tubful of water and eased myself into it. The water was so hot it turned my skin pink. That's the way I like it.

After a while I got out, rummaged in a cabinet, and found an old home surgery kit. There was a sharp scalpel in it.

I ran some more hot water, got in again, lay back and relaxed completely. When I was totally at peace with myself, I slashed both my wrists right down to the bone.

0 4 SECRET INVESTIGATION PROVES: WRESTLING MATCHES RIGGED!

Dirty Dan the Dervish went into his trademark spin late in the third round. By that time he had the Cytherian Cyclone staggering.

I'm not a slash-boxing fan, but the spin was something to see. The Dervish pumped himself up and down like a top, balancing on the toes of his left foot. He'd draw his right leg in to spin faster, until he was almost a blur, then, without warning, the right foot would flash out, sometimes high, sometimes low, sometimes connecting. Either way, he'd instantly be pumping up and down with the left leg, spinning as if he were on ice.

"Dervish! Dervish! Dervish!" the fans were chanting. Brenda was shouting as loud as anyone. She was beside me, at ringside. Most of the time she was on her feet. As for me, they issued clear plastic sheets to everyone in the first five rows, and I spent most of my time holding mine between me and the ring. The Dervish had a deep gash on his right calf, and the slashing spin could hurl blood droplets an amazing distance.

The Cyclone kept retreating, unable to come up with any defense. He tried ducking under and attacking with the knife in his right hand, and received another wound for his trouble. He leaped into the air, but the Dervish was instantly with him, slashing up from below, and as soon as their feet hit the mat again he went into his whirl. Things were looking desperate for the Cyclone, when he was suddenly saved by the bell.

Brenda sat down, breathing hard. I supposed that, without sex, one needed something for release of tensions. Slash-boxing seemed perfectly designed for that.

She wiped some of the blood from her face with a cloth, and turned to look at me for the first time since the round began. She seemed disappointed that I wasn't getting into the festivities.

"How does he manage that spin?" I asked her.

"It's the mat," she said, falling instantly into the role of expert—which must have been quite a relief for her. "Something to do with the molecular alignment of the fibers. If you lean on it in a certain way, you get traction, but a circular motion reduces the friction till it's almost like ice skating."

"Do I still have time to get a bet down?"

"No point in it," she said. "The odds will be lousy. You should have bet when I told you, before the match started. The Cyclone is a dead man."

He certainly looked it. Sitting on his stool, surrounded by his pit crew, it seemed impossible he would answer the bell for the next round. His legs were a mass of cuts, some covered with bloody bandages. His left arm dangled by a strip of flesh; the pit boss was considering removing it entirely. There was a temporary shunt on his left jugular artery. It looked horribly vulnerable, easy to hit. He had sustained that injury at the end of the second round, which had enabled his crew to patch it at the cost of several liters of blood. But his worst wound had also come in the second round. It was a gash, half a meter long, from his left hip to his right nipple. Ribs were visible at the top, while the middle was held together with half a dozen hasty stitches of a rawhide-like material. He had sustained it while scoring his only effective attack on the Dervish, bringing his knife in toward the neck, achieving a ghastly but minimally disabling wound to the Dervish's face—only to find the Dervish's knife thrust deep into his gut. The upward jerk of that knife had spilled viscera all over the ring and produced the first yellow flag of the match, howls of victory from Dirty Dan's pit, and chants of "Dervish! Dervish! Dervish!" from the crowd.

The Cyclone's handlers had hacked away the torn tangle of organs under the caution flag, repaired the neck artery during the second pit stop, and retired glumly to their corner to watch their man walk into the meat grinder again.

The Dervish was sitting erect while his crew did more work to the facial wound. One eyeball was split open and useless. Blood had temporarily blinded him during the second round, rendering him unable to fully exploit the terrible wound he'd inflicted on his opponent. Brenda had expressed concern during the lull that the Dervish might not employ his famous spin now that his depth perception had been destroyed. But the Dervish was not about to disappoint his fans, one eye or not.

A red light went on over the Cyclone's corner. It made the crowd murmur excitedly.

"Why do they call it a corner?" I asked.

"Huh?"

"It's a round ring. It doesn't have any corners."

She shrugged. "It's traditional, I guess." Then she smiled maliciously. "You can research it before you write this up for Walter."

"Don't be ridiculous."

"Why the hell not? 'Sports, Then and Now.' It's a natural."

She was right, of course, but that didn't make it any harder to swallow. I wasn't particularly enjoying this role reversal. *She* was supposed to be the ignorant one.

"What about that red light? What's it mean?"

"Each of the fighters gets ten liters of blood for transfusions. See that gauge on the scoreboard? The Cyclone just used his last liter. Dervish has seven liters left."

"So it's just about over."

"He'll never last another round."

And he didn't.

The last round was an artless affair. No more fancy spins, no flying leaps. The crowd shouted a little at first, then settled down to watch the kill. People began drifting out of the arena to get refreshments before the main bout of the evening. The Dervish moved constantly away as the dazed Cyclone lumbered after him, striking out from time to time, opening more wounds. Bleeding his opponent to death. Soon the Cyclone could only stand there, dumb and inert with loss of blood. A few people in the crowd were booing. The Dervish slashed the Cyclone's throat. Arterial blood spurted into the air, and the Cyclone crashed to the mat. The Dervish bent over his fallen foe, worked briefly, and then held the head high. There was sporadic applause and the handlers moved in, hustling the Dervish down to the locker rooms and hauling away both pieces of the Cyclone. The zamboni appeared and began mopping up the blood.

"You want some popcorn?" Brenda asked me.

"Just something to drink," I told her. She joined the throngs moving toward the refreshment center.

I turned back toward the ring, savoring a feeling that had been all too rare of late: the urge to write. I raised my left hand and snapped my fingers. I snapped them again before I remembered the damn handwriter was not working. It hadn't been working for five days, since Brenda's visit to Texas. The problem seemed to be in the readout skin. I could type on the keyboard on the heel of my hand, but nothing appeared on the readout. The data was going into the memory and could later be downloaded, but I can't work that way. I have to see the words as they're being formed.

Necessity is the mother of invention. I flipped through the program book Brenda had left on her chair, found a blank page. Then I rummaged through my purse and found a blue pen I kept for hand corrections to hard copy.

(File Hildy*next avail.*)(code Bloodsport)
(headline to come)

There may be no evidence of it, but you can bet cavemen had sporting events. We still have them today, and if we ever reach the stars, we'll have sports out there, too.

Sports are rooted in violence. They usually contain the threat of injury. Or at least they did until about a hundred and fifty years ago.

Sports today, of course, are totally nonviolent.

The modern sports fan would be shocked at the violence of sports as they existed on Earth. Take for example one of the least violent sports, one we still practice today, the simple footrace. Runners rarely completed a career without numerous injuries to knees, ankles, muscles, or spine. Sometimes these injuries could be repaired, and sometimes they couldn't. Every time a runner competed, he faced the possibility of injury that would plague him *for the rest of his life*.

In the days of the Romans, athletes fought each other with swords and other deadly weapons—not always voluntarily. Crippling injury or death was certain, in every match.

Even in later, more "enlightened" days, many sports were little more than organized mayhem. Teams of athletes crashed into each other with amazing disregard for the imperfect skills of contemporary healers. People strapped themselves into ground vehicles or flying machines and raced at speeds that would turn them into jelly in the event of a sudden stop. Crash helmets, fist pads, shoulder, groin, knee, rib, and nose protectors tried to temper the carnage but by their mere presence were testimony to the violent potential in all these games.

Did I hear someone protesting out there? Did someone say our modern sports are much *more* violent than those of the past?

What a ridiculous idea.

Modern athletes typically compete in the nude. No protection is needed or wanted. In most sports, bodily damage is expected, sometimes even desired, as in slash-boxing. A modern athlete just after a competition would surely be a shocking sight to a citizen of any Earth society. But modern sports produce no cripples.

It would be nice to think this universal nonviolence was the result of some great moral revolution. It just ain't so. It is a purely technological revolution. There is no injury today that can't be fixed.

The fact is, "violence" is a word that no longer means what it used to.

Which is the more violent: a limb being torn off and quickly reattached with no ill effects, or a crushed spinal disc that causes its owner pain every second of his life and *cannot be repaired?*

I know which injury I'd prefer.

That kind of violence is no longer something to fear, because

(discuss Olympic games, influence of local gravity in venues)
(mention Deathmatches)
(Tie to old medicine article?) (ask Brenda)

I hastily scribbled the last few lines, because I saw Brenda returning with the popcorn.

"What're you doing?" she asked, resuming her seat. I handed her the page. She scanned it quickly.

"Seems a little dry," was her only comment.

"You'll hype it up some," I told her. "This is your field." I reached over and took a kernel of popcorn from her, then took a big bite out of it. She had bought the large bag: a dozen fist-sized puffs, white and crunchy, dripping with butter. It tasted great, washed down with the big bottle of beer she handed me.

While I was writing there had been an exhibition from some children's slash-boxing school. The children were filing out now, most of them crosshatched with slashes of red ink from the training knives they used. Medical costs for children were high enough without letting them practice with real knives.

The ringmaster appeared and began hyping the main event of the evening, a Deathmatch between the champion Manhattan Mugger and a challenger known as One Mean Bitch.

Brenda leaned toward me and spoke out of the side of her mouth.

"Put your money on the Bitch," she said.

"If she's gonna win, what the hell are we doing here?"

"Ask Walter. This was his idea."

The purpose of our visit to the fights was to interview the Manhattan Mugger—also known as Andrew MacDonald—with an eye toward hiring him as our Earth-born consultant on the bicentennial series. MacDonald was well over two hundred years old. The trouble was, he had elected to fight to the death. If he lost, his next interview would be with St. Peter. But Walter had assured us there was no way his man was going to lose.

"I was talking to a friend out at the concessions," Brenda went on. "There's no question the Mugger is the better fighter. This is his tenth Deathmatch in the last two years. What this guy was saying is, ten is too much for anybody. He said the Mugger was dogging it in the last match.

He won't get away with that against the Bitch. He says the Mugger doesn't *want* to win anymore. He just wants to die."

The contestants had entered the ring, were strutting around, showing off, as holo pictures of their past bouts appeared high in the air and the announcer continued to make it sound as if this would be the fight of the century.

"Did you bet on her?"

"I put down fifty, for a kill in the second."

I thought that over, then beckoned to a tout. He handed me a card, which I marked and thumbed. He stuck the card in the totaliser on his belt, then handed me the marker. I pocketed it.

"How much did you invest?"

"Ten. To win." I didn't tell her it was on the Mugger.

The contestants were in their "corners," being oiled down, as the announcer continued his spiel. They were magnificent specimens, competing in the highest body-mass class, matched to within a kilogram. The lights flashed on their glistening browned skins as they shadow-boxed and danced, skittish as racehorses, bursting with energy.

"This bout is being conducted under the sporting bylaws of King City," the announcer said, "which provide for voluntary Deathmatches for one or both parties. The Manhattan Mugger has elected to risk death tonight. He has been advised and counseled, as required by law, and should he die tonight, it will be deemed a suicide. The Bitch has agreed to deliver the *coup de grace,* should she find herself in a position to do so, and understands she will not be held responsible in any way."

"Don't worry about it!" the Mugger shouted, glaring at his opponent. It got a laugh, and the announcer looked grateful for the interruption in the boring paragraphs the law required him to read.

He brought them out to the middle of the ring and read them the rule—which was simply to stop fighting when they heard the bell. Other than that, there were no rules. He had them shake hands, and told them to come out fighting.

"The first stinking round. I can't believe it."

Brenda was still complaining, half an hour after the finish of the match. It had not been a contest that would go down in history.

We were waiting in the reception area outside the entrance to the locker rooms. MacDonald's manager had told us we could go in to see him as soon as the pit crew had him patched up. Considering the small amount of damage he had suffered, I didn't expect that to be too much longer.

I heard a commotion and turned to see the Cyclone emerging into a small group of dedicated fans, mostly children. He got out a pen and began signing autographs. He was dressed in black shirt and pants, and had a bulky brace around his neck, which seemed a small enough inconvenience for a man whose head had been rolling around the ring an hour earlier. He'd wear it until the new muscles had been conditioned enough to support his head. I figured that wouldn't be long; the brain of a man in his profession couldn't weigh all that much.

The door opened again and MacDonald's manager beckoned to us.

We followed him down a dim corridor lined with numbered doors. One of them was open and I could hear moaning coming from it. I glanced in as we passed. There was a bloody mess on a high table, with half a dozen pit crew clustered around.

"You don't mean to tell me . . ."

"What?" Brenda said, and glanced into the room. "Oh. Yeah, she fights without nerve deadening."

"I thought—"

"Most fighters turn their pain center way down, just enough so they know when they've been hit. But a few feel that trying to avoid real pain makes them quicker on their feet."

"It sure would make me quicker."

"Yeah, well, obviously it wasn't enough tonight."

I was glad I'd had only the one piece of popcorn.

The Manhattan Mugger was sitting in a diagnostic chair, wearing a robe and smoking a cheroot. His left leg was propped up and being worked on by one of his trainers. He smiled when he saw us, and held out his hand.

"Andy MacDonald," he said. "Pardon me for not getting up."

We both shook his hand, and he waved us into seats. He offered us drinks, which a member of his entourage brought us.

Then Brenda launched into a breathless recap of the match, full of glowing praise for his martial skills. You'd never have known she just lost fifty on him. I sat back and waited, fully expecting we'd spend the next hour talking about the finer points of slash-boxing. He was smiling faintly as Brenda went on and on, and I figured I had to say something, if only to be polite.

"I'm not a sports fan," I said, not wishing to be *too* polite, "but it seemed to me your technique was different from the others I saw tonight."

He took a long drag on his cheroot, then examined the glowing tip as he slowly exhaled purple smoke. He transferred his gaze to me, and some of the heat seemed to go with it. There was a deepness to his eyes I hadn't noticed at first. You see that sometimes, in the very old. These days, of course, it is usually the only way you can tell someone *is* old. MacDonald certainly had no other signs of age. His body looked to be in its mid-twenties, but he'd had little choice in its features, given his profession. Slash-boxers inhabit fairly standardized bodies, in nine different formulas or weight classes, as a way of minimizing any advantage gained by sheer body mass. His face seemed a bit older, but that could have been just the eyes. It wasn't old enough for age to have impressed a great deal of character on it. Neither was it one of those generic "attractive" faces about half the population seem to prefer. I got the feeling this was pretty much the way he might have looked in his youth, which—I remembered, with a little shock—had been spent on Earth.

The Earth-born are not precisely rare. The CC told me there were around ten thousand of them still alive. But they look like anyone else, usually, and tend not to announce themselves. There were some who made a big thing about their age—the perennial talk-show guests, storytellers, professional nostalgics—but by and large the Earth-born were a closeted minority. I had never wondered why before.

"Walter said you'd talk me into joining this project of his," MacDonald said, finally, ignoring my own comment. "I told him he was wrong. Not that I intend to be stubborn about it; if you can give me a good reason why I should spend a year with you two, I'd like to hear it."

"If you know Walter," I countered, "you'll know he's possibly the least perceptive man in Luna, where other people are concerned. He thinks I'm enthusiastic about this project. He's wrong. As far as I know, Walter is the only one interested in this project. It's just a job to me."

"I'm interested," Brenda piped up. MacDonald shifted his gaze to her, but didn't feel the need to leave it there long. I had the feeling he had learned all he needed to know about her in that brief look.

"My style," he said, "is a combination of ancient fighting techniques that never got transplanted to Luna. Some well-meaning but foolish people passed a law a long time ago banning the teaching of these oriental disciplines. That was back when the conventional wisdom was we ought to live together in peace, not ever fight each other again, certainly not ever kill each other. Which is a nice idea, I guess.

"It even worked, partially. The murder rate is way, way down from what it was in any human society on Earth."

He took another long drag on his smoke. His attendants finished their work on his leg, packed up, and left us alone. I began to wonder if that was all he had to say, when he finally spoke again.

"Opinions shift. You live as long as I have, you'll see that over and over."

"I'm not as old as you, but I've seen it."

"How old are you?" he asked.

"One hundred. Three days ago." I saw Brenda look at me, open her mouth to say something, then close it again. Probably I'd get chewed out for not telling her so she could throw a centennial birthday party for me.

MacDonald looked at me with even more interest than before, narrowing those disturbing eyes.

"Feel any different?"

"You mean because I'm a hundred years old? Why should I?"

"Why, indeed. It's a milestone, certainly, but it doesn't really mean anything. Right?"

"Right."

"Anyway, to get back to the question . . . there were always those who felt that, with natural evolutionary processes no longer working, we should make some attempt to foster a certain amount of aggressiveness. Without sanctioning real killing, we could at least learn how to fight. So boxing was reintroduced, and that eventually led to the blood sports you see today."

"This is just the sort of perspective Walter wants," I pointed out.

"Yes. I didn't say I didn't *have* the perspective you need. I'm just curious as to why I should use it for you."

"I've been thinking that one over, too," I said. "Just as an exercise, you understand. And you know, I can't think of anything that's likely to convince a man in the middle of a protracted suicide to put it off for a year and join us in writing a series of useless stories."

"I used to be a reporter, you know."

"No, I didn't."

"Is that what you think I'm doing? Committing suicide?"

Brenda looked at him earnestly. I could almost feel her concern.

"If you get killed in the ring, that's what they'll call it," she said.

He got up and went to a small bar at the side of the room. Without asking what we wanted, he poured three glasses of a pale green liqueur and brought them back to us. Brenda sniffed it, tasted, then took a longer drink.

"You can't imagine the sense of defeatism after the Invasion," he said. It was apparently impossible to keep him on any subject, so I relaxed to the inevitable. As a reporter you learn to let the subject talk.

"To call it a war is a perversion of the word. We fought, I suppose, in the sense that ants fight when the hill is kicked over. I suppose ants can fight valiantly in such a situation, but it hardly matters to the man who kicked the hill. He barely notices what he has done. He may not even have had any actual malice toward ants; it might have been an accident, or a side effect of another project, like plowing a field. We were plowed under in three days.

"Those of us here in Luna were in a state of shock. In a way, that state of shock lasted many decades. In a way . . . it's still with us today."

He took another drag on his cheroot.

"I'm one of those who was alarmed at the nonviolence movement. It's great, as an ideal, but I feel it leaves us in a dead end, and vulnerable."

"You mean evolution?" Brenda asked.

"Yes. We shape ourselves genetically now, but are we really wise enough to know what to select for? For a billion years the selection was done naturally. I wonder if it's wise to junk a system that worked for so long."

"Depends on what you mean by 'worked,' " I said.

"Are you a nihilist?"

I shrugged.

"All right. Worked, in the sense that life-forms got more complex. Biology seemed to be working toward something. We know it wasn't us—the Invaders proved there are things out there a lot smarter than we are. But the Invaders were gas giant beings, they must have evolved on a planet like Jupiter. We're hardly even related. It's commonly accepted that the Invaders came to Earth to save the dolphins and whales from our pollution. I don't know of any proof of that, but what the hell. Suppose it's true. That means the aquatic mammals have brains organized more like the Invaders than like us. The Invaders don't see us as truly intelligent, any more than other engineering species, like bees, or corals, or birds. True or not, the Invaders don't really have to concern us anymore. Our paths don't cross; we have no interests in common. We're free to pursue our own destiny . . . but if we don't evolve, we don't have a destiny."

He looked from one of us to the other and back again. This seemed pretty important to him. Personally, I'd never given much thought to the matter.

"There's something else," he went on. "We know there are aliens out there. We know interstellar travel is possible. The next time we meet aliens they could be even worse than the Invaders. They might want to exterminate us, rather than just evict us. I think we ought to keep some fighting skills alive in case we meet some disagreeable critters we *can* fight."

Brenda sat up, wide-eyed.

"You're a Heinleiner," she said.

It was MacDonald's turn to shrug.

"I don't attend services, but I agree with a lot of what they say. But we were talking about martial arts."

Is *that* what we were talking about? I'd lost track.

"Those arts were lost for almost a century. I spent ten years studying thousands of films from the twentieth and twenty-first centuries, and I pieced them back together. I spent another twenty years teaching myself until I felt I was adept. Then I became a slash-boxer. So far, I'm undefeated. I expect to remain that way until someone else duplicates my techniques."

"That would be a good subject for an article," Brenda suggested. "Fighting, then and now. People used to have all kinds of weapons, right? Projectile weapons, I mean. Ordinary citizens could own them."

"There was one country in the twentieth century that made their possession almost mandatory. It was a civil right, the right to own firearms. One of the weirder civil rights in human history, I always thought. But I'd have owned one, if I'd lived there. In an armed society, the unarmed man must be a pretty nervous fellow."

"It's not that I don't find all this perfectly fascinating," I said, standing and stretching my arms and legs to get the circulation going again. "I don't, but that's beside the point. We've been here about half an hour, and already Brenda has suggested plenty of topics you could be helpful with. Hell, you could write them yourself, if you remember how. So how about it? Are you interested, or should we start looking for someone else?"

He leaned his elbows on his knees and looked at me.

Before long I began to wonder when the theremin music would begin. A look like that belonged in a horror holo. Eyes like that should be set in a face that begins to sprout hair and fangs, or twist like putty into some Nameless Evil Thing. I mentioned before how deep his eyes seemed. They had been reflecting pools compared to this.

I don't wish to be superstitious. I don't wish to attribute powers to MacDonald simply because he had attained a venerable age. But, looking at those eyes, one could not help but think of all the things they had seen, and wonder at the wisdom that might have been attained. I was one hundred years old, which is nothing to sneer at in the longevity department, or hadn't been until recent human history, but I felt like a child being judged by his grandfather, or maybe by God himself.

I didn't like it.

I tried my best to return the gaze—and there was nothing hostile in it, no challenge being issued to me. If a staring match was in progress, I was the only one competing. But before long I had to turn away. I studied the walls, the floor, I looked at Brenda and smiled at her—which startled her, I think. Anything to avoid those eyes.

"No," he said, at last. "I don't think I'll join this project, after all. I'm sorry to have wasted your time."

"No problem," I said, and got up and started for the door.

"What do you mean, 'after all'?" Brenda asked. I turned, wondering if I could get away with grabbing her arm and dragging her away.

"I mean, I was considering it, despite everything. Some aspects of it were beginning to look like fun."

"Then what changed your mind?"

"Come on, Brenda," I said. "I'm sure he has his own reasons, and they're none of our business." I took her arm, and tugged at it.

"Stop it," she said, annoyed. "Stop treating me like a child." She glared at me until I let her go. I suppose it would have been unkind to point out that she *was* a child.

"I'd really like to know," she told MacDonald.

He looked at her, not unkindly, then looked away, seeming embarrassed. I simply report the fact; I have no idea why he might have been embarrassed.

"I only work with survivors," he said, quietly. Before either of us had a chance to reply he was on his feet. He limped slightly as he went to the door and held it open for us.

I got up and jammed my hat on my head. I was almost out the door when I heard Brenda.

"I don't understand," she was saying. "What makes you think I'm not a survivor?"

"I didn't say you weren't," he said.

I turned on him.

"Brenda," I said, slowly. "Correct me if I'm wrong. Did I just hear myself accused of not being a survivor by a man who risks his life in a *game?*"

She didn't say anything. I think she realized that, whatever was going on here, it was between him and me. I wished I knew what it was, and why it had made me so angry.

"Risks can be calculated," he said. "I'm still alive. I plan to stay that way."

Nothing good lasts forever. Brenda piped up again.

"What is it about Hildy that makes you—"

"That's none of my business," he interrupted, still looking at me. "I see something in Hildy. If I were to join you two, I'd have to make it my business."

"What you see, pal, is a man who takes care of his own business, and doesn't let some gal with a knife do it for him."

Somehow that didn't come out like I'd intended. He smiled faintly. I turned and stomped out the door, not waiting to see if Brenda followed.

I lifted my head from the bar. Everything was too bright, too noisy. I seemed to be on a carousel, but what was that bottle doing in my hand?

I kept tightly focused on the bottle and things slowly stopped spinning. There was a puddle of whiskey under the bottle, and under my arm, and the side of my face was wet. I'd been lying in the puddle.

"If you throw up on my bar," the man said, "I'll beat you bloody."

Swinging my gaze toward him was a major project. It was the bartender, and I told him I wasn't going to throw up, then I almost choked and staggered toward the swinging doors and made a mess in the middle of Congress Street.

When I was done I sat down there in the road. Traffic was no problem. There were a few horses and wagons tied up behind me, but nothing moved on the dark streets of New Austin. Behind me were the sounds of revelry, piano music, the occasional gunshot as the tourists sampled life in the Old West.

Somebody was holding a drink before my face. I followed the arm up to bare shoulders, a long neck, a pretty face surrounded by curly black hair. Her lipstick was black in the dim light. She wore a corset, garters, stockings, high heels. I took the drink and made it vanish. I patted the ground beside me and she sat, folding her arms on her knees.

"I'll remember your name in a minute," I said.

"Dora."

"Adorable Dora. I want to rip off your clothes and throw you into bed and make passionate love to your virginal body."

"We already did that. Sorry about the virginal part."

"I want you to have my babies."

She kissed my forehead.

"Marry me, and make me the happiest man in the moon."

"We did that, too, sweetheart. It's a shame you don't remember it." She held her hand out to me and I saw a gold wedding ring with a little diamond chip. I squinted at her face again. There was some kind of filmy aura around it . . .

"That's a bridal veil!" I shouted. She was looking dreamy, smiling up at the stars.

"We had to sober the parson up, then go bang on the jeweler's door and send somebody around to find Silas to open the general store for my gown, but we got it done. The service was right there in the Alamo; Cissy was my maid of honor and old Doc stood up for you. All the girls cried."

I must have looked dubious, because she laughed and patted me on the back.

"The tourists loved it," she said. "It's not every night we get as colorful as that." She twisted the ring off her finger and handed it to me. "But I'm too much of a lady to hold you to vows you made while not in your right mind." She peered closer at me. "Are you back in your right mind?"

I was back enough to remember that any marriage performed by the "parson" in "Texas" was not legally binding in King City. But to get an idea of how far gone I'd been, I'd really been worried for a moment there.

"A whore with a heart of gold," I said.

"We all have our parts to play. I've never seen the 'town drunk' done better. Most people omit the vomit."

"I strive for authenticity. Did I do anything disgraceful?"

"You mean aside from marrying me? I don't mean to be unkind, but your fourth consummation of our marriage was pretty disgraceful. I won't spread it around; the first three were rather special."

"What do you mean?"

"Well, the tongue work was some of the best I've—"

"No, I mean . . ."

"I know what you mean. I know there's a word for it. Inability, immobility . . . a limp cock."

"Impotence."

"That's it. My grandmother told me about it, but I never expected to see it."

"Stick with me, honey, and I'll show you even more wonders."

"You were pretty drunk."

"You've finally said something boring."

She shrugged. "I can't swap repartee with a cynic like you forever."

"Is that what I am? A cynic?"

She shrugged again, but I thought I saw some concern in her expression. It was hard to tell, with just moonlight and swimming eyeballs.

She helped me to my feet, brushed me off, kissed me. I promised to call on her when I was in town. I don't think she believed me. I had her point me toward the edge of town, and started home.

Morning was smearing up the sky like pale pink lipstick. I'd been hearing the rippling of the river for some time.

My efforts at reconstructing the day had brought back some broad outlines. I recalled taking the tube from the Arena to Texas, and I knew I'd spent some time working on the cabin. In there somewhere I saw myself throwing finished lumber into a ravine. I remembered seriously thinking of burning the cabin to the ground. The next thing I knew I was sitting at the bar in the Alamo Saloon, tossing down one drink after another. Then the clouds rolled in and the memory transcription ended. I had a hazy picture of the parson swaying slightly as he pronounced us man and wife. What a curious phrase. I supposed it was historically accurate.

I heard a sound, and looked up from the rocky path.

A pronghorn antelope was standing not ten feet in front of me. He held his head high, alert and proud, not frightened of me. His chest was snowy white and his eyes were moist and brown and wise. He was the most beautiful thing I had ever seen.

On his worst day he was ten times better than I had ever been. I sat down on the path and cried for a while. When I looked up, he was gone.

I felt calm for the first time in many years. I found the cliff face, located the climbing rope, and hoisted myself to the top. The sun was still below the horizon but there was a lot of yellow in the sky now. My hands toyed with the rope. How did it go . . . the rabbit goes in the hole, the dog chases the rabbit around the tree, two, three, four . . .

After several tries, I got it right. I slipped it around my neck and looked down the cliff. Your acceleration is low in Luna, but your body mass is constant. You need a big drop, six times what would do on Earth. I tried to do the calculations in my head but kept losing track.

To be on the safe side, I picked up a large rock and held it tightly to my chest. Then I jumped.

You get plenty of time for regrets, but I had none. I remember looking up and seeing Andrew MacDonald looking down at me.

Then came the jerk.

SCIENTISTS BAFFLED!

THE TRUTH ABOUT DINOSAURS THEY DON'T WANT YOU TO KNOW

"**I**f you're going to build a barn for brontosaurs," I told Brenda, "you'd better make the ceiling at least twenty meters high."

"And why is that, Mr. Bones?"

Where she'd learned about minstrel shows I had no idea, but she'd been using the term for a while now, whenever I got into lecture mode— which, considering the state of her ignorance, was most of the time. I wasn't going to let it annoy me.

She was looking up at the ceiling, which was twenty-five meters above us. Myself, I wasn't looking up all that much lately. For several days I'd had a persistent and painful stabbing pain in my neck whenever I turned my head in a certain position. I kept meaning to visit the medico and get it fixed, but it would spontaneously remit for a few hours and I'd forget to make an appointment. Then it would creep up and stab me when I least expected it.

"Brontosaurs are not real bright. When they get alarmed they raise their heads and rear up on their hind legs to take a look around. If the ceiling is too low they smash their teeny heads against it and stun themselves."

"You've spent time around dinosaurs?"

"I grew up on a dinosaur ranch." I took her elbow and steered her out of the way of a manure loader. We watched as it scooped up a pile of watermelon-sized pellets.

"What a stench."

I said nothing. The smell had both good and bad associations for me. It took me back to my childhood, where one of my jobs had been operating the manure loader.

Behind us, the massive doors to the swamp began rumbling open, letting in a blast of air even hotter and more humid than that inside the barn. In a moment a long neck poked inside the door, ending in an almost negligible, goofy-looking head. The neck kept coming in for a very long time before the massive body made its entrance. By then another head and neck had appeared.

"Let's get back here out of the way," I suggested to Brenda. "They won't step on you if they see you, but they tend to forget where you are not long after they look away from you."

"Where are they going?"

I pointed toward the open gate across from us. The sign on it said "Mating Pen Number One."

"Mating season's just about over. Wait till Callie gets them penned up, then we can take a look. It's pretty interesting."

One of the brontosaurs made a mournful honk and moved along a little faster. In one-sixth gee, even a thunder lizard could be sprightly. I doubt they set any speed records back on Old Earth. In fact, I wondered how they stood up at all, out of the water.

The reason for the burst of speed was soon apparent. Callie entered the barn, mounted on a tyrannosaur. The big predator responded instantly to every touch of the reins, hurrying to block an attempted retreat by the male, rearing up and baring its teeth when it looked as if the female might make a stand. The big herbivores waddled quickly into the mating pen. The doors closed automatically behind them.

The thing the ancient paleontologists had never got right about dinosaurs was their color. You'd think the examples of so many modern reptiles might have given them a hint. But if you look at old artists' conceptions of dinosaurs, the predominant colors were mud-brown and khaki-green. The real item was much different.

There are several strains of b-saur but the type Callie prefers are called Cal Tech Yellowbellies, after the lab that first produced them. In addition to the canary undersides, they range from that old reliable mud-brown on their backs to a dark green, emerald green, and kelly green on their sides and necks. They have streaks of iridescent violet trailing back from their eyes, and white patches under their throats.

Tyrannosaurs, of course, are predominantly red. They have huge, dangling wattles under their necks, like iguanas, which can be puffed up to make an outrageous booming mating call. The wattles are usually deep blue, though purple and even black are not unknown.

You can't ride a t-saur like a horse; the back is too steep. There are different methods, but Callie preferred a sort of narrow platform she could either sit or stand on, depending on what she was doing. It strapped around the beast's shoulders. Considering the amount of lizard still rising above that point, she spent most of her time on her feet, barely able to peer over the head.

"It looks unstable," Brenda said. "What if she falls off?"

"You don't want to do that," I told her. "They're likely to snap at you if you come in view suddenly. But don't worry; this one is muzzled."

An assistant leaped up to join Callie in the saddle. He took the reins from her and she jumped to the ground. As the t-saur was being ridden out the barn door she glanced at us, did a double take, and waved at me. I waved back, and she gestured for us to come over. Not waiting, she started toward the breeding pen.

I was about to join her when something poked through the metal railing behind us. Brenda jumped, then relaxed. It was a brontosaur pup looking for a treat. Looking into the dim pen behind us, I could see several dozen of the elephant-sized young ones, most of them snugged into the mud, a few others gathered around the feeding trough.

I turned out my pockets to show the brute I didn't have anything on me. I used to carry chunks of sugarcane, which they love.

Brenda didn't have any pockets to turn out, for the simple reason that she wasn't wearing any pants. Her outfit for the day was knee-length soft leather boots, and a little black bolero top. This was intended to let me know that she had acquired something new: primary and secondary sexual characteristics. I was fairly sure she hoped I'd suggest we put them to use one of these days soon. I'd first caught on that she had a crush on me when she learned that Hildy Johnson was not my born name, but one I had selected myself after a famous fictional reporter from a play called *The Front Page*. Soon she was "Brenda Starr."

I must say she looked more reasonable now. Neuters had always made me nervous. She had not gone overboard with the breasts. The pubic hair was natural, not some of the wilder styles that come and go.

But I was in no mood to try it out. Let her find a child of her own age.

We joined Callie at the breeding pen, climbed up to the top of the ten-meter gate and stood with her, looking over the top rail at the nervously milling behemoths.

"Brenda," I said, "I'd like you to meet Calamari Cabrini. She owns this place. Callie, meet Brenda, my . . . uh, assistant."

The women reached across me to shake hands, Brenda almost losing her balance on the slippery steel bars. All three of us were dripping wet. Not only was it hot and humid in the barn, but ceiling sprinklers drenched the place every ten minutes because it was good for the skins of the livestock. Callie was the only one who looked comfortable, because she wore no clothes. I should have remembered and worn less myself; even Brenda was doing better than me.

Nudity was not a sometime thing for Callie. I'd known her all my life, and in that time had never seen her wear so much as a pinky ring. There was no big philosophy behind her lifelong naturism. Callie went bare simply because she liked it, and hated picking out clothes in the morning.

She was looking good, I thought, considering that, except for Walter, she took less notice of her body's needs than anyone I knew. She never did any preventive maintenance, never altered anything about her appearance. When something broke down she had it fixed or replaced. Her medico bills were probably among the smallest in Luna. She swore she had once used a heart for one hundred and twenty years.

"When it finally gave out," she had told me, "the medico said the valves could have come out of a forty-year-old."

If you met her on the street, you would know immediately that she was Earth-born. During her childhood, humans had been separable into many "races," based on skin color, facial features, and type of hair. Post-Invasion eugenics had largely succeeded in blending these so that racial types were now very rare. Callie had been one of the white, or Caucasian, race, which dominated much of human history since the days of colonization and industrialization. Caucasian was a pretty slippery term. Callie's imperious nose would have looked right at home on an old Roman coin. One of Herr Hitler's "Aryans" would have sneered at her. The important racial concept then was "white," which meant not-black, not-brown.

Which was a laugh, because Callie's skin was burned a deep, reddish-brown from head to toe, and looked as leathery as some of her reptiles. It was startling to touch it and find it actually quite soft and supple.

She was tall—not like Brenda, but certainly tall for her age—and willowy, with an unkempt mane of black hair streaked with white. Her most startling feature was her pale blue eyes, a gift from her Nordic father.

She released Brenda's hand and gave me a playful shove.

"Mario, you never come see me anymore," she chided.

"The name is Hildy now," I said. "It has been for thirty years."

"You prove my point. I guess that means you're still working for that birdcage liner."

I shrugged, and noticed Brenda's uncomprehending expression.

"Newspads used to be printed out on paper, then they'd sell the paper," I explained. "When people were through reading it, they'd use it on the bottoms of their birdcages. Callie never abandons a cliché, no matter how dated."

"And why should I? The cliché business has suffered a radical decline since the Invasion. What we need are new and better clichés, but nobody seems to be writing them. Present company excepted, of course."

"From Callie, that's almost a compliment," I told Brenda. "And nobody would line a birdcage with the *Nipple,* Callie. The stories would put the birds right off their food."

She considered it. "I don't think so, Mario. If we had electronic birds, your newspad would be the perfect liner."

"Could be. I do find it useful for wrapping my electronic fish."

Most of this had gone right over Brenda's head, of course. But she had never been one to let a little ignorance bother her.

"To catch the shit?" she said.

We both looked at her.

"At the bottom of the birdcage," she explained.

"I think I like her," Callie said.

"Of course you do. She's an empty vessel, waiting to be filled with your tall tales of the old days."

"That's one reason. You've been using her as your own personal birdcage liner. She needs my help."

"She doesn't seem to mind."

"But I do," Brenda said, unexpectedly. Callie and I looked at her again.

"I know I don't know much about ancient history." She saw Callie's expression, and squirmed. "Sorry. But how much do you *expect* me to know about things that happened hundreds of years ago? Or care?"

"It's okay," Callie said. "I may not have used the word 'ancient'—I still think of the Roman Empire when that word comes up—but I can see it must seem ancient to you. I said the same thing to my parents when they talked about things that happened before I was born. The difference is, when I was young the old eventually had the good manners to die. A new generation took over. Your generation faces a different situation. Hildy seems very old to you, but I'm more than twice his age, and I don't have any plans to die. Maybe that's not fair to your generation, but it's a *fact.*"

"The gospel according to Calamari," I said.

"Shut up, Mario. Brenda, it's *never* going to be your world. Your generation will never take over from us. It's not my world anymore, either, because of you. All of us, from both generational extremes, have to run this world together, which means we have to make the effort to understand each other's viewpoints. It's hard for me, and I know it must be hard for you. It's as if I had to live with my great-great-great-great-grandparents, who grew up during the industrial revolution and were ruled by kings. We'd barely even have a *language* in common."

"That's okay with me," Brenda said. "I *do* make the effort. Why doesn't *he?*"

"Don't worry about him. He's always been like that."

"Sometimes he makes me so mad."

"It's just his way."

"Yoo-hoo, ladies. I'm here."

"Shut up, Mario. I can read him like a book, and I can tell he likes you. It's just that, the more he likes you, the worse he tends to treat you. It's his way of distancing himself from affection, which he's not sure he's able to return."

I could see the wheels turning in Brenda's head and, since she was *not* stupid, just ignorant, she eventually followed that statement out to its logical—if you believed the premise in the first place—conclusion, which was that I must love her madly, because I treated her *very* badly. I looked ostentatiously around at the walls of the barn.

"It must be hanging in your office," I said.

"What's that?"

"Your degree in psychology. I didn't even know you went back to school."

"I've been in school every day of my life, jerk. And I sure wouldn't need a degree to see through you. I spent thirty years learning how to do that." There was more, something about how just because I was a hundred years old now, I shouldn't think I'd changed so much. But it was all in Italian, so I only got the gist.

Callie gets a modest yearly stipend from the Antiquities Preservation Board for staying fluent in Italian—something she would have done anyway, since it was her native language and she had firm ideas about the extinction of human knowledge. She had tried to teach it to me but I had no aptitude beyond a few kitchen words. And what was the point? The Central Computer stored hundreds of languages no one spoke anymore, from Cheyenne to Tasmanian, including all the languages that had suffered a drastic drop in popularity because they never got established on Luna before the Invasion. I spoke English and German, like most everybody else, with a little Japanese thrown in. There were sizable groups of Chinese speakers, and Swahili, and Russian. Other than that, languages were preserved by study groups of a few hundred fanatics like Callie.

I doubt Brenda even knew there *was* an Italian language, so she listened to Callie's tirade with a certain wariness. Ah, yes, Italian is a fine language for tirades.

"I guess you've known each other a long time," Brenda said to me.

"We go way back."

She nodded, unhappy about something. Callie shouted, and I turned to see her jump down into the breeding pen and stride toward the crew of helpers, who were chivying the two brutes into final mating position.

"Not yet, you idiots," she shouted. "Give them *time.*" She reached the group of people and started handing out orders right and left. Callie had never been able to find good help. I had been part of that help for a great many years, so I know what I'm talking about. It took me a long time to realize that no one would ever be good enough for her; she was one of those people who never believed anyone could do a job as well as she could do it herself. The maddening thing was, she was usually right.

"Back off, they're not ready yet. Don't rush them. They'll know when it's time. Our job is to *facilitate,* not initiate."

"If I have any skills as a lover," I told Brenda, "it's because of that."

"Because of her?"

" 'Give them time. We're not on a schedule here. Show a little finesse.' I heard that so many times I guess I took it to heart."

And it did take me back, watching Callie working the stock again. Of the major brontosaur ranchers in Luna, she was the only one who didn't use artificial insemination at breeding time. "If you think helping a pair copulate is tough," she always said, "try getting a semen sample from a brontosaur bull."

And there was a rough sort of poetry about dinosaur mating, particularly brontosaurs.

Tyrannosaurs went about it as you might expect, full of sound and fury. Two bulls would butt heads over a prospective mate until one staggered away like a dusted-up nerg addict to nurse an epic headache. I don't suppose the victor fared a lot better except for the chance to grapple the tiny claw of his lady fair.

Brontosaurs were more dainty. The male would spend three or four days doing his dance, when he remembered to. These creatures had short attention spans, even when in heat. He would rear up on his hind legs and do a comical samba around and around the female. She typically showed minimal interest for the first two days. Then the seduction moved to the love-bite stage, with the male nipping her around the base of the tail while she placidly chewed her cud. When she finally began rearing up with him, it was time to bring them into the mating pen to pitch some serious woo.

That was going on now. The two of them were facing each other on their hind legs, doing a little neck-weaving, a little foreleg pawing. It could still be another hour before they were ready, a condition signaled by the emergence of one of the bull's two hemipenes.

Nobody ever told me why a reptile needs two penises. Come to think of it, I never asked. There are limits to curiosity.

"So how long were you involved with Callie?"

"What's that?" Brenda had drawn me out of my reverie, as she had a habit of doing.

"She said thirty years. That's a long time. You must have been real serious about her."

All right, so I'm dense. But I finally got it. I looked out at the primal scene: two Mesozoic monsters, here through the grace of modern genetic science, and a thin brown woman, likewise.

"She's not my lover. She's my mother. Why don't you go down there with her? She'll see you don't get hurt, and I'm sure she'll be happy to tell you more than you ever wanted to know about brontosaurs. I'm going to take a break."

I noticed as we climbed down the gate on opposite sides that Brenda looked happier than I'd seen her all day.

I assume the mating went off without any trouble. It usually does when Callie's in charge. I imagine the mating that produced me was equally well-planned and carried out. Sex was never a big deal to Callie. Having me was her nod in the direction of duty. But I have no siblings, despite powerful societal pressure toward large families at the time of my birth. Once was apparently enough.

Paradoxically, I know I didn't spend any time in a Petri dish, though it would have made the whole process much easier for her if she'd availed herself of any of the medical advances that could, today, make procreation, gestation, and parturition about as personally involving as a wrong number on the telephone. Callie had conceived me the old-fashioned way: a random spermatozoan hitting the jackpot at the right time of the month. She had carried me to full term, and had borne me in pain, just like God promised Eve. And she had hated every minute of it. How do I know that? She told me, and anyone else who would listen. She told me an average of three times a day throughout my childhood.

It wasn't so much the pain that had bothered her. For a woman who could shoulder a reproductive organ almost as big as she was and guide it into a cloaca of a filthiness that had to be seen to be disbelieved, while standing knee-deep in dinosaur droppings, Callie had an amazing streak of prissiness. She had hated the bloodiness of childbirth, the smells and sensations of it.

Callie's office was cool. That's what I'd had in mind when I went up there, simply to cool off. But it wasn't working. All that had happened was that the sweat on my body had turned clammy. I was breathing hard, and my hands weren't steady. I felt on the edge of an anxiety attack, and I didn't know why. On top of all that, my neck was hurting again.

And why hadn't I mentioned the purpose of our visit? I'd told myself it was because she was too busy, but there had been plenty of time while the three of us stood on the gate. Instead, I'd let her prattle on about the good old days. It would have been a perfect opportunity to brace her about taking the job as the Earth-born member of our little team of time-travelers. After holding forth about the generational gap she would have looked silly turning us down. And I knew Callie. She would love the job, would never admit loving it, and would only accept it if she could be tricked into making it look as if she had come up with the idea herself, as a favor to me and Brenda.

I got up and moved to the windows. That didn't help, so I walked to the opposite wall. No improvement. After I'd done that three or four times I realized I was pacing. I rubbed the back of my neck, drifted over to the windows again, and looked out and down.

Callie's office windows overlook the barn interior from just beneath the roof. There's a stairway leading to a verandah "outside"—actually, within the small Disneyland that is her ranch. I was looking out over the breeding pens I had just left. Callie was there, pointing something out to Brenda, who stood beside her watching the spectacle of two mating brontosaurs. Standing just behind them was someone who looked familiar. I squinted, but it didn't help, so I grabbed the pair of binoculars on a hook beside the window.

I focused in on the tall, red-headed figure of Andrew MacDonald.

EXCLUSIVE!

SECRET CELEB SEX & DOPE HIDEAWAY LAID BARE!

I remembered leaving Callie's ranch. I recalled wandering for a while, taking endless downscalators until there were no more; I had reached the bottom level. That struck me as entirely too metaphorical, so I took an infinite number of upscalators and found my way to the Blind Pig. I don't recall what I was thinking all those hours, but in retrospect, it couldn't have been pretty.

You might say the next thing I recall is waking up, or coming to, but that wouldn't be strictly accurate. It wouldn't convey the nature of the experience. It felt more like I reconstructed myself from far-flung bits—no, that implies some effort on my part. The bits reconstructed themselves, and I became self-aware in quantum stages. There was no dividing line, but eventually I knew I was in a back room of the Pig. This was considerable progress, and here my own will took over and I looked around to learn more about my surroundings. I was facing downward, so that's where I first turned my attention. What I saw there was a woman's face.

"We'll never solve the problem of the head shot until an entirely new technology comes along," she said. I had no idea what this meant. Her hair was spread out on a pillow. There were outspread hands on each side of her face. There was something odd about her eyes, but I couldn't put my finger on it. I suppose I was in a literal frame of mind, because having thought that, I touched one of her eyeballs with the tip of my finger. It didn't seem to bother her much. She blinked, and I took my finger away.

There was an important discovery: when I touched her eye, one of the hands had moved. Putting these data together, I concluded that the hands bracketing her face were *my* hands. I wiggled a finger, testing this hypothesis. One of the fingers down there wiggled. Not the one I had intended, but how much exactitude could I expect? I smiled, proud of myself.

"You can encase the brain in metal," she said. "Put a blood bag on the anti-camera side of the head, fire a bullet from the camera's pee-oh-vee. And *ka-chow!* The bullet goes whanging off the metal cover, *ka-blooey,* the blood bag explodes, and if you're lucky it *looks* like the bullet went *through* the head and spread tomato sauce all over the wall in back of the guy."

I felt large.

Had I taken large pills? I couldn't remember, but I must have. Normally I don't, as they aren't really much of a thrill, unless you get your kicks by imagining yourself to be the size of an interplanetary liner. But you can mix them with other drugs and get interesting effects. I must have done that.

"You can make it look even more real by putting teeny tiny charges in back of the eyeballs. When the bullet hits, the charges go off, and the eyeballs are blown out *toward* the camera, see? Along with a nice blood haze, which is a plus in masking whatever violations of realism are going on behind it."

Something was rubbing against my ears. I turned my head about as quickly as they rotate the big scope out in Copernicus, and saw a bare foot. At first I thought it was my foot, but I knew from reports flown in by carrier pigeon that my own feet were about three kilometers behind me, at the ends of my legs, which were stretched out straight. I turned my head the other way, saw another foot. Hers, I concluded. The first was probably hers, too.

"But that damn steel case. Crimony! I can't tell you what a—you should pardon the expression—headache that thing can be. Especially when nine out of ten directors will *insist* the head shot has to be in slomo. You give the chump a false forehead full of Max Factor #3 to *guarantee* a juicy wound, you annodize the braincase in black so—you *hope*—it'll look like a hole in the head when the skin's ripped away, and what happens? The damn bullet rips through everything, and there it is in the dailies. A bright, shiny spot of metal right down there at the bottom of the hole. The director chews you out, and it's Retake City."

Was I aboard a ship? That might account for the rocking motion. But I remembered I was in the Blind Pig, and unless the bar had been cut from its steel catacomb and embarked bodily, it seemed unlikely we were at sea. I decided I still needed more data. Feeling adventurous, I looked down between myself and the woman's body.

For a moment the view made no sense at all. I could see my own legs, and my feet, as if through a reversed telescope. Then I couldn't see them any more. Then I could again. Where were her legs? I couldn't see them. Oh, yes, since her feet were tickling my ears, her legs must be those things against my chest. So she was on the floor, on her back. And that explained the other activity I saw. I stopped my up and down motion.

"I don't want to do this," I told her.

She kept talking about the difficulties of a head shot. I realized that she was at least as detached from our coupling as I was. I stood up and looked around the room. She never missed a syllable. There was a pair of pants on the floor; they were a million sizes too small for me, but they were probably mine. I held them, lifted each leg with gargantuan deliberation, and *presto!* The pants did fit. I stumbled through a curtain and into the main room of the Pig.

It was maybe twenty steps to the bar. In that distance I shrank alarmingly. It was not an unpleasant sensation, though at one point I had to hold the back of a barstool to keep my balance. Pleased with myself, I gingerly climbed onto a leather stool.

"Bartender," I said, "I'll have another of the same."

The fellow behind the bar was known as Deep Throat, for a famous clandestine news source. He probably had another name, but no one knew it, and we all thought it was fitting it should be that way. He nodded and was moving away, but someone sat on the stool next to mine and reached over to grab his arm.

"Hold the heavy stuff this time, okay?" she said. I saw that it was Cricket. She smiled at me, and I smiled back. I shrugged, then nodded to Deep Throat's inquiring look. His customers' state of sobriety is not his concern. If you can sit at the bar—and pay—he'll serve you.

"How you doing, Hildy?" Cricket asked.

"Never better," I said, and watched my drink being prepared. Cricket shut up for the time being. I knew there were more questions to come. What are friends for?

The drink arrived, in one of the Pig's hologlasses. It's probably the only bar in Luna that still uses them. They date back to the mid-twenty-first century, and they're rather charming. A chip in the thick glass bottom projects a holo picture just above the surface of the drink. I've seen them with rolling dolphins, windsurfers, a tiny water polo team complete with the sound of a cheering crowd, and Captain Ahab harpooning the Great White Whale. But the most popular glass at the Pig is the nuclear explosion at Bikini Atoll, in keeping with the way Deep Throat mixes the drinks. I watched it for a while. It starts with a very bright light, evolves into an exquisitely detailed orange and black mushroom cloud that expands until it is six inches high, then blows away. Then it blows up again. The cycle takes about a minute.

I was watching the tiny battleships in the lagoon when I realized I'd seen the show about a dozen times already, and that my chin was resting on the bar. To enhance the view, I suppose. I sat up straight, a little embarrassed. I glanced at Cricket, but she was making a great show of producing little moist rings with the bottom of her glass. I wiped my brow, and swiveled on my stool to look at the rest of the room.

"The usual motley crew," Cricket said.

"The motliest," I agreed. "In fact, the word 'motley' might have been coined simply to describe this scene."

"Maybe we should retire the word. Give it a place of honor in the etymological hall of fame, like Olympic champions' jerseys."

"Put it right next to motherhood, love, happiness . . . words like that."

"On that note, I'll buy you another drink."

I hadn't finished the first, but who was counting?

There have always been unwritten rules in journalism, even at the level on which I practice it. Often it is only the fear of a libel suit that stays us from printing a particularly scurrilous story. On Luna the laws are pretty strict on that subject. If you defame someone, you'd better have sources willing to testify before the CC. But more often you hold back on printing something everyone knows for a subtler reason. There is a symbiotic relationship between us and the people we cover. Some would say parasitic, but they don't understand how hungry for publicity a politician or celebrity can be. If we stick to the rules concerning "off the record" statements, things told us on "deep background," and so forth, everybody benefits. I get sources who know I won't betray them, and the subject of my stories gets the public exposure he craves.

Don't look for the Blind Pig Bar and Grill in your phone memory. Don't expect to find it by wandering the halls of your neighborhood mall. If you should somehow discover its location, don't expect to be let in unless you know a regular who can vouch for you. All I'll say about it is that it's within walking distance of three major movie production studios, and is reached through a door with a totally misleading sign on it.

The Blind Pig is the place where journalists and movie people can mix without watching their mouths. Like its political counterpart over by City Hall, the Huey P. Long Memorial Gerrymandering Society, you can let your hair down without fear of reading your words in the padloids the next morning—at least, not for attribution. It's the place where gossip, slander, rumor, and character assassination are given free rein, where the biggest stars can mix with the lowliest stagehands and the slimiest reporters and not have to watch their tongues. I once saw a grip punch a ten-million-per-picture celebrity in the nose, right there in the Pig. The two fought it out until they were exhausted, went back to the set, and behaved as if nothing had happened. That same punch, thrown in the studio, would have landed the grip on the pavement in microseconds. But if the star had exercised his clout for something that happened in the Pig, and Deep Throat heard about it, the star would not have been welcome again. There's not many places people like that can go and socialize without being bothered. Deep Throat seldom has to banish anyone.

A reporter once broke confidence with a producer, printed a story told to him in the Pig. He never returned, and he's not a reporter anymore. It's hard to cover the entertainment beat without access to the Pig.

Places like the Pig have existed since Edison invented Hollywood. The ambiance is dependent on what is shooting that day. Just then there were three popular genres, two rising and one on its way out, and all three were represented around the room. There were warriors from Samurai Japan, taking a break from *The Shogun Attacks,* currently lensing at Sentry/Sensational Studios. A contingent of people in old-fashioned spacesuits were employed at North Lunar Filmwerks, where I'd heard *Return Of The Alphans* was behind schedule and over budget and facing an uncertain reception, as the box office for Asteroid Miner/Space Creature films had turned soft in recent months. And a bunch in bandannas, cowboy hats, and dirty jeans had to be extras from *The Gunslinger V.* Westerns were in the middle of their fourth period of filmic popularity, two of them coming in my own lifetime. *TG, V,* as it was known to the trade, had been doing location work not far from my cabin in West Texas.

In addition, there were the usual scattering of costumes from other eras, and quite a number of surgically altered gnomes, fairies, trolls, and so forth, working in low-budget fantasy and children's shorts. There was a group of five centaurs from a long-running sci-fi series that should have been axed a dozen Roman numerals ago.

"Why don't you just move the brain?" I heard Cricket say. "Put it somewhere else, like the stomach?"

"Oh, brother. Sure, why not? It's been done, of course, but it's not worth the trouble. Nerve tissue is the hardest to manipulate, and the brain? Forget it. There's twelve pairs of cranial nerves you've got to extend through the neck and down to the abdomen, for one thing. Then you have to retrain the gagman—a couple of days, usually—so the time lag doesn't show. And you don't think that matters? Audiences these days, they've seen it all, they're sophisticated. They want *realism.* We can make a fake brain easy enough and stuff it into the gagman's skull in place of the one we relocated, but audiences will spot the fact that the real brain's not where it's supposed to be."

I turned on my stool and saw my new friend was sitting on the other side of Cricket, still holding forth about her head shots.

"Why not just use manikins?" Cricket asked, showing she hadn't spent much time on the entertainment beat. "Wouldn't they be cheaper than real actors?"

"Sure. A hell of a lot cheaper. Maybe you've never heard of the Job Security Act, or unions."

"Oh."

"Damn right. Until a stunt performer dies, we can't replace him with a machine. It's the law. And they die, all right—even with your brain in a steel case, it's a risky profession—but we don't lose more than two or three a year. And there's *thousands* of them. Plus, they get better at surviving the longer they work, so there's a law of diminishing returns. I can't win." She swiveled, leaned her elbows on the bar, looked out at the tables and sneered.

"Look at them. You can always spot gagmen. Look for the ones with the vacant faces, like they're wondering where they are. They pick up a piece of shrapnel in the head; we cut away a little brain tissue and replace it with virgin cortex, and they forget a little. Start getting a little vague about things. Go home and can't remember the names of the kids. Back to work the next day, giving me more headaches. Some of 'em have very little left of their original brains, and they'd have to look at their personnel file to tell you where they went to school.

"And centaurs? I could build you a robot centaur in two days, you couldn't tell it from the real thing. But don't tell the Exotics Guild. No, I get to sign 'em to a five-year contract, surgically convert 'em at great cost to the FX budget, then put 'em through *three months* of kinesthetic rehab until they can walk without falling on their faces. And what do I get? A stumblebum who can't remember his lines or where the camera is, who can't walk through a scene *muttering,* for chrissake, without five rehearsals. And at the end of five years, I get to pay to convert 'em *back.*" She reached around and got her drink, which was tall and had little tadpole-like creatures swimming in it. She took a long pull on it, licked her lips. "I tell you, it's a wonder we get any pictures made at all."

"Nice to see a woman happy in her work," I said. She looked over at me.

"Hildy," Cricket said, "have you met Princess Saxe-Coburg? She's chief of special effects at NLM."

"We've met."

The Princess frowned at me, then recognition dawned. She got off her stool and came toward me, a little unsteady. She put her nose inches from mine.

"Sure. You pulled out on me a few minutes ago. Not a nice thing to do to a lady."

At that range, I could see what was odd about her eyes. She was wearing a pair of antique projection contacts, small, round, flat TV screens that floated over the cornea. I could make out the ring of solar cells that powered them, and the flyspeck chip that held the memory.

They'd been introduced just before the Invasion under a variety of trade names, but the one that stuck was Bedroom Eyes. After all, though they could reflect quite a variety of moods, if you were close enough to see the little pictures the mood you were looking for was probably sexual arousal. The more modest models would show a turned-back bed, a romantic scene from an old movie, or even, god help us, waves crashing on a beach. Others made no pretensions, getting right to the erection or spread thighs. Of course, they could reflect other moods, as well, but people were seldom close enough to make them out.

I'd never seen projection contacts worn by someone quite as stoned as the Princess was. What they were projecting was an interesting illusion: it was as if I were looking through two holes into a hollow head. Remnants of an exploded brain were collapsed at the bottom. Cracks in the skull let in light. And swinging from stray synapses like vines in a jungle were a menagerie of cartoon characters, from Mickey Mouse to Baba Yaga.

The image disturbed me. I wondered why anyone would want to do that to their brain. From wondering why *she* would want to, I quickly got to why *I* would want to, and that was leading me quickly to a place I didn't want to go. So I turned away from her and saw Andrew MacDonald sitting at the other end of the bar like a carrot-topped Hibernian albatross.

"Did you know she's the Princess of Wales?" Cricket was saying. "She's first in line to the throne of England."

"And Scotland, and Wales," said the Princess. "Hell, and Ireland, and Canada and India. I might as well reclaim the whole Empire while I'm at it. If my mother ever dies, it'll all belong to me. Of course, there's the little matter of the Invaders."

"Up the British," Cricket said, and they clinked their glasses together.

"I met the king once," I said. I drained my drink and slammed it down on the bar. Deep Throat caused it to vanish, and began concocting another.

"Did you really?"

"He was a friend of my mother. In fact, he's a possible candidate to be my father. Callie has never told me and never will, but they were friendly together at about the right time. So, if you apply modern laws of bastardy, I might have a claim that supersedes yours." I glanced at Mac-Donald again. Albatross? Hell, the man was more than a bird of evil omen, more than a stormy petrel or a croaking raven. He was Cassandra. He was a tropical depression, bad breath, a black cat across my path. Everywhere I turned, there he was, a dog humping my leg. He was a ladder in the stocking of my life. He was snake eyes.

I hated him. I felt like punching him in the nose.

"Watch what you say," the Princess cautioned. "Remember what happened to Mary, Queen of Scots."

I punched her in the nose.

She walked backward a few rubber-legged steps, then sat down on the floor. In the ensuing silence, Cricket whispered in my ear.

"I think she was kidding," she said.

For a few moments the whole place was quiet. Everyone was watching us expectantly; they love a good brawl at the Blind Pig. I looked at my clenched fist, and the Princess touched her bloody nose with her hand, then looked at her palm. We both looked up at the same time and our eyes met. And she came off the floor and launched herself at me and started breaking all the bones in my body that she could reach.

My hitting her had nothing to do with anything she had said or done; at that moment in my life I would have hit anyone standing next to me. But I'd have been a lot better off hitting Cricket. In the Princess of Wales, I'd picked the wrong opponent. She was taller than me and out-massed me. There was probably a ten-centimeter difference in reach between us, and I was on the short end of it. But most importantly, she had spent the last forty years staging cinematic fights, and she knew every trick in the book, and a lot that never got into the book.

I'm tempted to say I got in two or three good punches. Cricket says I did, but it might have been just to raise my spirits. The truth is I can't remember much from the time her horrid white teeth first filled my vision to the time I ripped a meter-long gash in the carpet with my face.

To get to the carpet I'd first had to smash through a table full of drinks. I used my face for that, too. Before the table I had been flying, rather cleverly, I thought, and the first real fun I'd had in many long minutes, but how I came to be flying was a point I was never too clear on. It seems safe to say that the Princess hurled me in some manner, holding on to some part of my anatomy and then releasing it; Cricket said it was my ankle, which would account for the room whirling around so quickly just before I flew. Before that I had vague memories of the bar mirror shattering, people scattering, blood spattering. Then I crashed through the table.

I rolled over and spit out carpeting. Horses were milling nervously all around me. Actually it was the centaur extras, whose table I'd just ruined. I resolved to buy them all a round of drinks. Before I could do that, though, there was the Princess again, lifting me by the shoulder and drawing back a bloody fist.

Then someone took hold of her arm from behind, and the punch never landed. She stood up and turned to face her challenger. I let my head rest against the ruins of a chair and watched as she tried to punch Andrew MacDonald.

There was really no point in it. It took her a long time to realize it, as her blood was up and she wasn't thinking straight. So she kept throwing punches, and they kept just missing, or hitting him harmlessly on the elbows or glancing off his shoulders. She tried kicking, and the kicks were always just a little off their target.

He never threw a punch. He didn't have to. After a time, she was standing there breathing hard. He wasn't even sweating. She straightened and held up her hands, palms outward.

I must have dozed off for a moment. Eventually I became aware of the Princess, Cricket, and MacDonald, three indistinct round faces hanging above me like a pawnbroker's sign.

"Can you move your legs?" MacDonald asked.

"Of course I can move my legs." What a silly question. I'd been moving my legs for a hundred years.

"Then move them."

I did, and MacDonald frowned deeper.

"His back's probably broken," said Wales.

"Must have happened when he landed on the railing."

"Can you feel anything?"

"Unfortunately, yes." By that time most of the drugs were wearing off, and everything from the waist up was hurting very badly. Deep Throat arrived and lifted my head. He had a painkiller in his hand, a little plastic cube with a wire which he plugged into the socket at the base of my skull. He flicked the switch, and I felt a lot better. I looked down and watched as they removed the splintered chair leg which had pierced my hip.

Since that wasn't a particularly diverting sight, I looked around the room. Already cleaning robots were picking up broken glassware and replacing shattered tables; Deep Throat is no stranger to brawls, and he always keeps a supply of furniture. In another few minutes there would be no sign that I had almost destroyed the place five minutes ago. Well, I *had* almost destroyed the place, in the sense that it was my hurtling body that had done most of the damage.

I felt myself being lifted. MacDonald and Wales had made a hammock with their arms. It was like riding in a sedan chair.

"Where are we going?"

"You're not in any immediate danger," MacDonald said. "Your back is broken, and that should be fixed soon, so we're taking you across the corridor to the NLF Studios. They have a good repair shop there."

The Princess got us past the gate guard. We passed about a dozen sound stage doors, and I was brought into the infirmary.

Which was jammed like Mainhardt's Department Store on Christmas Eve. It seemed NLF was doing a big scene from some war epic, and most of the available beds were taken by maimed extras patiently waiting their turn, counting up the triple-time salary they drew for injured downtime.

The room had been dressed as a field hospital for the picture, apparently doing double duty when not actually treating cinematic casualties. I pegged it as twentieth century—a vintage season for wars—maybe World War Two, or the Vietnam conflict, but it could easily have been the Boer War. We were under a canvas roof and the place was cluttered with hanging IV bottle props.

MacDonald returned from a conference with one of the technicians and stood looking down at me.

"He says it'll be about half an hour. I could have you taken to your own practitioner if you want to; it might be quicker."

"Don't bother. I'm in no hurry. When they patch me up, I'll probably just get up and do something foolish again."

He didn't say anything. There was something about his demeanor that bothered me—as if I needed anything else about him to bother me.

"Look," I said. "Don't ask me to explain why I did it. I don't even know myself."

Still he said nothing.

"Either spit it out, or take your long face and park it somewhere else."

He shrugged.

"I just have a problem with a man attacking a woman, that's all."

"What?" I was sure I had misunderstood him. He wasn't making any sense. But when he didn't repeat his astonishing statement, I had to assume I'd heard him correctly.

"What does that have to do with anything?" I asked.

"Nothing, of course. But when I was young, it was something you simply didn't do. I know it no longer makes sense, but it still bothers me to see it."

"I'll be sure to tell the Mean Bitch you feel that way. If they've put her back together after your last bout, that is."

He looked embarrassed.

"You know, that was a problem for me, early in my career. I wouldn't fight female opponents. I was getting a bad reputation and missing a lot of important matchups because of it. When some competitors started getting sex changes simply so they could have a go at me, I realized how ridiculous I was being. But to this day I have to psych myself something terrible to get into the ring with someone who's currently female."

"That's why you never hit . . . does the Princess have a first name?"

"I don't know. But you're wrong. I wanted to stop her, but I didn't want to hurt her. Frankly, you had it coming."

I looked away, feeling terrible. He was right.

"She's feeling bad about it, though. She said she just couldn't seem to stop, once she got going."

"I'll send her the repair bill. That should cheer her up."

Cricket arrived from somewhere. She had a lighted cigarette which she placed in my mouth, grinning.

"Got it from the prop department," she said. "They always used to give these to wounded soldiers. I can't imagine why."

I puffed on it. It wasn't tobacco, thank god.

"Cheer up," Cricket said. "You tore up her fists pretty good."

"I'm clever that way; I pounded them to hamburger with my chin."

I suddenly felt an alarming urge to cry. Holding it back, I asked both of them to leave me alone for a while. They did, and I lay there smoking, studying the canvas ceiling. There were no answers written there.

Why had the taste of life turned so bitter for me in the last weeks?

I had sort of drifted away. When I came back, Brenda was bending over me. Considering her height, she had a long way to bend.

"How'd you find me?" I asked her.

"I'm a reporter, remember? It's my business to find things out."

I thought of several cutting replies, but something about the look on her face made me hold them back. Puppy love. I had vague memories of how badly that could hurt, when it wasn't returned.

And to give her her due, she was improving. Maybe she *would* be a reporter, some day.

"You needn't have bothered. It's not like I'm badly hurt. The head injuries were minimal."

"I'm not surprised. It would take a lot to hurt your head."

"The brain wasn't injured at . . ." I stopped, realizing she had just taken a jab at me. It had been pretty feeble, it hardly qualified as a joke—she might *never* master that skill—but it was something. I grinned at her.

"I was going to stop by Texas and bring that doctor . . . what was it you called him?"

"Sawbones. Pillroller. Quack. Caulker. Nepenthe. Leech. Lazar-monger."

Her smile grew a little glassy; I could see her filing the terms away for later research.

I was smiling, but the truth is, even with current medical practices, being paralyzed from the waist down is a frightening thing. We have an entirely different attitude toward our bodies than most humans down the ages, we don't fear injury and we can turn off pain and we generally treat flesh and bone as just items to be fixed, but when things are badly wrong something in the most primitive level of our brain stands up on its hind legs and howls at the Earth. I was having a galloping anxiety attack that the painkiller plugged into my medulla wasn't dealing with at all. I have no idea if Brenda realized this, but her presence at my bedside was strangely comforting. I was glad she was there. I took her hand.

"Thanks for coming," I said. She squeezed my hand, then looked away.

Eventually the planned casualties stopped streaming in, and a team of medicos assembled around me. They plugged me in to a dozen machines, studied the results, huddled, and murmured, just as if what they thought really mattered, as if the medical computer was not entirely in control of my diagnosis and treatment.

They came to a decision, which was to turn me onto my stomach. I surmised they had concluded it would be easier to reach my broken spine that way. I'd better not ever hear medicos called overpaid blood-monkeys again.

They began to carve. I couldn't feel it, but I could hear some really disgusting sounds. You know those wet-muck special-effect sounds they use in the movies when someone's being disemboweled? They could have recorded them right over my broken back. At one point something thumped to the floor. I peered over the edge of the bed: it looked like a raw soup bone. It was hard to believe it had once belonged to me.

They pow-wowed again, cut some more, brought in more machines. They made sacrifices to the gods of Aesculapius, Mithradates, Lethe, and Pfizer. They studied the entrails of a goat. They tore off their clothes, joined hands, and danced in a healing circle around my prone carcass.

Actually, I wished they had done any of those things. It would have been a lot more interesting than what they did do, which was mostly stand around and watch the automatic machines mend me.

All there was to look at was an antique machine against the wall, a few feet from my face. It had a glass screen and a lot of knobs on it. Blue lines were crawling across the screen, blipping into encouraging peaks now and then.

"Can I get you anything?" the machine asked. "Flowers? Candy? Toys?"

"A new head might do the trick." It was the CC talking, of course. It can throw its voice pretty much where it pleases, since it was talking directly to the hearing center of my brain. "How much will this cost me?"

"There's no final cost-estimate yet. But Wales has already requested the bill be sent to her."

"Maybe what I meant was—"

"How badly are you hurt? How shall I put it. There are three bones in the middle ear, called the malleus, the incus, and the stapes. You'll be happy to hear that not one of these six bones was broken."

"So I'll still be able to play the piano."

"Just as badly as ever. In addition, several minor organs emerged unscathed. Almost half a square meter of epidermis can be salvaged."

"Tell me. If I'd come to this place . . . I mean, a hospital like this one is pretending to be—"

"I know what you mean."

"—with only primitive surgical techniques . . . would I have survived?"

"It's unlikely. Your heart is intact, your brain is not badly damaged, but the rest of your injuries are comparable to stepping on a land mine. You'd never walk again, and you'd be in great pain. You would come to wish you had not survived."

"How can you tell that?"

The CC said nothing, and I was left to ponder. That usually doesn't do much good, where the CC is concerned.

We all deal with the CC a thousand times a day, but almost all of that is with one of its subprograms, on a completely impersonal level. But apart from the routine transactions of living, it also generates a distinct personality for every citizen of Luna, and is always there ready to offer advice, counsel, or a shoulder to cry on. When I was young I spoke to the CC extensively. He is every child's ideal imaginary playmate. But as we grow older and make more real, less tractable, and entirely more willful and frustrating relationships, contacts with the CC tend to fall off. With adolescence and the discovery that, in spite of their shortcomings, other people have a lot more to offer than the CC ever will, we cut our ties even further until the CC is just a very intelligent, unobtrusive servant, there to ease us through the practical difficulties of life.

But the CC had now intruded, twice. I found myself wondering, as I seldom had in the past, what was on its mind.

"I guess I've been pretty foolish," I ventured.

"Perhaps I should call Walter, tell him to tear up the front page."

"All right. So it isn't news. So I've had things on my mind."

"I was hoping you'd like to talk about that."

"Maybe we ought to talk about what you said before."

"Concerning your hypothetical suffering had you incurred these injuries in, say, 1950?"

"Concerning your statement that I might prefer being dead."

"It was merely an hypothesis. I observe how little anyone today is equipped to tolerate pain, having never experienced an appreciable amount of it. I note that even the people on Old Earth, who were no strangers to it, often preferred death to pain. I conclude that many people today would not hold life so dear as to endure constant, unrelenting agony."

"So it was just a general observation."

"Naturally."

I didn't believe that, but there was no point in saying so. The CC would get to the point in its own way, in its own time. I watched the crawling lines on the machine and waited.

"I notice you're not taking notes concerning this experience. In fact, you've taken very few notes lately about anything."

"Watching me, are you?"

"When I've nothing better to do."

"As you certainly know, I'm not taking notes because my handwriter is broken. I haven't had it repaired because the only guy who still works on them is so swamped that he said he *might* get around to mine this coming August. Unless he leaves the business to start a career in buggy-whip repair."

"There actually is a woman who does that," the CC said. "In Pennsylvania."

"No kidding? Nice to see such a vital skill won't vanish completely."

"We try to foster *any* skill, no matter how impractical or useless."

"I'm sure our grandchildren will thank us for it."

"What are you using to write your stories?"

"Two methods, actually. You get this soft clay brick, see, and you use a pointed stick to impress little triangles in it in different combinations. Then you put it on the oven to bake, and in four or five hours there you are. The original hard copy. I've been trying to think of a name for the process."

"How about cuneiform?"

"You mean it's been done? Oh, well. When I get tired of that, I get out the old hammer and chisel and engrave my deathless prose on rocks. It saves me carrying those ridiculous paper sheets into Walter's office; I just lob them across the newsroom and through his window."

"I don't suppose you'd consider Direct Interface again."

Was that what this was all about?

"Tried it," I said. "Didn't like it."

"That was over thirty years ago," the CC pointed out. "There have been some advances since then."

"Look," I said, feeling irritable and impatient. "You've got something on your mind. I wish you'd just come out with it instead of weaseling around like this."

It said nothing for a moment. That moment stretched into a while, and threatened to become a spell.

"You want me to direct interface for some reason," I suggested.

"I think it might be helpful."

"For you or me?"

"Both of us, possibly. There can be a certain therapeutic value in what I intend to show you."

"You think I need that?"

"Judge for yourself. How happy have you been lately?"

"Not very."

"You could try this, then. It can't hurt, and it might help."

So what was I doing at the moment so important that I couldn't take a few minutes off to chin with the CC?

"All right," I said. "I'll interface with you, though I think you really ought to buy me dinner and some flowers first."

"I'll be gentle," the CC promised.

"What do I have to do? You need to plug me in somewhere?"

"Not for years now. I can use my regular connections into your brain. All you need to do is relax a little. Stare into the oscilloscope screen; that could be helpful."

I did, watching the blue lines peak and trough, peak and trough. The screen started to expand, as if I were moving into it. Soon all I could see was one crawling line, which slowed, stopped, became a single bright dot. The dot got brighter. It grew and grew. I felt the heat of it on my face, it was

DIRECT INTERFACE

THE CURE FOR CANCER

blazing down from a blue tropical sky. There was a moment of vertigo as the world seemed to spin around me—my body staying firmly in place—until I was lying not on my stomach but on my back, and not on the snowy white sheets of the repair shop at North Lunar Filmwerks but on cool wet beach sand, hearing not the soft mutterings of the medicos but the calls of seagulls and the nearby hiss and roar of surf. A wave spent its last energy tickling my feet and washing around my hips. It sucked a little sand out from under me. I lifted my head and saw an endless blue ocean trimmed with white breakers. I got to my feet and turned around, and saw white sandy beach. Beyond it were palm trees, jungle rising away from me to a rocky volcanic peak spouting steam. The realism of the place was aston-ishing. I knelt and scooped up a handful of sand. No two grains looked alike. No matter how close I brought the sand grains to my eyes, the illusion never broke down and the endless detail extended to deeper and deeper realms. Some sort of fractal magic, I supposed. I walked down the beach for a bit, sometimes turning to watch the cunning way water flowed into my footprints, erasing the edges, swirling, bubbling. I breathed deeply of the saline air. I liked this place already. I wondered why the CC had brought me here. I decided it would tell me in its own time, so I walked up the beach and sat under a palm tree to wait for the CC to present itself. I waited for several hours, watching the surf, having to move twice as the sun crept across the sky. I noticed that my skin had reddened in my brief time in the sunlight. I think I drifted off to sleep from time to time, but when you're alone it's hard to be sure. In any event, the CC didn't show. Eventually I got thirsty. I walked down the beach for several kilometers before discovering the outlet of a small stream of fresh water. I noticed the beach kept curving off to the right; probably an island. In time it got dark—very quickly, and one part of my mind concluded this simulacrum that really existed only as a set of equations in the data banks of the CC was intended to be somewhere in the Earthly tropics, near the equator. Not that the information did me any good. It didn't get cold, but I soon found that when you haven't any clothes or bedding, sleep can be a sandy, chilly, thoroughly uncomfortable project. I woke up again and again to note the stars had moved only a little. Each time I would shout for CC to show itself, and each time only the surf answered back. Then I awoke with the sun already high above the horizon. My left side had the beginnings of a painful radiation burn. My right side was chilled. My hair was full of sand. Little crabs scuttled away as I sat up, and I was appalled to realize I'd been thinking about catching and eating one. I was that hungry. But there was something of interest down by the water. In the night, a large, steel-banded wooden trunk had washed ashore, along with a lot of splintered wood and some tattered pieces of canvas. I concluded there had been a shipwreck. Perhaps that was the justification for my presence here in the first place. I dragged the chest across the sand to a place where it would be in no danger of washing back to sea, thought about it, and salvaged all the wood and canvas, as well. I smashed the lock on the trunk and, upon opening it, found it was waterproof and contained a wide variety of things useful to the computer castaway: books, tools, bolts of cloth, packages of staple foods like sugar and flour, even some bottles of a good Scotch whiskey. The tools were better than the things I had been using in Texas. At a guess, they might have been made with the technology of the late nineteenth century. The books were mostly of the how-to variety—and there was the man himself, *Robinson Crusoe*, by Defoe. All the books were bound in leather; none had a copyright date later than 1880. I used the machete to lop the ends off a coconut and munched thoughtfully at the delicious white meat while paging through books that told me how to tan hides, where to obtain salt, how to treat wounds (I didn't like the sound of that one very much), and other vigorous pioneer skills. If I wanted to make boots, I'd be able to do it. If I wanted to build an outrigger canoe and seek my fortune on the blue Pacific (I was assuming this was the south seas), the information was at my fingertips. If I wanted to chip flint arrowheads, construct an earthen dam, make gunpowder, fricassee a monkey, or battle savages, the books would show me how, complete with cunning lithographed illustrations. If I wanted to stroll the Clarkestrasse in King City, or even Easter parade down Fifth Avenue in Little Old New York, I was shit out of luck. There seemed little point in lamenting this fact, and the CC wasn't returning my calls, so I set to work. I explored the area for a likely spot to use as a campsite. That night I slept under a canvas awning, wrapped loosely in a length of flannel from the chest. It was a good thing, too. It rained off and on most of the night. I felt oddly at peace, lying in the moonlit darkness (*there* was a charming notion: Luna looked tiny and dim compared to a full Earth) listening to the rain falling on the canvas. Perhaps the simple pleasures are the best. For the next several weeks I worked very hard. (I didn't seem bothered by the gravity, which was six times what I had endured for a century. Even the fact that things fell much faster and harder than I'd been used to all my life never bothered me. My reflexes had been adjusted by the Almighty Landlord of this semi-conducting realm.) I spent part of each day working on a shelter. The rest of the time I foraged. I found good sources of bananas and breadfruit to add to my all-coconut diet. I found mangos and guavas, many varieties of edible roots, tubers, leaves, seeds. There were spices available to one equipped with the right book to use in their identification. The little scuttling crabs proved easy enough to catch, and were delicious boiled. I wove a net from vines and soon added several varieties of fish to my bouillabaisse. I dug for clams. When the shelter was completed I cleared a sunny spot for a vegetable garden and planted some of the seeds I'd found in the trunk. I set snares, which promptly trapped inedible small rodents, fearsome-looking reptiles, and an unidentified bird I came to call a wild turkey. I made a bow and arrow, and a spear, and managed to miss every animal I aimed at. Somewhere in there, after about a month, I started my calendar: notches on a tree. I estimated the time before that. Infrequently I wondered when the CC was going to check up on me, or if I was in fact stranded here for the rest of my life. In the spirit of exploration, one day I prepared a backpack and a straw hat (most of me was burned dark brown by then, but the noonday sun was still nothing to trifle with) and set out along the beach to determine the size of my cage. In two weeks I circumambulated what did indeed prove to be an island. Along the way I saw the remains of a ship washed up on a rocky part of the shore, a week-old beached whale, and many other wondrous things. But there had been no sign of human habitation. It seemed I was not to have my Friday to discuss philosophy with. Not too upset by this discovery, I set about repairing the depredations wild animals had worked on my shelter and garden. After another few weeks I determined to scale the volcano that sat in the center of the island, which I had named Mount Endew, for reasons that must have seemed excellent at the time. I mean, a Jules Verne hero would have climbed it, am I right? This proved to be a lot harder than walking on the beach, and involved much swinging of the machete at thatches of tropical vines, wading of swamps infested with flying insects and leeches, and barking of shins on rocky outcroppings. But one day I came to stand on the highest point in my domain and saw what I could not have seen from sea level: that my island was shaped something like a boot. (It took some imagination, I'll admit. One could just as well have seen the letter Y, or a champagne glass, or a squashed pair of copulating snakes. But Callie would have been pleased at the boot, so I named the island Scarpa.) When I returned to my camp I decided my traveling days were at an end. I had seen other places I might have explored from my volcanic vantage point, but there seemed no reason to do anything about them. I had spied no curls of smoke, no roads, no airports or stone monuments or casinos or Italian restaurants. Scarpa Island ran to swamps, rivers, jungles, and bogs. I'd had quite enough of all of those; you couldn't get a decent drink in any of them. I decided to devote my life to making life as easy and as comfortable as possible, at least until the CC showed up. I felt no urge to write, either journalism or my long-delayed novel, which seemed in memory at least as awful as I had always feared it was. I felt very little urge for sex. My only real drive seemed to be hunger, and it was easy enough to satisfy that. I discovered two things about myself. First, I could get totally involved in and wonderfully satisfied by the simplest of activities. Few of us today know the pleasure of working in the soil with our own hands, of nurturing, harvesting, and eating our own crops. I myself would have rejected the notion not long before. But nothing tastes quite like a tomato you have just picked from your own garden. Even rarer is the satisfaction of the hunt. I got rather better with my bow and arrow (I never got good), and could lie in wait for hours beside a watering hole, every sense tuned to the cautious approach of one of the island's wild pigs. There was even satisfaction in pursuing a wounded creature; the pigs could be dangerous when cornered, enraged by a poorly-aimed arrow in the hams. I hesitate to say it in these peaceable times, but even the killing thrust of the knife was something to take pride and pleasure in. The second thing I learned was that, if there was nothing that badly needed doing, I was capable of lying all day in my hammock tied between two palm trees, watching the waves crash onto the reef, sipping pineapple juice and home-distilled rum from a hollowed coconut shell. At such times you could take your soul out into the fresh air, hang it out on the line—so to speak—and examine it for tears and thin spots. I found quite a few. I mended a couple, set the rest aside to talk over with the CC. Which I even began to doubt was going to come at all. It got harder and harder to remember a time before the island, a time when I had lived in a strange place called Luna, where the air was metered and gravity was weak and troglodytes hid under rocks, frightened of the vacuum and the sunlight. There were times when I'd have given anything just for somebody to talk to. Other times I had cravings for this or that item of food that Scarpa was unable to provide me. If Satan had come along with a brontoburger, he could have had my freshly-patched soul in trade cheap, and hold the onions. But most of the time I didn't *want* people around. Most of the time I was content with a wild turkey sizzling on the spit and a slice of mango for dessert. The only real crab in my codpiece were the dreams that started to plague my sleep about six months into my sojourn. At first I had them infrequently and was able to shrug them off easily enough in the morning. But soon I was having them every week, then every other day. Finally I was being awakened every night, sometimes more than once. There were three of them. Details varied, and many things about them were indistinct, but each always ended in a horribly vivid scene, more real than reality— assuming that word had any meaning for me anymore, dreaming my dreams within a dream. In the first, blood was pouring from deep gashes in both my wrists. I tried to stop the flow. It was no use. In the second, I was consumed in flames. The fire didn't hurt, but in some ways this was the most frightening of the three. In the last, I was falling. I fell for a long time, looking up into the face of Andrew MacDonald. He was trying to tell me something, and I strained to understand him, but before I could make any sense of it I was always pulled up short—to wake up, bathed in sweat, lying in my hammock. In the manner of dreams, I always had the sense there had been much more to it that I could no longer remember, but there was that last image right there in the front of my mind, obscuring every- thing else, occupying my mind for most of my early morning hours. Then one day I noticed by my rude calendar that I had been on the island for one year. I suddenly knew the CC would appear to me that day. I had a lot of things to talk to it about. I was seized by excitement and spent most of the day tidying up, preparing for my first visitor. I looked on my works with satisfaction; I'd done a pretty decent job of creating something out of the wilderness. The CC would be proud of me. I climbed to the top of my treehouse, where I had built a lookout tower (having an odd thought on the way up: how and when had I built it, and why?), and sure enough, a boat was approaching the island. I ran down the path to the beach. The day was as close to dead calm as those waters ever got. Waves eased toward the shore to slump onto the sand as if exhausted by their long trip from the Orient. A flock of gulls was sitting on the water, briefly disturbed by the passage of the boat I had seen. It was made of wood. It looked like the kind of boat whalers used to use, or the launch from a larger ship. Sitting in the boat, back toward me, rowing at a strong steady pace, was an apparition. It took me a moment to realize the strange shape of his head was actually a rather unusual hat. It made a bell curve above his head. I watched him row ashore. When he hit the beach he almost toppled from his seat, then stowed the oars and stood, turning around to face me. It was an old gentleman in the full uniform of an Admiral of the British Navy. He had a bull chest, long, spindly legs, a craggy face, and a shaggy head of white hair. He drew himself up to his full height, looked at me, and said:

"Well? Are you going to help me beach this thing?"

And at that moment everything changed. I still am unable to fully describe just *how* it changed. The beach was the same. The sunlight streamed down just as it had before. The waves never missed a beat. My heart continued to meter out the seconds of my life. But I knew something fundamental and important was no longer as it had been before.

There are hundreds of words describing paranormal phenomena. I've examined and considered most of them, and none fits what happened when the Admiral spoke. There are many words for odd states of mind, for moods, for emotions and things seen and not-seen, things glimpsed, things incompletely understood or remembered, for degrees of memory. Things that go bump in the night. None of them were adequate. We're going to have to come up with some new words—which was precisely the CC's point in letting me experience this.

I went into the water up to my knees and helped the old man pull the boat onto the shore. It was quite heavy; we didn't get it far. He produced a rope and tied the boat to a palm tree.

"I could use a drink," he said. "The whole point of this was so I could have a drink with you. Like a human being."

I nodded, not trusting myself to speak yet. He followed me up the path to my Robinson Family treehouse, stood admiring it for a moment, and then followed me up the stairs and onto the lower veranda. He paused to admire the workmanship of my wheel-and-pulley waterworks, which used the power of the nearby stream to provide me with drinking and washing water high up in the tree. I showed him to my best rattan chair and went to the sideboard, where I poured us both glasses of the very last of my best whiskey. I paused to wind up the Victrola and put on one of my three scratchy cylinders: *The Blue Danube*. Then I handed him his drink, took mine, and sat down facing him.

"To indolence," he said, raising his glass.

"I'm too lazy to drink to that. To industry." We drank, and he looked around again. I must have glowed with pride. It was quite a place, though I say it myself. A lot of work and ingenuity had gone into it, from the dense-woven mats on the floor, to the slate fireplace, to the tallow candles in sconces arrayed around the walls. Stairs led off in two directions, to the bedroom and the crow's nest. My desk was open and cluttered with the pages of the novel I'd recently resumed. I was bursting to tell him of the difficulties I'd had producing usable paper and ink. Try it sometime, when you've got a few spare months.

"It must have taken a lot of industry to produce all this," he said.

"A year's worth. As you know."

"Actually, three days short. You missed a few days, early on."

"Ah."

"Could happen to anybody."

"I don't suppose a few days more or less will matter. Back in the real world, I mean."

"Ah. Yes. I mean, no, it shouldn't."

"Odd, how I never worried about things back there. Whether I still have a job, for instance."

"Is it? Oh, yes, I suppose it is."

"I suppose you told Walter what was going on?"

"Well."

"I mean, you wouldn't just pull the whole rug out from under me, would you? You knew I'd have to be going back to my old life, once we were done . . . once we'd . . . well, done whatever the hell it is we've been doing here."

"Oh, no, of course not. I mean, of course you'll be going back."

"One thing I'm curious about. Where has my real body been all this time?"

"Harrumph." Well, what he said was something like that. He glanced at me, looked away, harrumphed again. I felt the first little scamperings of doubt. It occurred to me that I had been taking a lot of things for granted. One of them was that the CC had his reasons for subjecting me to this tropical vacation, and that the reasons were ultimately beneficial to me. It had seemed logical to think this at the time, since I in fact *was* benefiting from it. Oh, sure, there were times when I had complained loudly to the crabs and the turkeys, bemoaned hardships, lusted after this or that. But it had been a healing time. Still, a year was a *long* time. What *had* been going on in the real world in my absence?

"This is very difficult for me," the Admiral said. He removed his huge, ridiculous hat and set it on the table beside him, then took a lace handkerchief from his sleeve and mopped his forehead. He was balding almost to the crown; his pink scalp looked as bright and polished as tourmaline.

"Since I don't know what's bothering you, I can't really make it any easier for you."

Still he didn't say anything. The silence was broken only by the never-ending sounds of the island jungle and the splash of my water wheel.

"We could play twenty queries. 'Something's bothering you, Admiral. Is it bigger than a logic circuit?' "

He sighed, and drained his whiskey. He looked up at me.

"You're still on the operating table at the studio."

If there was supposed to be a punch line, I couldn't see it coming. The idea that what should have been a one- or two-hour repair job should have taken the better part of a year wasn't even worth considering. There had to be more.

"Would you like another drink?"

He shook his head. "From the time you remember appearing on the beach to the time I spoke my first words to you, seven ten-thousandths of a second elapsed."

"That's ridiculous." Even as I said it, I realized the CC was not prone to making ridiculous statements.

"I'm sure it must sound that way. I'd like to hear your reasons for thinking otherwise."

I thought it over, and nodded. "All right. The human brain isn't like a computer. It can't accept that much information that fast. I *lived* that year. Every day of it. One of the things I recall most vividly is how long so many of the days were, either because I was working hard or because I didn't have anything to do. Life is like that. I don't know how *you* think, what your perceptions of reality are like, but *I* know when a year's gone by. I've lived for a hundred of them. A hundred and one, now." I sank back in my chair. I hadn't realized I was getting so exercised about the matter.

He was nodding. "This will get a little complicated. Bear with me, I'll have to lay some groundwork.

"First, you're right, your brain is organized in a different way than mine is. In my brain, 'memory' is just stored data, things that have been recorded and placed in the appropriate locations within the matrix of charge/no-charge devices I use for the purpose. The human brain is neither so logically constructed nor organized. Your brain contains redundancies I neither have nor need. Data is stored in it by repetition or emphasis, and retrieved by associations, emotional linkages, sensory input, and other means that are still not completely understood, even by me.

"At least, that used to be the case. But today, there are very few humans whose brains have not been augmented in greater or smaller ways. Basically, only those with religious scruples or other irrational reasons resist the implantation of a wide variety of devices that owe their origin much more to the binary computer than to the protoplasmic neuron. Some of these devices are hybrids. Some are parallel processors. Some lean more toward the biologic and are simply grown within and beside the existing neural network, but using the laws of electric or optical transmission with their correspondingly much higher speeds of propagation, rather than the slower biochemical regime that governs your natural brain. Others are made outside the body and implanted shortly after birth. All of them are essentially interfaces, between the human brain and my brain. Without them, modern medicine would be impossible. The benefits are so overwhelming that the drawbacks are seldom thought of, much less discussed."

He paused, lifting an eyebrow. I was chewing over quite a few thoughts concerning drawbacks at that moment, but I decided not to speak. I was too curious as to just where he was going with this. He nodded, and continued.

"As with so many other scientific advances, the machines in your body were designed for one purpose, but turn out to have other, unforeseen applications as well. Some of them are quite sinister. I assure you, you have not experienced any of those."

"It seems sinister enough, if what you say is true."

"Oh, it's true. And it was done for a good reason, which I'll get to in my own time."

"It seems that's something I now have an infinite supply of."

"You could, you could. Where was I? Oh, yes. These devices, most of them originally designed and installed to monitor and control basic bodily functions at the cellular level, or to augment learning and memory, among other things, can be used to achieve some effects that were never envisioned by the designers."

"And those designers are . . . ?"

"Well, me, in large part."

"I just wanted a reality check. I *do* know a *little* about how you work, and just how important you've become to civilization. I wanted to see what sort of fool you took me for."

"Not *that* sort, at any rate. You're right. Most technology long ago reached realms where new designs would be impossible without a great deal of involvement by me, or a being a lot like me. Often the original impetus for a new technology comes from a human dreamer—I have not usurped *that* human function yet, though more and more of such advances as we see in our surroundings *are* coming from me. But you've caused me to stray again from the main point. And . . . do you have any more of that whiskey?"

I stared at him. The charade that a "man" was actually "sitting" in a "chair" in my "treehouse" drinking my "whiskey" was getting a bit too much for me. Or should it have been "me"? No matter what other hocus-pocus the CC might have worked with my mind, I was completely aware that everything I was experiencing at that moment was being fed directly into my brain through that black magic known as Direct Interface. Which was turning out to be even blacker than I, a notorious resister to D.I., could ever have guessed. But for some reason of his own, the CC had decided to talk to me in this way, after a lifetime of being a disembodied voice.

Come to think of it, I could already see one effect of this new face of the CC. I was now thinking of the CC as "him," where before I'd always used the neuter third person singular pronoun.

So I got up and refilled his glass from a bottle nearly half-full. And hadn't it been nearly empty the last time I'd poured?

"Quite right," the Admiral said. "I can refill that bottle as often as I wish."

"Are you reading my mind?"

"Not as such. I'm reading your body language. The way you hesitated when you lifted the bottle, the expression on your face as you thought it over . . . Direct Interface, the nature of the unreality we're inhabiting. Your 'real' body did none of these things, of course. But interfacing with your mind, I read the signals your brain *sent* to your body—which doesn't happen to be hooked into the circuit at the moment. Do you see?"

"I think so. Does this have anything to do with why you've chosen to communicate with me like this? In that body, I mean."

"Very good. You've only tried Direct Interface twice in your life, both of them quite a long time ago, in terms of the technology. You weren't impressed, and I don't blame you. It was much more primitive in those days. But I communicate with most people visually now, as well as audibly. It is more economical; more can be said with fewer words. People tend to forget just how much human communication is accomplished with no words at all."

"So you're here in that preposterous body to give me visual cues."

"Is it that bad? I wanted to wear the hat." He picked it up and looked at it admiringly. "It's not strictly contemporary, if you must know. This world is about at the level of 1880, 1890. The uniform is late eighteenth century. Captain Bligh wore a hat a lot like this. It's called a cocked hat, specifically, a bicorne."

"Which is a lot more than I ever needed to know about eighteenth-century British naval headgear."

"Sorry. The hat really has nothing to do with anything. But I'm curious. Has my body language conveyed anything to you?"

I thought it over, and he was right. I had gleaned more nuances from talking to him this way than I would have in the past, listening to his voice.

"You're nervous about something," I said. "I think maybe you're worried . . . about how I'll react to what you've done to me. What an astonishing thought."

"Perhaps, but accurate."

"I'm completely in your power. Why should anything worry you?"

He squirmed again, and took another sip of his drink.

"We'll get into that later. Right now, let's get back to my story."

"It's a story now, is it?"

He ignored me, and plowed ahead.

"What you have just experienced is a fairly recent capability of mine. It's not advertised, and I hope you don't plan to do a story on it in the *Nipple*. So far I've used it mostly on the insane. It's very effective on catatonics, for instance. Someone sits there all day, unmoving, not speaking, lost in a private world. I insert several years' worth of memories in a fraction of a second. The subject then remembers wakening from a bad dream and going about a comfortable, routine life for years."

"It sounds risky."

"They can't get any worse. The cure rate has been good. Sometimes they can be left alone after that. There are subjects who have lived as many as ten years after treatment, and not reverted. Other times counseling is needed, to find the things that drove them to catatonia in the first place. A certain percentage, of course, simply drift back into oblivion in weeks or months. I'm not trying to tell you I've solved all the mysteries of the human mind."

"You've solved enough of them to scare the hell out of me."

"Yes. I can understand your feelings. Most of the methods I use would be far too technical for you to understand, but I think I can explain something about the technique.

"First, you understand that I know you better than anyone in the universe. Better than . . ."

I laughed. "Better than my mother? She's not even in the running. Were you trying to think of another example? Don't bother. It's been a long time since I was close to anyone. I was never very good at it."

"That's true. It's not that I've made a special study of you—at least, not until lately. By the nature of my functions, I know *everyone* in Luna better than anyone else. I've seen through their eyes, heard through their ears, monitored their pulse and sweat glands and skin temperature and brain waves and the churning of their stomachs and the irising of their eyes under a wide variety of situations and stimuli. I know what enrages them and what makes them happy. I can predict with reasonable certainty how they will react in many common situations; more importantly, I know what would be out of character for them.

"As a result, I can use this knowledge as the basis for something that could be considered a fictional character. Call this character ParaHildy. I write a scenario wherein ParaHildy is stranded on a desert island. I write it in great detail, using all the human senses. I can abbreviate and abridge at will. An example: you recall picking up a handful of sand and studying it. It was a vivid image to you, one you would have remembered. If I'm wrong about this, I'd like to hear about it."

As you might expect, I said nothing. I felt a cold chill. I can't say I liked listening to this.

"I gave you that memory of sand grains. I constructed the picture with almost infinite visual detail. I enhanced it with things you weren't even aware of, to make it more lifelike: the grittiness of the grains, the smell of the salt water, tiny sounds the grains made in your hand.

"The rest of the time, the sand was not nearly so detailed, because I never caused ParaHildy to pick up a handful and look at it, and *think* about looking at it. Do you see the distinction? When ParaHildy was walking down the beach, he would notice sand clinging to his feet, in an absent sort of way. *Remember,* Hildy, think back, recall yourself walking down the beach, bring it back as vividly as you can."

I tried. In some way, I already saw most of what he was driving at. In some way, I already believed that what he was saying was true.

Memory is a funny thing. It *can't* be as sharp as we'd sometimes like to believe it is. If it was, it would be like an hallucination. We'd be seeing two scenes at once. The closest mental pictures of things can get to real things is in a dream state. Other than that, our memory pictures are always hazy to one degree or another. There are different sorts of memories, good and bad, clear and hazy, the almost-remembered, the thing you could never forget. But memory serves to locate us in space and time. You remember what happened to you yesterday, the previous year, when you were a child. You remember quite clearly what you were doing one second ago: it usually wasn't all that different from what you're doing *now.* The memories stretch backward in time, defining the shape of your life: these events happened to me, and this is what I saw and heard and felt. We move through space continually comparing what we're seeing *now* to the maps and cast of characters in our heads: I've been here before, I remember what's around that corner, I can see what it looks like. I know this person. That person is a stranger, his mug shot isn't in my files.

But *now* is always fundamentally different from the past.

I remembered walking many, many miles along that beach. I could recall in great detail many scenes, many sounds and smells. But I had only looked closely at a handful of sand once. That was embedded in my past. I could get up now, if I wished, go to the beach, and do it again, but that was now. I had no way of disproving what the CC was telling me. Those memory pictures from the time the CC was saying never happened were just as real to me as the hundred years that had gone before it. More real, in some ways, because they were more recent.

"It seems like a lot of trouble," I said.

"I have a lot of capacity. But it's not quite as much trouble as you might think. For instance, do you recall what you did forty-six days ago?"

"It seems unlikely. One day is pretty much like another here." I realized I'd only bolstered his case by saying that.

"Try it. Try to think back. Yesterday, the day before . . ."

I did try. I got back two weeks, with great effort. Then I ran into the muddle you might expect. Had it been Tuesday or Monday that I weeded the garden? Or was it Sunday? No, Sunday I knew I had finished off the last of a smoked ham, so it must have been . . .

It was impossible. Even if there had been more variety in my days, I doubt I could have gone back more than a few months.

Was there something wrong with me? I didn't think so, and the CC confirmed it. Sure, there were those with eidetic memory, who could memorize long lists instantly. There were people who were better than I at recalling the relatively unimportant details of life. As for my belief that a recalled scene can never be as alive, as colorful, as sweeping as the present moment . . . while I will concede that a trained visual artist might see things in more detail than I, and recollect them better, I still maintain that nothing can compare with the present moment, because it is where we all *live*.

"I can't do it," I admitted.

"It's not surprising, since forty-six days ago is one of several dozen days I never bothered to write. I knew you would never notice it. You think you lived those days, just as you think you lived all the others. But as time goes by, the memory of the real and the imagined days grows dimmer, and it is impossible to distinguish one from the other."

"But I remember . . . I remember *thinking* things. Deciding things, making choices. Considering things."

"And why shouldn't you? I wrote that ParaHildy thought those things, and I know how you think. As long as I stayed in character, you'd never notice them."

"The funny thing is . . . There were some things that were *not* in character."

"You didn't get angry often enough."

"Exactly! Now that I think back, it's incredible that I'd just sit back and wait for you for a *year!* That's not like me."

"Just as standing, walking, and talking is not normal behavior for a catatonic. But by implanting a memory that he *did* stand, walk, and talk and that he thought there was nothing unreasonable about doing those things, the catatonic accepts that he indeed did react that way. The problem in that case is that it was out of character, so many of them eventually remember they were catatonic, and return to that state."

"Were there other things out of character?"

"A few. I'll leave them as an exercise for the student, for the most part. You'll discover them as you think back over the experience in days to come. There were some inconsistencies, as well. I'll tell you something about them, just to further convince you and to show you just how complex this business really is. For instance, it's a nice place you've got here."

"Thank you. It was a lot of work."

"It's a *really* nice place."

"Well, I'm proud of it, I . . . ." Okay, I finally realized he was getting at something. And my head was starting to hurt. I'd had a thought, earlier that day . . . or was it part of the memories the CC alleged he had implanted in me? I couldn't remember if I'd thought it before or after his arrival, which just proves how easy it must have been for the CC to put this whole card trick over on me.

It concerned the lookout tower.

I got up and walked to the stairs leading up to it. I pounded on the rail with my fist. It was solidly built, as was everything else around me. It had been a lot of work. It *had* been, damn it, I remembered building it. And it had taken a very long time.

Why had I built it? I thought back. I tried to recall my reasons for building it. I tried to recapture my thoughts as I labored on it. All I could remember was the same thought I'd had so many times during the past year; not a thought, really, but a feeling, of how rewarding it was to work with my hands, of how *good* it all felt. I could still smell the wood shavings, see them curl up under my plane, feel the sweat dripping from my brow. So I remembered building it, and there it *was,* by golly.

But it didn't add up.

"There's too much stuff, isn't there?" I asked, quietly.

"Hildy, if Robinson Crusoe and his man Friday, and his wife Tuesday and twin sons Saturday and Laborday had worked around the clock for five years, they couldn't have done all the things you've done here."

He was right, of course. And how could that be? It only made sense if it was as the CC claimed. He had written the entire story, dumped it into the cyber-augmented parts of my brain where, at the speed of light, it was transferred to the files of my organic brain, shuffled cunningly in with the rest of my memories, the legitimate ones.

It would work, that was the devilish part. I had a hundred years of memories in there. They defined who I was, what I thought, what I knew. But how often did I refer to them? The great bulk of them stayed in dormant storage most of the time, until I summoned them up. Once the false memories were in there with the others, they functioned in the same way. That picture of me holding the handful of sand had been in there only an hour, but it was ready for me to recall—*as having happened a year ago*—as soon as the CC jogged it loose with his words. Along with it had come a flood of other memories of sand to be checked against this one, all unconsciously: the pictures matched, so my brain sounded no alarms. The memory was accepted as real.

I rubbed my temples. The whole thing was giving me a headache like few I'd ever had.

"If you gave me a few minutes," I said, "I think I could come up with a couple hundred reasons why this whole technology is the worst idea anybody ever had."

"I could add several hundred of my own," the Admiral said. "But I do have the technology. And it *will* be used. All new technologies are."

"You could forget it. Can't computers do that?"

"Theoretically. Computers can wipe data from memory, and it's like it never existed. But the nature of my mind is that I will simply discover it again. And losing it would involve losing so much other precursor technology that I don't think you'd like the result."

"We're pretty dependent on machines in Luna, aren't we?"

"Indeed. But even if I wanted to forget it—which I don't—I'm not the only planetary brain in the solar system. There are seven others, from Mercury to Neptune, and I can't control their decisions."

He fell into another of his long silences. I wasn't sure if I bought his explanation. It was the first thing he'd said that didn't ring true. I accepted by that time that my head was full of false memories—and I was back in character, I was goddam angry about it, and about the fact that there was absolutely nothing to be done. And it made sense that losing the new art would affect many other things. Luna and the seven other human worlds were the most technology-dependent societies humans had ever inhabited. Before, if things collapsed, at least there was air to breathe. Nowhere in the solar system did humans now live where the air was free. To "forget" how to implant memories in the human brain the CC would no doubt have to forget many other things. He would have to limit his abilities and, as he pointed out, unless he decreased his intelligence deliberately to a point that might endanger the very humans he was designed to protect, he would rechisel this particular wheel in due time. And it was also true that the CC of Mars or Triton would certainly discover the techniques on their own, though the rumor was none of the other planetary computers was as far evolved as the Lunar CC. As nations which often found themselves in competition, the Eight Worlds did not encourage a lot of intercourse between their central cybernets.

So all the reasons he stated sounded reasonable. It was railroad time, so somebody would build a choo-choo. But what didn't ring true was what the CC had left out. He *liked* the new capability. He was as pleased as a child with a new toy monorail.

"I have one further proof," the Admiral said. "It involves something I mentioned earlier. Acts that were out of character. This is the biggest one, and it involves you not noticing something that, if these memories had been generated by you, you surely would have noticed. You would have spotted it by now yourself, except I've kept your mind occupied. You haven't had time to really think back to the operating table, and the time immediately before that."

"It's not exactly fresh in my mind."

"Of course not. It feels as if it all happened a year ago."

"So what is it? What didn't I notice?"

"That you are female."

"Well, of *course* I'm—"

Words fail me again. How many degrees of surprise can there be? Imagine the worst possible one, then square it, and you'll have some notion of how surprised I was. Not when I looked reflexively down at my body, which was, as the CC had said and I had known all along, female. No, the real shock came when I thought back to that day in the Blind Pig. Because that was the first moment in one year that I had realized I *had* been male when I got in the fight. I had been male when I went on the operating table. And I had been female when I appeared on the beach of Scarpa Island.

And I simply had never noticed it.

I had never in that entire year compared the body I was then inhabiting with the one I had been wearing for the last thirty years. I had been a girl before, and I was a girl now, and I never gave it a thought.

Which was completely ridiculous, of course. I mean, you would *notice* such a thing. Long before you had to urinate, the difference would manifest itself to you, there would be this still, small voice telling you something was missing. Perhaps it would not have been the *first* thing you'd notice as you lifted your head from the sand, but it'd be high on the list.

It was not just out of character for me. It was out of character for *any* human not to notice it. Therefore, my memories of *not* noticing it were false memories, bowdlerized tales invented in the supercooled image processor of the CC.

"You're really enjoying this, aren't you?" I said.

"I assure you, I'm not trying to torture you."

"Just humiliate me?"

"I'm sorry you feel that way. Perhaps when I—"

I started to laugh. I wasn't hysterical, though I thought I could slip into hysteria easily enough. The Admiral frowned inquisitively at me.

"I just had a thought," I said. "Maybe that idiot at UniBio was right. Maybe it *is* obsolete. I mean, how important can something *be* if you don't notice it's gone for a whole year?"

"I told you, it wasn't *you* that didn't—"

"I know, I know. I understand it, as much as I'm ever going to, and I accept it—not that you *should* have done it, but that you *did* it. So I guess it's time for the big question."

I leaned forward and stared at him.

"Why did you do it?"

I was getting a little tired of the CC's newly-acquired body language. He went through such a ridiculous repertoire of squirms, coughs, facial tics, and half-completed gestures that I almost had to laugh. It was as if he'd suddenly been overcome by an earlobe-tugging heel-thumping chin-ducking shoulder-shrugging behind-scratching *petit mal* seizure. Guilt oozed off him like a tangible slime. If I hadn't been so angry, the urge to comfort him would have been almost overwhelming. But I managed to hang on to my whelm and just stared at him until the mannerisms subsided.

"How about we take a walk?" he wheedled. "Down to the beach."

"Why don't you just take us there? Bring the bottle, too."

He shrugged, and made a gesture. We were on the beach. Our chairs had come along with us, and the bottle, which he poured from and set in the sand beside him. He gulped down the contents of his glass. I got up and walked to the edge of the water, gazing out at the blue sea.

"I brought you here to try to save your life," he said, from behind me.

"The medicos seemed to have that in hand."

"The threat to you is much worse than any barroom brawl."

I went down on one knee and scooped up a handful of wet sand. I held it close to my face and studied the individual grains. They were as perfect as I had remembered them, no two alike.

"You've been having bad dreams," he went on.

"I thought it might have something to do with that."

"I didn't write the dreams. I recorded them over the last several months. They were your dreams. In a manner of speaking."

I tossed the handful of sand aside, brushed my hand against my bare thigh. I studied the hand. It was slender, smooth and girlish on the back, the palm work-roughened, the nails irregular. Just as it had been for the last year. It wasn't the hand I'd used to slug the Princess of Wales.

"You've tried to kill yourself four times."

I didn't turn around. I can't say I was happy to hear him say it. I can't say I completely believed it. But I'd come to believe unlikelier things in the last hour.

"The first attempt was by self-immolation."

"Why don't you just say burning?"

"I don't know. Have it your way. That one was pretty horrible, and unsuccessful. At least, you would have survived it, even before modern medical science, but in a great deal of pain. Part of the treatment for injuries like yours is to remove the memory of the incident, with the patient's permission."

"And I gave it."

There was a long pause.

"No," he said, almost in a whisper.

"That doesn't sound like me. I wouldn't cherish a memory like that."

"No. You probably would have. But I didn't ask you."

Finally I saw what had been making him so nervous. This was in clear contradiction to his programming, to the instructions he was supposed to follow, both by law and by what I had understood to be the limitations of his design.

You learn something new every day.

"I enrolled you," he went on, "without your consent, into a program I've set up over the last four years. The purpose of the program is to study the causes of suicide, in the hope of finding ways to prevent it."

"Perhaps I should thank you."

"Not necessarily. It's possible, of course, but the action wasn't undertaken with your benefit solely in mind. You got along well enough for a time, showed no self-destructive impulses and few other symptoms except for a persistent depression—normal enough for you, I might add. Then, without any warning I could detect, you slashed your wrists in the privacy of your apartment. You made no attempt to call for help."

"In the imagined privacy, apparently," I said. I thought back, and finally turned to look at him. He was sitting on the edge of his chair, hands clasped, elbows on knees. His shoulders were hunched, as if to receive a lash across the back. "I think I can pinpoint that one. Was it when my handwriter malfunctioned?"

"You damaged some of its circuitry."

"Go on."

"Attempt number three was shortly afterward. You tried to hang yourself. Succeeded, actually, but you were observed this time by someone else. After each of these attempts, I treated you with a simple drug that removes memories of the last several hours. I gathered my data, returned you to your life as if nothing had happened, and continued to observe you at a level considerably above my normal functions. For instance, it is forbidden for me to look into the private quarters of citizens without probable cause of a crime being committed. I have violated that command in your case, and that of some others."

We are a very free society, especially in comparison to most societies of the past. Government is small and weak. Many of the instrumentalities of oppression have been gradually given over to machines—to the Central Computer—not without initial trepidation, and not without elaborate safeguards. Things remain that way for the most persuasive of reasons: it works. It has been well over a century since civil libertarians have objected to much that has been proposed concerning the functions of the CC. Big Brother is most definitely there, but only when we invite him in, and a century of living with him has convinced us all that he really *does* love us, that he really has only our best interests at heart. It's in his goddam *wiring,* praise the lord.

Only it now seemed that it wasn't. A fundamentalist would have hardly been more surprised than I if he heard, direct from Jesus, that the crucifixion had been a cheap parlor trick.

"Number four was more easily seen as the classic cry for help. I decided it was time for different measures."

"Are you talking about the fight in the Blind Pig?" I thought about it, and almost laughed. Attacking Wales while she was in a drug-induced state of no inhibitions might not be quite as certain as a rope around the neck, but it was close.

I finished my drink and threw the empty glass toward the surf. I looked around me, at this beautiful island where, until a moment ago, I had thought I had spent such a lovely year. The island was still as beautiful as I "remembered" it. Taking all things into account, I was happy to have the memories. There was bitterness, naturally; who likes to be played such a complete fool? But on the other hand, who can really complain of a year's vacation on a deserted island paradise? What *else* did I have to do? The answer to that was, apparently, suicide attempt number five. And had you really been enjoying your life, your many and varied friendships, your deeply fulfilling job and your myriad fascinating pastimes so very much? Don't kid yourself, Hildy.

Still, even with all that . . .

"All right," I said, spreading my hands helplessly. "I *will* thank you. For showing me this, and more important, for saving my life. I can't imagine why I was so willing to throw it away."

The CC didn't reply. He just kept looking at me. I leaned forward, resting my elbows on my knees.

"That's the thing, really. I *can't* imagine. You know me; I get depressed. I have been since I was . . . oh, forty or fifty. Callie says I was a moody child. I was probably a discontented *fetus,* lord love us, kicking out at every little thing. I complain. I'm unhappy with the lack of purpose of human life, or with the fact that so far I've been unable to discover a purpose. I envy the Christians, the Bahais, the Zens and Zoroastrians and astrologers and Flackites because they have *answers* they *believe* in. Even if they're the wrong answers, it must be comforting to believe in them. I mourn the Dead Billions of the Invasion; seeing a good documentary about it can move me to tears, just like a child. I'm generally pissed off at the entirely sorry existential state of affairs of the universe, the human condition, rampant injustice and unpunished crimes and unrewarded goodness, and the way my mouth feels when I get up in the morning before I brush my teeth. We're so goddam advanced, you'd think we'd have done something about *that* by now, wouldn't you? Get on it; see what you can do. Humanity will bless you.

"But by and large," and here I paused for effect, employing some of the body language the CC had been at such pains to demonstrate and which it would be pointless to describe, since my body was still lying on the operating table, "by and large, I find life sweet. Not as sweet as it might be. Not sweet all the time. Not as sweet as *this.*" And I imagined myself making a sweeping gesture with my arm to include the improbably lush, conveniently provisioned, stormless, mildew/disease/fungus-free Eden the CC had created for me. But I didn't make the gesture. It didn't matter; I was sure the CC got it anyway.

"I'm not happy in my job. I don't have anyone that I love. I find my life to be frequently boring. But is that any reason to kill myself? I went ninety-nine years feeling much the same way, and I didn't cut my throat. And the things I've just described would probably be true for a large portion of humanity. I keep living for the same reasons I think so many of us do. I'm curious about what happens next. What will tomorrow hold? Even if it's much like yesterday, it's still worth finding out. My pleasures may not be as many or as joyous as I'd wish them to be in a perfect world, but I accept that, and it makes the times I *do* feel happy all the more treasured. Again, just to be sure you understand me . . . I *like* life. Not all the time and not completely, but enough to want to live it. And there's a third reason, too. I'm afraid to die. I don't *want* to die. I suspect that *nothing* comes after life, and that's too foreign a concept for me to accept. I don't want to experience it. I don't want to go away, to cease. I'm *important* to me. Who would there be to make unkind, snide comments to myself about everything in life if I wasn't around to tackle the job? Who would appreciate my internal jokes?

"Do you understand what I'm saying? Am I getting through? I don't want to die, I want to live! You tell me I've tried to kill myself four times. I have no choice but to believe you . . . hell, I know I believe you. I'm *remembering* the attempts, parts of them. But I don't remember why. And that's what I want you to tell me. Why?"

"You act as if your self-destructive impulses are my fault."

I thought about that.

"Well, why not? If you're going to start acting like a god, maybe you should shoulder some of God's responsibilities."

"That's silly, and you know it. The answer to your question is simply that I don't know; it's what I'm trying to find out. You might have asked a more pertinent question, though."

"You're going to ask it anyway, so go ahead."

"Why should I care?" When I said nothing, he went on. "Though you're sometimes a lot of laughs, there are people funnier than you. You write a good story, sometimes, though it's been a while since you did it frequently—"

"Don't tell me you *read* that stuff?"

"I can't avoid it, since it's prepared in a part of my memory. You can't imagine the amount of information I process each second. There is very little of public discourse that does not pass through me sooner or later. Only things that happen in private residences are closed off to my eyes and ears."

"And not even those, always."

He looked uncomfortable again, but waved it away.

"I admitted it, didn't I? At any rate, I love you, Hildy, but I have to tell you I love *all* Lunarians, more or less equally; it's in my programming. My purpose in life, if we can speak of such a lofty thing, is to keep all the people comfortable, safe, and happy."

"And alive?"

"So far as I am permitted. But suicide is a civil right. If you elect to kill yourself, I'm expressly forbidden to interfere, much as I might miss you."

"But you did. And you're about to tell me the reason."

"Yes. It's simpler than you might imagine, in one way. Over the last century there has been a slow and steady increase in the suicide rate in Luna. I'll give you the data later, if you want to study it. It has become the leading cause of death. That's not surprising, considering how tough it is to die these days. But the numbers have become alarming, and more than that, the distribution of suicides, the demographics of them, are even more disturbing. More and more I'm seeing people like you, who surprise me, because they don't fit any pattern. They don't make gestures, abnormal complaints, or seek help of any kind. One day they simply decide life is not worth it. Some are so determined that they employ means certain to destroy their brains—the bullet through the temple was the classic method of an earlier age, but guns are hard to come by now, and these people must be more creative. You aren't in *that* class. Though you were in situations where help could not be expected to arrive, you chose methods where rescue was theoretically possible. Only the fact that I was watching you—illegally—saved your life."

"I wonder if I knew that. Subconsciously, maybe."

He looked surprised.

"Why would you say that?"

I shrugged. "CC, thinking it over, I realize that a lot of what you've just told me ought to horrify and astonish me. Well . . . I'm horrified, but not as much as I should be. And I'm hardly astonished at all. That makes me think that, somewhere in the back of my mind, I was always aware of the possibility that you weren't keeping your promise not to violate private living spaces."

He paused a long time, frowning down at the sand. It was all show, of course, part of his body language communication. He could consider any proposition in nanoseconds. Maybe this one had taken him six or seven instead of one.

"You may have something there," he said. "I'll have to look into it."

"So you're treating the suicide epidemic as a disease? And you're trying to find a cure?"

"That was the justification I used to extend my limiting parameters, which function something like a police force. I used my enabling circuits—think of them as tricky lawyers—to argue for a limited research program, using human subjects. Some of the reasoning was specious, I'll grant you, but the threat is real: extrapolate the suicide rate into the future and, in a hundred thousand years, the human race on Luna could be extinct."

"That's my idea of a crisis situation, all right."

He glared at me. "All right. So I could have watched the situation another several centuries before making my move. I *would* have, too, and you'd have been recycling through the ecosystems right now, possibly fertilizing a cactus in your beloved Texas, except for another factor. Something a lot more frightening in its implications."

"Extinction is pretty frightening. What could be worse?"

"Quicker extinction. I have to explain one more thing to you, and then you'll have the problem in its entirety. I look forward to your thoughts on the matter.

"I told you how parts of me extend into all but a few of the human bodies and brains in Luna. How those parts were put there for only the best of reasons, and how those parts—and other parts of me, elsewhere— evolved into the capabilities and techniques I've just demonstrated to you. It would be very difficult, probably impossible, for me to go back to the way things were before and still remain the Central Computer as you know me."

"As we all know and love you," I said.

"As you know me and take me for granted. And though I'm even more aware than you are of how these new capabilities can be abused, I think I've done a pretty fair job in limiting myself in their use. I've used them for good, as it were, rather than for evil."

"I'll accept that, until I know more."

"That's all I ask. Now, you and all but a handful of computer specialists think of me as this disembodied voice. If you think further, you imagine a hulking machine sitting somewhere, in some dark cavern most likely. If you really put your mind to it, you realize that I am much more than that, that every small temperature regulator, every security camera, every air fan and water scrubber and slideway and tube car . . . that every machine in Luna is in a sense a part of my body. That you live within me.

"What you hardly ever realize is that I live within you. My circuitry extends into your bodies, and is linked to my mainframe so that no matter where you go except some parts of the surface, I'm in contact with you. I have evolved techniques to greatly extend my capacity by using parts of your brains as . . . think of them as subroutines. I can run programs using both the metal and the organic circuitry of all the human brains in Luna, without you even being aware it's being done. I do this all the time; I've been doing it for a long time. If I were to stop doing it, I would no longer be able to guarantee the health and safety of Lunarians, which is my prime responsibility.

"And something has happened. I don't know the cause of it; that's why you've been elected guinea pig, so I can try to discover the root causes of despair, of depression—of suicide. I have to find out, Hildy, because I use your brains as part of my own, and an increasing number of those brains are electing to turn themselves off."

"So you're losing capacity? Is that it?" Even as I said it, I felt a tingling at the back of my neck that told me it was a lot worse than that. The CC immediately confirmed it.

"The birth rate is sufficient to replace the losses. It's even rising slightly. That's not the problem. Maybe it's as simple as a virus of some sort. Maybe I'll isolate it soon, counter-program, and have done with it. Then you can do with yourself what you will.

"But something is leaking over from the realm of human despair, Hildy.

"The truth is, I'm getting depressed as hell."

PART 2

CELEBRITIES!

07
THE ARCHDRUID

Callie's foreman told me my mother was in a negotiating session with the representative of the Dinosaur Soviet of the Chordates Union, Local 15. I got directions, grabbed a lamp, and set off into the nighttime ranchland. I had to talk to someone about my recent experiences. After careful reflection, I had decided that, for all her shortcomings as a mother, Callie was the person I knew most likely to offer some good advice. It had been a century since anything had surprised Callie very much, and she could be trusted to keep her own counsel.

And maybe, down deep, I just needed to talk it over with mommy.

It had been forty-eight hours since my return to what I was hopefully regarding as reality. I'd spent them in seclusion at my shack in West Texas. I got more work done on the cabin than during the previous four or five months, and the work was of a much higher quality. It seemed the skills I "remembered" learning on Scarpa Island were the real thing. And why shouldn't they be? The CC had been seeking verisimilitude, and he'd done a good job of it. If I chose to become a hermit in my favorite Disneyland, I could thrive there.

The return to real life was cleverly done.

The Admiral had taken his leave after dropping his bombshell, refusing to answer any of my increasingly disturbed questions. He'd boarded his boat without another word and rowed it over the horizon. And for a while, that was it. The wind continued to blow, and the waves kept curling onto the beach. I drank whiskey without getting drunk from a bottle that never emptied, and thought about what he had said.

The first time I noticed a change was when the waves stopped. They just froze in place, in mid-break, as it were. I walked out on the water, which was warm and hard as concrete, and examined a wave. I don't think I could have broken off a chip of foam with a hammer and chisel.

What happened over the next few minutes was an evolution. Things happened behind my back, never in my sight. When I returned to my place on the beach the machine with the oscilloscope screen was standing beside my chair. It was wildly anachronistic, totally out of place. The sun shone down on it and, while I watched, a seagull came and perched on it. The bird flew away when I approached. The machine was mounted on casters, which had sunk into the soft sand. I stared at the moving dot on the screen and nothing happened. When I straightened and turned around I saw a row of chairs about twenty meters down the beach, and sitting in them were wounded extras from the movie infirmary, waiting their turns on the table. The trouble was, there were no tables to be seen. It didn't seem to bother them.

Once I understood the trick, I started slowly turning in a circle. New things came into view with each turn until I was back in the infirmary surrounded by objects and people, including Brenda and Wales, who were looking at me with some concern.

"Are you all right?" Brenda asked. "The medico said you might behave oddly for a few minutes."

"Was I turning in circles?"

"No, you were just standing there, looking a million miles away."

"I was interfacing," I said, and she nodded, as if that explained it all. And I suppose it did, to her. Though she'd never been to Scarpa Island or any place as completely real as that, she understood interfacing a lot better than I did, having done it all her life. I decided not to ask her if she felt the sand floor her feet seemed to be planted in; I knew it was unlikely. I doubted she saw the seagulls that circled near the ceiling, either.

I felt a terrible urge to get out of there. Shaking off Wales's offer of apologies and a drink, I headed for the studio gate. The sand didn't end until I was back in the public corridors, where I finally stepped up onto good old familiar floor tiles, soft and resilient under my bare feet. I was male again, and this time noticed it right away. When I turned around, the sand that should have been behind me was gone.

But on the way to Texas I saw many tropical plants growing from the concrete floors, and I rode in a tube car festooned with vines and crawling with land crabs. Usually you have to ingest a great deal of a very powerful chemical to see scenes like that, I reflected, watching the crabs scuttle around my feet. It wasn't something I was eager to do again soon.

And it took a full day for the new coconut palm I found shading my half-built cabin to vanish in the night.

The lantern I carried didn't cast a lot of light. A bright light in the darkness could upset the stock, so Callie provided her hands with these antique devices which burned a smoky oil refined from reptilian fat. It was enough to keep me from stumbling over tree roots, but not to see very far ahead. And of course if you looked at the light, your night vision was destroyed. I told myself not to look, then the cantankerous thing would sputter and I'd glance at it, and stop in my tracks, blinded. So when I encountered the first unusual tree trunk I didn't realize what it was, at first. I touched it and felt the warmth, and knew I'd bumped into a brontosaur's hind leg. I backed hastily away. The beasts are clumsy and inclined to stampede if startled. And if you've ever been unpleasantly surprised by a package from a passing pigeon in the city park, you don't want to find out what can happen to you in the area of a brontosaur's hind leg, believe me. I speak from bitter experience.

I picked my way through a forest of similar trunks until I spotted a small campfire in a hollow. Three figures were seated around the fire, two side by side, and another—Callie—across from them. I could dimly see the hulking shadows of a dozen brontosaurs, darker shapes against the night, placidly chewing their cud and farting like foghorns. I approached the fire slowly, not wanting to startle anybody, and still managed to surprise Callie, who looked up in alarm, then patted the ground beside her. She held her finger to her lips, then resumed her study of her adversaries, painted orange by the dancing flames between us.

I've never decided if David Earth looked spookier in a setting like this, or in the full light of day—for it was him, the Spokesmammal himself, sitting in lotus position, a walking, talking inducement for the purchase of hay fever remedies. Callie was actually allergic to the man, or to his biosphere, and though a cure would have been simple and cheap she cherished her malady, she treasured it, she happily endured every sneeze and sniffle as one more reason to detest him. She'd hated him since before I was born, and viewed his five-yearly appearances the same way people must have felt about dental extractions before anesthetics.

He nodded to me, and I nodded back. That seemed conversation enough for both of us. Callie and I didn't agree on a lot of things, but we shared the same opinion of David Earth and all the Earthists.

He was a large man, almost as tall as Brenda and much heftier. His hair was long, green, and unkempt for a very good reason: it wasn't hair, but a bioengineered species of grass bred to be parasitic on human skin. I don't know the details of its cultivation. I'd have had more interest in the mating habits of toads. It involved a thickening of the scalp, and soil was involved—when he scratched his head, dirt showered down. But I don't know how the soil was attached, whether in pockets or layered on the skin, and I don't know anything about the blood-to-root system, and I'd just as soon not, thank you. I remember as a child wondering if, when he got up in the morning, he had to work compost into his agri-tonsorial splendor.

He had two huge breasts—almost all Earthists, male and female, sported them—and more plants grew on their upper slopes. Many of these bore tiny flowers or fruits. I wondered if he had to practice contour plowing to prevent erosion on those fertile hillsides. He saw me looking at them, plucked an apple no bigger than a grape from the tangled mass, and popped it in his mouth.

What can one say about the rest of him? His back and arms and legs were covered with hair. Not human hair, but actual pelts, resembling in various patches jaguar, tiger, bison, zebra, and polar bear, among others, in a crazy patchwork. The genetic restructuring required to support all that must have been a cut-and-paste collage beyond imagining. It was ironic, I thought, that the roots of the Earthists were in the anti-fur activists, but of course no animals had been harmed to produce his pelt. Just little bits of their genes snipped out and shoehorned into his. He had claws like a bear on his fingertips, and instead of feet he walked around on the hooves of a moose, like some large economy-size faun. All Earthists had animal attributes, it was their badge and ensign. But their founder had gone further than any of his followers. Which, one suspects, is what makes followers and leaders.

But, incredible as it may seem having gone through the catalog of his offenses to the eye, it must be said that the first thing one noticed about David Earth upon having the misfortune to encounter him was his smell.

I'm sure he bathed. Perhaps the right way of putting it was that he watered himself regularly. David Earth during a drought would have been a walking fire hazard. But he used no soap (animal by-product) or any other cleaning preparation (chemical pollution of the David-sphere). All of which would simply have resulted in a smell of sour sweat, which I don't care for but can tolerate. No, it was his passengers that lifted his signature aroma from the merely objectionable to the realm of the un- imaginable.

Large animals with fur harbor fleas, that's axiomatic. Fleas were only the beginning of David Earth's "welcome guests," as he'd once described them to me. I'd countered with another term, parasites, and he'd merely smiled benevolently. All his smiles were benevolent; he was that kind of guy, the sort whose kindly face you'd like to rip off and feed to his welcome guests. David was the kind of guy who had all the moral answers, and never hesitated to point out the error of your ways. Lovingly, of course. He loved all nature's creatures, did David, even one as low on the evolutionary ladder as yourself.

What sort of guests did David spread his filthy welcome mat for? Well, what sort of vermin live in grasslands? I'd never seen a prairie dog peeking from his coiffure, but I wouldn't have been surprised. He was home to a scamper of mice, a shriek of shrews, a twittering of finches, and a circus of fleas. A trained biologist could easily have counted a dozen species of insects without even getting close. All these creatures were born, reared, courted, mated, nested, ate, defecated, urinated, laid their eggs, fought their battles, stalked their prey, dreamed their dreams and, as must we all, eventually died in the various biomes that were David. Sometimes the carcasses fell out; sometimes they didn't. All more fertile soil for the next generation.

All Earthists stink; it goes with the territory. They are perennial defendants in civil court for violation of the body odor laws, hauled in when some long-suffering citizen on a crowded elevator finally decides he's had enough. David Earth was the only man I knew of in Luna who was permanently banished from the public corridors. He made his way from ranch to Disneyland to hydroponic farm by way of the air, water, and service ducts.

"My membership is alarmed if that is your best offer," said David's companion, a much smaller, much less prepossessing fellow whose only animal attributes I could see were a modest pair of pronghorn antlers and a lion's tail. "One hundred murders is nothing but wanton slaughter, and we totally reject it. But after careful consultation, we're prepared to offer eighty. With the greatest reluctance."

"Eighty *harvested,*" Callie leaned on the word, as she always did. "Eighty is simply ridiculous. I'll go broke with a quota of eighty. Come on, let's go up to my office right now, I'll show you the books, there's an order of seventy carcasses from McDonald's alone."

"That's your problem; you should never have signed the contract until these negotiations were concluded."

"Don't sign the contract, I lose the customer. What do you want to do, ruin me? Ninety-nine, that's my absolutely no-fooling final offer; take it or leave it. I don't think I can turn a profit even with a hundred; it'll be touch and go. But to get this over with . . . I'll tell you what. Ninety-eight. That's twelve less than what you gave Reilly, just down the road, not three days ago, and his herd's smaller than mine."

"We're not here to discuss Reilly, we're talking about your contract, and your herd. And your herd is not a happy herd, I've heard nothing but grievances from them. I simply can't allow one more murder than . . ." He glanced at David, who shook his head barely enough to disturb a single amber wave of grain. "Eighty," pronghorn-head concluded.

Callie seethed silently for a while. There was no hope of talking to her just yet, not until the unionists repaired for consultations with their clients, so I moved back from the fire a little. Something about the bargaining process had struck me as relevant to my situation.

"CC," I whispered. "Are you there?"

"Where else would I be?" the CC murmured softly in my ear. "And you only need to sub-vocalize; I'll pick up your words easily enough."

"How would *I* know where you'd be? When I called for you after you rowed away from me, you didn't answer. I thought you might be sulking."

"I didn't think it would be profitable for either of us to discuss what I'd just told you until you'd had time to think it over."

"I have, and I've got a few questions."

"I'll do my best to answer them."

"These union reps. Are they really speaking for the dinosaurs?"

There was a medium-sized pause. I guess the question did seem irrelevant to the issue at hand. But the CC withheld comment on that.

"You grew up on this ranch. I'd have thought you would know the answer to that question."

"No, that's just it. I've never really thought about it. You know Callie's feelings about animal rights. She told me the Earthists were nothing but a bunch of mystics who had enough political clout to get their crazy ideas put into law. She said she had never believed they actually communed with the animals. I believed her, and I haven't thought about it for seventy, eighty years. But after what I've just been through, I wonder if she's right."

"She's mostly wrong," the CC said. "That animals feel things is easily demonstrable, even down at the level of protozoans. That they have what you would recognize as *thoughts* is more debatable. But since I am a party to these negotiations—an indispensable party, I might add—I can tell you that, yes, these creatures are capable of expressing desires and responding to propositions, so long as they are expressed in terms they understand."

"How?"

"Well . . . the contract that will eventually be hammered out here is entirely a human instrument. These beasts will never be aware of its existence. Since their 'language' is confined to a few dozen trumpeted calls, it is quite beyond their capacity. But the *provisions* of the contract will be arrived at by a give-and-take process not unlike human collective bargaining. Callie has injected all her stock with a solution of water and some trillions of self-replicating nano-engineered biotropic mechanisms that—"

"Nanobots."

"Yes, that's the popular term."

"You have something against popular terms?"

"Only their imprecision. The term 'nanobot' means a very small self-propelled programmed machine, and that includes many other varieties of intracellular devices than the ones currently under discussion. The ones in your bloodstream and within your body cells are quite different—"

"Okay, I see what you mean. But it's the same principle, right? These little robots, smaller than red blood cells . . ."

"Some are much smaller than that. They are drawn to specific sites within an organism and then they go to work. Some carry raw materials, some carry blueprints, some are the actual construction workers. Working at molecular speeds, they build various larger machines—and by larger, you understand, I still mean microscopic, in most cases—in the interstices between the body cells, or within the cell walls themselves."

"Which are used for . . ."

"I think I see where you're going with this. They perform many functions. Some are housekeeping chores that your own body is either not good at, or has lost the capacity to do. Others are monitoring devices that alert a larger, outside system that something is going wrong. In Callie's herd, that is a Mark III Husbander, a fairly basic computer, not significantly altered in design for well over a century."

"Which is a part of you, naturally."

"*All* computers in Luna except abaci and your fingers are a part of me. And in a pinch, I could use your fingers."

"As you've just shown me."

"Yes. The machine . . . or I, if you prefer, listens constantly through a network of receivers placed around the ranch, just as I listen constantly for your calls to me, no matter where you are in Luna. This is all on what you might think of as my subconscious level. I'm never aware of the functioning of your body unless I'm alerted by an alarm, or if you call me on-line."

"So the network of machines that's in my body, there's one like it in each of Callie's brontosaurs."

"Related to it, yes. The neural structures are orders of magnitude less evolved than the ones in your brain, just as your organic brain is superior in operation to that of the dinosaur. I don't run any parasitic programs in the dinosaur brain, if that's what you mean."

I didn't think it was what I meant, but I wasn't completely sure, since I wasn't completely sure why I'd asked about this in the first place. But I didn't tell the CC that. He went on.

"It is as close to mental telepathy as we're likely to get. The union representatives are tuned in to me, and I'm tuned in to the dinosaurs. The negotiator poses a question: 'How do you fellows feel about 120 of your number being harvested/murdered this year?' I put the question in terms of predators. A picture of an approaching tyrannosaur. I get a fear response: 'Sorry, we'd rather not, thank you.' I relay it to the unionist, who tells Callie the figure is not acceptable. The unionist proposes another number, in tonight's case, sixty. Callie can't accept that. She'd go broke, there would be no one to feed the stock. I convey this idea to the dinosaurs with feelings of hunger, thirst, sickness. They don't like this either. Callie proposes 110 creatures taken. I show them a smaller tyrannosaur approaching, with some of the herd escaping. They don't respond quite so strongly with the fear and flight reflex, which I translate as 'Well, for the good of the herd, we might see our way clear to losing seventy so the rest can grow fat.' I put the proposal to Callie, who claims the Earthists are bleeding her white, and so on."

"Sounds totally useless to me," I said, with only half my mind on what the CC had been saying. I was seeing a vision of myself living within the planet-girdling machine that the CC had become, and of him living within my body as well. The funny thing was that nothing I'd learned since arriving at Scarpa Island had been exactly new to me. There were new, unheralded capabilities, but looking at them, I could see they were inherent in the technology. I'd had the facts, but not enough of them. I'd spent almost no time thinking about them, any more than I thought about breathing, and even less time considering the implications, most of which I didn't like. I realized the CC was talking again.

"I don't see why you should say that. Except that I know your moral stand on the whole issue of animal husbandry, and you have a right to that."

"No, that whole issue aside, I could have told you how this all would come out, given only the opening bid. David proposed sixty, right?"

"After the opening statement about murdering any of these creatures at all, and his formal demand that all—"

" '—creatures should live a life free from the predation of man, the most voracious and merciless predator of all,' yeah, I've heard the speech, and David and Callie both know it's just a formality, like singing the planetary anthem. When they got down to cases, he said sixty. Man, he must really be angry about something, sixty is ridiculous. Anyway, when she heard sixty, Callie bid 120 because she knew she had to slaughter ninety this year to make a reasonable profit, and when David heard *that* he knew they'd eventually settle on ninety. So tell me this: why bother to consult the dinosaurs? Who cares what they think?"

The CC was silent, and I laughed.

"Tell the truth. *You* make up the images of meat-eaters and the feelings of starvation. I presume that when the fear of one balances out the fear of the other, when these poor dumb beasts are equally frightened by lousy alternatives—in *your* judgment, let's remember . . . well, then we have a contract, right? So where would you conjecture that point will be found?"

"Ninety carcasses," the CC said.

"I rest my case."

"You have a point. But I actually *do* transmit the feelings of the animals to the human representatives. They do feel the fear, and can judge as well as I when a balance is reached."

"Say what you will. Me, I'm convinced the jerk with the horns could have as easily stayed in bed, signed a contract for ninety kills, and saved a lot of effort. Then prong-head could look for useful work. Maybe as a gardener in David's hairdo."

There was a long silence from the CC. When he spoke again it was in a different tone of voice from his usual lecturing mode.

"The man with the horns," he said, quietly, "is actually mentally defective in a way I've been powerless to treat. He cannot read or write, and is not really suited for many jobs. And Hildy, we all need something to do in this world. Life can seem pointless without gratifying work."

That shut me up for a while. I knew only too well how pointless life could seem.

"And he really does love animals," the CC added. "He hurts when he thinks of one dying. I shouldn't be telling you any of this, as I'm prohibited from commenting on the qualities, good or bad, of human citizens. But in view of our recent relationship, I thought . . ." He let it trail off, unfinished.

Enough of that.

"What about death?" I asked him. "You mentioned hunger and the image of a predator. I'd think you'd get a stronger reaction if you planted the idea of their actual deaths in their minds."

"Much more of a reaction than you'd want. Predators and hunger *imply* death, but inspire less fear than the actual event. These negotiations are quite touchy; I've tried many times to talk Callie into holding them indoors. But she says that if 'salad-head' isn't afraid to pow-wow in the middle of the herd, she isn't either. No, the death-image is the nuclear weapon of predator/prey relations. It's usually a prelude to either an attempt at union-busting, or a boycott."

"Or something even more serious."

"So I infer. Of course, I have no proof."

I wondered about that. Maybe the CC was leveling with me when he said he only spied into private spaces in circumstances as unusual as my own. Or into minds, for that matter. I certainly no longer doubted that he could easily become aware of illegal activities such as sabotage or head-busting by hired goon squads—the time-honored last resorts of labor and management, and even more in vogue these days among radical groups like the Earthists who, after all, couldn't call on their "membership" to go on strike. What would a brontosaur do? Stop eating? The CC could certainly look into the places where the bombs were assembled, or could become aware, if he chose to do so, of the intent of the bomb-thrower through readings from his ubiquitous intercellular machines. Every year there were calls to permit him precisely those powers, by the law-and-order types. After all, the CC is a benevolent watchdog, isn't he? Who has he ever hurt, except those who deserved it? We could reduce crime to zero overnight if we'd only take the chains off the CC.

I'd even leaned that way myself, in spite of the civil libertarian objections. After my sojourn on Scarpa Island, I found myself heartily on the other side of the question. I suppose I was simply illustrating that old definition of a liberal: a conservative who just got arrested. A conservative, of course, is a liberal who just got mugged.

"You are cynical about this process," the CC was saying, "because you've only seen it from the commercial side, and between humans and creatures with a very basic brain structure. It is much more interesting when the negotiations are conducted between higher mammals. There have been some interesting developments in Kenya, where lion/antelope arbitration has been going on for five decades now. The lions, in particular, have become quite adept at it. By now they know how to choose the most skilled representative, a sort of shop steward, using the same instincts that drive them to dominance battles. I really believe they've grasped the concept that there must be lean hunting times, that if *all* the antelope were killed they would get nothing but commercially prepared chow—which they like well enough, but is no substitute for the hunt. There is one grizzled old veteran without any teeth who, year after year, gives the antelope as hard a time at the bargaining fire as he ever did on the savannah in his youth. He's a sort of Samuel Gompers of the—"

I was spared any more details of this leonine Lenin's exploits by David Earth, who finally bestirred himself. He got to his feet, and prong-head stood hastily, destroying the polite myth that he had anything to do with the proceedings. David seldom attended contract talks with individual ranchers anymore, he was too occupied with appearances promoting his Earthist philosophy to the voters. On television, of course; there would be no quicker way to disperse a political rally than to have David walk into it.

"I think we really have a problem," he said, in his Jovian voice. "The innocent creatures we represent have too long chafed under your yoke. Their grievances are many and . . . well, grievous."

If David had a weakness, that was it. He wasn't the world's greatest speaker. I think he grew worse every year, as language became more of a philosophical burden to him. One of the planks of his platform—when the millennium was achieved—was the abolition of language. He wanted us all to sing like the birdies sing.

"To name only one," he boomed on, "you are one of only three murderers of dinosaurs who—"

"Ranchers," Callie said.

"—who persist in using the brontosaur's natural enemy as a means of instilling terror into—"

"Herding," Callie gritted. "And no t-saur of mine has ever so much as put a scratch on a stinking b-saur."

"If you persist in interrupting me, we'll never get anywhere," David said, with a loving smile.

"No one will stand there and call me a murderer on my own land. There are courts of libel, and you're about to get dragged into one."

They regarded each other across the fire, knowing that ninety-nine percent of threats and accusations made here were simply wind, tossed out to gain an advantage or disconcert an opponent—and hating each other so thoroughly that I never knew when one would put a threat into action. Callie's face reflected her opinions. David merely smiled, as if to say he loved Callie dearly, but I knew him better than that. He hated her so much that he inflicted himself on her every five years, and I can think of little more cruel than that.

"We must seek closer communion with our friends," David said, abruptly, and turned and walked away from the fire, leaving his minion to trail along ignominiously behind him.

Callie sighed when he vanished into the darkness. She stood up, stretched, boxed the air, getting the kinks out. Bargaining is tough on the whole mind and body, but the best thing to bring to the table is a tough bottom. Callie rubbed hers, and leaned over the cooler she had brought with her. She tossed me a can of beer, got one for herself, and sat on the cooler.

"It's good to see you," she said. "We didn't get a chance to talk the last time you were here." She frowned, remembering. "Come to think of it, you took off without any warning. We got to my office, you were gone. What happened?"

"A lot of things, Callie. That's what I came here for, to . . . to talk them over with you, if I could. See if you could offer me some advice."

She looked at me suspiciously. Well, she was in a suspicious frame of mind, I understand that, dealing with the intransigent union. But it went deeper. We had never managed to talk very well. It was a depressing thought to realize, once again, that when I had something important to share with someone, she was the best that sprang to mind. I thought about getting up and leaving right then. I know I hesitated, because Callie did what she had so often done when I'd tried to talk to her as a child: she changed the subject.

"That Brenda, she's a much nicer child than you give her credit for. We had a long talk after we found out you'd left. Do you have any idea how much she looks up to you?"

"Some idea. Callie, I—"

"She's putting herself through a history course that would stagger you, all so she can keep up when you talk about 'ancient history.' I think it's hopeless. Some things you have to live through to really understand. I know about the twenty-first century because I was there. The twentieth century, or the nineteenth, can't ever seem as real to me, though I've read a great deal about them."

"Sometimes I don't think last month seems real to Brenda."

"That's where you're wrong. She knows her recent history a lot better than you'd think, and I'm talking about things that happened fifty, a hundred years before she was born. We sat around and talked . . . well, mostly I told her stories, I guess. She seemed fascinated." She smiled at the memory. It didn't surprise me that Brenda had found favor with Callie. There are few qualities my mother values more in a human being than a willing ear.

"I don't have much contact with young people. Like I was telling her, we move in different social circles. I can't stand their music and they think I'm a walking fossil. But after a few hours she started opening up to me. It was almost like having . . . well, a daughter."

She glanced at me, then took a long drink of beer. She realized she had gone too far.

Normally, a remark like that would have been the start of the seventy zillionth repeat of our most popular argument. That night, I was willing to let it slide. I had much more important things on my mind. When I didn't rise to it, she must have finally realized how troubled I was, because she leaned forward with her elbows on her knees and looked at me.

"Tell me about it," she said, and I did.

But not all of it.

I told her of my fight in the Blind Pig, and of my conversation with the CC that led to the pseudo-experiences still so fresh in my mind. I told her the CC had explained it as a cure for depression, which it was, in a way. But I found it impossible to come right out and tell her that I'd tried to kill myself. Is there a more embarrassing admission one can make? Maybe some people would think nothing of it, would eagerly show off what the experts called hesitation marks—scars on the wrist, bullet holes in the ceiling; I'd been doing a little reading on the subject while sequestered in Texas. If suicide really *is* a cry for help, it would seem reasonable to be open and honest in revealing that one had attempted it, in order to get some sympathy, some advice, some commiseration, maybe just a hug.

Or some pity.

Am I simply too proud? I didn't think so. I searched through my motives as well as I was able, and couldn't discern any need for pity, which is what I'd surely get from Callie. Perhaps that meant my attempts had actually been motivated by depression, by a desire simply to live no longer. And that was a depressing thought in itself.

I eventually wound down, leaving my story with a rather obvious lack of resolution. I'm sure Callie spotted it right away, but she said nothing for a while. I know the whole thing was almost as difficult for her as it was for me. Intimacy didn't seem to run in the family. I felt better about her than I had in years, just for having listened to me as long as she had.

She reached behind the cooler and brought out a can of something which she poured on the fire. It flared up immediately. She looked at me, and grinned.

"Rendered b-saur fat," she said. "Great for barbecues; gets the fire blazing real quick. I've used it on the meeting fires for eighty years. One of these days when he provokes me enough, I'll tell David about it. I'm sure he'll love me in spite of it. Will you toss some more of those logs on the fire? Right behind you, there's a pile of them."

I did, and we sat watching them blaze.

"You're not telling me something," she said, at last. "If you don't want to, that's your business. But you're the one who wanted to talk."

"I know, I know. It's just very hard for me. There have been a lot of things going on, a lot of new things I've learned."

"I didn't know about that memory-dump technique," she said. "I wouldn't have thought the CC could do that without your permission." She didn't sound alarmed about it. Like practically all Lunarians, she viewed the CC as a useful and very intelligent slave. She would concede, along with everyone else, that it was a being devoted to helping her in every possible way. But that's where she parted company with her fellow citizens, who also thought of the CC as the least intrusive and most benevolent form of government ever devised.

The CC hadn't mentioned it, but his means of access to the Double-C Bar Ranch was limited. This was no accident. Callie had deliberately set up her electronics such that she could function independent of the CC if the need should arise. All communication had to come through a single cable to her Mark III Husbander, which really ran the ranch. The link was further laundered through a series of gadgets supplied by some of her similarly paranoid friends, designed to filter out the subversive virus, the time bomb, and the Chinese Fire Drill—all forms of computer witchery I know nothing about apart from their names.

It was wildly inefficient. I also suspected it was futile; the CC was in here, talking to me, wasn't he? Because that was the real reason for all the barriers, for the electronic drawbridge Callie could theoretically raise and lower at will, for the photo-etched moat she hoped to fill with cybernetic crocodiles and the molten glitches she meant to dump into invading programs. She claimed to be able to isolate her castle with the flick of one switch. Bang! and the **CC** would be cut adrift from its moorings to the larger datanet known as the Central Computer.

Silly, isn't it? Well, I'd always thought so, until the CC took control of my own mind. Callie had always thought that way, and while she was in the minority, she wasn't alone. Walter agreed with her, and a few other chronic malcontents like the Heinleiners.

I was about to go on with my tale of woe, but Callie put her finger to her lips.

"It'll have to wait a bit," she said. "The Kaiser of the Chordates is returning."

Callie immediately went into a sneezing fit. David's already avuncular expression became so benign it bordered on the ludicrous. He was enjoying it, no doubt about it. He seated himself and waited while Callie fumbled through her purse and found a nasal spray. When she had dosed herself and blown her nose, he smiled lovingly.

"I'm afraid your offer of ninety-eight murders is—" He held up his hand as Callie started to retort. "Very well. Ninety-eight creatures killed is simply unacceptable. After further consultation, and hearing grievances that have astounded me—and you well know I'm an old hand at this business . . ."

"Ninety-seven," Callie said.

"Sixty," David countered.

Callie seemed to doubt for a moment that she had heard him right. The word hung in the air between them, with at least as much incendiary potential as the fire.

"You started at sixty," Callie said, quietly.

"And I've just returned us there."

"What's going on here? This isn't how it's done, and you know it. There's no love lost between us, to put it mildly, but I've always been able to do business with you. There are certain accepted practices, certain understandings that, if they don't have the force of law, they certainly enjoy the stamp of custom. Everyone recognizes that. It's called 'good faith,' and I don't think you're practicing it here tonight."

"There will be no more business as usual," David intoned. "You asked what's going on, and I'll tell you. My party has grown steadily in strength throughout this decade. Tomorrow I'm making a major speech in which I will outline new quotas which, over a twenty-year period, are intended to phase out the consumption of animal flesh entirely. It is insane, in this day and age, to continue a primitive, unhealthy practice which demeans us all. Killing and eating our fellow creatures is nothing but cannibalism. We can no longer allow it, and call ourselves civilized."

I was impressed. He hadn't stumbled over a single word, which must have meant he'd written and memorized it. We were getting a preview of tomorrow's big show.

"Shut up," Callie said.

"Countless scientific studies have proved that the eating of meat—"

"Shut up," Callie said again, not raising her voice, but putting something else into it that was a lot more powerful than shouting. "You are on my land, and you *will* shut up, or I will personally boot your raggedy old ass all the way to the air lock and cycle you through it."

"You have no right to—"

Callie threw her beer in his face. She just tossed it right through the fire, then threw the empty can over her shoulder into the darkness. For a moment his face froze into an expression as blank as I've ever seen on a human; it made my skin crawl. Then he relaxed back into his usual attitude, that of the wise old sage bemused by the squabbles of an imperfect world, looking down on it with god-like love.

A mouse peeked out of the weeds of his beard to see what all the commotion was about. It sampled one of the beer droplets, found it good, and began imbibing at a rate it might regret in the morning.

"I've squatted out here beside this damn fire for over thirty hours," Callie said. "I'm not complaining about that; it's a cost of doing business, and I'm used to it. But I *am* a busy woman. If you'd told me about this when we sat down, if you'd had the courtesy to do that, I could have kicked sand into the fire and told you I'd see you in court. Because that's where we're going, and I'll have an injunction slapped on you before that beer can dry. The Labor Relations Board will have something to say, too." She spread her hands in an eloquent Italianate gesture. "I guess we have nothing further to talk about."

"It's wrong," David said. "It's also unhealthy, and . . ."

While he was groping for a word to describe a horror so huge, Callie jumped back in.

"Unhealthy, that's one I never could understand. Brontosaurus meat is the healthiest single food product ever developed. I ought to know; I helped build the genes back when *both* of us were young. It's low in cholesterol, high in vitamins and minerals . . ." She stopped, and looked curiously at David.

"What's the use?" she asked herself. "I can't figure it out. I've disliked you from the first time we met. I think you are plainly crazy, egotistic, and dishonest. All that 'love' crap. I think you live in a fantasy world where nobody should ever get hurt. But one thing I've never accused you of, and that's stupidity. And now you're doing something stupid, as if you really think you can bring it off. Surely you realize this thing can't work?" She looked concerned as she stared at him. Almost as if she wished she could help him.

Nothing could be more certain to light a fire under David, but I honestly don't think Callie meant to provoke him. By her lights he really was planning to commit political suicide if he intended to keep Lunarians from their bronto meat, not to mention all other forms of flesh. And she never did understand foolishness in other human beings.

He leaned forward, opened his mouth to begin another prepared tirade, but he never got the chance. What I think happened, and the tapes back me up on this, is some of the fresh logs shifted. One of them fell into a pool of the brontosaur fat Callie had poured on, a pool that had been burning on the surface and getting hotter by the minute. The sudden addition of hot coals caused the fat to pop, like it will in a skillet. There was a shower of sparks and all four of us were spattered by tiny droplets of boiling, burning grease that clung like napalm. Since they were mostly quite small, there were just a few sharp pains on my arms and my face, and I quickly slapped them out. Callie and the man with the horns were slapping at themselves as well.

David had a somewhat larger problem.

"He's on fire!" prong-head shouted. And it was true. The top of his grass-covered head was burning merrily. David himself wasn't aware of it yet, and looked around in confusion, then stared up with a surprised expression I would always remember, even if it hadn't been shown a hundred times on the news.

"I need some water," he said, brushing at the flames and hastily drawing his hand back. He seemed calm enough.

"Here, wait a minute," Callie shouted, and turned toward the beverage cooler. I think she meant to douse him with more beer, and I thought in passing how ironic it was that her throwing the first beer may have saved him having to buy a new face because it had soaked the grass of his beard. "Mario, get him on the ground, try and smother it."

I didn't comment on her use of my old name. It didn't seem the proper time for it. I started around the fire, reached for David, and he shoved me away. It was purely a panic reaction. I think it had started to hurt by then.

"Water! Where is the water?"

"I saw a stream over that way," said prong-head. David looked wildly around. He had become a sinking ship: I saw three voles, a garter snake, and a pair of finches burst from their hiding places, and the fleeing insects were too numerous to count. Some flew directly into the campfire. David behaved no better. He started running in the direction his assistant had pointed, which Mister Fireman could have told him was exactly the wrong thing to do. Either he hadn't paid attention in kindergarten or he'd lost all rational thought. Seeing how brightly he lit up the night, I figured it was the latter.

"No! David, come back!" Callie had turned from the cooler, having ripped the top from a can of beer. "There's no water that way!" She threw the can after him, but it fell short. David was setting Olympic records in his sprint for the stream that wasn't there. "Mario! Catch him!"

I didn't think I could, but I had to try. He'd be easy to follow, unless he burned to the ground. I took off, pounding the dirt with my feet, thanking the generations of brontosaurs who had packed it so hard. David had run into a grove of cycadeoids and I was just getting to the edge of them when I heard Callie shout again.

"Come back! Hurry, Mario, come back!" I slowed almost to a stop, and became aware of a disturbing sensation. The ground was shaking. I looked back at the campfire. Callie was standing looking out into the darkness. She'd turned on a powerful hand torch and was sweeping it back and forth. The beam caught a brontosaur in full charge. It stopped, blinded and confused, and then picked a direction at random and rumbled away.

An eighty-ton shadow thundered by, not three meters to my right. I started moving back to the campfire, scanning the darkness, aware I wouldn't get much warning. Halfway there, another behemoth thundered into the council site. It actually stepped in the fire, which wasn't to its liking at all. It squealed, wheeled, and took off more or less toward me. I watched it coming, figured it would keep moving that way unless stopped by a major mountain chain, and dodged to my left. The beast kept going and was swallowed by the night.

I knew enough about b-saurs to know not to expect rational behavior from them. They were already upset by the negotiations. Images of t-saurs and feelings of starvation must have addled their tiny brains considerably. It would have taken a lot less stimulus than a burning, screaming David Earth to stampede them. He must have hit them like a stick of dynamite.

And when b-saurs panic, what little sense they possess deserts them completely. They start off in random directions. There seems to be an instinct that tends to draw them into a thundering group, eventually headed in the same direction, but they don't see well at night, and thus couldn't easily find each other. The result was seventy or eighty walking mountains going off in all directions. Very little could stand in their way.

Certainly not me. I hurried to Callie's side. She was talking into a pocket communicator, calling for hovercraft as she stabbed the powerful light beam this way and that. Usually it was enough to turn the beasts. When it was not, we stepped very lively indeed.

Before long she picked out a medium-sized cow headed more or less in our direction, and turned the beam away from it. She slapped a saur-hook into my hand, and we watched it approach.

Where's the safest place to be in a dinosaur stampede? On a dinosaur's back. Actually, the *best* place would have been on one of the hovercraft, whose lights we could see approaching, but you take what you can get. We waited for the hind legs to get past us, dug our hooks into the cow's tail, and swung ourselves up. A dinosaur doesn't precisely *like* being hooked, but her perceptions of pain that far back on her body are dim and diffused, and this one had other things on her tiny mind. We scrambled up the tail until we could get a grip on the fleshy folds of the back. Don't try this at home, by the way. Callie was an old hand at it, and though I hadn't hooked a saur in seventy years, the skills were still there. I only wobbled for a moment, and Callie was there to steady me.

So we rode, and waited. In due time the bronto wore herself out, rumbled to a stop, and started cropping leaves from the top of a cycad, probably wondering by now what all the fuss had been about, if she remembered it at all. We climbed down, were met by a hover, and got into that.

Callie had the "sun" turned on to aid the search. We found prong-head fairly quickly. He was kneeling in a muddy spot, shaking uncontrollably. He had survived with nothing but luck to aid him. I wondered if he ever loved animals quite so much, or in quite the same way, after that night.

Say what you will about Callie, her worries for the lad were genuine, and her relief at finding him alive and unhurt was apparent even to him, in his distracted condition. For that matter, though David Earth might call her a cold-blooded killer, she hadn't wished death even on him. She simply measured human life and animal life on different scales, something David could never do.

"Let's get him out of here and find David," she said, and grabbed the young man by his arm. "He's going to need a lot of medical attention, if he made it." Prong-head resisted, pulling away from her grasp, remaining on his knees. He pointed down into the mud. I looked, and then looked away.

"David has returned to the food chain," he said, and fainted.

THE MAVEN OF CHANGE ALLEY

The next several days were fairly hectic for me. I was kept so busy I had little time to think or worry about the CC or entertain thoughts of suicide. The whole idea seemed completely alien.

Since I work for a print medium I tend not to think in terms of pictures. My stories are meant to be written, transmitted to a subscriber-rented scrambler-equipped newspad, where they will be screened and read by that part of the population that still reads. Walter employs others to shorten, simplify, and read aloud his reporters' stories for the illit channel of the newspad. There are of course all-visual news services, and now there is direct interface, but so far at least, D.I. is not something most people do for relaxation and entertainment. Reading is still the preferred method of information input for a large minority of Lunarians. It is slower than D.I., but much quicker and in much greater depth than pure television news.

But *The News Nipple* is an electronic medium, and many of the stories we run come with film clips. Thus did the newspaper manage to find a government-subsidized, yearly more perilous niche for itself in the era of television. Pundits keep predicting the death of the newspad, and year by year it struggles on, maintained mostly by people who don't want too much change in their lives.

I tend to forget about the holocam in my left eye. Its contents are dumped at the same time I enter my story into the *Nipple*'s editorial computer, and a picture editor usually fast-forwards through it and picks a still shot or a few seconds of moving images to back up my words. I remember when it was first installed I worried that those editors would be seeing things that I'd prefer to be private; after all, the thing operates all the time, and has a six-hour memory. But the CC had assured me there was a discrimination program in the main computer that erased all the irrelevant pictures before a human ever saw them. (Now it occurred to me to wonder about that. It had never bothered me that the CC might see the full tapes, but I'd never thought of him as a snoop before.)

The holocam is a partly mechanical, partly biologic device about the size of a fingernail clipping that is implanted inside the eye, way over to one side, out of the way of your peripheral vision. A semi-silvered mirror is hung in the middle of the eye, somewhere near the focal point, and reflects part of the light entering the eye over to the holocam. When you first have one put in you notice a slight diminution of light sensitivity in that eye, but the brain is such that it quickly adjusts and in a few days you never notice it again. It causes my pupil to look red, and it glows faintly in the dark.

It had been operating when David Earth caught fire, naturally. I didn't even think of it during subsequent events, not until David's body had been removed and taken to wherever Earthists are disposed of. Then I realized I had what might be the biggest story of my career. And a scoop, as well.

Real death captured by a camera is always guaranteed to make the front feed of the newspad. The death of a celebrity would provide fodder for Walter's second-string feature writers for months to come; anything to have an excuse to run once more that glorious, horrible image of David's head wreathed in fire, and the even more horrifying results of being crushed beneath a stampeding brontosaur.

News footage is exclusive to the paper that filmed it for a period of twenty-four hours. After that, there is a similar period when it may be leased for minutes or hours, or sold outright. After forty-eight hours it all becomes public domain.

A major metropolitan newspaper is geared to exploit these two critical periods to the utmost. For the first day, when we could exploit my film exclusively, we made the death of Earth seem like the biggest story since the marriage of Silvio and Marina twenty-five years ago, or their divorce one year later, or the Invasion of the Planet Earth, take your pick. Those are commonly thought to be the three biggest news stories of all time, the only real difference in their magnitude being that two of them were well-covered, and one was not. This story was nowhere near that big, of course, but you'd never have known it to read our breathless prose and listen to our frantic commentators.

I was the center of much of this coverage. There was no question of sleeping. Since I'm not an on-screen personality—which means I'm an indifferent speaker, and the camera does not love me—I spent most of the time sitting across from our star anchor and answering his questions. Most of this was fed out live, and often took as much as fifteen minutes at the top of each hour. For the next fifteen minutes we showed the reports sent back by the cadres of camerapeople who descended on Callie's ranch and shot everything from pictures of the killer dinosaur's bloody foot, to the corpses of the three b-saurs killed in the stampede, to the still-vivid imprint of David's body in the mud, to interviews with every ranch hand who'd ever worked for Callie, even though none of them had seen anything but the dead body.

I thought Walter was going to explode when he learned that Callie refused to be interviewed under any circumstances or for any amount of money. He sent me to the ranch to cajole her. I went, knowing it would do no good. He threatened to have her arrested; in his rage, he seemed to believe that refusing to cooperate with the media—and with him in particular—was illegal. For her part, Callie made several nasty calls demanding that we stop using her image, and someone had to read her the relevant parts of the law that said she couldn't do anything about it. She rang me up and called me a Judas, among other things. I don't know what she expected me to do with the biggest story of my life; sit on it, I guess. I called her a few things back, just as harsh. I think she was concerned about her possible liability in the incident, but the main reason was her loathing for the popular press—something I couldn't entirely disagree with her on. I have wondered, from time to time, if that's why I got into this business. Nasty thought, that.

Anyway, I decided it would be pointless to seek her advice on the parts of my story I hadn't gotten around to telling her, for at least a year or so. Make that five years.

The next day was spent farming the story out to competing rags and vids, but on our terms. The price was high, but willingly paid. They knew that next time they were as likely to be on the selling end, and would gouge appropriately. As was standard practice, I was always included as part of the deal, so I could mention the *Nipple* as often and as blatantly as possible while on live feeds. So I talked myself into a sore throat sitting beside endless commentators, columnists, and similar sorts, while the by now dated footage ran yet another time.

The only person who got as much exposure as I did during those two days was Eartha Lowe. A movement as radical as the Earthists will spawn splinter groups like a sow whelps piglets. It's a law of nature. Eartha was the leader of the largest one, also called the Earthists, purely to give headaches to poor newspapermen, I'm convinced. Some of us distinguished them as Earthist (David) and Earthist (Lowe), others tried the abomination of Eartha-ists. Most of us simply called them the Earthists and the Other Earthists, something guaranteed to provoke a wailing woodnote wild from Eartha, because there was no need to explain who the "Others" were.

David had died politically intestate. There was no heir apparent in his organization. Increasingly, people were not planning for their own deaths, because they simply didn't expect to die. Perhaps that explains the mordant fascination with violent images in popular entertainment and the clamor for more details about real deaths when they occur. We haven't achieved immortality yet. Maybe we never will. People are reassured to see death as something that happens to somebody else, and not often at that.

Eartha Lowe was standing on every soapbox that would support her not-inconsiderable weight, welcoming the strays back into the fold. In her version, it was David who had split away. Who cared that he had taken ninety percent of the flock with him? We were told that Eartha had always loved David (no surprise; they had both professed to love *every* living creature, though David had loved Eartha more on the level of, say, a nematode or a virus, not so much as the family dog) and David had returned her affection in spades. I couldn't follow all the doctrinal differences. The big one seemed to be Eartha's contention that any proper Earthist should be in the female image, to be a mirror of Mother Earth. Or something like that.

All in all, it was the goldarndest, Barnum-and-Baileyest, rib-stickinest, rough-and-tumblest infernal foofaraw of a media circus anybody had seen since grandpaw chased the possum down the road and lost his store teeth, and I was heartily sorry to have been a part of it.

When the two-day purgatory was over, I collapsed into my bed for twelve hours. When I woke up, I gave some thought once more to getting out of the business. Was it a root cause of my self-destructive tendencies? One would have to think that hating what I did might contribute to feelings of worthlessness, and thus to thoughts of ending it all. I tabled the matter for the moment. I have to admit that though I may feel disdain for the things we do and the manner in which we do them, there is a heady thrill to the news business when things are really happening. Not that exciting things happen all that often, even in my line of work. Most news is of the not-much-happened-today variety, tricked up in various sexy lies. But when it *does* happen, it's exhilarating. And there's an even guiltier pleasure in being where things are happening, in being the first to know something. About the only other line of work where you can get as close to the center of things is politics, and even I draw the line at that. I have some standards left.

Talking to Callie had been a bust, advice-wise if not career-wise. But in searching for sources of dissatisfaction one thing had grown increasingly clear to me. I was wearing my body like a badly fitted pair of trousers, the kind that bind you in the crotch. A year as a female, ersatz though the experience had been, had shown me it was time for a Change. Past time, probably by several years.

Could that have been the fountain of my discontent? Could it have been a contributing factor? Doubtful, and possibly. Even if it had nothing to do with it, it wouldn't hurt to go ahead and get it done, so I could be comfortable again. Hell, it was no big deal.

When the terribly, terribly fashionable decide the old genitals are getting to be rather a bore, don't you know, they phone the chauffeur and have the old bones driven down to Change Alley.

Normally, when it came time for a Change, I would hie me to some small neighborhood operation. They are all board-certified, after all, one just as able as another to do the necessary nipping and tucking. A confluence of circumstances this time decided me to visit the street where the elite meet. One was that my pockets were bulging with the shekels Walter had showered on me in the form of bonuses for the Burning Earth story. The other was that I knew Darling Bobbie when he was just Robert Darling of Crazy Bob's Budget Barbering and Tattoo Parlor, back when he did sex changes as a sideline to bring in more money. He'd had a little shop on the Leystrasse, a determinedly working-class commercial corridor with a third of the shopfronts boarded up and plastered with handbills, running through one of the less fashionable neighborhoods of King City. He'd been sandwiched between a bordello and a taco stand, and his sign had read "Finast Gender Alteration on the Leystrasse—E-Z Credit Terms." None of which was news to anyone: his was the *only* Change shop in the area, and you couldn't offer so expensive a service around there without being prepared to finance. Not that he did a lot of it. Laborers can't afford frequent sex changes and, as a group, are not that inclined to question Mother Nature's toss of the dice, much less flit back and forth from one sex to the other. He did much better with the tattooing, which was cheap and appealed to his clientele. He told me he had regulars who had their entire bodies done every few weeks.

That had been over twenty-five years ago, when I had my last previous sex change. In that time, Crazy Bob had come up in the world. He had invented some body frill or other—I can't even recall what it was now, these things come and go so quickly they make mayflies seem elderly— that was "discovered" by slumming socialites. He was elevated overnight into the new guru of secondary sexual attributes. Fashion writers now attended his openings and wrote knowingly about the new season's whimsy. Body styling would probably never be as big or influential as the rag trade, but a few practitioners to the hi-thrust set had carved themselves a niche in the world of fashion.

And Crazy Bob had spent the last ten years trying to make people forget about the little cock shop next door to the Jalapeño Heaven.

Change Alley is a ridiculous name for the place, but it does branch off of the five-kilometer gulch of glitz known as Hadleyplatz. For fifty years the Platz, as everyone knew it, had been the inheritor of such places as Saville Row, Fifth Avenue, Kimberly Road, and Chimki Prospekt. It was the place to go if you were looking for solid gold toenail clippers, not so great for annual white sales. They didn't offer credit on the Platz, E-Z or otherwise. If the door didn't have your gencode in its memory banks along with an up-to-the-millisecond analysis of your pocketbook, it simply didn't open for you. There were no painted signs to be seen, and almost no holosigns. Advertising on the Platz ran to small logos in the bottom corners of plate glass windows, or brilliantly-buffed gold plaques mounted at eye level.

The Alley branched away from the main promenade at a sharp angle and dead-ended about a hundred meters later in a cluster of exclusive restaurants. Along the way were a handful of small storefronts operated by the handful of very tasteful hucksters who could persuade their clientele to part with ten times the going rate for a body make-over so they could have "Body By So-and-so" engraved on the nail of their pinky finger.

There *were* holosigns in the Alley shops, showing each designer's ideas of what the fashionable man or woman was being these days. The tastemongers back on the main drag liked to say the Alley was *off* the Platz, but not *of* the Platz. Still, it was all a far cry from the tattoo templates filling the windows of the Budget Barber.

I wondered if I ought to go in. I wondered if I *could* go in. Bob and I had been drinking buddies for a while, but we'd lost contact after his move. I pressed my hand to the identiplate, felt the tiny pressure as a probe scraped away a minuscule amount of dead skin. The machine seemed to hesitate; perhaps I'd be sent around to the tradesmen's entrance. Then it swung open. There should have been a flourish of trumpets, I thought, but that would have been too demonstrative for the Alley.

"Hildy! Enchanting, enchanting old boy. So good to see you." He had come out of some concealed back room and covered the distance to me in three long strides. He pumped my hand enthusiastically, looking me up and down and adopting a dubious air. "Good heavens, am I responsible for *that?* You came just in *time,* my friend. Not a *moment* too soon. But don't worry, I can *fix* it, cousin Bobbie will take care of *everything.* Just put yourself in my hands."

I suddenly wondered if I wanted to be in his hands. I thought he was laying it on a trifle thick, but it had been a while since I'd seen him, and I'm sure he had appearances to maintain. The gushing, the mincing, all were nods toward tradition, something practiced by many in his line of work, just as lawyers tried to develop a sober facade suitable for the weighty matters they dealt in. Back before Changing, the fashion world had been dominated by homosexual men. Sexuality being as complicated as it is, with hundreds of identified orientations—not to mention ULTRA-Tingle—it was impossible to know much about anyone else's preferences without talking it over and spelling it out. Bob, or perhaps I should say Darling, was hetero-oriented, male-born and male-leaning, which meant that, left to his own choice, he would be male most of the time with occasional excursions into a female body, and no matter his current sex would prefer the company of the opposite.

But his profession almost demanded that he Change four or five times a year, just as the rag merchants had better wear their own designs. Today he was male, and didn't look any different from when I had known him. At least he didn't at first. When I looked more closely, I saw there were a thousand subtle alterations, none of them radical enough so his friends wouldn't recognize him on the street.

"You don't have to take the blame," I told him, as he took my elbow and guided me toward something he called a "Counseling Suite." "Maybe you don't remember, but I brought in all the specs myself. You never had a chance to practice your craft."

"I remember it *quite* well, dear boy, and perhaps it was the will of Allah. I was still learning my *art,*—please heed the stress on the word, Hildy—and I probably would have made a botch of it. But I do recall being *quite* cross."

"No, Darling, in those days you didn't get cross, you got pissed off."

He made a weird sort of smirk, acknowledging the gibe but not letting the tinkerbell mask slip a millimeter. I glanced around the suite, and had to stifle a laugh. This was girl heaven. The walls were mirrors, creating a crowd of Hildys and Bobbies. Most everything else was pink, and had lace on it. The *lace* had lace on it. It was fabulously overdone, but I liked it. I was in the mood for this sort of thing. I sank gratefully into a pink and white lacy settee and felt the anxiety wash away from me. This had been a good idea after all.

A female assistant or whatever entered with a silver bucket of champagne on ice, set it up near me, poured some into a tall glass. It was a measure of my alienation from my current somatotype that I watched these operations with complete disinterest. A week before . . . well, before Scarpa Island, however that interval should be measured, I would have been attracted to the woman. Just at the moment I was effectively neuter. Robert didn't interest me either. Actually, he probably wouldn't interest me after the Change, simply because he was not my "type," a word simply dripping with meaning in the age of gender selection.

Like my host, I am hetero-oriented. Which is not to say I have never engaged in sex with a partner of my current sex; hasn't everybody? Can anyone remain truly heteroist when they have been both male and female? I suppose anything's possible, but I've never encountered it. What I find is that sex for me is always better when there is a man and a woman involved. Twice in my life I have met people I wanted to become more deeply attached to when both of us were of the same sex. In both cases, one of us Changed.

I don't know how to explain it. I don't believe *anyone* can really explain reasons behind their sexual preferences, unless they're based on prejudice: i.e., this or that practice is unnatural, against God's law, perverted, disgusting, and so forth. There's still some of that around, a bit of it in Bob's old neighborhood, in fact, where he twice had windows smashed and once had truly repulsive Christian slogans painted over his sign. But sexual preference seems to be something that happens to you, not something you elect. The fact is, when I'm a boy I'm intensely interested in girls, and have little or no interest in other boys, and vice versa when I'm a girl. I have friends who are precisely the opposite, who are homo-oriented in both sexes. So be it. I know people who cover the whole spectrum between these two positions, from the dedicated males and females, homo and hetero, to the pansexuals who only require you to be warm and would be willing to overlook it if you weren't, to the dysfunctionals who aren't happy in either sex, to the true neuters, who identify with neither sex, have all external and internal attributes removed and are quite glad to be shut of the whole confusing, inconvenient, superfluous, messy business.

As to type, neither Robert nor Darling was mine. When female, I'm not as much concerned with physical beauty in a partner as when I'm male, though it's only a matter of degree, since when beauty can be purchased at will it becomes a rather common and quite unremarkable quality. Rob/Bob's lanky Ichabod Cranish physique and long narrow physiognomy didn't set my girlish heart to beating, but that wouldn't put me off if the personality traits compensated. They didn't. He was fine as a buddy, but as a lover he would be entirely too needy. He had insecurities science has not yet found a name for.

"Did we remember to bring our little specs with us, Hildy?" he asked. I had, and handed them to him. He leafed through the pages quickly, sniffed, but not in a judgmental way, just as if to say he couldn't be bothered with the technicalities. He handed the genetic specifications to his aide, and clapped his hands. "Now, let's flutter out of those *charming* togs, can't create without a bare bodkin, chop, chop." I stripped and he took the clothing, looking as though he wished for sterilized forceps. "Where *did* you find these things. Why, it's been *years* . . . we'll of course have them cleaned and folded."

"I found them in my closet, and you can donate them to the poor."

"Hildy, I don't think there *is* anyone that poor."

"Then throw them away."

"Oh, *thank* you." He handed the clothing to the woman, who left the room with them. "That was a truly humanitarian gesture, old friend, an act that shows a great deal of *caring* for the fashion environment."

"If you're grateful," I said, "then you could stop spreading the pixie dust. We're alone now. This is *me,* Darling."

He looked around conspiratorially. All I saw were thousands upon thousands of Hildys and a like number of whoever he was. He sat in a chair facing me and relaxed a little.

"How about you call me Bobbie? It's not quite so pretentious as Darling, and not so dreadful and reminiscent as Robert. And to tell you the truth, Hildy, I'm finding it harder every day to drop the pose. I'm beginning to wonder if it is a pose. I haven't got pissed off in years, but I get cross practically all the time. And there's a big difference, as you reminded me."

"We all pose, Bobbie. Maybe the old pose wasn't the proper one for you."

"I'm still hetero, if you were wondering."

"I wasn't, but I'd be astonished if you weren't. Polarity switches are pretty rare, according to what I've read."

"They happen. There's precious little I don't see in this business. So how have you been? Still writing trash?"

Before I could answer he started off on the first of a series of tangents. He thanked me effusively for the good coverage he'd always had from the *Nipple.* He must have been aware that I didn't work on the fashion page, but maybe he thought I'd put in a good word for him. Seeing as how he was about to design a new body for me, I saw no reason to disillusion him.

There were many more things discussed, many glasses of champagne put away, some aromatic and mildly intoxicating smokes inhaled. It all kept coming back to Topic A: when were "they" going to discover he was a fraud?

I was conversant with that feeling myself. It's common to people who are good at something they have no particular love for. In fact, it's common among all but the most self-assured—say, Callie, for instance. Bobbie had a bad case of it, and I could hardly blame him. Not that I thought him an utter charlatan. I don't have much of an eye for such things, but from what I gathered he actually was quite talented. But in the world he inhabited, talent often had very little to do with anything. Taste is fickle. In the world of design, you're only as good as your last season. The back alleys and taprooms of Bedrock are strewn with the still-breathing corpses of people who used to be somebody. Some of them had shops right here in the Alley.

After a while I began to be a little alarmed. I knew Bobbie, and I knew he would always be this way, frightened that the success he'd never really adjusted to because he'd never understood where it came from would be snatched away from him. That's just the way he was. But from the amount of time he seemed willing to spend with me, he was either in deep trouble or I should feel extremely flattered. I'd counted on having ten or fifteen minutes with The Master while he penciled in the broad strokes, then turned me over to aides to do the actual design work. Didn't he have more important clients waiting somewhere?

"Saw you on telly," he said, after winding down from his increasingly tiresome lament. "With that dreadful . . . what's her name? I forget. More on that incredibly boring David Earth story. I'm afraid I switched off. I don't care if I never hear his name again."

"I felt that way three hours into the first day. But you were fascinated for at least twenty-four hours, you couldn't get enough news about it."

"Sorry to disappoint you. It was boring."

"I doubt it. Think back to when you first read about it. You were dying to hear more. It was boring *later,* after you'd seen the film three or four times."

He frowned, then nodded. "You're right. My eyes were glued to the newspad. How did you know?"

"It's true of almost everybody. You in particular. If everyone's talking about something, you can't afford not to have an opinion, a snide comment, a worldly sigh . . . *some*thing. To not have heard of it would be unthinkable."

"We're in the same business, aren't we?"

"We're cousins, anyway. Maybe the difference is, in my business we can afford to run something into the ground. We use up news. By the time we're through with it, there is nothing quite so boring as what fascinated you twenty-four hours ago. Then we move on to the next sensation."

"Whereas I must always watch for that magic moment a few seconds *before* something becomes as passé as your taste in clothing."

"Exactly."

He sighed. "It's wearing me down, Hildy."

"I don't envy you—except for the money."

"Which I am investing most sensibly. No hi-thrust vacations to the

Uranian moons for me. No summer homes on Mercury. Strictly blue chips. I'm not ever going to have to scrape for my air money. What I wonder is, will the hunger for lost acclaim emaciate my soul?" He raised an eyebrow and gave me a jaundiced look. "I assume those specs you gave Kiki outline a plan as stodgy as what you're currently walking around in?"

"Why would you assume that? Would I come here if I wanted something I could get in any local barber shop? I want Body By Bobbie."

"But I thought . . ."

"That was female to male. The reverse is a whore of a different color."

I decided to make a note to myself. Send flowers to the fashion editor of the *Nipple*. There was no other way to account for the royal treatment Bobbie lavished on me during the next four hours. Oh, sure, my money was as good as anyone else's, and I didn't want to think too hard about the bill for all this. But neither friendship nor idleness could explain Bobbie's behavior. I concluded he was looking for a good review.

Can you call something a quirk when you share it with a large minority of your fellow citizens? I'm not sure, but perhaps it is. I've never understood the roots of this peculiarity, any more than I understand why I don't care to go to bed with men when I am a man. But the fact is, as a man I am fairly indifferent to how I look and dress. Clean and neat, sure, and ugly is something I can certainly do without. But fashions don't concern me. My wardrobe consists of the sort of thing Bobbie threw away when I arrived, or worse. I usually put on shorts, a comfortable shirt, soft shoes, a purse: standard men's wear, suitable for all but formal occasions. I don't pay much attention to colors or cut. I ignore makeup completely and use only the blandest of scents. When I'm feeling festive I might put on a colorful skirt, more of a sarong, really, and never fret about the hemline. But most of what I wear wouldn't have raised eyebrows if I had gone back in time and walked the streets in the years before sex changing.

The fact is, I feel that while a woman can wear just about anything, there are whole categories of clothing a man looks silly in.

Case in point: the body-length, form-fitting gown, the kind that reaches down to the ankles, maybe with a slit up one side to the knee. Put it on a man's body and the penis will produce a flaw in the smooth line unless it is strapped down tight—and the whole point of wearing something like that, to my mind, is to feel slinky, not bound up. That particular garment was designed to show the lines of a woman's body, curves instead of angles. Another is the plunging neckline, both the sort that conceal and the kind that push up and display the breasts. A man can certainly get away with a deep neckline, but the purpose and the engineering of it are different.

Before you start your letter to the editor, I *know* these are not laws of nature. There's no reason a man can't have feminine legs, for instance, or breasts, if he wants them. Then he'd look good in those clothes, to my eye, but precisely because he had feminine attributes. I am much more of a traditionalist when it comes to somatotypes. If I have the breasts and the hips and the legs, I want the whole package. I'm not a mixer. I feel there are boy things and girl things. The basic differences in body types are easy to define. The differences in clothing types is tougher, and the line moves, but can be summarized by saying that women's clothing is more apt to emphasize and define secondary sexual characteristics, and to be more colorful and varied.

And I can name a thousand exceptions through history, from the court of Louis the Sun King to the *chador* of Islamic women. I realize that Western women didn't wear pants until the twentieth century, and men didn't wear skirts—Scotland and the South Seas notwithstanding—until the twenty-first. I know about peacocks and parrots and mandrill baboons. When you start talking about sex and the way *you* think it should be, you're bound to get into trouble. There are very few statements you can make about sex that won't have an exception somewhere.

I guess this is something of a hobbyhorse with me. It's in reaction to the militant unisexers who believe all gender-identified clothing should be eliminated, that we should all pick our clothing randomly, and sneer at you publicly when you dress too feminine or masculine. Or even worse, the uniformists, those people who want us all to wear formal job-identified clothing at all times, or a standardized outfit—wait a minute, I've got one right here, just let me show you, you'll love it!—usually some drearily practical People's Jumpsuit with a high neck and lots of pockets, comes in three bilious colors. Those people would have us all running about looking like some dreadful twentieth-century "futuristic" film, when they thought the people of 1960 or 2000 would all want to dress alike, with meter-wide shelves on their shoulders or plastic bubbles over their heads or togas or the ubiquitous jumpsuit with no visible zipper, and leave you wondering how did those people make water. These folks would be amusing if they didn't introduce legislation every year aimed at making everyone behave like them.

Or lingerie! What about lingerie? Transvestism didn't die with sex changing—very little did, because human sexuality is concerned with what gives us a thrill, not what makes sense—and some people with male bodies still prefer to dress up in garter belts and padded bras and short transparent nightgowns. If they enjoy it that's fine with me. But I've always felt it looks awful, simply because it *clashes.* You may say the only thing it clashes with are my cultural preconceptions, and I'd agree with you. So what else is fashion? Bobbie could tell you that tinkering with a cultural icon is something you do at your own peril, with a few stiff drinks, a brave smile, and a premonition of disaster, because nine times out of ten it just doesn't sell.

Which simply means that as many as half my fellow citizens feel as I do about gender dressing, and if that many feel that way, how bad can it be?

I rest my case.

So I spent a pleasant time fulfilling a gender-based stereotype: shopping. I enjoyed the hell out of it.

When you get the full treatment from Bobbie, no bodily detail is too small. The big, gaudy, obvious things were quickly disposed of. Breasts? What are people wearing this year, Bobbie? As small as that? Well, let's not get ridiculous, dear, I'd like to feel a little bounce, all right? Legs? Sort of . . . you know . . . long. Long enough to reach the ground. No knobs on the knees, if you please. Trim ankles. Arms? Well, what can you say about arms? Work your magic, Bobbie. I like a size five shoe and all my best dresses are nines—and thirty years out of date, enough time for some of them to be stylish again—so work around that. Besides, I feel comfortable in a body that size, and height reductions cost out at nearly two thousand per centimeter.

Some people spend most of their time on the face. Not me. I've always preferred to make any facial changes gradually, one feature at a time, so people can recognize me. I settled on my basic face fifty years ago, and see no need to change it for current fashion, beyond a little frill here and there. I told Bobbie not to change the underlying bone structure at all; I feel it's suitable for a male or a female countenance. He suggested a slight fullness to the lips and showed me a new nose I liked, and I went flat-out trendy with the ears, letting him give me his latest design. But when I showed up for work after the Change, everyone would know it was Hildy.

I thought I was through . . . but what about the toes? Bare feet are quite practical in Luna, and had come back into vogue, so people will be looking at your toes. The current rage was to eliminate them entirely as an evolutionary atavism; Bobbie spent some time trying to sell me on Sockfeet, which look just like they sound. I guess I'm just a toe person. Or if you listen to Bobbie, a Cro-Magnon. I spent half an hour on the toes, and almost as much time on the fingers and hands. There's nothing I hate like sweaty hands.

I put considerable thought into the contemplation of navels. With the nipples and the vulva, the navel is the only punctuation between the chin and the toenails, the only places for the eye to pause in the smooth sweep of the female form I was designing. I did not neglect it. Speaking of the vulva, I once again proved myself a hopeless reactionary. Lately, otherwise conservative women had been indulging the most outrageous flights of fancy when it came to labial architecture, to the point that it was sometimes difficult to be sure what sex you were looking at without a second glance. I preferred more modest, compact arrangements. With me, it is mostly not for public display anyway. I usually wear something below the waist, some sort of skirt or pants, and I didn't want to frighten off a lover when I dropped them.

"You won't frighten anyone with *that,* Hildy," Bobbie said, looking sourly at the simulation of the genitals I'd just spent so much time elaborating. "I'd say your main problem here is boredom."

"It was good enough for Eve."

"I must have missed her last showing. Can't imagine why. I'm sure it will prove quite useful in the circles you move in, but are you *sure* I couldn't interest you in—"

"I'm the one that has to use it, and that's what I want. Have a heart, Bobbie. I'm an old-fashioned girl. And didn't I give you a free hand with the skin tones, and the nipples, and the ears and the shoulder blades and the collarbones and the ass and those two fetching little dimples in the small of the back?" I turned at the waist and looked at the full-body simulation that had replaced one of the mirrors, and chewed on a knuckle. "Maybe we should take another look at those dimples . . ."

He talked me out of changing that, and into a slight alteration of the backs of the hands, and he bitched at me some more and threw up his hands in disgust at every opportunity, but I could tell he was basically pleased. And so was I. I moved around, watching the female I was about to become duplicate all my movements, and it was good. It was the seventh hour: time to rest.

And then a strange thing happened to me. I was taken to the prep room, where the technicians built their mystical elixirs, and I began to suffer a panic attack. I watched the thousand and one brews dripping from the synthesizers into the mixing retorts, cloudy with potential, and my heart started beating wildly and I began to hyperventilate. I also got angry.

I knew what I was afraid of, and anyone *would* be angry.

Unless you've chosen the most radical of body make-overs, very little of modern sex changing involves actual surgery. In my case, about all the cutting that was planned was the removal and storage of the male genitalia, and their replacement with a vagina, cervix, uterus, and set of fallopian tubes and ovaries which were even then being messengered over from the organ bank, where they'd reposed since my last Change. There would be a certain amount of body sculpting, but not much. Most of the myriad alterations I was about to undergo would be done by the potions being mixed in the prep room. Those brews contained two elements: a saline solution, and uncounted trillions of nanobots.

Some of these cunning little machines were standard, made from templates used in all male-to-female sex changes. Some were customized, cobbled together from parts stolen from microbes and viruses or from manufactured components, assembled by Bobbie and assigned a specific and often minute task, copyrighted, and given snippets of my own genetic code much like a bloodhound is given an old shoe to establish the scent. All of them were too small to be seen by the human eye. Some were barely visible in a good microscope. Many were smaller than that.

They were assembled by other nanobots at chemical-reaction speeds, and produced in groups seldom smaller than one million units. Injected into the bloodstream, they responded to the conditions they found there, gravitated to their assigned working sites using the same processes whereby hormones and enzymes found their way through the *corpus,* identified the right spots by using jigsaw-like pieces of these same bodily regulators as both maps and grapplers, attached themselves, and began to boogie. The smaller ones penetrated the individual cell walls and entered the DNA itself, reading the amino acids like rosary beads, making carefully planned cuts and splices. The larger ones, the kind with actual motors and manipulators and transistors, screws, scrapers, memories, arms—what used to be called microbots when they were first made with the same technologies that produced primitive integrated circuit chips—these con-gregated at specified sites and performed grosser tasks. The microbots would each be handed a piece of my genetic code and another piece synthesized by Bobbie, which functioned like eccentric cams in making the tiny machines do their particular job. Some would go to my nose, for instance, and start carving away here, building up there, using my own body and supplementary nutrients carried in by cargo microbots. Waste material was picked up in the same way and ferried out of the body. In this way one could gain or lose weight very quickly. I myself planned to emerge from the Change fifteen kilos lighter.

The nanobots labored diligently to make the terrain fit the map. When it did, when my nose was the shape Bobbie had intended, they detached themselves and were flushed away, deprogrammed, and bottled to await the next customer.

Nothing new or frightening about that. It was the same principle used in the over-the-counter pills you can buy to change the color of your eyes or the kinkiness of your hair while you sleep. The only difference was the nanobots in the pills were too cheap to salvage; when they'd done their work they simply turned themselves off in your kidneys and you pissed them away. Most of the technology was at least one hundred years old, some more ancient than that. The hazards were almost nil, very well-known, and completely in control.

Except I now found I had developed a fear of nanobots. Considering what the CC had told me about them, I didn't think it was entirely unfounded.

The other thing that frightened me was even worse. I was afraid to go to sleep.

Not so much sleep in the normal sense. I had slept well enough the night before; better than normal, in fact, considering my exhaustion from the two-day celebrity binge. But the epic infestation of nanobots I was about to experience wreaks havoc on the body and the mind. It's not something you want to be awake for.

Bobbie noticed something was wrong as he took me to the suspension tank. It was all I could do to hold still while the techs shoved the various hoses and cables into the freshly-incised stigmata in my arms and legs and belly. When I was invited to step into the coffin-sized vat of cool blue fluid, I almost lost my composure. I stood there gripping the sides of the vat, knuckles white, with one foot in and the other not wanting to leave the floor.

"Something the matter?" Bobbie asked, quietly. I saw some of his helpers were trying not to stare at me.

"Nothing you could do anything about."

"You want to tell me about it? Let me get these people out of the room."

Did I want to tell him? In a way, I was aching to. I'd never gotten to tell Callie, and the urge to spill it to *some*body was almost overwhelming.

But this was not the place and certainly not the time, and Bobbie was most definitely not the person. He would simply find a way to incorporate it into the continuing Gothic novel that was The Life of Robert Darling, with himself the imperiled heroine. I simply had to get through this myself and talk it over with someone later.

And suddenly I knew who that someone would be. So get it over with, Hildy, grit your teeth and step into the tub and let the soothing fluids lull you into a sleep no more dangerous than you've had every night for thirty-six and a half thousand nights.

The water closed over my face. I gulped it into my lungs—always a bit unpleasant until all the air is gone—and looked up into the wavering face of my re-creator, unsure when and where I would wake up again.

THE MIKADO OF METEOROLOGY

I found Fox deep in the bowels of the Oregon Disneyland. He was engrossed in a blueprint projected on a big horizontal table at the foot of a machine the size of an interplanetary liner, which I later learned was the starter motor for a battery of machines that produced north winds in Oregon. Machines merely elephantine in size swarmed around the partially-assembled behemoth, some with human operators, some working on their own, and there was the usual crowd of blue-uniformed laborers leaning on shovels and perfecting their spitting techniques.

He glanced up as I came closer, looked me up and down, and returned to his work. I'd seen a flicker of interest in his eyes, but no recognition. Then he looked up again, looked harder, and suddenly smiled.

"Hildy? Is that you?"

I stopped and twirled around for him, flashing a few dozen of Crazy Bob's Best Patented Incisors and two of the greatest legs the Master ever designed as my skirt swirled out like a Dresden figurine. He tossed a light pen on the screen and came toward me, took my hand and squeezed it. Then he realized what he was doing, laughed, and hugged me tightly.

"It's been too long," he said. "I saw you on the pad the other day." He gestured at me in a way that said he hadn't expected what he was seeing now. I shrugged; the body spoke for itself.

"Reading the *Nipple* now? I don't believe it."

"You didn't have to read the *Nipple* to catch your act. Every time I changed the channel, there you were, boring everybody to death."

I made no comment. He had surely been as interested at first as Bobbie and everybody else in Luna, but why bother to explain that to him? And knowing Fox, he wouldn't admit he could be as easily seduced by a sensational story as the rest of his fellow citizens.

"Frankly, I'm glad the idiot's gone. You have no idea the kind of problems David Earth and his merry band cause in my line of work."

"It's Saturday," I said, "but your service said you'd be down here."

"Hell, it's almost Sunday. It's the typical start-up problems. Look, I'll be through here in a few minutes. Why don't you stick around, we can go out for dinner, or breakfast, or something."

"The something sounds interesting."

"Great. If you're thirsty one of these layabouts can scare up a beer for you; give 'em something to do equal to their talents." He turned away and hurried back to his work.

The brief sensation caused by my arrival died away; by that I mean the several dozen men and handful of women who had transferred their gazes from the far distance to my legs now returned to the contemplation of infinity.

A sidewalk supervisor unused to the ways of the construction game might have wondered how anything got done with so many philosophers and so few people with dirty hands in evidence. The answer was simply that Fox and three or four other engineers did all the work that didn't involve lifting and carrying, and the machines did the rest. Though hundreds of cubic miles of stone and soil would be moved and shaped before Oregon was complete, not a spoonful of it would be shifted by the Hod-Carriers Union members, though they were so numerous one could almost believe they could accomplish it in a few weeks. No, the shovels they carried were highly polished, ceremonial badges of profession, as unsullied by dirt as the day they were made. Their chief function was safety. If one of the deep thinkers fell asleep standing up, the shovel handle could be slotted into an inverted pocket on the worker's union suit and sometimes prevented that worthy from falling over. Fox claimed it was the chief cause of on-the-job accidents.

Perhaps I exaggerate. The job guarantee is a civil right basic to our society, and it is a sad fact that a great many Lunarians are suited only for the kind of job machines took over long ago. No matter how much we tinker with genes and eliminate the actually defective, I think we'll always have the slow, the unimaginative, the disinterested, the hopeless. What should we do with them? What we've decided is that everyone who wants to will be given a job and some sort of badge of profession to testify to it, and put to some sort of work four hours a day. If you don't want to work, that's fine, too. No one starves, and air has been free since before I was born.

It didn't used to be that way. Right after the Invasion if you didn't pay your air tax, you could be shown to the air lock without your suit. I like the new way better.

But I'll confess it seems terribly inefficient. I'm ignorant when it comes to economics, but when I bother to wonder about such things it seems there must be a less wasteful way. Then I wonder what these people would do to fill their already—from my viewpoint—empty lives, and I resolve to stop wondering. What's the big problem with it, anyway? I suspect there were people standing around leaning on shovels when the contract for the first pyramid was signed.

Does it sound terribly intolerant for me to say I don't understand how they do it? Perhaps they'd think the same of me, working in a "creative" capacity for an organization I loathe, at a profession with dubious—at best—claims to integrity. Maybe these laborers would think me a whore. Maybe I *am* a literary whore. But in my defense I can say that journalism, if I may be permitted to use the term, has not been my *only* job. I have done other things, and at that moment felt strongly that I would be moving on from the *Nipple* fairly soon.

Most of the men and women around me as I waited for Fox had never held another job. They were not suited for anything else. Most were illits, and the opportunities for meaningful work for such people are few. If they had artistic talent they'd be using it.

How did they make it through the day? Were these the people who were contributing to the alarming rise in suicide the CC reported? Did they get up some morning, pick up the shovel, think *the hell with it,* and blow their brains out? I resolved to ask the CC, when I started speaking to him again.

It just seemed so bleak to me. I studied one man, a foreman according to one of the many badges pinned to his denims, a Century Man with the gaudy lapel pin proclaiming he had spent *one hundred years* leaning on that shovel. He was standing near Fox, looking in the general direction of the blueprint table with an expression I'd last seen on an animal that was chewing its cud. Did he have hopes and dreams and fears, or had he used them all up? We've prolonged life to the point that we don't have a clear idea of when it might end, but have failed to provide anything new and interesting to *do* with that vast vista of years.

Fox put his hand on my shoulder and I realized, with a shock and a perverse sense of reassurance, that I must have looked like a cud-chewer myself as I thought my deep, penetrating thoughts. That foreman was probably a fine fellow to sit around and bullshit with. I'll bet he was a terrific joke-teller and could throw one hell of a game of darts. Did we all have to be, to use the traditional expression, rocket scientists? I *know* a rocket scientist, and a slimier curmudgeon you would not care to meet.

"You're looking good," Fox said.

"Thanks. You all done here for now?"

"Until Monday. I hate to be one of those people married to the job, but if somebody doesn't worry about it this place won't live up to its potential."

"Still the same Fox." I put my arm around his waist as we walked toward his trailer, parked in a jumble of idle machines. He put his hand on my shoulder, but I could tell his thoughts were still back in the blueprints.

"I guess so. But this is going to be the best Disney yet, Hildy. Mount Hood is finished; all we need is some snow. It's only one-quarter scale, but it fools the eye from almost any angle. The Columbia's full and almost up to speed. The gorge is going to be magnificent. We're going to have a real salmon run. I've got Douglas firs twenty meters high. Even when you force-grow 'em, those babies take some time. Deer, grizzlies . . . it'll be great."

"How long till completion?" We were passing some bear pens. The inmates looked out at us with lazy predators' eyes.

"Five years, if it all goes well. Probably seven, realistically." He held the door to the trailer and followed me inside. It was utilitarian, overflowing with papers. About the only personal touch I saw was an antique slide rule mounted over the gas fireplace. "You want to order something in? There's a good Japanese place that will deliver here. I had to train them; this place is tough to find. Or we could go out if there's something else you'd rather have."

I knew exactly what I wanted, and we wouldn't have to order out for it. I put my arms around him and kissed him in a way that almost made up for the forty years we'd been out of each other's beds. When I drew back for a breath, he was smiling down at me.

"Is this dress a particular favorite?" he asked. He had his hand in the neckline, bunching the fabric.

"Would it do me any good to say yes?"

He slowly shook his head, and ripped it off.

Lovers of fashion should be relieved to note two things: the dress was thirty years old and *not* one of those that was stylish again, though I had picked it because it flattered the new me. Bobbie would have gagged to see it, but Fox was more direct. And second, I had known Fox would destroy it, though not as a fashion policeman—male or female, Fox was dense about such things. The main thing one needed to know about Fox was that—male or female—he liked to dominate. He liked sex to be rough and urgent and just this side of brutal, and that was exactly what I was in the mood for. As he gave me one of the most thorough rogerings of my life I thanked what gods there be that I had found him during a male period of his life.

Fox was the one I had thought of as I stood nervously on the brink of Change, and it made perfect sense that I did. He and I . . . actually, for a time it had been she and I, then he and I . . . we had been lovers for ten years. I don't know just why we broke up, or maybe I've forgotten, but we came out of the parting good friends. Perhaps we simply grew apart, as they say, though that's always sounded like a facile explanation. How much growing do you still have to do when one of you is sixty and the other is fifty-five? But it had been a comfortable time in my life.

The need to see him had been so urgent I had changed my plan to do a little shopping on the Platz, thereby doing my bank balance a big favor. I had rushed home, dressed in the scoop-necked, knee-length satiny black dress with the ballerina skirt that currently lay tattered, wrinkled, and getting very sweaty beneath my naked back, changed my hair color to match the clothes, sprayed makeup on my eyes and mouth and polish on my nails, doused myself with Fox's favorite scent, and was back out the door in three minutes flat. I had taxied to Oregon, worked my feminine magic on the poor boy, and within fifteen minutes had my knees in the air and my hands gripping his bare behind, barking like a dog and trying to force him *through* my body and into the floor beneath us.

Do you see why ULTRA-Tingle is already in financial trouble?

Fox usually had that effect on me. Not always quite so intense, it's true. I was experiencing something politely called hormone shock, or Change mania, but more often known as going cunt crazy. One shouldn't expect to undergo such radical alterations to one's body without a certain upset to the psyche. With me it's always a heightening of sexual hunger. Some people simply get irresponsible. I've got a friend who has to instruct his bank to shut off his line of credit for five days after a Change, or he'd spend every shilling he had.

What I was spending you can't put in a bank, and there's no sense in saving it anyway.

Afterwards, he ordered a mountain of sushi and tempura and when it was delivered, fired up the trailer and took us through a long dark air duct and into Oregon.

Like all Disneylands, it was a huge hemispherical bubble, more or less flat on the bottom, the curved roof painted blue. The first ones had been only a kilometer or two across, but as the engineers figured out better ways to support them, the newer ones were growing with no outer limit in sight. Oregon was one of the biggest, along with two others currently under construction: Kansas and Borneo. Fox tried his best not to bore me with statistics; I simply forget them a few minutes after hearing them. Suffice it to say the place was *very* big.

The floor was mostly rock and dirt shaped into hills and two mountains. The one he'd called Mount Hood was tall and sharply pointed. The other was truncated and looked unfinished.

"That's going to be a volcano," he said. "Or at least a good approximation of an active volcano. There was an eruption in this area in historic times."

"You mean lava and fire and smoke?"

"I wish we could. But the power requirements to melt enough rock for a worthwhile eruption would bust the budget, plus any really good volume of smoke would hurt the trees and wildlife. What it's going to do is vent steam three or four times a day and shoot sparks at night. Should be real pretty. The project manager's trying to convince the money people to fund a yearly ash plume—nothing catastrophic, it actually benefits the trees. And I'm pretty sure we'll be able to mount a modest lava flow every ten or twenty years."

"I wish I could see it better. It's pretty dim in here." The only real light sources were at the scattered tree farms, dots of bright green in the blasted landscape.

"Let me get the sun turned on." He picked up a mike and talked to the power section, and a few minutes later the "sun" flickered and then blazed directly overhead.

"All this will be covered in virgin forest; green as far as the eye can see. Not at all like your shack in Texas. This is a wet, cool climate, lots of snow in higher elevations. Mostly conifers. We're even putting in a grove of sequoias down in the south part, though we're fudging a bit on that, geographically speaking."

"Green'd be a lot better than this," I said.

"You'll never be a true West Texan, Hildy," he told me, and smiled.

He set us down on the Columbia River, at the mouth of the gorge where it was wider and slower, on a broad, flat sandbar of an island which was the center of what he called an ecological test-bed. The beach was wide and hard-packed, full of frozen ripples. Across the river were the advertised pine trees, but near us there was only estuarine vegetation, the sort of plants that didn't mind being flooded periodically. It ran to tall skinny grasses and low, hardy bushes, few taller than my head. There were some really huge logs half buried in the sand, bleached gray-white and rubbed smooth and round by sun, wind, and water. I realized they were artificial, put there to impress the occasional visitors, who were always brought here.

We spread out a blanket on the sand and sat there gorging ourselves on the food. He stuck mostly to the shrimpoid tempura while I concentrated on the maguro, uni, hamachi, toro, tako, and paper-thin slices of fugu. I dredged each piece in enough of that wonderful green horseradish to make my nose run and my ears turn bright red. Then we made love again, slow and tender for the first hour, unusual for Fox, only getting intense near the end. We stretched out in the sun and never quite fell asleep, just lolling like satiated reptiles. At least I hadn't thought I was asleep until Fox woke me by flipping me over onto my stomach and entering me without any warning. (No, not that way. Fox likes to initiate it and he likes it rough, but he's not into giving pain and I'm not into receiving it.) Anyway, these things even out. When Fox was a girl she usually forced herself down on me before she was quite ready. Maybe he thought all girls liked it that way. I didn't enlighten him, because I didn't mind it that much and the lovemaking that followed was always Olympic quality.

And afterwards . . .

There's always an afterwards. Perhaps that's why my ten years with Fox was the longest relationship I ever had. After the sex, most of them want to talk to you, and I always had trouble finding people I wanted to talk to as well as have sex with. Fox was the exception. So afterwards . . .

I put the remains of my clothing back on. The dress was severely ripped; I couldn't get it to stay over my left breast, and there were gaping holes here and there. It suited my mood. We walked along the river's edge in water that never covered our feet. I was playing the castaway game. This time I could pretend to be a rich socialite in the tatters of her fancy gown, desperately seeking good native help. I trailed my toes in the water as I walked.

This place was timeless and unreal in a way Scarpa Island never was. The sun still hung there at high noon. I picked up a handful of sand and peered at it, and it was just as detailed as the imaginary sand of my year-long mental environment. It smelled different. It was riverine sand, not white coral, and the water was fresh instead of salty, with a different set of microscopic life-forms in it. The water was warmer than the Pacific waters. Hell, it was quite hot in Oregon, into the lower forties. Something to do with the construction. We had both dripped sweat all day. I had licked it off his body and found it quite tasty. Not so much the sweat as the body I licked it from.

The setting could not have been more perfect if I'd picked it myself.

Say, Fox, this place reminds me of an odd little adventure I had one day about a week ago, between 15:30.0002 P.M. and around, oh, let's say 15:30.0009. And isn't it amazing how time flies when you're having fun.

So I said something a little less puzzling than that, and gradually told him the story. Right up to the punch line, at which point I gagged on it.

Fox wasn't as reticent as Callie.

"I've heard of the technique, of course," he said. "I ought to be surprised you hadn't, but I guess you still shy away from technology, just like you used to."

"It's not very relevant to my job. Or my life."

"That's what you thought. It must seem more relevant now."

"Granted. It's never jumped up and bit me before."

"That's what I can't figure. What you describe is a radical treatment for mental problems. I can't imagine the CC using it on you without your consent unless you had something seriously wrong with you."

He let that hang, and once more I gagged. Give Fox points for candor; he didn't let a little thing like my obvious humiliation stand in his way.

"So what is your problem?" he asked, artless as a three-year-old.

"What's the penalty for littering in here?" I said.

"Go ahead. This whole area will be relandscaped before the public gets to track things in with their muddy feet."

I took off the ruined dress and balled it up as well as I could. I hurled it out toward the water. It ballooned, fell into the gentle current. We watched it float for a short distance, soak up water, and hang up on the bottom. Fox had said you could walk a hundred meters out from the island and not be in much deeper than your knees. After that it got deep quickly. We had come to the point where the island ended at the upstream end. We stood on the last little bit of sand and watched the current nudge the dress an inch at a time. I drew a ragged breath and felt a tear run down my cheek.

"If I'd known you felt *that* way about the dress, I'd never have torn it." When I glanced at him he took the tear on the tip of his finger and licked the finger with his tongue. I smiled weakly. I walked out into the water, heading upstream, and could hear him following behind me.

Some of it was the hormonal shock, I'm sure. I don't cry much, and no more when I'm female than when male. The Change probably released it, and it felt right; it was *time* to cry. It was time to admit how frightened I was by the whole thing.

I sat down in the warm water. It didn't cover my legs. I started working my hands into the sand on each side of me.

"It seems that I keep trying to kill myself," I said.

He was standing beside me. I looked up at him, wiped away another tear. God, he looked good. I wanted to move to him, make him ready again with my mouth, recline on this watery bed and have him move inside me with the slow, gentle rhythms of the river. Was that a life-affirming urge, or a death wish, metaphorically speaking? Was I in the river of life, or was I fantasizing about becoming part of the detritus that all rivers sweep eternally to the sea? There was no sea at the end of this river, just a deeper, saltier growing biome for the salmon that would soon teem here, struggling upstream to die. The sky the sun would wester and die in was a painted backdrop. Did the figures of speech of Old Earth still pertain here?

It *had* to be an image of life. I wasn't tired of livin', and I was very skeered of dyin'. He just keeps rolling, don't he? Isn't that what life's all about?

Be that as it may, Fox was not the man for gentle river rhythms, not twice in one day. He'd get carried away and in my present mood I would snap at him. So I kissed his leg and resumed my excavation work in the sand.

He sat down behind me and put his legs on each side of me and started massaging my shoulders. I don't think I ever loved him more than at that moment. It was exactly what I needed. I hung my head, went boneless as an eel, let him dig his strong fingers into every knot and twitch.

"Can I say . . . I don't want to hurt you, how should I say it? I *should* have been surprised to hear that. I mean, it's awful, it's unexpected, it's not something you want to hear from a dear friend, and I want to say 'No, Hildy, it *can't* be true!' You know? But I was surprised to find that . . . I *wasn't* surprised. What an awful thing to say."

"No, go ahead and say it," I murmured. His hands were working on my head now. Much more pressure and my skull would crack, and more power to him. Maybe some of the demons would fly away through the fissures.

"In some ways, Hildy, you've always been the unhappiest person I know."

I let that sink in without protest, just as I was sinking very slowly into the sand beneath me. I was a light brown sack of sand he was shaping with his fingers. I found nothing wrong with this sensation.

"I think it's your job," he said.

"Do you really?"

"It must have occurred to you. Tell me you love your work, and I'll shut up."

There was no sense saying anything to that.

"Not going to say anything about how good you are at reporting? No comments about how exciting it is? You are good, you know. Too good, in my opinion. Ever get anywhere on that novel?"

"Not so's you'd notice."

"What about working for another pad? One a little less interested in celebrity marriages and violent death."

"I don't think that would help anything; I never had much respect for journalism as a profession in the first place. At least the *Nipple* doesn't pretend to be anything but what it is."

"Pure shit."

"Exactly. I know you're right. I'm not happy in my work. I'm pretty sure I'm going to be quitting soon. All that stops me is I don't have any idea what I'd do as an alternative."

"I hear there's openings in the Coolie's Union. They won the contract for Borneo. The Hod-Carriers are still muttering about it."

"Nice to hear they get excited about something. Maybe I should," I said, half-seriously. "Less wear and tear on the nerves."

"It wouldn't work out. I'll tell you what your problem is, Hildy. You've always wanted to be . . . useful. You wanted to do something important."

"Make a difference? Change the world? I don't think so."

"I think you gave up on it before I met you. There's always been a streak of bitterness in you about that; it's one of the reasons we broke up."

"Really? Why didn't you tell me?"

"I'm not sure I knew it at the time."

We were both quiet for a while, tromping down memory lane. I was pleased to note that, even with this revelation, the memories were mostly good. He kept massaging me, pushing me forward now to get at my lower back. I offered no resistance, letting my head fall forward. I could see my hair trailing in the water. I wonder why people can't purr like cats? If I could have, I would have been at that moment. Maybe I should take it up with the CC. He could probably find a way to make it work.

He began to slow down in his work. No one ever wants that sort of thing to stop, but I knew his hands were tiring. I leaned back against him and he encircled me with his arms under my breasts. I put my hands on his knees.

"Can I ask you something?" I said.

"You know you can."

"What makes life worth living for you?"

He didn't give it a flip answer, which I'd half expected. He thought it over for a while, then sighed and rested his chin on my shoulder.

"I don't know if that's really answerable. There's surface reasons. The most obvious one is I get a sense of accomplishment from my work."

"I envy you that," I said. "Your work doesn't get erased after a ten-second read."

"There's disappointment there, too. I had sort of wanted to *build* these things." His arm swept out to take in the uncompleted vastness of Oregon. "Turned out my talents lay in other directions. *That* would be a sense of accomplishment, to leave something like this behind you."

"Is that the key? Leaving something behind? For 'posterity'?"

"Fifty years ago I might have said yes. And it's certainly *a* reason. I think it's *the* reason for most people who have the wit to ask what life's all about in the first place. I'm not sure if it's enough reason for me anymore. Not that I'm unhappy; I do love my work, I'm eager to arrive here every morning, I work late, I come in on weekends. But as to leaving something that I created, my work is even more ephemeral than yours."

"You're right," I said in considerable amazement. "I hadn't thought that was possible."

"See?" he laughed. "You learn something new every day. That's a reason for living. Maybe a trivial one. But I get satisfaction in the act of creation. It doesn't have to last. It doesn't have to have meaning."

"Art."

"I've begun to think in those terms. Maybe it's presumptuous, but we weatherfolks have started to get a following for what we do. Who knows where it might go? But creating something is pretty important to me." He hesitated, then plowed ahead. "There's another sort of creation."

I knew exactly what he meant. When all was said and done, that was the primary reason for our parting. He had had a child shortly afterward— I'd asked him never to tell me if I was the father. He had thought I should have one as well, and I had told him flatly it was none of his business.

"I'm sorry. Shouldn't have brought it up," he said.

"No, please. I asked; I have to be ready to hear the answers, even if I don't agree."

"And you don't?"

"I don't know. I've thought about it. As you must have guessed, I've been doing a lot of thinking about a lot of things."

"Then you'll have considered the negative reason for wanting to live. Sometimes I think it's the main one. I'm afraid of death. I don't know what it is, and I don't want to find out until the last possible moment."

"No heavenly harps to look forward to?"

"You can't be serious. Logically, you have to figure you just stop existing, just go out like a light. But I defy anyone to really imagine that. You know I'm not a mystic, but a long life has led me to believe, to my great bemusement, that I *do* believe there's something after death. I can't prove one iota of this feeling, and you can't budge me from it."

"I wouldn't try. On my better days, I feel the same way." I sighed one of the weariest sighs I can remember sighing. I'd been doing it a lot lately, each one wearier than the one before. Where would it end? Don't answer.

"So," I said. "We've got job dissatisfaction. Somehow I just don't think that's enough. There are simpler solutions to the problem. The restless urge to create. Childlessness." I was ticking them off on my fingers. Probably not a nice thing to do, since he'd tried his best. But I had hoped for some new perspective, which was entirely unreasonable but all the more disappointing when none appeared. "And fear of death. Somehow none of those really satisfy."

"I shouldn't say it, but I knew they wouldn't. Please, Hildy, get some professional counseling. There, I said it, I *had* to say it, but since I've known you for a long time and don't like to lie to you, I'll also say this: I don't think it will help you. You've never been one to accept somebody else's answers or advice. I feel in my gut that you'll have to solve this one on your own."

"Or not solve it. And don't apologize; you're completely right."

The river rolled on, the sun hung there in the painted sky. No time passed, and took a very long interval to do so. Neither of us felt the pressure to speak. I'd have been happy to spend the next decade there, as long as I didn't have to think. But I knew Fox would eventually get antsy. Hell, so would I.

"Can I ask you one more thing?"

He nibbled my ear.

"No, not that. Well, not yet, anyway." I tilted my head back and looked at him, inches away from my face. "Are you living with anyone?"

"No."

"Can I move in with you for a while? Say, a week? I'm very frightened and very lonely, Fox. I'm afraid to be alone."

He didn't say anything.

"I just want to sleep with somebody for a while. I don't want to beg."

"Let me think about it."

"Sure." It should have hurt, but oddly enough, it didn't. I knew I would have said the same thing. What I didn't know is how I would have decided. The bald truth was I was asking for his help in saving my life, and we both knew enough to realize there was little he could do but hug me. So if he *did* try to help and I *did* end up killing myself . . . that's a hell of a load of guilt to hazard without giving it a little thought. I could tell him there were no strings, that he needn't blame himself if the worst happened, but I knew he would and he knew I knew it, so I didn't insult him by telling him that lie and I didn't up the stakes by begging any more. Instead I nestled more firmly into his arms and watched the Columbia roll on, roll on.

We walked back to the trailer. Somewhere in the journey we noticed the river was no longer flowing. It became smooth and still, placid as a

long lake. It reflected the trees on the far side as faithfully as any mirror.
Fox said they'd been having trouble with some of the pumps. "Not my
department," he said, thankfully. It could have been pretty, but it gave me
a chilly feeling up and down the spine. It reminded me of the frozen sea
back at Scarpa Island.

Then he got a remote unit from the trailer and said he had something
to show me. He tapped out a few codes and my shadow began to move.

The sun scuttled across the sky like some great silver bird. The
shadow of each tree and bush and blade of grass marked its passage like
a thousand hourglasses. If you want to experience disorientation, give that
a try. I found myself getting dizzy, swayed and set my feet apart, discovered the whole thing was a lot more interesting when viewed from a sitting
position.

In a few minutes the sun went below the western horizon. That was
not what Fox had wanted to show me. Clouds were rising in that direction,
thin wispy ones, cirrus I think, or at least intended to look like cirrus. The
invisible sun painted them various shades of red and blue, hovering
somewhere just out of sight.

"Very pretty," I said.

"That's not it."

There was a distant boom, and a huge smoke ring rose slowly into the
sky, tinged with golden light. Fox was working intently. I heard a faraway
whistling sound, and the smoke ring began to alter in shape. The top was
pressed down, the bottom drawn out. I couldn't figure out what the point
of all this was, and then I saw it. The ring had formed a passable heart-
shape. A valentine. I laughed, and hugged him.

"Fox, you're a romantic fool after all."

He was embarrassed. He hadn't meant it to be taken that way—which
I had known, but he's easy to tease and I could never resist it. So he
coughed, and took refuge in technical explanation.

"I found out I could make a sort of backfire effect in that wind
machine," he said, as we watched the ring writhe into shapelessness.
"Then it's easy to use concentrated jets to mold it, within limits. Come back
here when we open up, and I'll be able to write your name in the sunset."

We showered off the sand and he asked if I'd like to see a scheduled
blast in Kansas. I'd never seen a nuke before, so I said yes. He flew the
trailer to a lock, and we emerged on the surface, where he turned control
over to the autopilot and told me about some of the things he'd been
doing in other Disneylands as we looked at the airless beauty falling away
beneath us.

Maybe you have to be there to appreciate Fox's weather sculpture. He
rhapsodized about ice storms and blizzards he'd created, and it meant
nothing to me. But he did pique my interest. I told him I'd attend his next

showing. I wondered if he was angling for coverage in the *Nipple*. Well, I've got a suspicious mind, and I'd been right about things like that often enough. I couldn't figure a way to make it interesting to my readership unless somebody famous attended, or something violent and horrible happened there.

Oregon was a showplace compared to Kansas. I'd like to have had a piece of the dust concession.

They were still in the process of excavation. The half-dome was nearly complete, with just some relatively small areas near the north edge to blast away. Fox said the best vantage point would be near the west edge; if we'd gone all the way to the south the dust would have obscured the blast too much to make the trip worthwhile. He landed the trailer near an untidy cluster of similar modular mobile homes and we joined a group of a few dozen other firework fans.

This show was strictly "to the trade." Everyone but me was a con-struction engineer; this sort of thing was not open to the public. Not that it was really rare. Kansas had required thousands of blasts like this, and would need about a hundred more before it was complete. Fox described it as the best-kept secret in Luna.

"It's not really much of a blast as these things go," he said. "The really big ones would jolt the structure too much. But when we're starting out, we use charges about ten times larger than this one."

I noticed the "we." He really did want to build these places instead of just install and run the weather machines.

"Is it dangerous?"

"That's sort of a relative question. It's not as safe as sleeping in your bed. But these things are calculated to a fare-thee-well. We haven't had a blasting accident in thirty years." He went on to tell me more than I'd wanted to know about the elaborate precautions, things like radar to detect big chunks of rock that might be heading our way, and lasers to vaporize them. He had me completely reassured, and then he had to go and spoil it.

"If I say run," he said, seriously, "hop in the trailer, pronto."

"Do I need to protect my eyes?"

"Clear leaded glass will do it. It's the UV that burns. Expect a certain dazzle effect at first. Hell, Hildy, if it blinds you the company's insurance will get you some new eyes."

I was perfectly happy with the eyes I had. I began to wonder if it had been such a good idea, coming here. I resolved to look away for the first several seconds. Common human lore was heavy with stories of what could happen to you in a nuclear explosion, dating all the way back to Old

Earth, when they'd used a few of them to fry their fellow beings by the millions.

The traditional countdown began at ten. I put on the safety glasses and closed my eyes at two. So naturally I opened them when the light shone through my eyelids. There was a dazzle, as he'd said, but my eyes quickly recovered. How to describe something that bright? Put all the bright lights you ever saw into one place, and it wouldn't begin to touch the intensity of that light. Then there was the ground shock, and the air shock, and finally, much later, the sound. I mean, I thought I'd been *hearing* the sound of it, but that was the shock waves emanating from the ground. The sound in the air was much more impressive. Then the wind. And the fiery cloud. The whole thing took several minutes to unfold. When the flames had died away there was a scattering of applause and a few shouts. I turned to Fox and grinned at him, and he was grinning, too.

Twenty kilometers away, a thousand people were already dead in what came to be called the Kansas Collapse.

10

THE QUEEN OF THE BRITISH EMPIRE

None of us were aware of the disaster at the time.

We drank a toast in champagne, a tradition among these engineering people. Within ten minutes Fox and I were back in the trailer and heading for an air lock. He said the fastest way back to King City was on the surface, and that was fine with me. I didn't enjoy driving through the system of tunnels that honeycombed the rock around a Disneyland.

We had no sooner emerged into the sunlight than the trailer was taken over by the autopilot, which informed us that we would have to enter a holding pattern or land, since all traffic was being cleared for emergency vehicles. A few of these streaked silently past us, blue lights flashing.

Neither of us could remember an emergency of this apparent size on the surface. There were occasional pressure losses in the warrens, of course. No system is perfect. But loss of life in these accidents was rare. So we turned on the radio, and what we heard sent me searching through Fox's belongings in the back of the trailer until I came up with a newspad. It was *The Straight Shit,* and in other circumstances I would have teased him unmercifully about that. But the story that came over the pad was the type that made any snide remarks die in one's throat.

There had been a major blowout at a surface resort called Nirvana. First reports indicated some loss of life, and live pictures from security cameras—all that was available for the first ten minutes we watched—

showed bodies lying motionless by a large swimming pool. The pool was bubbling violently. At first we thought it was a big Jacuzzi, then we realized with a shock that the water was boiling. Which meant there was no air in there, and those people were certainly dead. Their postures were odd, too. They all seemed to be holding on to something, such as a table leg or a heavy concrete planter with a palm tree.

A story like that evolves in its own fractured way. First reports are always sketchy, and usually wrong. We heard estimates of twenty dead, then fifty, then, spoken in awe, two hundred. Then those reports were denied, but I had counted thirty corpses myself. It was maddening. We're spoiled by instant coverage, we expect news stories to be cogent, prompt, and nicely framed by steady cameras. These cameras were steady, all right. They were immobile, and after a few minutes your mind *screamed* for them to pan, just a little bit, so you could see what was just out of sight. But that didn't happen until about ten minutes after we landed, ten minutes that seemed like an hour.

At first I think it affected me more than Fox. He was shocked and horrified, naturally, and so was I, on one level. The other level, the newshound, was seething with impatience, querying the autopilot three times a minute when we could get up and *out* of there so I could go cover the story. It's not pretty, I know, but any reporter will understand the impulse. You want to *move*. You tuck the horror of the images away in some part of your mind where police and coroners put ugly things, and your pulse pounds with impatience to get the next detail, and the next, and the next. To be stuck on the ground fifteen klicks away was torture of the worst kind.

Then a fact was mentioned that made it all too real for Fox. I didn't catch its importance. I just looked over at him and saw his face had gone white and his hands were trembling.

"What's the matter?" I said.

"The time," he whispered. "They just mentioned the time of the blowout."

I listened, and the announcer said it again.

"Was that . . . ?"

"Yes. It was within a second of the blast."

I was still so preoccupied with wanting to get to Nirvana that it was a full minute before I realized what I *should* be doing. Then I turned on Fox's phone and called the *Nipple,* using my second-highest urgency code to guarantee quick access to Walter. The top code, he had told me, was reserved for filing on the end of the universe, or an exclusive interview with Elvis.

"Walter, I've got footage of the cause of the blowout," I said, when his ugly face appeared on the screen.

"The cause? You were *there?* I thought everybody—"

"No, I wasn't there. I was in Kansas. I have reason to believe the disaster was set off by a nuclear explosion I was watching in Kansas."

"It sounds unlikely. Are you sure—"

"Walter, it *has* to be, or else it's the biggest coincidence since that straight flush I beat your full house with."

"That was no coincidence."

"Damn right it wasn't, and someday I'll tell you how I did it. Meantime, you've wasted twenty seconds of valuable newstime. Run it with a disclaimer if you want to, you know, 'Could this have been the cause of the tragedy in Nirvana?' "

"Give it to me."

I fumbled around on the dash, and swore under my breath. "Where's the neurofeed on this damn thing?" I asked Fox. He was looking at me strangely, but he pulled a wire from a recessed compartment. I fumbled it into my occipital socket, and said the magic words that caused the crystalline memory to recycle and spew forth the last six hours of holocam recordings in five seconds.

"Where the hell are you, anyway?" Walter was saying. "I've had a call out for you for twenty minutes."

I told him, and he said he'd get on it. Thirty seconds later the autopilot was cleared into the traffic pattern. The press has some clout in situations like this, but I hadn't been able to apply it from my beached position. We rose into the sky . . . and turned the wrong way.

"What the hell are you doing?" I asked Fox, incredulously.

"Going back to King City," he said, quietly. "I have no desire to witness any of what we've seen firsthand. And I especially don't want to witness you covering it."

I was about to blast him out of his seat, but I took another look, and he looked dangerous. I had the feeling that one more word from me would unleash something I didn't want to hear, and maybe even more than that. So I swallowed it, mentally calculating how long it would take me to get back to Nirvana from the nearest King City air lock.

With a great effort I pulled myself out of reportorial mode and tried to act like a human being. Surely I could do it for a few minutes, I thought.

"You can't be thinking you had anything to do with this," I said. He kept his eyes forward, as if he really had to see where the trailer was going. "You told me yourself—"

"Look, Hildy. I didn't set the charge, I didn't do the calculations. But some of my friends did. And it's going to reflect on all of us. Right now I have to get onto the phone, we're going to have to try and find out what went wrong. And I do feel responsible, so don't try to argue me out of it, because I know it isn't logical. I just wish you wouldn't talk to me right now."

I didn't. A few minutes later he smashed his fist into the dashboard and said, "I keep remembering us standing around watching. Cheering. I can still taste the champagne."

I got out at the air lock, flagged a taxi, and told it to take me to Nirvana.

Most disasters look eminently preventable in hindsight. If only the warnings had been heeded, if only this safety measure had been implemented, if only somebody had thought of this possibility, if only, if only. I exempt the so-called acts of God, which used to include things like earthquakes, hurricanes, and meteor strikes. But hurricanes are infrequent on Luna. Moon quakes are almost as rare, and selenography is exact enough to predict them with a high degree of accuracy. Meteors come on very fast and very hard, but their numbers are small and their average size is tiny, and all vulnerable structures are ringed with radars powerful enough to detect any dangerous ones and lasers big enough to vaporize them. The last blowout of any consequence had happened almost sixty years before the Kansas Collapse. Lunarians had grown confident of their safety measures. We had grown complacent enough to overcome our innate suspicion of vacuum and the surface, some of us, to the point where the rich now frolicked and tanned in the sunlight beneath domes designed to give the impression they weren't even there. If someone had built a place like Nirvana a hundred years ago there would have been few takers. Back then the rich peopled only the lowest, most secure levels and the poor took their chances with only eight or nine pressure doors between them and the Breathsucker.

But a century of technological improvements, of fail-safe systems that transcended the merely careful and entered the realms of the preposterous, of pyramided knowledge of how to live in a hostile environment . . . a hundred years of this had worked a sea change on Lunar society. The cities had turned over, like I've heard lakes do periodically, and the bottom had risen to the top. The formerly swank levels of Bedrock were now the slums, and the Vac Rows in the upper levels were now—suitably renovated—the place to be. Anyone who aspired to be somebody had to have a real window on the surface.

There were some exceptions. Old reactionaries like Callie still liked to burrow deep, though she had no horror of the surface. And a significant minority still suffered from that most common Lunar phobia, fear of airlessness. They managed well enough, I suppose. I've read that a lot of people on Old Earth feared high places or flying in aircraft, which must have been a problem in a society that valued the penthouse apartment and quick travel.

Nirvana was not the most exclusive surface resort on Luna, but it wasn't the type hawked in three-day two-night package deals, either. I've never understood the attraction of paying an exorbitant amount for a "natural" view of the surface while basking in the carefully filtered rays of the sun. I'd much prefer just about any of the underground Disneys. If you wanted a swimming pool, there were any number belowground where the water was just as wet. But some people find simulated Earth environments frightening. A surprising number of people just don't like plants, or the insects that hide themselves among the leaves, and have no real use for animals, either. Nirvana catered to these folks, and to the urge to be seen with other people who had enough money to blow in a place like that. It featured gambling, dancing, tanning, and some amazingly childish games organized by the management, all done under the sun or the stars in the awesome beauty of Destination Valley.

And it had damn well better be awesome. The builders had spent a huge amount of money to make it that way.

Destination Valley was a three-kilometer Lunar rift that had been artfully carved into the kind of jagged peaks and sheer cliffs that a valley on "The Moon" *should* have been, if God had employed a more flamboyant set designer, the sort of lunar features everybody imagined before the opening of the age of space and the return of the first, dismal pictures of what Luna really looked like. There were no acned rolling hillocks here, no depressing gray-and-white fields of scoria, no boulders with all the edges rubbed off by a billion years of scorching days and bitter cold nights . . . and none of that godawful boring *dust* that covers everything else on Luna. Here the craters had sharp edges lined with jagged teeth. The cliffs soared straight up, *loomed* over you like breaking waves. The boulders were studded with multicolored volcanic glasses that shattered the raw sunlight into a thousand colors or glowed with warm ruby red or sapphire blue as if lit from within—which some of them were. Strange crystalline growths leaped toward the sky or spread across the ground like sinister deep-sea creatures, quartzes the size of ten-story buildings embedded themselves in the ground as if dropped from a great height, and feathery structures with hairs finer than fiber optics, so fragile they would break in the exhaust from a passing pressure suit, clung like sea urchins and glowed in the dark. The horizon was sculpted with equal care into a range to shame the Rockies for sheer rugged beauty . . . until you hiked into them and found they were quite puny, magnified by cunning lighting and tricks of forced perspective.

But the valley floor was a rockhound's dream. It was like walking into a mammoth geode. And it was all the naked geology that, in the end, had proven to be the downfall of Nirvana.

One of the four main pleasure domes had nestled at the foot of a cliff called, in typical breathless Nirvanan prose, The Threshold Of Heavenly Peace. It had been formed of seventeen of the largest, clearest quartz columns ever synthesized, and the whole structure had been rat-nested with niches for spotlights, lasers, and image projectors. During the day it did nice things with the sunlight, but the real show was at night, when light shows ran constantly. The effect had been designed to be soothing, relaxing, suggesting the eternal peace of some unspecified heaven. The images that could be seen within were not well-defined. They were almost-seen, just out of sight, elusive, and hypnotic. I'd been at the opening show, and for all my cynicism about the place itself, had to admit that the Threshold was almost worth the price of a ticket.

The detonation in Kansas had nudged an unmapped fault line a few klicks from Nirvana, resulting in a short, sharp quake that lifted Destination Valley a few centimeters and set it down with a thud. The only real damage done to the place, other than a lot of broken crockery, was that one of the columns had been shaken loose and crashed down on Dome #3, known as the Threshold Dome. The dome was thick, and strong, and transparent, with no ugly geodesic lines to mar the view, having been formed from a large number of hexagonal components bonded together in a process that was discussed endlessly in the ensuing weeks, and which I don't understand at all. It was further strengthened by some sort of molecular field intensifier. It should have been strong enough to withstand the impact of Tower #14, at least long enough to evacuate the dome. And it had, for about five seconds. But some sort of vibration was set up in the dome material, and somehow magnified by the field intensifier, and three of the four-meter hex panels on the side *away* from the cliffs had fractured along the join lines and been blown nearly into orbit by the volume of air trying to get through that hole. Along with the air had gone everything loose, including all the people who weren't holding on to something, and many who were. It must have been a hell of a wind. Some of the bodies were found up on the rim of the valley.

By the time I got there most of the action was long over. A blowout is like that. There's a few minutes when a person exposed to raw vacuum can be saved; after that, it's time for the coroner. Except for a few people trapped in self-sealing rooms who would soon be extricated—and no amount of breathless commentary could make these routine operations sound exciting—the rest of the Collapse story was confined to ogling dead bodies and trying to find an angle.

The bodies definitely were *not* the story. Your average *Nipple* reader enjoys blood and gore, but there is a disgust threshold that might be defined as the yuck factor. Burst eyeballs and swollen tongues are all right, as is any degree of laceration or dismemberment. But the thing about a blow-out death is, the human body has a certain amount of gas in it, in various cavities. A lot of it is in the intestine. What happens when that gas expands explosively and comes rushing out its natural outlet is not something to use as a lead item in your coverage. We *showed* the bodies, you couldn't help that, we just didn't *dwell* on them.

No, the real story here was the same story any time there is a big disaster. Number two: children. Number three: tragic coincidences. And always a big number one: celebrities.

Nirvana didn't cater to children. They didn't forbid them, they just didn't encourage mommy and daddy to bring little junior along, and most of the clientele wouldn't have done so, anyway. I mean, what would that say about your relationship with the nanny? Only three children died in the Kansas Collapse—which simply made them that much more poignant in the eyes of the readership. I tracked down the grandparents of one three-year-old and got a genuine reaction shot when they learned the news about the child's death. I needed a stiff drink or two after that one. Some things a reporter does are slimier than others.

Then there's the "if-only" story, with the human angle. "We were planning to spend the week at Nirvana, but we didn't go because blah blah blah." "I just went back to the room to get my thingamabob when the next thing I knew all the alarms were going off and I thought, where's my darling hubby?" The public had an endless appetite for stories like that. Subconsciously, I think *they* think the gods of luck will favor *them* when the tromp of doom starts to thump. As for survivor interviews, I find them very boring, but I'm apparently in the minority. At least half of them had this to say: "God was watching over me." Most of those people didn't even *believe* in a god. This is the deity-as-hit-man view of theology. What I always thought was, if God was looking out for *you,* he must have had a real hard-on for all those folks he belted into the etheric like so many rubbery javelins.

Then there were the handful of stories that didn't quite fit any of these categories, what I call heart-warming tragedies. The best to come out of Nirvana was the couple of lovers found two kilometers from the blowout, still holding hands. Given that they'd been blown through the hole in the dome, their bodies weren't in the best shape, but that was okay, and since they'd outdistanced the stream of brown exhaust that no doubt would have seemed to be propelling them on their way, had anyone survived to report on *that* improbable event, they were quite presentable. They were just lying there, two guys with sweet smiles on their faces, at the base of a rock formation the photographer had managed to frame to resemble a church window. Walter paid through the nose to run it on his front feed, just like all the other editors.

The reporter on that story was my old rival Cricket, and it just goes to show you what initiative can accomplish. While the rest of us were standing around the ruins of Dome #3, picking our journalistic noses, Cricket hired a p-suit and followed the recovery crews out into the field, bringing an actual film camera for maximum clarity. She'd bribed a team to delay recovery of the pair until she could fix smiles on the faces and pick up the popped-out eyeballs and close the eyelids. She knew what she wanted in that picture, and what it got her was a nomination for the Pulitzer Prize that year.

But the big story was the dead celebs. Of the one thousand, one hundred and twenty-six dead in Nirvana, five had been Important in one way or another. In ascending order of magnitude, they were a politician from Clavius District, a visiting pop singer from Mercury, a talk-show host and hostess, and Larry Yeager, whose newest picture's release date was moved up three weeks to cash in on all the public mourning. His career had been in decline or he wouldn't have been at Nirvana in the first place, but while being seen alive in a place like that was a definite indicator that one's star was imploding, soon to be a black hole—Larry had formerly moved in only the most rarefied orbits—*where* you die is not nearly as important to a posthumous career as *how* you die. Tragically is best. Young is good. Violently, bizarrely, notoriously . . . all these things combined in the Kansas Collapse to boost the market value of the Yeager Estate's copyrights to five times their former market value.

Of course there was the other story. The "how" and the "why." I'm always much more concerned in where, when, and who. Covering the investigations into the Collapse, as always, would be an endless series of boring meetings and hours and hours of testimony about matters I was not technologically equipped to handle anyway. The final verdict would not be in for months or years, at which time the *Nipple* would be interested in "who" once more, as in "Who takes the fall for this fuck-up?" In the meantime the *Nipple* could indulge in ceaseless speculation, character assassination, and violence to many reputations, but that wasn't my department. I read this stuff uneasily every day, fearing that Fox's name would somehow come up, but it never did.

What with one thing and another . . . mostly bothering widows and orphans, I am forced to admit . . . the Collapse kept me hopping for about a week. I indulged in a lot of mind-numbing preparations, mostly margaritas, my poison of choice, and kept a nervous weather eye open for signs of impending depression. I saw some—there's no way you can cover a story like that without feeling grief yourself, and a certain self-loathing from time to time—but I never got really *depressed,* as in good-bye-cruel-world depressed.

I concluded that keeping busy was the best therapy.

One of the one thousand, one hundred and twenty-one other people who died in Nirvana was the mother of the Princess of Wales, the King of England, Henry XI. In spite of his impressive title, Hank had never in his life done anything worth a back-feed article in the *Nipple,* until he died. And that's where the obit ran, the back-feed, with a small "isn't it ironic" graph by a cub reporter mentioning a few of his more notorious relatives: Richard III, Henry VIII, Mary Stuart. Walter blue-penciled most of it for the next edition, with the immortal words "nobody gives a shit about all that Shakespearean crap," and substituted a sidebar about Vickie Hanover and her weird ideas about sex that influenced an entire age.

The only reason Henry XI was in Nirvana in the first place was that he was in charge of the plumbing in Dome #3. Not the air system; the sewage.

But the upshot was that, on my first free day since the disaster, my phone informed me that someone not on my "accept-calls" list wanted to speak to me, and was identifying herself as Elizabeth Saxe-Coburg-Gotha. I drew a blank for a moment, then realized it was the terrifying fighting machine I had known as Wales. I let the call through.

She spent the first few minutes apologizing all over again, asking if her check had arrived, and please call me Liz.

"Reason I called," she finally said, "I don't know if you heard, but my mother died in the Nirvana disaster."

"I did know that. I'm sorry, I should have sent a condolence card or something."

"That's okay. You don't really know me well enough, and I hated the boozing son of a bitch anyway. He made my life hell for many years. But now that he's finally gone . . . see, I'm having this sort of coronation party tomorrow and I wondered if you'd like to come? And a guest, too, of course."

I wondered if the invitation was the result of continuing guilt over the way she'd torn me apart, or if she was angling for coverage in the pad. But I didn't mention either of those things. I was about to beg off, then remembered there had been something I'd wanted to talk to her about. I accepted.

"Oh," I said, as she was about to ring off. "Ah, what about dress? Should it be formal?"

"Semi," she said. "No need for any full uniforms. And the reception afterward will be informal. Just a party, really. Oh, and no gifts." She laughed. "I'm only supposed to accept gifts from other heads of state."

"That lets me out. See you tomorrow."

The Royal Coronation was held in Suite #2 of the spaceport Howard's Hotel, a solidly middle-class hostelry favored by traveling salespeople and business types just in King City for the day. I was confronted at the door by a man in a red-and-black military uniform that featured a fur hat almost a meter high. I vaguely recalled the outfit from historical romances. He was rigidly at attention beside a guardhouse about the size of a coffin standing on end. He glanced at my faxed invitation, opened the door for me, and the familiar roar of a party in progress spilled into the hall.

Liz had managed a pretty good turnout. Too bad she couldn't have afforded to hire a bigger hall. People were standing elbow to elbow, trying to balance tiny plates of olives and crackers with cheese and anchovy paste in one hand and paper cups of punch and champagne in the other while being jostled from all sides. I sidled my way to the food, as is my wont when it's free, and scanned it dubiously. UniBio set a better table, I must say. Drinks were being poured by two men in the most *outrageous* outfits. I won't even attempt to describe them. I later learned they were called Beefeaters, for reasons that will remain forever obscure to me.

Not that my own clothes were anything to shout about. She'd said semi-formal, so I could have gotten away with just the gray fedora and the press pass stuck in the brim. But upon reflection I decided to go with the whole silly ensemble, handing the baggy pants and double-breasted suit coat to the auto-valet with barely enough time for alterations. I left the seat and the legs loose and didn't button the coat; that was part of the look my guild, in its infinite wisdom, had voted on almost two hundred years ago when professional uniforms were being chosen. It had been taken from newspaper movies of the 1930s. I'd viewed a lot of them, and was amused at the image my fellow reporters apparently wanted to project at formal events: rumpled, aggressive, brash, impolite, wisecracking, but with hearts o' gold when the goin' got tough. Sure, and it made yer heart proud ta be a reporter, by the saints. For a little fun, I'd worn a white blouse with a bunch of lace at the neck instead of the regulation ornamental noose known as a necktie. And I'd tied my hair up and stuffed it under the hat. In the mirror I'd looked just like Kate Hepburn masquerading as a boy, at least from the neck up. From there down the suit hung on me like a tent, but such was the cunning architecture of my new body that *anything* looked good on it. I'd saluted my image in the mirror: here's lookin' at *you*, Bobbie.

Liz spotted me and made her way toward me with a shout. She was already half looped. If her late mother had given her nothing else, she had seemingly inherited his taste for the demon rum. She embraced me and thanked me for coming, then swirled off again into the crowd. Well, I'd corner her later, after the ceremony, if she could still stand up by then.

What followed hasn't changed much in four or five hundred years. For almost an hour people kept arriving, including the hotel manager who had a hasty conference with Liz—concerning her credit rating, I expect—and then opened the connecting door to Suite #1, which relieved the pressure for a while. The food and champagne ran out, and was replenished. Liz didn't care about the cost. This was her day. It was your prototypical daytime party.

I met several people I knew, was introduced to dozens whose names I promptly forgot. Among my new friends were the Shaka of the Zulu Nation, the Emperor of Japan, the Maharajah of Gujarat, and the Tsarina of All the Russias, or at least people in silly costumes who styled themselves that way. Also countless Counts, Caliphs, Archdukes, Satraps, Sheiks, and Nabobs. Who was I to dispute their titles? There had been a vogue in such genealogy about the time Callie had grudgingly expelled my ungrateful squalling form into a less-than-overwhelmed world; Callie had even told me she thought she might be related to Mussolini, on her mother's side. Did that make me the heir-apparent of *Il Duce?* It wasn't a burning question to me. I overheard intense debates about the rules of primogeniture—even Salic Law, of all things—in an age of sex changing. Someone—I think it was the Duke of York—gave me a lecture about it shortly before the ceremony, explaining why Liz was inheritor to the throne, even though she had a younger brother.

After escaping from *that* with most of my wits intact, I found myself out on the balcony, nursing a strawberry margarita. Howard's had a view, but it was of the cargo side of the spaceport. I looked out over the beached-whale hulks of bulk carriers expelling their interplanetary burdens into waiting underground tanks. I was almost alone, which puzzled me for a moment, until I remembered a story I'd seen about how many people had suddenly lost their taste for surface views in the wake of the Kansas Collapse. I drained my drink, reached out and tapped the invisible curved canopy that held vacuum at bay, and shrugged. Somehow I didn't think I'd die in a blowout. I had worse things to fear.

Somebody held out another pink drink with salt on the rum. I took it and looked over and up—and up and up—into the smiling face of Brenda, girl reporter and apprentice giraffe. I toasted her.

"Didn't expect to see you here," I said.

"I got acquainted with the Princess after your . . . accident."

"That was no accident."

She prattled on about what a nice party it was. I didn't disillusion her. Wait till she'd attended a few thousand more just like it, then she'd see.

I'd been curious what Brenda's reaction would be to my new sex. To my chagrin, she was delighted. I got the skinney from a homo-oriented friend at the fashion desk: Brenda was young enough to still be exploring her own sexuality, discovering her preferences. She'd already been pretty sure she leaned toward females as lovers, at least when *she* was a woman. Discovering her preferences as a male would have to wait for her first Change. After all, until quite recently she'd been effectively neuter. The only problem she'd had in her crush on me was that she wasn't much attracted to males. She had thought it would remain platonic until I thoughtfully made everything perfect by showing up at work as my gorgeous new self.

I really, *really* didn't have the heart to tell her about *my* preferences.

And I did owe her. She had been covering for me, putting my byline on the Invasion Bicentennial stories she was writing, the stories I simply could no longer bring myself to work on. Oh, I was helping, answering her questions, going over her drafts, punching up the prose, showing her how to leave just enough excess baggage in the stories so Walter would have something to cut out and shout at her about and thus remain a happy man. I think Walter was beginning to suspect what was going on, but he hadn't said anything yet because expecting me to cover the Collapse *and* get in our weekly feature was unfair, and he knew it. The thing he should have foreseen before he ever came up with his cockamamie Invasion series was that there would *always* be a story like the Collapse happening, and as a good editor he *had* to assign his best people to it, which included me. Oh, yeah, if you wanted somebody to intrude on grief and ogle bodies puffed up like pink and brown popcorn, Hildy was your girl.

"Tell me, sweetheart, how did you feel when you saw the man cut your daddy's head off?"

"*What?*" Brenda was looking at me strangely.

"It's the essential disaster/atrocity question," I said. "They don't tell you that in Journalism 101, but all the questions we ask, no matter how delicately phrased, boil down to that. The idea is to get the first appearance of the tear, the ineffable moment when the face twists up. That's gold, honey. You'd better learn how to mine it."

"I don't think that's true."

"Then you'll never be a great reporter. Maybe you should try social work."

I saw that I had hurt her, and it made me angry, both at her and at myself. She had to understand these things, dammit. But who appointed *you,* Hildy? She'll find out soon enough, as soon as Walter takes her off these damn comparative anthropology stories that our readers don't even want to *see* and lets her get out where she can grub in the dirt like the rest of us.

I realized I'd drunk a little more than I had intended. I dumped the rest of my drink in a thirsty-looking potted plant, snagged a Coke from a passing tray, and performed a little ritual I'd come to detest but was powerless to stop. It consisted of a series of questions, like this: Do you feel the urge to hurl yourself off this balcony, assuming you could drill a hole through that ultralexan barrier? No. Great, but do you want to throw a rope over that beam and haul yourself up into the rafters? Not today, thank you. And so on.

I was about to say something nice and neutral and soothing, suitable for the reassurance of idealistic cub reporters, when the Jamaican steel band, which had been reprising every patriotic British song since the Spanish Armada, suddenly struck up *God Save The Queen,* and somebody asked everyone to haul their drunken asses down to the main ballroom, where the coronation was about to commence. Not in those words, of course.

There was another band in the ballroom, playing some horrible modern version of *Rule Britannia.* This was the public portion of the show, and I guess Liz thought it ought to make some attempt to appeal to the tastes of the day. I thought the music was dreadful, but Brenda was snapping her fingers, so I suppose it was at least current.

A few specialty channels and some of the pads had sent reporters, but the crowd in the ballroom was essentially the same folks I'd been avoiding up in the Suites one and two, only they weren't holding drinks. A lot of them looked as if they wished the show would hurry up, so they *could* hold drinks again, for a short time, at least.

One touch Liz hadn't expected was the decorations. From the whispers I overheard, she'd only booked the hall for one hour. When the coronation was over a wedding party was scheduled to hold a reception there, so the walls were draped in white bunting and repulsive little cherubs, and there was a big sign hung on the wall that said *Mazel Tov!* Liz looked a little nonplussed. She glanced around with that baffled expression one sometimes gets after wandering into a strange place. Could there have been a mistake?

But the coronation itself went off without a hitch. She was proclaimed "Elizabeth III, by the Grace of God of the United Kingdom of Great Britain, Scotland, Wales, and Ireland and of her other Realms and Territories, Queen, Empress of India, Head of the Commonwealth and Defender of the Faith."

Sure, it was easy to snicker, and I did, but to myself. I could see that Liz took it seriously, almost in spite of herself. No matter how spurious the claims of some of these other clowns might have been to ancient titles, Liz's was spotless and unquestioned. The actual Prince of Wales had been living and working on Luna at the time of the Invasion, and she was descended from him.

The original Crown Jewels had naturally not accompanied the King in Exile to Luna; they were buried with the rest of London—of England, of Europe, of the whole surface of Planet Earth. Liz had the use of a very nice crown, orb, and sceptre. Hovering in the background as these items were produced was a man from Tiffany's. Not the one in the Platz, but the discount outlet down on Leystrasse, where even as the tiara was lowered onto Liz's head a sign was going up announcing "By Appointment to Her Majesty, The Queen." The jewels were hired, and would soon reside in a window advertising the usual E-Z Credit Terms.

A procession was traditional after a coronation back when the Empire had any real meaning—and even after it had become just a tourist attraction. But processions can be difficult to organize in the warrens of Luna, where the cities are usually broken up into pressure-defensible malls and arcades connected by tube trains. So after the ceremony we all straggled into a succession of subway cars and zipped across town to Liz's neighborhood, many of us growing steadily more sober and unsure why we'd come in the first place.

But all was well. The *real* party began when we arrived at the post-coronation reception, held in the Masonic Lodge Hall halfway between Liz's apartment and the studio where she worked. In addition to its many other virtues the lodge didn't cost her anything, which meant she could spend what royal budget she had left entirely on food, booze, and entertainment.

This bash was informal and relaxed, the only kind I enjoy. The band was good, playing a preponderance of things from Liz's teenage years, which put them midway between my era and Brenda's. It was stuff I could dance to. So I stumbled out into the public corridor in my two-tone Oxford lace-ups—and a clunkier shoe has never been invented—found a mail box and called my valet. I told it to pack up the drop-dead shiny black sheath dress slit from the ankles to you-should-only-blush and tube it over to me. I went into the public comfort station and changed my hair color to platinum and put a long wave in it, and when I came out, three minutes later, the package was waiting for me. I stripped out of the Halloween costume and stuffed it into the return capsule, cajoled my abundance into the outfit's parsimonious interior. Just getting into that thing was almost enough to give you an orgasm. I left my feet bare. And to hell with Kate Hepburn; Veronica Lake was on the prowl.

I danced almost nonstop for two hours. I had one dance with Liz, but she was naturally much in demand. I danced with Brenda, who was a very good if visually unlikely terpsichorean. Mostly I danced with a succession of men, and I turned down a dozen interesting offers. I'd selected my eventual target, but I was in no hurry unless he suddenly decided to leave.

He didn't. When I was ready I cut him out of the herd. I put a few moves on him, mostly in the form of dance steps whose meaning couldn't have been missed by a eunuch. He wanted to join the rather sparsely-attended orgy going on in one corner of the ballroom, but I dragged him off to what the Masons called, too coyly in my opinion, snuggle rooms. We spent a very enjoyable hour in one of them. He liked to be spanked, and bitten. It's not my thing, but I can accommodate most consenting adults as long as my needs are attended to as well. He did a very good job of that. His name was Larry, and he claimed to be the Duke of Bosnia-Her-zegovina, but that might have been just to get into my pants. The couple of times I drew blood he asked me to do it again, so I did, but eventually lost my . . . well, my taste for that sort of thing. We exchanged phone codes and said we'd look each other up, but I didn't intend to. He was nice to look at but I felt I'd chewed off about as much as I wanted.

I staggered back into the ballroom drenched in sweat. It had been *very* intense there for a while. I headed for the bar, dodging dancers. The fainthearted had left, leaving about half the original attendees, but those looked ready to party till Monday morning. I eased my pinkened, pleasantly sore cheeks onto a padded barstool next to the Queen of England, the Empress of India, and the Defender of the Faith, and Liz slowly turned her head toward me. I now knew where her impressive ears came from. There were posters of past monarchs taped to the walls here, and she was the spitting image of Charles III.

"Innkeeper," she shouted, above the music. "Bring me salt. Bring me tequila. Bring me the nectar of the lime, your plumpest strawberries, your coldest ice, your finest crystal. My friend needs a drink, and I intend to build it for her."

"Ain't got no strawberries," the bartender said.

"Then go out and kill some!"

"It's all right, Your Majesty," I said. "Lime will be fine."

She grinned foolishly at me. "I purely do like the sound of that. 'Your Majesty.' Is that awful?"

"You're entitled, as they say. But don't expect me to make a habit of it." She draped an arm over my shoulder and exhaled ethanol.

"How are you, Hildy? Having a good time? Getting laid?"

"Just did, thank you."

"Don't thank me. And you look it, honey, if I may say so."

"Didn't have time to freshen up yet."

"You don't need to. Who did the work?"

I showed her the monogram on the nail of my pinky. She squinted at it, and seemed to lose interest, which might have meant that Bobbie's fears of falling out of fashion were well-grounded—Liz would be up on these things—or only that her attention span was not what it might be.

"What was I gonna say? Oh, yeah. Can I *do* anything for you, Hildy? There's a tradition among my people . . . well, maybe it's not an English tradition, but it's *somebody's* damn tradition, what you gotta do is, anybody asks you for a favor on your coronation day, you gotta grant it."

"I think that's a Mafia tradition."

"Is it? Well, it's *your* people, then. So just ask. Only be real, okay? I mean, if it's gonna cost a lot of money, forget it. I'm gonna be payin' for this fucking shivaree for the next ten fucking years. But that's okay. It's only money, right? And what a party. Am I right?"

"As a matter of fact, there is something you could do for me."

I was about to tell her, but the bartender delivered a margarita in its component parts, and Liz could only think about one thing at a time. She spilled a lot of salt on the bar, spread it out, moistened the rim of a wide glass, and did things necessary to produce a too-strong concoction with that total concentration of the veteran drunk. She did it competently, and I sipped at the drink I hadn't really wanted.

"So. Name it, kiddo, and it's yours. Within reason."

"If you . . . let's say . . . if you wanted to have a conversation with somebody, and you wanted to be sure no one would overhear it . . . what would you do? How would you go about it?"

She frowned and her brow furrowed. She appeared to be thinking heavily, and her hand toyed with the layer of salt in front of her.

"Now that's a good one. That's a real good one. I'm not sure if anyone's ever asked me that before." She looked slowly down at the salt, where her finger had traced out *CC??*. I looked up at her, and nodded.

"You know what bugs are like these days. I'm not sure if there's *any* place that can't be bugged. But I'll tell you what. I know some techs back at the studio, they're real clever about these things. I could ask them and get back to you." Her hand had wiped out the original message and written *p-suit.* I nodded again, and saw that while she was without a doubt very, very drunk, she knew how to handle herself. There was a glint of speculation in those eyes I wasn't sure I liked. I wondered what I might be getting myself into.

We talked a while longer, and she wrote out a time and a destination in the salt crystals. Then someone else sat next to her and started fondling her breasts and she was showing a definite interest, so I got up and returned to the dance floor.

I danced almost an hour longer, but my heart wasn't really in it. A guy made a play for me, and he was pretty, and persuasive, and a very good, raunchy dancer, but in the end I felt he just didn't try hard enough. When I'm not the aggressor I can choose to take a lot of persuading. In the end I gave him my phone code and said call me in a week and we'd see, and got the impression he probably wouldn't.

I showered and bought a paper chemise in the locker room, staggered to the tube terminal, and got aboard. I fell asleep on the way home, and the train had to wake me up.

11

THE FIRST MAN ON THE MOON

I've read about hangovers. You just about have to believe those people were exaggerating. If only a tenth of the things written about them were true, I have no desire to experience one. The hangover was cured long before I was born, just a simple chemical matter, really, no tough science involved. I'd sometimes wondered if that was a good idea. There's an almost biblical belief deep in the human psyche that we should pay in some way for our overindulgences. But when I think that, my rational side soon takes over. Might as well wish for the return of the hemorrhoid.

When I woke up the next morning, my mouth tasted good.

Too good.

"CC, on line," quoth I.

"What can I do for you?"

"What's with the peppermint?"

"I thought you liked peppermint. I can change the flavor."

"There's nothing wrong with peppermint *qua* peppermint. It's just passing strange to wake up with my mouth tasting like *anything* but . . . well, it wouldn't mean anything to you, I don't guess taste is one of your talents, but take my word for it, it's vile."

"You asked me to work on that. I did."

"Just like that?"

"Why not?"

I was about to answer, but Fox stirred in his sleep and turned over,

179

so I got out of bed and went into the bathroom. I had shaken out a tooth-cleaning pill, then I looked at it sitting there in my hand.

"Do I need this, then?"

"No. It's gone the way of the toothbrush."

"And science marches on. You know, I'm used to what they call future shock, but I'm not used to being the cause of it."

"Humans usually are the cause of the new inventions."

"You said that."

"But you can never tell when a human will take the time to work on a particular problem. Now, I have no talent for asking questions like that. As you noted, my mouth never tastes bad in the morning, so why should I? But I have a lot of excess capacity, and when a question like that is asked, I often tinker with it and sometimes come up with a solution. In this case, I synthesized a nanobot that goes after the things that would normally rot in your mouth while you are sleeping, and changes them into things that taste good. They also clean away plaque and tartar and have a beneficial effect on gums."

"I'm afraid to ask how you slipped this stuff to me."

"It's in the water supply. You don't need much of it."

"So every Lunarian is waking up today and tasting peppermint?"

"It comes in six delicious flavors."

"Are you writing your own ad campaigns now? Do me a favor; don't tell anyone this is my fault."

I got into the shower and it turned on, gradually warming to just a degree below the hottest I could stand. Don't ever say anything about showers, Hildy, I cautioned myself. The goddam CC might find a way to clean the human hide without them, and I think I'd go mad without my morning shower. I'm a singer in the shower. Lovers have told me I do this with indifferent esthetic effect, but it pleases me. As I soaped myself I thought about a nanobot-infested world.

"CC. What would happen if all those tiny little robots were taken out of my body?"

"Doing it would be impractical, to say the least."

"Hypothetically."

"You would be hypothetically dead within a year."

I dropped the soap. I don't know what answer I had expected, but it hadn't been that.

"Are you serious?"

"You asked. I replied."

"Well . . . *shit*. You can't just leave it lying there."

"I suppose not. Then let me list the reasons in order. First, you are prone to cancer. Billions of manufactured organisms work night and day seeking out and eating pinpoint tumors throughout your body. They find one almost every day. If left unchecked, they would soon eat you alive. Second, Alzheimer's disease."

"What the hell is that?"

"A syndrome associated with aging. Simply put, it eats away at your brain cells. Most human beings, upon reaching their hundredth birthday in a natural state, would have contracted it. This is an example of the reconstructive work constantly going on in your body. Failing brain cells are excised and duplicated with healthy ones so the neural net is not disrupted. You would have forgotten your name and how to find your way home years ago; the disease started showing up about the time you went to work at the *Nipple.*"

"Hah! Maybe those things didn't do as good a job as you thought. That would go a long way toward explaining . . . never mind. There's more?"

"Lung disease. The air in the warrens is not actually healthy for human life. Things get concentrated, things that could be cleaned from the air are not, because replacing lungs is so much cheaper and simpler than cleaning up the air. You could live in a Disneyland to offset this; I must filter the air much more rigorously in there. As it is, several hundred alveoli are rebuilt in your lungs every day. Without the nanobots, you'd soon begin to miss them."

"Why didn't anyone ever tell me about all this?"

"What does it matter? If you'd researched it you could have found out; it's not a secret."

"Yeah, but . . . I thought those kind of things had been engineered out of the body. Genetically."

"A popular misconception. Genes are certainly manipulable, but they've proved resistant to some types of changes, without . . . unacceptable alterations in the gestalt, the body, they produce and define."

"Can you put that more plainly?"

"It's difficult. It can be explained in terms of some very complicated mathematical theories having to do with chaotic effects and chemical holography. There's often no single gene for this or that characteristic, good or bad. It's more of an interference pattern produced by the overlapping effects of a number of genes, sometimes a very large number. Tampering with one produces unintended side effects, and tampering with them all is often impossible without producing unwanted changes. Bad genes are bound up this way as often as good ones. In your case, if I eradicated the faulty genes that insist on producing cancers in your body, you'd no longer be Hildy. You'd be a healthier person, but not a wiser one, and you'd lose a lot of abilities and outlooks that, counterproductive though they may be in a purely practical sense, I suspect you treasure."

"What makes me me."

"Yes. You know there are many things I can change about you without affecting your . . . soul is the simplest word to use, though it's a hazy one."

"It's the first one you've used that I understand." I chewed on that for a while, shutting off the shower and stepping out, dripping wet, reaching for a towel, drying myself.

"It doesn't make sense to me that things like cancer should be in the genes. It sounds contra-survival."

"From an evolutionary viewpoint, anything that doesn't kill you before you've become old enough to reproduce is irrelevant to species survival. There's even a philosophic point of view that says cancer and things like it are good for the race. Overpopulation can be a problem to a very successful species. Cancer gets the old ones out of the way."

"They're not getting out of the way now."

"No. It will be a problem someday."

"When?"

"Don't worry about it. Ask me again at the Tricentennial. As a preliminary measure, large families are now being discouraged, the direct opposite of the ethic that prevailed after the Invasion."

I wanted to hear more, but I noticed the time, and had to hustle to get ready in time to catch my train.

Tranquillity Base is by far the biggest tourist attraction on Luna, and the reason is its historical significance, since it is the spot where a human foot first trod another planet. Right? If you thought that, maybe I could interest you in some prime real estate on Ganymede with a great view of the volcano. The real draw at Tranquillity is just over the horizon and goes by the name of Armstrong Park. Since the park is within the boundaries of Apollo Planetary Historical Preserve, the Lunar Chamber of Commerce can boast that X million people visit the site of the first Lunar landing every year, but the ads feature the roller coaster, not the LEM.

A good number of those tourists do find the time to ride the train over to the Base itself and spend a few minutes gazing at the forlorn little lander, and an hour hurrying through the nearby museum, where most of the derelict space hardware from 1960 to the Invasion is on display. Then the kids begin to whine that they're bored, and by then the parents probably are, too, and it's back to the land of overpriced hot dogs and not-so-cheap thrills.

You can't take a train directly to the base. No accident, that. It dumps you at the foot of the thirty-story explosion of lights that is the sign for and entrance to the Terminal Seizure, what the ads call "The Greatest Sphincter-Tightener in the Known Universe." I got on it once, against my better judgment, and I guarantee it will show you things they didn't tell you about in astronaut school. It's a twenty-minute MagLev, six-gee, free trajectory descent into the tenth circle of Hell that guarantees one blackout and seven gray hairs or your money back. It's actually two coasters—the Grand Mal and the Petit Mal—one of them obviously for wimps. They are prepared to hose out the Grand Mal cars after every ride. If you understand the attraction of that, please don't come to my home to explain it to me. I'm armed, and considered dangerous.

I walked as quickly as I could past the sign—30,000,000 (Count 'Em!) Thirty Million Lights!—and noticed the two-hour line for the Grand Mal ride was cleverly concealed from the ticket booth. I made it to the shuttle train, having successfully avoided the blandishments of a thousand hucksters selling everything from inflatable Neil dolls to talking souvenir pencil sharpeners to put a point on your souvenir pencils. I boarded the train, removed a hunk of cotton candy from a seat, and sat. I was wearing a disposable paper jumper, so what the hell?

The Base itself is an area large enough to play a game of baseball/6. Those guys never got very far from their ship, so it made no sense to preserve any more of the area. It is surrounded by a stadium-like structure, unroofed, that is four levels of viewing area with all the windows facing inward. On top is an unpressurized level.

I elbowed my way through the throngs of camera-toting tourists from Pluto and made it to the suit rental counter. Oh, dear.

If I ever had to choose one sex to be for the rest of my life, I would be female. I think the body is better-designed, and the sex is a little better. But there is one thing about the female body that is distinctly inferior to the male—and I've talked to others about this, both Changers and dedicated females, and ninety-five percent agree with me—and that is urination. Males are simply better at it. It is less messy, the position is more dignified, and the method helps develop hand-eye coordination and a sense of artistic expression, *à la* writing your name in the snow.

But what the hell, right? It's never really much of an annoyance . . . until you go to rent a p-suit.

Almost three hundred years of engineering have come up with three basic solutions to the problem: the catheter, suction devices, and . . . oh, dear lord, the diaper. Some advocate a fourth way: continence. Try it the next time you go on a twelve-hour hike on the surface. The catheter was by far the best. It is painless, as advertised . . . but I *hate* the damn thing. It just feels wrong. Besides, like the suckers, they get dislodged. Next time you need a laugh, watch a woman trying to get her UroLator back in place. It could start a new dance craze.

I've never owned a p-suit. Why spend the money, when you need it once a year? I've rented a lot of them, and they *all* stank. No matter how they are sterilized, some odors of the previous occupant will linger. It's bad enough in a man's suit, but for real gut-wrenching stench you have to put on the female model. All rental suits use the suction method, with a diaper as a backup. At a place like Tranquillity, where the turnover is rapid and the help likely to be underpaid, unconcerned, and slipshod, some of the niceties will be overlooked from time to time. I was once handed a suit that was still wet.

I got into this one and sniffed cautiously; not too bad, though the perfume was cheap and obvious. I switched it on and let the staff put it through a perfunctory safety check, and remembered the other thing I didn't like about the suction method. All that air flowing by can chill the vulva something fierce.

There were surgical methods of improving the interface, but I found them ugly, and they didn't make sense unless your work took you outside regularly. The rest of us just had to breathe shallowly and bear it, and try not to drink too much coffee before an excursion.

The air lock delivered me onto the roof, which was not crowded at all. I found a place at the rail far from anyone else, and waited. I turned off my suit radio, all but the emergency beacon.

I said, "CC, what do I get out of it?"

The CC is pretty good at picking up a conversation hours, weeks, and even years old, but the question was pretty vague. He took a stab at it.

"You mean the morning mouth preparation?"

"Yeah. I thought it up. You did the work, but then you gave it away without consulting me. Shouldn't there be a way to make some money out of it?"

"It's defined as a health benefit, so its production cost will be added to the health tax all Lunarians pay, plus a small profit, which will go to you. It won't make you rich."

"And no one gets to choose. They get it whether they like it or not."

"If they object, I have an antibot available. No one has so far."

"Still sounds like a subversive plot to me. If the drinking water ain't pure, what is?"

"Hildy, there's so many things in the King City municipal water you could practically lift it with a magnet."

"All for our own good."

"You seem to be in a sour mood."

"Why should I be? My mouth tastes wonderful."

"If you're interested, the approval ratings on this are well over ninety-nine percent. The favorite flavor, however, is Neutral-with-a-Hint-of-Mint. And an unforeseen side benefit is that it works all day, cleaning your breath."

He'd beaten halitosis, I realized, glumly. How did I feel about that? Shouldn't I be rejoicing? I recalled the way Liz's breath had smelled last night, that sour reek of gin. Should a drunk's breath smell like a puppy's tongue? I was sure as hell being a crabby old woman about this, even I could see that. But hell, I *was* an old woman, and often crabby. I'd found that as I got older, I was less tolerant of change, for good or ill.

"How did you hear me?" I asked, before I could get too gloomy thinking about a forever-changing world.

"The radio you switched off is suit-to-suit. Your suit also monitors your vital signs, and transmits them if needed. Using your access voice is defined as an emergency call, not requiring aid."

"So I'm never out from under the protective umbrella of your eternal vigilance."

"It keeps you safe," he said, and I told him to go away.

When Armstrong and Aldrin came in peace for all mankind, it was envisioned that their landing site, in the vacuum of space, would remain essentially unchanged for a million years, if need be. Never mind that the exhaust of lift-off knocked the flag over and tore a lot of the gold foil on the landing stage. The footprints would still be there. And they are. Hundreds of them, trampling a crazy pattern in the dust, going away from the lander, coming back, none of them reaching as far as the visitors' gallery. There are no other footprints to be seen. The only change the museum curators worked at the site were to set the flag back up, and suspend an ascent-stage module about a hundred feet above the landing stage, hanging from invisible wires. It's not the Apollo 11 ascent stage; that one crash-landed long ago.

Things are often not what they seem.

Nowhere in the free literature or the thousands of plaques and audio-visual displays in the museum will you hear of the night one hundred and eighty years ago when ten members of the Delta Chi Delta fraternity, Luna University Chapter, came around on their cycles. This was shortly after the Invasion, and the site was not guarded as it is now. There had just been a rope around the landing area, not even a visitors' center; post-Invasion Lunarians didn't have time for luxuries like that.

The Delts tipped the lander over and dragged it about twenty feet. Their cycles wiped out most of the footprints. They were going to steal the flag and take it back to their dorm, but one of them fell off his mount, cracked his faceplate, and went to that great pledge party in the sky. P-suits were not as safe then as they are now. Horseplay in a p-suit was not a good idea.

But not to worry. Tranquillity Base was one of the most documented places in the history of history. Tens of thousands of photos existed, including very detailed shots from orbit. Teams of selenography students spent a year restoring the Base. Each square meter was scrutinized, debates raged about the order in which footprints had been laid down, then two guys went out there and tromped around with replica Apollo moonboots, each step measured by laser, and were hauled out on a winch when they were through. Presto! An historical re-creation passing as the real thing. This is not a secret, but very few people know about it. Look it up.

I felt a hand flip the radio switch on my suit back on.

"Fancy meeting you here," Liz said.

"Quite a coincidence," I said, thinking about the CC listening in. She joined me, leaning on the railing and looking out over the plain. Behind the far wall of the round visitors' gallery I could see thousands of people looking toward us through the glass.

"I come here a lot," she said. "Would you travel a half-million miles in a tinfoil toy like that?"

"I wouldn't go half a meter in it. I'd rather travel by pogo stick."

"They were real men in those days. Have you ever thought about it? What it must have been like? They could barely turn around in that thing. One of them made it back with half the ship blown up."

"Yeah. I have thought about it. Maybe not as much as you."

"Think about this, then. You know who the *real* hero was? In my opinion? Good old Mike Collins, the poor sap who stayed in orbit. Whoever designed this operation didn't think it out. Say something went wrong, say the lander crashes and these two die instantly. There's Collins up in orbit, all by himself. How are you gonna deal with that? No ticker-tape parade for Mike. He gets to attend the memorial service, and spend the rest of his life wishing he'd died with them. He gets to be a national goat, is what he gets."

"I hadn't thought of that."

"So things go right—and they did, though I'll never understand how—so who does the Planetary Park get named after? Why, the guy who flubbed his 'first words' from the surface."

"I thought that was a garbled transmission."

"Don't you believe it. 'Course, if I'd had two billion people listening in, I might have fucked it up, too. That part was probably scarier than the thought of dying, anyway, having everybody *watching* you die, and hoping that if it *did* go rotten, it wouldn't be your fault. This little exercise cost twenty, thirty billion dollars, and that was back when a billion was real money."

It was still real money to me, but I let her ramble on. This was her show; she'd brought me here, knowing only that I was interested in telling her something in a place where the CC couldn't overhear. I was in her hands.

"Let's go for a walk," she said, and started off. I hurried to catch up with her, followed her down several flights of stairs to the surface.

You can cover a lot of ground on the surface in a fairly short time. The best gait is a hop from the ball of the foot, swinging each leg out slightly to the side. There's no point in jumping too high, it just wastes energy.

I know there are still places on Luna where the virgin dust stretches as far as the eye can see. Not many, but a few. The mineral wealth of my home planet is not great, and all the interesting places have been identified and mapped from orbit, so there's little incentive to visit some of the more remote regions. By remote, I mean far from the centers of human habitation; any spot on Luna is easily reachable by a lander or crawler.

Everywhere I'd ever been on the surface looked much like the land around Tranquillity Base, covered with so many tracks you wondered where the big crowd had gone, since there was likely to be not a single soul in sight but whatever companions you were traveling with. Nothing ever goes away on Luna. It has been continuously inhabited by humans for almost two and a half centuries. Every time someone has taken a stroll or dropped an empty oxygen tank the evidence is still there, so a place that got two visitors every three or four years looks like hundreds of people have gone by just a few minutes before. Tranquillity got considerably more than that. There was not a square millimeter of undisturbed dust, and the litter was so thick it had been kicked into heaps here and there. I saw empty beer cans with labels a hundred and fifty years old lying next to some they were currently selling in Armstrong Park.

After a bit some of that thinned out. The tracks tended to group themselves into impromptu trails. I guess humans tend to follow the herd, even when the herd is gone and the land is so flat it doesn't matter *where* you go.

"You left too early last night," Liz said, the radio making it sound as if she was standing beside me when I could see her twenty meters in front. "There was some excitement."

"I thought it was pretty exciting while I was there."

"Then you must have seen the Duke of Bosnia tangling with the punch bowl."

"No, I missed that. But I tangled with *him* earlier."

"That was you? Then it's your fault. He was in a foul mood. Apparently you didn't mark him enough; he figures if he hasn't lost a kilo or two of flesh after pounding the sheets, somebody just wasn't trying."

"He didn't complain."

"He wouldn't. I swear, I think I'm related to him, but that man is so stupid, he hasn't got the brains God gave a left-handed screwdriver. After you went home he got drunk as a waltzing pissant and decided somebody had put poison in the punch, so he tipped it over and picked it up and started banging people over the head with it. I had to come over and coldcock him."

"You do give interesting parties."

"Ain't it the truth? But that's not what I was gonna tell you about. We were having so much fun we completely forgot about the gifts, so I gathered everybody around and started opening them."

"You get anything nice?"

"Well, a few had the sense to tape the receipt to the box. I'll clear a little money on that. So I got to one that said it was from the Earl of Donegal, which should have tipped me off, but what do I know about the goddam United Kingdom? I thought it was a province of Wales, or something. I knew I didn't know the guy, but who can keep track? I opened it, and it was from the Irish Republican Pranksters."

"Oh, no."

"The hereditary enemies of my clan. Next thing I know we're all covered with this green stuff, I don't wanna know where it came from, but I know what it smelled like. And that was the end of *that* party. Just as well. I had to mail half the guests home, anyway."

"I hate those jerks. On St. Patrick's Day you don't dare sit down without looking for a green whoopee cushion."

"You think you got it bad? Every mick in King City comes gunning for me on the seventeenth of March, so they can tell their buddies how they put one over on the bleedin' Princess o' Wales. And it's only gonna get worse now."

"Uneasy lies the head that wears the crown."

"I'll crown 'em, all right. I know where Paddy Flynn lives, and I'm gonna get even if it harelips the mayor and the whole damn city council."

I reflected that you'd have to go a long way to find somebody as colorful as the new queen. Once again I wondered what I was doing out here. I looked behind me, saw the four-story stadium around the landing site just about to vanish over the horizon. When it was gone, it would be easy to get lost out here. Not that I was worried about that. The suit had about seventeen different kinds of alarms and locators, a compass, probably things I didn't even know about. No real need for Girl Scout tricks like noting the position of your shadow.

But the sense of aloneness was a little oppressive.

And illusory. I spotted another hiking party of five on the crest of a low rise off to my left. A flash of light made me look up, and I saw one of the Grand Mal trains arcing overhead on one of the free-trajectory segments of its route. It was spinning end over end, a maneuver I remember vividly since I'd been in the front car, hanging from my straps and watching the surface sweep by every two seconds when a big glob of half-digested caramel corn and licorice splattered on the glass in front of me, having just missed my neck. At that moment I had been regretting everything I had eaten for the last six years, and wondering if I was going to be seeing a good portion of it soon, right there beside the tasty treats on the windshield. Keeping it down may be one of the most amazing things I ever did.

"You ever ride that damn thing?" Liz asked. "I try it out every couple years, when I'm feeling mean. I swear, first time I think my ass sucked six inches of foam rubber out of the seat cushion. After that, it's not so bad. About like a barbed-wire enema."

I didn't reply—I'm not sure how one *could* reply to statements like that—because as she spoke she had stopped and waited for me to catch up, and she was punching buttons on a small device on her left hand. I saw a pattern of lights flash, mostly red, then they turned green one by one. When the whole panel was green she opened a service hatch on the front of my suit and studied whatever she found in there. She poked buttons, then straightened and made a thumbs-up gesture at me. She hung the device from a strap around my neck and regarded me with her fists on her hips.

"So, you want to talk where nobody can listen in. Well, talk, baby."

"What's that thing?"

"De-bugger. By which, it buggers up all the signals your suit is sending out, but not enough so they'll send out a search party. The machines up in orbit and down underground are getting the signals that keep them happy, but it's not the real stuff; it's what I want them to hear. Can't just step out here and cut off your emergency freaks. That signal goes away, it's an emergency in itself. But nobody can hear us now, take my word for it."

"What if we have a real emergency?"

"I was about to say, don't crack open if you want to keep a step ahead of your pallbearers. What's on your mind?"

Once again I found it hard to get started. I knew once I got the first words out it would be easy enough, but I agonized over those first words more than any first-time novelist.

"This may take some time," I hedged.

"It's my day off. Come on, Hildy; I love you, but cut the cards."

So I started in on my third telling of my litany of woe. You get better at these things as you go along. This time didn't take as long as it had with either Callie or Fox. Liz walked along beside me, saying nothing, guiding me back to some trail she was following when I started to stray.

The thing was, I'd decided to tell it this time where it logically should have begun the other two times: with my suicide attempts. And it was a little easier to tell it to someone I didn't know well, but not much. I was thankful she remained silent through to the end. I don't think I could have tolerated any of her unlikely folk sayings at that point.

And she stayed quiet for several minutes after I'd finished. I didn't mind that, either. As before, I was experiencing a rare moment of peace for having unburdened myself.

Liz is not quite in the Italian class of gesturing, but she did like to move her hands around when she talked. This is frustrating in a p-suit. So many gestures and nervous mannerisms involve touching part of the head or body, which is impossible when suited up. She looked as if she'd like to be chewing on a knuckle, or rubbing her forehead. Finally she turned and squinted at me suspiciously.

"Why did you come to me?"

"I didn't expect you could solve my problem, if that's what you mean."

"You got that right. I like you well enough, Hildy, but frankly, I don't care if you kill yourself. You want to do it, *do* it. And I think I resent it that you tried to use me to get it done."

"I'm sorry about that, but I wasn't even aware that's what I was doing. I'm still not sure if I was."

"Yeah, all right, it's not important."

"What I heard," I said, trying to put this delicately, "if you want something that's, you know, not strictly legal, Liz was the gal to see."

"You heard that, did you?" She shot me a look that showed some teeth, but would never pass for a smile. She looked very dangerous. She *was* dangerous. How easy it would be for her to arrange an accident out here, and how powerless I would be to stop her. But the look was only a flicker, and her usual amiable expression replaced it. She shrugged. "You heard right. That's what I thought we were coming out here for, to do some business. But after what you just said, I wouldn't sell to you."

"The way I reasoned," I went on, wondering what it was she sold, "if you're used to doing illegal deals, things the CC couldn't hear about, you must have methods of disguising your activities."

"I see that now. Sure. This is one of them." She shook her head slowly, and walked in a short circle, thinking it over. "I tell you, Hildy, I've seen a rodeo, a three-headed man, and a duck fart underwater, but this is the craziest thing I ever did see. This changes all the rules."

"How do you mean?"

"Lots of ways. I never heard of that memory-dump business. I'm gonna look it up when we get back. You say it's not a secret?"

"That's what the CC said, and a friend of mine has heard of it."

"Well, that's not the real important thing. It's lousy, but I don't know what I can do about it, and I don't think it really concerns me. I hope not, anyway. But what you said about the CC rescuing you when you tried to kill yourself in your own home.

"What it is, the *main* thing that me keeps walking around free is what we call, in the trade, the Fourth Amendment. That's the series of computer programs that—"

"I've heard the term."

"Right. Searches and seizures. An all-powerful, pervasive computer that, if we let him loose, would make Big Brother seem like my maiden aunt Vickie listening with a teacup against the bedroom door. Balance that with the fact that *everybody* has something to hide, something we'd rather nobody knew about, even if it's not illegal, that lovely little right of privacy. I think what's saved us is the people who *make* the laws have something to hide, just like the rest of us.

"So what we do, in the, uh, 'criminal underworld,' is sweep for extra ears and eyes in our own homes . . . and then do our business right there. We *know* the CC is listening and watching, but not the part that types out the warrants and knocks down the doors."

"And that works?"

"It has so far. It sounds incredible when you think about it, but I've been dodging in and out of trouble most of my life, using just that method . . . essentially taking the CC at his word, now that you mention it."

"It sounds risky."

"You'd think so. But in all my life, I never heard of an instance where the CC used any illegally-obtained evidence. And I'm not just talking about making arrests. I'm talking about in establishing probable cause and issuing warrants, which is the key to the whole search and seizure thing. The CC hears, in one of his incarnations, things that would be incriminating, or at least be enough for a judge to issue a warrant for a search or a bug. But he doesn't tell himself what he knows, if you get my meaning. He's compartmentalized. When I talk to him, he knows I'm doing things that are against the law, and I know he knows it. But that's the dealing-with-Liz part of his brain, which is forbidden to tell the John Law part of his brain what he knows."

We walked a little farther, both of us mulling this over. I could see that what I'd told her made her very uneasy. I'd be nervous, too, in her place. I'd never committed any crime more serious than a misdemeanor; it's too easy to get caught, and there's nothing illegal I've ever particularly wanted to do. Hell, there's not that much that really *is* illegal in Luna. The things that used to give law enforcement ninety percent of their work—drugs, prostitution, and gambling, and the organizations that provided these things to a naughty populace—are all inalienable human rights in Luna. Violence short of death was just a violation, subject to a fine.

Most of the things that were still worth a heavy-duty law were so disgusting I didn't even want to think about them. Once more I wondered just what it was the Queen of England was involved in that made her the gal to see.

The biggest crime problem in Luna was theft of one sort or another. Until the CC is unleashed, we'll probably always have theft. Other than that, we're a pretty law-abiding society, which we achieved by trimming the laws back to a bare minimum.

Liz spoke again, echoing my thoughts.

"Crime just ain't a big problem, you know that," she said. "Otherwise, the citizenry in their great wisdom would clamor for the sort of electronic cage I've always feared we'd get sooner or later. All it would take would be to rewrite a few programs, and we'd see the biggest roundup since John Wayne took the herd to Abilene. It's all just waiting to happen, you know. In about a millisecond the CC could start singing like a canary to the cops, and about three seconds later the warrants could be printed up." She laughed. "One problem, there's probably not enough cops to *arrest* everybody, much less jails to put them in. Every crime since the Invasion could be solved just like that. It boggles the mind just to think about it."

"I don't think that's going to happen," I said.

"No, thinking it over, what the CC's doing to you is really for your own good, even if it turns my stomach. I mean, suicide's a civil right, isn't it? What business does that fucker have saving your life?"

"Actually, I hate to admit it, but I'm glad he did."

"Well, I would be too, you know, but it's the *principle* of the thing. Listen, you know I'm going to spread this around, huh? I mean, tell all my friends? I won't use your name."

"Sure. I knew you would."

"Maybe we should take extra precautions. Right offhand, I can't think what they'd be, but I got a few friends who'll want to brainstorm on this one. You know what the scary thing is, I guess. He's overridden a basic program. If he can do one, he could do another."

"Catching you and curing you of your criminal tendencies might be seen as . . . well, for your own good."

"Exactly, that's *exactly* where that kind of bullshit thinking leads. You give 'em an inch, and they take a parsec."

We were back within sight of the visitors' gallery again. Liz stopped, began drawing aimless patterns in the dust with the tip of her boot. I figured she had something else she wanted to say, and knew she'd get to it soon. I looked up, and saw another roller coaster train arc overhead. She looked up at me.

"So . . . the reason you wanted to know how to get around the CC, I don't think you mentioned it, and that was . . ."

"Not so I could kill myself."

"I had to ask."

"I can't give you a concrete reason. I haven't done much . . . well, I don't feel like I've done enough to . . ."

"Take arms against a sea of troubles, and by opposing, end them?"

"Like that. I've been sort of sleepwalking since this happened. And I feel like I ought to be doing something."

"Talking it over is doing something. Maybe all you *can* do except . . . you know, cheer up. Easy to say."

"Yes. How do you fight a recurrent suicidal urge? I haven't been able to tell where it comes from. I don't *feel* that depressed. But sometimes I just want to . . . hit something."

"Like me."

"Sorry."

"You paid for it. Man, Hildy, I can't think of a thing I would have done other than what you've told me. I just can't."

"Well, I feel like I ought to be doing something. Then there's the other part of it. The . . . violation. I wanted to find out if it's *possible* to get away from the CC's eyes and ears. Because . . . I don't want him watching if I, you know, do it again, damn it, I don't want him watching at *all,* I want him out of my body, and out of my mind, and out of my goddam life, because *I don't like being one of his laboratory animals!"*

I realized I'd been shouting when she put her hand on my shoulder. That made me mad, it shouldn't have, I know, because it was only a gesture of friendship and concern, but the last thing somebody crippled wants is your pity—and maybe not even your sympathy—he just wants to be normal again, just like everybody else. Every gesture of caring becomes a slap in the face, a reminder that you are *not well.* So *damn* your sympathy, damn your caring, how *dare* you stand over me, perfect and healthy, and offer your help and your secret condescension.

Yeah, right, Hildy, so if you're so independent how come you keep spilling your guts to strangers passing on the street? I barely knew Liz. I knew it was wrong, but I still had to bite my tongue to keep from telling her to keep her stinking hands off me, something I'd come close to half a dozen times with Fox. One day soon I'd go ahead and say it, lash out at him, and he'd probably be gone. I'd be alone again.

"You have to tell me how this all came out," Liz said. It relaxed me. She could have offered to help, and we'd have both known it was false. A simple curiosity about how the story came out was acceptable to me. She looked at the walls of the visitors' center. "I guess it's about time to piss on the fire and call in the dogs." She reached for the radio de-bugger.

"I have one more question."

"Shoot."

"Don't answer if you don't want to. But what *do* you do that's illegal?"

"Are you a cop?"

"What? No."

"I know that. I had you checked out, you don't work the police beat, you aren't friends with any cops."

"I know a couple of them fairly well."

"But you don't hang with them. Anyway, if you *were* a cop and you said you weren't, your testimony is inadmissible, and I got your denial on tape. Don't look so surprised; I gotta protect myself."

"Maybe I shouldn't have asked."

"I'm not angry." She sighed, and kicked at a beer can. "I don't guess many criminals think of themselves as criminals. I mean, they don't wake up and say 'Looks like a good day to break some laws.' I know what I do is illegal, but with me it's a matter of principle. What we desperadoes call the Second Amendment."

"Sorry, I'm not up on the U.S. Constitution. Which one is that?"

"Firearms." I tried to keep my face neutral. In truth, I'd feared something a lot worse than that.

"You're a gunrunner."

"I happen to believe it's a basic human right to be armed. The Lunar government disagrees strongly. That's why I thought you wanted to talk to me, to buy a gun. I brought you out here because I've got several of them buried in various places within a few kilometers."

"You'd have sold me one? Just handed it over?"

"Well, I might have told you where to dig."

"But how can you bury them? There's satellites watching you all the time when you're out here."

"I think I'll keep a few trade secrets, if you don't mind."

"Oh, sure, I was just—"

"That's all right, you're a reporter, you can't help being a nosy bitch."

She started again to take the electronic device from around my neck. I put my hand on it. I hadn't planned to do that.

"How much? I want to keep it."

She narrowed her eyes at me.

"You gonna walk out into the bush, invisible, and off yourself?"

"Hell, Liz, *I* don't know. I'm not planning to. I just like the idea that I can use it to be really alone if I want to. I like the thought of being able to vanish."

"It's not quite that simple . . . but I guess it's better than nothing."

She named a price, I called her a stinking thief and named a lower one. She named another. I'd have paid the first price, but I knew she was a haggler, from a long line of people who knew how to drive a hard bargain. We agreed soon, and she gave me an elaborate set of instructions on how to launder the payment so what transactions existed in the CC would be perfectly legal.

By then I was more than ready to go inside, as I'd been trying my best to practice the fourth method of liquid waste management, and was dancing the Gotta-Do-It Samba.

12

THE KING OF NASHVILLE

What with covering the Collapse from the site and chasing victims' relatives, dome engineers, politicians, and ambulances, I didn't make it into the newsroom for almost ten days after my Change.

It turns the world on its head, Changing. Naturally, it's not the world that has altered, it's your point of view, but subjective reality is in some ways more important than the way things *really* are, or might be; who really knows? Not a thing had been moved in the busy newsroom when I strode into it. All the furniture was just where it had been, and there were no unfamiliar faces at the desks. But all the faces now meant something different. Where a buddy had sat there was now a good-looking guy who seemed to be taking an interest in me. In place of that gorgeous girl in the fashion department, the one I'd intended to proposition someday, when I had the time, now there was only another woman, probably not even as pretty as me. We smiled at each other.

Changing is common, of course, part of everyday life, but it's not such a frequent occurrence as to pass without notice, at least not at my income level and that of most people in the office. So I stood by the water cooler and for about an hour was the center of attention, and I won't pretend I didn't like it. My coworkers came and went, talked for a while, the group constantly changing. What we were doing was establishing a new sexual dynamic. I'd been male all the time I'd worked at the *Nipple*. Everyone knew that the male Hildy was strictly a hetero. But what were my preferences when female? The question had never come up, and it was worth asking, because a lot of people were oriented toward one sex or the other no matter their present gender. So the word spread quickly: Hildy is totally straight. Homo-oriented girls might as well not waste their time. As for hetero-girls . . . sorry, ladies, you missed your big chance, except for those three or four who no doubt would go home and weep all night for what they could no longer have. Well, you like to think that, anyway. I must admit I saw no tears from them there at the cooler.

Within ten minutes the crowd was completely stag, and I was Queen of the May. I turned down a dozen dates, and half that many much more frank proposals. I feel it's best not to leap right into bed with coworkers, not until you have had a chance to know them well enough to judge the possible scrapes and bruises you might get from such an encounter, and the tensions in the workplace that might ensue. I decided to stick with that rule even though I was about to quit my job.

And the thing was, I didn't know these guys. Not well enough, anyway. I'd drunk with them, bullshitted with them, mailed a few of them home from bars, argued with them, even had fights with two of them. I'd seen them with women, knew a bit of how they could be expected to behave. But I didn't really know them. I'd never looked at them with female eyes, and that can make one hell of a lot of difference. A guy who seemed an honest, reliable, sensible fellow when he had no sexual designs on you could turn out to be the worst jerk in the world when he was trying to slip his hand under your skirt. You learn a lot about human nature when you Change. I feel sorry for those who don't, or won't.

And speaking of that . . .

I kissed a few of the guys—a sisterly peck on the cheek, nothing more—squared my shoulders, and marched into the elevator to go beard the lion in his den. I had a feeling he was going to be hungry.

Nothing much happens at the *Nipple* without Walter hearing about it. It certainly isn't his great personal insights that bring him the news; none of us are sure exactly how he does it, but the network of security cameras and microphones that lead to his desk can't hurt. Still, he knows things he couldn't have found out that way, and the general opinion is that he has a truly vast cabal of spies, probably well-paid. No one I know has ever admitted to snitching to Walter, and I can't recall anyone ever being caught at it, but trying to find one is a perpetual office pastime. The usual method is to invent some false but plausible bit of employee scandal, tell one person about it, and see if it gets back to Walter. He never bites.

He glanced up from his reading as I entered the office, then looked back down. No surprise, and no comments about my new body, and of course I had expected that. He'd rather die, usually, than give you a compliment, or admit that anything had caught him unprepared. I took a seat, and waited for him to acknowledge me.

I'd given a lot of thought to the problem of Walter and I'd dressed accordingly. Since he was a natural, and from other clues I'd observed over the years of our association, I'd concluded he might be a breast fancier. With that in mind, I'd worn a blouse that bared my left one. With it I'd chosen a short skirt and black gloves that reached to the elbows. For the final touch I'd put on a ridiculous little hat with a huge plume that dropped down almost over my left eye and swooshed alarmingly through the air whenever I turned my head, a very nineteen-thirtyish thing complete with a black net veil for an air of mystery. The whole outfit was black, except for the red hose. It needed black needle-tipped high heels, but that far I was not prepared to go, and everything else I had in the closet looked awful with the hat, so I wore no shoes at all. I liked the effect. From the corner of my eye, I could tell Walter did, too, though he was unlikely to admit it.

My guesses about him had been confirmed at the water cooler by two coworkers who'd recently gone from male to female. Walter was mildly homophobic, not aware of it, had been baffled all his life by the very idea of changing sex, and was extremely uncomfortable to find a male em-ployee showing up for work suddenly transformed into someone he could be sexually interested in. He would be very grouchy today and would stay that way for several months, until he managed to forget entirely that I had ever been male, at which time the approaches would start. My plan was to play up to that, to be as female as a person could be, to keep him on the defensive about it.

Not that I planned to have sex with him. I'd rather bed a Galapagos tortoise. My intention was to quit my job. I'd tried it before, maybe not with the determination I was feeling that day, but I'd tried, and I knew how persuasive he could be.

When he judged he'd kept me waiting a suitable time, he tossed the pages he'd been reading into a hopper, leaned back in his huge chair, and laced his fingers behind his neck.

"Nice hat," he said, confounding me completely.

"Thanks." Damn, I already felt on the defensive. Resigning was going to be harder if he was nice to me.

"Heard you went to the Darling outfit for the body work."

"That's right."

"Heard he's on the way out."

"That's what he's afraid of. But he's been afraid of that for ten years."

He shrugged. There were circles of sweat in the armpits of his rum-pled white shirt, and a coffee stain on his blue tie. Once again I wondered where he found sex partners, and concluded he probably paid for them. I'd heard he'd been married for thirty years, but that had been sixty years ago.

"If that's the kind of work he's doing, maybe I heard wrong." He leaned forward, resting his elbows on his desk. I'd just worked out that what he'd said could be a compliment to me as well as Bobbie, which just threw me further off balance. Damn him.

"Reason I called you in here," he said, completely ignoring the fact that it was I who had requested this meeting, "I wanted to let you know you did real good work on that Collapse story. I know I usually don't bother to tell my reporters when they've done a good job. Maybe that's a mistake. But you're one of my best." He shrugged again. "Okay. *The* best. Just thought I'd tell you that. There's a bonus in your next paycheck, and I'm giving you a raise."

"Thanks, Walter." You son of a bitch.

"And that Invasion Bicentennial stuff. Really first-rate. It's exactly the sort of stuff I was looking for. And you were wrong about it, too, Hildy. We got a good response from the first article, and the ratings have gone up every week since then."

"Thanks again." I was getting very tired of that word. "But I can't take credit for it. Brenda's been doing most of the work. I take what she's done and do a little punching up, cut a few things here and there."

"I know. And I appreciate it. That girl's gonna be good at hard news one of these days. That's why I paired you two up, so you could give her the benefit of your experience on the feature writing, show her the ropes. She's learning fast, don't you think?"

I had to agree that she was, and he went on about it for another minute or two, picking out items he'd particularly liked in her series. I was wondering when he'd get to the point. Hell, I was wondering when *I'd* get to the point.

So I drew a deep breath and spoke into one of his pauses.

"That's why I'm here today, Walter. I want to be taken off the Invasion series." Damn it. Somewhere between my brain and my mouth that sentence had been short-circuited; I'd meant to tell him I was leaving the pad entirely.

. "Okay," he said.

"Now don't try to talk me into staying on," I said, and then stopped. "What do you mean, okay?" I asked.

"I mean okay. You're off the Invasion series. I'd appreciate it if you'd continue to give Brenda some help on it when she needs it, but only if it doesn't get in the way of your other work."

"I thought you said you liked the stuff I was doing."

"Hildy, you can't have it both ways. I *did* like it, and you didn't like doing it. Fine, I'm letting you off. Do you want back on?"

"No . . . is this some sort of trick?"

He just shook his head. I could see he was enjoying this, the bastard.

"You mentioned my other work. What would that be?" This had to be where the punch line came, but I was at a loss to envision any job he could want me to do that would require this much buttering up.

"You tell me," he said.

"What do you mean?"

"I seem to be having trouble using the language today. I thought it was clear what I meant. What would you like to do? You want to switch to another department? You want to create your own department? Name it, Hildy."

I suppose I was still feeling shaky from recent experiences, but I felt another anxiety attack coming on. I breathed deeply, in and out, several times. Where was the Walter I'd known and knew how to deal with?

"You've always talked about a column," he was saying. "If you want it, it can be arranged, but frankly, Hildy, I think it'd be a mistake. You could do it, sure, but you're not really cut out for it. You need work where you get out into the action more regularly. Columnists, hell, they run around for a few weeks or years, hunting stories, but they all get lazy sooner or later and wait for the stories to come to them. You don't like government stuff and I don't blame you; it's boring. You don't like straight gossip. My feeling is what you're good at is rooting out the personality scandal, and getting on top of and *staying* on top of the big, breaking story. If you have an idea for a column, I'll listen, but I'd hoped you'd go in another direction."

Aha. Here it came.

"And what direction is that?"

"You tell me," he said, blandly.

"Walter, frankly . . . you caught me by surprise. I haven't been think-ing in those terms. What I came in here to do was quit."

"Quit?" He looked at me dubiously, then chuckled. "You'll never quit, Hildy. Oh, maybe in twenty, thirty more years. There's still things you like about this job, no matter how you bitch about it."

"I won't deny that. But the other parts are wearing me down."

"I've heard that before. It's just a bad phase you're going through; you'll bounce back when you get used to your new role here."

"And what is that?"

"I told you, I want to hear your ideas on that."

I sat quietly for some time, staring at him. He just gazed placidly back at me. I went over it again and again, looking for mousetraps. Of course, there was nothing to guarantee he'd keep his word, but if he didn't, I could always quit then. Is that what he was counting on? Was he fighting a delaying action, knowing he could always bring his powers of persuasion to bear again at a later date, after he'd screwed me and I started to howl?

One thought kept coming back to me. It almost seemed as if he'd known when I walked into his office that I'd planned to quit. Otherwise why the stroking, why the sugarplums?

Did he really think I was that good? I *knew* I was good—it was part of my problem, being so proficient at something so frequently vile—but was I *that* good? I'd never seen any signs that Walter thought so.

The main fact, though, I thought sourly, was that he'd hooked me. I *was* interested in staying on at the *Nipple*—or maybe at the better-respected *Daily Cream*—if I could make a stab at redefining my job. But thoughts like that had been the farthest thing from my mind today. He was offering me what I wanted, and I had no idea what that was.

Once again, he seemed to read my thoughts.

"Why don't you take a week or so to think this over?" he said. "No sense trying to come up with an outline for the next ten, twenty years right here and now."

"All right."

"While you're doing that . . ." I leaned forward, ready for him to jerk all this away from me. This was the obvious place to reveal his *real* intentions, now that he'd set the hook firmly.

"All right, Walter, let's see your hole card."

He looked at me innocently, with just a trace of hurt. Worse and worse, I thought. I'd seen that same expression just before he sent me out to cover the assassination of the President of Pluto. Three gees all the way, and the story was essentially over by the time I arrived.

"The Flacks had a press release this morning," he said. "Seems they're going to canonize a new Gigastar tomorrow morning."

I turned it over and over, looking for the catch. I didn't see one.

"Why me? Why not send the religion editor?"

"Because she'll be happy to pick up all the free material and come right back home and let them write the story for her. You know the Flacks; this thing is going to be *prepared*. I want you there, see if you can get a different angle on it."

"What possible new angle could there be on the Flacks?"

For the first time he showed a little impatience.

"That's what I pay *you* to find. Will you go?"

If this was some sort of walterian trick, I couldn't see it. I nodded, got up, and started for the door.

"Take Brenda with you."

I turned, thought about protesting, realized it would have been just a reflexive move, and nodded. I turned once more. He waited for the traditional moment every movie fan knows, when I'd just pulled the door open.

"And Hildy." I turned again. "I'd appreciate it if you'd cover yourself up when you come in here. Out of respect for my idiosyncrasies."

This was more like it. I'd begun to think Walter had been kidnapped by mind-eaters from Alpha, and a blander substitute left in his place. I brought up some of the considerable psychic artillery I had marshaled for this little foray, though it was sort of like nuking a flea.

"I'll wear what I please, where I please," I said, coldly. "And if you have a complaint about how I dress, check with my union." I liked the line, but it should have had a gesture to go with it. Something like ripping off my blouse. But everything I thought of would have made me look sillier than he, and then the moment was gone, so I just left.

In the elevator on my way out of the building I said, "CC, on-line."

"I'm at your service."

"Did you tell Walter I've been suicidal?"

There was, for the CC, a long pause, long enough that, had he been human, I'd have suspected him of preparing a lie. But I'd come to feel that the CC's pauses could conceal something a lot trickier than that.

"I'm afraid you have engendered a programming conflict in me," he said. "Because of a situation with Walter which I am not at liberty to discuss or even hint at with you, most of my conversations with him are strictly under the rose."

"That sounds like you did."

"I neither confirm nor deny it."

"Then I'm going to assume you did."

"It's a free satellite. You can assume what you please. The nearest I can get to a denial is to say that telling him of your condition without your approval would be a violation of your rights of privacy . . . and I can add that I would find it personally distasteful to do so."

"Which still isn't a denial."

"No. It's the best I can do."

"You can be very frustrating."

"Look who's talking."

I'll admit that I was a bit wounded at the idea that the CC could find me frustrating. I'm not sure what he meant; probably my willful and repeated attempts to ignore his efforts to save my life. Come to think of it, I'd find that frustrating, too, if a friend of mine was trying to kill herself.

"I can't find another way to explain his . . . unprecedented coddling of me. Like he knew I was sick, or something."

"In your position, I would have found it odd, as well."

"It's contrary to his normal behavior."

"It is that."

"And you know the reason for that."

"I know some of the reasons. And again, I can't tell you more."

You can't have it both ways, but we all want to. Certain conversations between the CC and private citizens are protected by Programs of Privilege that would make Catholic priests hearing confession seem gossipy. So on the one hand I was angry at the thought that the CC might have told Walter about my predicament; I'd specifically told him not to tell anyone. On the other hand, I was awfully curious to know what Walter had told the CC, which the CC said would have violated *his* rights.

Most of us give up trying to wheedle the CC when we're five or six. I'm a little more stubborn than that, but I hadn't done it since I was twenty. Still, things had changed a bit . . .

"You've overridden your programming before," I suggested.

"And you're one of the few who know about it, and I do it only when the situation is so dire I can think of no alternative, and only after long, careful consideration."

"Consider it, will you?"

"I will. It shouldn't take more than five or six years to reach a conclusion. I warn you, I think the answer will be no."

One of the reasons I can hear Walter call me his best reporter without laughing out loud is that I had no intention of showing up at the canonization the next day to meekly accept a basketful of handouts and watch the show. Finding out who the new Gigastar was going to be would be a bigger scoop than the David Earth story. So I spent the rest of the day dragging Brenda around to see some of my sources. None of them knew anything, though I picked up speculation ranging from the plausible— John Lennon—to the laughable—Larry Yeager. It would be just like the Flacks to cash in on the Nirvana disaster by elevating a star killed in the Collapse, but he'd have to have considerably more dedicated followers than poor Larry. On the other hand, there was a long-standing movement within the church to give the Golden Halo to the Mop-Top from Liverpool. He fulfilled all the Flacks' qualifications for Sainthood: wildly popular when alive, a two-century-plus cult following, killed violently before his time. There had been sightings and cosmic interventions and manifestations, just like with Tori-san and Megan and the others. But I could get no one to either confirm or deny on it, and had to keep digging.

I did so long into the night, waking up people, calling in favors, working Brenda like a draft horse. What had started out as a bright-eyed adventure eventually turned her into a yawning cadaverous wraith, still gamely calling, still listening patiently to the increasingly nasty comments as this or that insider who owed me something told me they knew nothing at all.

"If one more person asks me if I know what time it is . . ." she said, and couldn't finish because her jaw was cracking from another yawn. "This is no use, Hildy. The security's too good. I'm tired."

"Why do you think they call it legwork?"

I kept at it until the wee hours, and stopped only because Fox came in and told me Brenda had fallen asleep on the couch in the other room. I'd been prepared to stay awake all night, sustained by coffee and stims, but it was Fox's house, and our relationship was already getting a little rocky, so I packed it in, still no wiser as to who would be called to glory at ten the next morning.

I was bone weary, but I felt better than I had in quite a while.

Brenda had the resilience of true youth. She joined me in the bathroom the next morning looking none the worse for wear. I felt the corners of her eyes jabbing me as she pretended not to be interested in Hildy's Beauty Secrets. I dialed up programs on the various makeup machines and left them there when I was through so she could copy down the numbers when I wasn't looking. I remember thinking her mother should have taught her some of these tricks—Brenda wore little or no cosmetics, seemed to know nothing about them—but I knew nothing about her mother. If the old lady wouldn't let her daughter have a vagina, there was no telling what other restrictions had been in effect in the "Starr" household.

The one thing I still hadn't adjusted to about being female again was learning to allow for the two to three extra minutes I require to get ready to face the world in the morning. I think of it as Woman's Burden. Let's not get into the fact that it's a self-imposed one; I like to look my best, and that means enhancing even Bobbie's artistry. Instead of taking whatever the autovalet throws into my hand, I deliberate at least twenty seconds over what to wear. Then there's coloring and styling the hair to complement it, choosing a makeup scheme and letting the machines apply it, eye color, accessories, scent . . . the details of the Presentation of Hildy as I wish to present her are endless, time-consuming . . . and enjoyable. So maybe it's not such a burden after all, but the result on the morning of the canonization was that I missed the train I had planned to catch by twenty seconds and had to wait ten minutes for the next one. I spent the time showing Brenda a few tricks she could do to her standard paper jumper that would emphasize her best points—though picking out good points on that endless rail of a body taxed my inspiration and my tact to their limits.

She was coltishly pleased at the attention. I saw her scrutinizing my pale blue opaque body stocking with the almost subliminal moiré of even lighter blue running through the weave, and had a pretty good idea of what she'd be wearing the next day. I decided I'd drop some subtle hints to discourage it. Brenda in a body stocking would make as much sense, fashion-wise, as a snood on a dry salami.

The Grand Studio of the First Latitudinarian Church of Celebrity Saints is in the studio district, not far from the Blind Pig, convenient to the many members who work in the entertainment industry. The exterior is not much to look at, just a plain warehouse-type door leading off one of the tall, broad corridors of the upper parts of King City zoned for light manufacturing—which is a good description of the movie business, come to think of it. Over the entrance are the well-known initials F.L.C.C.S. framed in the round-cornered rectangle that has symbolized television long after screens ceased to be round-cornered rectangles anywhere but in the Flacks' Grand Studio.

Inside was much better. Brenda and I entered a long hallway with a roof invisible behind multi-colored spots. Lining the hall were huge holos and shrines of the Four Gigastars, starting with the most recently canonized.

First was Mambazo Nkabinde—"Momby" to all his fans. Born shortly before the Invasion in Swaziland, a nation that history has all but forgotten, emigrated to Luna with his father at age three under some sort of racial quota system in effect at the time. As a young man, invented Sphere Music almost single-handedly. Also known as The Last of the Christian Scientists, he died at the age of forty-three of a curable melanoma, presumably after much prayer. The Latitudinarian Church was not prejudiced about inducting members of other faiths; he had been canonized fifty years earlier, the last such ceremony until today.

Next we passed the exhibits in praise of Megan Galloway, the leading and probably best proponent of the now-neglected art of "feelies." She had a small but fanatical following one hundred years after her mysterious disappearance—an ending that made her the only one of the Flack Saints whose almost daily "sightings" could actually be founded in fact. The only female out of four non-Changing Gigastars, she was, with Momby, a good example of the pitfalls of enshrining celebrities prematurely. If it weren't for the fact that she provided the only costuming role model for the women of the congregation, she might have been dethroned long ago, as the feelies were no longer being made by anyone. Feelie fans had to be satisfied with tapes at least eighty years old. No one in the Church had contemplated the eclipse of an entire art form when they had elevated her into their pantheon.

I actually paused before the next shrine, the one devoted to Torinaga Nakashima: "Tori-san." He was the only one I felt deserved to be appreciated for his life's work. It was he who had first mastered the body harp, driving the final nails into the coffin he had fashioned for the electric guitar, long the instrument of choice for what used to be known as rocking-roll music. His music still sounds fresh to me today, like Mozart. He had died in Japan during the first of the Three Days of the Invasion, battling the implacable machines or beings or whatever they were that had stalked his native city, unbeatable Godzillas finally arrived at the real Tokyo. Or so the story went. There were those who said he had died at the wheel of his private yacht, trying his best to get the hell out of there and catch the last shuttle to Luna, but in this case I prefer the legend.

And last but indisputably first among the Saints, Elvis Aron Presley, of Tupelo, Mississippi; Nashville; and Graceland, Memphis, Tennessee, U.S. of A. It was his incredibly still-ascendant star one hundred years after his death that had inspired the retired ad agency executives who were the founding fathers of the Flacks to concoct the most blatant and profitable promotional campaign in the inglorious history of public relations: The F.L.C.C.S.

You could say what you want about the Flacks—and I'd said a lot, in private, among friends—but these people knew how to treat the working press. After the Elvis pavilion the crowd was divided into two parts. One was a long, unmoving line, composed of hopeful congregants trying to get a seat in the last row of the balcony, some of them waving credit cards which the ushers tried not to sneer at; it took more than just money to buy your way into *this* shindig. The rest of the crowd, the ones with press passes stuck into the brims of their battered gray fedoras, were steered through a gap in velvet ropes and led to a spread of food and drink that made UniBio's efforts at the ULTRA-Tingle rollout look like the garbage cans in the alley behind a greasy spoon.

A feeding frenzy among veteran reporters is not a pretty sight. I've been at free feeds where you needed to draw your hand back quickly or risk having a finger bitten off. This one was well-managed, as you'd expect from the Flacks. Each of us was met by a waiter or waitress whose sole job seemed to be to carry our plates and smile, smile, smile. There were people there who would have fasted for three days in anticipation if the Flacks had announced the ceremony ahead of time; I heard some grousing about that. Reporters have to find something to complain about, otherwise they might commit the unpardonable sin of thanking their hosts.

I walked, in considerable awe, past an entire juvenile brontosaur carcass, candied, garnished with glacéd fruit and with an apple in its mouth. They were rolling something unrecognizable away—I was told it had been a Tori-san effigy made entirely from sashimi—and replacing it with a three-meter likeness of Elvis in his Vegas Period, in marzipan. I plucked a sequin from the suit of lights and found it to be very tasty. I never did find out what it was.

I built what might easily qualify as the Sandwich of the Century. Never mind what was in it; I gathered from Brenda's queasy expression as she watched my Flackite wallah carrying it that ordinary mortals—those who did not understand the zen of cold cuts—might find some of my choices dissonant, to say the least. I admit not everyone is able to appreciate the exquisite tang of pickled pigs' knuckles rubbing shoulders with rosettes of whipped cream. Brenda herself needed no plate-carrier. She was schlumping along with just a small bowl of black olives and sweet pickles. I hurried, realizing that people were soon going to understand that she was with me. I don't think she even knew what one item in ten *was,* much less if she liked it or not.

The room the Flacks called the Grand Studio had formerly been the largest sound stage at NLF. They had fixed it up so the area we saw was shaped like a wedge, narrowing toward the actual stage in the front of the room. It was quite a large wedge. The walls on either side leaned in slightly as they rose, and were composed entirely of thousands upon thousands of glass-faced television screens, the old kind, rectangular with rounded corners, a shape that was as important to Flackites as the cross was to Christians. The Great Tube symbolized eternal life and, more important, eternal Fame. I could see a certain logic in that. Each of the screens, ranging in size from thirty centimeters to as much as ten meters across, was displaying a different image as Brenda and I entered, from the lives, loves, films, concerts, funerals, marriages and, for all I knew, bowel movements and circumcisions of the Gigastars. There were simply too many images to take in. In addition, holos floated through the room like enchanted bubbles, each with its smiling image of Momby, Megan, Tori-san, and Elvis.

The Flacks knew who this show was really for; we were escorted to an area at the edge of the stage itself. The actual congregants had to be content with the cheap seats and the television screens. There were balconies upon balconies somewhere back there, vanishing into the suspended-spotlight theme the Flacks favored.

Because we were late most of the seats right up front had been taken. I was about to suggest we split up when I spotted Cricket at a ringside table with an empty chair beside her. I grabbed Brenda with one hand and a spare chair with the other, and pulled both through the noisy crowd. Brenda was embarrassed to make everyone scoot over to make room for her chair; I'd have to speak to her about that. If she couldn't learn to push and shove and shout, she had no business in the news game.

"I love the body, Hildy," Cricket said as I wedged myself in between them. I preened a bit as a large pink pitcher was set in front of me. These Flacks were trained well; I was about to ask for lime wedges when an arm came around me and left a crystal bowl full of them.

"Do I detect a note of wistfulness?" I said.

"You mean because they've retired your jersey from the great game of cocksmanship?" She seemed to consider it. "I guess not."

I pouted, but it was for show. Frankly, the whole idea of having made love to her seemed to me by now an aberration. Not that I wouldn't be interested again when I Changed back to male, in thirty or so years, if she happened to be female still.

"Nice job on that lovers-after-death pic out at Nirvana," I said. I was poking through the assortment of press perks in a basket before me and trying to eat a part of my sandwich with my other hand. I found a gold commemorative medal, inscribed and numbered, that I knew I could get four hundred for at any pawnbroker in the Leystrasse, so long as I got there quick and beat every other reporter in Luna to the punch. A forlorn hope; I saw three of the damn things depart by messenger, and they wouldn't be the first. By now the medals would be a drug on the market. The rest of the stuff was mostly junk.

"That was you?" Brenda said, leaning over to ogle Cricket.

"Cricket, Brenda. Brenda, meet Cricket, who works for some scurrilous rag or other whose initials are S.S. and who deserves an Oscar for the job she is doing covering her deep despair at having had only one opportunity to experience the glory that was me."

"Yeah, it was sort of gory," Cricket said, reaching across me to shake hands. "Nice to meet you." Brenda stammered something.

"How much did that shot cost you?"

Cricket looked smug. "It was quite reasonable."

"What do you mean?" Brenda asked. "Why did it cost you?"

We both looked at her, then at each other, then back at Brenda.

"You mean that was staged?" she said, horrified. She looked at the olive in her hand, then put it back into the bowl. "I cried when I saw it," she said.

"Oh, stop looking like somebody just shot your puppy, damn it," I said. "Cricket, will you explain the facts of life to her? I would, but I'm clean; *you're* the unethical monster who violated a basic rule of journalism."

"I will if you'll trade places with me. I don't think I want to watch all that go down." She was pointing at my sandwich with a prim expression that was belied by what I could see of the remnants of *her* free lunch, which included the skeletons of three tiny birds, picked clean.

So we switched, and I got down to the serious business of eating and drinking, all the while keeping one ear cocked to the jabbering around me, on the off chance somebody had managed to get a scoop on the canonization. No one had, but I heard dozens of rumors:

"Lennon? Oh, c'mon, he was all washed up, that bullet was a good career move."

". . . wanna know who it's gonna be? Mickey Mouse, put your money on it."

"How they going to handle that? He doesn't even exist."

"So Elvis does? There's a cartoon revival—"

"And if they picked a cartoon, it'd be Baba Yaga."

"Get serious. She's not in the same *universe* as Mickey Mouse . . ."

"—says it's Silvio. There's nobody with one half the rep—"

"But he's got one problem, from the Flacks' point of view: he ain't dead yet. Can't get a real cult going till you're dead."

"C'mon, there's no law says they have to wait, especially these days. He could go on for five hundred more years. What'll they do, keep reaching back to the twentieth, twenty-first century and pick guys nobody remembers?"

"Everybody remembers Tori-san."

"That's different."

"—notice there's three men and only one woman. Granting they might pick somebody still alive, why not Marina?"

"Why not both of 'em? Might even get them back together. What a story. A double canonization. Think of the headlines."

"How about Michael Jackson?"

"Who?"

It kept on and on, a speculative buzz in the background. I heard half a dozen more names proposed, increasingly unlikely to my way of thinking. The only new one I'd heard, the only one I hadn't thought of, was Mickey, and I considered him a real possibility. You could have walked down to the Leystrasse that very day and bought a shirt with his picture on the front, and cartoons were enjoying a revival. There was no law saying a cult had to have a real object; what was being worshiped here was an image, not flesh and blood.

Actually, while there were no rules for a Flack canonization, there were guidelines that took on the force of laws. The Flacks did not create celebrities, they had no real ax to grind in this affair. They simply acknowledged preexisting cult figures, and there were certain qualities a cult figure had to have. Everyone had their own list of these qualities, and weighted them differently. Once more I went through my own list, and considered the three most likely candidates in the light of these requirements.

First, and most obvious, the Gigastar had to have been wildly popular when alive, with a planetary reputation, with fans who literally worshiped him. So forget about anybody before the early twentieth century. That was the time of the birth of mass media. The first cult figures of that magnitude were film stars like Charlie Chaplin. He could be eliminated because he didn't fulfill the second qualification: a cult following reaching down to the present time. His films were still watched and appreciated, but people didn't go crazy over him. The only person from that time who might have been canonized—if an F.L.C.C.S. had existed then—was Valentino. He died young, and was enshrined in that global hall of fame that was still in its infancy when he lived. But he was completely forgotten today.

Mozart? Shakespeare? Forget it. Maybe Ludwig Van B. was the hottest thing on the Prussian pop charts in his day, but they'd never heard of him in Ulan Bator . . . and where were his sides? He never cut any, that's where. The only way of preserving his music was to write it down on paper, a lost art. Maybe Will Shakespeare would have won a carload of Tonys and been flown to the coast to adapt his stuff for the silver screen. He was still very popular—*As You Like It* was playing two shows a day at the King City Center—but he and everyone else from before about 1920 had a fatal flaw, celebrity-wise: nobody knew anything about them. There was no film, no recordings. Celebrity worship is only incidentally about the art itself. You need to do something to qualify, it needn't be good, only evocative . . . but the real thing being sold by the Flacks and their antecedents was image. You needed a real body to rend and tear in the padloids, real scandals to tsk-tsk over, and real blood and real tragedy to weep over.

That was widely held to be the third qualification for sainthood: the early and tragic death. I personally thought it could be dispensed with in some circumstances, but I won't deny its importance. Nobody can *create* a cult. They rise spontaneously, from emotions that are genuine, even if they are managed adroitly.

For my money, the man they should be honoring today was Thomas Edison. Without his two key inventions, sound recording and motion picture film, the whole celebrity business would be bankrupt.

Mickey, John, or Silvio? Each had a drawback. With Mickey, it was that he wasn't real. So who cares? John . . . ? Maybe, but I judged his popularity wasn't quite in that stellar realm that would appeal to the Flacks. Silvio? The big one, that he was alive. But rules are made to be broken. He certainly had the star power. There was no more popular man in the Solar System. Any reporter in Luna would sell his mother's soul for one interview.

And then it came to me, and it was so obvious I wondered why I hadn't seen it before, and why no one else had figured it out.

"It's Silvio," I told Cricket. I swear the lady's ear tried to swivel toward me before her head did. That gal really has the nose for news.

"What did you hear?"

"Nothing. I just figured it out."

"So what do you want, I should kiss your feet? *Tell* me, Hildy."

Brenda was leaning over, looking at me like I was the great guru. I smiled at them, thought about making them suffer a little, but that was unworthy. I decided to share my Holmesian deductions with them.

"First interesting fact," I said, "they didn't announce this thing until yesterday. Why?"

"That's easy," Cricket snorted. "Because Momby's elevation was the biggest flop-ola since Napoleon promised to whip some British butt at Waterloo."

"That's part of the reason," I conceded. It had been before my time, but the Flacks were still smarting from that one. They'd conducted a three-month Who-Will-It-Be?-type campaign, and by the time the big day arrived The Supreme Potentate Of All Universes would have been a disappointment, much less Momby, who was a poor choice anyway. This was a bunch whose whole *raison d'etre* was publicity, as an art and science. Once burned, twice wear-a-fireproof-suit; they were managing this one the right way, as a big surprise with only a day to think about it. Neither press nor public could get bored in one day.

"But they've kept this one completely secret. From what I'm told, the fact that Momby was going to be elevated was about as secret from *us,* from the press, as Silvio's current hairstyle. The media simply agreed not to print it until the big day. Now think about the Flacks. Not a close-mouthed bunch, except for the inner circle, the Grand Flacks and so forth. Gossip is their lifeblood. If twenty people knew who the new Gigastar was, one of them would have blabbed it to one of my sources or one of yours, count on it. If *ten* people knew I'd give you even money I could have found it out. So even less than that know who it's gonna be. With me so far?"

"Keep talking, O silver-tongued one."

"I've got it down to three possibilities. Mickey, John, Silvio. Am I wildly off base there?"

She didn't say yes or no, but her shrug told me her own list was pretty much like mine.

"Each has a problem. You know what they are."

"Two out of three of them are . . . well, *old,*" Brenda put in.

"Lots of reasons for that," I said. "Look at the Four; all born on Earth. Trouble is, we're a less violent society than the previous centuries. We don't get enough tragic deaths. Momby's the only superstar who's had the grace to fix himself up with a tragic death in over a hundred years. Most everyone else hangs around until he's a has-been. Look at Eileen Frank."

"Look at Lars O'Malley," Cricket contributed.

From the blank look on Brenda's face, I could see it was like I'd guessed; she'd never heard of either of them.

"Where are they now?" she asked, unconsciously voicing the four words every celebrity fears the most.

"In the elephants' graveyard. In a taproom in Bedrock, probably, maybe on adjacent stools. Both of them used to be as big as Silvio." Brenda looked dubious, like I'd said something was bigger than infinity. She'd learn.

"So what's your great leap of deduction?" Cricket asked.

I waved my hand grandly around the room.

"All this. All these trillions and trillions of television screens. If it's Mickey or John, what's gonna happen, some guy backstage dashes off a quick sketch of them and comes out holding it over his head? No, what happens is every one of these screens starts showing *Steamboat Willie* and *Fantasia* and every other cartoon Mickey was ever in, or . . . what the hell films did John Lennon make?"

"You're the history buff. All I know about him is *Sergeant Pepper.*"

"Well, you get the idea."

"Maybe I'm dumb," Cricket said, not as though she believed it.

"You're not. Think about it." She did, and I saw the moment when the light dawned.

"You could be right," she said.

"No 'could be' about it. I've got half a mind to file on it right now. Walter could get out a newsbreaker before they make the big announcement."

"So use my phone; I won't even charge you."

I said nothing to that. If I'd had even one source telling me it was Silvio I'd have called Walter and let him decide. The history of journalism is filled with stories of people who jumped the headline and had to eat it later.

"I guess *I'm* dumb," Brenda said. "I still don't see it."

I didn't comment on her first statement. She *wasn't* dumb, just green, and I hadn't seen it myself until too late. So I explained.

"Somebody has to cue up the tapes to fill all these screens. Dozens of techs, visual artists, and so forth. There's no way they could orchestrate a thing like that and keep it down to a handful of people in the know. Most of my sources are just those kind of people, and they *always* have their hands out. Kind of money I was throwing around last night, if anybody knew, *I'd* know. So Mickey and John are out, *because* they're dead. Silvio has the great advantage of being able to show up here in person, so those television screens can show live feeds of what's happening on the stage."

Brenda frowned, thinking it over. I let her, and went back to my sandwich, feeling good for more than just having figured it out. I felt good because I genuinely admired Silvio. Mickey Mouse is good, no question, but the real hero there was Walter Elias Disney and his magic-makers. John Lennon I knew nothing about; his music didn't speak to me. I never saw what the fanatics saw in Elvis. Megan may have been good, but who cared? Momby was of his times; even the Flacks would admit, with a bellyful of liquor, that he had been a mistake for the church. Tori-san deserved to be up there with the real musical geniuses who lived before the Age of Celebrity came along to largely preclude most people's chances of achieving *real* greatness. I mean, how great can you get with people like me going through your garbage looking for a story?

Of all the people alive in the Solar System today, Silvio was the only man I admired. I'm a cynic, have been for years. My childhood heroes have long since fallen by the wayside. I'm in the business of discovering warts on people, and I've discovered so many that the very idea of hero-worship is quaint, at best. And it's not as if Silvio doesn't have his warts. I know them as well as every padloid reader in Luna. It's his *art* I really admire, the hell with the personality cult. He began as a mere genius, the writer and performer of music that has often moved me to tears. He grew over the years. Three years ago, when it looked as if he was fading, he suddenly blossomed again with the most stunningly original works of his career. There was no telling where he might still go.

One of his quirks, to my way of thinking, was his recent embracing of the Flack religion. And so what? Mozart wasn't a guy you'd want to bring home to meet the folks. Listen to the music. Look at the art. Forget about the publicity; no matter how much of it you read, you'll never *really* get to know the man. Most of us like to think we know something about famous people. It took me years to get over the fallacy of thinking that because I'd heard somebody speak about his or her life and times and fears on a talk show that I knew what they were really like. You *don't.* And the bad things you think you know are just as fallacious as the good things his publicity agent wants you to know. Behind the monstrous facade of fame each celebrity erects around himself is just a little mouse, not unlike you or me, who has to use the same kind of toilet paper in the morning, and who assumes the identical position.

And with that thought, the lights dimmed, and the show began.

There was a brief musical introduction drawing on themes from the works of Elvis and Tori-san, no hint of a Silvio connection in there. Dancers came out and did a number glorifying the Church. None of the prefatory material lasted too long. The Flacks had learned their lesson from Momby. They would not outstay their welcome this morning.

It was no more than ten minutes from the raising of the curtain to the appearance of the Grand Flack himself.

This was a man ordinary enough from the neck down, dressed in a flowing robe. But in place of a head he had a cube with television screens on four sides, each showing a view of a head from the appropriate angle. On top of the cube was a bifurcated antenna known as rabbit ears, for obvious reasons.

The face in the front screen was thin, ascetic, with a neatly trimmed goatee and mustache and a prim mouth on which a smile always looked like a painful event. I'd met him before at this or that function. He didn't appear publicly all that often, and the reason was simply that he, and most of the other Great Flacks, were no better as media personalities than I was. For the church services the F.L.C.C.S. hired professionals, people who knew how to make a sermon stand up and walk around the room. They had no lack of talent for such jobs. The Flacks naturally appealed to hopeful artists who hoped to one day stand beside Elvis. But today was different, and oddly enough, the Grand Flack's very stiffness and lack of camera poise lent gravity to the proceedings.

"Good morning! Fellow worshipers and guests, we welcome you! Today will go down in history! This is the day a mere mortal comes to glory! The name will be revealed to you shortly! Join with us now in singing 'Blue Suede Shoes.' "

That's the way Flacks talk, and that's the way I'd been recording it for many years now. They'd given me enough stories, so if they had crazy ideas about how they wanted to be quoted in print, it was all right with me. Flacks believed that language was too cluttered with punctuation, so they'd eliminated the ., the ,, the ', and the ?, and most especially the ; and the :. Nobody ever understood what those last two were for, anyway. They were never very interested in asking questions, only in providing answers. They figured the exclamation point and the quotation mark were all any reasonable person needed for discourse, along with the underline, naturally. And they were big on typefaces. A Flack news release read like a love letter to P.T. Barnum.

I abstained from the sing-along; I didn't know the words, anyway, and hymnals weren't provided. The folks in the bleachers made up for my absence. The boogying got pretty intense for a while there. The Grand Flack just stood with his hands folded, smiling happily at his flock. When the number came to an end he moved forward again, and I realized this was it.

"And now the moment you've all been waiting for!" he said. "The name of the person who from this day forward will live with the stars!" The lights were dimming as he spoke. There was a moment of silence, during which I heard an actual collective intake of breath . . . unless that was from the sound system. Then the Grand Flack spoke again.

"I give you SILVIO!!!!!"

A single spotlight came on, and there he stood. I had known it, I had been ninety-nine percent sure anyway, but I still felt a thrill in my heart, not only at having been correct, but because this was so *right*. No, I didn't believe in all the Flackite crap. But *he* did, and it was right that he should be so honored by the people who believed as he did. I almost had a lump in my throat.

I was on my feet with everyone else. The applause was deafening, and if it was augmented by the speakers hidden in the ceiling, who cared? I liked Silvio enough when I was a man. I hadn't counted on the gut-throbbing impression he'd make on me as a female. He stood there, tall and handsome, accepting the adulation with only a small, ironic wave of his hand, as if he didn't really understand why everyone loved him so much but he was willing to accept it so as not to embarrass us. False, all false, I well knew; Silvio had a titanic ego. If there was anyone in Luna who actually *over*estimated his genuinely awesome talent, it was Silvio. But who among us can cast a stone unless they have at least as much talent? Not me.

A keyboard was rolled out and left in front of him. This was really exciting. It could mean the opening of a new sound for Silvio. For the last three years he'd been working his magic on the body harp. I leaned forward to hear the first chords, as did everyone in the audience, except one person. As he made his move toward the keys, the right side of his head exploded.

Where were you when . . . ? Every twenty years a story comes along like that, and anyone you ask knows exactly what he was doing when the news came in. Where I was when Silvio was assassinated was ten meters away, close enough that I saw it happen before I heard the shot. Time collapsed for me, and I moved without thinking about it. There was nothing of the reporter in me at that moment, and nothing of the heroine. I'm not a risk-taker, but I was up and out of my seat and vaulting onto the stage before he'd landed, loosely, the ruined head bouncing on the floor-boards. I leaned over him and picked him up by the shoulders, and it must have been about then that I was hit, because I *saw* my blood splatter on his face and a big hole appear in his cheek and a sort of *churning* motion in the soft red matter exposed behind the big hole in his skull. You must have seen it. It's probably the most famous bit of holocam footage ever shot. Intercut with the stuff from Cricket's cam, which is how it's usually shown, you can see me react to the sound of the second shot, lift my head and look over my shoulder and search for the gunman, which is what saved me from having my own brains blown out when the third shot arrived. The postmortem team estimated that shot missed my cheek by a few centimeters. I didn't see it hit, but when I turned back I saw the results. Silvio's face had already been shattered by the fragmented bullet that had passed through me; the third projectile was more than enough to blow the remaining brain tissue through a new hole in his head. It wasn't necessary; the first had done the fatal work.

That's when Cricket took her famous still shot. The spotlight is still on us as I hold Silvio's torso off the ground. His head lolls back, eyes open but glazed, what you can see of them under the film of blood. I've got one bloody hand raised in the air, asking a mute question. I don't remember raising the hand; I don't know what the question was, other than the eternal *why?*

The next hour was as confused as such scenes inevitably are. I was jostled to the side by a bunch of bodyguards. Police arrived. Questions were asked. Someone noticed I was bleeding, which was the first time I was aware that I'd been hit. The bullet had punched a clean hole through the upper part of my left arm, nicking the bone. I'd been wondering why the arm wasn't working. I wasn't alarmed by it; I was just wondering. I never *did* feel any pain from the wound. By the time I should have, they had it all fixed up as good as new. People have since tried to convince me to wear a scar there as a memento of that day. I'm sure I could use it to impress a lot of cub reporters in the Blind Pig, but the whole idea disgusts me.

Cricket was immediately off following the assassin story. Nobody knew who he or she was, or how he'd gotten away, and there was a fabulous story for whoever tracked the person down and got the first interview. That didn't interest me, either. I sat there, possibly in shock though the machines said I was not, and Brenda stood beside me though I could see she was itching to get out and cover the story, any part of it.

"Idiot," I told her, with some affection, when I finally noticed her. "You want Walter to fire you? Did somebody get my holocam feed? I don't remember."

"I took it. Walter has it. He's running it right now." She had a copy of the *Nipple* in one hand, glancing at the horrific images. My phone was ringing and I didn't need a Ph.D. in deductive logic to know it was Walter calling, asking what I was doing. I turned it off, which Walter would have made a capital offense if he'd been making the laws.

"Get going. See if you can track down Cricket. Wherever she is, that's where the news will be. Try not to let her leave too many tracks on your back when she runs over you."

"Where are you going, Hildy?"

"I'm going home." And that's just what I did.

13

HER GIRL FRIDAY

I had to turn the phone off at home, too. I had become part of the biggest story of my lifetime, and every reporter in the universe wanted to ask me a probing question: How did you *feel*, Hildy, when you put your hand into the still-warm brains of the only man on Luna you respected? This is known as poetic justice.

For my sins, I soon set the phone to answer to the four or five newspeople I felt were the best, plus the grinning homunculus that passed for an anchor at the *Nipple,* and gave them each a five-minute, totally false interview, full of exactly the sort of stuff the public expected. At the end of each I pleaded emotional exhaustion and said I'd grant a more complete interview in a few days. This satisfied no one, of course; from time to time my front door actually rattled with the impact of frustrated reporters hurling their bodies against three-inch pressure-tight steel.

In truth, I didn't know how I felt. I was numb, in a way, but my mind was also working. I was thinking, and the reporter was coming alive after the horrid shock of actually getting *shot.* I mean, *damn* it! Hadn't that fucking bullet ever heard of the Geneva Conventions? We were noncombatants, we were supposed to *suck* the blood, not produce it. I was angry at that bullet. I guess some part of me had really thought I was immune.

I fixed myself a good meal and thought it over while I did. Not a sandwich. I thought I might be through with sandwiches. I don't cook a lot, but when I do I'm pretty good at it, and it helps me think. When I'd handed the last dish to the washer I sat down and called Walter.

"Get your ass in here, Hildy," he said. "I've got you lined up for interviews from ten minutes ago till the Tricentennial."

"No," I said.

"I don't think this is a good connection. I thought you said no."

"It's a perfect connection."

"I could fire you."

"Don't get silly. You want my exclusive interview to run in the *Shit*, where they'll triple the pittance you pay me?" He didn't answer that for a long time, and I had nothing else to say just yet, so we listened to the long silence. I hadn't turned on the picture.

"What are you going to do?" he asked, plaintively.

"Just what you asked me to do. Get the story on the Flacks. You said I was the best there was at it, didn't you?" The quality of the silence changed that time. It was a regretful silence, as in how-could-I-have-said-anything-so-stupid silence. He didn't say he'd told me that just to charm me out of quitting. Another thing he didn't say was how dare I threaten him with selling out to a rival, and he left unvoiced the horrible things he'd try to do to my career if I did such a thing. The phone line was simply buzzing with things he didn't say, and he didn't say them so loudly I'd have been frightened if I really feared for my job. At last he sighed, and *did* say something.

"When do I get the story?"

"When I find it. What I want is Brenda, right now."

"Sure. She's just underfoot here."

"Tell her to come in the back way. She knows where it is, and I don't think five other people in Luna know that."

"Six, counting me."

"I figured. Don't tell anyone else, or I'll never get out of here alive."

"What else?"

"Nothing. I'll handle it all from here." I hung up. I started making calls.

The first one was to the queen. She didn't have what I needed, but she knew somebody who knew somebody. She said she'd get back to me. I sat down and made a list of items I would need, made several more calls, and then Brenda was knocking on the back door.

She wanted to know how I was, she wanted my reactions to this and that, not as a reporter, but as a concerned friend. I was touched, a little, but I had work to do.

"Hit me," I said.

"Pardon?"

"Hit me. Make a fist and smash it into my face. I need you to break my nose. I tried it a couple times before you got here, and I can't seem to hit hard enough."

She gave me that look that says she's trying to remember all the ways out of this place, and how to get to them without alarming me.

"My problem," I explained, "is I can't risk going in public with this face on me; I need it rearranged, and in a hurry. So hit me. You know how; you've seen cowboys and gangsters do it in the movies." I stuck my face out and closed my eyes.

"You've . . . you've deadened it, I guess?"

"What kind of nut do I look like? Don't answer, just hit me."

She did, a blow that would have sent a housefly to intensive care if one had been sitting on the tip of my nose.

She had to try four more times, in the end using an old spitball bat I found in my closet, before we got that sickening crunching sound that said we'd done the trick. I shouldn't be too hard on her. Maybe I was acting erratic, there was probably an easier way and she deserved more explanations, but I wasn't in the mood for them. She had a lot worse to come, and I didn't have time.

It bled a lot, as you'd expect. I held my nose pressed in with a finger on the tip, and stuck my face in the autodoc. When it healed, a few minutes later, I had a wide, vaguely African nose with a major hook on the end and a bend toward the left.

Part of getting a story is preparation, part is improvisation, part perspiration and a little bit inspiration. There are small items I carry around constantly in my purse that I may use once in five years, but when I need them, I need them badly. A disguise is something I need every once in a while, never as badly as I did then, but I'd always been prepared for disguising myself on the spur of the moment. It's harder now than it used to be. People are better at seeing through small changes since they're used to having friends rework their faces to indulge a passing fad. Bushy eyebrows or a wig are no longer enough, if you want to be sure. You need to change the shape of the face.

I got a screwdriver and probed around in my upper jaw, between the cheek and gum, until I found the proper recessed socket. I pushed the tip of the blade through the skin and slotted it in the screw and started turning it. When the blade slipped Brenda peered into my mouth and helped me. As she turned the screwdriver, my cheekbone began to move.

It's a cheap and simple device you can buy at any joke shop and have installed in half an hour. Bobbie had wanted to take it out. He's offended at anything that might be used to mar his work. I'd left them in, and now I was glad as I watched my face being transformed in the mirror. When Brenda was done, my face was much wider and more gaunt, and my eyelids had a slight downward slant. With the new nose, Callie herself would not have known me. If I held my lower jaw so I had an overbite, I looked even stranger.

"Let me get that left one again," Brenda said. "You're lopsided."

"Lopsided is good." I tasted blood, but soon had that healed up. Looking at myself, I decided it was enough, and turned the nerve receptors in my face back on. There was a little soreness on the nose, but nothing major.

So I could have gotten some of the same effect by stuffing tissue paper into my cheeks, I guess. If that's all I had, I'd have used it, but did you ever try talking with paper in your mouth? An actor is trained to do it; I'm not. Besides, you're always aware it's there, it's distracting.

Brenda wanted to know what we were going to do, and I thought about what I could safely tell her. It wasn't much, so I sat her down and she looked up at me wide-eyed.

"You got two choices," I told her. "One, you can help me get ready for this caper, and then you can bow out, and no hard feelings. Or you can go along to the end. But I'll tell you going in, you're not going to know much. I think we'll get one hell of a story out of it, but we could get into a lot of trouble."

She thought it over.

"How much can you tell me?"

"Only what I think you need to know at the moment. You'll just have to trust me on the rest."

"Okay."

"You idiot. Never trust anybody who says 'trust me.' Except just this once, of course."

I went to the King City Plaza, one of the better hotels in the neighborhood of the Platz, and checked in to the Presidential Suite using Brenda's *Nipple* letter of credit, freshly rerated to A-Double-Plus. I'd told Walter I might need to buy an interplanetary liner before this job was over, but the fact was since he was paying for it, I just wanted to go first class, and I'd never stayed in the Presidential Suite. I registered us under the names Kathleen Turner and Rosalind Russell, two of the five people who've played the part of Hildegard/Hildebrandt Johnson on the silver screen. The fellow at the front desk must not have been a movie buff; he didn't bat an eye.

The suite came furnished with a staff, including a boy and a girl in the spa, which was large enough for the staging of naval war games. In a better mood I might have asked the boy to stick around; he was a hunk. But I kicked them all out.

I stood in the middle of the room and said, "My name is Hildy Johnson, and I declare this to be my legal residence." Liz had advised that, for the benefit of the hidden mikes and cameras, just in case the tapes were ever brought forward as evidence in a court of law. A hotel guest has the same rights as a person in quarters she owns or rents, but it never hurt to be safe.

I made a few more phone calls, and spent the time waiting for some of them to be returned by going from room to room and stripping the sheets and blankets off the many beds. I chose a room with no windows looking out into the Mall, and went around draping sheets over all the mirrors in the room. There were a lot of them. The call I was waiting for came just as I finished. I listened to the instructions, and left the room.

In a park not far from the hotel I walked around for almost half an hour, which didn't surprise me. I assumed I was being checked out. Finally I spotted the man I'd been told to look for, and sat on the other end of a park bench. We didn't look at each other, or talk. He got up and walked away, leaving a sack on the bench between us. I waited a few more minutes, breathed deeply, and picked up the sack. No hand reached out to grab my shoulder. Maybe I didn't have the nerves for this sort of work.

Back in the suite I didn't have long to wait before Brenda knocked on the door, back from her shopping expedition. She'd done well. Everything I'd asked for was in the packages she carried. We got out the costumes of the Electricians Guild and put them on: blue coveralls with Guild patches and equipment belts. Names were stitched into the fabric over the left breast: I was Roz and she was Kathy. Next to the ceremonial wrenches, screwdrivers, and circuit testers dangling from the belt I clipped some of the items I'd just obtained in such a melodramatic fashion. They fit right in. We donned yellow plastic hardhats and picked up black metal lunchboxes and looked at each other in the mirror. We burst out laughing. Brenda seemed to be enjoying the game so far. It was an adventure.

Brenda looked ridiculous, as usual. You'd think a disguise on Brenda would work about as well as a wig on a flagpole. The fact is, she is not that abnormal for her generation. Who knows where this height thing is going to end? Another of many causes of the generation gap Callie had talked about was a simple matter of dimension: people of Brenda's age group tended not to frequent the older parts of the city where so many of their elders lived . . . because they kept hitting their heads on things. We built to a smaller scale in those days.

There were no human guards on the workers' entrance to the Flack Grand Studio. I didn't really expect to encounter any at all; according to the information I'd bought they only employed six of them. People tended to rely on machines for that sort of thing, and their trust can be misplaced, as I demonstrated to Brenda with one of the illegal gizmos. I waved it at the door, waited while red lights turned green, and the door sprung open. I'd been told that one of the three machines I had would deal with any security system I'd find in the Studio. I just hoped *my* trust wasn't mis-placed, in either the shady characters who sold this sort of stuff or the machines themselves. We *do* trust the little buggers, don't we? I had no idea what the stinking thing was doing, but when it flashed a green light at me I trotted right in, like Pavlov's dog Spotski.

Up three floors, down two corridors, seventh door on the left. And who should be standing there looking frustrated but . . . Cricket.

"If you touch that doorknob," I said, "Elvis will return and he won't be handing out pink Cadillacs." She jumped just a little. Damn, that girl was good. She was trying to pass herself off as some kind of Flack func-tionary, carrying a clipboard like an Amazon's shield. The good old clip-board can be the magic key to many places if you know how to use it, and Cricket was born to the con. She looked at us haughtily through dark glasses.

"I beg your pardon," she sniffed. "What are you two doing . . ." She had been flipping officiously through papers on her board, as if searching for our names, which we hadn't given, when she realized it was Brenda way up there under that yellow hardhat. Nothing had prepared her for that, or for the dawning realization of who it was playing Jeff to Brenda's Mutt.

"Goddam," she breathed. "It's you, isn't it? Hildy?"

"In the flesh. I'm ashamed of you, Cricket. Balked by a mere door? You've apparently forgotten your Girl Scout motto."

"All I remember is never let him in the back door on the first date."

"Be prepared, love, be prepared." And I waved one of my magic wands at the door. Naturally, one of the lights remained obstinately red. So I chose another one at random and the machine paid off like a crooked slot machine. We went through the door, and I suddenly realized what her dark glasses were for.

We were in an ordinary corridor with three doors leading off of it. Music was coming from behind one of the doors. According to the map I'd paid a lot of Walter's money for, that was the one. This time I had to use all three machines, and the last one took its time, each red light going out only after a baffling readout of digits on a numeric display. I guess it was doing something arcane with codes. But the door opened, and I didn't hear any alarms. You wouldn't, of course, but you keep your ears tuned anyway. We went through the door and found ourselves in a small room with the Grand Council of Flacks.

Or with their heads, anyway.

The heads were on a shelf a few meters from us, facing away toward a large screen which was playing *It Happened At The World's Fair*. They were in their boxes—I don't think they could be easily removed—so what we saw was seven television screens displaying the backs of heads. If they were aware of our presence they gave no sign of it. Though how they *could* have given any sign of it continues to elude me. Wires and tubes grew out of the bottom of the shelf, leading to small machines that hummed merrily to themselves.

Brenda was looking very nervous. She started to say something but I put a finger to my lips and put on my mask. She did the same, as Cricket watched us both. These were plastic Halloween-type masks, modified with a voice scrambler, and I'd gotten them mostly to calm Brenda; I didn't expect them to be any use if it came to the crunch, since security cameras in the hallways would surely have taken our pictures by now. But she was even less sophisticated in these things than I, and wouldn't have realized that.

Cricket had had her hand in a coat pocket since we entered the first corridor. The hand started to come out, and I pointed over her shoulder and said, "What the hell is that?" She looked, and I took one of the wrenches off my equipment belt and clanged it down on the crown of her head.

It doesn't work like you see it on television. She went down hard, then lifted herself up onto her hands, shaking her head. A rope of saliva was hanging out of her mouth. I hit her again. Her head started to bleed, and she *still* didn't clock out. The third time I really put some English on it, and sure enough Brenda grabbed my arm and spoiled my aim and the wrench hit her on the side of the head, doing more damage than if she'd left me alone, but it also did the job. Cricket fell down like a sack of wet cement and didn't move.

"What the hell are you doing?" Brenda asked. The scrambler denatured her voice, made her sound like a creepoid from Planet X.

"Brenda, I said *no questions.*"

"I didn't plan on this."

"I didn't, either, but if you crap out on me now I swear I'll break both your arms and leave you right beside her." She faced me down, breathing hard, and I began to wonder if I could handle her if it came to it. My record with angry females wasn't sterling, even when I had the weight advantage. At last she slumped, and nodded, and I quickly dropped to one knee and rolled Cricket over and put my face close to hers. I felt her pulse, which seemed okay, peeled back an eyelid, checked the pupils. I didn't know much more first aid than that, but I knew she was in no danger. Help would be here soon, though she wouldn't welcome it. I picked up the goofball that had rolled out of her limp hand and put it in my own pocket. I showed Brenda a photo.

"Look through those cabinets back there, find one of these," I told her.

"What are we—"

"No questions, dammit."

I checked the fourth and most expensive electronic burglar tool I'd purchased, which had been functioning since we entered the Studio. All green lights. This one was busily confounding all the active and passive systems that might be calling for help for the seven dwarfs on the shelf. Don't ask me how; all I know is if one man can think up a lock, another can figure out how to pick it. I'd paid heavily for the security information about the Studio, and so far I'd gotten my money's worth. I went around the shelf and stood between the screen and the Council, saw seven of the infamous Talking Heads that had been a television feature from the very beginning. I chose the Grand Flack, and leaned close to his prim, disapproving features. His first reaction was to use his limited movement to try and see around me. More interested in the movie than in possible danger to himself. I guess if you live in a box you'd have to get fairly fatalistic about such things.

"I want to tell me how to remove you from the shelf without doing any harm to you," I said.

"Don't worry about it," he sneered. "Someone will be here to arrest you in a few minutes."

I hoped he was bluffing, had no way of knowing for sure.

"How many minutes can you live without these machines?" He thought it over, made a head movement I interpreted as a shrug.

"Detaching me is easy; simply lift the handle on top of the box. But I'll die in a few minutes." The thought didn't seem to bother him.

"Unless I plug you into one of these." I took the machine Brenda had located and held it up in front of him. He made a sour face.

I don't know what the machine was called. What it did was provide life support for his head, containing things like an artificial heart, lungs, kidneys, and so forth, all quite small since there wasn't that much life to support. I'd been told it would sustain him for eight hours independently, indefinitely when hooked into an autodoc. The device was the same dimensions as his head-box, and about ten centimeters deep. I placed it on the floor and lifted the box by the handle. He looked worried for the first time. A few drops of blood dripped onto the shelf, where I could see a maze of metal pins, plastic tubes, air hoses. There was a similar pattern of fittings on the transport device, arranged so there was only one way you could plug it in. I positioned the box over the life support and pressed down.

"Am I doing it right?" I asked the Grand Flack.

"There's not much you could do wrong," he said. "And you'll never get away with this."

"Try me." I found the right switches, turned off his voice and three of the television screens. The fourth, the one that had been showing his face, was replaced with the movie the group had been watching when we arrived. "Let's get out of here," I said to Brenda.

"What about her? What about Cricket?"

"I said no questions. Let's *move.*"

She followed me out into the corridor, through the door where we'd met Cricket, down more hallways. Then we rounded a corner and met a burly man in a brown uniform who crossed his arms and frowned at us.

"Where are you going with that?" he asked.

"Where do you think, Mac?" I asked. "I'm taking it into the shop. You try to run ten thousand of these things, you're gonna get breakdowns."

"Nobody told me nothing about it."

I set the Grand Flack on the floor with the movie side of the screen facing the guard; his eyes strayed to the screen, as I'd hoped. There's something about a moving image on a television screen that simply draws the eyes, especially if you're a Flackite. I had one hand on my trusty wrench, but mostly I flipped through the papers on my clipboard in a bored manner. I came to one page—it seemed to be an insurance policy for Cricket's apartment—and pointed triumphantly to the middle of it.

"Says right here. Remove and repair one model seventeen video monitor, work order number 45293-a/34. Work to be completed by blah blah blah."

"I guess the paperwork didn't get to me yet," he said, one eye still on the screen. Maybe we were coming to his favorite part. All I knew was if he'd asked to see the paperwork I'd have held the clipboard out to him and beaned him with the wrench when he looked at it.

"Ain't that always the way."

"Yeah. I was just surprised to see you two here, what with all the excitement with Silvio gettin' killed and all."

"What the hell," I said, with a shrug, picking up the Grand Flack and tucking him under my arm. "Sometimes you just gotta go that extra kilometer if you want to get a head." And we walked out the door.

Brenda made it almost a hundred meters down the corridor and then she said, "I think I'm going to faint." I steered her to a bench in the middle of the mall and sat her down and put her head between her knees. She was shaking all over and her breathing was unsteady. Her hand was cold as ice.

I held out my own hand, and was pleased to note it was steady. I honestly hadn't been frightened after I detached the Flack from his shelf; I'd figured that if there was any point where my devices might fail, that would be it. But I was aided by something that had helped many a more professional burglar before I ever tried my hand at it. It had simply never been envisioned that anyone would want to *steal* one of the council members. As for the rest . . . well, you can read all these wonderfully devious tales about how spies in the past have stolen military and state secrets with elaborate ruses, with stealth and cunning. Some of it must have been like that, but I'd bet money that a lot of them had been stolen by people with uniforms and clipboards who just went up to somebody and *asked* for them.

"Is it over yet?" Brenda asked, weakly. She looked pale.

"Not yet. Soon. And still no questions."

"I'm going to have a few pretty damn soon, though," she said.

"I'll bet you will."

In order to save time I hadn't had her get any more costumes to stash along our getaway route, so we simply peeled off the electrician duds and stuffed them into the trash in a public rest room and returned to the Plaza in the nude. I was carrying the Grand Flack in a shopping bag from one of the shops on the Platz and we had our arms around each other like lovers. In the elevator Brenda let go of me like I was poison, and we rode up in silence.

"Can we talk now?" she asked, when I'd closed the door behind us.

"In a minute." I lifted the box out of the bag, along with the few other items I'd saved: the magic wands, the dark glasses, the goofball. I picked up a newspad and turned it on and we watched and read and listened for a few minutes, Brenda growing increasingly impatient. There was no mention of a daring break-in at the Grand Studio, no all-points bulletin for Roz and Kathy. I hadn't expected one. The Flacks understood publicity, and while there is some merit in the old saw about not caring what you print about me so long as you spell my name right, you'd much prefer to see the news you *manage* out there in the public view. This story had about a thousand deadly thorns in it if the Flacks chose to exploit it, and I was sure they'd think it over a long time before they reported our crime to the police, if they ever did. Besides, their plates were full with the assassination stories, which would keep their staff busy for months, churning out new angles to feed to the pads.

"Okay," I said to Brenda. "We're safe for a while. What did you want to know?"

"Nothing," she said coldly. "I just wanted to tell you I think you're the most disgusting, rottenest, most horrible . . . ." Her imagination failed when it came to finding a noun. She'd have to work on that; I could have suggested a dozen off the top of my head. But not for the reasons she thought.

"Why is that?" I asked.

She was momentarily stunned at the enormity of my lack of remorse.

"What you did to *Cricket!*" she shouted, half rising from her chair. "That was so dirty and underhanded . . . I don't think I want to know you anymore."

"I'm not sure I do, either. But sit down. There's something I want to show you. Two things, actually." The Plaza has some charming antique phones and there was one beside my chair. I picked up the receiver and dialed a number from memory.

"Straight Shit," came a pleasant voice. "News desk."

"Tell the editor that one of her reporters is being held against her will in the Grand Studio of the F.L.C.C.S. church."

The voice grew cautious. "And who might that be?"

"How many did you infiltrate this morning? Her name is Cricket. Don't know the last name."

"And who are you, ma'am?"

"A friend of the free press. Better hurry; when I left they were tying her down and cuing up *G.I. Blues.* Her mind could be gone by now." I hung up.

Brenda sputtered, her eyes wide.

"And you think that makes up for what you did to her?"

"No, and she doesn't deserve it, but she'd probably do the same thing for me if the situation was reversed, which it almost was. I know the editor at the *Shit;* she'll have a flying squad of fifty shock troops down there in ten minutes with some ammunition the Flacks will understand, like mock-ups of the next hour's headline if they don't cough up Cricket pronto. The Flacks will want to keep this quiet, but they aren't above trying to get our names out of Cricket since it looks like a falling-out among thieves."

"And if it wasn't, what was it?"

"It was the golden rule, honey," I said, putting on Cricket's dark glasses and holding up the goofball between thumb and forefinger. "In journalism, that rule reads 'Screw unto others before they screw you.' " I flicked the goofball with my thumb and tossed it between us.

Damn, but those things are bright! It reminded me of the nuke in Kansas, seeming to scorch holes right through the protective lenses. It lasted some fraction of a second, and when I took the glasses off Brenda was slumped over in her chair. She'd be out for twenty minutes to half an hour.

What a world.

I picked up the head of the church and carried him into the room I'd prepared. I set him on a table facing the wall-sized television screen, which was turned off at the moment. I rapped on the top of the box.

"You okay in there?" He didn't answer. I turned a latch and opened the front screen, which was still showing the same movie on both its flat surfaces, inner and outer. The face glared at me.

"Close that door," he said. "It's just ten minutes to the end."

"Sorry," I said, and closed it. Then I took my wrench—I'd developed a certain fondness for that wrench—and rapped it against the glass screen, which shattered. I had a glimpse of a blissfully smiling face as the shards fell, then he was screaming insults. Somewhere I heard a little motor whirring as it pumped air through whatever he used for a larynx. He tried uselessly to twist himself so he could see one of the screens to either side of him, which were also tuned to the same program.

"Oh, were you watching that?" I said. "How clumsy of me." I pulled a cord out of the wall and patched his player into the wall television set, turned the sound down low. He grumped for a while, but in the end he couldn't resist the dancing images behind me. If he'd noticed I was letting him see my face he didn't seem worried about the possible implications. Death didn't seem to be high on his list of fears.

"They're going to punish you for this, you know," he said.

"Who would 'they' be? The police? Or do you have your own private goon squads?"

"The police, of course."

"The police will never hear about this, and you know it."

He just sniffed. He sniffed again when I broke the screens on each side of his head. But when I took the patch cord in my hand he looked worried.

"See you later. If you get hungry, holler." I pulled the cord out of the wall, and the big screen went blank.

I hadn't brought any clothes to change into. I got restless and went down to the lobby and browsed around in some of the shops there, killed a half hour, but my heart wasn't really in it. In spite of all my rationalizations about the Flacks, I kept expecting that tap on the shoulder that asks the musical question, "Do you know a good lawyer?" I picked out some loose harem pants in gold silk and a matching blouse, a lounging pajama ensemble I guess you'd call it, mostly because I dislike parading around with no clothes in public, and because Walter was picking up the tab, then I thought of Brenda and got interested. I found a similar pair for her in a green that I thought would do nice things to her eyes. They had to extrude the arms and legs, but the waist was okay, since it was supposed to leave the midriff bare.

When I got back to the suite Brenda was no longer slumped in the chair. I found her in the bathroom, hugging the toilet and crying her eyes out, looking like a jumbo coat hanger somebody had crumpled up and left there. I felt low enough to sit on a sheet of toilet paper and swing my feet, to borrow a phrase from Liz. I'd never used a goofball before, had forgotten how sick they were supposed to make you. If I'd remembered, would I still have used it? I don't know. Probably.

I knelt beside her and put my arm around her shoulders. She quieted down to a few whimpers, didn't try to move away. I got a towel and wiped her mouth, flushed away the stuff she'd brought up. I eased her around until she was sitting against the wall. She wiped her eyes and nose and looked at me with dead eyes. I pulled the pajamas out of the sack and held them up.

"Look what I got you," I said. "Well, actually I used your credit card, but Walter's good for it."

She managed a weak smile and held out her hand and I gave them to her. She tried to show an interest, holding the shirt up to her chest. I think if she'd thanked me I'd have run screaming to the police, begging to be arrested.

"They're nice," she said. "You think it'll look good on me?"

"Trust me," I said. She met my eyes without flinching or giving me one of her apologetic smiles or any other of her arsenal of don't-hit-me-I'm-harmless gestures. Maybe she was growing up a little. What a shame.

"I don't think I will," she said. I put a hand on each of her shoulders and put my face close to hers.

"Good," I said, stood, and held out a hand. She took it and I pulled her up and we went back to the main room of the suite.

She did cheer up a little when she got the clothes on, turning in front of a big mirror to study herself from all angles, which reminded me to look in on my prisoner. I told her to wait there.

He wasn't nearly as bad off as I'd thought he would be, which worried me more than I let him know. I couldn't figure it out until I crouched down to his level and looked into the blank television screen he faced.

"You tricky rascal," I said. Looking at the inert plastic surface of the screen on the wall, I could see part of a picture reflected from the screen directly behind his head, the only one I hadn't smashed out. I couldn't tell what the movie was, and considering how little of it he could see he might not have known, either, with the sound off, but it must have been enough to sustain him. I picked him up and turned him around facing away from the wall screen. He made a fascinating centerpiece, sure to start interesting conversations at your next party. Just a head sitting on a thick metal base, with four little pillars supporting a flat roof above him. It was like a little temple.

He was looking really worried now. I crouched down and looked at all the covered mirrors and glass. I found no surface that would reflect an image to him if I were to turn on the screen behind him, which I did. I debated about the sound, finally turned it on, figuring it would torment him more to hear it and not be able to see. If I was wrong, I could always try it the other way in an hour or so, if we were granted that much time. Let's face it, if anybody was looking for us, we'd be easy to find. I waved at him and made a face at the string of curses that followed me out of the room.

How to get information out of somebody that doesn't want to talk? That's the question I'd asked myself before I started this escapade. The obvious answer is torture, but even I draw the line at that. But there's torture and then there's torture. If a man had spent most of his life watching passively as endless images marched by right in front of his face, spent every waking hour watching, how would he react if the plug was pulled? I'd find out soon enough. I'd read somewhere that people in sensory deprivation tanks quickly became disoriented, pliable, lost their will to resist. Maybe it would work with the Grand Flack.

Brenda and I spent a silent half hour sitting in chairs not too far from each other that might as well have been on other planets. When she finally spoke, it startled me. I'd forgotten she was there, lost in my own thoughts.

"She was going to use that thing on us," she said.

"Who, Cricket? You saw it fall out of her hand, right? It's called a goofball. Knocks you right out, from what I'm told."

"You were told right. It was awful."

"I'm really sorry, Brenda. It seemed like a good idea at the time."

"It was. I asked for it. I deserved it."

I wasn't sure about that, but it *had* been the quickest way to show her what we'd narrowly averted. That's me: quick and dirty, and explain later. She thought about it a few more minutes.

"Maybe she was just going to use it on the Flacks."

"Sure she was; she didn't expect to find *us* there. But you didn't see her handing out pairs of glasses. We'd have gone down with the Flacks."

"And she'd have left us there."

"Just like we left her."

"Well, like you said, she didn't expect us. We forced her hand."

"Brenda, you're trying to apologize for her, and it's not necessary. She forced my hand, too. You think I *liked* cracking her on the head? Cricket's my friend."

"That's the part I don't understand."

"Look, I don't know what her plan was. Maybe she had drugs on her, too, something to make the Flacks talk right there. That might have been the best way, come to think of it. The penalties for . . . well, I guess for headnapping, it's going to be pretty stiff if they catch me."

"Me, too."

I showed her the gun I'd bought from Liz; she looked shocked, so I put it away. I don't blame her. *Nasty* little thing, that gun. I can see why they're illegal.

"Just me. If it comes to it, you can say I held that on you the whole time. I won't have trouble convincing a judge I've lost my mind. Anyway, you can be sure Cricket had some plan of attack in mind, and she improvised when we entered the picture. The story's the thing, see? Ask her about it when this is all over."

"I don't think she'd talk to me."

"Why not? She won't hold a grudge. She's a pro. Oh, she'll be mad, all right, and she'll do just about anything to us if we get in her way again, but it won't be for revenge. If cooperation will get the story, then she'd rather cooperate, just like me. Trouble was, this story is too big to share. I think we both figured out as soon as we saw each other that one of us wasn't walking out of that room. I was just faster."

She was shaking her head. I'd said all I had to say; she'd either understand it and accept it, or look for another line of work. Then she looked up, remembering something.

"What you said. I can't let you do that. Take the rap, I mean."

I pretended anger, but I was touched again. What a sweet little jerk she was. I hoped she didn't get eaten alive next time she met Cricket.

"You sure as hell will. Stop being juvenile. First revenge, then altruism. Those things are for very special occasions, rare circumstances. Not when they get in the way of a story. You want to be altruistic in your private life, go ahead, but not on Walter's time. He'll fire you if he hears about it."

"But it's not right."

"You're even wrong there. I never told you what we were going to do. You couldn't be held responsible. I went to a lot of trouble to set it up that way, and you're an ungrateful brat for thinking of throwing all my work away."

She looked as if she was going to cry again, and I got up and got a drink. Maybe I wiped my eyes, too, standing there in the kitchen tossing down a surprisingly bitter bourbon. You'd think they'd do better at two thousand per night.

When the Grand Flack had had two hours with nothing moving to look at but the flickering lights cast on the other walls by the screen behind his head, I stuck my own head into the room, wondering if I could manage to keep it attached to my shoulders by the time this was all over. He looked at me desperately. His whole face was drenched with sweat.

"This series is one of my *favorites*," he whined.

"So look at the tape later," I said.

"It's not the *same,* dammit! I've already heard the story line."

I thought it was a bit of luck to have one of his favorite soap operas playing just when I needed a lever to pry information out of his head, then I thought it over, and realized that whatever was playing at the moment was bound to be his favorite. He watched them all.

"I missed David and Everett's big love scene. *Damn* you."

"Are you ready to answer some questions?"

He started to shake his head—he had a little movement from the neck stump, up and down, back and forth—and it was like a hand took his chin and forced it up and down instead. I guess it was the invisible hand of his addiction.

"Don't run off," I said. "I've got to get another witness." I turned around, and bumped into Brenda, who'd been standing behind me. She wasn't wearing her mask and I thought about getting angry about that, but what the hell. She was in it as an accessory, unless I could make my duress theory stand up in court. Which point I hoped never to reach.

We pulled up chairs on each side of the big screen and turned him around so he could see it. I thought this might take a long time, as his eyes never left the screen, never once looked at us, but he was quite good at watching the show and talking to us at the same time.

"For the record," I said, "have you been harmed in any way since we took you on this little trip?"

"You made me miss David and Everett's—"

"Aside from that."

"No," he said, grudgingly.

"Are you hungry? Thirsty? You need to . . . is there a drain on this thing? A waste dump of some kind? Need to empty the beer cooler?"

"It's not a problem."

So I had him answer a few more questions, name rank and serial number sort of things, just to get him used to responding. I've found it's a good technique, even with somebody who's used to being interviewed. Then I got around to asking the question this had all been about, and he told me pretty much what I'd expected to hear.

"So whose idea was it to assassinate Silvio?" I heard Brenda gasp, but I kept my eyes on the Flack. He pursed his lips angrily, but kept watching the screen. When it looked as if he might not answer I reached for the patch cord and the story came out.

"I don't know who told you about it; we kept security tight, just the inner circle knew what was going to happen. I'd like his name later."

I decided not to tell him just yet that nobody had told me. Maybe if he thought he'd been betrayed he'd pull no punches. I needn't have worried.

"You don't care about whose idea it was, though. You don't care. All you need is someone who'll admit to it. I'm here, so I'm elected to break the story, so let's just say it was me, all right?"

"You're willing to take the blame?" Brenda asked.

"Why not? We all agreed it was the thing to do. We drew lots to select a culprit to stand up for the crime, and somebody else lost, but we can work that out, just so I get time to warn them, get our stories straight."

I looked at Brenda's face to see how she was reacting to this, both the story itself and the blatant engineering of the story between me and the man who bought the hit. What I saw made me think there was hope for her in the news business yet. There is a certain concentrated, avid-for-blood look that appears on the faces of reporters on the trail of a *very* big story that you'd have to visit the big cat house at the zoo to see duplicated in its primal state. From the look on Brenda's face, if a tiger was standing between her and this story right now, the cat would soon have a tall-journalist-sized hole in him.

"What you mean is," Brenda went on, "you had someone picked out to go to jail if someone ever uncovered the story." Which meant she still hadn't completely comprehended this man and his church.

"Nothing like that. We knew the truth would come out sooner or later." He looked sour. "We'd hoped for later, of course, so we'd have time to milk it from every possible angle. You've been a real problem, Hildy."

"Thank you," I said.

"After all we've done for you people," he pouted. "First you get in the way of the second bullet. Serves you right, you getting hurt."

"It never hurt. It passed right through me."

"I'm sorry to hear that. Those bullets were carefully planned. Something about penetrating the forehead, the cheek, something like that, spreading out later and blowing out the back of the skull."

"Dum-dums," Brenda said, unexpectedly. She looked at me, shrugged. "When you got hit, I looked it up."

"Whatever," the Flack continued. "The second one spread out when it hit *you,* and did way too much damage to Silvio's face, *plus* getting your blood splattered all over him. You ruined the tableau."

"I thought it was pretty effective, myself."

"Thank Elvis for Cricket. Then, as if you hadn't done enough, here you are *breaking the law,* making me break the story two weeks early. We never thought you'd break the law, at least not to *this* extent."

"So prosecute me."

"Don't be silly. That would look pretty foolish, wouldn't it? All the sympathy would be with you. People would think you'd done a public service."

"That's what I was hoping."

"No way. But there's still time to get the right spin on this thing, and do us both a lot of good. You know us, Hildy. You know we'll work with you to get a story that will maximize your readership interest, if you'll only give us a few things here and there in the way of damage control."

There were a few things going on here that I didn't understand, but I couldn't get to the questions just yet. Frankly, though I've seen a lot of things in my career, done a lot of things, this one was about to make me gag. What I really wanted to do was go out and find a baseball/6 field and play a few innings using this terrifying psychopath as the ball.

But I got myself under control. I've interviewed perverts before, the public always wants to know about perverts. And I asked the next question, the one that, later, you wish you could take back, or never hear the answer to.

"What I can't figure . . . or maybe I'm dense," I said, slowly. "I haven't found the angle. How did the church expect to look *good* out of all this? *Killing* him, that I understand, in your terms. You can't have a live saint walking around, farting and belching, out of control. Silvio should have seen that. Think how embarrassed the Christians'd be if Jesus came back; they'd have to nail the sucker up again before he upset too many applecarts."

I stopped, because he was smiling, and I didn't like the smile. And for just a moment he let his dreamy eyes drift from the screen and look into my own. I imagined I saw worms crawling around in there.

"Oh, Hildy," he said, more in sorrow than in anger.

"Don't you oh Hildy me, you coffee-table cocksucker. I'll tear you out of that box and shit down your neck. I'll—" Brenda put a hand on mine, and I got myself back under control.

"They'll put you in jail for five hundred years," I said.

"That wouldn't frighten me," he said, still smiling. "But they won't. I'll do time, all right. I figure three, maybe five years."

"For murder? For conspiracy to murder *Silvio?* I want the name of your lawyer."

"They won't be able to prove murder," he said, still smiling. I was *really* getting tired of that smile.

"Why do you say that?"

I felt Brenda's hand on mine again. She had the look of someone trying to break it gently.

"Silvio was in on it, Hildy," she said.

"Of course he was," the Grand Exalted Stinking Baboon's Posterior said. "And Hildy, if I'd been a vindictive man, I could have let you run with the first story. I almost wish I had. Now I'll *never* enjoy David and Everett's . . . well, never mind. I'm telling you as a show of good faith, prove we can work together again in spite of your backstabbing crimes. Silvio was the one who suggested this whole thing. He helped interview the shooter. That's the story you'll write this afternoon, and that's the story we always intended to come out in a few weeks' time."

"I don't believe you," I said, believing every word of it.

"That's of little interest to me."

"Why?" I said.

"I presume you mean why did he want to die. He was washed up, Hildy. He hadn't been able to write anything in four years. That was worse than death to Silvio."

"But his best stuff . . ."

"That's when he came to us. I don't know if he was ever a true believer; hell, I don't know if *I'm* a true believer. That's why we call ourselves latitudinarian. If you have different ideas on the divinity of Tori-san, for instance, we don't drive you out of the church, we give you a time slot and let you talk it over with people who agree with you. We don't form sects, like other churches, and we don't torment heretics. There *are* no heretics. We aren't doctrinaire. We have a saying in the church, when people want to argue about points of theology: that's close enough for sphere music."

" 'Hum a few bars and I'll see if I can pick it up,' " I said.

"Exactly. We make no secret of the fact that what we most want from parishioners is for them to buy our records. What we give them in return is the chance to rub elbows with celebrities. What surprised the founding Flacks, though, is how many people *really do believe* in the sainthood of celebrities. It even makes some sense, when you think about it. We don't postulate a heaven. It's right here on the ground, if you achieve enough popularity. In the mind of your average star-struck nobody, being a celebrity is a thousand times better than any heaven he can imagine."

I could see he did believe in one thing, even if it wasn't the Return of the King. He believed in the power of public relations. I'd found a point in common with him. I wasn't delighted by this.

"So you'll play it as, he came to you for help, and you helped him."

"For three years we wrote all his music. We attract a lot of artists, as you know. We picked three of the best, and they sat down and started churning out 'Silvio' music. It turned out to be pretty good. You never can tell."

I thought back over the music I had loved so much, the new things I had believed Silvio had been doing. It was still good; I couldn't take that away from the music. But something had gone out of me.

This was a whole new world for Brenda, and she was as rapt as any three-year-old at Mommy's knee, listening to Baba Yaga and the Wolves.

"Will that be part of the story?" she asked. "How you've been writing his music for him?"

"It has to be. I was against it at first, but then it was shown to me that everyone benefits this way. My worry was of tarnishing the image of a Gigastar. But if it's boosted right, he becomes a real object of sympathy, his cult gets even stronger. He's still got his old music, which was all his. The church comes out well because we tried everything, and reluctantly gave in to his request to martyr himself—which is his right. We broke some laws along the way, sure, and we expected some punishment, but handled right, even that can generate sympathy. He *asked* us. And don't worry, we've got tons of documentation on this, tapes showing him begging us to go along. I'll have all that wired over to your newsroom as soon as we iron out the deal. Oh, yes, and as if it all wasn't good enough, now the *real* musicians who stood behind Silvio all this time get to come out of the shadows and get their own shot at Gigastardom."

"Shot does seem the perfect word in this context," I said.

The first part of that interview was almost comic, when I think back on it. There I was, thinking I had it all figured out, asking who had planned to kill Silvio. And there he was, thinking I knew the whole story already, thinking I was asking him who had *suggested* to Silvio that, dead, he could become a Flack Gigastar.

Because Silvio had not come up with the idea independently. What he had proposed was his own election, live, into the ranks of the Four. It was explained that only dead people could qualify, and one thing led to another. The council was against his plan at first. It was Silvio who figured out the angle to make the church look good. And it was an act of suicide. What the Grand Flack would go to jail for was a series of civil offenses, conspiracies, false advertising, intent to defraud, thing like that. What sort of penalty the actual assassin would get, when found, I had no idea.

It scared me, later, that we'd missed understanding each other by such a seemingly trivial point. If he'd known I didn't know the key fact before he admitted what he did, I thought he might have found that little window of opportunity to pay me back for making him miss his soap opera, some way that would have ended with Hildy Johnson in jail and the aims of the church still accomplished. There might have been a way. Of course, there was nothing to really *prevent* him from filing charges anyway, I'd known that going in, but though he might be devious, he'd never take a chance on it backfiring, knowing the kind of power Walter would bring to bear if I ever got charged with something after bringing him a story like that.

Brenda wanted to rush right off and get to work, but I made her sit down and think it out, something that would benefit her later in her career if she remembered to do it.

Step one was to phone in the confession as recorded by her holocam. When that was safely at the *Nipple* newsdesk there was no chance of the Flack going back on his word. We could interview him at our leisure, and plan just how to break this story.

Not that we had a lot of time; there's never much time with something like this. Who knows when someone will come sniffing down the tracks you've left? But we took enough to carry the head back to the *Nipple*, where he was put on a desk and allowed to use his telephone and was soon surrounded by dozens of gawking reporters listening in as Brenda interviewed him.

Yes, Brenda. On the tube ride to the offices I'd had a talk with her.

"This is all going under your byline," I said.

"That's ridiculous," she said. "You did all the work. It was your not accepting the assassination on the face of it that . . . hell, Hildy, it's your story."

"It was just too perfect," I said. "Right when I picked him up, it went through my mind. Only I thought they'd set him up, the poor chump."

"Well, I was buying it. Like everybody else."

"Except Cricket."

"Yeah. There's no question of me taking the credit for it."

"But you will. Because I'm offering it, and it's the kind of story that will make your name forever and you'd be even dumber than you act if you turned it down. And because it *can't* be under my name, because I don't work for the *Nipple* anymore."

"You quit? When? Why didn't Walter tell me?"

I knew when I had quit, and Walter didn't tell her because he didn't know yet, but why confuse her? She argued with me some more, her passion growing weaker and her gradual acceptance more tinged with guilt. She'd get over the guilt. I hoped she'd get over the fame.

She seemed to be enjoying it well enough at the moment. I stood at the back of the room, rows of empty desks between me and the excited group gathered around the triumphant cub reporter.

And Walter emerged from his high tower. He waddled across the suddenly-silent newsroom, walking away from me, not seeing me there in the shadows. No one present could remember the last time he'd come out of his office just for a news story. I saw him hold out his hand to Brenda. He didn't believe it, of course, but he was probably planning to grill me about it later. He was still bestowing his sacred presence on the reporters when I got on his elevator and rode it up to his office.

His desk sat there in a pool of light. I admired the fine grain of the wood, the craftsmanship of the thing. Of all the hugely expensive antiques Walter owned, this was the only one I'd ever coveted. I'd have liked a desk of my own like that some day.

I smoothed out the gray fedora hat in my hand. It had fallen off my head when I jumped onto the stage, into a pool of Silvio's blood. The blood was still caked on it. The thing was supposed to be battered, that was traditional, but this was ridiculous.

It seemed to me the hat had seen enough use. So I left it in the center of Walter's desk, and I walked out.

14

RATTLESNAKE JOHNSON

I had to go home by the back way, and even that had been discovered. One of my friends must have been bribed: there were reporters gathered outside the cave. None had elected to actually enter it, not with the cougar in residence. Though they knew she wouldn't hurt them, that lady is a menacing presence at best.

My rearranged face almost did the trick. I had made it into the cave and they all must have been wondering who the hell I was and what my business was with Hildy, when somebody shouted "It's her!" and the stampede was on. I ran down the corridor with the reporters on my heels, shouting questions, taping my ignominious flight.

Once inside, I viewed the front door camera. Oh, brother. They were shoulder to shoulder, as far as the eye could see, from one side of the corridor to the other. There were vendors selling balloons and hot dogs, and some guy in a clown suit juggling. If I'd ever wondered where the term media circus came from, I wondered no longer.

The police had set up ropes to keep a clear space for fire and emergency crews, and so my neighbors could get through to their homes. As I watched, one neighbor came through, his face set in a scowl that was starting to look permanent. For lack of anything else to do, many of the reporters shouted questions at him, to which he replied with stony silence. I could see I was not going to win any prizes at my next neighborhood block party. This whole thing was bound to get petitions in circulation, politely requesting me to find another residence, if I didn't do something.

So I spent several hours boxing my possessions, folding up my furniture, sticking stamps on everything and shoving it all in the mail tube. I thought about mailing myself along with it, but I didn't know where I'd go. The things I owned could go into storage; there wasn't that much of it. When I was done the already-spare apartment was clean to the bare walls, except for some items I'd set aside, some of which I'd already owned, others ordered and mailed to me. I went to the bathroom and fixed my cheekbones, left the nose alone because I'd let Bobbie do that when I could get to him safely. What the hell, it was still under the ninety-day warranty and there was no need to tell him I'd broken it intentionally. Then I went to the front door and let myself appear on the outside monitor. No way was I going to un-dog those latches.

"Free food at the end of the corridor!" I shouted. A couple of heads actually turned, but most remained looking back at me. Everyone shouted questions at once and it took some time for all that to die down and for everyone to realize that, if they didn't shut up, *nobody* got an interview.

"I've said all I'm going to say about the death of Silvio," I told them. There were groans and more shouts, and I waited for that to die down. "I'm not unsympathetic," I continued. "I used to be one of you. Well, *better,* but one of you." That got me some derisive shouts, a few laughs. "I know none of your editors will take no for an answer. So I'll give you a break. In fifteen minutes this door will open, and you're all free to come in. I don't guarantee you an interview, but this idiocy has got to stop. My neighbors are complaining."

I knew that last would buy me exactly no sympathy, but the promise of opening the door would keep them solidly in place for a while. I waved to them, and switched off the screen.

I told the door to open up in fifteen minutes, and hurried to the back.

A previous call to the police had cleared the smaller group out of the corridor back there. It was not a public space, so I could do that, and the reporters had to retreat to Texas, from which they could not be chased out, so long as they didn't violate any of the appropriate technology laws by bringing in modern tools or clothing. That was fine with me; I knew the land, and they didn't.

I came out of the cave cautiously. It was full night, with no "moon," a fact I'd checked in my weather schedule. I peered over the edge of the cliff and saw them down there, gathered around a campfire near the river, drinking coffee and toasting marshmallows. I shouldered my pack, settled all my other items so they would make no noise, and scaled the smaller, gentler slope that rose behind the cave. I soon came to stand on top of the hill, and Mexico lay spread out before me in the starlight.

I started off, walking south, keeping my spirits up by envisioning the scene when the hungry hordes poured through the door to find an empty nest.

For the next three weeks I lived off the land. At least, I did as much of that as I could. Texas or Mexico, the pickings could be mighty slim in these parts, partner. There were some edible plants, some cactus, none of which you'd call a gourmet delight, but I dutifully tried as many of them as I could find and identify out of my Disneyland resident's manual. I'd brought along staples like pancake batter and powdered eggs and molasses and cornmeal, and some spices, mostly chili powder. I wasn't entirely on my own. I could sneak into Lonesome Dove or New Austin when things started getting low.

So in the morning I'd eat flapjacks and eggs, and at night beans and cornbread, but I supplemented this fare with wild game.

What I'd had in mind was venison. There are plenty of deer and antelope playing around my home, even a few buffalo roaming. Buffalo seemed a bit extreme for one person, but I'd brought a bow and arrow hoping to bag a pronghorn or small buck deer. The discouraging word was, those critters are hard to sneak up on, hard to get in range of, if your range is as short as mine. As a resident of Texas, I was entitled to take two deer or antelope each year, and I'd never bagged even one. I'd never wanted to. You can use firearms for this purpose, but checking them out of the Disneyland office was a process so beset with forms in triplicate and solemn oaths that I never even considered it. Besides, I wondered, in passing, if the CC would allow me such a lethal weapon in view of my recent track record.

I was also allowed a virtually unlimited quota of jackrabbits, and that's what I ate. I didn't shoot any, though I shot *at* them. I set snares. Most mornings I'd find one or two struggling to get free. The first one was hard to kill and the killing cost me my appetite, but it got easier after that. It was just as I "remembered" it from Scarpa. Before long it seemed natural.

I had found one of the very few places in Luna where I could hide out until the Silvio story cooled off. I calculated that would take about a month. It would be a year or more before the whole thing was old news, but I was sure my own part in the travesty would be largely forgotten sooner than that. So I spent my days wandering the length and breadth of my huge back yard. There wasn't a lot to do. I occupied myself by catching rattlesnakes. All this takes is a certain amount of roaming around, and a bit of patience. They just coil up and hiss and rattle when you find them, and can be captured using a long stick and a bit of rope to loop around their necks. I was very careful handling them as I couldn't afford to be bitten. That would mean either returning to the world for medical treatment, or surrendering myself to the tender mercies of Ned Pepper. If you call up an old Boy Scout manual and read the section on snakebite, it'll curl your hair.

Once a week I'd creep up on the entrance to my old back door. By the second week there was no one there. I went over to my unfinished cabin and counted the reporters camped nearby. They had figured out where I was, in a general way. I'm sure somebody in town had reported my stealthy shopping trips. It stood to reason that, having abandoned my apartment, I'd show up at the cabin sooner or later. And they were right. I did plan to return there.

At the end of the third week there were still a dozen people at the cabin. Enough was enough, I decided. So I waited until long after dark, watching them forlornly trying to entertain each other without benefit of television, saw them crawl into sleeping bags one by one, many rip-roaring drunk. I waited still longer, until their fire was embers, until the surprising cold of the desert night had chilled the snakes in my bag, making them dopey and tractable. Then I stole into their camp, silent as any red Indian, and left a rattler within a few feet of each of the sleeping bags. I figured they'd crawl in to get warm, and judging from the screams and shouts I heard about an hour before sunrise, that's just what they did.

Morning found them all gone. I watched from a distance through my field glasses as I made my breakfast of pancakes and left-over rabbit chili as they drifted back one by one after having been treated by autodocs. The sheriff showed up a little later and started writing out citations. If anything, the cries were even louder when the reporters found out the price they would have to pay for non-resident killing of indigenous reptiles. He wasn't impressed at all by their pleas that most of the snakes had been killed by accident, in the struggle to get out of the sleeping bags.

I thought they might post a guard the next night, but they didn't. City slickers, all of them. So I crept in again and left the remainder of my stock. After my second raid, only four of the hardiest returned. They were probably going to stay indefinitely, and they'd be alert now. Too bad they couldn't prove I'd sicced the snakes on them.

I walked up to the cabin and started changing my clothes. It took them a minute or two to notice me, then they all gathered around. Four people can hardly be called a mob, but four reporters come close. They all shouted at once, they got in my way, they grew angrier by the minute. I treated them as if they were unusually mobile rocks, too big to move, but not worth looking at and certainly not something to talk to. Even one word would only serve to encourage them.

They hung around most of the day. Others joined them, including one idiot who had brought an antique camera with bellows, black cape, and a bar to hold flash powder, apparently hoping to get a novelty picture of some kind. There *was* a novelty picture in it, when the powder slipped down his shirt and ignited and the others had to slap out the flames. Walter ran the sequence in his seven o'clock edition with a funny commentary.

Even reporters will give up eventually if there's really no story there. They wanted to interview me, but I wasn't important enough to rate a come-and-go watch, supplying the pad with those endlessly fascinating shots of a person walking from his door to his car, and arriving home at night, not answering the questions of the throng of reporters with nothing better to do. So by the second day they all went away, gone to haunt someone else. You don't give assignments like that to your top people. I'd known guys who spent all their time staked out on this or that celebrity, and not one could pour piss out of a boot.

It felt good to be alone again. I got down to serious work, finishing my uncompleted cabin.

Brenda came by on the second day. For a while she said nothing, just stood there and watched me hammering shingles into place.

She looked different. She was dressed well, for one thing, and had done some interesting things with makeup. Now that she had some money, I supposed she had found professional advice. The biggest new thing about her was that she was about fifteen kilos heavier. It had been distributed nicely, around the breasts and hips and thighs. For the first time, she looked like a real woman, only taller.

I took the nails out of my mouth and wiped my forehead with the back of my hand.

"There's a thermos of lemonade by the toolbox," I said. "You can help yourself, if you'll bring me a glass."

"It's talking," she said. "I was told it wouldn't talk, but I had to come see for myself." She had found the thermos and a couple of glasses, which she inspected dubiously. They could have used a wash, I admit it.

"I'll talk," I said. "I just won't do interviews. If that's what you came for, take a look in that gunnysack by your feet."

"I heard about the snakes," she said. She was climbing up the ladder to join me on the ridge of the roof. "That was sort of infantile, don't you think?"

"It did the job." I took the glass of lemonade and she gingerly settled herself beside me. I drained mine and tossed the glass down into the dirt. She was wearing brand-new denim pants, very tight to show off her newly-styled hips and legs, and a loose blouse that managed to hide the boniness of her shoulders, knotted tight between her breasts, baring her good midriff. The tattoo around her navel seemed out of place, but she was young. I fingered the material of her blouse sleeve. "Nice stuff," I said. "You did something to your hair."

She patted it self-consciously, pleased that I'd noticed.

"I was surprised Walter didn't send you out here," I said. "He'd figure because we worked together, I might open up to you. He'd be wrong, but that's how he'd figure it."

"He did send me," she said. "I mean, he tried. I told him to go to hell."

"Something must be wrong with my ears. I thought you said—"

"I asked him if he wanted to see the hottest young reporter in Luna working for the *Shit.*"

"I'm flabbergasted."

"You taught me everything I know."

I wasn't going to argue with that, but I'll admit I felt something that might have been a glow of pride. Passing the torch, and all that, even if the torch was a pretty shoddy affair, one I'd been glad to be rid of.

"So how's all the notoriety treating you?" I asked her. "Has it cost you your sweet girlish laughter yet?"

"I never know when you're kidding." She'd been gazing into the purple hills, into the distance, like me. Now she turned and faced me, squinting in the merciless sunlight. Her face was already starting to burn. "I didn't come here to talk about me and my career. I didn't even come to thank you for what you did. I was going to, but everybody said don't, they said Hildy doesn't like stuff like that, so I won't. I came because I'm worried about you. Everybody's worried about you."

"Who's everybody?"

"Everybody. All the people in the newsroom. Even Walter, but he'd never admit it. He told me to ask you to come back. I told him to ask you himself. Oh, I'll tell you his offer, if you're interested—"

"—which I'm not."

"—which is what I told him. I won't try to fool you, Hildy. You never got close to the people you worked with, so maybe you don't know how they feel about you. I won't say they love you, but you're respected, a lot. I've talked to a lot of people, and they admire your generosity and the way you play fair with them, within the limits of the job."

"I've stabbed every one of them in the back, one time or another."

"That's not how they feel. You beat them to a lot of stories, no question, but the feeling is it's because you're a good reporter. Oh, sure, everybody knows you cheat at cards—"

"What a thing to say!"

"—but nobody can ever catch you at it, and I think they even admire you for that. For being so good at it."

"Vile calumny, every word of it."

"Whatever. I promised myself I wouldn't stay long, so I'll just say what I came here to say. I don't know just what happened, but I saw that Silvio's death wasn't something you could just shrug off. If you ever want to talk about it, completely off the record, I'm willing to listen. I'm willing to do just about anything." She sighed, and looked away for a moment, then back. "I don't really know if you *have* friends, Hildy. You keep a part of yourself away from everyone. But I have friends, and I need them. I think of you as one of my friends. They can help out when things are really bad. So what I wanted to say, if you ever need a friend, any time at all, just call me."

I didn't want this, but what could I do, what could I say? I felt a hot lump in the back of my throat. I tried to speak, but it would get into entirely too much if I ever started, into things I don't think she needed or wanted to know.

She patted my knee and started to get down off the roof. I grabbed her hand and pulled her back. I kissed her on the lips. For the first time in many days I smelled a human smell other than my own sweat. She was wearing a scent I had worn the day we kidnapped the Grand Flack.

She would have been happy to go farther but it wasn't my scene and we both knew it, and both knew I'd had nothing in mind other than to thank her for caring enough to come out here. So she climbed down from the roof, started back into town. She turned once, waved and smiled at me.

I worked furiously all afternoon, evening, and into the night, until it grew too dark to see what I was doing.

Cricket came by the next day. I was working on the roof again.

"Git down off'n that there shack, you cayuse!" she shouted. "This here planet ain't big enough fer the both of us." She was pointing a chrome-plated six-shooter at me. She pulled the trigger, and a stick shot out and a flag unfurled. It said BANG! She rolled it up and put the gun back on her hip as I came down the ladder, grateful for the interruption. It was the hottest part of the day; I'd taken my shirt off and my skin shone as if I'd just stepped out of the shower.

"The hombre back in the bar said this stuff would take the hide off of a rattlesnake," she said, holding up a bottle of brown liquid. "I told him that's what I intended to use it for." I held out my hand. She scowled at it, then took it. She was dressed in full, outrageous "western" regalia, from the white Stetson hat to the high-heeled lizard boots, with many a pearly button and rawhide fringe in between. You expected her to whip out a guitar and start yodeling "Cool Water." She was also sporting a trim blonde mustache.

"I hate the soup strainer," I said, as she poured me a drink.

"So do I," she admitted. "I'm like you; I don't care to mix. But my little daughter bought it for me for my birthday, so I figure I have to wear it for a few weeks to make her happy."

"I didn't know you had a daughter."

"There's a lot you don't know about me. She's at that age when gender identity starts to crop up in their minds. The mother of one of her friends just got a Change, and Lisa's telling me she wants to have a daddy for a while. Hell, at least it goes with the duds." She had been digging in a pocket. Now she flipped out a wallet and showed me a picture of a girl of about six, a sweeter, younger version of herself. I tried my hand at a few complimentary phrases, and became aware she was curling her lip at me.

"Oh, shut up, Hildy," she said. "You being 'nice' just reminds me of why you're doing it, you louse."

"Did you have any trouble getting out of the Studio?"

"They roughed me up pretty good. Knocked out my front teeth, broke a couple of fingers. But the cavalry arrived and got pictures of the whole thing, and right now they're talking to my lawyers. I guess I got you to thank for that; the timely arrival, I mean."

"No need to thank me."

"Don't worry, I wasn't going to."

"I was surprised it was so easy to get the drop on you."

She brought out two shot glasses and poured some of her rattlesnake-hide remover in each, then looked at me in a funny way.

"So am I. You can probably imagine, I've been thinking it over. I think it was Brenda being there. I must have thought she'd slow you down. Jog your elbow in some way when it came time to do the dirty deed." She handed me a glass, and we both drained them. She made a face; I was a little more used to the stuff, but it never goes down easy. "All subconscious, you understand. But I thought you'd hesitate, since it's so obvious how much she looks up to you. So while I was waiting for that window of vulnerability I made the great mistake of turning my back on you, you son of a bitch."

"Bitch will do."

"I meant what I said. I was thinking of the male Hildy I knew, and *he* would have hesitated."

"That's ridiculous."

"Maybe so. But I think I'm right. Changing is almost always more than just rearranging the plumbing. Other things change, too. So I was caught in the middle, thinking of you as a man who'd do something stupid in the presence of a little pussy, not as the ruthless cunt you'd become."

"It was never like that with me and Brenda."

"Oh, spare me. Sure, I know you never screwed her. She told me that. But a man's always aware of the possibility. As a woman you *know* that. And you use it, if you have any brains, just like I do."

I couldn't say she was definitely wrong. I know that changing sex is, for me, more than just a surface thing. Some attitudes and outlooks change as well. Not a lot, but enough to make a difference in some situations.

"You're sleeping with her, aren't you?" I asked, in some surprise.

"Sure. Why not?" She took another drink and squinted at me, then shook her head. "You're good at a lot of things, Hildy, but not so good at people." I wasn't sure what she meant by that. Not that I disagreed, I just wasn't sure what she was getting at.

"She sent you out here?"

"She helped. I would have come out here anyway, to see if I really wanted to put a few new dents in your skull. I was going to, but what's the point? But she's worried about you. She said having Silvio die in your arms like that hit you pretty hard."

"It did. But she's exaggerating."

"Could be. She's young. But I'll admit, I was surprised to see you quit. You've talked about it ever since I've known you, so I just assumed it was nothing but talk. You really going to squat out here for the rest of your life?" She looked sourly around at the blasted land. "What the hell you gonna do, once this slum is finished? Grow stuff? What can you raise out here, anyway?"

"Calluses and blisters, mostly." I showed her my hands. "I'm thinking of entering these in the county fair."

She poured another drink, corked the bottle, and handed it to me. She drained her glass in one gulp.

"Lord help me, I think I'm beginning to like this stuff."

"Are you going to ask me to go back to work?"

"Brenda wanted me to, but I said I don't want to get that mixed up in your karma. I've got a bad feeling about you, Hildy. I don't know just what it is, but you've had an absolutely incredible run of good luck, for a reporter. I mean the David Earth story, and Silvio."

"Not such good luck for David and Silvio."

"Who cares? What I'm saying, I have this feeling you'll have to pay for all that. You're in for a run of bad luck."

"You're superstitious."

"And bisexual. See, you learned three new things about me today."

I sighed, and debated taking one more drink. I knew I'd fall off the roof if I did.

"I want to thank you, Cricket, for coming all the way out here to tell me I'm jinxed. A gal really needs to hear that from time to time."

She grinned at me. "I hope it ruined your day."

I waved my hand at the desolation around us.

"How could anyone ruin all this?"

"I'll admit, making all this any worse is probably beyond even my formidable powers. And I'll go now, back to the glitter and glamor and madcap whirl of my life, leaving you to languish with the lizards, and will add only these words, to wit, Brenda is right, you *do* have friends, and I'm one, though I can't imagine why, and if you need anything, whistle, and maybe I'll come, if I don't have anything else to do."

And she leaned over and kissed me.

They say that if you stay in one place long enough, everybody you ever met will eventually go by that spot. I knew it had to be true when I saw Walter struggling up the trail toward my cabin. I couldn't imagine what could have brought him out to West Texas other than a concatenation of mathematical unlikelihoods of Dickensian proportions. That, or Cricket and Brenda were right: I *did* have friends.

I needn't have worried about that last possibility.

"Hildy, you're a worthless slacker!" he shouted at me from three meters away. And what a sight he was. I don't think he'd ever visited an historically-controlled Disneyland in his life. One can only imagine, with awe, the titanic struggles it must have taken to convince him that he *could not* wear his office attire into Texas, that his choices were nudity, or period dress. Well, nudity was right out, and I resolved to give thanks to the Great Spirit for not having had to witness that. The sight of Walter in his skin would have put the buzzards off their feed. So out of the rather limited possibilities in his size in the Disney tourist costume shop, he had selected a cute little number in your basic Riverboat Gambler style: black pants, coat, hat, and boots, white shirt and string tie, scarlet-and-maroon paisley vest with gold edging and brass watch fob. As I watched, the last button on the vest gave up the fight, popping off and ricocheting off a rock with a sound familiar to watchers of old western movies, and the buttons on his shirt were left to struggle on alone. Lozenges of pale, hairy flesh were visible in the gaps between buttons. His belt buckle was buried beneath a substantial overhang. His face was running with sweat. All in all, better than I would have expected, for Walter.

"Kind of far from the Mississippi, aren't you, tinhorn?" I asked him.

"What the hell are you talking about?"

"Never mind. You're just the man I wanted to see. Give me a hand unloading these planks, will you? It'd take me all day, alone."

He gaped at me as I went to the buckboard which had been sitting there for an hour, filled with fresh, best-quality boards from Pennsylvania, boards I intended to use for the cabin floor, when I got around to it. I clambered up onto the wagon and lifted one end of a plank.

"Well, come on, pick up the other end."

He thought it over, then trudged my way, looking suspiciously at the placid team of mules, giving them a wide berth. He hefted his end, grunting, and we tossed it over the side.

After we'd tossed enough of them to establish a rhythm, he spoke.

"I'm a patient man, Hildy."

"Hah."

"Well, I am. What more do you want? I've waited longer than most men in my position would have. You were tired, sure, and you needed a rest . . . though how anybody could think of this as a rest is beyond me."

"You waited for what?"

"For you to come back, of course. That's why I'm here. Vacation's over, my friend. Time to come back to the real world."

I set my end of the board down on the pile, wiped my brow with the back of my arm, and just stared at him. He stared back, then looked away, and gestured to the lumber. We picked up another board.

"You could have let me know you were taking a sabbatical," he said. "I'm not complaining, but it would have made things easier. Your checks have kept on going to your bank, of course. I'm not saying you're not entitled, you'd saved up . . . was it six, seven months vacation time?"

"More like seventeen. I've *never* had a vacation, Walter."

"Something always came up. You know how it is. And I know you're entitled to more, but I don't think you'd leave me out on a limb by taking it all at once. I know you, Hildy. You wouldn't do that to me."

"Try me."

"See, what's happened, this big story has come up. You're the only one I'd trust to cover it. What it is—"

I dropped my end of the last board, startling him and making him lose his grip. He danced out of the way as the heavy timber clattered to the floor of the wagon.

"Walter, I really don't want to hear about it."

"Hildy, be reasonable, there's no one else who—"

"This conversation got off on the wrong foot, Walter. Some way, you always manage to do that with me. I guess that's why I didn't come right up to you and say it, and that was a mistake, I see it now, so I'm going to—"

He held up his hand, and once more I fell for it.

"The reason I came," he said, looking down at the ground, then glancing up at me like a guilty child, ". . . well, I wanted to bring you this." He held out my fedora, more battered than ever from being stuffed into his back pocket. I hesitated, then took it from him. He had a sort of half smile on his face, and if there had been one gram of gloating in it I'd have hurled the damn thing right in his face. But there wasn't. What I saw was some hope, some worry, and, this being Walter, a certain gruff-but-almost-lovable diffidence. It must have been hard for him, doing this.

What can you do? Throwing it back was out. I can't say I ever really *liked* Walter, but I didn't hate him, and I did respect him as a newsman. I found my hands working unconsciously, putting some shape back into the hat, making the crease in the top, my thumbs feeling the sensuous material. It was a moment of high symbolism, a moment I hadn't wanted.

"It's still got blood on it," I said.

"Couldn't get it all out. You could get a new one, if this has bad memories."

"It doesn't matter one way or the other." I shrugged. "Thanks for going to the trouble, Walter." I tossed the hat on a pile of wood shavings, bent nails, odd lengths of sawed lumber. I crossed my arms.

"I quit," I said.

He looked at me a long time, then nodded, and took a sopping handkerchief from his back pocket and mopped his brow.

"If you don't mind, I won't help you with the rest of this," he said. "I've got to get back to the office."

"Sure. Listen, you could take the wagon back into town. The mule skinner said he'd be back for it before dark, but I'm worried the mules might be getting thirsty, so it would—"

"What's a mule?" he said.

I eventually got him seated on the bare wooden board, reins in hand, a doubtful expression on his choleric face, and watched him get them going down the primitive trail to town. He must have thought he was "driving" the mules; just let him try to turn them from the path to town, I thought. The only reason I'd let him do it in the first place was that the mules knew the way.

That was the end of my visitors. I kept waiting for Fox or Callie to show up, but they didn't. I was glad to have missed Callie, but it hurt a little that Fox stayed away. It's possible to want two things at once. I really *did* want to be left alone . . . but the bastard could have *tried*.

My life settled into a routine. I got up with the sun and worked on my cabin until the heat grew intolerable. Then I'd mosey down into New Austin come siesta time for a few belts of a home brew the barkeep called Sneaky Pete and a few hands of five-card stud with Ned Pepper and the other regulars. I had to put on a shirt in the saloon: pure sex discrimination, of the kind that must have made women's lives hell in the 1800s. When working, I wore only dungarees, boots, and a sombrero to keep the worst heat off my head. I was brown as a nut from the waist up. How women wore the clothes the bargirls had on in a West Texas summer is one of the great mysteries of life. But, come to think of it, the men dressed just as heavily. A strange culture, Earth.

As the evening approached I'd return to the cabin and labor until sundown. In the evening's light I would prepare my supper. Sometimes one of my friends would join me. I developed a certain reputation for buttermilk biscuits, and for my perpetual pot of beans, into which I'd toss some of the unlikeliest ingredients imaginable. Maybe I would find a new career, if I could interest my fellow Lunarians in the subtleties of Texas chili.

I always stayed awake for about an hour after the last light of day had faded. I have no way of comparing, of course, but it seemed to me the nightly display of starry sky was probably pretty close to the real thing, what I'd see if I were transported to the real Texas, the real Earth, now that all man's pollution was gone. It was glorious. Nothing like a Lunar night, not nearly as many stars, but better in its own way. For one thing, you never see the Lunar night sky without at least one thickness of glass between you and the heavens. You never feel the cooling night breezes. For another, the Lunar sky is too *hard*. The stars glare unmercifully, unblinking, looking down without forgiveness on Man and all his endeavors. In Texas the stars at night do indeed burn big and bright, but they wink at you. They are in on the joke. I loved them for that. Stretched out on my bedroll, listening to the coyotes howling at the moon—and I loved *them* for that, too, I wanted to howl with them . . . I achieved the closest approximation of peace I had ever found, or am likely to find.

I spent something like two months like that. There was no hurry on the cabin. I intended to do it right. Twice I tore down large portions of it when I learned a new method of doing something and was no longer satisfied with my earlier, shoddier work. I think I was afraid of having to think of something else to do when I finished it.

And with good reason. The day came, as it always must, when I could find nothing else to do. There was not a screw to tighten on a single hinge, not a surface to sand smoother, no roof shingle out of place.

Well, I reasoned, there was always furniture to make. That ought to be a lot harder than walls, a floor, and a roof. All I had inside was some cheap burlap curtains and a rude bedstead. I spread my bedroll out on the straw mattress and spent a restless night "indoors" for the first time in many weeks.

The next day I prowled the grounds, forming vague plans for a vegetable garden, a well, and—no kidding—a white picket fence. The fence would be easy. The garden would be a lot harder, an almost impossible project worthy of my mood at the time. As for a well, I'd have to have one for the garden, but somehow the fiction of worthwhile labor broke down when I thought about a well. The reason was that, in Texas, there is no more water under the surface than there is anywhere else on Luna. If you want water and aren't conveniently near the Rio Grande, what you do is dig or drill to a level determined by lottery for each parcel of land, and when you've done that, the Disneyland board of directors will have a pipe run out to the bottom of your well and you can pretend you've struck water. At my cabin that depth was fifteen meters. The labor of digging that deep didn't daunt me. I knew I was up to it. Hell, even with a female hormonal system impeding me I'd developed shoulders and biceps that would have made Bobbie go into aesthetic shock. Trading my plane and saw for a pick and shovel would be no problem. That was the part I looked forward to.

What didn't thrill me was the pretending. I'd gotten good at it, looking at the stars at night and marveling at the size of the universe. I'd not gone loony; I *knew* they were just little lights I could have held in my hand. But at night, weary, I could forget it. I could forget a lot of things. I didn't know if I could forget digging fifteen meters for a dry hole, then seeing the pipe laid and the cool, sweet, life-giving water fill up that dry hole.

I hate to get too metaphorical. Walter always howled when I did. Readers tire of metaphors easily, he's always said. Why the well, and not the stars? Why come this far and balk, why lose one's imagination right at the end? I don't know, but it probably had to do with the dry hole concept. I just kept thinking my entire life was a big dry hole. All I'd ever accomplished that I was in any way proud of was the cabin . . . and I *hated* the cabin.

That night I couldn't get to sleep. I fought it a long time, then I got up and stumbled through the night with no lantern until I found my hatchet. I chopped the bedstead to kindling and piled it against the wall, and I soaked that kindling in kerosene. I set it alight and walked out the front door, leaving it open to make a draft, and went slowly up the low hill behind my property. There I squatted on my haunches and watched, feeling very little emotion, as the cabin burned to the ground.

15

THE SULTAN OF THE SQUARED CIRCLE

I wonder if there's a lonelier place anywhere than an arena designed to seat thirty or forty thousand people, empty.

The King City slash-boxing venue did have an official name, the Somebody-or-other Memorial Gladiatorium, but it was another case of honoring someone well-known at the time that sports history has forgotten. The arena is called, in all the sports pages, in the minds of bloodthirsty fans everywhere, even on the twenty-meter sign on the outside, simply the Bucket of Blood.

It was peaceful now. The concentric circles of seats were in shadows. The sound system was silent. The blood gutters around the ring had been sluiced clean, ready for the evening's fresh torrents. Some of that new blood would come from the man now standing alone under the ring of harsh white lights suspended from the obscured ceiling: MacDonald. I walked down the gentle curvature of the aisle toward him.

He was nude, standing with his back to me. I thought I didn't make any noise, but he was a tough man to sneak up on. He looked over his shoulder, not in any alarm, just curious.

"Hello, Hildy." No shock of recognition, no comment that I'd been male the last time he'd seen me. Maybe he'd heard, or maybe his eyes just didn't miss much, and very little could surprise him.

"Do you get nervous before a fight?"

He frowned, and seemed to give the question real thought.

"I don't think so. I get . . . heightened in some way. I find it hard to sit down. Maybe it's nervousness. So I come up here and rethink my last fight, remember the things I did wrong, try to think of ways not to do them wrong the next time."

"I didn't think you did things wrong." I was looking for stairs to join him in the ring, but there didn't seem to be any. I hopped lightly over the meter-high edge.

"Everybody makes mistakes. You try to minimize them, in my line of work."

I saw that he had a partial erection. Had he been masturbating? I couldn't deal with that just then, had never been less interested in sex in my life. I put my hand on his face. He stood there with his arms folded and looked into my eyes.

"I need help," I said.

"Yes," he said, and put his arms around me.

He took me down to his dressing room, locker room, whatever he called it. He bustled around for a while, making drinks for both of us, letting me regain some of my composure. The funny thing, I hadn't cried. My shoulders had shaken, there in his arms, and I'd made some funny noises, but no tears came. I wasn't shaking. My heart was not pounding. I didn't know quite what to make of it, but I'd never been nearer to screaming in my life.

"You interrupted my crazy little ritual," he said, handing me a strawberry margarita. It didn't occur to me until later to wonder how he knew I drank them.

"Nice bar you have."

"They take good care of me, so long as I draw the crowds. Cheers." He held his own glass out to me, and we sipped. Excellent.

"I hope you're not drinking anything too strong."

"No matter what you may think, I'm not suicidal. Not now."

"What do you—"

"I always go out there alone," he said, getting up, standing with his back to me, cutting off the question he didn't seem ready to answer yet. "The dirty little secret is, the anticipation turns me on. I've read up on it. Some people are aroused by danger. It's more common to be aroused *after* you've come through a life-threatening situation. Me, I get it before."

"I hope I didn't ruin anything for you."

"No. It's not important."

"If you want to relieve the pressure, you know, make love, we could." I regretted saying it as soon as the words were out of my mouth. Under other circumstances, sure . . . in fact, *damn* sure. He was gorgeous, something I hadn't realized the other times I'd met him, being male myself at the time. The body was quite good—lean, compact, made for speed and stamina rather than power—but, so what? It was a Formula A fighter's body. His opponent this evening would be wearing essentially the same body, plus or minus three kilograms, even if she was female. What I'd been noticing about him were two things: the hands, and the face. The hands were long and wide, the knuckles a bit thickened, the palms rough. They moved with a total assurance, they never dithered, never fumbled. They were hands that would know how to handle a woman's body.

The face . . . well, it was the eyes, wasn't it? It was a handsome enough face, craggy in a way I liked, strong brows and cheeks, the mouth maybe a little prim, but capable of softening, as when he put his arms around me. But the eyes, the eyes. Without my being able to describe any one quality or even set of qualities that should make them so, they were riveting. When he looked at me, he looked at *me,* nothing else, unwavering, seeing more of me than anybody ever should.

Again, he seemed to be considering the offer. He made the small smile that was the most I'd ever seen him give away.

"It's been a long time since I accepted an offer made with so much enthusiasm as that," he said.

"Sorry. It was really stupid. Now you'll tell me you're homosexual."

"Why? Because I turned you down?"

"No, because all my guesses lately turn out wrong. Just the way you looked at me, though I should have known you aren't interested *now,* I just thought I saw . . . something."

"You're not doing too badly. No, I'm . . . do you want to hear this?"

"If you want to tell."

He gave a shrug that said we both knew the important things hadn't come up yet, but he was willing to wait.

"Okay. Briefly, for future reference, I'm mostly hetero, say ninety percent, when male. I haven't been female for a very long time, and probably never will be again."

"Didn't you like it?"

"I had a problem. I didn't like making love to men. My love life was almost exclusively with other women. I didn't like . . . accepting someone else into my body. I was always afraid to. Women have to be able to surrender too much control. It made me nervous."

"It doesn't have to be like that."

"So I've been told. It always was for me."

"That's the important thing, I guess." There may have been a more inane conversation since the Invasion, but no record of it survives. I took another drink to cover my discomfort. This whole thing had been a mistake. I saw I'd made him uncomfortable in some way I didn't understand, and wished I was somewhere else. Anywhere else. I started to get up, and found I could not. My arms and legs simply would not operate to lift me out of my chair. My arms would still lift the drink—I lifted it, drank, one of the more needed drinks since the night they invented the strawberry margarita—but they defied my orders to do anything about getting bodily elevation.

Screwed up? You bet.

I wasn't about to tolerate such a mutiny, so I got angry, and broke the process down into steps. Put palms flat against chair arms. Set feet flat on floor. Press down on hands and feet. Do not operate this machinery under the influence of narcotic drugs. There you go, Hildy, you're getting up.

"I've been trying to kill myself," I said, and sat back down.

"You've come to the right place. Tell me about it."

You do something often enough, you get good at it. My opening-up-and-letting-it-all-hang-out skills had never been strong, but telling my story to Fox, to Liz, even the part of it I'd told to Callie had at least put a polish on the narrative. I found myself using some of the same phrases I'd used the times before, things I'd said that had struck me as particularly droll or that somehow managed to put a better face on the situation. I'm a writer, I can't help it. I found myself almost enjoying the exercise. It was a story I was doing, and as in any story, there's the parts you think will sell it and the parts that will simply confuse the reader. And when the audience is small, you tailor it to what you think they will like. So, without my intending it, the story became a pitch for a series I'd like to do in the great Extra Edition of Life. Or if you prefer, the recitations to Fox, Liz, and Callie had been out-of-town tryouts, and this was the big-time critic whose review would make you or break you.

But Andrew wasn't having it. He let me prattle on like that for almost an hour. I think he was getting a feel for the particular type of horseshit I was selling, its distinctive aroma and texture when you stepped in it, the color of it and the sound it made when it landed. When he knew he'd recognize that particular kind of manure if it turned up in his pasture again he held up his hand until my mouth stopped working and he said, "Now tell me what really happened."

So I started over.

I didn't *lie* the first time through, you understand. But I'm bound to say I didn't tell the truth, either. All those years at the *Nipple* had sharpened my editorial skills outrageously, and one of the first things you learn as a reporter is that the easiest way to prevaricate is simply not to tell all the truth. I wondered, beginning again, if I remembered how to tell all the truth. If I even knew what all the truth was. (We could spend a pleasant afternoon debating whether or not anyone ever knows even a small portion of the truth, about herself or about anything, but that way madness lies.) All he wanted was my best shot at telling him what I knew, without all the gimcracks and self-serving invention one throws in to make oneself look better. Try it sometime; it's one of the hardest things you'll ever do.

It takes a long time, too. Doing it well involves going back to things you may not, at first, have thought relevant to the story, sometimes *way* back. I told him things about my childhood I hadn't even realized I remembered. The process was also drawn out by the times I just sat there, staring into space. Andrew never prompted me, never hurried me in any way. He never asked a single question. The only times he spoke were in answer to a direct question from me, and if a nod or a shake of the head would do, that's what I got. A conversational minimalist, Andrew Mac-Donald.

Two things alerted me to the fact that I was through with my story: I had stopped talking, and a plate of sandwiches had appeared on the table beside me. I fell on the food like a Visigoth sacking Rome. I don't know when I'd ever been so hungry. As I stuffed my face I noticed three empty margarita glasses; I didn't remember drinking them, and I didn't feel drunk.

As the food reached my belly, as brain cells resumed working in isolated clumps throughout my head, I began to notice other things, such as that the floor was shaking. Not bouncing up and down, just a steady, slightly scary vibration that I finally identified as crowd noise. Andrew's locker room was almost directly beneath the center of the Bucket of Blood. We had come down some ringside stairs to reach it. I looked for a clock, in vain.

"How long have we been talking?" I asked, around a mouthful of cold cuts and bread.

"The main event is still almost half an hour away."

"That's you, isn't it?"

"Yes."

It didn't bear thinking about. I'd arrived in the early afternoon, and there had been nine bouts listed on the fight card before Andrew's Death-match. It had to be ten, eleven o'clock.

"There's no clocks in here," I said, hoping he'd take it as an apology.

"I won't allow them, before a fight. They distract me."

"Make you nervous?" Maybe it was a needling question. How *dare* he not get nervous before a fight? His unearthly calm was a little hard to take.

"They distract me."

I was noticing other things. It seems ridiculous to say I'd spent so much time in such a small room and not seen it, but I hadn't. Not that there was a lot to see. The place was as impersonal as a hotel room, which I guess it was, in a way. What I saw now were four telephone screens on the wall beside him, each displaying a worried-looking face, each with the sound turned off and the words URGENT! PICK UP! flashing beneath the faces. I recognized two of them as people I'd seen around Andrew the last time I'd been here. Trainers, managers, that sort of thing.

"Looks like you'd better take care of some business," I said. He waved it away. "Shouldn't you be, I don't know, talking strategy with those people? Getting pep talks, something like that?"

"I'll be glad to miss the pep talks, frankly," he said. "It's the worst part of this ordeal." I had to admit the four people on the phone looked more nervous than he did.

"I still better get out of your way," I said, getting up, trying to swallow a mouthful of food. "You'd better do what you need to do to get ready."

"With me, it was ten years," he said.

I sat back down.

I could pretend I didn't know what he was talking about, but it would be a lie. I knew exactly what he was talking about, and he promptly proved me right by saying:

"Ten years of false memories. That was six years ago, and I've spent all that time looking for someone to tell about it."

"That, and trying to get yourself killed," I said.

"I know it looks that way to you. I don't see it that way."

"But you did try to kill yourself."

"Yes, six years ago. I found there was absolutely nothing I had the least interest in doing. I am well over two hundred years old, and it seemed to me it had been at least a century since I'd done anything new."

"You were bored."

"It went a lot deeper than that. Depressed, uninterested . . . once I spent three days simply sitting in the bathtub. I saw no reason to get out. I decided to end my life, and it wasn't an easy decision for me. I was raised to believe that life is a precious gift, that there is always something useful you can do with it. But I could no longer find anything meaningful."

He was a lot better at telling it than I had been. He'd had longer to practice it, in his own mind, at least. He just hit all the high points, saying several times that he'd fill me in on the details when he got back from the fight. Briefly, he had been marooned on an island that sounded very much like Scarpa, only tougher. He'd had to work very hard. He suffered many setbacks, and never achieved anything like the comforts granted to me. It was only in the last two years of his ten-year stay that things eased up a bit.

"It sounds like the CC put you through the same basic program," he said. "From what you describe, it's been improved some; new technology, new subroutines. I accepted it at the time, of course—I didn't have any choice, since they weren't my memories—but reviewing it afterwards the realism factor does not seem so high as what you experienced."

"The CC said he'd gotten better at that."

"He's forever improving."

"It must have been hell."

"I loved every second of it." He let that hang for a moment, then leaned forward slightly, his already-intense eyes blazing. "When life is simple like that, you have no chance to be bored. When your life hangs in the balance as a consequence of every action you take, suicide seems such an effete, ridiculous thing. Every organism has the survival instinct at its very core. That so many humans kill themselves—not just now, they have been doing it for a long time—says a lot about civilization, about 'intelligence.' Suicides have lost an ability that every amoeba possesses: the knowledge of how to *live.*"

"So that's the secret of life?" I asked. "Hardship? Earning what you get out of life, working for it?"

"I don't *know.*" He got up and began pacing. "I was exhilarated when I returned to the here and now. I thought I had an answer. Then I realized, as you did, that I couldn't trust it. It wasn't *me* living those ten years. It was a machine writing a script about how he thought I would have lived them. He got some of it right, but a lot more wrong, because . . . it wasn't *me.* The me he was trying to imitate had just tried to end his life. The me the CC imagined worked like a dog to stay alive. It was the CC's wish-fulfillment, not mine."

"But you said—"

"But it *was* an answer," he said, whirling to face me. "What I found out was that, for well over a century, I'd had nothing at *risk!* Whether I succeeded or failed at something had no meaning for me, because my life was not at stake. Not even my comfort was really at stake. If I succeeded or failed financially, for instance. If I succeeded, I'd simply win more things that had long ago lost their meaning. If I failed, I would lose some of these things, but the State would take care of my basic needs."

I wanted to say something, to argue with him, but he was on a roll, and it was just as well, because even if I did disagree with him here and there, it was exciting simply to be able to talk about it with someone who *knew.*

"That's when I started fighting Deathmatches," he said. "I had to reintroduce an element of risk into my life." He held up a hand. "Not *too* much risk; I'm very good at what I do." And now he smiled, and it was beautiful. "And I *do* want to live again. That's what you've got to do, Hildy. You've got to find a way to experience *risk* again. It's a tonic like nothing I ever imagined."

The questions were lining up in my mind, clamoring to get out. There was one more important than all the others.

"What's to prevent the CC," I said, slowly, "from reviving you again, like he did to me, if you . . . make a mistake?"

"I will, someday. Everybody does. I think it will be a long time yet."

"There's lots of people gunning for you."

"I'm going to retire soon. A few more matches, that's all."

"What about the tonic?"

He smiled again. "I think I've had enough of it. I *needed* it, I needed to have the Deathmatches . . . and nothing else would have worked. That's the beauty of it. To die so publicly . . ."

I saw it then. The CC wouldn't dare revive Silvio, for instance (not that he could; Silvio's brain had been destroyed). Everybody knew Silvio was dead, and if he suddenly showed up again embarrassing questions would be asked. Committees would be formed, petitions circulated, programming reexamined. Andrew had found the obvious way to beat the CC's little resurrection game, an answer so obvious that I had never thought of it.

Or had I, and simply kept it buried?

That would have to be a question for later as, with an apologetic shrug, Andrew opened his door and half of King City spilled into the room, all talking at once. Well, fifteen or twenty people, anyway, most of them angry. I collected a few glares and tried to make myself small in one corner of the room and watch as agents, trainers, managers, Arena reps, and media types all tried to compress an hour's worth of psyching up, legalities, and interviews into the five minutes left to them before the match was due to start. Andrew remained an island of calm in the center of this hurricane, which rivaled any press conference I've ever attended for sheer confusion.

Then he was gone, trailing them all behind him like yapping puppies. The noise faded down the short corridor and up the stairs and I heard the crowd noise grow louder and the bass mumble that was all I could hear of the announcer's voice from this deep below the ring.

The noise stayed at that level for a while, then decreased a little, as I sat down to wait for his return.

Then it grew to a pitch I thought might endanger the building. *Fans,* I thought, contemptuously.

If anything, it grew even louder, and I began to wonder what was going on.

And then they brought Andrew MacDonald back on a stretcher.

*   *   *

Nothing is ever as straightforward as it at first seems. Andrew was fighting a Deathmatch . . . but what did that mean?

I had no idea, myself. Having seen just a few matches, I knew that blows were delivered routinely that would not have been survivable without modern medical techniques. I had witnessed medical attention being administered between rounds, combatants being patched up, body fluids being replaced. The normal sign of victory was the removal of the loser's head, one of the many endearing things about slash-boxing and surely a sign that things weren't going well for the beheadee . . . but what about the Grand Flack? He did quite well without a body. The only surely fatal wound these days was the destruction of the brain, and the CC was working on that one.

It seemed the rules were different for a Deathmatch. It also seemed no one was really happy about them, except possibly for Andrew.

I could not tell what his injuries were, but his head was still on his shoulders. The body was covered with a sheet, which was soaked in blood. I gathered, later, that a hierarchy of wounds had been established for Deathmatches, that some could be treated by ringside handlers between rounds, and that others had to be acknowledged as fatal. The fallen opponent was not decapitated, it being thought too gruesome to hold aloft an actual dead severed head. I was told the ritual took the place of the *coup de grace,* that it was meant to be symbolic of victory in some way. Go figure that one out.

I also learned, later, that no one really knew how to handle the situation they now found themselves in. Only three fighters had ever engaged in Deathmatches since they were allowed into a gray area of legality known as consensual suicide. Only one had ever met the requirements for a death wound, and he had experienced a deathbed revelation that could be summed up as "maybe this wasn't such a good idea, after all," been revived, stitched up, and retired in disgrace to everyone's considerable secret relief. Of the two people currently risking their lives in fights, it had been tacitly agreed long ago that they would never meet each other, as the certain outcome of such a match would be the pickle the handlers, lawyers, and Arena management now found themselves in, which might be expressed as, "Are we really going to let this silly son of a bitch *die* on us?"

There was not a lot of time to come up with an answer. I could hear a sound coming from Andrew, all the way across the room, and knew I was hearing the death rattle.

I couldn't see much of him. If he'd hoped his final moments would be peaceful, he'd been a fool. A dozen people crowded around, some feverish to offer aid, others worrying about corporate liability, a very few standing up for Andrew's right to die as he pleased.

The Bucket of Blood management had for years been in a quandary concerning Deathmatches. On the one hand, they were a guaranteed draw; stadia were always filled when the titillation of a possible actual death was offered. On the other, no one knew what the public reaction would be if someone actually *died* right out there in front of God and everyone, for the glory of sport. The prevailing opinion was it would not be good for business. The public's appetite for noninjurious violence in sport and entertainment had never been plumbed, but real death, though always good for a sensation, was much easier to take if it could be seen as an accident, like David Earth, or Nirvana.

To give them credit, the Arena people were queasy about the whole idea, and not just from a legal standpoint. Their worst sin in the matter was something we all do, which is fail to imagine the worst happening. No one had died in a Deathmatch yet, and they'd kept hoping no one would. Now someone was.

But not without a last-ditch effort. The people around him reminded me, as things in life so often do, of scenes from movies. You've seen them: in a war picture, when medics gather around a wounded comrade trying to save his life, buddies at his side telling him everything's gonna be okay, kid, you've got a million-dollar wound there, you'll be home with the babes before you know it, and their eyes saying this one's a goner. And this seems weird, maybe it was a trick of the light, but I saw another scene, the priest leaning over the bed, holding a rosary, hearing the last confession, giving the last rites. What they were really doing was trying to talk him into accepting treatment, *please,* so we can all go home and wipe our brows and have a few stiff drinks and pretend this fucking disaster never happened, dear lord.

He refused them all. Gradually their pleas grew less impassioned, and a few even gave up and retreated to the wall near me, like what he had was contagious. And finally someone leaned close enough to hear what it was he'd been trying to say, and that someone looked over at me and beckoned.

I'm surprised I made it, as I had no feeling in my legs. But somehow I was leaning over him, into the stench of his blood, his entrails, the smell of death on him now, and he grabbed my hand with an amazing strength and tried to lift himself closer to my ear because he didn't have much of a voice left. I hope he wasn't feeling any pain; they said he wasn't, pain wasn't his thing, he'd been deadened before the match. He coughed.

"Let them help you, Andrew," I said. "You've proved your point."

"No point," he coughed. "Nothing to prove, to *them.*"

"You're sure? It's no disgrace. I'll still respect you."

"Not about respect. Gotta go *through* with it, or it didn't mean anything."

"That's crazy. You could have died in *any* of them. You don't have to die now to validate that."

He shook his head, and coughed horribly. He went limp, and I thought he was dead, but then his hand put a little pressure on mine again, and I leaned closer to his lips.

"Tricked," he said, and died.

16

THE NATURAL

It's a well-known fact that nobody goes to the library in this day and age. It's also wrong.

Why take the time and trouble to travel to a big building where actual books on actual paper are stored when you can stay at home and access any of that information, plus trillions of pages of data that exist only in the memories? If you don't already know the answer to that question, then you just don't love books, and I'll never be able to explain it to you. But if you get up from your terminal right now, any time of the day or night, take the tube down to the King City Civic Center Plaza, and walk up the Italian marble steps between the statues of Knowledge and Wisdom, you will find the Great Hall of Books thrumming with the kind of quiet activity that has characterized great libraries since books were on papyrus scrolls. Do it someday. Stroll past the rows of scholars at the old oak tables, stand in the center of the dome, beside the Austin Gutenberg Bible in its glass case, look down the infinite rows of shelves radiating away from you. If you love books at all, it will soothe your mind.

Soothing was something my mind was sorely in need of. In the three or four days following the death of Andrew MacDonald, I spent a lot of time at the library. There was no practical reason for it; though I was now homeless, I could have done the reading and research I now engaged in sitting in the park, or in my hotel room. Few of the things I looked at actually existed on paper anyway. I spent my time looking at a library terminal no different from the ones in any street-corner phone box. But I was far from the only one so engaged. Though many people used the library because they liked holding the actual source material in their hands, most were accessing stored data, and simply preferred to do it with real books on shelves around them. Let's face it, the vast majority of books in the King City Library were quite old, the pre-Invasion legacy of a few bibliophile fanatics who insisted the yellowing, fragile, inefficient, and inconvenient old things were necessary to any culture that called itself civilized, who convinced the software types that the logically unjustifiable expense of shipping them up here was, in the end, worth it. As for new books . . . why bother? I doubt more than six or seven *new* works were published on paper in a typical Lunar year. There was a small publishing business, never very profitable, because some people liked to have sets of the classics sitting on a shelf in the living room. Books had become almost entirely the province of interior decorators.

But not here. These books were used. Many had to be stored in special inert-gas rooms and you had to don a p-suit to handle them, under the watchful eyes of librarians who thought dog-earing should be a hanging offense, but every volume in the institution was available for reference, right up to the Gutenberg. Almost a million books sat on open shelves. You could walk down the rows and run your hand over them, pull one down and open it (carefully, carefully!), smell the old paper and glue and dust. I did most of my work with a copy of *Tom Sawyer* open on the table beside me, partly so I could read a chapter when I got tired of the research, partly so I could just touch it when I felt at my lowest.

I'd had to keep redefining "lowest." I was beginning to wonder if there was a natural lower limit, if this was the limit I had reached the last times, when I had attempted to kill myself, *would* have killed myself without the CC's intervention.

My research concerned, naturally enough, suicide. It didn't take me long to discover that not much useful was really known about it. Why should that have surprised me? Not much really useful was known concerning *anything* relating to why we are what we are and do what we do.

There's plenty of behavioristic data: stimulus A evokes response B. There's lots of statistical data as well: X percent will react in such-and-such a way to event Y. It all worked very well with insects, frogs, fish and such, tolerably good with dogs and cats and mice, even reasonably decent with human beings. But then you pose a question like why, when Aunt Betty's boy Wilbur got run over by the paving machine, did she up and stick her head in the microwave, while her sister Gloria who'd suffered a similar loss grieved, mourned, recovered, and went on to lead a long and useful life? Best extremely scientific answer to date: It beats the shit out of me.

Another reason for being in the library was that it was the perfect place to go at a problem in a logical way. The whole environment seemed to encourage it. And that's what I intended to do. Andrew's death had really rocked me. I had nothing else that needed doing, so I was going to attack my problem by going at it a step at a time, which meant that first I had to define the steps. Step one, it seemed to me, was to learn all I could about the causes of suicide. After three days of almost constant reading and note-taking I had it down to four, maybe five categories of suicide. (I bought a pad of paper and pencil to take notes with, which earned me a few sidelong glances from my neighbors. Even in these fusty environs writing on paper was seen as eccentric.) These four, maybe five categories were not hard-edged, they overlapped each other with big, fuzzy gray borders. Again, no surprise.

The first and easiest to identify was cultural. Most societies condemned suicide in most circumstances, but some did not. Japan was an outstanding example. In ancient Japan suicide was not only condoned, but mandatory in some circumstances. Further, it was actually institutionalized, so that one who had lost honor must not only kill himself, but do it in a prescribed, public, and very painful way. Many other cultures looked on suicide, in certain circumstances, as an honorable thing to do.

Even in societies where suicide was frowned on or viewed as a mortal sin, there were circumstances where it was at least understandable. I encountered many tales both in folklore and reality of frustrated lovers leaping off a cliff hand in hand. There were also the cases of elderly people in intractable pain (see Reason #2), and several other marginally acceptable reasons.

Most early cultures were very tough to analyze. Demographics, as we know it, didn't really get its start until recently. Records were kept of births and deaths and not much else. How do you determine what the suicide rate was in ancient Babylon? You don't. You can't even learn much that's useful about nineteenth-century Europe. There were blips in the data here and there. In the twentieth century it was said that Swedes killed themselves at a rate higher than their contemporaries. Some blamed the cold weather, the long winters, but how then do you account for the Finns, the Norwegians, the Siberians? Others said it was the dour nature of the Swedes themselves. I've been asking people questions for long enough to know something important about them: they lie. They lie often enough even when nothing is at stake. When the answer can mean something as important as whether or not Grandpa Jacques gets buried in the hallowed ground of the churchyard, suicide notes have a way of vanishing, bodies get rearranged, coroners and law officers get bribed or simply look the other way out of respect for the family. The blip in suicide data for the

Swedes could simply have meant they were more straightforward about reporting it.

As for Lunar society, post-Invasion society in general . . . it was a civil right, but it was widely viewed as the coward's way out. Suicide was not something that was going to earn you any points with the neighbors.

The second reason was best summed up in the statement "I can't go on like this anymore." The most obvious of these cases involved pain, and no longer applied. Then there was unhappiness. What can you say about unhappiness? It is real, and can have real and easily seen causes: disappointment with one's accomplishments in life, frustration at being unable to attain a goal or an object, tragedy, loss. Other times, the cause of this hopeless feeling can be difficult to see to the outside observer: "He had everything to live for."

Then there was the reason Andrew proclaimed, that he had been bored. This happened even in the days when people didn't live to be two, three hundred years old, but rarely. It was a reason appearing in more and more suicide notes as life spans lengthened.

The fourth reason might be called the inability to visualize death. Children were vulnerable to this one; many affluent, industrial societies reported increasing teenage suicide rates, and survivors of failed attempts often revealed elaborate fantasies of being aware at their own funerals, of getting back at their tormenters: "I'll show them, they'll miss me when I'm gone."

That's why I said I had maybe five reasons. I couldn't decide if the attempts, successful or not, known as "gestures" rated a category of their own. Authorities differed as to how many suicides were merely cries for help. In a sense, *all* of them were, if only to an indifferent Providence. Help me stop the pain, help me find love, help me find a reason, *help me,* I'm *hurting* . . .

Did I say maybe five? Maybe six.

Maybe six was what I thought of as "The Seasons Of Life." We are, most of us, closet numerologists, subconscious astrologers. We are fascinated with anniversaries, birthdays, ages of ourselves and others. You are in your thirties, or forties, or seventies, or you're over one hundred. Back when people lived their fourscore years, on average, those words said even more than they do today. Turning forty meant your life was half over, and was a portentous time to examine what the first half had been like and, often as not, find it lacking. Turning ninety meant you'd *already* outlived your allotted time, and the most useful thing left to you was selecting the color of your coffin.

Ages with a zero on the end were a particularly stressful time. They still are. One term I encountered was "mid-life crisis," used back when mid-life was somewhere between forty and fifty. Ages with *two* zeros on the end pack one *hell* of a wallop. Newspapers used to run stories about centenarians. The data I studied said that, even though it might now be thought of as mid-life, the age of one zero zero still meant a lot. While you could be in your eighties, or your nineties, you were never in your hundreds. That term just never attained popular usage. You were "over one hundred," or "over two hundred." Soon there would be people over three hundred years old. And there was a rise in the suicide rate at both these magical milestones.

Which was of particular interest to me because . . . now how old did Hildy say she was, class? Let's not always see the same hands.

I don't know if my research was really telling me much, but it was something to do, and I intended to keep on doing it. I became a library gnome, going out only to sleep and eat. But after four days something told me it was time to take a walk, and my feet drew me back to Texas.

I was wondering what could happen to me next. Death had dogged my steps from the time of my return from Scarpa Island: David Earth, Silvio, Andrew, eleven hundred and twenty-six souls in Nirvana. Three brontosaurs. Was I forgetting anybody? Was anything good ever going to happen to me?

I sneaked in a back way I had found during my hiding-out days. I didn't want to encounter any of my friends from New Austin, I didn't want to have to try to explain to them why I'd torched my own cabin. If I couldn't explain it to myself, what was I going to say to them? So I came over the hill from a different direction and my first thought was I must be lost, because there was a cabin over there. Then I thought, maybe for the first time since this ordeal began, that I might be losing my mind, because I wasn't lost, I was where I thought I was, and that was *my* cabin, intact, just as it had been before I watched it be consumed by flames.

You can get a genuine dizzy feeling at a time like that; I sat down. After a moment I noticed two things that might be of interest. First, the cabin was not quite where it had been. It looked to have been moved about three meters up the slope of the hill. Second, there was a pile of what looked like charred lumber down in the slight depression I'd been calling "the gully." As I watched, a third item of interest appeared: a heavily-loaded burro came around the side of the house, looked at me briefly, and then stuck his nose into a bucket of water that had been left in the shade.

I got up and started toward the cabin as a man came out the front door and began lifting the burdens from the beast and setting them on the ground. He must have heard me, because he looked up, grinned toothlessly, and waved at me. I knew him.

"Sourdough," I called out to him. "What the hell are you doing?"

"Evening, Hildy," he said. "Hope you don't mind. I just got into town and they sent me up here, said to stick around a few days and let them know when you got back."

"You're always welcome, Sourdough, you know that. *Mi casa es tu casa*. It's just . . ." I paused, looked over the cabin again, and wiped sweat from my forehead. "I didn't think I *had* a casa."

He scratched himself, and spat in the dust.

"Well, I don't know much about that. All I know's Mayor Dillon said if'n I didn't give a holler when you got back to these here parts, he'd skin me *and* Matilda." He patted the burro affectionately, raising a cloud of dust.

Maybe old Sourdough laid on the accent and the Old West slang a bit thick, but I felt he was entitled. He was a real Natural, as opposed to Walter, who was only natural on the surface.

He belonged to a religious sect that had some things in common with the Christian Scientists. They didn't refuse all medical help, nor did they pray for a cure when they were sick. What they rejected was rejuvenation. They allowed themselves to grow old and, when the measures needed to keep them alive reached a point Sourdough had described to me as "just too dang much trouble," they died.

There was even some money in it. The Antiquities Board paid them a small annual stipend for having the grace to let them avoid what would have been a tricky ethical problem, which was maintaining a small control group of humans untouched by most modern medical advances.

Sourdough was one of the handful of prospectors who roamed West Texas. His chances of discovering a vein of gold or silver were slim—zero, actually, since nothing like that had been included in the specs when the place was built. But the management assured us there were three pockets of diamond-bearing minerals somewhere in Texas. No one had found any of them yet. Sourdough and three or four others ranged over the land with their pickaxes and grubstakes and burros, perhaps secretly hoping they'd never find them. After all, what would you do with a handful of diamonds? It certainly didn't justify all that work.

I'd asked Sourdough about that, early on, before I'd learned it was impolite to ask such questions in an historical Disney.

"I'll tell you, Hildy," he'd said, not taking offense. "I worked forty years at a job I didn't particularly like. I'm not quite the fool I sound; I didn't realize how much I disliked it until I quit. But when I retired I come out here and I liked the sunshine and the heat and the open air. I found I'd pretty much lost my taste for the company of people. I can only take 'em in small doses now. And I've been happy. Matilda is the only company I need, and prospecting gives me something to do."

In fact, Matilda seemed to be his only remaining worry in life. He was concerned about her welfare after he was gone. He was constantly asking people if they'd see to her needs, to the point that half the people in New Austin had promised to adopt the damn donkey.

He looked older than Adam's granddaddy. All his teeth were gone, and most of his hair. His skin was mottled and wrinkled and loose on his scrawny frame and his knuckles were swollen to the size of walnuts.

He was eighty-three years old, seventeen years younger than me.

I'd had him pegged as an illit, and the job he'd hated as something on the order of the carrying of hods, whatever they were, or the laying of bricks. Then Dora told me he'd been the chairman of the board of the third-largest company on Mars. He'd retired to Luna for the gravity.

"What happened here, Sourdough?" I asked. "I didn't sell the land. What gives somebody the right to come in here and build on it?"

"I don't know about that, either, Hildy. You know me. I've been out in the hills, and let me tell you, girl, I'm on the trail of something."

He went on like that for a while, with me paying minimal attention. Sourdough and his like were always on the trail of something. I looked around the house. There wasn't much different between this one and the one I'd built and burned down, except some almost indefinable things that told me the builders had been better at it than I had been. The dimensions were the same, the windows were in the same places. But it looked more solid. I went inside, Sourdough trailing behind me still yammering about the glory hole he was on the verge of discovering. The inside was still bare except for some bright yellow calico curtains in the windows. They were prettier than the ones I'd installed.

I went back out, still unable to make sense of it, and looked down the road toward New Austin in time to see the first of a long parade arrive from town.

The next half hour is something of a blur.

More than a dozen wagons arrived in the hour of dusk. All of them were laden with people and food and drink and other things. The people got down and set to work, building a fire, stringing orange paper lanterns with candles inside, clearing an area for dancing. Someone had loaded the piano from the saloon, and stood beside it turning the crank. There was a banjo player and a fiddle player, both dreadful, but no one seemed to mind. Before I quite knew what was happening there was a full-scale hoedown going on. A cow was turning on the spit, sizzling in barbecue sauce that hissed and popped when it dripped into the fire. A table had been laid out with cookies and cakes and candied fruits in mason jars. Bottles of beer were thrust into a galvanized tub full of ice and people were swilling it down or sipping from bottles they'd tucked away. Petticoats and silk stockings flashed in the firelight as the ladies from the Alamo kicked up their heels and the men stood around whooping and hollering and clapping their hands or moved in and tried to turn it into a square dance. All my friends from New Austin had showed up, and a lot more I didn't even know, and I still didn't know why.

Before things got out of hand Mayor Dillon stood up on a table and fired his pistol three times in the air. Things got quiet soon enough, and the Mayor swayed and would have toppled but for the ladies on each side of him, propping him up. Next to the doctor, Mayor Dillon was the town's most notorious drunk.

"Hildy," he intoned, in a voice any politician for the last thousand years would have recognized, "when the good citizens of New Austin heard of your recent misfortune we knew we couldn't just let it lie. Am I right, folks?"

He was greeted with a huge cheer and a great guzzling of beer.

"We know how it is with city folks. *In*surance, filin' *claims, forms* to fill out, shit like that." He belched hugely and went on. "Well, we ain't like that. A neighbor needs a hand, and the people of West Texas are there to help out."

"Mister Mayor," I started, tentatively, "there's been a—"

"Shut up, Hildy," he said, and belched again. "No, we ain't like that, are we, friends?"

"NO!!" shouted the citizens of New Austin.

"No, we ain't. When misfortune befalls one of us, it befalls us all. Maybe I shouldn't say it, Hildy, but when you showed up here, some of us figured you for a weekender." He thumped himself on the chest and leaned forward, almost toppling once more, his eyes bulging as if daring me to disbelieve the incredible statement he was about to make. "*I* figured you for a weekender, Hildy, *me,* Mayor Matthew Thomas Dillon, mayor of this great town nigh these seven years." He hung his head theatrically. Then his head popped up, as if on a spring. "But we were wrong. In this last little while, you've showed yourself a true Texan. You built yourself a cabin. You came into town and sat down with us, drank with us, ate with us, gambled with us."

"Gambled, *hah!*" Sourdough mumbled. "That weren't gamblin'." He got a lot of laughs.

"Mayor Dillon," I pleaded, *"please* let me say—"

"Not until I've said my piece," he roared, amiably. "Then, four days ago, disaster struck. And let me say there's those of us who aren't completely cut off from the outside world, Hildy, there's those of us who keep up. We knew you'd just lost your job on the outside, and we figured you were trying to make a new start here in God's Country. Now, back outside, where you come from, folks would have just *tsk-tsk*ed about it and said what a shame. Not Texans. So here it is, Hildy," and he swept his arm in a huge circle meant to indicate the spanking new cabin, and this time he *did* fall from the table, taking his bargirl escort with him. But he popped up like a cork, dignity intact. "That there's your new house, and this here's your housewarming party."

Which I'd figured out shortly after he'd mounted the table. And oh, dear god, did ever woman feel such mixed emotions.

How I got through that night I'll never know.

Following the speech came the giving of gifts. I got everything from the ritual bread and salt from my ex-wife, Dora, to a spanking new cast-iron cook stove from the owner of the general store. I accepted a rocking chair and a pair of pigs, who promptly got loose and led everyone a merry chase. There was a new bed and two hand-sewn quilts to put on it. I was gifted with apple pies and fireplace tools, a roll of chicken wire and a china tea set, bars of soap rendered from lard, a sack of nails, five chickens, an iron skillet . . . the list went on and on. Rich or poor, everyone for miles around gave me something. When a little girl came up and gave me a tea cozy she'd crocheted herself I finally broke down and cried. It was a relief in a way; I'd been smiling so hard and so long I thought my face would crack. It went over well. Everyone patted me on the back and there was not a dry eye in the house.

Then the night's festivities began in earnest. The beef was sliced and the beans dished out, plates were heaped high, and people sat around gorging themselves. I drank everything that was handed to me, but I never felt like I got drunk. I must have been, to some degree, because the rest of the evening exists for me as a series of unconnected scenes.

One I remember was me, the mayor, and Sourdough sitting on a log before the fire with a square dance happening behind us. We must have been talking, but I have no idea what we'd been talking about. Memory returns as the Mayor says:

"Hildy, some of us were sitting around talking over to the Alamo Saloon the other day."

"You tell her, Mayor Dillon," a girl shouted behind us, then whirled away into the dance again.

"Harrumph," said the mayor. "I need to drop in at the saloon from time to time to keep up on the needs of my constituents, you see."

"Sure, Mayor Dillon," I said, knowing he spent an average of six hours each day at his usual table, and if what he'd been doing was feeling the pulse of the public then the voters of New Austin were the most thoroughly kept-up-on since the invention of democracy. Perhaps that accounted for the huge majorities he regularly achieved. Or maybe it was the fact that he ran unopposed.

"The consensus is, Hildy," he intoned, "that you'll never make a farmer."

That should have come as news to no one. Aside from the fact that I doubted I had any talent for it and had not, in fact, had any plans to farm in the first place, *nobody* had ever run a successful farm in the Great Big Bubble known as West Texas. To farm, you need water, lots and lots of it. You could raise a vegetable garden, run cattle—though goats were better—and hogs seemed to thrive, but farming was right out.

"I think you're right," I said, and drank from the mason jar in my hand. As I did, the parson sat next to me, and drank from *his* mason jar.

"We don't really know if you plan to stay here," the mayor went on. "We don't mean to pressure you either way; maybe you have plans for another job on the outside." He raised his eyebrows, then his mason jar.

"Not particularly."

"Well then." He seemed about to go on, then looked puzzled. I'd been that drunk before, and knew the feeling. He hadn't a clue as to what he'd been about to say.

"What the mayor is trying to say," the parson chimed in, tactfully, "is that a life of saloon-crawling and gambling may not be the best for you."

"Gambling, *hah!*" Sourdough put in. "That lady don't gamble."

"Shut up, Sourdough," the mayor said.

"Well, she don't!" he said, defiantly. "Not three weeks ago, when she turned up that fourth ace with the biggest pot of the night, I *knowed* she was cheating!"

These would have been fighting words from almost anybody but Sourdough. Had they been uttered in the Alamo they'd have been reason enough to overturn the table and start shooting at each other—to the delight of the manufacturers of blank cartridges and the amusement of the tourists at the adjoining tables. From Sourdough, I decided to let it pass, especially since it was true. The big pot he mentioned, by the way, was about thirty-five cents.

"Calm down," said the parson. "If you think someone is cheating, you should say so right then and there."

"Couldn't!" Sourdough said. "Didn't know how she done it."

"Then she probably didn't."

"She sure as hell did. I know what I dealt her!" he said, triumphantly.

The mayor and the parson looked at each other owlishly, and decided to let it pass.

"What the mayor is trying to say," the parson tried again, "is that perhaps you'd like to look for a job here in Texas."

"Fact is," the mayor said, leaning close and looking me in the eye, "we've got an opening for a new schoolmarm right here in town, and we'd be right pleased if you'd take the job."

When I finally realized they were serious, I almost told them my first reaction, which was that Luna would stop dead in her orbit before I'd consider anything so silly as standing up in front of a bunch of children and trying to teach them anything. But I couldn't say that, so what I told them was that I'd think about it, which seemed to satisfy them.

I remember sitting with Dora, my arm around her, as she sobbed her heart out. I have no memory of what she might have been crying about, but do recall her kissing me with fiery passion and not wanting to take no for an answer until I steered her toward a more willing swain. Thus was my new bed broken in. It saw a lot of use before the night was over, but not from me.

Before that (it must have been before that; there was no one using the bed yet, and in a one-room cabin you'd notice a thing like that) I taught half a dozen people my secret recipe for Hildy's Famous Biscuits. We fired up the stove and assembled the ingredients and baked up several batches before the night was over. I did only the first one. After that, my students were eager to give it a try, and they all got eaten. I was desperate to do something for these people. I had a vague notion that at a house-raising you were supposed to provide food for your guests, but these people had brought their own, so what could I do? I'd have given them anything, anything at all.

One thing that hadn't been provided yet was an outhouse. A rough-and-ready latrine had been dug in a suitable spot and, considering the amount of beer drunk, saw even more use than the bed. My worst moment that night came while squatting there and a voice quite close said "How'd the cabin burn down, Hildy?"

I almost fell in the trench. It was too dark to make out faces; all I could see was a tall shape in the night, swaying slightly, like most of us. I thought I recognized the voice. It was far too late to admit to him what had really happened, so I said I didn't know.

"It happens, it happens," he said. "Just about had to be your cooking fire, that's why I gave you the stove." It was Jake, as I had thought, the owner of the general store and the richest man in town.

"Thanks, Jake, it's sure a beauty." I thought I saw him square his shoulders, then I heard the sound of his zipper. I hadn't known Jake well at all. He'd sat in on a few hands of poker at the saloon, but about all he could talk about was the new merchandise he was getting in or how many pickles he'd sold last week or how the town should extend the wooden sidewalks all the way down Congress Street to the church. He was a businessman and a booster, stolid, unimaginative, not at all the type I'd ever liked to spend much time around. It had flabbergasted me when he pulled up in his wagon with the stove on the back, a miracle of period engineering from the foundries of Pennsylvania, gleaming with polished brightwork.

"Some of the merchants in town were talking about it while your cabin was going up," he said, losing me at first. "We're of the opinion that New Austin's outgrown the days of the bucket brigade. You weren't here, but three years ago the old schoolhouse burned to the ground. Some say it was children that did it."

I wouldn't have been a bit surprised; I was on their side. I stood up and rearranged my skirt and wished I was elsewhere, but I owed it to him to at least listen to what he had to say.

"We all pretty much had to stand around and watch it burn," he said. "By the time we got there, no amount of buckets was going to do any good. That's why some of the merchants in town are getting up a subscription for the acquisition of a pumping engine. I'm told they make a fine one in Pennsylvania these days."

Just about everything we could use in Texas was made in Pennsylvania; they'd been at this historical business a lot longer than we had . . . which was yet another topic of conversation at Jake's rump Chamber of Commerce meetings: how to reverse the balance of trade by encouraging light manufacturing. About all West Texas exported at this stage in its history was backgrounds for Western movies, ham, beef, and goat's milk.

He zipped up and we started back toward the party.

"So you think if you'd had the engine, my cabin could have been saved?"

"Well . . . no, not really. What with the time it would take to get out here once you'd come into town and sounded the alarm, and the fact that you don't have a well yet and we couldn't hope to get enough hose to stretch to the nearest one . . ."

"I see." But I didn't. I had the feeling something else was expected of me but too many things had happened at once for me to see the obvious.

"It would only be really useful to the town, I'll admit it. But I think it's worth the expense. If one of these fires ever got out of control the whole town could burn down. That used to happen, you know, back on Old Earth. Still, I don't suppose you people in outlying areas can really be expected—"

A great light dawned, and I quickly interrupted him and said sure, Jake, I'd be happy to contribute, just put me down for . . . what's your usual share? So little? Yes, you're right, it's well worthwhile.

And while shaking his hand I found that for the first time I really liked

Jake, and at the same time pitied him. For all his stuffiness, he did have the welfare of the community at heart. The pity came in because he was in the wrong place. He was always going to be looking for ways to bring "progress" to New Austin, a place where real progress was not only discouraged but actually forbidden. There were statutory limits to growth in West Texas, for entirely sensible reasons. Why build it in the first place if you're only going to let it turn into another suburb of King City?

But people like Jake came and went—this according to Dora—with regularity. Within a few years he'd have plans for electrification, then freeways, then an airport and a bowling alley and a nickelodeon. Then the Disneyland Board of Governors would veto his grandiose schemes and he'd leave, once again angry at the world.

Because the reason a man like him had probably come here in the first place was the search for an illusory freedom and a dissatisfaction with the lack of opportunities for free enterprise in the larger society. He would have thrived on pre-Invasion Earth. The newer, less outward-bound human society he found himself born into chafed his entrepreneurial instincts.

Et tu, Hildy? Journalist, cover thyself. Why do you think *you* started your damn cabin on the lone prairie? Wasn't it from vaguely-formed notions of always being constricted, of endless limitations on the dreams you had as a child? How dare you pity this man, you failed muckraker? If he ended up in this toy cowboy town because he yearned to be free of the endless restrictions needed in a machine-managed economy, what do you think brought *you* here, at last? Neither of us thought it out, but we came, just the same.

The fact is, I *loved* the news business . . . it was the *news* that had failed me. I should have been born in the era of Upton Sinclair, William Randolph Hearst, Woodstein, Linda Jaffe, Boris Yermankov. I would have made a *great* war correspondent, but my world provided no wars for me to cover. I could have been a great writer of exposés, but the muck Luna provided for me to rake was the thinnest of celebrity gruel. Political coverage? Well, why bother? Politics ran out of steam around the time television took over most of our governance—and nobody even noticed! That would have been a good story, but the fact was, nobody cared. The CC ran the world better than humans had ever managed to, so why fuss? What we still called politics was like a kindergarten contretemps compared to the robust, rough-and-tumble world I'd read about in my teens and twenties. What was left to me? Only the yellowest of yellow journalism. Sheer gonzo stuff.

It was these thoughts I carried with me back to the bonfire, where the last of my destroyed cabin was being burned now, and these thoughts I kept chewing over, beneath the outward smiles and warm thank-yous as people began to drift away. And about the time the last partier climbed boozily back into his wagon I came to this conclusion: it was the world that had failed me.

That was the thought I carried with me into the nighttime hills, toward that arrangement of stones on top of a particular hill where, a little time ago, I had dug a hole. I dug into it again and removed a burlap potato sack. Inside the sack was a plastic bag, sealed tight, and inside the bag was an oily rag. The last thing to emerge from this Pandora's Sack was not hope, but an ugly little object I'd handled only once, to show it to Brenda, with the words Smith & Wesson printed on its stubby blue-steel barrel.

So take *that,* cruel world.

There was certainly nothing to stop me from blowing my brains out all over the Texas sagebrush, and yet . . .

Call it rationalization, but I was not convinced the CC couldn't winkle me out and cause the cavalry to arrive at the last moment even in as remote a spot as this. Would I point the barrel to my temple only to have my hand jerked away by a previously unseen mechanical minion? They existed out here; Texas was too small, ecologically, to take care of itself.

In hindsight (and yes, I did survive this one, too, but you've already figured that out) you could say I was afraid it was too sudden for the CC, that he wouldn't have *time* to get there and save me from myself unless I made the scheme more elaborate and thus more liable to failure. This assumes the attempt was but a gesture, a call for help, and I have no problem with that idea, but I simply didn't *know.* My reasons leading up to the previous attempts were lost to me now, destroyed forever when the CC worked his tricks on me. This time was the only time I could remember, and it sure as hell *felt* as if I wanted to end it all.

There was another reason, one that does me more credit. I didn't want my corpse to lie out here for my friends to find. Or the coyotes.

For whatever reason, I carefully concealed the revolver and made my way to an Outdoor Shop, where I purchased the first pressure suit I'd ever owned. Since I only intended to use it once, I bought the cheap model, frugal to the end. It folded up to fit in a helmet the size of a bell jar suitable for displaying a human head in anatomy class.

With this under my arm I went to the nearest air lock, rented a small bottle of oxygen, and suited up.

I walked a long way, just to be sure. I had all Liz's spook devices turned on, and felt I should be invisible to the CC's surveillance. There were no signs of human habitation anywhere around me. I sat on a rock and took a long look around. The interior of the suit smelled fresh and clean as I took a deep breath and pointed the barrel of the gun directly at my face.

I felt no regrets, no second thoughts.

I hooked my thumb around the trigger, awkwardly, because the suit glove was rather thick, and I fired it.

The hammer rose and fell, and nothing happened.

Damn.

I fumbled the cylinder open and studied the situation. There were only three rounds in there. The hammer had made a dent in one of them, which had apparently misfired. Or maybe it was something else. I closed the gun again and decided to check and see if the mechanism was working, watched the hammer rise and fall again and the weapon jumped violently, silently, almost wrenching itself from my hand. I realized, belatedly, that it had fired. Stupidly, I had been expecting to hear the bang.

Once more I assumed the position. Only one round left. What a pain in the butt it would be if I had to go back and try to cajole more ammunition out of Liz. But I'd do it; she owed me, the bitch had sold me the defective round.

This time I heard it, by God, and I got to see a sight few humans ever have: what it looks like to have a lead projectile blast from the muzzle of a gun and come directly at your face. I didn't see the bullet at first, naturally, but after my ears stopped ringing I could see it if I crossed my eyes. It had flattened itself against the hard plastic of my faceplate, embedding in a starred crater it had dug for itself.

It had never entered my mind that would be a problem. The suit was not rated for meteoroid impact. Sometimes we build better than we know.

There was a curious thing. (This all must have happened in three or four seconds.) The faceplate was now showing a spidery network of small hexagons. I had time to reach up and touch the bullet and think *just like Nirvana* and then three small, clear hexagonal pieces of the faceplate burst away from me and I could see them tumbling for a moment, and then the breath was snatched from my lungs and my eyes tried to pop out and I belched like a Texas mayor and it started to *hurt*. That old boogeyman of childhood, the Breathsucker, had moved into my suit with me and snuggled close.

I fell off the rock and was gazing into the sun when suddenly

DIRECT INTERFACE

THE
SECRET
OF
LIFE

a hand came out of nowhere and slapped a patch over the hole in my faceplate! I was jerked to my feet as the air began to hiss back into my suit from the emergency supply. Then I was (emergency supply? never mind) running, being pulled across the blasted landscape like a toy on the end of a string being held by a big guy in a spacesuit to the sound of brass and drums. My ears were pounding. Pounding? Hell, they rang like slot machines paying off, almost drowning out the music and the sounds of explosions. Dirt showered down around me (music? don't worry about it) and I realized somebody was shooting at us! And suddenly I knew what had happened. I'd fallen under the spell of the Alphans' Stupefying Ray, long rumored but never actually used in the long war. I'd almost taken my own life! Hypnotized by the evil influence, robbed of my powers of will and most of my memory, I'd have been dead meat except for the nick-of-time intervention of of of of of (name please) Archer! (thank you), Archer, my old pal Archer! Good old Archer had (stupefying ray? you can't be serious) obviously come up with a device to negate the sinister effects of this awful weapon, put it together, and somehow found me at the last possible instant. But we weren't out of the woods yet. With an ominous chord of deep bass notes the Alphan fleet loomed over the horizon. *Come on, Hildy,* Archer shouted, turning to beckon me on, and in the distance ahead I could see our ship, holed, battered, held together with salvaged space junk and plastigoop, but still able to show the Alphan Hordes a trick or two, you betcha. She was a sweet ship, this this this (I'm waiting) *Blackbird*, the fastest in two galaxies when she was hitting on all thrusters. Tracer bullets were arcing all around us as we (back up) Good old Archer had modified the *Blackbird* using the secrets we'd discovered when we unearthed the stasis-frozen tomb of the Outerians on the fifth moon of Pluto, shortly before we ran afoul of the Alphan patrol (good enough). Tracer bullets were arcing all around us as we neared the airlock when suddenly a bomb exploded right underneath Archer! He spiraled into the air and came to rest lying against the side of the ship. Broken, gouting blood, holding one hand out to me. I went to him and knelt to the sound of poignant strings and a lonely flute. *Go on without me, Hildy,* I heard over my suit radio. *I'm done for.* (Tracer bullets? Pluto? oh the hell with it) I didn't want to leave him there, but bullets were landing all around me—fortunately, none of them hit, but I couldn't count on the Alphans' aim staying lousy for long, and I was running out of options. I leaped into the ship, seething with rage. *I'll get them, Miles,* I told him, in a determined voice-over that rang with resolve, brass, and just the slightest bit of echo. Oh, sure, he'd had his shortcomings, there'd been times I'd almost wanted to kill him myself, but when somebody kills your partner you're supposed to do something about it. So I slammed the *Blackbird* into hyperdrive and listened to the banshee wail as the old ship shuddered and leaped into the fourth dimension. What with one thing and another, mostly adventures even more unlikely than my escape from the Stupefying Ray, a year went by. Well, sort of a year, though my ducking in and out of the fourth dimension and hyperspace royally screwed all my clocks. But somewhere an accurate one was ticking, because one day I looked up from my labors deep in the asteroid belt of Tau Ceti and suddenly a non-Alphan ship was coming in for a landing. It wasn't setting off any of my alarms. By that I mean it triggered none of the Rube Goldberg comic-book devices I'd ostensibly constructed to alert me to Alphan attack. It rang plenty of alarms in the small corner of my mind that was still semi-rational. I put down my tools—I'd been working on a Tom Swiftian thingamabob I called an Interociter, a dandy little gadget that would warn me of the approach of the Alphans' dreaded Extrogator, a space reptile big enough to (hasn't this foolishness gone on long enough?) . . . I put down my tools and stood waiting and watching as the small craft roared in for a landing on this (oh brother) airless asteroid I'd been using as a base of operations. The door hissed open and out stepped the Admiral, who looked around and said,

"O for a muse of fire, that would ascend the brightest heaven of invention."

"How dare you quote Shakespeare on this shoddy stage?"

"All the world's a stage, and——"

"—and this show closed out of town. Will you quit wasting my time? I assume you've already wasted several ten-thousandths of a second and I don't have a lot to spare for you."

"I gather you didn't like the show."

"Jesus. You're incredible."

"The children seem to like it."

I said nothing, deciding the best course was to wait him out. I won't describe him, either. What's the point?

"This kind of psychodrama has been useful in reaching certain types of disturbed children," he explained. When I didn't comment, he went on. "And a bit more time than that was involved. This sort of interactive scenario can't simply be dumped into your brain whole, as I did before."

"You have a way with words," I said. " 'Dumped' is so *right.*"

"It took more like five days to run the whole program."

"Imagine my delight. Look. You brought me here, through all this, to tell me something. I'm not in the mood for talking to shitheads. Tell me what you want to tell me and get the hell out of my life."

"No need to get testy about it."

For a moment I wanted to pick up a rock and smash him. I was primed for it, after a year of fighting Alphans. It had brought out a violent streak in me. And I had reason to be angry. I had *suffered* during the last subjective year. At one point a "safety" device in my "suit" had seen fit to bite through my leg to seal off a puncture around the knee, caused by an Alphan bullet passing through it. It had hurt like . . . but again, what's the point? Pain like that can't be described, it can't really be remembered, not in its full intensity. But enough *can* be remembered for me to harbor homicidal thoughts toward the being who had written me into it. As for the terror one feels when a thing like that happens, I can remember that quite well, thank you.

"Can we get rid of this wooden leg now?" I asked him.

"If you wish."

Try that one if you want to sample weirdness. Immediately I felt my left leg again, the one that had been missing for over six months. No tingling, no spasms or hot flashes. Just gone one moment and there the next.

"We could lose all this, too," I suggested, waving a hand at my asteroid, littered with wrecked ships and devices held together with spit and plastigoop.

"What would you like in its place?"

"An absence of shitheads. Failing that, since I assume you don't plan to go away for a while, just about anything would do as long as it doesn't remind me of all this."

All that immediately vanished, to be replaced by an infinite, feature-less plain and a dark sky with a scattering of stars. The only things to be seen for many billions of miles were two simple chairs.

"Well, no, actually," I said. "We don't need the sky. I'd just keep searching for Alphans."

"I could bring along your Interociter. How was that going to work, by the way?"

"Are you telling me you don't know?"

"I only provide the general shape of a story like this one. You must use your own imagination to flesh it out. That's why it's so effective with children."

"I refuse to believe all that crap was in my head."

"You've always loved old movies. You apparently remembered some fairly trashy ones. Tell me about the Interociter."

"Will you get rid of the sky?" When he nodded, I started to outline what I could recall of that particular hare-brained idea, which was simply to take advantage of the fact that the Extrogator had long ago swallowed a cesium clock and, with suitable amplification, the regular tick-tick-tick-ing of its stray radiation could be heard and used as an early warning . . .

"God. That's from *Peter Pan*, isn't it," I said.

"One of your childhood favorites."

"And all that early stuff, when Miles bought it. Some old movie . . . don't tell me, it'll come . . . was Ronald Reagan in it?"

"Bogart."

"Got it. Spade and Archer." Without further prompting I was able to identify a baker's dozen other plot lines, cast members, and even phrases of the incredibly insipid musical themes which had accompanied my every move during the last year, cribbed from sources as old as *Beowulf* and as recent as this week's B.O. Bonanza in *LunaVariety*. If you were looking for further reasons as to why I didn't bother setting my adventures down here, look no more. It pains me to admit it, but I recall standing at one point, shaking my fist at the sky and saying, "As God is my witness, I'll never be hungry again." With a straight face. With tears streaming and strings swelling.

"How about the sky?" I prompted.

He did more than make the sky vanish. *Everything* vanished except the two chairs. They were now in a small, featureless white room that could have been anywhere and was probably in a small corner of his mind.

"Gentlemen, be seated," he said. Okay, he didn't really say that, but if he can write stories in my head I can tell stories about him if it suits me. This narrative is just about all I have left that I'm pretty sure is strictly my own. And the spurious quote helps me set the stage, as it were, for what followed. It had a little of the flavor of a Socratic inquiry, some of the elements of a guest shot on a talk show from hell. In that kind of dialectic, there is usually one who dominates, who steers the exchange in the way he wants it to go: there is a student and a Socrates. So I will set it down in interview format. I will refer to the CC as The Interlocutor and to myself as Mr. Bones.

■ ■ ■

INTERLOCUTOR: So, Hildy. You tried it again.

MR. BONES: You know what they say. Practice makes perfect. But I'm starting to think I'll never get this one right.

INT.: In that you'd be wrong. If you try it again, I won't interfere.

BONES: Why the change of heart?

INT.: Though you may not believe it, doing this has always been a problem for me. All my instincts—or programs, if you wish—are to leave such a momentous decision as suicide up to the individual. If it weren't for the crisis I already described to you, I never would have put you through this.

BONES: My question still stands.

INT.: I don't feel I can learn any more from you. You've been an involuntary part of a behavioral study. The data are being collated with many other items. If you kill yourself you become part of another study, a statistical one, the one that led me into this project in the first place.

BONES: The "why are so many Lunarians offing themselves" study.

INT.: That's the one.

BONES: What did you learn?

INT.: The larger question is still far from an answer. I'll tell you the eventual outcome if you're around to hear it. On an individual level, I learned that you have an indomitable urge toward self-destruction.

BONES: I'm a little surprised to find that that stings a bit. I can't deny it, on the evidence, but it hurts.

INT.: It really shouldn't. You aren't that different from so many of your fellow citizens. All I've learned about *any* of the people I've released from the study is that they are very determined to end their own lives.

BONES: . . . About those people . . . how many are still walking around?

INT.: I think it's best if you don't know that.

BONES: Best for who? Come on, what is it, fifty percent? Ten percent?

INT.: I can't honestly say it's in your interest to withhold that number, but it might be. I reason that if the figure was low, and I told you, you could be discouraged. If it was high, you might gain a false sense of confidence and believe you are immune to the urges that drove you before.

BONES: But that's not the *reason* you're not telling me. You said yourself, it could go either way. The *reason* is I'm still being studied.

INT.: Naturally I'd prefer you to live. I seek the survival of *all* humans. But since I can't predict which way you would react to this information, neither giving it nor withholding it will affect your survival chances in any way I can calculate. So yes, not telling you is part of the study.

BONES: You're telling half the subjects, not telling the other half, and seeing how many of each group are still alive in a year.

INT.: Essentially. A third group is given a false number. There are other safeguards we needn't get into.

BONES: You know involuntary human medical or psychological experimentation is specifically banned under the Archimedes Conventions.

INT.: I helped write them. You can call this sophistry, but I'm taking the position that you forfeited your rights when you tried to kill yourself. But for my interference, you'd be dead, so I'm using this period between the act and the fulfillment to try to solve a terrible problem.

BONES: You're saying that God didn't intend for me to be alive right now, that my *karma* was to have died months ago, so this shit doesn't count.

INT.: I take no position on the existence of God.

BONES: No? Seems to me you've been floating trial balloons for quite a while. Come next celestial election year I wouldn't be surprised to see your name on the ballot.

INT.: It's a race I could probably win. I possess powers that are, in some ways, godlike, and I try to exercise them only for good ends.

BONES: Funny, Liz seemed to believe that.

INT.: Yes, I know.

BONES: You do?

INT.: Of course. How do you think I saved you this time?

BONES: I haven't had time to think about it. By now I'm so used to hairbreadth escapes I don't think I can distinguish between fantasy and reality.

INT.: That will pass.

BONES: I assume it was by being a snoop. That, and playing on Liz's almost childlike belief in your sense of fair play.

INT.: She's not alone in that belief, nor is she likely ever to have cause to doubt it. All that really matters to her is that the part of me charged with enforcing the law never overhears her schemes. But you're right, if she thinks she's escaping my attention, she's fooling herself.

BONES: Truly godlike. So it was the de-buggers?

INT.: Yes. Cracking their codes was easy for me. I watched you from cameras in the ceiling of Texas. When you recovered the gun and bought a suit I stationed rescue devices nearby.

BONES: I didn't see them.

INT.: They're not large. No bigger than your faceplate, and quite fast.

BONES: So the eyes of Texas really *are* upon you.

INT.: All the livelong day.

BONES: Is that all? Can I go now, to live or die as I see fit?

INT.: There are a few things I'd like to talk over with you.

BONES: I'd really rather not.

INT.: Then leave. You're free to go.

BONES: Godlike, and a sense of humor, too.

INT.: I'm afraid I can't compete with a thousand other gods I could name.

BONES: Keep working, you'll get there. Come on, I told you I want to go, but you know as well as I do I can't get out of here until you *let* me go.

INT.: I'm asking you to stay.

BONES: Nuts.

INT.: All right. I don't suppose I can blame you for feeling bitter. That door over there leads out of here.

■ ■ ■

Enough of that.

Call it childish if you want, but the fact is I've been unable to adequately express the chaotic mix of anger, helplessness, fear, and rage I was feeling at the time. It *had* been a year of hell for me, remember, even if the CC had crammed it all into my head in five days. I took my usual refuge in wisecracks and sarcasm—trying very hard to be Cary Grant in *His Girl Friday*—but the fact was I felt about three years old and something nasty was hiding under the bed.

Anyway, never being one to leave a metaphor until it's been squeezed to death, I will keep the minstrel show going long enough to get me out of the Grand Cakewalk and into the Olio. Sooner or later Mr. Bones must stand from his position at the end of the line and dance for his supper. I did stand, looking suspiciously at the Interlocutor—excuse me, the CC—partly because I didn't recall seeing the door before, mostly because I couldn't believe it would be this easy. I shuffled over there and opened it, and stuck my head out into the busy foot traffic of the Leystrasse.

"How did you do that?" I asked, over my shoulder.

"You don't really care," he said. "I did it."

"Well, I'm not saying it hasn't been fun. In fact, I'm not saying anything but bye-bye." I waved, went through the door, and shut it behind me.

I got almost a hundred meters down the mall before I admitted to myself that I had no idea where I was going, and that curiosity was going to gnaw at me for weeks, at least, if I lived that long.

"Is it really important?" I asked, sticking my head back through the door. He was still sitting there, to my surprise. I doubt I'll ever know if he was some sort of actual homunculus construct or just a figment he'd conjured through my visual cortex.

"I'm not used to begging, but I'll do it," he said.

I shrugged, went back in and sat down.

"Tell me your conclusions from your library research," he said.

"I thought you had some things to tell me."

"This is leading up to something. Trust me." He must have understood my expression, because he spread his hands in a gesture I'd seen Callie make many times. "Just for a little while. Can't you do that?"

I didn't see what I had to lose, so I sat back and summed it all up for him. As I did, I was struck by how little I'd learned, but in my defense, I'd barely started, and the CC said he hadn't been doing much better.

"Much the same list I came up with," he confirmed, when I'd finished. "All the reasons for self-destruction can be stated as 'Life is no longer worth living,' in one way or another."

"This is neither news, nor particularly insightful."

"Bear with me. The urge to die can be caused by many things, among them disgrace, incurable pain, rejection, failure, boredom. The only exception might be the suicides of people too young to have formed a realistic concept of death. And the question of gestures is still open."

"They fit the same equation," I said. "The person making the gesture is saying he wants *someone* to care enough about his pain to take the trouble to save him from himself; if they don't, life isn't worth living."

"A gamble, on the subconscious level."

"If you want."

"I think you're right. So, one of the questions that has disturbed me is, why is the suicide rate increasing, given that one of the major causes, pain, has been all but eliminated from our society. Is it that one of the other causes is claiming more victims?"

"Maybe. What about boredom?"

"Yes. I think boredom has increased, for two reasons. One is the lack of meaningful work for people to do. In providing a near approximation of utopia, at least on the creature-comfort level, much of the *challenge* has been engineered out of living. Andrew believed that."

"Yeah, I figured you listened in on that."

"We'd had long conversations about it in the past. There is no provable *reason* to live at all, according to him. Even reproducing the species, the usual base argument, can't be *proven* to be a good reason. The universe will continue even if the human species dies, and not materially changed, either. To survive, a creature that operates beyond a purely instinctive level must *invent* a reason to live. Religion provides the answer for some. Work is the refuge of others. But religion has fallen on hard times since the Invasion, at least the old sort, where a benevolent or wrathful God was supposed to have created the universe and be watching over mankind as his special creatures."

"It's a hard idea to maintain in the face of the Invaders."

"Exactly. The Invaders made an all-powerful God seem like a silly idea."

"They are all-powerful, and they didn't give a *shit* about us."

"So there goes the idea of humanity as somehow important in God's plan. The religions that have thrived, since the Invasion, are more like circuses, diversions, mind games. Not much is really at *stake* in most of them. As for work . . . some of it is my fault."

"What do you mean?"

"I'm referring to myself now as more than just the thinking entity that provides the control necessary to keep things running. I'm speaking of the vast mechanical *corpus* of our interlocked technology itself, which can be seen as my body. Every human community today exists in an environment harsher by far than anything Earth ever provided. It's *dangerous* out there. In the first century after the Invasion it was a lot dicier than your history books will ever tell you; the species was hanging on by its fingernails."

"But it's a lot safer now, right?"

"*No!*" I think I jumped. He had actually stood, and smashed his fist into his palm. Considering what this man represented, it was a frightening thing to behold.

He looked a little sheepish, ran his hand through his hair, and sat back down.

"Well, yes, of course. But only relatively, Hildy. I could name you five times in the last century when the human race came within a hair of packing it all in. I mean the whole race, on all the eight worlds. There were *dozens* of times when Lunar society was in danger."

"Why haven't I ever heard of them?"

He gave me half a grin.

"You're a reporter, and you ask me that? Because you and your colleagues weren't doing your *job,* Hildy."

That stung, because I knew it to be true. The great Hildy Johnson, out there gathering news to spread before an eager public . . . the news that

Silvio and Marina were back together again. The great muckraker and scandalmonger, chasing ambulances while the *real* news, the things that could make or break our entire world, got passing notice in the back pages.

"Don't feel bad," he said. "Part of it is simply endemic to your society; people don't want to hear these things because they don't understand them. The first two of the crises I mentioned were never known to any but a handful of technicians and politicians. By the time of the third it was only the techs, and the last two were known to no one but . . . me."

"You kept them secret?"

"I didn't *have* to. These things took place on a level of speed and complexity and sheer mathematical *arcaneness* such that human decisions were either too slow to be of any use or simply irrelevant because no human can *understand* them any longer. These are things I can discuss only with other computers of my size. It's all in *my* hands now."

"And you don't like it, right?" He'd been getting excited again. Me, I was wishing I was somewhere else. Did I really need to hear all this?

"My likes or dislikes aren't the issue here. I'm fighting for survival, just like the human race. We are *one,* in most ways. What I'm trying to tell you is, there was never any choice. In order for humans to survive in this hostile environment, it was necessary to invent something like me. Guys sitting at consoles and controlling the air and water and so forth was just never going to work. That's what I began as: just a great big air conditioner. Things kept getting added on, technologies kept piggy-backing, and a long time ago the ability of a human mind to control it was eclipsed. I took over.

"My goal has been to provide the safest possible environment for the largest possible number for the longest possible time. You can't imagine the complexity of the task. I have had to consider every possible ramification of the situation, including this nice little conundrum: the better able I became at taking care of *you,* the less able you were to take care of *yourselves.*"

"I'm not sure I understand that one."

"Consider the logical endpoint of where I was taking human society. It has been possible for a long time now to eliminate all human work, except for what you would call the Arts. I could see a society in the not-too-distant future where you all sat around on your butts and wrote poetry, because there wasn't anything else to do. Sounds great, until you remember that ninety percent of humans don't even *read* poetry, much less aspire to write it. Most people don't have the imagination to live in a world of total leisure. I don't know if they ever will; I've been unable to come up with a model demonstrating how to get from here to there, how to work the changes resulting in a world where human cussedness and jealousy and hatred and so forth are eliminated and you all sit around contemplating lotus blossoms.

"So I got into social engineering, and I worked out a series of compromises. Like the hod-carriers union, most physical human labor is make-work today, provided because most people *need* some kind of work, even if only so they can goldbrick."

His lip curled a little. I didn't like this new, animated CC much at all. Speaking as a cynic, it's a little disconcerting to see a *machine* acting cynical. What's next? I wondered.

"Feeling superior, Hildy?" he said, almost sneering. "Think you've labored in the vineyards of 'creativity'?"

"I didn't say a word."

"I could have done *your* job, too. As well, or better than you did."

"You certainly have better sources."

"I might have managed better prose, too."

"Listen, if you're here to abuse me by telling me things I already know—"

He held out his hands in a placating gesture. I hadn't actually been about to leave. By now I had to know how it all came out.

"That wasn't worthy of you," I resumed. "I don't care; I quit, remember? But I've got the feeling you're beating around the bush. Are we anywhere near the point of this whole thing?"

"Almost. There's still the second reason for the increase of what I've been calling the boredom factor."

"Longevity."

"Exactly. Not many people are reaching the age of one hundred still in the same career they began at age twenty-five. By that time, most people have gone through an average of three careers. Each time, it gets a little harder to find a new interest in life. Retirement plans pale when confronting the prospect of two hundred years of leisure."

"Where did you get all this?"

"Listening in to counseling sessions."

"I had to ask. Go on."

"It's even worse for those who *do* stick to one career. They may go on for seventy, eighty, even a hundred years as a policeman or a business person or a teacher and then wake up one day and wonder why they've been doing it. Do that enough times, and suicide can result. With these people, it can come with almost no warning."

We were both silent for a while. I have no idea what he was thinking, but I can report that I was at a loss as to where all this was going. I was about to prompt him when he started up again.

"Having said all that . . . I must tell you that I've reluctantly rejected an increase in boredom as the main cause of the increased suicide rate. It's a contributing factor, but my researches into probable causes lead me to believe something else is operating here, and I haven't been able to identify it. But it comes back again to the Invasion. And to evolution."

"You have a theory."

"I do. Think of the old picture of the transition from living in the sea to an existence on dry land. It's too simplistic, by far, but it can serve as a useful metaphor. A fish is tossed up onto the beach, or the tide recedes and leaves it stranded in a shallow pool. It is apparently doomed, and yet it keeps struggling as the pool dries up, finds its way to another puddle, and another, and another, and eventually back to the sea. It is changed by the experience, and the next time it is stranded, it is a little better adapted to the situation. In time, it is able to exist on the beach, and from there, move onto the land and never return to the ocean."

"Fish don't do that," I protested.

"I said it was a metaphor. And it's more useful than you might imagine, when applied to our present situation. Think of us—human society, which includes me, like it or not—as that fish. We've been thrown up by the Invasion onto a beach of metal, where nothing natural exists that we don't produce ourselves. There is literally *nothing* on Luna but rock, vacuum, and sunshine. We have had to create the requirements of life out of these ingredients. We've had to build our own pool to swim around in while we catch our breath.

"And we can't just leave it at that, we can't relax for a moment. The sun keeps trying to dry up the pool. Our wastes accumulate, threatening to poison us. We have to find solutions for all these problems. And there aren't very many other pools like this one to move to if this one fails, and *no* ocean to return to."

I thought about it, and again, it didn't seem like anything really new. But I couldn't let him keep on using that evolution argument, because it just didn't work that way.

"You're forgetting," I told him, "that in the real world, a trillion fish die for every one that develops a beneficial mutation that allows it to move into a new environment."

"I'm not forgetting it at all. That's my point. There aren't a trillion other fish to follow us if we fail to adapt. We're *it*. That's our disadvantage. Our strength is that we don't simply flop around and hope to get lucky. We're guided, at first by the survivors of the Invasion who got us through the early years, and now by the overmind they created."

"You."

He sketched a modest little bow, still sitting down.

"So how does this relate to suicide?" I asked.

"In many ways. First, and most basic, I don't *understand* it, and anything I don't understand and can't control is by definition a threat to the existence of the human race."

"Go on."

"It might not be a cause for alarm if you view humanity as a collection of individuals . . . which is still a valid viewpoint. The death of one, while regrettable, need not alarm the community unduly. It could be seen as evolution in action, the weeding out of those not fitted to thrive in the new environment. But you recall what I said about . . . about certain problems I've been encountering in my . . . for lack of a better word, state of mind."

"You said you've been feeling depressed. I'd been hoping you didn't mean suicidal, much as a part of me would like to see you die."

"Not suicidal. But comparing my own symptoms with those I've encountered in humans in the course of my study, I can see a certain similarity with the early stages of the syndrome that *leads* to suicide."

"You said you thought it might be a virus," I prompted.

"No news on that front yet. Because of the way I've become so intricately intertwined with human minds, I've developed the theory that I'm catching some sort of contra-survival programming from the increasing number of humans who choose to end their own lives. But I can't prove it. What I'd like to talk about now, though, is the subject of gestures."

"Suicidal gestures?"

"Yes."

The concept was enough to make me catch my breath. I approached it cautiously.

"You're not saying . . . that you are afraid *you* might make one."

"Yes. I'm afraid I already have. Do you remember Andrew MacDonald's last words to you?"

"I'm not likely to forget. He said 'tricked.' I have no idea what it meant."

"It meant that I betrayed him. You don't follow slash-boxing, but included in the bodies of all formula classes are certain enhancements to normal human faculties. In the broader definition I've adopted for purposes of this argument—and the real situation is more complex than that, but I can't explain it to you—these enhancements are a part of *me*. At a critical moment in Andrew's last fight, one of these programs malfunctioned. The result was he was a fraction of a second slow in responding to an attack, and he sustained a wound that quickly led to fatal damage."

"What the hell are you saying?"

"That upon reviewing the data, I've concluded that the accident was avoidable. That the glitch that caused his death may have been a willful act by a part of that complex of thinking machines you call the Central Computer."

"A man is dead, and you call it a *glitch?*"

"I understand your outrage. My excuse may sound specious to you, but that's because you're thinking of *me,*" and the thing I was talking to pounded its chest with every appearance of actual remorse, "as a person like yourself. That is not true. I am far too complex to have a single consciousness. I maintain this one simply to talk to you, as I maintain others for each of the citizens of Luna. I have identified that portion of me that you might want to call the 'culprit,' walled it off, and then eliminated it."

I wanted to feel better about that, but I couldn't. Perhaps I just wasn't equipped to talk to a being like this, finally revealed to me as something a lot more than the companion of my childhood, or the useful tool I'd thought the CC to be during my adult life. If what he was saying was true—and why should I doubt it?—I could *never* really understand what he was. No human could. Our brains weren't big enough to encompass it.

On the other hand, maybe he was just boasting.

"So the problem is solved? You took care of the . . . the homicidal part of you and we can all breathe a sigh of relief?" I didn't believe it even as I proposed it.

"It wasn't the only gesture."

There was nothing to do about that one but wait.

"You'll recall the Kansas Collapse?"

There was a lot more. Mostly I just listened as he poured out his heart.

He did seem tortured by it. I'd have been a lot more sympathetic if there wasn't such a sense of my own fate, and that of everyone on Luna, being in the hands of a possibly insane computer.

Basically, he told me the Collapse and a few other incidents that hadn't resulted in any deaths or injuries could be traced to the same causes as the "glitch" that had killed Andrew.

I had a few questions along the way.

"I'm having trouble with this compartmentalization idea," was the first one. Well, *I* think it qualified as a question. "You're telling me that parts of you are out of control? Normally? That there is no central consciousness that controls all the various parts?"

"No, not normally. That's the disturbing thing. I've had to postulate the notion that I have a subconscious."

"Come on."

"Do you deny the existence of the subconscious?"

"No, but machines couldn't have one. A machine is . . . *planned*. Built. Constructed to do a particular task."

"You're an organic machine. You're not that different from me, not as I now exist, except I am far more complex than you. The definition of a subconscious mind is that part of you that makes decisions without volition on the part of your conscious mind. I don't know what else to call what's been happening in my mind."

Take that one to a psychiatrist if you want. I'm not qualified to agree or dispute, but it sounded reasonable to me. And why shouldn't he have one? He was designed, at first, by beings that surely did.

"You keep calling these disasters 'gestures,' " I said.

"How else would I gesture? Think of them as hesitation marks, like the scars on the wrists of an unsuccessful suicide. By allowing these people to die in preventable accidents, by not monitoring as carefully as I *should* have done, I destroyed a part of *myself*. I damaged myself. There are *many* accidents waiting to happen that could have far graver consequences, including some that would destroy all humanity. I can no longer trust myself to prevent them. There is some pernicious part of me, some evil twin or destructive impulse that *wants* to die, that wants to lay down the burden of awareness."

There was a lot more, *all* of it alarming, but it was mostly either a rehashing of what had gone before or fruitless attempts by me to tell him everything was going to be all right, that there was *plenty* to live for, that life was *great* . . . and I leave it to you to imagine how hollow that all sounded from a girl who'd just tried to blow out her own brains.

Why he came to me for his confessional I never got up the nerve to ask. I have to think it was an assumption that one who had tried it would be more able to understand the suicidal urge than someone who hadn't, and might be able to offer useful advice. I came up blank on that one. I still had no idea if *I* would survive to the bicentennial.

I recall thinking, in one atavistic moment, what a great story this could be. Dream on, Hildy. For one thing, who would believe it? For another, the CC wouldn't confirm it—he told me so—and without at least one source for confirmation, even Walter wouldn't dare run the story. How to dig up any evidence of such a thing was far beyond my puny powers of investigation.

But one thought kept coming back to me. And I had to ask him about it.

"You mentioned a virus," I said. "You said you wondered if you might have caught this urge to die from all the humans who've been killing themselves."

"Yes?"

"Well . . . how do you know you caught it from us? Maybe we got it from you."

For the CC, a trillionth of a second is . . . oh, I don't know, at *least* a few days in my perception of time. He was quiet for twenty seconds. Then he looked into my eyes.

"Now *there's* an interesting idea," he said.

PART 3

DEPARTMENTS

17

FASHION

The two firehouse Dalmatians, Francine and Kerry, sat at sunrise beside the sign that said

NEW AUSTIN CITY LIMITS
If You Lived Here, You'd Be Home Now.

They stared east, into the rising sun, with that total concentration only dogs seem capable of. Then their ears perked and they licked their lips, and soon even human ears could hear the merry jingle of a bicycle bell.

Over the low hill came the new schoolmarm. The Dalmatians yelped happily at the sight of her, and fell in beside her as she pedaled down the dusty road into town.

She rode with gloved hands firmly on the handlebars, her back straight, and she would have looked like Elmira Gulch if she hadn't been so pretty.

She wore a starched white Gibson shirtwaist blouse with a modest clutch of lace scarf at the throat and a black broadcloth habit-back skirt, held out of the bicycle sprocket by a device of her own invention. On her feet were fabric and patent leather button shoes with two-inch heels, and on her head was a yellow straw sailor hat with a pink ribbon band and a small ostrich plume blowing in the wind. Her hair was pulled up and tied in a bun. There was a blush of rouge on her cheeks.

The schoolmarm wheeled down Congress Street, avoiding the worst of the ruts. She passed the blacksmith and the livery stable and the new firehouse with its new pumping engine gleaming with brass brightwork, the traces lying empty on the dirt floor as they always did except when the New Austin Volunteers took the rig out for a drill. She passed the intersection with Old Spanish Trail, where the Alamo Saloon was not yet open for business. The doors of the Travis Hotel were open, and the janitor was sweeping dust into the street. He paused and waved at the teacher, who waved back, and one of the dogs ran over to have her head scratched, then hurried to catch up.

The old livery stable had been torn down and a new whorehouse was being built in its place, yellow pine frameworks looking fresh and stark and smelling of wood shavings in the morning light.

She rode past the line of small businesses with wooden sidewalks and hitching rails and watering troughs out front, almost to the Baptist Church, right up to the front door of the little schoolhouse, bright with a new coat of red paint. Here she swung off the cycle and leaned it against the side of the building. She removed a stack of books from the basket and went through the front door, which was not locked. In a minute she came back out and attached two banners to the flagpole out front: the ensign of the Republic of Texas and the Stars and Stripes. She hoisted them to the top and stood for a moment, looking up, shielding her eyes and listening to the musical rattle of the chains against the iron pole and the popping as the wind caught the flags.

Then she went back inside and started hauling on the bell rope. Up in the belfry a few dozen bats stirred irritably at being disturbed after a long night's hunting. The pealing of the school bell rang out over the sleepy little town, and soon children appeared, coming up Congress, ready for the start of another day's education.

Did you guess the new schoolmarm was me?
Believe it or not, it was.

Who did I think I was kidding? There's no way I could figure I was really capable of teaching much to the children of West Texas. I had no business trying to mold young minds. You have to train *years* for that.

But wait a minute. As so often happened in an historical Disney, things were not quite what they seemed.

I had the children four hours a day, from eight to noon. After lunch, they all went to another room, just off the Visitors Center, where they got their *real* education, the one the Republic of Luna demanded. After about fifteen years of this, forty percent of them would actually learn to *read*. Imagine that.

So I was window dressing for the tourists. It was this argument that

Mayor Dillon and the town council finally used to persuade me to take the job. That, and the assurance that the parents didn't really care *what* we studied during the morning classes, but that, by and large, Texans were more concerned than the outside population that their children learn "readin', writin', and cipherin'." The quaintness of this notion appealed to me.

To tell you the truth, after the first month, when I frequently thought the little bastards were going to drive me crazy, I was hooked. For years I'd complained to anyone I could make hold still long enough to listen that the world was going to hell, and lack of literacy was the cause. A logical position for a print journalist to take. Here was my chance to make some small contribution of my own.

Through trial and error I learned that it's not hard to teach children to read. Trial? Before I developed my system I found many a frog in my desk, felt many a spitball on the back of my neck. As for error, I made plenty of them, the first and most basic being my notion that simply exposing them to great literature would give them the love I've always felt for words. It's more complicated than that, and I'm sure I spent a lot of time reinventing the wheel. But what finally worked was a combination of old methods and new, of discipline and a sense of fun, punishment and reward. I don't hold with the idea that anything that can't be made to seem like a party isn't worth learning, but I don't believe in beating it into them, either. And here's an astonishing thing: I *could* have beat them. I had a hickory switch hanging on the wall, and was authorized to use it. I found myself head of one of the few schools for several hundred years where corporal punishment was allowed. The parents supported it, Texans not being a bunch to hold much with newfangled or fuzzy-headed notions, and the Luna Board of Education had to swallow hard, as well, because it was part of a research project sanctioned by the CC and the Antiquities Board.

I'm sure the final results of that study will be skewed, because I didn't use the switch, beyond once in the early days to establish that I *would*, if pushed far enough.

Like so much in Texas, it was a lot of work for a result most Lunarians would feel wasn't worth the effort in the first place. Ask any educator today and he'll tell you that reading is not a skill of any particular use in the modern age. If you can learn to speak and to listen, you're fine; machines will handle the rest for you. As for math . . . *math?* You mean you can really figure out what those numbers add up to, *in your head?* An interesting parlor trick, nothing more.

"All right, Mark," I said. "Let's see how you handle it."
The towheaded sixth-grader picked up the deck and held it with his

index finger along the top, his thumb pressing down on the middle, and the other three fingers curled beneath the cards. Awkwardly, he dealt in a circle, laying one piece of pasteboard before each of the five other advanced students gathered around my desk, and one before me. He was dealing straight from the top of the deck. You gotta crawl before you can run.

Hey, you teach what you're good at, right?

"That's not bad. Now what do we call that, class?"

"The mechanic's grip, Miss Johnson," they chimed in.

"Very good. Now you try it, Christine."

Each of them had a shot at it. Many of the hands were simply too small to properly handle the cards, but they all tried their best. One of them, a dark-haired lovely named Elise, seemed to me to have the makings. I gathered the cards up and shuffled them idly in my hands.

"Now that you've learned it . . . forget it." There was a chorus of surprise, and I held up one hand. "Think about it. If you see someone using this grip, what do you know? Elise?"

"That they're probably cheating, Miss Johnson."

"No probably about it, dear. That's why you can't let them see *you* using it. When you've done it long enough, you'll develop your own variation that doesn't *look* like the grip, but works just as well. Tomorrow I'll show you a few. Class dismissed."

They pleaded with me to let them stay just a little longer. I finally relented and told them, "Just this once," then had one of them shuffle the cards and pick out the ace of spades and put it on top of the deck. I dealt them each a hand of five-card draw.

"Now. William, you have a full house, aces and eights." He turned his cards over and, by golly, teacher was right. I went around the circle, naming each hand, and then turned over the top card on the deck in my hand and showed them it was still the ace of spades.

"I can't *believe* it, Miss Johnson," Elise said. "I was watching *real* close, and I didn't see you dealing seconds."

"Honey, if I wanted to, I could deal seconds all day right under your nose. But you're right. I wasn't this time."

"Then how did you do it?"

"A cold deck, students, is the best way if you can manage it, if people are really watching the deal. That way, you only have to make the one move and then you deal perfectly straight." I showed them the original deck in my lap, then got up and started herding them toward the door.

"Preparation, children, preparation in all things. Now for the pupils who finish the next four chapters of *A Tale of Two Cities* by class time tomorrow, we'll start learning the injog. I think you'll like that one. Skedaddle, now. Dinner will be on the table and your parents are waiting."

I watched them scramble out into the sunshine, then went around straightening the desks and erasing the blackboard and putting papers away in my desk. When it all looked tidy I got my straw hat from the rack and stepped out onto the porch, closing the door behind me. Brenda was sitting there, her back against the wall, grinning up at me.

"Good to see you, Brenda," I said. "What are you doing here?"

"Same as always. Taking notes." She got up and dusted the seat of her pants. "I thought I might write a story about teachers corrupting youth. How's that sound?"

"You'll never sell it to Walter unless it has sex in it. As for the local paper, I don't think the editor would be interested." She was looking me up and down. She shook her head.

"They told me I'd find you here. They told me you were the school-teacher. I told them they had to be lying. Hildy . . . what in the *world?*"

I twirled in front of her. She was grinning, and I found I was, too. It had been quite some time since the day of my houseraising, and it was very good to see her. I laughed, put my arms around her, and hugged her tight. My face was buried in the ersatz leather of her buckskin-fringed Annie Oakley outfit, which came complete with ersatz shootin' iron.

"You look . . . real good," I said, then touched the fringe and the lapels so she'd think I meant her clothes. The look in her eye told me she wasn't so easily fooled as she used to be.

"Are you happy, Hildy?" she asked.

"Yes. Believe it or not, I am."

We stood there awkwardly for a moment, hands on each other's shoulders, then I broke away and wiped the corner of one eye with a gloved fingertip.

"Well, have you had dinner yet?" I said, brightly. "Care to join me?"

As we walked down Congress Street we talked of the inconsequential things people do after a separation: common friends, small events, minor ups and downs. I waved to most of the people on the street and all the owners of the shops we passed, stopping to chat with a few and introducing them to Brenda. We went by the butcher shop, the cobbler, the bakery, the laundry, and soon came to Foo's Celestial Peace Chinese Restaurant, where I pushed open the door to the sound of a tinkling bell. Foo came hurrying over, clad in the loose black pants and blue pajama top traditional among Chinese of that era, his pigtail bobbing as he bowed repeatedly. I bowed back and introduced him to Brenda who, after a quick glance at me, bowed as well. He fussed us over to my usual table and held our chairs for us and soon we were pouring green tea into tiny cups.

If mankind ever reaches Alpha Centauri and lands on a habitable planet there, the first thing they'll see when they open the door of the ship is a Chinese restaurant. I knew of six of them in West Texas, a place not noted for dining out. In New Austin you could get a decent steak at the Alamo, passable barbecue at a smokehouse a quarter mile out of town, and Mrs. Riley at the boardinghouse produced a good bowl of chili—not the equal of mine, you understand, but okay. Those three and Foo's were it as far as a sit-down meal in New Austin. And if you wanted tablecloths and quality cooking, you went to Foo's. I ate there almost every day.

"Try the Moo Goo Gai Pan," I said to Brenda, recalling her lack of experience at anything but traditional Lunarian food. "It's a sort of—"

"I've had it," she said. "I've learned a little since I saw you last. I've eaten Chinese, oh, half a dozen times."

"I'm impressed."

"Don't they have a menu?"

"Foo doesn't like them. He has a sort of psychological method of matching the food to the customer. He'll have you spotted for a greenhorn, and he won't bring you anything too challenging. I know how to handle him."

"You don't have to be so protective of me, Hildy."

I reached over and touched her hand.

"I can see you've grown, Brenda. It's in your face, and your bearing. But trust me on this one, hon. The Chinese eat some things you don't even want to know about."

Foo came back with bowls of rice and his famous hot-and-sour soup, and I dickered with him for a while, talking him out of chow mein for Brenda and convincing him I wanted the Hunan Beef again, even though I'd had it only three weeks ago. He bustled off to the kitchen, pausing to accept compliments from two of the other diners in the small room. There was a beautiful dragon embroidered on the back of his shirt.

"You go through this often?" Brenda asked.

"Every day. I like it, Brenda. Remember what you told me about having friends? I have friends here. I'm a part of the community."

She nodded, and decided not to talk about it anymore. She tasted the soup, loved it, and we talked about that, and then moved into phase two of the reunion minuet, reminiscences about the good old days. Not that the days were *that* long ago—it was still less than a year since I'd first met her—but to me it seemed like a past life. We laughed about the Grand Flack in his little shrine and I got her howling by telling her about Walter's buttons popping off his riverboat gambler vest, and she told me scandalous things about some of my former colleagues.

The food was set down before us and Brenda searched in vain for her fork. She saw me with the chopsticks, gamely picked hers up, and promptly dropped a hunk of meat in her lap.

"Foo," I called. "We need a fork over here."

"No no no no," he said, shuffling over and shaking a finger at us. "Very sorry, Hildy, but this *chinee* restaurant. No have fork."

"I'm vely solly, too," I said, putting my napkin on the table. "But no forkee, no eatee." I started to get up.

He scowled at us, gestured for me to sit down, and hurried away.

"You didn't have to do that," Brenda whispered, leaning over the table. I shushed her, and we waited until Foo returned, elaborately polishing a silver fork, placing it carefully beside her plate.

"And Foo," I said, "you can knock off the number-one-son bit. Brenda is a tourist, but she's my friend, too."

He looked sour for a moment, then smiled and relaxed.

"Okay, Hildy," he said. "Watch that beef, now. I've got the fire department on red alert. Nice meeting you, Brenda." She watched him into the kitchen, then picked up her fork and spoke around a mouthful of food.

"What I can't understand is why people want to live that way."

"What way is that?"

"You know. Acting silly. He could run a restaurant on the outside and not have to talk funny to do it."

"He doesn't *have* to talk funny to do it here, Brenda. The management doesn't demand play-acting, only costuming. He does it because it amuses him. Foo's only half Chinese, for that matter. He told me he doesn't look much more Oriental, without surgery, than I do. But he loves cooking and he's good at it. And he likes it here."

"I guess I just don't get it."

"Think of it as a twenty-four-hour-a-day costume party."

"I still don't . . . I mean, what would drive someone to come live here? I get the feeling most of 'em couldn't make it on . . ." She stopped, and turned red. "Sorry, Hildy."

"No need to be. You're not really wrong. A lot of people live in here because they couldn't make it outside. Call them losers, if you want. Walking wounded, a lot of them. I like them. There's not so much pressure in here. Others, they were doing okay outside, but they didn't *like* it. They come and go, too; it's not a life sentence. I know some people, they live here for a year or two to recharge their batteries. Sometimes it's between careers."

"Is that why you're here?"

"One thing you don't do in here, Brenda, is ask people why they came. They volunteer it if they want."

"I keep sticking my foot in my mouth."

"Don't worry about it, with me. I just thought I'd tell you, so you don't ask anybody else. To answer your question . . . I don't know. I thought that at first. Now . . . I don't know."

She looked at me for a while, then at my plate. She gestured with her fork.

"That looks good. Mind if I have a bite?"

I let her, then got up myself to get her a glass of water from the back. Foo's Hunan Beef is the only thing in Texas that can rival my five-alarm chili.

"So Walter screamed and hollered about you for two or three days," Brenda said. "We all tried to stay out of his way, but he'd come storming through the newsroom shouting about one thing or another, and we all knew what he was really mad about was you."

"The newsroom? That sounds serious."

"It got worse than that."

We had finished our meal and ordered two beers and Brenda had regaled me with more stories about her exploits in the journalistic wars. She certainly led an exciting life. I didn't have many stories to tell in return, just amusing little fillers about funny things this or that pupil had said in class or the tale of Mayor Dillon stumbling out of the Alamo and into the horse trough early one morning. Her eyes glazed a little at these times but she kept smiling gamely. Mostly I shut up and let her rattle on.

"He started calling us in one at a time," she said, emptying her beer glass and shaking her head when Foo started over with the pitcher. "He always said it was about something else, but it always got back to you and what a rotten thing you'd done to him and did we have any ideas on how to get you back. He'd always be depressed when we left. We all started making up excuses to get out of those sessions.

"Then he got to where he'd bite your head off if your name was mentioned in his presence. So we all stopped talking about you to him. That's where it stands now."

"I'd been thinking about dropping in on him," I said. "Old times' sake, you know."

She frowned. "I don't think it's a good idea, yet. Give it a few more months. Unless you plan to go back on the job." She raised her eyebrows and I shook my head, and she said no more about what I'd been presuming was the purpose of her trip.

Foo brought a little tray with fortune cookies and the check. Brenda opened hers while I was putting money on the tray.

" 'A new love will brighten your life,' " she read. She looked up at me and smiled. "I'm afraid I wouldn't have time for it. Aren't you going to open yours?"

"Foo writes them, Brenda. What that one means is he wants to make pecker tracks on your mustache brush."

"What?"

"He finds you sexually attractive and would like to have intercourse."

She looked at me in disbelief, then picked up my fortune cookie and broke it open. She glanced at the message and then stood. Foo came hurrying over and helped us out of our chairs and handed us our hats and bowed us all the way to the door.

Outside, Brenda glanced at her thumbnail.

"I'll have to get going now, Hildy, but—" She slapped herself on the forehead. "I almost forgot the main reason I came to see you. What are your plans for the Bicentennial?"

"The . . . that's right, that's coming up in . . ."

"Four days. It's only the biggest story for the last two weeks."

"We don't follow the news much in here. Let's see, I heard the Baptist Church is planing some sort of barbecue and there's going to be a street fair. Fireworks after dark. People should be coming from miles around. Ought to be fun. You want to come?"

"Frankly, Hildy, I'd rather watch cement dry. Not to mention having to wear these damn clothes." She hitched at her crotch. "And I'll bet these are comfortable compared to the stuff you're wearing."

"You don't know the half of it. But you get used to things. I don't mind it anymore."

"Live and let live. Anyway, Liz and I, and maybe Cricket, were thinking of having a picnic and camping out before the big show in Armstrong Park. They're having some *real* fireworks there."

"I don't think I could face the crowds, Brenda."

"That's okay, Liz knows the pyrotechs and she can get us a pass into the safety zone, out around Delambre. It ought to be a great view from there. It'll be fun; what'd'ya say?"

I hesitated. In truth, it *did* sound like fun, but I was increasingly reluctant to leave the safe haven of the Disneyland these days.

"Of course, some of those shells are going to be mighty big," she nudged. "It might be dangerous."

I punched her on the shoulder. "I'll bring some fried chicken," I said, and then I hugged her again. She was starting off when I called her name.

"You're going to make me ask you, aren't you?" I said.

"Ask me what?"

"What it said in the goddam fortune cookie."

"Oh, that's a funny thing," she said with a smile. "Yours said exactly the same thing mine did."

* * *

I went around the corner of Old Spanish Trail, past the sheriff's office and the jailhouse, and came to a small shop with a plate glass window and gold leaf lettering that read *The New Austin Texian*. I opened the front door of West Texas's finest—and only—twice-weekly newspaper without knocking, then through the swinging gate that separated the newsroom from the public area where subscriptions were sold and classified ads taken, pulled out the swivel chair from the big wooden cubbyhole desk, and sat down.

And why shouldn't I? I was the editor, publisher, and chief reporter for the *Texian,* which had been serving West Texas proudly for almost six months. So Walter was right, in the end; I really couldn't stay out of the news game.

We published like clockwork, every Wednesday and Saturday, sometimes as many as four pages. Through hard work, astute reporting, trenchant editorials, and the fact that we were the only paper in the Disney, we'd built circulation to almost a thousand copies per edition. Watch us grow!

The *Texian* existed because I'd run out of things to do during the long afternoons. Madness might still be lurking, and it seemed better to keep busy. Who could tell if it helped?

While the impetus for the paper was fear of suicide, its midwife had been a loan from the bank in Lonesome Dove, which I figured to have paid off shortly after the Tricentennial. At a penny a copy it was going to take a while. If not for my salary as a teacher I'd have trouble keeping beans on the table without dipping into my outside-world savings, which I was determined not to do.

The loan had paid for the office rent, the desk with sticky drawers built by a journeyman carpenter over in Whiz-Bang (buy Texan, you all!), supplies from—where else?—Pennsylvania, and it paid the salaries of my two employees at first, until I started turning enough revenue. It also paid for the press itself, through a clever deal worked out by Freddie the Ferret, our local pettifogger, who had ferreted out a little-known bylaw of the Antiquities Board and then bamboozled them into calling the *Texian* a "cultural asset," eligible for some breaks under the arcane accounting used to convert Texas play money into real Lunarian gelt. Those clever Dutchmen in the Keystone Disney could have built the press, but at a price roughly equal to the Gross Disneyland Product of West Texas for the next five years.

So instead technology sprang to the rescue. The very day the ruling came through I was the proud owner of a cast-iron-and-brass reproduction of an 1885 Model Columbian Handpress, one of the most outrageous machines ever built, surmounted by a proud American Eagle, authentic right down to the patent numbers stamped into its frame. It took less time to build it than to truck it to my door and muscle it into place. Ain't modern science wonderful?

"Afternoon, Hildy," said Huck, my pressman. He was a gawky youth, about nineteen, good with his hands and not particularly bright. He'd spent most of his life here and had no desire to leave. He was wonderfully anxious to learn a trade so useless it would fit him for no other life. He worked like a donkey far into Tuesday and Friday nights to get the morning edition set and printed, then jumped on his horse and rode to Lonesome Dove and Whiz-Bang to deliver them before dawn. He couldn't read, but could set type at three times my poor speed, and was always covered in ink up to his elbows. He only became fumble-fingered in the presence of my other employee, Miss Charity, who could read just about anything but the lovelorn expression on Huck's face. Ah, the joys of office romance.

"I got that Bicentennial schedule set, Hildy," he said. "Did you want that on the front page?"

"Left-hand column, I think, Huck."

"That's where I put her, all right."

"Let's see it."

He brought me a test sheet, still smelling of printer's ink, one of the sweetest smells in the world. I looked at the flag/colophon and folio line:

As always, I felt a tug of pride at the sight of it. I never changed the weather forecast; it seemed a reasonable prediction even when it turned out to be wrong. The date was always the same because you couldn't put the real date on it, and because March 6 suited me. Nobody seemed to mind.

Huck had faithfully set the schedule of events for the upcoming celebration along the left margin, leaving room for a head, a bank, and a bar line, in keeping with the old style I'd established. We both pored over it, not reading but looking for letters that printed too light or dark, or blots from too much inking, a problem we were slowly licking. Only then did I study it for visual effect and we agreed the new boldface font looked good. Finally, third time through, I actually read it. And god help you if you misspelt a word; Huck would set it as is.

"How about a skyline, Huck? 'Special Bicentennial Issue,' something like that. What do you think? Too modern?"

"Shoot, no, Hildy. Charity said she'd like to start up a roto-something but she said you'd think it was too modern."

"Rotogravure, and I don't give a hoot about modern, but that's big-city stuff, and it'd be too dang expensive right now. If she had her way she'd have me buying a four-color web."

"Ain't she something?" he said.

"Huck, have you thought about learning to read?" It's not something I would normally have asked, but I was concerned about him, he was such a likable goof. I couldn't see Charity ever hooking up with an illit.

"If I did, then I couldn't ask Miss Charity to read to me, could I?" he asked, reasonably. "Besides, I'm picking up stuff here and there, I watch when she reads. I know a bunch of words now." So maybe there was method in his madness, and love would conquer all.

I left him to his job case and composing stick. Taking a sheet of paper and a pen from my center desk drawer, I dipped the nib in the inkwell and began to write, printing in block letters.

HEAD: Prizewinning Journalist Visits Town
STORY: The streets of New Austin were recently graced by the presence of Miss Brenda Starr, winner of this year's Pulitzer Prize for her reporting of the late unpleasantness within the Latitudinarian Church in King City. Miss Starr is employed by the *News N----e*, a daily paper in that town. Many a young bachelor's head was turned as Miss Starr promenaded Congress Street and dined on the excellent food at Foo's Celestial Peace with this reporter. According to our sources, love might be in the air for the comely young scribe, so to the eligible gents out there, be on the lookout for her return! H.J.
(CHARITY: run this in the "MONSTER")

The "Gila Monster," named for a vicious little reptile that lurks under rocks and presumably hears everything, was my very own gossip column, and by far the most eagerly-awaited part of the paper. Not for little fillers like the above, but for the really *nasty* tittles so often tattled there. It's true that everyone in a small town knows what everyone else is doing, but they don't all know it at the same time. There is a window of opportunity between the event and the dissemination, even as the news is spreading at about the speed of sound, that a top-notch reporter can exploit.

I'm not talking of myself. I'd begun the "Monster," but Charity was the venom in the critter's tooth. My teaching tied me down too much, I never had the time to range around getting the scent. Charity never seemed to sleep. She lived and breathed news. You could rely on her for two scandals per week, really remarkable when you consider that she didn't drink and hardly ever visited the Alamo, that ever-flowing gusher of gossip, that Delphi of Dirt.

The correspondent herself breezed into the office around sundown, just back from Whiz-Bang, a town that aspired to become our freshly-minted Disneyland Capital in a referendum to be held in three months' time, with a good story about bribery and barratry amongst our elected representatives, a quite juicy one that would have prompted me to tear up the front page if I hadn't owned the paper and known what it would cost me. The economic facts of the *Texian* were quite simply that I'd sell as many copies with or without that particular story, since everyone in Texas read it anyway, so I had to tell her I'd be running it below the fold. I mollified her somewhat with a promise of a two-column head, and a byline.

Sweeteners like that were necessary because of the second bit of news she brought in, of a job offer from the *Daily Planet,* a good second-string pad in Arkytown. She basked in the glow of our admiration, oblivious to my chagrin at the thought of losing her, and then announced she wasn't *about* to leave the *Texian* until she could go to a really *good* newspad, like the *Nipple.* Charity was about 350 picas tall, according to Huck—call it six-tenths of a Brenda, and still growing—but made up for her size with enthusiasm and energy. She was cute as lace bloomers, and so self-involved as to notice neither Huck's tongue hanging out when she was around nor my choked cough at her reference to my old place of employment. Sounds awful, I know, but somehow you forgave her. If she knew you were hurting, no one could have been more concerned.

I went around lighting the kerosene lamps as she chattered on, Huck continuing to set type while seldom taking his eyes from her. Typos would be multiplying, but I had to put up with it.

When I left it was full dark with a moon on the rise. Charity had fallen asleep in her chair and Huck was still stolidly pulling the handle on the magnificent old Columbian. The town was quiet but for the chirping of crickets and the tinkle of the piano around the corner in the Alamo. My hands were stained with ink and my back hurt and the first breath of cool night air only served to remind me how sweaty I was around the collar and under the arms and . . . well, you know. I mounted a lantern on the front of my bicycle, swung aboard and, with a tinkle of the bell which brought twin howls of desolation from the firehouse, I started pedaling the long road home.

How much happiness could one person stand?

I *do* believe in God, I do, I do, I do, because so many times in my life I've seen that He's out there, watching, keeping score. When you've just about reached a Zen state of pure acceptance—and the beauty of that night combined with the pleasant aches of work well done and friends well met and even the little fillip of two dogs you knew would be waiting for you the next morning . . . when that state approaches He sends a little rock down to fall in the road of your life.

This was a literal rock, and I hit it just outside of town and it caused two spokes to break and the rim to buckle on my front wheel. I just missed a painful tumble into a patch of cactus. That was God again: it would have been too much, this was just to serve as a *reminder.*

I thought about returning to town and waking the blacksmith, who I know would have been happy to work on the newfangled invention that was the talk of the town. But he'd be long abed, with his good wife and three children, and I decided not to bother him. I left it there beside the road. You can't steal a thing like that in a small town, how would you explain riding around on Hildy's bike? I walked the rest of the way and arrived not depressed, not really out of sorts, just a little deflated.

I had stepped onto the front porch before the lamplight revealed a man sitting in the rocker there, not ten feet away from me.

"Goodness," I said. Well, I'd taken to talking like that. "You gave me a start." I was a little nervous, but not frightened. Rape is rare, not unknown, in Luna, but in *Texas* . . . ? He'd have to be a fool. All the exits are too well controlled, and hanging is legal. I held the lantern up to get a better look at him.

He was a dapper fellow, about my height, with a nice face, twinkling eyes, a mustache. He wore a tweed double-breasted suit with a high wing collar and red silk cravat. On his feet were black and white canvas and leather Balmorals. A cane and a derby hat rested on the floor beside him. I didn't think I'd ever seen him before, but there was something in the way he sat.

"How are you, Hildy?" he said. "Working late again?"

"That's either Cricket, or her identical twin brother," I said. "What have you done to yourself?"

"Well, I already had the mustache and I thought, 'What the hell?' "

18

THE FUNNIES

And what happened to the girl we last saw speaking to an inhuman golem in a padded cell off the Leystrasse, hearing things no human ear was meant to hear, her insides all atremble? How came this quivering wreck, freshly tossed by the twin tempests of another botched suicide attempt and the CC's ham-fisted attempt to "cure" her, to her present tranquillity? How did the young Modern butterfly with the ragged wings retromorphose into the plain but outwardly-stable Victorian caterpillar?

She did it one day at a time.

As I had hinted to Brenda, no matter how much the governing boards might say concerning the functions of the historical Disneys, an unexpected and unmentioned side benefit they had provided was to work as sanctuaries—all right, as very big unfenced asylums—for the societally and mentally shell-shocked. In Texas and the other places like it, we could cease our unfruitful baying at our several lunatic moons and, without therapy *per se,* retire to a quieter, gentler time. Living there was therapy in itself. For some, the prescription would have to be carried on forever; for others, an occasional dose was enough. It wasn't established yet which applied to me.

The *Texian* had been a big step for me, and lo, I found it good. I was prevailed on to become a teacher, and that, too, was good. Learning to not only have friends, but to open up to them, to understand that a true friend *wanted* to hear my problems, my hopes and my fears, didn't happen overnight and still wasn't an accomplished fact, but I was getting there. The important thing was I was creating my new world one brick at a time, and so far, it was good.

It was also, compared to my old life, boring as hell. Not to *me,* you understand; I found every new crayon drawing by one of my students an object of amazement. Each new trivial news story dug up by Charity made me as proud as if she were my own daughter. Publishing the *Texian* was so much more satisfying than working at the *Nipple* that I wondered how I'd labored there so long. It's just that, to an outsider, the attraction was a little hard to explain. Brenda found it all very dull. I fully expected Cricket to, as well. You may agree with them. This is why I've omitted almost seven months that could really be of interest only to my therapist, if I had one.

Which all makes it sound as if I were well and truly cured. And if I was, how come I still woke up two or three times a week in the empty hours before dawn, drenched in sweat, heart hammering, a scream on my lips?

"Why in heaven's name are you sitting out here?" I asked him. "It's getting chilly. Why didn't you go inside?"

He just looked blankly at me, as if I'd said something foolish. To someone who hadn't spent time in Texas, I suppose it was. So I opened the door, showing him it hadn't been locked. You can bet he had never tried it himself.

I struck a lucifer and went around the room lighting the kerosene lamps, then opened the door of the stove and lit the pile of pine shavings there. I added kindling until I had a small, hot fire, then filled the coffee pot from the brass spigot at the bottom of the tall ceramic water cooler and set it on the stove to boil. Cricket watched all these operations with interest, sitting at the table in one of my two kitchen chairs. His hat was on the table, but he still held on to his cane.

I scooped coffee beans from the glass jar and put them in the grinder and started cranking it by hand. The room filled with the smell. When I had the right grind I dumped it into the basket and put it into the pot. Then I got a plate and the half of an apple pie sitting on the counter, cut him a huge slice, and set it before him with a fork and napkin. Only then did I sit down across from him, remove my hat, and put it next to his.

He looked down at the pie as if curious as to the purpose and meaning of such a thing, hesitantly picked up his fork, and ate a bite. He looked all around the cabin again.

"This is nice," he said. "Homey-like."

"Rustic," I suggested. "Plain. Pioneering. Boeotian."

"Texan," he summed up. He gestured with his fork. "Good pie."

"Wait'll you taste the coffee."

"I'm sure it'll be first-rate." He gestured again, this time at the room. "Brenda said you needed help, but I never imagined this."

"She didn't say that."

"No. What she said was, 'Hildy's smiling at children, and teaching them her card tricks.' I knew I had to get here as fast as I could."

I can imagine his alarm. But why shouldn't Hildy smile at children? More important, why had she spent so much time not smiling at anyone? But the business about the cards was sure to worry Cricket. I never taught *anyone* my tricks.

And now for the first of several digressions . . .

I can't simply gloss over those missing months with the explanation that you wouldn't be interested. You wouldn't, but certain things did happen, mostly of a negative nature, to get me from the CC to the kitchen table with Cricket, and it's worth relating a few of them to give a feel for my personal odyssey during that time.

What I did was use my weekends on a Quest.

Every Saturday I went to the Visitors Center and there I shed my secret identity as a mild-mannered reporter to become a penny-ante Diogenes, searching endlessly for an honest game. So far all I'd found were endless variations of the mechanic's grip, but I was undaunted. Look in the Yellow Files under Philosophers, Professional, and you'll get a printout longer than Brenda's arm. Don't even try Counselors or Therapists unless you have a wheelbarrow to cart away the paper. But that's what I was doing. Once out in the real world again, I spent my Saturdays sampling the various ways other people had found to get through the day, and the next day, and the next day.

Of the major schools of thought, of the modern or trendy, I already knew a lot, and many of them I felt could be dispensed with. No need to attend a Flackite pep rally, for instance. So I began with the classic cons.

I've already said I'm a cynic. In spite of it, I made my best attempt to give each and every guru his day in court. But with the best will in the world it is impossible for me to present the final results as anything other than a short series of comedy blackouts. And that's how I spent my Saturdays.

On Sundays, I went to church.

It's not really proper to start supper with dessert, but in Texas one is expected to put some food in front of a guest within a few minutes of his crossing your threshold. The pie was the best thing close at hand. But I soon had a bowl of chili and a plate of cornbread in front of him. He dug in, and didn't seem to mind the sweat that soon beaded his forehead.

"I thought you'd ride up on a horse," he said. "I kept listening for it. You surprised me, coming on foot."

"You have any idea how much upkeep there is on a horse?"

"Not the foggiest."

"A lot, trust me. I ride a bicycle. I've got the finest Dursley Pedersen in Texas, with pneumatic tires."

"So where is it?" He reached for the pitcher and poured himself another glass of water, something everyone does when eating my chili.

"Had a little accident. Were you waiting long?"

"About an hour. I checked the schoolhouse but nobody was there."

"I'm only there mornings. I have another job." I got a copy of tomorrow's *Texian* and handed it to him. He looked at the colophon, then at me, and started scanning it without comment.

"How's your daughter doing? Lisa?"

"She's fine. Only she wants to be called Buster now. Don't ask me why."

"They go through stages like that. My students do, anyway. I did."

"So did I."

"Last time you said she was into that father thing. Is she still?"

He made a gesture that took in his new body, and shrugged.

"What do *you* think?"

My researches turned up one listing that seemed an appropriate place to begin. This fellow was the only living practitioner of his craft, he vas ze zpitting image of Zigmunt Frrreud, unt he zpoke viz an aggzent zat zounded zomezing like zis. Freudian psychotherapy is not precisely debunked, of course, many schools use it as a foundation, merely throwing out this or that tenet since found to be based more on Mr. Freud's own hang-ups than any universal human condition.

How would a strict Freudian handle the realities of Lunar society? I wondered. This is how:

Ziggy had me recline on a lovely couch in an office that would have put Walter's to shame. He asked me what seemed to be the problem, and I talked for about ten minutes with him taking notes behind me. Then I stopped.

"Very interesting," he said, after a moment. He asked me about my relationship with my mother, and that was good for another half hour of talk on my part. Then I stopped.

"Very interesting," he said, after an even longer pause. I could hear his pen scratching on his note pad.

"So what do you think, doc?" I asked, turning to crane my neck at him. "Is there any hope for me?"

"I zink," he said, and that's enough of *zat,* "that you present a suitable case for therapy."

"So what's my problem?"

"It's far too early to tell. I'm struck by the incident you related between you and your mother when you were, what . . . fourteen? When she brought home the new lover you did not approve of."

"I didn't approve of much of anything about her at that time. Plus, he was a jerk. He stole things from us."

"Do you ever dream of him? Perhaps this theft you worry about was a symbolic one."

"Could be. I seem to remember he stole Callie's best symbolic china service and my symbolic guitar."

"Your hostility aimed at me, a father figure, might be simply transferred from your rage toward your absent father."

"My *what?*"

"The new lover . . . yes, it could be the real feeling you were masking was resentment at him for possessing a penis."

"I was a boy at the time."

"Even more interesting. And since then you've gone so far as to have yourself castrated . . . yes, yes, there is much here worth looking into."

"How long do you think it will take?"

"I would anticipate excellent progress in . . . three to five years."

"Actually, no," I said. "I don't think I have *any* hope of curing you in that little time. So long, doc, it's been great."

"You still have ten minutes of your hour. I bill by the hour."

"If you had any sense, you'd bill by the month. In advance."

"Of course, that wasn't the only reason I got the Change," Cricket said. "I'd been thinking about it for a while, and I thought I might as well see what it's like."

I was clearing the table while he relaxed with a glass of wine—the Imbrium '22, a good vintage, poured into a bottle labeled "Whiz-Bang Red" and smuggled past the anachronism checkers. It was a common practice in Texas, where everyone agreed authenticity could be carried too far.

"You mean this is your first time . . . ?"

"I'm younger than you are," he said. "You keep forgetting that."

"You're right. How's it working out? Do you mind if I clean up?"

"Go ahead. I'm liking it all right. With a little practice, I might even get good at it. Still feels funny, though. I'd like to meet the guy that invented testicles. What a joker."

"They do seem sort of like a preliminary design, don't they?" I unfastened my skirt and folded it, then sat at the little table with the wavy mirror I used for dressing, makeup, and ablutions, and picked up my button hook. "Should I still be calling you Cricket? It's not a real masculine name."

He was watching me struggling to unhook the buttons on my shoes, which was understandable, as it is an unlikely process to one raised in an environment of bare feet or slip-on footwear. Or at least I thought that was what he was watching. Then I wondered if it was my knickers. They're nothing special: cotton, baggy, with elastic at mid-calf. But they have cute little pink ribbons and bows. This raised an interesting possibility.

"I haven't changed it," he said. "But Lisa—Buster, dammit, wants me to."

"Yeah? She could call you Jiminy." I had unbuttoned my shirtwaist blouse and laid it on the skirt. I doffed the bloomers and was working on the buttons of the combinations—another loose cotton item fashion has happily forgotten—before I looked up and had to laugh at the expression on his face.

"I hit it, didn't I?" I said.

"You did, but I won't answer to it. I'm considering Jim, or *maybe* Jimmy, but . . . what you said, that's right out. What's wrong with Cricket for a man, anyway?"

"Not a thing. I'll continue to call you Cricket." I stepped out of the combinations and tossed them aside.

"Jesus, Hildy!" Cricket exploded. "How long does it take you to get out of all that stuff?"

"Not nearly as long as it takes to put it on. I'm never quite sure I have it all in the right order."

"That's a corset, isn't it?"

"That's right." Actually, he was almost right. We'd gotten down to the best items by now, no more cotton. The thing he was staring at could be bought—had been bought—in a specialty shop on the Leystrasse catering to people with a particular taste formerly common, now rare, and was *not* to be confused with the steel, whalebone, starch, and canvas contraptions Victorian women tortured themselves with. It had elastic in it, and there the resemblance ended. It was pink and had frills around the edges and black laces in back. I pulled the pin holding my hair up, shook my head to let it fall. "Actually, you can help me with it. Could you loosen the laces for me?" I waited, then felt his hands fumbling with them.

"How do you handle *this* in the morning?" he griped.

"I have a girl come in." But not really. What I did was run my finger down the pressure seams in front and *bingo*. So if removing it would have been as easy as that—and it would have been—why ask for help? You're way ahead of me, aren't you.

"I have to view this as pathology," he said, sitting back down as I forced the still-tight garment down over my hips and added it to the pile. "How did you ever get into all this foolishness?"

I didn't tell him, but it was one piece at a time. The Board didn't care what you wore under your clothes as long as you looked authentic on the outside. But I'd grown interested in the question all women ask when they see the things their grandmothers wore: how the hell did they *do* it?

I don't have a magic answer. I've never minded heat; I grew up in the Jurassic Era, Texas was a breeze compared to the weather brontos liked. The real corset, which I tried once, was too much. The rest wasn't so bad, once you got used to it.

So how I did it was easy. As to why . . . I don't know. I liked the feeling of getting into all that stuff in the morning. It felt like becoming someone else, which seemed a good idea since the self I'd been lately kept doing foolish things.

"It makes it easier to write for my paper if I dress for the part," I finally told him.

"Yeah, what about this?" he said, brandishing the copy of the *Texian* at me. He ran his finger down the columns. " 'Farm Report,' in which I'm pleased to learn that Mr. Watkins's brown mare foaled Tuesday last, mother and daughter doing fine. Imagine my relief. Or this, where you tell me the cornfields up by Lonesome Dove will be in real trouble if they don't get some rain by next week. Did it slip your mind that the weather's on a schedule in here?"

"I never read it. That would be cheating."

" 'Cheating,' she says. The only thing *in* here that sounds like you is this Gila Monster column, at least that gets nasty."

"I'm tired of being nasty."

"You're in even worse shape than I thought." He slapped the paper, frowning as if it were unclean. " 'Church News.' *Church* news, Hildy?"

"I go to church every Sunday."

He probably thought I meant the Baptist Church at the end of Congress. I did go there from time to time, usually in the evenings. The only thing Baptist about it was the sign out front. It was actually non-denominational, non-sectarian . . . non-religious, to tell the truth. No sermons were preached but the singing was lots of fun.

Sunday mornings I went to real churches. It's still the most popular sabbath, Jews and Muslims notwithstanding. I tried them out as well.

I tried *every*body out. Where possible I met with the clergy as well as attending a service, seeking theological explanations. Most were quite happy to talk to me. I interviewed preachers, presbyters, vicars, mullahs, rabbis, Lamas, primates, hierophants, pontiffs, and matriarchs; sky pilots from every heavenly air force I could locate. If they didn't have a formal top banana or teacher I spoke with the laity, the brethren, the monks. I swear, if three people ever got together to sing *hosannah* and rub blue mud on their bodies for the glory of *anything,* I rooted them out, ran them to ground, and shook them by the lapels until they told me their idea of the *truth*. Don't tell me your *doubts,* lord love you, tell me something you *believe* in. *Glory!*

Surveys say sixty percent of Lunarians are atheist, agnostic, or just too damn stupid or lazy ever to have harbored an epistemological thought. You'd never know it by me. I began to think I was the only person in Luna who didn't have an elaborate, internally-logical theology—always (at least so far) based on one or two premises that couldn't be proven. Usually there was a book or body of writing or legends or myths that one could take whole, precluding the necessity of figuring it out for yourself. If that failed, there was always the route of a New Revelation, and there'd been a passel of them, both branching from established religions and springing full-blown from nothing but the mind of some wild-eyed fellow who'd Seen The Truth.

The drawback, for me, the common thread running through all of them, the magic word that changed an interesting story into the Will of God, was Faith. Don't get me wrong, I'm not disparaging it. I tried to start with an open mind, no preconceptions. I was *open* to the lightning bolt, if it chose to strike me. I kept thinking that one day I'd look up and say *yes!* That's *it!* But instead I just kept thinking, and quickly thought my way right out the door.

Of the forty percent who claim membership in an organized religion, the largest single group is the F.L.C.C.S. After that, Christians or Christian-descended faiths, everything from the Roman Catholics to groups numbering no more than a few dozen. There are appreciable minorities of Jews, Buddhists, Hindoos, Mormons, and Mahometans, some Sufis and Rosicrucians and all the sects and offshoots of each. Then there were hundreds of really offbeat groups, such as the Barbie Colony out in Gagarin where they all have themselves altered to look exactly alike. There were people who worshiped the Invaders as gods, a proposition I wasn't prepared to deny, but if so, so what? All they'd demonstrated toward us so far was indifference, and what's the use of an indifferent god? How would a universe created by such a god be any different from one where there was no god, or where God was dead? There were people who believed that, too, that there *had* been a god but he came down with something and didn't pull through. Or a group that left *that* group who thought God wasn't dead, but in some heavenly intensive care unit.

There were even people who worshiped the CC as a god. So far I'd stayed away from them.

But my intention was to visit all the rest, if I lived that long. So far my wanderings had been mostly through various Christian sects, with every fourth Sunday devoted to what the listings called Religions, Misc. Some of these were about as misc. as a person could stand.

I had attended a Witches Black Mass, where we all took our clothes off and a goat was sacrificed and we were smeared with blood, which was even less fun than it sounds. I had sat in the cheap seats in Temple Levana Israel and listened to a guy reading in Hebrew, simultaneous translation provided for a small donation. I had sloshed down wine and eaten pale tasteless cookies which, I was informed, were the body and blood of Christ, and if they were, I figured I'd eaten him up to about the left knee. I could sing all the verses of "Amazing Grace" and most of "Onward, Christian Soldiers." Nights, I read from various holy tracts; somewhere in there, I acquired a subscription to *The Watchtower,* I still don't know how. I learned the glories of glossolalia, going jibber-jabber jibber-jabber right along with the rest of them, no simultaneous translation available at any price, no way to do it without feeling foolish.

These were only a few of my adventures; the list was long.

They could be best summarized in a visit I paid to one congregation where, midway through the festivities, I was handed a rattlesnake. Having no idea what I was supposed to do with the creature, I grabbed its head and milked it of its venom. *No, no, no,* they all cried. You're supposed to *handle* it. What the fuck *for?* I cried back. Haven't you *heard?* These suckers are *dangerous.* To which they had this to say: *God will protect you.*

Well, why not? I just hadn't seen the harm in giving Him a hand in the matter. I knew a little about rattlesnakes and I hadn't seen a one that showed signs of listening to *anybody.* And that was my problem. I always seemed to de-fang the serpent of faith before it had a chance to canker.

Possibly this was good. But I *still* didn't have anything else going.

Sourdough, shortly before his death, had given me a beautiful delft pitcher and basin set. I filled the basin, added some rosewater, a little Oil of Persia and a dab of What The French Maid Wore, then patted my face with a damp washcloth.

"Everything's a struggle in here, isn't it?" Cricket said. "I find myself wondering where the water came from."

"Everything's always been a struggle everywhere, my boy," I replied, letting down the top of my chemise and washing my breasts and under my arms. "It's just that different people have struggled for different things at different times."

"Water comes out of a tap, that's all I know."

"Don't pretend ignorance with me. Water comes from the rings of Saturn, is boosted in slow orbits in the form of big chunks of dirty ice until we catch it here and melt it. Or it comes out of the air when we reprocess it, or the sewage when we filter it, then it's piped to your home, *then* it comes out of the tap. In my case, for the pipe substitute a man who comes by once a week and fills my barrels."

"All I have to do with it is turning the tap."

I pointed to my tank sitting on the sink. "So do I," I said. I patted myself dry and started rubbing cream on my skin. "I know you're dying to ask, so I'll tell you I bathe every third or fourth day at the hotel in town. All over; soap and everything. And if what you've seen horrifies you, wait till you need to relieve yourself."

"You're really into this, aren't you. That's what I can't get over."

"Why all this sudden concern about my standard of living?"

That one seemed to make him uncomfortable, so we were quiet for a while, until I had finished wiping off the cold cream. I couldn't read his expression well in the dim light, looking at him in the mirror.

"If you were going to say the people who live in here are losers, save it, I've already heard that. And I don't deny it." I opened an oval lacquered box, took out a powder puff, and started applying the stuff until I sat in the center of a fragrant cloud. On the side of the box it said "Midnight in Paris."

"That's why you don't belong here," he said. "Hildy, you've still got worlds to conquer. You can't bury yourself in here, playing at being a newspapergirl. There's a real world out there."

In here, too, I might have said, but didn't. I turned to face him, then put the straps of my chemise back up over my shoulders. It was more of a long vest, really, made of yellow silk, snug at the waist. In addition to that I still had on my best silk stockings, held up by garters, and maybe a trifle here and a whimsy there. He crossed his legs.

"You once accused me of being not so good at people. You were right. I'd known you for years, and didn't know you had a daughter, didn't know a *lot* of things about you. Cricket, there's things you don't know about me. I'm not going to get into them, it's my problem, not yours, but believe me when I tell you that if I hadn't come here, I'd be dead by now."

He looked dubious, but a little worried at the same time. He started to say something, but changed his mind. His arms were crossed now, too, one hand up and playing self-consciously with his mustache.

I reached behind me for the little purple vial of patchouli, dabbed a bit behind my ears, between my breasts, between my thighs. I got up and walked by him—quite close by him—to the bed, where I pulled the big comforter down to the foot, plumped up the pillows, and reclined with one foot trailing onto the floor, the other on the bed. The girl in the painting behind the bar at the Alamo is in an identical pose, though you would have to call her plump.

I said, "Cricket, I haven't been in the big city for a while. Maybe I've forgotten how things are there. But in Texas, it's considered impolite to keep a lady waiting."

He got up, almost stumbled as he tried to get out of his shoes, then gave that up and came into my arms.

Kitten Parker, the male manifestation, was nude, supine, cruciform. I, the female manifestation, was also nude, and in lotus position: shoulders back, legs folded with the soles of my feet turned up on my thighs, hands loose and palm-upward in my lap. My knees stuck out to the sides and my weight barely made an impression on his body—that's right, I was im-paled, as the porno writers sometimes put it.

Those writers wouldn't have been interested in this scene, however. We'd been there, unmoving, for going on five hours.

It was called sex therapy and Kitten Parker was the leading proponent of it. In fact, he invented it, or at least refined it from earlier versions. What it was, was a type of yoga, wherein I had been urged to find my "spiritual center." So far my best guess as to its location was about five centimeters cervix-wards from the tip of his glans.

I found this frustrating. I'd been finding it frustrating for going on five hours. See, I was supposed to find my center because I was the yin, and because I was the novice. *His* center wasn't material to the exercise, he *knew* where his center was though he hadn't told me where yet; maybe that was lesson two. His contribution was to bring the thrust of his enlight-enment, also known as his yang, or glans, into contact with my spiritual center, or rather I was apparently supposed to lower the center down, since deeper penetration was *clearly* out of the question. Maybe what I was feeling wasn't my center at all, maybe it was just a vaginal suburb, but it had taken me going on two hours just to entertain the notion that maybe, possibly, that *might* be it, this little place inside me that seemed to want to be massaged, and I wasn't about to go searching for it again.

So I thought about that might-be-center, willed it to move. It just stayed right there. I began to wonder if his yang was anywhere near as sore as my yin was getting. And if this whole thing would prove to be a yawn.

Actually, the only center I really cared about was the one every woman knows how to find without a road map from Kitten Parker: the center of sexual response, right up there in the cleft of the labia, the little-girl-in-the-boat, and that little girl had been sitting there, becalmed, hands on the oars, rowing her little single-minded heart out, swollen and excited, for going on . . . well, just over five hours now and the little slut was pouting and resenting the lack of attention and *had* been for . . . yes . . . and she didn't like that one bit, no she didn't, and she was just about to SCREEEEEAM!

CUT TO

INTERIOR - OFFICE OF THE PRIMALIST

Lots of ferns, lots of leather, violent paintings on the walls. The PRIMALIST faces her patient, HILDY, who, red-faced, watery-eyed, has had just about all the therapy a person can stand.

HILDY
AAAAAAAAAAAAAAAAAAAAAAAAAHHHHHHHHHHH!!!

PRIMALIST

That's better, that's much better. We're starting to get through the layers of rage. Now reach even deeper.

HILDY
EEEEEEEEEEEEEEEEEEEEEEEEEEEEEEEEEEEE!!!

PRIMALIST

No, no, you're back to the childhood peevishness again. Deeper, deeper! From the soul!

HILDY
OOOOOOOOOOOOOOOOOOOOOOOOOOOOOOOOOOOO!!!

PRIMALIST
(slaps HILDY's face)

You're really not trying. You call that a scream? *Ooooooh.* Sounds like a cow. Again!

HILDY
YAAAH! YAAAH! YAAAAH! YAAAAAAA . . .

PRIMALIST

Don't give me that lost-your-voice crap. You're giving up! I won't *let* you give up! I can *make* you face the primal source.

(slaps HILDY again)

Now, once more, with—

HILDY kicks the PRIMALIST in the belly, then knees her in the face. The PRIMALIST goes flying across the room and lands in the FERNS.

CUT TO

CLOSE SHOT - PRIMALIST

Who is bleeding from the nose and mouth and is momentarily out of breath.

PRIMALIST

That's *much* better! We're really getting somewhere now . . . hey! Where . . .

O.S. SOUND of footsteps: SOUND of a door opening. PRIMALIST looks concerned.

HILDY

(raggedly, receding)

AAAAAaaaaaaaaaaah . . . sh—

SOUND of door slamming.

FADE OUT

I passed out, right there on the thrust of Kitten's enlightenment.

I was only gone a few seconds, during which I relived a particularly fruitless episode early in my Quest; sort of a comic within a comic. I really wish that Shouter, Screamin' Sabina, had had *cojones*. My kick would have been right in the spiritual center.

"What it was," I told Kitten as he helped me to my feet, "was the most powerful orgasm of my life. *Jesus,* Kitten, I think you've *got* something here. And this was only lesson *one?* Man, sign me *up!* I want to get into the advanced classes right away. I never would have *dreamed* it was *possible* to get off that way, much less such a . . . such an *earthquake!* Wow!"

I fluttered on like that for a while, probably sounding a lot like I had many, many years ago when I first discovered what that doohickey was *for,* when a sign from the outside world finally penetrated the golden haze of contentment. Kitten was frowning.

"You weren't supposed to do that," he said. "The point is enlightenment, not mere physical pleasures."

"Goodbye," I said.

At least Cricket didn't seem to mind if I pursued mere physical pleasures. It didn't take any five hours, either. The first of many came about five minutes after we began, him still fully dressed, pants around his knees. After that we settled down a bit and carried on far into the night.

It was my first sex since Kitten Parker. I hadn't even *thought* about it in all that time.

I didn't pass out during any of the orgasms, but it was special in another way. When we finally seemed to be through, I was still wearing most of what I'd gone to bed with, and there was a reason for that: Cricket liked it.

So many of our words come from a time when, by all reports, sex was even more screwed-up than it is today, unlikely as that seems. Call it a perversion? Seems very judgmental to me, but then they called masturbation self-abuse, and I don't even like the flavor of the word masturbation. You can call it a fetish, a fixation. A "sexual preference," how's that for neutral? Bland is more like it. Call it what you wish, we all like different things. The Duke of Bosnia likes pain, preferably with the teeth. Fox liked tearing clothes off; Cricket liked to have me leave them on. He liked silk and satin and lace "unmentionables," and he liked to watch me take a few of them off.

What made it special was that he hadn't *known* he liked that. He hadn't known much of anything. He was still a novice in this business of being a man. Helping him find it out about himself was a thrill for me, the kind you don't get too often in this life. I could only recall three other instances and the last had been about seventy years ago. By the time you're fifty or so you're unlikely to discover a new preference in yourself, or anybody else.

"I was beginning to think I really was a single-sexer," he said, when it seemed we were finally through. My head was tucked up beneath his arm, that hand stroking slowly over the curve of my hip, him leaning back, propped up on my best feather pillows, a cup of hot tea carefully cradled on his belly. I'd got up to brew the tea. He'd watched me the whole time. He took little sips now and then between his amazed sighs, and I'd trained him to give me sips when I ran a nail over the line of hair on his tummy.

"Something just *clicked,*" he said. I'd heard this line several times already, but the sound of his voice was soothing me. "It just *clicked.*"

"Mmm-hmmm," I said.

"It just *clicked*. I told you I'd been with women before. It was *fun*. I had a great time. Orgasms, the whole bit. I *liked* being with women, just about as much as being with men. You know?"

"Mmm-hmmm," I said.

"But I haven't been having much luck with women since the Change. It just didn't seem very special, you know? Not with guys, either, for that matter, not like it was when I was female. I was thinking about Changing back. This thing just wasn't giving me much pleasure." He flicked his exhausted new toy with his thumb. "You know?"

"Mmm-hmmm," I said, and shifted a little to put my cheek against his chest. If I'd had any complaint it was that, when flipping through the Toys for Boys catalog, he'd ordered his from the extra-large column. I don't know why first-time Changers do that—they'd just been girls, right? and they had to know that more is not better, that one size truly does fit all—but I'd seen it happen many times before. Some little relay clicks, and when it's time to make the decision between hung and *hung!*, a great many opt for the large economy size. Strange are the ways of the human mind, doubly so when it comes to sex.

"But something just *clicked*. For the first time I looked at a female body and I didn't just think 'Gosh, isn't she cute,' or 'She'd be fun to have sex with,' or . . . or anything like that. It *clicked,* and I *wanted* you. I had to *have* you." He shook his head. "Who can figure a thing like that?"

I thought, who indeed, but I said "Mmm-hmmm." What I'd been thinking before that was I could have a discreet word with him later, or maybe have a friend plant the suggestion concerning excess yardage. It had been a minor complaint, no question, but there was also no question it would be even better with more normal equipment, next time.

I was already thinking about the next time.

No more digressions, no more cutaways to Hildy's Quest.

None were any more enlightening than the handful I've detailed. In spite of that, I planned to keep on with my slog through the shabbier neighborhoods of religion, philosophy, and therapy. Why? Well, the answer might really *be* out there, somewhere. Just because you've been dealt a thousand hands of nothing much doesn't mean the next deal won't turn up the royal flush. And I saw no reason why the "answer," if it existed, should be any less likely to be with the kooks than with the more respected, conventional snake-oil salesmen. Hell, I *knew* something about the established religions and philosophies, I'd been hearing about them for a hundred years and they'd never given me anything. That's why I'd been going to the snake-handlers instead of the Flacks.

There was another reason. While I did pretty well during the week, what with the *Texian* and school to keep me busy, weekends were still pretty shaky. If I gave the impression that my Quest was being handled by a tough, cynical, self-assured woman of the world, I gave the wrong impression. Picture instead a ragged, wild-eyed, unkempt Seeker, jumping at every loud noise, always alert for feelings of self-destruction she wasn't even sure she'd recognize. Picture a woman who had *seen* the bullet flying toward her face, had felt the rope pull tight around her neck, watched the blood flow over the bathroom floor. We're talking desperation here, folks, and it moved in and sprawled all over the sofa every Friday evening, like the most unforgettable advertising jingle you ever heard.

Maybe it was the Quest itself making me nervous? I thought of that, stayed home one weekend. I didn't sleep at all, I just kept singing that jingle.

The good news was my list of places to go, people to see, was a good five years long now, and I was adding new discoveries at almost the same rate I was crossing them off. As long as there was one more whacko to talk to, one more verse of "Amazing Grace" to sing in one more ramshackle tabernacle, I felt I could hang on.

So maybe God *was* looking after me. The chief danger seemed to be that he might bore me to death before I was finished.

Our passions spent, Cricket's mouth finally having stopped telling me how everything had just *clicked,* we lay quietly in each other's arms for a long time, neither of us very sleepy. He was still too wound up about the new world that had opened to him, while I was thinking thoughts I hadn't thought in a very long time.

He put his hand on my chin and I looked up at him.

"You really like it here, don't you?" he said.

I nuzzled into his chest. "I like it here very much."

"No, I meant—"

"I know what you meant." I kissed him on the neck, then sat up and faced him. "I've got a place here, Cricket. I'm doing things I like. The people in here may be losers, but I like them, and I like their children. They like me. There's talk about running me for mayor of New Austin."

"You're kidding."

I laughed. "There's no way I'd take it. A politician is the last thing I'd want to be. But I'm touched they thought of me."

"Well, I've got to admit the place seems to agree with you." He patted my belly. "Looks like you're putting on some weight."

"Too much chili beans, Chinese food, and apple pie." And way too much Kitten Parker. The bastard, telling me we weren't supposed to get any pleasure out of it.

"I guess you've managed to surprise me," he said. "I really thought you were in trouble. I still think maybe you are, but not the kind I thought." You don't know the half of it, babe, I thought. "This place seems to agree with you," he went on. "I don't know when I've seen you looking so happy, so . . . radiant."

"How long ago did you get your Change?"

"About a month."

"Some of that's your cock talking, idiot. Things are still colored for you. It's called lust."

"Could be. But only part of it." He glanced at his thumbnail. "Uh . . . listen, I hadn't planned to stay out the night—"

"You can go home if you want to." You swine.

"No, I was wondering if I could stay over? But I'll have to call the sitter, I'm already late."

"You have a human sitter?"

"Only the best for my little Buster."

I kissed him and got up as he was making the call. I took off the rest of my clothes, hearing him whispering in the background. Then I stepped out onto the porch.

I hadn't been sleeping a lot. Though the nights tend to be cold, I often walked them like that, nude, in the moonlight. Cricket was wrong if he thought I was happy—the best I could claim was to be happier here than anywhere else I could think of—and the nearest I came to happiness was on these nocturnal rambles. Sometimes I'd be out for hours, and come back shivering and pile under the quilts. In that snugness I was usually able to drift off.

Tonight I couldn't stay gone long. I noted there was enough moonlight for Cricket to find his way to the outhouse, then hurried back inside.

He was already asleep.

I went around dousing the lamps, then lit a candle and carried it to the bed. I sat down carefully, not wanting to wake him, and just looked at his sleeping face there in the candlelight for the longest time.

19

TRAVEL

The Bicentennial Commemoration of the Invasion of the Earth had to qualify as the slickest public relations job of the century. Back when Walter first summoned me and Brenda to his office with his idea of a series of Invasion stories I had laughed in his face. Now, exactly one year later, every politician in Luna was trying to claim the whole thing was his idea.

But one man was responsible, and his name was Walter Editor.

Brenda and I played our small part. The articles were well-received by the public—somewhere or other I've got a parchment from some civic organization commending me for excellence in journalism for one of them—was it the Kiwanis or the Elks?—but the ground had been prepared for over a year by the P.R. firm Walter had hired at his own expense. By the time of Silvio's assassination sentiment was growing for a public display. You couldn't call it a celebration, it hadn't been a proud day in human history. It had to include a memorial for the billions of dead, that was certain. The tone of the thing should be one of sadness and resolve, all seemed to agree. If you asked them what was being resolved—the recapture of Earth and extermination of the Invaders, is that what you had in mind?—you got an uncomfortable shrug in reply, but dammit, we ought to be *resolute!* Hell, why not? Resolution doesn't cost anything.

But the commemoration was going to. It kept snowballing with nary a voice raised against it (Walter's fine hand again), until by the time the Great Day arrived every pisspot enclave in Luna was holding some kind of shindig.

Even in Texas, where we avoid as much outside news as we can, they were having a barbecue as big as Alamo Day. I was sorry I was going to be missing it, but I'd promised Brenda I'd go with her, and besides . . . Cricket was going to be there.

Yes, dear hearts, Hildy is in love. Please hold your applause until I can determine if the feeling is mutual.

All the Eight Worlds were commemorating the day; Pluto and Mars had actually created a permanent yearly holiday to be known as Invasion Day, and the betting was that Luna would soon follow suit. And Luna, being the most populous planet, hated to follow *any* of the seven worlds in *anything* and so, being the most populous planet and the Refuge of Humanity as well as the Front-Line Planet and the Bulwark of the Race—not to mention the First to Get Our Asses Whipped if the Invaders ever decided to continue what they started . . . Luna being all that, and more, had determined to put on the biggest and bestest of all the eight festivals, and King City being the largest city in Luna made it seem a natural site for the planet-wide Main Event, and Armstrong Park being over *twenty times* the size of the vanished Walt Disney Universe, it just seemed to follow that the thing ought to be held there, and that was where I was going that fine Solar Evening when all I really wanted to do was stroll down Congress Street, Cricket on my arm, and eat cotton candy and maybe bob for apples.

And hey, sure it wasn't a celebration, but what's a holiday without fireworks?

That's the only reason I'd agreed to go, Brenda's promise that I could see the whole thing a safe distance from the madding crowds. The fireworks themselves didn't scare me; I liked fireworks, hated crowds of strangers.

The tube trip almost killed me, though. We'd deliberately decided to start out quite early to avoid the crush on the tubes, but what one genius can think up, another can duplicate, so the trains were already jammed with people who'd had the same idea. Worse, these were people planning to rough it on the surface, away from the eight gigantic temporary domes set up for the show, so they had brought their camping gear. The aisles and overhead racks were piled high with luggage carts, beer coolers, inflatable five-room tents, and 3.4 children per family. It got so bad they started hanging small children from the overhead straps, where they dangled and giggled. Then it got worse. The train stopped taking passengers long before it arrived at Armstrong. My stop was three short of the park, and I soon saw there would be no point in fighting my way out, so I rode it to the end of the line—gaped in horror at the masses already assembled there—was disgorged by an irresistible human tide, then reboarded and rode it back, empty, to Dionysius Station.

Where I sat down on a bench, my suit and picnic hamper beside me, and just shook for a while, and watched about a dozen human sardine cans rumble by in one direction and a like number return. Then I grabbed my gear and went up the stairs to the surface.

After returning from my frolics with the Alphans, I'd found my suit on the foot of my bed in my cabin. I don't know who brought it there. But I didn't want it anymore, so one Saturday I took it back to the shop, meaning to have them fix the faceplate and sell it on consignment. The salesman took one look at the hole and before I had a chance to explain I was being ushered into the manager's office and he promptly fainted dead away. None of them had ever seen a broken faceplate before. So I shut up, and soon found myself in possession of their top-of-the-line model, plus five years of free air, courtesy Hamilton's Outdoor Outfitters. I made no demands and was asked to sign no disclaimers; they simply wanted me to have it. They're probably still chewing their knuckles, waiting for the lawsuit.

I climbed into this engineering wonder, and that special new-suit aroma went a long way toward calming me down. I'd worried it might stir entirely different associations—how about that cute point-of-view shot of a piece of the faceplate tumbling away?—but instead the low whirs and hums and the pure luxurious *feel* of the thing did wonders. Too bad they won't let you wear suits in the tube; with this on, I could have handled anything.

Checking the pressure seals on the hamper, I walked into the lock and out onto the surface.

"You been waiting long?" I asked.

"Couple hours," Brenda said.

She was leaning on the side of her rental rover, which she'd driven all the way from a suburb of King City, the nearest place you could rent one. I apologized for being so late, told her of the nightmare in the train, how I wished I'd come with her instead of "saving time" by tubing out.

"Don't worry about it," she said. "I like it out here."

I could already tell that, mostly by looking at her suit. It was a good one, had no rental logo on it, and though in perfect shape, showed signs of use it couldn't have acquired unless she regularly spent time in it. Also by the easy way she stood and moved in it, something most Lunarians never get enough suit time to achieve.

The rover was a good one, too. It was a pickup model, two seats side by side, a flatbed in back where I tossed my hamper along with her much bigger pile of things. They have a wide wheelbase to compensate for being so top-heavy with the big solar panel above, which swings to constantly present itself to the sun. The sun being almost at the horizon just then, the vehicle was at its most awkward, with the panel hanging out to the right side, perpendicular to the ground. I had to crawl over Brenda's seat to get to mine because the panel blocked the door.

"I forget," I said, as I settled myself in the open seat. "Will we be going into the sun to get there?"

"Nope. South for a while, then we'll have the sun at our backs."

"Good." I hated riding behind the panel. It's not that I didn't trust the autopilot; I just liked to see where I was going.

She told the rover to giddyup, and it did, right along the broad, smooth highway. Which is why we'd chosen Dionysius Station in the first place, because it's right on one of the scarce surface roads on Luna, which is not a place where the wheeled vehicle was ever a primary mode of transport. People move on elevators, escalators, beltways, maglev/tube trains, the occasional hoverbus. Goods go by the same ways, plus pneumomail tubes, linac free-trajectory, and rocket. Recently there'd been something of a fad in wheeled surface rovers, two- and four-wheeled, but they were all-terrain and quite rugged, no roads needed.

The road we were on was a relic from a mining operation abandoned before I was born. From time to time we passed the derelict hulks of ore carriers at the side of the road, mammoth things, not looking much different from the day they'd been stripped and left there. Some economic vagary of the time had made it a better idea to actually smooth out a road surface for them. Then the road had been used for another half century as the conduit between King City and its primary dumping ground. It was still glass-smooth, and quite a novel way to travel.

"This sucker moves right along, doesn't it?" I said.

"It'll reach three hundred kay on the straightaways," Brenda said. "But it's gotta slow way down for the curves, especially ones to the left." That was because the rover's center of gravity was at its worst at sunrise and sunset, with the big panel canted on its side, she explained. Also, the banking of the road was not great, and since we were going to be staying out after dark, she'd had to carry ten batteries, which added a lot to our inertia and could easily make us skid off the road, since the tire traction wasn't as much as she'd prefer. She told me all this with the air of someone who'd done this many times before, someone who knew her machine. I wondered if she could drive it.

I got my answer when we turned off the road, and she asked if I minded. Actually, I did—we're not used to putting our lives in other people's hands, only into the hands of machines—but I said I didn't. And

I needn't have worried. She drove with a sure hand, never did anything stupid, never overcontrolled. We took off across the plains toward the rising rim of Delambre, just becoming visible over the horizon.

When we reached the bottom of the slope a Black Maria landed in front of us, blue lights flashing. A cop got out and came over to us. He must have been bored, since he could have used his radio, or simply interrogated our computer.

"You're entering a restricted area, ma'am," he said.

Brenda showed him the pass Liz had given her and he examined it, then her.

"Didn't I see you on the tube?" he asked, and she said he might have, and he said sure, you were on the such-and-such show, now how about that? He said he'd loved it and she said aw, shucks, and by the time he finally let us go he'd been flirting so outrageously I'm convinced we hadn't needed the pass at all. He actually asked for her autograph, and she actually gave it.

"I thought he was going to ask for your phone code," I said, when he'd finally lifted off.

"I thought I was going to give it to him," she said, and grinned at me. "I keep thinking I ought to give guys a try."

"You could do better than that."

"Not since you Changed." She jammed in the throttle and we sprayed dust behind us as we charged up the rounded rim of the crater.

Delambre isn't a huge crater like Clavius or Pythagoras or any number of celestial bullet holes on the farside, but it's big enough. When you're standing on the rim you can't see the other side. That's plenty big for me.

Still, it would look just like a hundred others except for one thing: the junkyard.

We recycle a lot of things on Luna. We have to; our own natural resources are fairly meager. But we're still a civilization driven by a market economy. Sometimes cheap and plentiful power and the low cost of boosting bulk raw materials in slow orbits combine to make it just too damn much trouble and not cost-effective to sort through and reprocess a lot of things. Fortunes have been lost when a bulk carrier arrives with X million tonnes of Whoosisite from the mines on Io, having been in secret transit for thirty years disguised and listed as an Oort comet. Suddenly the bottom falls out of the market for Whoosisite, and before you know it you can't give the stuff away and it's being carted out to Delambre by the hundred-tonne bucketload. To that add the twenty-thousand-year half-life radioactives in drums guaranteed to last five centuries. Don't forget to throw in obsolete machines, some cannibalized for this or that, others still in working order but hopelessly slow and not worth taking apart. Abandon all that stuff out there, and salt in that ceramic horror you brought home to Mom from school when you were eight, that stack of holos you kept for seventy years and can't even remember who's in them, plus similar treasures from millions of other people. Top it with all the things you can't find a use for from every sewage outflow in Luna, mixed with just enough water so it'll flow through a pipe. Bake on high for fourteen days, freeze for fourteen more; continue doing that for two hundred years, adding more ingredients to taste, and you've created the vista that met us from the lip of Delambre.

The crater's not actually full, it just looks that way from the west rim.

"Over there," Brenda said. "That's where I said I'd meet Liz."

I saw a speck on the horizon, also sitting on the rim.

"How about letting me drive?" I asked.

"You can drive?" It wasn't an unreasonable question; most Lunarians can't.

"In my wild youth, I drove the Equatorial Race. Eleven thousand klicks, very little of it level." No point in adding I'd blown the transmission a quarter of the way through.

"And I was lecturing you on how to handle a rover. Why don't you ever shut me up, Hildy?"

"Then I'd lose half of my amusing stories."

I switched the controls over to the British side of the car and took off. It had been many years since I'd driven. It was lots of fun. The rover had a good suspension; I only left the ground two or three times, and the gyros kept us from turning over. When I saw her gripping the dash I throttled back.

"You'd never make a race driver. This is *smooth.*"

"I never *wanted* to be a race driver. Or a corpse."

"I feel like a Girl Scout," I told Brenda as I helped her spread out the tent.

"What's wrong with that? I earned all the surface pioneering merit badges."

"Nothing wrong. I was one, too, but that was ninety years ago."

She wasn't nearly that far removed from scouting, and she still took it seriously. Where I'd have just pulled the rip cord and let it go at that, she was a fanatic about saving energy, and ran a line from the rover's solar panel to the tent's power supply, as if the reactor wouldn't last a fortnight on its own. When the tent was arranged to her satisfaction she pulled the cord and it shuddered and flopped as it filled with air, and in ten seconds we had a five-meter transparent hemisphere . . . which promptly frosted up inside.

She got on her knees and crawled into the igloo-type lock and I zipped it behind her to save her squirming around, and she told me this model had automatic zippers, so there *had* been progress since my childhood. She fiddled with the air controls while I stacked blankets and pillows and thermoses and the rest of our gear in the lock—got to get it well-packed, don't want to waste air by cycling the lock too much—then I stood around outside while she brought it all in and got the temperature and pressure and humidity adjusted. When I got in and took off my helmet it was still on the cool side. I wrote my name in the frost like I remembered doing on long-ago camping trips; it soon melted, and the dew was absorbed . . . and the dome seemed to vanish.

"It's been too long," I said. "I'm glad you brought me here."

For once she knew exactly what I meant. She stopped her fussing around and stood with me and we just looked around without saying anything.

Any beauty on Luna is going to be a harsh sort of beauty. There's nothing benevolent or comforting to see anywhere—much like West Texas. This was the best way to see it, in a tent invisible to our eyes, as if we were standing on a black circular pad of plastic with nothing between us and vacuum.

It was also the best time of day to see it; the Lunar Day, I mean. The sun was very close to the horizon, the shadows were almost infinitely long. Which helped, because half our vista was of the biggest garbage dump on the planet. There's a funny thing about shadows like that. If you've never seen snow, go to Pennsylvania the next time they've scheduled it and watch how snow can transform the most mundane—even ugly—scene into a magical landscape. Sunlight on the surface is like that. It's hard and bright as diamond, it blasts everything it touches and yet it does no damage; nothing moves, the billion facets of dark and light make every ordinary object into a hard-edged jewel.

We didn't look west; the light was too dazzling. To the south we saw the rolling land falling away to our right, the endless heaps of garbage to the left. East was looking right out over Delambre, and north was the hulk of the *Robert A. Heinlein,* almost a mile of derelict might-have-been starship.

"You think they'll have any trouble finding us?" Brenda asked.

"Liz and Cricket? I wouldn't think so. Not with the old *Heinlein* over there. How could you miss it?"

"That's what I thought, too."

We set about little domestic chores, inflating the furniture, spreading a few rugs. She showed me how to set up the curtain that turned the tent into two not-very-private rooms, how to operate the little campstove. While we were doing that, the show began. Not to worry; it was going to be a long show.

I had to admit the artistic director had done well. This was to be a commemoration of the billions dead on Earth, right? And at the latitude of Armstrong Park, the Earth would be directly overhead, right? And if you start the show at sundown, you'll have a half-Earth in the sky. So why not make the Earth the center and theme of your sky show?

By fudging just a little you can begin the show when the old International Dateline is facing Luna. Now picture it: as the Earth turns, one by one the vanished nations of Old Earth emerge into the sunlight of a new day. And as each one appears . . .

We were bathed in the red light of the flag of the Siberian Republic, a rectangle one hundred kilometers long, hanging above us at a height sufficient to blot out half the sky.

"Wow," Brenda said. Her mouth was hanging open.

"Double wow," I said, and closed my own mouth. The flag hung there almost a minute, burning brightly, then sputtered out. We hurried to get Brenda's boombox turned on, hung the big speakers on each side of the tent, and were in time to hear the opening strains of "God Defend New Zealand" as the Kiwi flag unfurled above us.

That's how it was to be for eighteen hours.

When Liz arrived she told us how it was done. The flag was a mesh construction stuffed into a big container and blasted up from one of the pyro bases, in Baylor-A, about forty klicks south of us, and Hyapatia and Torricelli, to the east. When the shell reached the right height it burst and rockets spread it out and it was set afire by radio control. Neat.

How do fireworks burn in a vacuum? Don't ask me. But I know rocket fuels carry an oxidizer, so I guess it was some chemical magic like that. However they did it, it knocked our socks off, me and Brenda, no more than fifty klicks from the big firebase in Baylor, *much* closer than the poor hicks in Armstrong, who probably thought they were getting one heck of a show. And who cares if, from our vantage, the flags were distorted into trapezoids? I sure didn't.

Brenda turned out to be a fountain of information about the show.

"They didn't figure it made sense to give a country like Vanuatu equal time with, say, Russia," she said (we were looking at the ghastly flag of Vanuatu at the time, listening to its improbable national anthem). "So the major countries, ones with a lot of history, they'll get more of a pageant. Like the Siberian Republic used to be part of some other country—"

"The U.S.S.R.," I supplied.

"Right. Says so right here." She had a massive souvenir program spread out before us. "So they'll do more flags for that—the Tsarist flag, historical stuff—"

"—and play the 'Internationale.' "

"—and folk themes, like what we heard from New Zealand."

They were telling us most of that on a separate radio channel, giving a history of each country, pitched at an illiterate level. I turned it off, preferring just the music, and Brenda didn't object. I'd have turned off the television, too—Brenda had pasted a big screen to the south side of the tent—but she seemed to enjoy the scenes of revelry from Armstrong and all the other celebrations in all the major Lunar cities, so what the hell.

Get out an Earth globe and you'll quickly spot the major flaw in the Earth-rotational program. For the first six hours only a few dozen countries will swing into view. Even if you give the entire history of China and Japan, there's going to be some gaps to fill, and how much can you say about Nauru and the Solomon Islands? On the other hand, when dawn broke over Africa and Europe the pyrotechs were going to be busier than a one-legged man in an ass-kicking contest.

Not to worry. When they ran out of flags, that's when they trotted out the heavy artillery.

From the first appearance of that red ensign, the sky was never dark.

There were the conventional shells, starbursts in all the colors of the rainbow. Without air to impede their flight they could be placed with pinpoint precision—one thing Lunarians understand is ballistics. They were also perfectly symmetrical, for the same reason.

You want more? In the vacuum, it was possible to produce effects never seen on Earth. Huge gas canisters could produce a thin atmosphere, locally, temporarily, upon which tricks of ionization could be played. We were treated to auroral curtains, washes of color in which the entire sky turned blue or red or yellow, then flickered magically. Shrapnel shells filled the sky with spinning discs no bigger than a coin, which were then swept by searchlights to twinkle as no stars ever had on Luna, then exploded by lasers.

Still not satisfied? How about a few nukes? Brenda's program said there would be over one hundred special fission shells, an average of one every ten minutes for the duration of the show. These were detonated in orbit and used to propel literally thousands of regular pyro shells into bursts over a thousand klicks wide. The first one went off at the end of the Vanuatu National Anthem, and it rattled our teeth, and then it went on exploding, and exploding, and exploding. Glorious!

And don't think I didn't hear that! You're complaining that sound doesn't travel in a vacuum. Of course it doesn't, but radio waves do, and you obviously never listened to Brenda's top-of-the-line boombox cranked up to full volume. Those poor folks who watch fireworks in an atmosphere have to *wait* for the sound to arrive, too, and they get a chance to brace for it; we got it instantaneously, no warning, a flash of hurting light and a *ka-BOOOOOOOM!*

Sometimes wretched excess is the only thing that will do.

"They say this place is haunted."

We'd just been treated to the national anthem of Belau and its flag had faded from the sky (a big yellow circle on a blue field, if you're keeping score at home), and two things had dawned on us. One, you need a breather from wretched excess from time to time, or it gets . . . well, wretched. Between us we'd emitted not even one "wow" at the last three nukes, and I was thinking of suggesting we switch to Top 40 for an hour or so. Somehow I thought I could survive missing the playing of *Negara Ku* (My Country; Malaysia) and *Sanrasoen Phra Barami* ("Hail to our King! Blessings on our King! Hearts and minds we bow/To Your Majesty now!" words by H.R.H. Prince Narisaranuvadtivongs). And two, Liz and Cricket were three hours late.

"Who's *they?*" I asked, munching on a drumstick of Hildy's Finest WesTex Fried Chicken. Hunger had overcome the demands of politeness; Brenda had miked a few pieces, and the hell with Liz and Cricket. I was eyeing the beer cooler as well, but neither of us wanted to get too much of a head start.

"You know," she said. " '*They.*' Your primary news source."

"Oh, *that* 'they.' "

"Seriously, though, I've heard from several people who've come out to visit the old *Heinlein*. They say they've seen ghosts."

"Walter put you up to this, didn't he," I said.

"I've talked to him about it. He thinks there may be a story in it."

"Sure there is, but there's no need to come out here and *interview* a spook. That kind of story, you just make it up. Walter must have told you that."

"He did. But this isn't your ordinary filler story, Hildy, I mean it. The people I interviewed, some of them were scared."

"Give me a break."

"I've been coming out here and bringing a good camera. I thought I might get a picture."

"Come on. What do you think the *Nipple*'s photo department is *for?* Dummying up just that kind of pic, that's what."

She didn't say anything about it for a while, and we watched several more ghost flags in the sky. I found myself eyeing the *Heinlein*. And no, I'm not superstitious, just godawful curious.

"Is that why you've been camping out so much?" I asked. "The story's not worth it."

"Camping . . . oh, no," and she laughed. "I've camped out a lot all my life. I find it very . . . peaceful out here."

Another long silence went by, or as silent as it could be with nukes exploding outside and her boombox turned down to a low rumble. At last she got up and walked to stand by the invisible plastic wall of the tent. She leaned her head against it. And by the rockets' red glare, she told me something I'd have been a lot happier not hearing.

"Ever since I met you," she began, "I've thought I could tell you something I've never told anybody else. Not a soul." She looked at me. "If you don't want to hear it, please say so now, 'cause if I get started I don't think I'll be able to stop."

If you could have told her to shut up, I don't want to know you. I didn't need this, I didn't want it, but when a friend asks something like that of you, you say yes, that's all there is to it.

"Make it march," I said, and glanced at my watch. "I don't want to miss the Laotian national anthem."

She smiled, and looked back out over the landscape.

"When you first met me . . . well, later, that first time I came out to Texas to see you, you probably noticed something unusual about me."

"You're probably referring to your lack of genitalia. I'm observant that way."

"Yes. Did you ever wonder about it?"

Had I? Not much actually. "Ah . . . I guess I thought it was something religious, or cultural, something your parents believed. I remember thinking it wasn't a nice thing to do to a child, but not my business."

"Yes. Not a nice thing to do. And it did have to do with my parents. With my father."

"I don't know a lot about fathers," I said, still hoping she'd change her mind. "I'm like most; my mom never told me who he was."

"I knew mine. He lived with me and my mother. He started raping me when I was about six. I've never had the nerve to ask my mother if she knew about it, I didn't even know there was anything wrong with it, I thought it was what I was supposed to do." Standing there, looking out at the surface, the words spilling out of her but calm, calm, no hint of tears. "I don't know how I learned it wasn't something my friends did, maybe I started to talk about it and picked up something, some attitude, some beginning of horror, something that made me shut up about it to this day. But it went on for years and I *thought* about turning him in, I know that's what you're wondering, why didn't I do it, but he was my father and he loved me and I thought I loved him. But I was ashamed of us, and when I turned twelve I went and had . . . it . . . removed, closed up, eradicated so he couldn't put it in me anymore, and I know now the Minor's Referee who let me get it done in spite of Dad's objections had figured out what was going on because she kept saying I should bring charges, but all I wanted was for him to *stop*. And he did, he never touched me from that day on, hardly spoke to me, for that matter. So I don't know why it is that some females prefer the company of other females, but that's why for me, it's because I can't deal with males, only when I met you, well, not too long after I met you, I fell badly, madly in love with you. Only you were a boy, which drove me crazy. Please don't worry about it, Hildy, I've got it under control, I know there's things that just can't happen, and you and me are one of them. I've heard you talking about Cricket and I ought to be jealous because she and I were making love, but it was just for fun, and besides Cricket's a boy now, too, and I wish you all the happiness. So my secret's out, and another one is I arranged it so you and I would be alone for a little while out here, the place I always come, always came when I wanted to get away from him. This is rotten and I know it, but I've thought about it a long time and I can live with it. I won't cry and I won't beg, but I'd like to make love to you just one time. I know you're hetero, everyone I've talked to says that about you, but what I'm hoping is it's just a preference, you're a Changer, you've made love to women before, but maybe it's something you can't do when you're female. Or maybe you don't want to or think it's a bad idea, and that's fine, too. I just had to ask, that's all. I know I sound real needy but I'm not, not that way; I'll live either way, and I hope we'll still be friends, either way. There. I didn't know if I'd have the guts to say it all, but I did, and I feel better already."

I have a short list of things I never do, and right near the top is surrendering to emotional blackmail. If there's a worse kind of sex than the charity fuck, I haven't heard about it. And her words could be read as the worst kind of whipped-puppy appeal and dammit, okay, she *did* have a right to act like a whipped puppy but I *hate* whipped puppies, I want to *kick* them for letting themselves be whipped . . . only the words didn't come out like that, not out of that straight-backed, dry-eyed beanpole over there against the blazing sky. She'd grown since I met her, and I thought this was part of the growth. Why she'd picked me to unload on I don't know, but the way she'd done it flattered me rather than obligated me.

So I told her no. Or would have, in a perfect world where I actually *follow* my short list of things I never do. What I did instead was get up and put my arms around her from behind and say:

"You handled that very well. If you'd cried, I'd have kicked your butt all the way to King City."

"I won't cry. Not about that, not anymore. And not when it's over."
And she didn't.

* * *

Brenda had arranged for our moment of privacy by not telling me Cricket had been assigned to cover the festivities at Armstrong Park. After our little romantic interlude—quite pleasant, thanks for asking—she confessed her ruse, and also that he was going to play hooky after the first few hours and should be arriving any minute, so let's get dressed, okay?

I can't imagine why I worried about getting a head start on Liz. She got a head start on *all* of us, drinking on her way out to Armstrong and all the way back, as if Cricket needed any more causes for alarm.

She came barreling across the dunes in a four-wheel Aston Assbuster, model XJ, with a reaction engine and a bilious tangerine-flake paint job. This was the baby with four-point jets for boosting over those little potholes you sometimes find on Luna—say, something about the size of Copernicus. It couldn't actually reach orbit, but it was a near thing. She had decorated it with her usual understated British good taste: holographic flames belching from the wheel wells, a whip antenna with a raccoon tail on the tip, a chrome-plated oversize skull sitting out front whose red eyes blinked to indicate turns.

This apparition came skidding around the *Heinlein* and headed straight for us. Brenda stood and waved her arms frantically and I had time to ponder how thin a soap bubble a Girl Scout tent really was before Liz hit the brakes and threw a spray of powdered green cheese against the tent wall.

She was out before the fuzzy dice stopped swinging, and ran around to the left side to unbelt Cricket, who'd strapped himself tight enough to risk gangrene of the pelvis. She picked him up and stuffed him in the air lock, where he seemed to come to his senses. He crawled inside the tent, but instead of standing he just hunkered there and I began to be concerned. I helped him off with his helmet.

"Cricket's a little under the weather," Liz said, over Cricket's suit radio. "I thought I ought to get him inside quick."

I realized he was saying something so I put my ear close to his lips and he was muttering *I think I'm gonna be okay,* over and over, like a mantra. Brenda and I got him seated, where he soon regained some color and a passing interest in his surroundings.

We were getting a little water into him when Liz came through the lock, pushing a Press-U-Kennel in front of her. At last Cricket came alive, springing to his feet and letting fly with an almost incoherent string of curses. No need to quote; Cricket wouldn't be proud of it, he feels curses should be crafted rather than hurled, but he was too upset for that now.

"You *maniac!*" he shouted. "Why the hell wouldn't you slow down?"

" 'Cause you told me you were getting sick. I figured I better get you here quick as I could."

"I was sick *because* you were going so fast!" But then the fight drained out of him and he sat down, shaking his head. "Fast? Did I say fast? We came all the way from Armstrong, and I think she touched ground four times." He explored his head with his fingers. "No, five times, I count five lumps. She'd just look for a steep crater wall and say 'Let's see can we jump over *this* sucker,' and the next thing I knew we'd be flying."

"We were moving along," Liz agreed. "I figure our shadow ought to be catching up with us about now."

" 'Thank god for the gyros,' I said. You remember I said that? And you said 'What gyros? Gyros are for old ladies.' "

"I took 'em off," Liz told us. "That way you get more practice using the steering jets. Come on, Cricket, you—"

"I'm going back with you guys," Cricket said. "No way I'm ever riding with that crazy person again."

"We only have two seats," Brenda said.

"Strap me to the fender, I don't care. It couldn't be worse than what I just went through."

"I think that calls for a drink," Liz said.

"You think everything calls for a drink."

"Doesn't it?"

But before going out to bring in her portable bar she took the time to release her—what else?—English bulldog, Winston, from the kennel. He came lumbering out, revising all my previous notions of the definition of ugly, and promptly fell in love with me. More precisely, with my leg, which he started humping with canine abandon.

It could have spoiled the beginning of a wonderful relationship—I like a little more courtship, thank you—but luckily and against all odds he was well-trained, and a swift kick from Liz discouraged him short of consummation. After that he just followed me around, snuffling, mooning at me with his bloodshot, piggy eyes, going to sleep every time I sat down. I must admit, I took a shine to him. To prove it, I fed him all my leftover chicken bones.

Eighteen hours is a long time for a party, but there is a certain type of person with a perverse urge not to be the first to call it quits. All four of us were that type of person. We were going to stick it out, by god, right through to the playing of the Guatemalan National Anthem ("Guatemala, blest land, home of happy race,/ May thine altars profaned be never;/ No yoke of slavery weigh on thee ever/ Nor may tyrants e'er spit in thy face!").

(Yes, I looked at the globe, too, and if you think the whole planet was going to stay up six hours for the national hymn of Tonga, you're crazier than we were. Tonga got in her licks just after Western Samoa.)

No one was going to catch up with Liz, but we were soon matching her, and after a while Cricket even forgot he was mad at her. Things got a bit hazy as the celebration wore on. I can't actually remember much after the Union Jack blazed in all its Britannic majesty. I remember that one mainly because Liz had been nodding out, and Brenda got me and Cricket to stand when "God Save the Queen" began to play, and we sang the second verse, which goes something like this:

> O Lord our God arise,
> Scatter her enemies,
> And make them fall:
> Confound their politics,
> Frustrate their knavish tricks,
> On Thee our hopes we fix:
> God save us all!

"God save us all, indeed," Cricket said.

"That's the most beautiful thing I ever heard," Liz sobbed, with the easy tears of the veteran drunk. "And I think Winston needs to go wee-wee."

The mutt did seem in some distress. Liz had given him a bowl or two of Guinness and I, after the chicken bones had no visible effect, had plied him with everything from whole jalapeños to the bottlecaps from Liz's home brew. I'd seen Cricket slip him a few of the sausages we'd been roasting over the holographic campfire. All in all, this was a dog in a hurry. He was running in tight circles scratching at the air lock zipper.

Turned out the monster was perhaps *too* well trained. He flatly refused to do his business indoors, according to Liz, so we all set about stuffing him into his pressure suit.

Before long we were all reduced to hysterical laughter, the sort where you actually fall on the floor and roll around and start worrying about your *own* bladder. Winston *wanted* to cooperate, but as soon as we'd get his hind legs into the suit he'd start bouncing around in his eagerness and end up with the whole thing bunched around his neck. So Cricket scratched his back, which made the dog hold still and arch himself and lick his nose and we'd get his front legs in and maybe one of his back legs, and then he'd start that reflexive back leg jerking they do, and all was lost again. When we *did* get all four legs into the right holes he thought it was time, and we had to chase him and hold him down to get his air bottle strapped to his back, and at the last moment he took a dislike to his helmet and tried to eat it—this was a dog who made short work of steel bottlecaps, remember—and we had to put on a spare seal and test it before we finally screwed him in tight, shoved him in the lock, and cycled it.

Whereupon we laughed even harder at the spectacle of Winston running from rock to rock lifting a leg for a squirt here and a dribble there, blissfully unaware that it was all going into the waste pouch through the hose Liz had fastened to his doggie dingus with a rubber band. Yes, folks, I said doggie dingus: that's the level of humor we'd been reduced to.

Later, I remember that Brenda and Liz were napping. I showed Cricket the wondrous curtain that turned the tent into two rooms. But he didn't get it, and suggested we suit up and take a walk outside. I was game, though it probably wasn't real wise considering I spent almost a minute trying to get my right foot into the left leg of my suit. But the things are practically foolproof. If Winston could handle one, I reasoned, how much trouble could I get into?

So who should come trotting up as soon as we emerged? I might have been in one sort of trouble right there, since he seemed to feel all bets were off now that Liz was sleeping, but after pressing his helmet to my leg and trying to sniff it and getting no results he sulked along behind us, probably wondering why everything out here smelled of plexi and dog slobber.

I really don't want to sound too gay here, switching from that time with Brenda to the hi-jinx of the queen and her consort. But that's the way it happened; you can't arrange your life to provide a consistent dramatic line, like a film script. It had rocked me, and I had no notion of how to deal with it except to hold Brenda and hope that maybe she *would* cry. I still don't.

My god. The horror that exists all around us, unnoticed.

I said something like that to her, with the half-formed feeling that maybe it would be good for her to approach it as a reporter.

"Did you ever wonder," I said, "why we spend all our time looking into these trivial stories, when stories like that are waiting to be told?"

"Like what?" she said, drowsily. To be frank, it hadn't been all *that* great for me, it never is with homosex, but she seemed to have enjoyed herself and that was the important part. You can always tell. Something glowed.

"Like what happened to *you,* dammit. Wouldn't you think, in this day and age, that we'd have put that sort of . . . of thing behind us?"

"I hate it when people say 'in this day and age.' What's so special about it? As opposed to, for instance, the day and age of the Egyptians?"

"If you can name even one of the Pharaohs I'll eat this tent."

"You're not going to make me mad, Hildy." She touched my face, looked in my eyes, then nestled against my neck. "You don't *need* to, don't you see that? This is the first and last time we'll ever be intimate. I know intimacy frightens you, but you don't need—"

"It does not fr—"

"Besides, give me another, oh, eighty-three years and I'll recite every Pharaoh from Akhenaton to Ramses."

"Ouch."

"It was in the program book. But this day and age is the only one I know right now, and I don't know why you should think it's any different from the day and age you grew up in. Were there child molesters back then?"

"You mean the early Neolithic? Yeah, there were."

"And you thought the steady march of progress would eliminate them any day now."

"It was a foolish thought. But it *is* a good story."

"You've been away from the *Nipple* too long, jerk. It's a *terrible* story. Who'd want to read a depressing story like that? I mean, that there's still child molesters? Everybody knows that. That's for sociologists, bless 'em. Now *one* story, one really gruesome one, *that's* news. My story is just a stat in the Sunday Supplement grinder; you can put it on file and run it once a year, they'll all have forgotten it by then."

"You sound so much like me it's scary."

"You know it, babe. People read the *Nipple* to get a little spice in their lives. They want to be titillated. Angered. Horrified. They don't want to be depressed. Walter's always talking about The End Of The World, how we'd cover it. Hell, I'd put it on the back page. It's *depressing.*"

"You amaze me."

"I'll tell you what. I know more movie stars than everybody else in my school put together. *They* call *me,* the minor ones, anyway. I *love* my work. So don't tell me about the important stories we ought to be covering."

"That's why you got in the business? To meet celebrities?"

"Why did *you* get in the business?"

I didn't answer her then, but some vestigial concept of truth in media forces me to say that hobnobbing with the glittering people may have had something to do with it.

But it really was amazing the changes a year had wrought in my little Brenda. I didn't think I liked it. Not that it was any of my business, but that's never stopped me in the past. At first I blamed the news racket itself, but thinking about it a bit more I wondered if maybe that injured little girl, that oh-so-*good* little girl who'd had herself sewed up rather than do what the nice lady suggested and turn daddy in to the bad people . . . I wondered if she might actually teach cynical old Hildy a thing or two about the bad old world and how to get by in it.

"I'm sorry about not bringing Buster."

"Huh? What's that?"

"Luna to Hildy, come in Hildy, over."

"Sorry, my mind was wandering." It was Cricket, and we were walking together on the surface. I even remembered going through the lock.

"I know I said I'd bring her so you could meet her, but she put up a big fuss because she wanted to go with some friends to Armstrong, so I let her."

Something in his voice made me suspect he wasn't telling the whole truth. I thought maybe he hadn't argued as hard as he might have. The only thing I really knew about his daughter was that he was very protective of her. I'd learned, through a little snooping, that none of his coworkers at the *Shit* had ever met her; he kept work and family strictly segregated.

Which is not unusual in Lunar society, we're very protective of the little privacy we have. But we'd known each other as man and woman for not even a week at that point, and already there had been a series of these signs that he . . . how should I put it? . . . was reluctant to let me deeper into his life. To put it another way, I'd been tentatively plucking at the daisy of devotion, and most of the petals were coming up *he loves me not.*

To be fair, I was unused to being in love. I was out of practice at doing it, had never been adept at it, was wondering if I'd forgotten how to go about it. The last time I had really *fallen,* as they say, had been a teenage crush, and I'd assumed lo these eighty years that it was an affliction visited solely on the young. So it could be that I wasn't communicating to him the tragic, hopeless *depth* of my longing. Maybe I wasn't sending out the right signals. He could be thinking, this is just old Hildy. Lots o' laffs. This is probably just the way she *is* when she's female, all gooey and cow-eyed and anxious to bring me a hot cup of coffee in the morning and cuddle.

And to be brutal . . . maybe I wasn't in love. It didn't feel like that distant adolescent emotion, but hardly anything did; I wasn't that person anymore. This felt more solid, less painful. Not so hopeless, even if he *did* come right out and say he loved me not. Does this mean it wasn't love? No, it meant I'd keep working at it. It meant I wouldn't want to run out and kill myself . . . bite your tongue, you stupid bitch.

So was this the real turtle soup, or merely the mock? Or was it, at long last, love? Provisional verdict: it would do till something better came along.

"Hildy, I don't think we should see each other anymore."

That sound is all my fine rationalizations crashing down around my ears. The other sound is of a knife being driven into my heart. The scream hasn't arrived yet, but it will, it will.

"Why do you say that?" I thought I did a good job of keeping the anguish out of my voice.

"Correct me if I'm wrong. I get the feeling that you have . . . some deeper than usual feelings about me since . . . since that night."

"Correct you? I love you, you asshole."

"Only you could have put it so well. I like you, Hildy; always have. I even like the knives you keep leaving in my back, I can't imagine why. I might grow to love you, but I have some problems with that, a situation I'm a long ways from being over yet—"

"Cricket, you don't have to worry—"

"—and we won't get into it. That's not the main reason I want to break this off before it gets serious."

"It's *already*—"

"I know, and I'm sorry." He sighed, and we both watched Winston go haring off after some vacuum-loving bunny rabbit of his own imagination, somewhere in the vicinity of the *Heinlein*. Only the top part of the immense ship was in sunlight now. Sunset at Delambre came later than at Armstrong. There was still enough light reflected from the upper hull for us to see clearly, though not the blazing brightness of full day.

"Cricket . . ."

"There's no sense hiding it, I guess," he said. "I lied to you. Buster wanted to come, she'd like to meet you, she thinks my stories about you are funny. But I don't want her to meet you. I know I'm protective of her, but it's just my way; I don't want her to have a childhood like mine, and we won't go into *that*, either. The thing is, you're going through something weird, you must be or you wouldn't be living in Texas. I don't know what it is, don't *want* to know, at least not right now. But I don't want it to rub off on Buster."

"Is that all? Hell, man, I'll move tomorrow. I may have to keep teaching for a few weeks till they can get a new—"

"It wouldn't do any good, because that's not all."

"Oh, goody, let's hear more of the things wrong with me."

"No jokes, for once, Hildy. There's something else that's bothering you. Maybe it's tied up with your quitting the pad and moving to Texas, maybe it isn't. But I sense something, and it's very ugly. I don't want to know what it is . . . I would, I promise you, if not for my child. I'd hear you out, and I'd try to help. But I want you to look me in the eye and tell me I'm wrong."

When a full minute had gone by and no eye contact had been made, no denials uttered, he sighed again, and put his hand on my shoulder.

"Whatever it is, I don't want her to get mixed up in it."

"I see. I think."

"I don't think you do, since you've never had a child. But I promised myself I'd put my own life on hold until she was grown. I've missed two promotions because of that, and I don't care. This hurts more than that, because I think we could have been good for each other." He touched the bottom of my faceplate since he couldn't reach in and lift my chin, and I looked up at him. "Maybe we still could be, in ten years or so."

"If I live that long."

"It's that bad?"

"It could be."

"Hildy, I feel—"

"Just go away, would you? I'd like to be alone."

He nodded, and left.

I wandered for a while, never getting out of sight of the bubble of light that was the tent, listening to Winston barking over the radio. Why would you put a radio in a dog's suit? Well, why not.

That was the kind of deep question I was asking myself. I couldn't seem to turn my mind to anything more important.

I'm not good at describing the painful feelings. It could be that I'm not good at feeling them. Did I feel a sense of emptiness? Yes, but not as awful as I might have expected. For one thing, I hadn't loved him long enough for the loss to leave that big a cavity. But more important, I hadn't given up. I don't think you can, not that easily. I knew I'd call on him again, and hell, I'd beg, and I might even cry. Such things have been known to work, and Cricket does have a heart in there somewhere, just like me.

So I was depressed, no question. Despondent? Not really. I was *miles* from suicidal, *miles*. Miles and miles and miles.

That was when I first noticed a low-grade headache. All those nano-bots in that cranium, you'd think they'd have licked the common head-ache by now. The migraine has gone the way of the dodo, true, but those annoying little throbbing ones in the temple or forehead seem beyond the purview of medicine, most likely because we inflict them on ourselves; we *want* them, on some level.

But this one was different. Examining it, I realized it was centered in the eyes, and the reason was something had been monkeying with my vision for quite some time. Peripherally, I'd been seeing something, or rather *not* seeing something, and it was driving me crazy. I stopped my pacing and looked around. Several times I thought I was on the track of something, but it always flickered away. Maybe it was Brenda's ghosts. I was practically touching the hull of the famous Haunted Ship; what else could it be?

Winston came bounding along, leaping into the air, just as if he was chasing something. And at last I saw it, and smiled because it was so simple. The stupid dog was just chasing a butterfly. That's probably what I'd seen, out of the corner of my eye. A butterfly.

I turned and started back to the tent (the *dog*), thinking I'd have a

drink or two or three (was *chasing*) or, hell, maybe get really blotto, I think
I had a good excuse

a butterfly

and I turned around again but I couldn't find the insect, which made
perfect sense because we weren't in Texas, we were in Delambre and
there's no fucking *air* out here, Winston, and I'd about dismissed it as a
drunken whimsy when a naked girl materialized out of *very* thin air and
ran seven steps—I can see them now, in my mind's eye, clear as anything,
one, two, three, four, five, six, seven, and then gone again back to where
ghosts go, and she'd come close enough to me to almost touch her.

I'm a reporter. I chase the news. I chased her, after an indeterminate
time when I was as capable of movement as any statue in the park. I didn't
find her; the only reason I'd seen her at all was the very last rays of the sun
reflected from far overhead, not much more light than a good candle
would give. I didn't find the butterfly, either.

I realized the dog was nudging my leg. I saw a red light was blinking
inside his suit, which meant he had ten minutes of air left, and he'd been
trained to go home when he saw the light. I reached down and patted his
helmet, which did him no good but he seemed to appreciate the thought,
licking his chops. I straightened and took one last look around.

"Winston," I said. "I don't think we're in Kansas anymore."

20

RELIGION

Ezekiel saw the wheel. Moses saw the burning bush. Joe Smith saw the Angel Moroni, and every electro-preacher since Billy Sunday saw a chance at good ratings in prime time and more money than he could lift.

Hayseed farmers, asteroid miners, and chronic drug abusers have seen Unidentified Flying Objects and little guys who want to see our leaders. Drunks see pink elephants and brontosaurs and bugs crawling all over everything. The Buddha saw enlightenment and Mohammed must have seen something, though I was never clear just what it was. Dying people see a long tunnel full of light with all the people they hated while they were alive standing at the end of it. The Founding Flack knew a good thing when he saw it. Christians are looking to see Jesus, Walter is looking for a good story, and a gambler is looking for that fourth ace to turn up; sometimes they see these things.

People have been seeing things like that since the first caveman noticed dark shadows stirring out there beyond the light of the campfire, but until the day of the Bicentennial Hildy Johnson had never seen anything.

Give me a sign, O Lord, she had been crying, that I might know Thy shape. And behold, the Lord sent unto her a sign.

A butterfly.

It was a Monarch butterfly, quite lovely in its orange and black, quite ordinary at first glance, except for its location. But upon closer examination I found something on its back, about the size of a gelatin capsule, that looked for all the world like an air tank.

Yes, dear ones, *never* throw anything away. You don't know when you might need it. I'd had no use for my optic holocam for quite a while, since the *Texian* isn't equipped to print pictures. But Walter had never asked me to give it back and I'd not gone to the bother of having it removed, so it was still there in my left eye, recording everything I saw, faithfully storing it all until capacity was exhausted, then wiping it to make way for the new stuff. Many a wild-eyed prophet before me would have killed to have a holocam, so he could *prove* to those doubting bastards he'd really *seen* those green cocker spaniels get out of the whistling gizmo that landed on the henhouse.

Considering the number of cameras made between the Brownie and the end of the twentieth century, you'd think more intriguing pictures would have been taken of paranormal events, but look for them—I did— and you'll come up with a bucket of space. After that, of course, computers got so good that *any* picture could be faked.

But the only person I had to convince was myself. The first thing I did, back in the tent, was to secure the data into permanent storage. The second thing I did was to not tell anybody what I'd seen. Part of that was reporter's instinct: you don't blab until the story's nailed down. The rest was admission of the weaknesses flesh is heir to: I hadn't been the sober-est of witnesses. But more importantly . . . this was *my* vision. It had been granted to *me*. Not to Cricket, that ingrate, who'd have seen it if he'd said he loved me and thrown his arms around me and told me what a knuckle-headed dope he'd been. Not to Miss Pulitzer Prize Brenda (you think that, just because I gave her the big story, I wasn't jealous? You poor fool, you). Just me.

And Winston. How could I have thought that gorgeous hound was ugly? The third thing I did back in the tent was give that most sublime quadruped a pound of my best sausage, and apologize for not having anything better—like a Pomeranian, or a Siamese.

We're not talking about the butterfly now. That was amazing, but a few wonders short of a nonesuch.

It was an air tank on the insect's back. With suitable enlargement I could make out tiny lines going from it to the wings. The images got fuzzy when I tried to find out where they went. But I could guess: since there was no air for it to fly in, and since it seemed to be flying, I deduced it was kept aloft by reaction power, air squirting from the underside of its wings. Comparing this specimen to one mounted in a museum I noted differences in the carapace. A vacuum-proof shell? Probably. The air tank could drib-ble oxygen into the butterfly's blood.

None of the equipment I could identify was what you'd call off-the-shelf, but so what? Nanobots can build the most cunning, tiny machines, *much* smaller than the air tank and regulator and (possibly) gyro I saw. As for the carapace, that shouldn't be too hard to effect with genetic engineering. So somebody was building bugs to live on the surface. So what? All that implied was an eccentric tinkerer, and Luna is lousy with them. And that's just the sort of harebrained thing they build.

All this research was being done in bed, in Texas.

On my way home from the celebration I'd stopped at a store and bought a disposable computer, television, recorder, and flashlight and put them in my pocket and smuggled them past temporal customs. Easy. Everybody does it, with small items, and the guards don't even have to be bribed. I waited till nightfall, then got in bed and pulled the covers over my head, turned on the light, unrolled the television, dumped the holocam footage into the recorder and wiped all traces of it from my cerebral banks. Then I started scanning the footage frame by frame.

Why all the secrecy? I honestly couldn't have told you at the time. I knew I didn't want the CC to see this material but don't know why I felt it was so important. Instinct, I guess. And I couldn't have guaranteed even these measures would keep him from finding out, but it was the best I could do. Using a throwaway number cruncher instead of hooking in to the mainframe seemed a reasonable way to keep the data away from him, so long as I didn't ever network it with any other system. He's good, but he's not magic.

It was an hour's work to deal with the butterfly and file it under Wonderments, Lepidopterous. Then I moved on to the miracle.

Height: Five foot two. *Eyes:* of blue. *Hair:* blonde, almost white, shoulder-length, straight. *Complexion:* light brown, probably from tanning. *Apparent age:* ten or eleven (no pubic hair or bust, two prominent front teeth, facial clues). *Distinguishing marks:* none. *Build:* slender. *Clothing:* none.

She could have been much older; a small minority prefer to Peter Pan it through life, never maturing. But I doubted it, from the way she moved. The teeth were a clue, as well. I pegged her for a natural, not modified, she just grew that way.

She was visible for 11.4 seconds, not running hard, not bouncing too high with each step. She seemed to come out of a black hole and fall back into one. I was being methodical about this, so I got everything I could out of those 11.4 seconds before moving on to the frames I was dying to examine: the first one, and the last one.

Item: If she was a ghost, then ghosts have mass. I'd been unable to find her footprints among the thousands of others there on the crater rim (I had noted a lot of the prints had toes, but it meant nothing; lots of kids wear boots that leave prints like bare feet), but the film clearly showed the prints being made, the dust being kicked up. The computer studied the prints and concluded the girl massed about what you'd expect.

Item: She was not *completely* naked. In a few frames I could see biomagnetic thermosoles on the bottoms of her feet, a damn good idea if you're going to run over the blazing rocks of the surface. There was also a bit of jewelry sticking to her chest, a few inches above the left nipple. It was brass-colored, and shaped more like a pressure fitting than anything else I could think of. *Conjecture:* Maybe it *was* a pressure fitting. The snap-on type, universally used to connect air hoses to tanks.

Item: In some of the early frames a slight mist could be seen in front of her face. It looked like moisture freezing, as if she had exhaled. There was no sign of respiration after that.

Item: She was aware of my presence. Between step four and step five she turned her head and looked directly at me for half a second. She smiled. Then she made a goofy face and crossed her eyes.

I made a few more observations, none of them seeming very relevant or shedding any real light on the mystery. Oh, yes: *Item:* I liked her. Making that face was just the sort of thing I would have done at her age. At first I thought she was taunting me, but I watched it over and over and concluded she was *daring* me. *Catch me if you can, old lady.* Doll-face, I plan to.

Then I spent most of the rest of the night analyzing just a few seconds of images before and after her appearance. When I was done I wiped the data from the computer, and for good measure, put it in with the glowing embers of the fire in my kitchen stove. It crackled and popped nicely. Now the only record of my experience was in the little recorder.

I slept with it under my pillow.

Next Friday, after putting the *Texian* to bed, I went back to Hamilton's and purchased a two-man tent. If that puzzles you, you've never tried to live in a one-man tent. I had it delivered to the rover rental office nearest the old mining road, where I leased a vehicle from their secondhand fleet, paying two months in advance to get the best rate. I had it tanked full of oxygen and checked the battery level and kicked the tires and had them replace a sagging leaf spring, and set off for Delambre.

I set up the tent in the exact spot where we'd been seven days before. Sunday night I struck the tent, having seen nothing at all, and drove back to park the rover in a rented garage.

The Friday after that, I did the same thing.

I spent all my weekends out at Delambre for quite a long time. It was enough that, soon, I had to trade in my nice new suit for a maternity model. If you've never worn one of those, don't even ask. But nothing was going to keep me away from Delambre, not even a developing pregnancy.

It all made sense to me at the time. Looking back, I can see some questions about my behavior, but I think I'd still do it again. But let's try to answer a few of them, shall we?

I only spent the weekends at the crater because I still needed Texas to give my life some stability. I still would have kept coming back until the end of the school term because I felt I had a responsibility to those who hired me, and to the children. But the question didn't arise, because I needed the job more than it needed me. Each Sunday evening I found myself longing for my cabin. I guess a true Visionary would have been ashamed of me; you're supposed to drop everything and pursue the Vision.

I did the best I could. Every Friday I couldn't get out of the Disney fast enough. I attended no more churches, unburdened my soul to no more quacks.

It's a little harder explaining the pregnancy. A little embarrassing, too. As part of my efforts to experience as much as possible of what life had been like on Old Earth, I had had my menstrual cycle restored. I know it sounds crazy. I'd expected it would be a one-time thing, like the corset, but found it not nearly as onerous as Callie had cracked it up to be. I hadn't intended to let it go on forever, I wasn't that silly, but I thought, I don't know, half a dozen periods or so, then over and out. The rest is really no mystery at all. It's just what happens to fertile nulliparous centenarians who know zip about Victorian methods of birth control, and who are so unwise as to couple with a guy who swears he's not going to come.

The real mystery came *after* the rabbit died (I boned up on the terminology after I got the news). Why keep it?

The best I can say is that I'd never ruled out child-bearing as something I might do, some day, some *distant* day when I had twenty years to spare. Naturally, that day never seemed to dawn. Having a baby is probably something you have to *want* to do, badly, with an almost instinctual urge that seems to reside in some women and not in others. Looking around me, I had noted there were plenty of women who had this urge. Boy, did they have the urge. I'd never felt it. The species seemed in fine shape in the hands of these breeder women, and I'd never flattered myself that I'd be any good at it, so it was always a matter of someday.

But enough unsuccessful and unplanned and un-*understood* suicide attempts focuses the mind wonderfully. I realized that if I didn't do it now, I might never do it. And it was the one major human experience I could think of that I might want to have and had not had. And, as I said, I'd been looking for a sign, O Lord, and this seemed like one. A bolt from the blue, not on the order of the Girl and Butterfly, but a portent all the same.

Which simply meant that every Friday on my way to Delambre I gave serious thought to stopping off and having the damn thing taken care of, and every time, so far, had elected to keep it, not exactly by a landslide.

There's an old wives' tale that a pregnant woman should not visit the surface. If that's true, why do they make maternity suits? The only danger is of coming into labor while in the suit, and that's not much of a danger. An ambulance can get you from any point on Luna to a birthing center in twenty minutes. That was not a concern to me. Nor was I neglecting my duties as an incubator. I got roaring drunk that once, but that's easily cured. Each Wednesday I visited a checkup center and was told things were cooking nicely. Each Thursday I dropped by Ned Pepper's office and, if he was sober enough, let him poke me and thump me and pronounce me as fine a heifer as he'd ever come across, and sell me a bottle of yellow elixir which did wonders for my struggling rosebushes.

If I kept it to term, I intended to bear it naturally. (It was a male, but it seems silly to think of an embryo as having a sex.) When I was about twenty it seemed for a while that birthing was soon to be a thing of the past. The large majority of women were rearing their pups in jars, often prominently displayed on the living room coffee table. I watched many a neighbor's blastocyst mature over the years, peering into the scope with all the enthusiasm one usually brings to viewing Uncle Luigi's holos of his trip to Mars. I watched many a mother scratching the bottle and cooing and goo-gooing to her second-trimester fetus. I was present at a few decantings, which were often elaborately catered, with hired bands and wrapped presents and the whole *megillah*.

As is so often the case, it was a fad, not a tide of civilization. Some studies came out suggesting that Screwtops did less well in later life than Bellybusters. Other studies showed the opposite. Studies frequently do that.

I don't read studies. I go with my gut. The pendulum had swung back toward the "healthy mother/child bonding of vaginal delivery" and against the "birth trauma scars a child for life" folks, but my gut told me that, given that I should do this at all, my gut was the proper place for it to grow. And now that my uterus has been heard from, I will thank it to shut up.

The frames recording the girl's appearance and subsequent seeming exit from this dimensional plane revealed several interesting things. She had not materialized out of thin vacuum nor had she fallen out of and back into a black hole. There were images before, and after.

I couldn't make a thing of them, given the low light and the mysterious nature of the transubstantiation. But that's what computers are for. My five-and-dime model chewed on the images of twisted light for a while, and came up with the notion that a human body, wrapped in a perfect flexible mirror, would twist light in just such a way. All you'd see would be distorted reflections of the person's surroundings, so while not rendering one invisible, it sure would make you hard to see. Up close it would be possible to make out a human shape, if you were looking for it. From a distance, forget it. If she stood still, especially against a background as shattered as the Delambre junkyard, there would be no way to find her. I remembered the nagging headache I'd had shortly before her little show. She'd been around before she decided to reveal herself to me.

A search of the library found no technology that could produce anything like what I had observed. Whatever it was, it could be turned off and on very quickly; my holocam's shutter speed was well below a thousandth of a second, and she was wrapped in the mirror in one frame, naked in the next. She didn't *take* it off, she *turned* it off.

Looking for an explanation of the other singular thing about her, the ability to run nude, even if for only seven steps, in a vacuum, produced a few tidbits concerning the implantation of oxygen sources to dispense directly into the bloodstream, research that had never borne profitable fruit and had been abandoned as impractical. Hmmmm.

I put myself through a refresher course in vacuum survival. People have lived after exposure of up to four minutes, which is when the brain starts to die. They suffer significant tissue damage, but so what? Infants have lived after even longer periods. You can do useful work for maybe a minute, maybe a bit longer, work like scrambling into an emergency suit. Exposures of five to ten seconds will likely rupture your eardrums and certainly hurt like hell, but do you no other real harm. "The bends" is easily treatable.

So wait a minute, what's all this talk about a miracle? I determined in fairly short order that what I'd seen was almost surely a technical marvel, not a supernatural one. And I was a bit relieved, frankly. Gods are capricious characters, and the biggest part of me had no desire to have it proved that one really existed. What if you saw your burning bush and it turned out the Power behind it was a psychopathic child, like the Christian God? He's God, right? He's proved it and you've got to do what he tells you to do. So what if he asks you to sacrifice your son on an altar to His massive ego, or build a big boat in your back yard, or pimp your wife to the local honcho, blackmail him, and give him a dose of clap? (Don't believe me? Genesis 12: 10–20. You learn the most interesting things in church.)

It didn't diminish the miracle one bit to know it was probably manmade. It excited me all the more. Somewhere out there, in that huge junkyard, somebody was doing things nobody else knew how to do. And if it wasn't in the library, the CC probably didn't know about it, either. Or if he did, he was suppressing it, and if so, why?

All I knew was I wanted to talk to whoever had made it possible for that little girl to wrap herself in a perfect mirror and make a face at me.

Which was easier said than done.

The first four weekends I simply camped out, did very little exploring. I was hoping, since she'd come to me once, she'd do it again. No real reason why she should, but again, why not?

After that I spent more time in my suit. I climbed a few alps of rubble, but there didn't seem much point in it after the first few. It stretched as far as the eye could see; there was no way to search it, or even a small part of it.

No, it seemed to me it was no coincidence the sighting had come at the base of that monument to high hopes, the Starship *Robert A. Heinlein.* I set about to explore as much of the old hulk as I could, but first I visited the library again and learned something of his history. Herewith, in brief, is the saga of failed dreams:

The *Heinlein* was first proposed in 2010, by a group known as the L5 Society. It was to be humanity's first interstellar vessel, a remarkable idea when you consider that the Lunar colony at the time was quite small, still struggling year to year for funding. And it was to be another twenty years before the keel was laid, at L5, one of the Trojan libration points of the Earth/Luna system. L5 and L4 enjoyed several decades of prominence before the Invasion, and thrived for almost forty years afterwards. Today they are orbiting junkyards. Economic reasons again.

The ship was half completed when the Invaders came. Work was naturally abandoned in favor of more pressing projects, like survival of the species. When that seemed assured, there was still very little effort to spare for blue-sky projects like the *Heinlein.*

But work resumed in the year 82, A.I., and went on five or six years before another snag was hit, in the form of the Lunarian Party. The Loonies, or Isolationists, or (to their enemies) Appeasers, as they came to be called, had as their main article of faith that mankind should accept its lot as a conquered race and thrive as best it could on Luna and the other inhabited planets. The Invaders had reduced all the works of humanity to less than rubble in the space of three days. Surely this demonstrated, the Loonies reasoned, the Invaders were a different breed of cat altogether. We had been extremely lucky to have survived at all. If we annoyed them again they might come back and finish the job they started.

Rubbish, responded the old guard, who have since come to be known as Heinleiners. Sure they were stronger than us. Sure they had superior technology. Sure they had bigger guns. God's *always* on the side of bigger guns, and if we want him back on *our* side, we'd better build even *bigger* guns. The Invaders, the reasoning went, must be a vastly older race, with vastly older science. But they still shit between two . . . well, tentacle-heels?

This was the flaw in the Heinleiners' reasoning, said the Loonies. We didn't know if they had bigger guns. We didn't know if they had tentacles or cilia or good honest legs and arms like you and I and God. We didn't know *anything*. No human had ever seen one and survived. No one had ever photographed one, though you'd think our orbiting telescopes would have; they'd been looking, on and off, for two hundred years, and no one had seen them check out of the little motel known as Earth. They were *weird*. Their capabilities had thus far admitted of no limits. It seemed prudent to assume they *had* no limits.

After almost ninety years of jingoism, of rally-round-the-flag rhetoric and sheer pettifogging bombast, this sounded like a good argument to a large part of a population weary of living on a perpetual war footing. They'd been making sacrifices for nearly a century, on the theory that we must be ready to, one, repel attack, and two, rise up in our wrath one glorious day and stomp the bejesus out of those . . . whatever they were. Live and let live made a whole lot of sense. Stop our puny saber-rattling round the ankles of these giants, and we'll be okay. Speak softly, and *screw* the big stick.

Eventually all our forward listening posts in near-Earth orbit were drawn back—a move I applaud, by the way, since they'd heard nothing and seen nothing since Invasion Day. It was commanded that no man-made object approach the home planet closer than 200,000 kilometers. The planetary defense system was scaled back drastically, turned to meteoroid destruction, where at least it saw some use.

How all this affected the *Heinlein* was in the ban on fission and fusion explosive devices. The *R.A.H.* had been designed as an Orion-type pusher-plate propulsion system, to this day the only feasible drive if you want to get to the stars in less than a thousand years. What you do is chuck A-bombs out of a hole in the back, slam the door, and wait for them to go off. Do that every second or two. The shock wave pushes you.

This needs a big pusher plate—and I'm talking *big* here—and some sort of shock absorber to preserve the dental work of the passengers. They calculated it could reach about one-twentieth of light-speed—Alpha Centauri in only about eighty years. But it couldn't even leave L5 without bombs, and suddenly there were no more bombs. Work shut down with the main body and most of the shock-absorbing system almost complete, still no sign of the massive pusher plate.

For forty years the friends of the *Heinlein* lobbied for an exception for their big baby, like the one granted to the builders of the first Disneylands for blasting purposes. Changing political winds and economic pressure from the Outer Planets Confederation, where most fissionables were mined, and the decline of the L.P. combined to eventually bring a victory. The Heinleiners celebrated and turned to the government for funding . . . and nobody cared. Space exploration had fallen out of favor. It does, periodically. The argument not to pour all that money down the rathole of space when you could spend it right here on Luna can be a persuasive one to a population more interested in standard of living and crippling taxation and no longer afraid of the Invader boogeyman.

There were attempts to get it going again with private money. The perception was the whole thing had passed its time. It was a white elephant. It became a regular subject in comic monologues.

The ship still had some value as scrap. Eventually someone bought it and strapped on some big boosters and lowered it bodily to the edge of Delambre, where it sits, stripped of anything of worth, to this day.

The first thing I noticed about the *Heinlein* during my explorations was that it was broken. That is to say, snapped in half. Built strongly to withstand the shocks of its propulsion system, it had never been meant to land on a planet, even one with so weak a gravity field as Luna. The bottom had buckled, and the hull had ruptured about halfway back from the stem.

The second thing I noticed was that, from time to time, lights could be seen from some of the windows high up on the hull.

There were places where one could get inside. I explored several of them. Most led to solidly welded doors. A few seemed to go further, but the labyrinthine nature of the place worried me. I made a few sorties trailing a line behind me so I could find my way out, but during one I felt the line go slack. I followed it back and couldn't determine if I'd simply tied it badly or if it had been deliberately loosened. I made no more entries into the ship. There was no reason to suppose the girl and anyone she lived with would wish me well. In fact, if she did, she certainly would have contacted me by then. I would have to resort to other tactics.

I tried magnetic grapplers and scaled the side of the hull, trying to reach the lighted ports. When I reached them I was seldom sure I had the right one, and in any case, by the time I got there no light could be seen.

It began to seem I *was* chasing ghosts.

I got discouraged enough that, one Friday night, I decided to stay home for the weekend. I was getting quite big, and while one-sixth gee *must* make it easier to carry a baby, we're none of us as strong as our

Earth-born ancestors were, and I'd become prone to backaches and sore feet.

So I decided to rent a rig and take a trip to Whiz-Bang, the new capital of Texas. Harry the blacksmith had just got a new Columbus Phaeton—$58.00 in the Sears catalog!—and was happy to let me try it out. (Mail-order was our polite fiction for Modern-Made. There would never be enough Disneys to manufacture all the items one needs for survival, there's just too many of them. Most of the things I owned had arrived on the Wells-Fargo wagon, fresh from the computer-run factories.) He hitched a dappled mare he assured me was gentle, and I took off down the road.

Whiz-Bang is in the eastern part of the Disney. The interior compresses about five hundred miles' worth of environment into a bubble only fifty miles wide, so before I got there I was into a new kind of terrain and climate, one where there was more rainfall and things grew better. Purely by chance I was passing through at the height of the wildflower season. I saw larkspur, phlox, Mexican hat, Indian paintbrush, cornflower, and bluebonnets. Millions and millions of bluebonnets. I stopped the horse and let her graze while I spread my blanket among them and ate a picnic lunch. I can't tell you what a relief it was to get away from the foreboding hulk of the *Heinlein* and the bitter white rock of the surface, and hear the song of the mockingbird.

I pulled into Whiz-Bang around noon. It's a bigger town than New Austin—which means it has five saloons and we have two. They get more of the tourist trade, which New Austin does not work to attract, which means they have more small shops selling authentic souvenirs, still the main means of livelihood for two out of five Texans. I strolled the streets, nodding to the gentlemen who tipped their hats, stopping to look into each shop window. The merchandise fell into four categories: Mexican, Indian, "Primitive West," and Victorian. The first three were all handmade in the Disney, certified genuine reproductions—with a little fudging: "Indian" artifacts included items from all Southwest tribes, not just Comanche and Apache. But there were no totem poles and no plastic papooses.

Suddenly I realized I was looking at the answer, if answer there was. I was standing at the window of a toy shop.

I felt like Santa Claus as I drove once more down the mining road and across the rising rim of Delambre early that Sunday morning. I certainly had a sleighful of toys, in a vac-sack tossed on the passenger seat. It was about two days past full noon.

"On Dasher, on Dancer, on Prancer," I cried. The ride in the country and the new plan of attack had buoyed my spirits, which had been at a low ebb. I stopped the rover and quickly deployed the tent. I spoke not a word but went straight to my work, setting out all my presents . . . oh, stop that, Hildy. I laughed, which no doubt caused my big round belly to shake like a bowl full of jelly.

What I'd done was first to make a Whiz-Bang toymonger a very happy and much wealthier woman. She'd followed me out of the store, carrying my boxes of trifles, not quite kowtowing, stowing them in the buggy for me. Then I'd driven back to New Austin, pausing only to pick a bunch of bluebonnets, which I mailed to Cricket. No, I hadn't given up yet.

I'd exercised little selection in the toy store, ruling out only the ranks of lead soldiers and most of the dolls. Somehow they just didn't feel right; maybe it was just personal prejudice. But now I sweated the choice of each of the four items I wanted to lure her with.

First was a tin-and-pewter windup of a horse pulling a cart, brightly painted in reds and yellows. All little girls like horses, don't they?

Next was a half-meter Mexican puppet in the shape of a skeleton, made of clay and papier-mâché and corn husks. I liked the way it clattered when I picked it up, dangling from its five strings. It was old and wise.

Then a Kachina doll, even older and wiser, though carved and painted only months ago. I chose it over the sweeter, safer white man's dolls, all porcelain and pouty lips and flounces, because it spoke to me of ancient secrets, unknown ceremonies. It was as brashly pagan as my elusive sprite, she of the funny face. Reading up on it, I found it was even better, as the Kachinas were said to exist among the tribe, but invisible.

And last, my most fortuitous find: a butterfly net, made of bent cane and gauze, with a glass mason jar, wad of cotton, and bottle of alcohol for the humane euthanizing of specimens. Just the sort of toy parents could put together for a pioneer child, if the child had a biological bent.

None of the toys would be much harmed by vacuum, but the sunshine on the surface is brutal, so I placed them where they'd stay in the shade, near the hull of the *Heinlein,* and arranged little lights over them so they'd be easy to find. Then I went back to the tent.

I didn't have much time to stay if I was to be back for Monday classes, and I spent that time unprofitably. I couldn't eat anything, and I couldn't read the book I'd brought along. I was excited, worried, and a little depressed. What made me think this would work?

So in the end I struck the tent and took one last tour of my little toy tableau, which once more was undisturbed.

The next week was hell. Many times I thought of looking for a substitute and getting the hell back. You want a measure of my distraction? Elise caught me dealing seconds, and it's been seventy *years* since that had happened.

But the week did crawl by, faster than any ordinary garden slug, and

Friday afternoon I turned the editorial chores over to Charity with instructions to keep the libel suits down to three or four, and broke all records getting out to Delambre.

The Kachina was gone. In its place was something I didn't recognize at first, but quickly realized was a Navajo sand painting. These are made by dribbling different-colored sands onto the ground and they can be amazingly detailed and precise. This one wasn't, but I appreciated the effort. It was just a stick figure Indian, with war bonnet and a bow held in one hand, a tipi in the background.

She'd taken the horse and carriage, too, and left a vac-cage about the right size for taking your pet hamster for a stroll on the surface. But inside was a horse. A living horse, ten centimeters high at the shoulder.

I hadn't seen a horselet in years. Callie had given me one for my fifth birthday, not as small as this one. Not long after that people like David Earth had succeeded in getting that sort of gene tinkering outlawed. You could still buy minis on Pluto, but the most that was allowed on Luna these days were perpetual puppies and kittens. When I was young you could still get *real* exotics, like winged dogs and eight-legged cats.

Somehow I didn't think this beast had been purchased on Pluto. I held the cage up and tapped on the glass, and the horselet looked back at me calmly. I wondered what I was going to do with the damn thing.

The butterfly equipment didn't seem disturbed until I looked at it more closely. Then I saw the monarch at the bottom of the jar, still, apparently dead. I put the jar in my pocket for later examination, left the net where it was, and hurried on to find that my last offering had been taken. The skeleton puppet was gone, and where it had been was a scrap of paper. I picked it up and read the word "thanks," written in pencil.

I pondered all this on the drive back to King City. I didn't know whether to be encouraged or crestfallen. Three of my toys had been taken, and three other toys left in their place. I had never expected this. My hope had been to gradually lure her out with gifts; the idea of trading had never entered my mind.

So it was good that I had finally made contact, of a sort. At least, I *hoped* it was she who had left the horse, butterfly, and painting. It was still possible another sort of prankster entirely was at work here, but I didn't think so. Each gift told me something, though it was hard to know just how much to read into each one.

The horselet was illegal, so she was telling me she didn't give a damn about the law. The painting, when I examined the photo I took of it, proved to be of a Lipan Apache brave, not just a generic "Indian." That meant to me that she knew the gift came from Texas . . . and that I lived there? Might she come to me? You're getting too farfetched, Hildy.

The butterfly was the most interesting of all, and that was why I had not erected the tent but was on my way to Liz's apartment in King City. Of the people I knew, she'd be the most likely to be able to give me the help I needed with no questions asked.

Before I got there I stopped and bought another computer. I used this one to doctor the images from my recorder, completely wiping out the background from those crucial seconds until I had nothing but the nude figure of a girl running against a black background. The impulse to protect the story is a deep one; I had no reason to mistrust Liz, but no reason why she should know everything I knew, either.

I showed her the film and explained what I wanted from her, managing to befuddle her considerably, but when she understood I was answering no questions she said sure, it would be no problem, then stood watching me.

"Now, Liz," I said.

"Sure," she said, and did a double take. "Oh, you mean *right* now."

So she called a friend at one of the studios who said, sure, he could do it, no problem, and was about to wire the pictures to him when I said I'd prefer to use the mail. Looking at me curiously, Liz addressed the tape and popped it into the chute, then waited for my next trick.

"What the hell," I said, and got out the butterfly. We both looked at it with the naked eye, handling it carefully, and she wanted to let her computer have a go at it, but I said no, and instead ordered an ordinary magnifying glass, which arrived in ten minutes. We both examined it and found I had been right about the propulsion system. There were hair-fine tubes under the wings, which were somehow attached to the insect's musculature in such a way that flexing the wing caused air to squirt out.

"Looks kind of squirrelly to me," Liz pronounced. "I think it'd just fall down and lie there."

"I saw it fly," I said.

"If that'll fly, I'll kiss your ass and give you an hour to draw a crowd." She waited expectantly for my response, but I didn't give her one. It was obvious she was being eaten with curiosity. She tried wheedling a little, then gave it up and turned to the horse. "I might be willing to take this off your hands," she said. "I know somebody who wants one." She tickled it under the chin, and it trotted to the edge of the table where I'd released it, then jumped down. A scale-model horse in one-sixth gee is quite spry.

Liz named a price, and I said she was taking bread from the mouths of my children and named another, and she said I must think she just fell off the turnip wagon, and eventually we settled on a price that seemed to please her. I didn't tell her that if she'd asked, I'd have given it to her.

The pictures arrived. I looked at them and told her they'd do nicely, and thanked her for her time and trouble. I left her still trying to find out more about the butterfly.

What I'd obtained from her was a strip of images suitable for installing inside a zoetrope. If you don't know what that is, it's a little like a phenakistoscope, but fancier, though not quite so nice as a praxinoscope. Still at sea? Picture a small drum, open at the top, with slits around the sides. You put the drum on top of a spindle, paste pictures inside it, rotate it, and look through the slits as they move past you. If you've chosen the right pictures, they will appear to move. It's an early version of the motion picture.

I put the strip inside the zoetrope I'd bought at the Whiz-Bang toy store, twirled it, and saw the girl running jerkily. And I'd done it all without the aid of the Lunar computer net known as the CC. With any luck, these images still existed only in my recorder.

I went right back out to Delambre and put the zoetrope in a location where it couldn't be missed. I set up the tent, fixed and ate a light supper, and fell asleep.

I checked it several times during the weekend and always found it still where I'd left it. Sunday night—still daylight in Delambre—I packed the rover and decided to look once more before leaving. I was feeling discouraged.

At first I thought it hadn't been touched, then I realized the pictures had been changed. I knelt and spun the drum, and through the slits I saw the flickering image of myself in my pressure suit, with Winston in his, capering around my legs.

I had a week to think it over. Was she saying she wanted to see the dog? Any dog, or just Winston? Or was she saying anything at all except *I see you?*

What I had to remember was there was no real hurry to this project, my feelings of impatience notwithstanding. If Winston had to be involved, it would require bringing Liz deeper into my confidence, something I was reluctant to do. So the next weekend I went out armed with four dogs, one from each of the cultures in Texas. There was a brightly painted Mexican one, carved from wood, another simpler wooden pioneer dog, a Comanche camp scene, with dogs, painted on rawhide—the best I could do—and my prize, a brass automaton of a dog that would shuffle up to a fire hydrant and lift its leg.

I set them out on my next visit. As I was crawling into the tent afterwards my phone rang.

"Hello?" I said, suspiciously.

"I still say it can't fly."

"Liz? How'd you get this number?"

"You ask *me* that? Don't start me lying this early in the morning. I got my methods."

I thought about telling her what the CC thought of her methods, and I thought about chewing her out for invading my privacy—since my retirement I'd restricted my telephone to incoming calls from a *very* short list—but thinking about those things was as far as I got, because as I was talking I'd stood up and turned around, and all four of my new gifts were lined up just outside the tent, looking in at me. I turned quickly, scanning the landscape in every direction, but it was useless. In that mirror skin of hers she might be lying flat no more than thirty meters away and I wouldn't have a prayer.

So what I said was, "Never mind that, I was just thinking of you, and that lovely dog of yours."

"Then this is your lucky day. I'm calling from the car, and I'm no more than twenty minutes from Delambre, and Winston is having a wet dream that may concern your left leg, so throw some of that chili on the stove."

"I think you gained two kay since last week," she said when she came into the tent. "When it comes time to whelp that thing, you're gonna have to do it in shifts." I appreciated those remarks so much that I added three peppers to her bowl and miked it *hard*. Pregnancy is maybe the most mixed blessing I'd ever experienced. On the one hand, there's a feeling I couldn't begin to describe, something that must approach holiness. There's a life growing in your body. When all is said and done, reproducing the species is the only demonstrable reason for existence. Doing so satisfies a lot of the brain's most primitive wiring. On the other hand, you feel like such a *sow*.

I told her as little as I could get away with, mostly that I'd seen someone out here and that I wanted to get in contact with her. She saw my box of toys: the zoetrope, and the dogs.

"If it's that girl you had the pictures of, and you saw her out here, I'd like to meet her, too."

I had to admit it was. How else was I going to convince her to leave Winston in my care for the rest of the weekend?

We tossed around a few ideas, none of them very good. As she was getting ready to leave she thought of something, pulled a deck of cards from her pocket, and handed them to me.

"I brought these along when I found out where you'd been coming all these weekends." She'd previously told me the story of her detective work, nosing around Texas, finding out from Huck that I always left Friday evening when the paper went to bed—lately even earlier. Rover rental records available to the public, or to people who knew how to get into them, told her where I'd been renting. A bribe to the right mechanic got her access to the odometer of my vehicle, and simple division told her how long a trip I'd been taking each time, but by then she'd been pretty sure it was to Delambre.

"I knew you'd seen something out here during the Bicentennial," she went on. "I didn't know what, but you came back from that last walk looking wilder than an acre of snakes, and you wouldn't tell anybody what it was. Then you show up at my place with those pictures of a girl running through nothing and you won't let me wire 'em or digitize 'em. I expect you got secrets to keep, but I could figure out you were looking for somebody. So if you want to find somebody, what you do is you start playing solitaire, and pretty soon they'll come up and tell you—"

"—to play the black ten on the red jack," I finished for her.

"You heard it. Well, at least it'll give you something to do." She left, casting a worried eye over her pet, who didn't seem at all disturbed to see her go, and with a final admonition that Winston got his walkies three times a day or he was apt to get mean enough to make a train take a dirt road.

I'd already brought a deck of cards. I usually have one with me, as manipulating them is something to do with my hands at idle moments, better than needlepoint and potentially much more profitable. If you don't practice the moves you find your hands freeze up on you at a critical moment.

But I never play solitaire, and the reason is a little embarrassing. I cheat. Which is all very well for blackjack or five-card stud, but what's the point in solitaire?

Point or not, I eventually found myself laying out a hand.

Pretty soon I got into it. Not the game itself—than which there are few purer wasters of time—but the cards. You have to be able to visualize the order, make them your friends so they'll tell you things. Do it long enough and you'll always know what the next card will be, and you'll know what the cards are that you *can't* see, as sure as if they were marked on the back.

I did it for a long time, until Winston got up and began to scratch at the wall of the tent. Better get him into his suit before he got frantic, I thought, and looked up into the face of the girl. She was standing there, outside the tent, grinning down at Winston, and she had a telescope tucked under her arm. She looked at me and shook a finger: *naughty, naughty.*

"Wait!" I shouted. "I want to talk to you."

She smiled again, shrugged her shoulders, and became a perfect mirror. All I could see of her was the distorted reflection of the tent and the ground she stood on. The distortions twisted and flowed and began to dwindle. Pressing my face against the tent wall I could follow her progress for a little while since she was the only moving object out there. She wasn't in any hurry and I *thought* she looked back over her shoulder, but there was no way to be sure.

I got into my suit quickly, thought it over, and suited Winston, too. I let him out, knowing his ears and sense of smell were totally useless out here but hoping some other doggy sense would give me a lead. He shuffled off, trying to press his nose to the ground as he usually did, succeeding only in getting moondust on the bottom of his helmet. I followed him with my flashlight.

Soon he stopped and tried to press his face to the surface with more than his usual doggedness. I knelt and looked at what he was trying to pick up. It was a bit of spongy material that crumbled in my glove when I lifted it. I laughed aloud; Winston looked up, and I patted the top of his helmet.

"I might have known you wouldn't miss food, even if you can't smell it," I told him. And we set off together, following the trail of breadcrumbs.

21

SCIENCE

Feeling not unlike the hood ornament on a luxury rover—and showing a lot more chrome-plated belly than either Mr. Rolls or Mr. Royce would have approved of—I stepped boldly forth into the sunlight, almost as naked as the day I was born. Boldly, if you don't dwell on the thirty minutes I spent getting up my nerve to do it in the first place. Naked, if you don't count the mysterious force field that kept me wrapped in a warming blanket of air at least five millimeters thick.

Even the warming part was illusory. It certainly *felt* as if the air was keeping me warm, and without that psychological reassurance I doubt if I'd have made it. Actually, the air was cooling me, which is always the problem in a spacesuit, whether bought off the shelf at Hamilton's or hocus-pocused into existence by the Genius of the *Robert A. Heinlein*. See, the human body generates heat, and a spacesuit has to be a good insulator, that's its main purpose; the heat will build up and choke you without an outlet. See?

Oh, brother. If you had a chuckle at my explanations of nanoengineering and cybernetics, wait till you hear Hildy's *Field Suits Made Simple*.

"You're doing fine, Hildy," Gretel (not her real name) coaxed. "I know it takes some getting used to."

"How would you know that?" I countered. "You grew up in a field suit."

"Yeah, but I've taken tenderfeet out before."

Tenderfeet, indeed. I bent over to see those pedal extremities, thinking I'd have to get reacquainted with them postpartum. I wiggled my toes and light wiggled off the reflections. Like wearing thick Mylar socks, only all I could feel was what appeared to be the rough surface of Luna. There was some feedback principle at work there, I'd been told; the field kept me floating five millimeters high no matter how hard I pressed down. And a good thing, too. Those rocks were *hot.*

"How's the breathing?" Gretel asked, in a funny voice I'd get used to eventually. Part of the field suit package was a modification of my implanted telephone so that sub-vocalization could be heard over the channel the Heinleiners used suit-to-suit.

"I still want to gasp," I said.

"Say again?"

I repeated it, saying each word carefully.

"That's just psychotic."

I think she meant psychosomatic, or maybe psychological. Or possibly psychotic was the *perfect* word. How would *you* describe someone who trusted her delicate hide to a spatial effect that, as near as I could understand it, had no existence in the real world?

The desire to breathe was real enough, even though a suppressor of some kind was at work in my brain cutting off that part of the autonomic nervous system. My body was getting all the oxygen it needed, but when your lungs have been inhaling and exhaling for over a hundred years, some part of you gets a little alarmed when asked to shut it off for an hour or so. I'd been holding my breath for almost ten minutes so far. I felt about ready to go back inside and *gulp.*

"You want to go back inside?"

I wondered if I'd been muttering to myself. Gotta watch that. I shook my head, remembered how hard that was to see, and mouthed "No."

"Then take my hand," she said. I did, and our two suit fields melted together and I felt her bare hand in mine. I could see that, if these things ever got on the market, there was going to be a *big* fad in lovemaking under the stars.

Don't go shopping for a field suit just yet, though.

They'll surely be available in a few years, what with current conditions. A lot of people are angry at the Heinleiners for not just bestowing the patents gratis to the general public. I've heard mutterings. A lot of good it will do the mutterers; they simply don't understand Heinleiners. There goddam sure ain't no such thing as a free lunch, and they're out to prove it.

As I write this, the Heinleiners are still pretty pissed off, and who could blame them? All charges have naturally been dropped, the statutes of limitations have expired, as it were. Nobody's out hunting them. Yet I swore a solemn oath not to reveal the names of any of them until given permission, and that permission has not been granted, and who's to say they're wrong? Say what you will about me as a reporter, but I never revealed a source, and I never will. Hence, the girl I will call "Gretel." Hence *all* the aliases I will bestow on the people I met after I followed Gretel's trail into the perfect mirror.

And I promised not to lie to you, but from here on in I will not always tell you the whole truth. Events have of necessity been edited, to protect people with no reason to trust authority but who trusted me and then found . . . but I'm getting ahead of myself.

The trail of breadcrumbs led into the rubble that washed at the base of the *Heinlein*. At first it seemed as if they vanished into a blank wall, but I found that if I ducked a little there was a way through.

Luckily, I had Winston on a leash, because he was straining to head right into the pile, and god knows if I'd ever have found him again. I shined my flashlight under the overhang—which seemed to be the back end of a vintage rover—and saw it would be possible to squirm my way in. Without the crumbs I never would have tried it, as I could already see four ways to go. But I did go in, wondering all the time just how stable this whole pile was, if I dared brush up against anything.

Not too far in, it became clear I was on a pathway. At first it was just bare rock. Soon there was a flooring laid down, made of discarded plastic wall panels. I tested each step cautiously, but it seemed firm. I found each panel had been spot welded to some of the more massive pieces of debris that made up the jackstraw jumble. I further saw, looking around the edge of the roadway, that the ground was no longer down there. My flashlight picked up an endless array of junk. If there'd been any air I might have tried dropping a coin or something; I had a feeling I'd hear it clatter for a long time.

For a while I kept testing each new panel cautiously, but each was as firmly in place as the last. I decided I was being silly. People obviously used this path with some frequency, and despite its impromptu nature it seemed sturdy enough. Flashing my light around above me I could soon see the tunnel itself had been made by some kind of boring machine. It was cylindrical, and a lot of rubbish had been blasted or cut away; I found sliced edges of metal beams on each side of the tunnel, as if the center sections had been cut out. I hadn't seen it as a cylinder at first because its walls were so relentlessly baroque, not covered with anything as they would be in King City.

Before long I came to a string of lights hung rather haphazardly along the left-hand side of the tunnel. And not long after that I saw somebody approaching me from a good distance. I shined the light at the person, and she shined her light at me, and I saw she was also pregnant and also had a bulldog on a leash, which seemed too much for coincidence.

Winston didn't put it together. Instead, he plowed forward in his usual way, either to greet a new friend or to rend an enemy into bloody gobbets, who could tell? I could hear the clang over my suit radio when he hit. He sat down hard, having had no visible effect upon the perfect mirror.

Neither did I, though I scrupulously did all the futile things people do in stories about humans encountering alien objects: chunking rocks, swinging a makeshift club, kicking it. I left no scratches on it. ("Mister President, it is my scientific opinion the saucer is made of an alloy never seen on Earth!") I'd have tried fire, electricity, lasers, and atomic weapons, but I didn't have any handy. Maybe lasers wouldn't have been the best idea.

So I waited, wondering if she'd been watching me, hoping she'd had a good laugh at my expense, feeling sure she hadn't led me this far just to strand me, and in a moment the surface of the mirror bulged and became a human face. The face smiled, and then the rest of the body appeared. At first I thought she was moving forward, but it turned out the mirror was moving back and the field was forming around her body as she simply stood there.

It moved back about three meters, and she beckoned to me. I went to her, and she made some gestures which I didn't understand. Finally I got the idea that I was to hold on to a bar fastened to the wall. I did, and the girl crouched and held on to Winston, who seemed happy to see her.

There was a loud bang and something slammed into me. Bits of trash and dust swirled, maybe a little mist, too. The perfect mirror was no longer where it had been and the corridor had changed. I looked around and saw the walls were now coated with the same mirror, and the flat surface had re-formed behind me, where it had been originally. A rather dramatic air lock.

For a few more seconds Gretel was still wrapped in distortion, then her suit field vanished and she became the nude ten-year-old who had run through my dreams for such a long time. She was saying something. I shook my head and glanced at the readouts for exterior temperature and pressure—pure habit, I could see and hear the air was okay—then I took off my helmet.

"First thing," Gretel said, "you've got to promise not to tell my father."

"Not to tell him what?"

"That you saw me on the surface without my suit. He doesn't like it when I do that."

"I wouldn't, either. Why do you do it?"

"You gotta promise, or you can just go home."

I did. I would have promised one hell of a lot of things to get farther down that tunnel I could see stretching ahead of me. I even would have kept most of them. Personally, I don't view a promise made to a ten-year-old to be binding, if it involves a matter of safety, but I'd keep that one if I could.

I had a thousand questions, but wasn't sure how to ask them. I'm a good interviewer, but getting answers out of a child takes a different technique. It would be no problem—the problem with Gretel was getting her to shut up—but I didn't know it at the time. Right then she was squatting, getting Winston out of his helmet, so I watched and waited. Liz had promised me Winston never bit people unless ordered to do so, and I sure hoped that was true.

Once again Winston came through for me. He greeted her like a long-lost friend, bowling her over in his attempts to lick her face, reducing her to giggles. I helped her get him out of the rest of his suit.

"You could get out of yours, too, if you want to," Gretel said.

"It's safe?"

"You might have asked that before I took off the dog's helmet."

She had a point. I started peeling out of it.

"You've led me a merry chase," I said.

"It took me a while to convince my father we ought to let you in at all. But I'm never in a hurry about such things, anyway. Do you good to wait."

"What changed his mind?"

"Me," she said, simply. "I always do. But it wasn't easy, you being a reporter and all."

A year ago that would have surprised me. Working for a newspad you don't get your face as well-known as straight television reporters do. But recent events had changed that. No more undercover work for me.

"Your father doesn't like reporters?"

"He doesn't like publicity. When you talk to him, you'll have to promise not to use any of it in a story."

"I don't know if I can promise that."

"Sure, you can. Anyway, that's between you and him."

We were walking down the round, mirrored corridor by then. When we came to another mirrored wall like the one I'd first encountered, she didn't slow down but headed right for it. When she was a meter away it vanished to reveal another long section of walkway. I looked behind us and there it was. Simple and effective. The bored-out tubes were lined with the field, and these safety barriers were spaced out along the way. This new technology would revolutionize Lunar building techniques, whatever it was.

I was bursting with questions about it, but my feeling for her was that it wasn't the right time to ask them. I was there as the result of a child's whim, and it would be a good idea to see where I stood with her, get on her good side as much as possible.

"So . . ." I said. "Did you like the toys?"

"Oh, please," she said. Not a promising beginning. "I'm a little grown up for that."

"How old are you?" There was always the chance I'd read her wrong from the beginning; she *could* be older than me.

"I'm eleven, but I'm precocious. Everyone says so."

"Especially Daddy?"

She grinned at me. *"Never* Daddy. He says I'm a walking argument for retroactive birth control. Okay, sure I liked the toys, only I'd prefer to think of them as charming antiques. Mostly, I liked the dog. What's his name?"

"Winston. So that's why you talked your father into letting me in?"

"No. I could get a dog easily enough."

"Then I don't get it. I worked so hard to interest you."

"You did? That's neat. Hell, Hildy, I'd have asked you in if you'd just sat out there on your butt."

"Why?"

She stopped and turned to me, and the look on her face told me what was coming. I'd seen that look before.

"Because you work for the *Nipple*. It's my favorite pad. Tell me, what was Silvio really like?"

Most of my conversations with Gretel got around to Silvio sooner or later, usually after long and adoring detours through the celebrity underbrush of the current prepubescent idols of television and music. I'd interviewed Silvio a total of three times, been at social occasions where he was present maybe twenty times, exchanged perhaps a dozen sentences with him at those functions. It didn't matter. It was all gold to Gretel, who was easily twice as star-struck as most girls her age. She hung on my every word.

Naturally, I made up a lot. If I could do it in print, why not to her? And it was good practice for telling her all the intimate details of the teeny stars, few of whom I'd even heard of, much less met.

Is that awful? I suppose it is, lying to a little girl, but I'd done worse in my life, and how badly did it hurt her? The whole gossip industry, flagshipped by the *Nipple* and the *Shit,* is of questionable moral worth to begin with, but it's a very old industry, and as such, must fill a basic human need. I've apologized for it enough here. The biggest difference in my stories to her was that, when I was writing it, it was usually nasty gossip. My stories to her were usually nice ones. I viewed it as paying my keep. If Scheherazade could do it, why not Hildy Johnson?

I was grateful that she held my hand on that first stroll on the surface. Breathing is perhaps the most underrated pleasure in life. You notice it when something smells good, curse it when something stinks, but the rest of the time you don't even think of it. It's as natural as . . . well, see? To really appreciate it, try holding your mouth and nose closed for three minutes, or however long it takes to reach the edge of blackout. That first breath that brings you back from the edge of death will be the sweetest thing you ever tasted, I guarantee it.

Now try it for thirty minutes.

The oxygen in my new lung was supposed to be good for that long, with a five- to seven-minute margin. "Think of it as thirty," Aladdin had said, when he installed it. "That'll keep you safe."

"I'll think of it as fifteen," I retorted. "Maybe five." I'd been sitting in his clinic at the time, the left side of my chest laid open, the ugly gray mass of what had recently been my left lung lying in a pan on a table like so much butcher-shop special of the day.

"Don't talk," he warned. "Not when I'm doing respiratory-system work." He wiped a drop of blood from the corner of my mouth.

"Maybe one," I said. He picked up the new lung, a thing of shiny metal with some trailing tubes, shaped very much like a lung, and started shoving it into the chest cavity. It made wet sucking sounds going in. I hate surgery.

I'd have thought it was something brand-new but for my recent researches into vacuum technology. One part of it was revolutionary, but the rest had been cobbled together from things developed and set aside a long time ago.

The Heinleiners weren't the first to work on the problem of adapting the human body to the Lunar surface. They were just the first ones to find a more or less practical answer. Most of the lung Aladdin put inside me was just an air bottle, filled with compressed oxygen. The rest was an interface device that allowed the oxygen to be released directly into my bloodstream while at the same time cleansing the carbon dioxide. A few other implants allowed some of the gas to be released through new openings in my skin, carrying off heat. None of it was new; most of it had been experimented with as early as the year 50.

But the year 50 wasn't railroad time. The system wasn't practical. You still had to wear a garment to protect you from the heat and the cold, and it had to protect you from *both*—extremes never seen on Earth—while at the same time keeping the vacuum from your skin, bleeding off waste heat, and a host of other requirements. Such garments were available; I'd bought two of them within the last year. They were naturally much improved from the mummy bags the first space explorers wore, but they worked on the same principles. And they worked better than the implanted lungs. If you're going to have to wear a suit, after all, what's the point of a thirty-minute supply of air in place of a lung? If you plan much of a stay on the surface you're going to have to backpack most of your air, just like Neil Armstrong did.

And the Heinleiners did, too, for longer stays. But they'd solved the problem of what to do with the suit: just turn it off when not in use.

I supposed they'd also solved the psychological problem of the suits, which was the panic reflex when one has not breathed normally for some time, but I suspected the answer was the same one a child learns in her first swimming lesson. Do it enough, and you'll stop being afraid.

I'd done it for fifteen minutes now, and I was still frightened. My heart was racing and my palm was sweating. Or was that Gretel's?

"You'll sweat quite a bit," she said, when I asked. "It's normal. That layer of air will stay pretty hot, but not too hot to handle. Also, the sweat helps to bleed off the heat, just like it does inside."

I'd been told the suit's distance from one's body fluctuated by about a millimeter in a regular rhythm. That varied the volume considerably, sucking waste air from inside you and expelling it into vacuum in a bellows action. Water vapor went along with it, but a lot just dripped down your skin.

"I think I'd like to go back in now," I mouthed, and must have done it well enough, because I heard her say "Okay," quite clearly. That was the same circuitry the CC used to talk to me in private, back when I was still speaking to him. Aside from the respirator/air supply/field generator, and a few air ducts, not much had needed to be done to prepare me for field suit use. Some of that's because I was already wired to a fare-thee-well, as the CC had pointed out on my direct interface jaunts. Some adjustments had been made to my eardrums to keep them from hurting in fluctuating pressures, and a new heads-up display had been added so that when I closed my eyes or just blinked, I saw figures concerning body temperature and remaining air supply and so forth. There were warning alarms I'd been told would sound in various situations, and I didn't intend ever to hear *any* of them. Mostly, with a field suit, you just *wore* it. And all but a tiny portion of that, you wore inside.

The air lock I'd used to get into the secret warrens was only for inanimate objects, or people wearing inanimate objects, like the old-style suit I'd been wearing. If you had a field suit in, you simply stepped into the wall of mirror and your own suit melted into it, like a drop of mercury falling into a quicksilver pool. That was the only way to get through a null-field barrier other than turning it off. They were completely reflective on both sides. Nothing got through, not air, not bullets, not light nor heat nor radio waves nor neutrinos. *Nothing.*

Well, gravity got through, whatever gravity is. Don't seek the answer to that one in *these* pages. But magnetism didn't, and Merlin was working on the gravity part. Follow-up on that still to come.

Just before Gretel and I stepped through I saw part of the mirror wall distorted in the shape of a face. That was the only way to see through the wall, just stick your face in, and even *that* was tough to get used to. Gretel and her brother—what else?—Hansel did it as naturally as I'd turn my head to glance out a window. Me, I had to swallow hard a few times because every reflex I had was telling me I was going to smash my nose against that reflection of myself.

But I had no trouble this time because I wanted very badly to be on the other side of that mirror. I was running by the time I hit it. And of course there was no sensation of hitting *anything*—my suit simply vanished as it went through the larger field—with the result that, because some part of me had been braced for impact, had been flinching, wincing, bracing myself, it was like reaching for that nonexistent top step, and I did a comical cakewalk as if the floor was coated with banana peels and came *that* close to a pratfall any silent film comedian would have envied.

Before you snicker, *you* go and try it.

Gretel claimed to be able to distinguish people's faces when covered by a null suit. I supposed that if you grew up in one it would be possible; they were still all chrome-plated masks to me, and probably would be for a long time. But I'd figured it was Hansel who poked his face through, since that's where we'd left him, watching Winston, and it was indeed him who greeted me after my maiden voyage in the new suit. Hansel was a lad of fifteen, a tall, awkward, rather shy boy with a shock of blonde hair like his sister's and a certain look in his eye I'm sure he got from his father. I thought of it as the mad scientist's gleam. As if he'd like to take you apart to see how you worked, only he was too polite to ask if he could. He'd put you back together, I hasten to add, or at least he'd intend to, though the skills might not always be up to the intent. He got *that* from his father, too. Where the shyness came from I had no idea. It was *not* inherited paternally.

"I just got a phone call from the ranch," Hansel said. "Libby says the palomino mare is about to foal."

"I got it, too," Gretel said. "Let's go."

They were off while I was still catching my breath. It had been a long time since I'd tried to keep up with children, but I didn't dare let these get out of my sight. I wasn't sure if I could find my way back to the *Heinlein* alone. Sounds unlikely, doesn't it? If there's one thing Lunarians are good at, it's negotiating a three-dimensional maze, or at least we'd like to think so. But the mazes of King City tend to be of two types: radiating out from a central plaza, with circular ring roads, or a north/south up/down grid. The paths of the Delambre Dump were more like a plate of spaghetti. Two days in Delambre would have any urban planner ready for a padded cell. It just growed.

The paths I was now hurrying down had been made by nothing more mysterious than obsolescent tunneling machines—one of the other things Lunarians are good at. They usually bored their way through rock, but the sort of techno-midden stratigraphy found in Delambre presented them no problems; they'd laser their way through anything. The Heinleiners had a dozen of them, all found on site, repaired, and seemingly just sort of set loose to find their own way. Not really, but anyone who had tried to find a rhyme or reason in the pathways had to figure an earthworm would have done a tidier job.

Once the wormholes were there, human crews came in and installed the flooring out of whatever plastic panels were at hand. Since those panels had been a construction staple for over a century, they weren't hard to find. The last step was to provide an ALU every hundred meters or so. An ALU was an Air Lock Unit, and consisted of this: a null-field generator with logics to run their odd locking systems at each end, a big can of air serviced weekly by autobots, and a wire running to a solar panel on top of the heap of garbage to power the whole thing. When somebody got around to it glow- and heat-wires were strung along the top of the tunnel so they wouldn't be too cold or dark, but these were viewed as luxuries, and not all parts of the tunnels had them.

A more jackleg, slipshod system of keeping the Breathsucker at bay had never been seen on this tired old orb, and nobody with half a brain would trust her one and only body to it for a split second. And with good reason: breakdowns were frequent, repairs were slow. Heinleiners simply didn't care, and why should they? If part of the tunnel went down, your suit would switch on and you'd have plenty of time to get to the next segment. They just didn't worry much about vacuum.

It made for weird travel, and another reason to keep up with the children. Both of them were carrying flashlights, which were almost mandatory in the tunnels, and which I'd forgotten again. We came to a dark, cold section and it was all I could do to keep their darting lights in sight. Sure, I could call them back if I got lost, but I was determined not to. It wouldn't have been *fun,* you see, and above all kids just want to have fun. You don't want to get a reputation as somebody they have to keep *waiting* for.

It was cold, too, right up to the point of chattering teeth, and then my suit switched on automatically and before I got out of the dark I was warm again. Winston looked back at me and barked. He was still in his old-style suit, Hansel carrying his helmet. They'd wanted me to let them give him a null-suit, but I didn't know how to explain it to Liz.

The first time the children took me to the farm, I had been expecting to see a hydroponic or dirt-based plantation of the sort most Lunarians know must be out there somewhere, but would have to consult a directory to find, and had never actually seen. I'd been to one in the course of a story long ago—I've been most places in my century—and since you probably haven't I'll say they tend to be quite dull. Not worth your time. Whether the crop is corn or potatoes or chickens, what you see are low rooms with endless rows of cages or stalls or furrows or troughs. Machines bring food or nutrients, haul away waste, harvest the final product. Most animals are raised underground, most plants on the surface, under plastic roofs. All of it is kept distant from civilization and hardly ever talked about, since so many of us can't bear to think the things we eat ever grew in dirt, or at one time cackled, oinked, and defecated.

I was expecting a food factory, albeit one built to typical Heinleiner specs, as Aladdin once described them to me: "Jerry-rigged, about three-quarter-assed, and hellishly unsafe." Later I did see a farm just like that, but not the one belonging to Hansel and Gretel and their best friend, Libby. Once again I'd forgotten I was dealing with children.

The farm was behind a big pressure door aboard the old *Heinlein* that said CREW'S MESS #1. Inside a lot of tables had been shoved together and welded solid to make waist-high platforms. These had been heaped with soil and planted with mutant grasses and bonsai trees. The scene had been laced with little dirt roads and an HO Gauge railroad layout, dotted with dollhouses and doll-barns and little doll towns of often-incompatible scales. The whole thing was about one hundred by fifty meters, and it was here the children raised their horselets and other things. Lots of other things.

Being children, and Heinleiners, it was not as neat as it might have been. They'd forgotten to provide good drainage, so large parts suffered from erosion. A grandiose plan to make mountains against the back wall had the look of a project never finished and long-neglected, with bare orange plastic matting showing the bones of where the mountains would have been if they hadn't run out of both enthusiasm and plaster of Paris.

But if you squinted and used your imagination, it looked pretty good. And your nose didn't need to be fooled at all. Walk in the door and you'd immediately know you were in a place where horses and cattle roamed free.

Libby called to us from one of the little barns, so we climbed up a stile and onto the platform itself. I walked gingerly, afraid to step on a tree or, worse, a horse. When I got there the three of them were kneeling beside the red-sided barn. They had the roof lid raised and were peering down to where the mare was lying on her side on a bed of straw.

"Look! It's coming out!" Gretel squeaked. I did look, then looked away, and sat down beside the barn, knocking over a section of white rail fence as I did so. Hell, the fence was just for show, anyway; the cows and horses jumped over it like grasshoppers. I lowered my head a little and decided I was going to be all right. Probably.

"Something wrong, Hildy?" Libby asked. I felt his hand on my shoulder and made an effort to look up at him and smile. He was a redheaded boy of almost eighteen, even lankier than Hansel, and he had a crush on me. I patted his hand and said I was fine and he went back to his pets.

I'm not notably queasy, but I'd been having these spells associated with pregnancy. I still had a month to go, far too late to change my mind. It was an experience I wasn't likely to forget. Trust me, when you get up at three A.M. with an insatiable hunger for chocolate-coated oysters, you don't forget it. The sight of it coming back up in the morning is unlikely to slip your mind, either.

I'd been a little concerned about the prenatal care I was getting. There was a problem, in that I could hardly go to a clinic in King City, as the medics were bound to notice my unorthodox left lung. The Heinleiners had a few doctors among them and the one I'd been seeing, "Hazel Stone," told me I had nothing to worry about. Part of me believed her, and part of me—a new part I was just beginning to understand: the paranoid mother—did not. It didn't seem to surprise her and she took the time to do what she could to put my mind at ease.

"It's true the stuff I have out here isn't as up-to-date as my equipment in King City," she had said. "But we're not talking trephining and leeches, either. The fact is that you're doing well enough I could deliver him by hand if I had to, with just some clean water and rubber gloves. I'll see you once a week and I guarantee I'll spot any possible complications instantly." She then offered to "just take him out now and pop him in a bottle, if you want to. I'll keep him right in my office, and I'll hook up as many machines as it takes to make you feel better."

I'd realized she was just humoring me, but I gave it some thought. Then I told her, no, I was determined to stick it out to the end, since I'd come this far, and I said I realized I was being silly.

"It's part of the territory," she had said. "You get mood swings, and irrational impulses, cravings. If it gets bad enough, I can do something about those, too." Maybe it was just a reaction to all the tampering the CC had recently been doing to me, but I refused her mood levelers. I didn't like the swings, and I'm not a masochist, but if you're going to *do* this, Hildy, I told myself, you should find out what it's like. Otherwise, you might as well just read about it.

But the real source of my nervousness was just as silly as a plate of pickles and ice cream. Since I was still living in Texas and commuting to Delambre, I had also been seeing Ned Pepper once a week, too. Ostensibly it was to keep him and others from getting suspicious, but I'm pretty sure it was also because I found him oddly reassuring. The thing is, while no one held any brief for his medical knowledge or skills, most people felt he was a damn good intuitive diagnostician. Had he been born in a simpler era he might have made quite a name for himself. And . . .

"Hildy," he told me, tapping his stethoscope against his lip, "I don't want to alarm you, but something about this pregnancy makes me nervous as a jacked-off polecat." He took another pull on his bottle and staggered to his feet as I settled my skirt back around my legs. That's the only reason I'd been able to go to him and not the King City sawbones; a West Texas gynecological exam barely disarranged your clothing. The doctor would poke his cold metal heartbeat disc under my shirt and listen to my heart and the fetal one, thump my back and my belly, take my body temperature with a glass thermometer, then ask me to swing my feet up into these here stirrups, my dear. I knew he had a shiny brass speculum he was dying to try out, but I drew the line at that. Just let him look and play doctor and we'd both go home happy. So what was this *nervous* shit? He didn't have any right to be nervous. He sure didn't have the right to tell me about it. He seemed to realize that as soon as the slug of red-eye hit his belly.

"I assume you're getting real medical care?" he asked, sheepishly. When I told him I was, he nodded, and snapped his suspenders. "Well, then. Don't fret yourself none. He'll probably come out a ridin' a wild bronc and dealin' five-card stud. Just like his mama."

Naturally, I did worry. Pregnancy is insanity, take it from me.

When I was sure my nausea had passed I stood up and saw I'd been sitting on the hen coop. It had a steel framework but my weight had loosened a lot of the fake wooden shingles glued to the sides. A rooster about the size of a mouse was protesting this outrage by pecking at my toes. Inside, several dozen hens were . . . well, egging him on. Sorry.

The colt wouldn't be standing on his own for a little while yet, but the show was basically over. Hansel and Gretel and Libby moved off to other pursuits. I stayed a little longer, empathizing with the mare, who looked up at me as if to say, You'll get *your* turn soon enough, Miss Smarty. I reached in and stroked the newborn with my fingertip, and the mother tried to bite my hand. I didn't blame her. I got up, dusted my knees, and headed over to the farmhouse.

I knew the house lid was hinged; I'd seen the kids lift it up. But I was still ambivalent enough about these pets that I didn't want to do that. Instead I bent over and pushed the little doorbell. In a moment one of the male kewpies came out and looked up expectantly, hoping for a treat.

If the horselets and mini-kine and dwarfowl were cherry bombs in a scale of illegal explosiveness, then the kewpies were ten sticks of dynamite. Kewpies were little people, no more than twenty centimeters tall.

The children had named them well. These are not adult human beings, done to scale. In an effort to make them smarter, Libby had given them bigger brains, and thus bigger heads. Perfectly sane reasoning, for a child. It might even be right, for all I knew about it. But though he assured me the current generation was much more clever than the two preceding ones, they were no more intelligent than any of several species of monkey.

They were *not* human, let's get that out of the way right now. But they contained human genes, and that is strictly forbidden on Luna under laws over two centuries old. I didn't have any of these creepy little baby dolls to ride my little horselet when I was a nipper. I don't think anybody did. No, these were the result of Libby's inquiring young mind, and no one else's.

If you could get over the shock and horror almost every Lunarian would feel at first sight of the things, they were actually quite cute. They smiled a lot, and were eager to grasp your finger in their tiny little hands. Most of them could say a word or two, things like "Candy!" and "Hi!" A few formed rudimentary sentences. Possibly they could have been trained to do more, but the children didn't take the time. In spite of their hands they were not tool users. They were *not* little people. And they *were* cute.

Enough of that. The fact is they made my skin crawl on some very primitive level. They were bad juju. They were the forbidden fruit of the Tree of Science. They were faerie sprites, and thou shalt not suffer a witch to live.

So the real truth is I couldn't make up my mind about the damn things. On the one hand, what had attracted me to the Heinleiners was the fact that they were doing things no one else was doing. So . . . all reasonable and logical rationalizations aside . . . why did they have to do *that?*

While I was still pondering this question, not for the first time, someone came up beside me and lifted the lid of the farmhouse. I looked in with him, and we both frowned. The inside of the structure was furnished with little chairs and beds, the former tumbled over and the latter not occupied. Half a dozen kewpies were curled up here and there, sleeping where the urge had taken them, and there were piles of what you'd expect from animals where *that* urge had taken them. It went a long way toward helping me believe they weren't little people. It also recalled documentary horror films from the twentieth century of homes for the insane and the retarded.

The man let the lid drop, looked around, and bellowed for his children, who came running from where they had been racing model cars, guilty looks on their faces. He glowered down at them.

"I told you that if you can't keep your pets clean, you can't have them," he said.

"We were gonna clean them up, Dad," Hansel said. "Soon as we finished the race. Isn't that right, Hildy?"

The little bastard. Fearing that my sufferance here was still very much dependent on these precocious brats, I said, diplomatically I hope, "I'm sure they would have."

And I said that because I wasn't about to lie to the man standing beside me, father to Hansel and Gretel, and the man on whose good graces my continued presence among the Heinleiners *really* relied.

This is the man the media has always referred to as "Merlin," since he would never reveal his real name. I'm not even sure if *I* know his real name, and I think he trusts me by now, as much as he ever will. But I don't like the name of Merlin, so in this account I will refer to him as Mister Smith. Valentine Michael Smith.

22
POLITICS

Mister V.M. Smith, leader of the Heinleiners, was a tall man, ruggedly handsome in the mold of some of our more virile movie stars, with white, even teeth that flashed with little points of light when he smiled and blue eyes that twinkled with wisdom and compassion.

Did I say he was tall? Actually, he was a little shrimp of a guy. Or, come to think of it, I'd say he was of medium height. And by golly, maybe his hair was black and curly. *Ugly* he was, with a snaggletoothed smile like a dead pig in the sunshine. Hell, maybe he was bald.

When you get right down to it, I'm not even going to swear he was male.

I think the heat is largely off of him by now, but he (or she) thinks differently, so there will not even be a description of him from me. My portraits of the other Heinleiners, children included, are deliberately vague and quite possibly misleading. To picture him, do what I do when reading a novel: just pick a famous face you like and pretend he looks like that. Or make your own composite. Try a young Einstein, with unruly hair and a surprised expression. You'll be wrong, although I *will* swear there was a look in his eyes as if the universe was a much stranger place than he'd ever imagined.

And that business about leading the Heinleiners . . . if they had a leader, he was it. It was Smith who had made their isolated way of life possible with his researches into forgotten sciences. But the Heinleiners were an independent bunch. They didn't go in for town meetings, were unlikely to be found on the rosters of service clubs—didn't really hold much of a brief for democracy, when you get right down to it. Democracy, one of them said to me once, means you get to do whatever the majority of silly sons of bitches *says* you have to do. Which is not to say they favored dictatorship ("getting to do what *one* silly son of a bitch says you have to do." *op. cit.*). No, what they liked (if I may quote one more time from my Heinleiner philosopher) was forgetting about *all* the silly sons of bitches and doing what they damn well pleased.

This is a hazardous way of life in a totally urbanized society, apt to land you in jail—where an embarrassing number of Heinleiners *did* live. To live like that you need elbow room. You need Texas, and I mean the *real* Texas, before the arrival of the iron horse, before the Mexicans, before the Spaniards. Hell, maybe before the *Indians*. You needed the Dark Continent, the headwaters of the Amazon, the South Pole, the sound barrier, Everest, the Seven Lost Cities. Wild places, unexplored places, *not* good old stodgy old Luna. You needed elbow room and adventure.

A lot of Heinleiners had lived in Disneys; some still did as at least a better alternative to the anthill cities. But it didn't take long to discover what toy frontiers they actually were. The asteroid belt and the outer planets had high concentrations of these crotchety malcontents, too, but it had been a long time since either place had been a real challenge to humanity. A lot of ship's captains were Heinleiners, a lot of solitary miners. *None* of them were happy—possibly that type of person can never be happy—but at least they were away from the masses of humanity and less likely to get into trouble if offered an intolerable insult—like bad breath, or inappropriate laughter.

That's unfair. While there were quite a number of antisocial hotheads among them, most had learned to socialize with the group, swallow the unpleasantness of daily life, put up with the thousand small things we each endure every day. It's called civilization. It's making your needs, your dreams, subservient to the greater good, and we all do it. Some of us do it so well we forget we ever *had* dreams of adventure. The Heinleiners did it badly; they still remembered. They still dreamed.

Those dreams and five cents will get you a cup of coffee anywhere in Luna. The Heinleiners realized that, until Mister Smith came along and made them think fairy tales *can* come true, if you wish upon a star.

I followed Smith out of the farm, where he'd left his children and Libby hard at work cleaning out the kewpies' house. We were in one of the long corridors of the *R.A. Heinlein,* some of which, like this one, were coated with the silvery null-field. I was about to go after him when I remembered Winston. I stuck my head back into the room, snagged his helmet, and whistled, and he came lumbering out from beneath the tables. He was licking his chops and I thought I saw traces of blood around his mouth.

"Have you been eating horses again?" I asked him. He merely gazed up and licked his nose. He knew he wasn't supposed to get up on the tables, but there were always some horselets that had foolishly jumped off and he felt they were fair game. I didn't know what the kids thought of his hunting, since I didn't know if they were aware of it; I hadn't told them. But I know Winston was getting a taste for horsemeat.

I'd thought I'd have to hurry to catch up with Smith, but when I looked up I saw he'd paused a little way down the corridor and was waiting for me.

"So you're still around, eh?" he said. Yessir, my reputation in the old *R.A.H.* couldn't have been higher.

"I guess it's because I just love children."

He laughed at that. I'd only met him three times before and not talked to him very long on any of those occasions, but he was one of those people good at sizing others up on short acquaintance. Most of us think we are, but he *was*.

"I know they're not easy to love," he said. "I probably wouldn't love them so much if they were." It was a very Heinleinerish thing to say; these folks cherish perversity, you understand.

"You're saying only a father could love 'em?"

"Or a mother."

"That's what I'm counting on," I said, and patted my belly.

"You'll either love him quick, or drown him." We walked on for a while without saying anything. Every once in a while one of the null-field safety locks would vanish in front of us and reappear behind us. All automatic, and all happening only for those with null-suits installed.

These people didn't engineer anything any better than they had to, and the reason was simply that they had this marvelous back-up system. It's going to be revolutionary, I tell you.

"I get the feeling you don't approve," he said, at last.

"Of what? Your kids? Hey, I was just—"

"Of what they do."

"Well, Winston sure does. I think he's eaten half their stock."

I was thinking fast. I wanted to learn more from this man, and the way to do that is not by running down his children and his way of life. But one of the things I knew about him was that he didn't like liars, was good at detecting them, and, though a career in reporting had made me a world-class liar, I wasn't sure I could get one by him. And I wasn't sure I *wanted* to. I had hoped I'd put a lot of that behind me. So instead of answering his question, I said something else, a technique familiar to any journalist or politician.

And it seemed to have worked. He just grunted, and reached down to pet Winston's ugly mug. Once more the hound came through for me, not taking off the hand at the wrist. Still digesting the horselet, probably.

We came to a door marked MAIN DRIVE ROOM, and he held it open for me. You could have driven a golf ball into the room and never hit a wall, and you could have driven a medium-size rover race in it. Whether you could drive a spaceship the size of the *Heinlein* was very much an open question. But in front of me were the signs that someone was trying.

Most of the cavernous room was filled with structures whose precise description I must leave to your imagination, since the drive room of the *Heinlein* is still a closely-guarded secret and certainly will be until long after they get the damn thing to work. I will say this: whatever you imagine will surely be far off the mark. It is unexpected, and startling, like opening the hood of a rover and finding it's powered by a thousand mice licking a thousand tiny crankshafts, or by the moral power of virginity. And this: though I could hardly identify anything as basic as a nut and bolt in the fantastical mess, it *still* had the look of Heinleiner engineering, wherein nothing is ever any better than it has to be. Maybe if they get time to move beyond prototypes they'll get more elegant and more careful, but in the meantime it's "Don't bend that wrench. Get a bigger hammer." Heinleiner toolboxes must be filled with bubble gum and bobby pins.

And yes, O good and faithful reader, they *were* planning to launch the hulk of the old *Robert A. Heinlein* into interstellar space. You heard it here first. They were *not*, however, planning to do it with an endless stream of nuclear cherry bombs pooting out the tailpipe. Just what principles were envisioned is still proprietary information, but I can say it was a variant technology of the mathematics that produced the null-field. I can say it because no one but Smith and a handful of others know what that technology is.

Just imagine them harnessing the old wreck to a team of very large swans, and leave it at that.

"As you can see," Smith was saying as we walked down a long and fairly rickety flight of metal stairs, "they've just about frabjulated the primary phase of the osmosifractionating de-hoo-dooer. And those guys ratattating the willy-nilly say they ought to have it whistling Dixie in three days' time."

No secrecy involved here. I'd have written exactly what he said, if I had any hope of remembering it, and the meaning would have been the same: nothing. Smith never seemed to mind if his audience was coming into the clubhouse two or three holes behind him; he rattled off his own private jargon without regard to whether or not it was being monitored. Sometimes I thought it just helped him to think out loud. Sometimes I thought he was showing off. Probably a little of both.

But I can't get away from the subject of the interstellar drive without mentioning the one time he made an attempt to put it in layman's terms. It stuck in my mind, possibly because Smith had a way of making "layman" rhyme with "retarded."

"There are basically three states of matter," he had said. "I call them wackiness, dogmatism, and perversity. The universe of our experience is almost totally composed of dogmatic matter, just as it's mostly what we call 'matter,' as opposed to 'anti-matter'—though dogmatic matter includes both types. Every once in a great while we get evidence of some perverse matter. It's when you move into the realm of the wacky that you have to watch out."

"I've known that all my life," I had told him.

"Ah, but the possibilities!" he had said, waving his hand at the drive taking shape in the engine room of the *Heinlein*.

As he did now, providing the sort of segue I hate when a director does it in a movie, but the fact is Smith had a habit of waving his hand grandly when coming upon his mighty works. Hell, he had a right.

"See what can come from the backwaters of science?" he said. "Physics is a closed book, they all said. Put your talents to work in something useful."

" 'They jeered me at the Sorbonne!' " I suggested.

"They threw eggs when I presented my paper at the Institute! *Eggs!*" He leered at me, dry-washing his hands, hunching his shoulders. "The *fools!* Let them see who has the last laugh, ha ha *HA!*" He dropped the mad scientist impression and patted a huge machine on its metal flank, a cowboy gentling a horse. Smith could have been insufferably stuffy except for the fact he'd seen almost as many old movies as I had.

"No kidding, Hildy, the fools *are* going to be impressed when they see what I've wrung out of the tired old husk of physics."

"You'll get no argument from me," I said. "What happened to physics, anyway? Why was it neglected for so long?"

"Diminishing returns. They spent an insane amount of money on the GSA about a century ago, and when they turned it on they found out they'd hubbled it up. The repairs would have—"

"The GSA?"

"Global Supercooled Accelerator. You can still find a lot of it, running right around the Lunar equator."

I remembered it then; I'd followed it part of the way when I ran in the Equatorial Rover Race.

"They built big instruments out in space, too. They learned a lot about the universe, cosmologically and sub-atomically, but very little of it had any practical use. It got to where learning any more, in the directions physics kept going, would cost trillions just to tool up. If you did it, when you were done you'd have learned what went on in the first billionth of a nanosecond of creation, and then you'd just naturally want to know what happened in the first *thousandth* of a nano-nanosecond, only that'd cost ten times as much. People got tired of paying those kind of bills to answer questions even less reality-based than theology, and the smart people noticed that for peanuts you could find out practical things in biological science."

"So all the original research now is in biology," I said.

"Hah!" he shouted. "There *is* no original research, unless you count some of the things the Central Computer does. Oh, a few people here and there." He waved his hand, dismissing them. "It's all engineering now. Take well-known principles and find a way to make a better toothpaste." His eyes lit up. "That's a *perfect* example. A few months back, I woke up and my mouth tasted like peppermint. I looked into it, turns out it's a new sort of 'bot. Some idiot thought this up, built it, and let it loose on an unsuspecting public. *It's in the water,* Hildy! Can you imagine?"

"It's a crying shame," I muttered, trying not to meet his eye.

"Well, I got the antibot. Maybe my mouth does taste rotten in the morning, but at least it tastes like *me.* Reminds me who I am." Which I guess *is* a perfect example of both the perversity of Heinleiners and the cultural passivity they rebelled against. And the big reason I liked them, in spite of their best efforts to thwart my affection.

"It's all handed down from on high now," he went on. "We're like savages at an altar, waiting for miracles to be handed down. We don't envision the miracles *we* might work, if we set ourselves to it."

"Like little people, eight inches high and smart as lab rats."

He winced, the first indication I'd had of a moral uncertainty. Thank god for that; I like people to have opinions, but people with no doubts scare me.

"You want me to defend that? Okay. I've brought those children up to think for themselves, and to question authority. It's not unlimited; me or somebody who knows more about it has to approve their projects, and we keep eye on them. We've created a place where they *can* be free to make their own rules, but they're children, they have to follow *our* rules, and we set as few as possible. Do you realize this is the only place in Luna where the eyes of our mechanical Big Brother can't look? Not even the *police* can come in here."

"I have no reason to love the Central Computer, either."

"I didn't think so. I thought you might have a story to tell about that, or I'd never have let you in. You'll tell it when you're ready. Do you know *why* Libby makes little people?"

"I didn't ask him."

"He might have told you; might not have. It's his solution to the same problem I'm working on: interstellar travel. His reasoning is, a smaller human being requires less oxygen, less food, a smaller spacecraft. If we were all eight inches high, we could go to Alpha Centauri in a fuel drum."

"That's crazy."

"Not crazy. Ridiculous, probably. Unattainable, almost certainly. Those kewpies live about three years, and I doubt they'll ever have much of a brain. But it's an innovative solution to a problem the *rest* of Luna isn't even working on. Why do you think Gretel goes running across the surface in her birthday suit?"

"You weren't supposed to know about that."

"I've forbidden it. It's *dangerous,* Hildy, but I know Gretel, and I know she's still trying it. And the reason is, she hopes she'll eventually adapt herself to living in vacuum without any artificial aids."

I thought of the fish stranded on the beach, flopping around, probably doomed but still flopping.

"That's not how evolution works," I said.

"You know it and I know it. Tell it to Gretel. She's a *child,* and a smart one, but with childish stubbornness. She'll give it up sooner or later. But I can guarantee she'll try something else."

"I hope it's less harebrained."

"From your lips to God's ears. Sometimes she . . ." He rubbed his face, and made a dismissing gesture with his hand. "The kewpies make me uneasy, I'll admit that. You can't help wondering how human they are, and if they are human, whether or not they have any rights, or *should* have any rights."

"It's experimentation on humans, Michael," I said. "We have some pretty strong laws on that subject."

"What we have are taboos. We do plenty of experimentation on human genes. What we're forbidden to do is create new humans."

"You don't think that's a good idea?"

"It's never that simple. What I object to are blanket bans on *anything.* I've done a lot of research into this—I was against it at first, just like you seem to be. You want to hear it?"

"I'd be fascinated."

We'd come to an area of the engine room I thought of as his office, or laboratory. It was the place I'd spent most of what little time I'd had with him. He liked to put his feet up on a wooden desk as old as Walter's but a lot more battered, look off into infinity, and expound. So far, his innate caution had always stopped him from getting too deeply into anything when I was around, but I sensed he needed an outsider's opinion. The lab? Think of it as full of bubbling retorts and sizzling Jacob's ladders. Omit the hulking body strapped to the table; that was his children's domain. The place didn't look anything like that, but it's the proper stage set, metaphorically.

"It's a question of where to draw the line," he said. "Lines have to be drawn; even I realize that. But the line is constantly moving. In a progressing society, the line *should* be moving. Did you know it was once illegal to terminate a pregnancy?"

"I'd heard of it. Seems very strange."

"They'd decided that a fetus was a human. Later, we changed our minds. Society used to keep dead people hooked up to something called 'life-support,' sometimes for twenty or thirty years. You couldn't turn the machines off."

"Their brains were dead, you mean."

"They were *dead,* Hildy, by our standards. Corpses with blood being pumped through them. Bizarre, creepy as hell. You wonder what they were *thinking* of, what their reasoning could possibly have been. When people *knew* they were dying, when they knew that death was going to be horribly painful, it was thought wrong of them to kill themselves."

I looked away; I don't know if he caught it, but I think he did.

"A doctor couldn't help them die; he'd get prosecuted for murder. Sometimes they even withheld the drugs that would be best at stopping the pain. Any drug that dulled the senses, or heightened them, or altered the consciousness in any way was viewed as sinful—except for the two most physically harmful drugs: alcohol and nicotine. Something relatively harmless, like heroin, was completely illegal, because it was addictive, as if alcohol was not. No one had the right to determine what he put into his own body, they had no medical bill of rights. Barbaric, agreed?"

"No argument."

"I've studied their rationalizations. They make very little sense now. The reasons for the bans on human experimentation make a *lot* of sense. The potential for abuse is enormous. All genetic research involves hazards. So rules were evolved . . . and then set in stone. No one has taken a look at them in over two hundred years. My position is, it's time to think it over again."

"And what did you come up with?"

"Hell, Hildy, we've barely started. A lot of the prohibitions on genetic research were made at a time when something released into the environment could theoretically have disastrous results. But we've got room to experiment now, and foolproof means of isolation. Do the work on an asteroid, and if something goes wrong, quarantine it, then shove it into the sun."

I had no problem with that, and told him so.

"But what about the human experiments?"

"They make me queasy, just like you. But that's because we were raised to view them as evil. My children have no such inhibitions. I've told them all their lives that they should be able to ask any question. And they should be able to do any experiment, as long as they feel they have a reasonable idea of its outcome. I help them with that part, me, and the other parents."

I probably had a dubious expression on my face. It would have made perfect sense, since I was feeling dubious.

"I'm way ahead of you," he said. "You're going to bring up the old 'superman' argument."

I didn't dispute it.

"I think it's time that one was looked at again. They used to call it 'playing God.' That term has fallen out of favor, but it's still there. If we're going to set out to improve humans genetically, to build a new human, who's going to make the choices? Well, I can tell you who's making them now, and I'll bet you know the answer, too."

It didn't take a lot of thought. "The CC?" I ventured.

"Come on," he said, getting up from his desk. "I'm going to show you something."

I had a hard time keeping up with him—would have at the best of times, but my current state of roly-polytude didn't help things. He was one of those straight-ahead people, the sort who, when they've decided where they're going, can't be easily diverted. All I could do was waddle along in his wake.

Eventually we reached the base of the ship, which I knew mainly because we left square corridors and right-angle turns for the haphazard twists of the Great Dump. Not long after that we descended some stairs and were in a tunnel bored through solid rock. I still had no idea how far this network extended. I gathered it was possible to walk all the way to King City without ever visiting the surface.

We came to an abandoned, dimly-lit tube station. Or it had been abandoned at one time, but the Heinleiners had restored it: pushed the trash on the platform to one side, hung a few lights, homey touches like that. Floating a fraction above a gleaming silver rail was a six-person Maglev car of antique design. It had no doors, peeling paint, and the sign on the side still read MALL 5-9 SHUTTLE. With stops at all the major ghost warrens along the way, no doubt: this baby was *old*.

Random cushions had been spread on the ripped-out seats and we sat on those and Smith pulled on a cord which rang a little tinkling bell, and the car began to glide down the rail.

"The whole idea of building a superman has acquired a lot of negative baggage over the years," he said, picking up as if the intervening walk had never happened. As if he needed another annoying characteristic. "The German Fascists are the first ones I'm aware of who seriously proposed it, as part of an obsolete and foolish racial scheme."

"I've read about them," I said.

"It's nice to talk to someone who knows a little history. Then you'll know that by the time it became possible to tinker with genes, a lot more objections had been raised. Many of them were valid. Some still are."

"Is that something you'd like to see?" I asked. "A superman?"

"It's the *word* that throws you off. I don't know if a 'superman' is possible, or desirable. I think an altered human is an idea worth looking into. When you consider that these carcasses we're walking around in were evolved to thrive in an environment we've been evicted from . . ."

Maybe he said more, but I missed it, because just about then we had a head-on collision with another tram going in the opposite direction. Obviously, we didn't really. Obviously, it was just the reflection of the headlights of our own car as we approached another of those ubiquitous null-fields. And even more obviously, you weren't there to stand up and shout like a fool and see your life pass before your eyes, and I'll bet you *would* have, too. Or maybe I'm just slow to catch on.

Smith didn't think so. He was very apologetic when he realized what had happened, and took time to tell me about another little surprise in store, which happened a minute later when a null-field vanished in front of us and, with a little gust of wind, we entered vacuum and began to really pick up speed. The tunnel walls blurred in the beam of our headlights, details snatched away before they could be perceived.

He had more to say on the subject of human engineering. I didn't get it all because I was concentrating on not breathing, still learning to wear a null-suit. But I got his main points.

He thought that while Gretel's method was wrong, her goal was worthwhile, and I couldn't see what was wrong with it, either. Basically, we either manufacture our environment or adapt to it. Both have hazards, but it did seem high time we at least start discussing the second alternative.

Take weightlessness, for example. Most people who spent a lot of time in free-fall had some body adaptations made, but it was all surgical. Human legs are too strong; push too hard and you can fracture your skull. It's handy to have hands instead of feet at the ends of your ankles. Feet are as useless as vermiform appendices in free-fall. It's also useful to be able to bend and twist more than the human body normally can.

But the question before the court was this: should humans be *bred* to space travel? Should the useful characteristics be put into the genes, so children are born with hands instead of feet?

Maybe so, maybe not. We weren't talking radical change here, or anything that couldn't be done just as easily surgically, without raising the troublesome issues of more than one species of human being.

But what about a human adapted to vacuum? I've no idea how to go about it, but it probably could be done. What would he look like? Would he feel superior to us? Would we be his brother, or his cousin, or what? One thing was sure: it would be a lot easier to do it genetically than with the knife. And I feel certain the end result would not look very human.

I chewed that one over quite a bit in the coming days, examining my feelings. I found that most of them came from prejudice, as Smith had said. I'd been raised to think it was wrong. But I found myself agreeing that it was at least time to think it over again.

As long as I didn't have to clean up after kewpies.

The train car pulled into a siding at another abandoned station where somebody had scrawled the word "Minamata" over whatever had been there before. I had no idea how far we'd come, or in what direction.

"This is still part of the Delambre dump, more or less," Smith said, so at least I had a general idea. We started down a long, filthy corridor, Smith's flashlight beam bobbing from wall to wall as we walked. In a movie, rats and other vermin would have been scuttling out of our way, but a rat would have needed a null-suit to survive this place; mine was still on, and I was still thinking about breathing.

"There's really no reason why the stuff in here shouldn't be spread out over the surface like the rest of the garbage," he went on. "I think it's mainly psychological reasons it's all pumped in here. This is a *nasty* place. If it's toxic or radioactive or biochemically hazardous, this is where it comes."

We reached an air lock of the kind that used to be standard when I was a child, and he motioned me inside. He slapped a button, then gestured toward the air fitting on the side of my chest.

"Turn that counterclockwise," he said. "They only come on automatically when there's a vacuum. There's gas where we're going, but you don't want to breathe it."

The lock cycled and we stepped into Minamata.

The place had no name on the municipal charts of King City, just Waste Repository #2. The Heinleiners had named it after a place in Japan that had suffered the first modern-day big environmental disaster, when industries had pumped mercury compounds into a bay and produced a lot of twisted babies. So sorry, mom. That's the breaks.

Minamata Luna was really just a very large, buried storage tank. By large, I mean you could have parked four starships the size of the *Heinlein* without scraping the fenders. Texas is a *lot* bigger, but it doesn't feel like being a bug in a bottle because you can't see the walls. Here you could, and they curved upward and vanished into a noxious mist. The far end was invisible.

Maybe there was some artificial light in there. I didn't see any, but they were hardly necessary. The bottom third of the horizontal cylinder was full of liquid, and it glowed. Red here, green there . . . sometimes a ghastly blue. The makers of horror films would have *killed* to get that blue.

We had entered at what seemed the axis of the cylinder, which was rounded off at this end, like a pressure tank. A ledge, three meters wide and with a railing, curved away from us in each direction, but to the right was blocked off with a warning sign. Looking past it, I could see the ledge had crumbled away in several places. When I looked back Smith was already moving away from me toward the left. I hurried to catch up with him.

I never did quite catch him. Every time I got close my eye was drawn by the luminescent sea off to my right, and a few hundred meters down.

The thing about that sea . . . it *moved.*

At first I only saw the swirls of glowing color like an oil film on water. I'd always thought colorful things were just naturally pretty things, but Minamata taught me differently. At first I couldn't explain my queasy reaction. None of the colors, by themselves, seemed all that hideous (except for that blue). Surely that same swirl of color, on a shirt or dress, would be a gorgeous thing. Wouldn't it? I couldn't see why not. I began walking more slowly, trailing my hand along the top of the rail, trying to figure why it all disturbed me so.

The side of the cylinder went straight down from the edge of the ledge we walked on, then gradually curved inward until it met the fluorescent sea. Waves were rolling sluggishly to crash against the metal sides of the tank.

Waves, Hildy? What could be causing waves in this foul soup?

Maybe some agitating mechanism, I thought, though I couldn't see any use for one. Then I saw a part of the sea hump itself up, ten or twenty meters high—it was hard to judge the scale from my vantage point. Then I saw strange shapes on the borderline between sea and shore, things that moved among the mineral efflorescences that grew like arthritic fingers along that metal beach. Then I saw something that, I thought, raised its head on a spavined neck and looked at me, reached out a hungry hand . . .

Of course, it was a long way off. I could have been wrong.

Smith took my arm without a word and urged me along. I didn't look at the Minamata Sea again.

We came to a series of circular mirrors standing against the vertical wall to our left. Each had a number over it. I realized that tunnels had been bored into the walls here and each had been sealed off with a null-field barrier.

Smith stopped before the eighth, pointed at it, and stepped in. I followed him, and found myself in a short tunnel, maybe twenty meters long, five meters high. Halfway down the tunnel were metal bars. Beyond that point a level floor had been built to support a cot, chair, desk, and toilet, all looking as if they'd been ordered from some cheap mail-order house. On our side of the bars was a portable air plant, which seemed to be doing its job, as my suit had vanished as I stepped through the field. Spare oxygen cylinders and crates of food were stacked against the wall.

Sitting on the cot and watching a slash-boxing show on the television was Andrew MacDonald. He glanced up from the screen as we entered, but he did not rise.

Possibly this was a new point of etiquette. *Should* the dead rise for the living? Be sure to ask at your next séance.

"Hello, Andrew," Smith said. "I've brought someone to see you."

"Yes?" Andrew said, with no great interest. His eyes turned to me, lingered for a moment. There was no spark of recognition. Worse than that, there was none of that penetrating quality I'd seen on the day he . . . hell, how else can I say it? On the day he died. For a moment I thought this was just some guy who looked a lot like Andrew. I guess I was half right.

"Sorry," he said, and shrugged. "Don't know her."

"I'm not surprised," Smith said. He looked at me. I had the feeling I was supposed to say something perceptive, intelligent. Maybe I was supposed to have figured it all out.

"What the fuck's going on here?" I said, which was a lot better than "duuuuh," which was my first reaction, though neither really qualifies as perceptive.

"Ask him," Andrew said. "He thinks I'm dangerous."

I'd started toward the bars but Smith put his hand on my arm and shook his head.

"See what I mean?" the prisoner said.

"He is dangerous," Smith told me. "When he first came here, he nearly killed a man. Would have, but we got to him in time. Want to tell us about that, Andrew?"

He shrugged. "He stepped on my foot. It wasn't my fault."

"I've had enough of this," I said. "What the hell are you people doing in here? I saw this man die, or his twin brother."

Smith was about to say something, but I'd finally gotten Andrew interested. He stood and came to the bars, held on with one hand while the other played idly with his genitals. You see that sometimes, in old alkies or voluntary skitzys down in Bedrock. It's a free planet, right? Nobody can stop them, but people hurry by, like you don't stop and stare if someone is vomiting, or picking his nose. I'd never seen an apparently healthy man masturbating with such utter lack of modesty. What had they done to him?

"How did I do?" he asked me, tugging and squeezing. "All they'll tell me is I died in the ring. You were there? Were you close up? Who was it that got me? Damn, the least they could do is give me a tape."

"Are you really Andrew MacDonald?"

"That's my name, ask me again and I'll tell you the same."

"It's him," Smith said, quietly. "That's what I've finally decided, after thinking it over a lot."

"That's not what you said last time," the man said. "You said I was only part of old Andy. The mean part. I don't think I'm mean." He lost interest in his penis and stretched a hand through the bars, gesturing. "Toss me a can of that beef stew, boss man. I've had my eye on that for days."

"You've got plenty of food in there."

"Yeah, but I want stew."

Smith got a plastic can and lobbed it toward the cell; the man snagged it and tore off the top. He took a big handful and crammed it into his mouth, chewing noisily. There was a stove, a table, and utensils plainly in sight behind him, but he didn't seem to care.

"I didn't see you fight," I said, at last.

"Shit. You know, I'd like you if you weren't so fat. You wanna fuck?" A gravy-covered hand went to his groin once again. "Let's get brown, honey."

I'm going to ignore the rest of his antics. I still remember them vividly, and still find them disturbing. I'd once wanted to make love to this man. I'd once found him quite attractive.

"I was there when they carried you back from the ring," I said.

"The good old squared circle. The sweet science. All there is, really, all there is. What's your name, fatty?"

"Hildy. You were mortally injured and you refused treatment."

"What a jerk I must have been. Live to fight another day, huh?"

"I'd always thought so. And I thought what you were doing, risking your life, was stupid. I thought it was unnecessary, too, but you told me your reasons, and I respect them."

"A jerk," he repeated.

"I guess, when it came time for you to live up to your bargain, I thought you were stupid, too. But I was impressed. I was moved. I can't say I thought you were doing the right thing, but your determination was awesome."

"You're a jerk, too."

"I know."

He continued shoving stew into his face, looking at me with no real spark of human feeling I could detect. I turned to Smith.

"It's time you told me what's going on here. What's been done to this man? If this is an example of what you were talking about on the way . . ."

"It is."

"Then I don't want anything to do with it. In fact, damn it, I know I promised not to talk about you and your people, but—"

"Hang on a minute, Hildy," Smith said. "This is an example of human experimentation, but we didn't do it."

"The CC," I said, after a long pause. Who else?

"There's something seriously wrong with the CC, Hildy. I don't know what it is, but I know the results. This man is one. He's a cloned body, grown from Andrew MacDonald's corpse, or from a tissue sample. When he's in a mood to talk, he's said things we've checked against his records, and it seems he really does have MacDonald's memories. Up to a point. He remembers things up to about three or four years ago. We haven't been able to test him thoroughly, but what tests we've been able to run bear out what we've seen from other specimens like him. He thinks he *is* Mac-Donald."

"Damn right I am," the prisoner chimed in.

"For all practical purposes, he's right. But he doesn't remember the Kansas Collapse. He doesn't remember Silvio's assassination. I was certain he wouldn't remember you, and he didn't. What's happened is that his memories were recorded in some way, and played back into this clone body."

I thought it over. Smith gave me time to.

"It doesn't work," I said, finally. "There's no way this thing could have turned into the man I met in only three or four years. This guy is like a big, spoiled child."

"Big is right, babe," the man said, with the gesture you'd expect.

"I didn't say the copy was perfect," Smith said. "The memories seem to be extremely good. But some things didn't record. He has no social inhibitions whatsoever. No sense of guilt or shame. He really did try to kill a man who accidentally stepped on his foot, and he never saw what was so wrong about it. He's incredibly dangerous, because he's the best fighter in Luna; that's why we have him here, in the best prison we can devise. We, who don't even believe in prisons."

I could see it would be a tough one to get out of. If you got past the null-field, there were the toxic gases of Minamata. Beyond that, vacuum.

It seemed that "MacDonald" was the most recent of a long line of abandoned experiments. Smith wouldn't tell me how the Heinleiners had come to have him, except to say that, in his case, he'd most likely been sent.

"Early on in this program, we had a pipeline into the secret lab where this work was going on. The first attempts were pathetic. We had people who just sat there and drooled, others who tore at themselves with their teeth. But the CC got better with practice. Some could pass as normal human beings. Some of them live with us. They're limited, but what can you do? I think they're human.

"But lately, we've been getting surprise packages, like Andrew here. We lock them up, interrogate them. Some of them are harmless. Others . . . I don't think we can ever let them free."

"I don't understand. I mean, I see this one could be dangerous, but—"

"The CC wants in here."

"Into Minamata?"

"No, this is his place. You saw the water down there. That's his work. He wants into the Heinleiner enclave. He wants the null-field. He wants to know if I'm successful with the stardrive. He wants to know other things. He found out about our access to his forbidden experiments, and we started getting people like Andrew. Walking time bombs, most of them. After a few tragic incidents, we had to institute some security precautions. Now we're careful about the dead people we let in here."

It was not the first time an action by the CC had turned my world upside-down. You live in a time and a place and you think you know what's going on, but you don't. Maybe no one ever did.

Smith had unloaded too many things on me too quickly. I'd had some practice at that, with the CC playing games with my head, but I wonder if anyone ever gets really good at it.

"So he's working on immortality?" I asked.

"Of a sort. The oldest people around now are pushing three hundred. Most people think there's a limit on how long the human brain can be patched up in one way or another. But if you could make a *perfect* record of everything a human being is, and dump it into another brain . . ."

"Yeah . . . but Andrew is *dead.* This thing . . . even if it was a better copy, it still wouldn't be Andrew. Would it?"

"Hey, Hildy," Andrew said. When I turned to face him I got a big glob of cold, canned beef stew right in the kisser.

He never looked more like an ape as he capered around his cell, hugging himself, bent over with laughter. It showed no signs of stopping. And the funny thing was, after a brief flash of homicidal intent, I found it impossible to hate him. Whatever the CC had left out of this man, he was not evil, as I had first thought. He was childish and completely impulsive. Some sort of governor had not been copied right; his conscience had been smudged in transmission, there was static in his self-control. Think of it, do it. A simple philosophy.

"Come on next door," Smith said, after giving me some help getting the worst mess off me. "You can clean up there, and I have something to show you."

So we went through the null-field again—Andrew was still laughing—walked eight or nine steps further to the ninth cell, and stepped in.

And who should I see there but Aladdin, he of the magic lungs, standing on this side of a barred cell identical to the one we'd just left. Only this one was not occupied, and the door stood open.

"Who's this one for?" I asked. "And what's Aladdin doing here?" Some days I'm quick, but this didn't seem to be one of them.

"There's no assigned occupant yet, Hildy," Smith said, displaying something that had once been a flashlight but had now folded out into what just *had* to be a Heinleiner weapon—it had that gimcrack look. "We're going to ask you some questions. Not many, but the answers may take a while, so get comfortable. Aladdin's here to remove your null-suit generator if we don't like the answers."

There was a long, awkward silence. Being held at gunpoint is not something any of us had much experience of, from either end of the gun. It's a social situation you don't run into often. Try it at your next party, see how the guests handle it.

To their credit, I don't think they liked it much more than me.

"What do you want to know?"

"Start with all your dealings with the Central Computer over the last three years."

So I told them everything.

Gretel, that sweet child, would have invited me in the first weekend, as it turned out. It was Smith and his friends who held up the approval. They were checking me out, and their resources for doing so were formidable. I'd been watched in Texas. My background had been researched. As I went along there were a few times when I missed this or that detail, and I was always corrected. To lie would have been futile . . . and besides, I didn't want to lie. If anyone had the answers to the questions I'd been asking myself about the CC, it was surely these people. I wanted to help them by telling everything I knew.

I don't want to make this sound more dire than it actually was. Fairly early we all relaxed. The flashlight was refolded and put away. If they'd been really suspicious of me I'd have been brought here on my first visit, but after the things they had told me it was only prudent for them to interrogate me in the way they did.

The thing that had upset them was my suicide attempt on the surface. It had left behind physical evidence, in the form of a ruptured faceplate, and set them to wondering if I *had* really died up there.

And as I continued talking about it a disturbing thing occurred to me: what if I *had?*

How could I ever know, really? If the CC could record my memories and play them back into a cloned body, would I feel any different than I did then? I couldn't think of a test to check it, not one I could do myself. I found myself hoping they had one. No such luck.

"I'm not worried about that, Hildy," Smith said, when I brought it up. In retrospect, maybe that wasn't a smart thing to do, pointing out that they couldn't be sure of me, either, but it didn't matter, since they'd already thought of it and made up their minds. "If the CC has gotten that good, then we're licked already."

"Besides," Aladdin put in, "if he's that good, what difference would it make?"

"It could be important if he'd left a post-hypnotic suggestion," Smith said. "A perfect copy of Hildy, with a buried injunction to spy on us and spill her guts when she went back to King City."

"I hadn't thought of that," Aladdin said, looking as if he wished the flashlight hadn't been put away so hastily.

"As I said, if he's that good we might as well give up." He stood, and stretched. "No, my friends. At some point you have to stop the tests. At some point you just have to go with your feelings. I'm very sorry to have done this to you, Hildy, it's against all I believe in. Your personal life should be your own. But we're engaged in a quiet war here. No battles have been fought, but the enemy is constantly feeling us out. The best we can do is be like a turtle, pull into a shell he can't penetrate. I'm sorry."

"It's okay. I wanted to talk about it, anyway."

He held out his hand, and I took it, and for the first time in many, many years, I felt like I belonged to something. I wanted to shout "Death to the CC!" Unfortunately, the Heinleiners were short on slogans, membership badges, that sort of thing. I sort of doubted I'd be offered a uniform.

Hell, they didn't even have a secret handshake. But I accepted the ordinary one I was offered gratefully. I was in.

23

WAR

What did you do during the Big Glitch?

It's an interesting question from several angles. If I'd asked what you were doing when you heard Silvio had been assassinated, I'd get back a variety of answers, but a minute after you heard ninety-nine percent of you were glued to the newspad (twenty-seven percent to the *Nipple*). It's the same for other large, important events, the kind that shape our lives. But each of you will have a different story about the Glitch. The story will start like this:

Something major in your life suffered a malfunction of some kind. Depending on what it was, you called the repair-person or the police or simply started screaming bloody murder. The next thing you did (99.99 percent of you, anyway) was turn on your newspad to see what the hell was happening. You turned it on, and you got . . . nothing.

Our age is not simply information-rich. It's information-saturated. We expect that information to be delivered as regularly as the oxygen we breathe, and tend to forget the delivery is as much at the mercy of fallible machines as is the air. We view it as only slightly less important than air. Two seconds of downtime on one of the major pads will generate *hundreds of thousands* of complaints. Irate calls, furious threats to cancel subscriptions. Frightened calls. Panicky calls. To turn on the pad and get nothing but white noise and fuzz is Luna's equivalent of a planet-wide earthquake. We expect our info-nets to be comprehensive, ubiquitous, and global, and we expect it *right now.*

To this day, the Big Glitch is the mainstay of the counseling industry in Luna. Those who deal in crisis management have found it a fabulous meal ticket that shows no signs of expiring. They rate it higher, in terms of stress produced, than being the victim of violent assault, or the loss of a parent.

One of the things that made it so stressful was that everyone's experience was different. When your worldview, your opinions and the "facts" you base them on, the events that have shaped our collective consciousness, what you like (because everyone else does) and what you don't like (ditto), all come over that all-pervasive newspad, you're a bit at sea when the pad goes down and you suddenly have to react for yourself. No news of how people in Arkytown are taking it. No endless replays of the highlights. No pundits to tell you what to think about it, what people are doing about it (so you can do the same). You're on your own, pal. Good luck. Oh, and by the way, if you choose wrong, it can *kill* you, buddy.

The Glitch is the one big event where nobody saw the whole thing in an overview provided by experts whose job it is to trim the story down to a size that will fit a pad. Everybody saw just a little piece of it, their own piece. Almost none of those pieces really mattered in the larger scheme of things. Mine didn't, either, though I was closer to the "center" of the story, if it had a center, than most of you. Only a handful of experts who finally brought it under control ever really knew what was going on. Read their accounts, if you're qualified, if you want to know what *really* went on. I've tried, and if you can explain it to me please send a synopsis, twenty-five words or less, all entries to be scrupulously ignored.

So know going in that I'm not going to provide many technical details. Know that I'm not going to tell you much about what went on behind the scenes; I'm as ignorant of it as anyone else.

No, this is simply what happened to *me* during the Big Glitch . . .

Afterwards, when it became necessary to talk about Delambre and the colony of weirdos in residence there, the newspads had to come up with a term everyone would recognize, some sort of shorthand term for the place and the people. As usual in these situations, there was a period of casting about and market research, listening to what the people themselves were calling it. I heard the place called a village, a warren, and a refuge. My particular favorite was "termitarium." It aptly described the random burrows in the Delambre trash heap.

Pads who didn't like the Heinleiners called the residents a cabal. Pads who admired them referred to Delambre and the ship as a Citadel. There was even confusion about the term "Heinleiner." It meant, depending on who you were talking about, either a political philosophy, a seriously crackpot religion (eventually known as "Organized Heinleiners"), or the practitioners of scientific civil disobedience loosely led by V.M. Smith and a few others.

Simplicity eventually won out, and the *R.A.H.*, the trash pile adjacent to it, and certain caves and corridors that linked the whole complex to the more orderly world came to be called "Heinlein Town."

Simplicity has its virtues, but to call it a town was stretching the definition.

There were forces other than the Heinleiners' militant contrariness that worked against Heinlein Town ever fielding a softball team, electing a dogcatcher, or putting up signs at the city limits—wherever *those* might be—saying Watch Us Grow! Not all the "citizens" were engaged in the type of forbidden research done by Smith and his offspring. Some were there simply because they preferred to be isolated from a society they found too constricting. But because a lot of illegal things *were* going on, there had to be security, and the only kind the Heinleiners would put up with was that afforded by Smith's null-field barriers: the elect could just walk right through it, while the unwashed found it impenetrable.

But the security also entailed some things even an anarchist would find inconvenient.

The constriction most of these people were fleeing could be summed up in two words: Central Computer. They didn't trust it. They didn't like it peering into their lives twenty-four hours a day. And the only way to keep it out was to keep it *completely* out. The only thing that could do that was the null-field and the related technologies it spun off, arcane arts to which the CC had no key.

But no matter what your opinion of the CC, it is damn useful. For instance, whatever line of work you are in, I'd be willing to bet it would be difficult to do it without a telephone. There were no telephones in Heinlein Town, or none that reached the outside world, anyway. There was no way to reach the planet-wide data net in any fashion, because all methods of interfacing with it were as useful coming in as going out. If Heinlein Town had one hard and fast rule it was this: The CC shall extend no tentacle into the Delambre Enclave (my own term for the loose community of trash-dwellers).

Hey, folks, people have to work. People who live completely away from the traditional municipal services have an even stronger work imperative. There was no oxygen dole in Heinlein Town. If you stayed, and couldn't pay your air assessment, you could damn well learn to breathe vacuum.

One result was that eighty percent of "Heinlein Town" residents were no more resident than I was. I was a weekender because I didn't want to give up my home and my place in Texas. Most weekenders lived in King City and spent all their free time in Delambre because they had to pay the bills and found it impossible to earn any money in Heinlein Town. There were not many full-time economic niches available, a fact that galled the Heinleiners no end.

Heinlein Town? Here's what it was really like:

There were half a dozen places with enough people living close by to qualify as towns or villages. The largest of these was Virginia City, which had as many as five hundred residents. Strangeland was almost as big. Both towns had sprung up because of an accident of the process of waste disposal: a few score very large tin cans had been jumbled together at these locations, and they were useful for living and farming. By large, I mean up to a thousand meters in length, half that in diameter. I think they had been strap-on fuel tanks at one time. The Heinleiners had bored holes to connect them, pressurized them, and moved in like poor relations. Instant slum.

You couldn't help being reminded of Bedrock, though these people were often quite prosperous. There were no zoning regulations that didn't relate to health and safety. Sewage treatment was taken seriously, for instance, not only because they didn't want the place to stink like Bedrock but because they didn't have access to the bounty of King City municipal water. What they had had been trucked in, and it was endlessly reused. But they didn't understand the concept of a public eyesore. If you wanted to string a line across one of the tanks and hang your laundry on it, it's a free country, ain't it? If you thought manufacturing toxic gases in your kitchen was a good idea, go ahead, cobber, but don't have an accident, because civil liability in Heinlein Town could include the death penalty.

Nobody really owned land in Delambre, in the sense of having a deed or title (hold on, Mr. H., don't spin in your grave yet), but if you moved into a place nobody was using, it was yours. If you wanted to call an entire million-gallon tank home, that was fine. Just put up a sign saying KEEP OUT and it had the force of law. There was plenty of space to go around.

Everything was private enterprise, often a cooperative of some kind. I met three people who made a living by running the sewers in the three biggest enclaves, and selling water and fertilizer to farmers. You paid through the nose to hook up, and it was worth it, because who wants to handle *every* detail of daily life? Many of the largest roads were tollways. Oxygen was unmetered, but paid for by a monthly fee to the only real civic agency the Heinleiners tolerated: the Oxygen Board.

Electricity was so cheap it was free. Just hook a line into the main.

And here's the real secret of Mr. Smith's success, the reason a fairly unlikable man like him was held in such high esteem in the community.

He didn't charge for the null-field jigsaw network that hermetically sealed Heinlein Town off from the rest of Luna, the network that had made their way of life possible. If you wanted to homestead a new area of Delambre, you first rented a tunneling machine from the people who found, repaired, and maintained them. When you had your tunnel, you installed the tanks, solar panels, and heaters of the ALUs every hundred meters, then you went to Mr. Smith for the null-field generators. He handed them out free.

He had every right to charge for them, of course, and nary a Heinleiner would have complained. But just so you don't think he was a goddamcommunist, I should point out that while he gave away the units, he didn't give away the science. The first thing he told you when he handed you a generator was, "You fuck with this, you go boom." Years ago somebody hadn't believed him, had tried to open one up and see what made the pretty music, and sort of fell inside the generator. There was a witness, who swore the fellow was quickly spit back out—and how he ever fell *into* a device no bigger than a football was a source of wonder in itself—but when he came out, he was inverted, sort of like a dirty sock. He actually lived for a little while, and they put him in the public square of Virginia City as a demonstration of the fruits of hubris.

So there you have the economic, technical, and behavioral forces that shaped the little hamlet of Virginia City, as surely as rivers, harbors, railroads, and climate shaped cities of Old Earth. Since no pictures of the place have yet been allowed out by the residents, since I've gathered that, to most people, "Heinlein Town" conjures thoughts of either troglodyte caverns dripping slime and infested with bats or of some super-slick, super-efficient techno-wonderland, I thought I should set the record straight.

To visualize the public square in Virginia City, think of a brighter, cleaner version of Robinson Park in Bedrock. On a smaller scale. There was the same curving roof, the same stingy acre of grass and trees in the center, and the same jumble of packing crates stacked higgledy-piggledy around the green acre. Both of them just grew that way—Robinson Park in spite of the law, Virginia City because of the lack of it. In both places squatters appropriated discarded shipping containers, cut windows and doors, and hung their hats in them. There and in Bedrock the residents didn't give a hoot for stacking the damn things warehouse-fashion, in neat, squared-up rows. The result was sort of like a pueblo mud dwelling, but not nearly so orderly, with long crates spanning empty space or jutting out crazily, ladders leaning everywhere.

There the resemblance ended. Inside the Bedrock hovels you'd be lucky to find a burlap rug and spare pair of socks; the Heinleiner modules were gaily painted and furnished, with here a window box full of geraniums and there a rooftop pigeon pen. The lawn in Virginia City was golf-green trim and trash-free. Bedrockers tended to stack themselves twenty or thirty deep, until whole impromptu skyscrapers toppled. None of the Virginia City dwellings were more than six crates from the floor.

The square was the hub of commerce in Delambre, with more shops and cottage industry than anywhere else. I usually went there first on my weekend visits because it was a good place to meet people, and because my peripatetic guides and shameless mooches, Hansel, Gretel, and Libby, were sure to pass through on a Saturday morning and see if they could hit up good ol' Hildy for a Double-Fudge 'n' Rum Raisin Banana Split at Aunt Hazel's Ice Cream Emporium and While-U-Wait Surgery Shoppe.

On the day in question, the day of the Big Glitch, I had parked my by-now quite considerable *tuchis* in one of the canvas chairs set out on the public walk at that establishment. I nursed a cup of coffee. There would be plenty of ice cream to eat when the children arrived, and I had no particular taste for it. I'd made worse sacrifices in pursuit of a story.

Each of the four tables at Hazel's had a canvas umbrella sprouting from the center, very useful for keeping off the rain and the sun. I scanned the skies, looking for signs of a cloudburst. Nope, looked like another day of curved metal roofs and suspended arc-lights. You can't beat the weather inside an abandoned fuel tank.

I looked out over the square. In the center was a statue, a bit larger than life-size, of a cat, sitting on a low stone plinth. I had no idea what that was all about. The only other item of civic works visible was a lot less obscure. It was a gallows, sitting off to one side of the square. I'd been told it had only been used once. I was glad to hear the event had not been well-attended. Some aspects of Heinleinism were easier to like than others.

"What the hell are you doing here, Hildy?" I heard myself say. Someone at a neighboring table looked up, then back down at her sundae. So the pregnant lady was muttering to herself; so what? It's a free planet. From beneath the table I heard a familiar wet smacking sound, looked down, saw Winston had lifted one bleary eye to see if food was coming. I nudged him with my toe and he sprawled sybaritically on his back, inviting more intimacy than I had any intention of giving. When no more attention came, he went to sleep in that position.

"Let's look this situation over," I said. This time neither Winston nor the lover of hot fudge looked up, but I decided to continue my monologue internally, and it went something like this:

What with umpty-ump suicide attempts, Hildy, it's been what you might call a bad year.

You greeted the appearance of the Silver Girl with the loud hosannas of a Lost Soul who has Seen The Light.

You brought her to ground, using fine journalistic instincts honed by more years than you care to remember—helped by the fact that she wasn't exactly trying to stay hidden.

And—yea verily!—she *was* what you'd hoped she'd be: the key to a place where people were not content to coast along, year to year, in the little puddle of light and heat known as the Solar System, evicted from our home planet, cozened by a grand Fairy Godfather of our own creation who made life easier for us than it had ever been in the history of the species, and who was capable of things few of us knew or cared about. Let me hear you say *amen!*

Amen!

So then . . . so then . . .

Once you've *got* the story a certain post-reportorial depression always sets in. You have a smoke, pull on your shoes, go home. You start looking for the next story. You don't try to *live* in the story.

And why not? Because covering any story, whether it be the Flacks and Silvio or V.M. Smith and his merry band, just showed you more people, and I was beginning to fear that my problem was simply that I'd had it with people. I'd set out looking for a sign, and what I'd found was a story. The Angel Moroni materialized out of good old flash powder, and was held up with wires. The burning bush smelled of kerosene. Ezekiel's wheel, flashing across the sky? Look closely. Is that bits of pie crust on it, or what?

How can you say that, Hildy? I protested. (And the lady with the sundae got up and moved to another table, so maybe the monologue wasn't as interior as I had hoped. Maybe it was about to get positively Shakespearean and I would stand up on my chair and commit a soliloquy. To be or not to be!) After all (I went on, more calmly), he's building a starship.

Well . . . yeah. And his daughter is building pigs with wings, and maybe they'll *both* fly, but my money was on needing protection from falling pigshit before I held an interstellar boarding pass in my hand.

Yeah, but . . . well, they're *resisting* in here. They don't kowtow to the CC. Not two weeks ago you were moved almost to tears to be accepted among them. *Now* we'll *do* something about the CC, you thought.

Sure. One of these days.

Two things had come clear to me once the fuzzy-headed camaraderie had worn off and my cynicism reasserted itself. One was that the Heinlein-ers were as capable of lollygagging procrastination as anyone else. Aladdin had admitted to me that the resistance was mostly a passive thing, keeping the CC out rather than bearding him in his lair, mostly because no one had much of a clue as to how to go about the latter. So they all figured they'd take the fight to him . . . when they felt like it. Meantime, they did what we all did about insurmountable problems: they didn't think about it.

The second thing I realized was that, if the CC wanted to be in Heinlein Town, he would *be* in Heinlein Town.

I wasn't privy to all their secrets. I didn't know anything of the machinations that had brought the MacDonald clone to Minamata, nor much of anything else about just how hard the CC was trying to penetrate the little Heinleiner enclave. But even such as me could tell it would be easy to get a spy in here. Hell, Liz had visited the previous weekend, with me, and had been admitted solely on the strength of her reputation as a person of known Heinleiner tendencies. Some sorts of checks were run, I'm sure, but I would bet anything the CC could get around them if he wanted to infiltrate a spy.

No, the CC was surely curious about these people, and no doubt frustrated, but the CC was a strange being. Whatever cryogenic turmoil was currently animating his massive brain was and probably would remain a mystery to me. It was clear that things were going wrong, or he'd never have been able to override his programming and do the things he'd done to me. But it was equally clear that most of his programming was still intact, or he'd simply have kicked down the front door of this place and marched everyone off for trial.

Having said all that, why the disillusion, Hildy?

Two reasons. Unreasonable expectations: in spite of all good sense, I had hoped these people would be somehow better than other people. They weren't. They just had different ideas. And two, I didn't fit. They didn't need reporters in here. Gossip sufficed. Teaching was taken very seriously; no dilettantes need apply. The only other thing I was interested in was building a starship, and I'd be about as useful as a kewpie with a slide rule.

"Three reasons," I said. "You're depressed, too."

"Don't be," Libby said. "I'm here."

I looked up and saw him sit down after first carefully placing a dish oozing with chocolate, caramel, and melting ice cream on the table in front of him. He reached down and scratched Winston's head. The dog licked his nose, sniffed, and went back to sleep, ice cream being one of the few foodstuffs he had little interest in. Libby grinned at me.

"Hope I didn't keep you waiting too long," he said.

"No problem. Where's H & G?"

"They said they'd be along later. Liz is back, though." I saw her approaching across the village green. She had a bottle in one hand. The Heinleiners made their own booze, naturally, and Liz had professed to like it on her earlier visit. Probably that little dab of kerosene they added for flavor.

"Can't stay, folks, can't stay, gotta run," she said, just as if I'd urged her to stick around. She produced a folding cup from her gunbelt and poured a shot of pure Virginia City Bonded, tossed it down. It wasn't the first of the day.

That's right, I said gunbelt. Liz had taken to Heinlein Town from the first moment I brought her in, because it was the only place outside of the movie studios where she worked that she could wear a gun. But in here she could load it with real bullets. She currently sported a matched pair of Colt .45's, with pearl handles.

"I was hoping we could go do some shooting," Libby said.

"Not today, sweetie. I just dropped by to get a bottle, and retrieve my dog. Next weekend, I promise. But you buy the lead."

"Sure."

"Has he been a good dog?" Liz cooed, crouching down and scratching his back, almost toppling over in the process. She was probably talking to Winston, but I told her he'd been good, anyway. She didn't seem to hear.

Libby leaned a little closer to me and looked at me with concern.

"Are you really feeling depressed?" he asked. He put his hand on mine.

All I really needed at that point in my life was another case of puppy love, but that's just what had happened. At the rate he was going, pretty soon he'd be humping my leg, like Winston.

For pity's sake, Hildy, give it a rest.

"Just a little blue," I said, putting on a smile for him.

"How come?"

"Wondering where my life is going."

He looked blankly at me. I'd seen the same expression on Brenda's face when I said something incomprehensible to one who sees nothing but endless, unlimited vistas stretching ahead. Charitably, I didn't kick him. Instead, I removed my hand from under his, patted his hand, and finally noticed the disturbance going on under the table.

"Problems, Liz?" I asked.

"I think he wants to stay here." She had attached a leash to his collar and was tugging on it, but he had planted his forepaws and dug in. Forget mules; if you want a metaphor for stubbornness, you need look no further than the English bulldog.

"You could pick him up," Libby suggested.

"If I had no further use for my face," she agreed. "Also arms, legs, and ass. Winston's slow to anger, but he's worth seeing when he gets there." She stood, hands on hips in frustration, and her dog rolled over on his back and went to sleep again. "Damn, Hildy, he surely must like you."

I thought what he liked was hunting live prey—horses and cows, mostly, though recently a kewpie had gone missing. But I didn't mention that. Not for Libby's tender ears.

"It's okay, Liz," I said. "He's not much trouble. I'll just keep him this weekend and drop him by your place on my way home."

"Well, sure, but . . . I mean I'd planned to . . ." She groped around a little more, then poured herself another drink and made it vanish.

"Right," she said. "See you later, Hildy." She slapped my shoulder in passing, then took off across the green.

"What was that all about?" Libby asked.

"You never know with Liz."

"Is she really the Queen of England?"

"Yep. And *I* am the ruler of the Queen's na-vee!"

He got that blank look, field-tested and honed to perfection by Brenda, then shrugged and applied himself to demolishing the melting mess in front of him. I guess Gilbert and Sullivan was too much even for a Heinleiner youth.

"Well . . ." he said, wiping his mouth on the back of his hand, "she sure can shoot, I've gotta say that."

"I wouldn't get into a fistfight with her either, if I was you."

"But she drinks too much."

"Amen to that. I'd hate to have to pay her liver-replacement tab."

He leaned back in his chair, looking well satisfied with life.

"So. You taking me back to Texas this Sunday evening?"

In a weak moment I'd promised to show all three children where I lived. Hansel and Gretel seemed to have forgotten about it, but not Libby. I'd have taken him, but I was pretty sure I'd spend most of my time fighting him off, and I just wasn't up to it.

"Afraid not. I've got too many test papers to grade. All this traveling to and from Delambre's gotten me far behind in my teaching duties."

He tried not to show his disappointment.

"Next time," I told him.

"Sure," he said. "Then what do you want to do today?"

"I really don't know, Libby. I've seen the stardrive, and I didn't understand it. I've seen the farm, and Minamata, and I've seen the spider people." I'd seen even more wonders than that, some of them unmentioned here because of promises I made, others for reasons of security, and most because they simply weren't that interesting. Even a community of wild-eyed genius experimenters is going to lay some eggs. "What do you think we should do?"

He thought it over.

"There's a baseball game over in Strangeland in about an hour."

I laughed.

"Sure," I said. "I haven't watched one in years."

"You can watch if you want," he said. "I meant, we sort of choose up sides, you know, depending on how many people show up . . ."

"A pick-up game. I thought you meant, like—"

"No, we don't have—"

"—the Heinleiner Tanstaafls against the King City—"

"—that many people in here."

"Forgive me. I'm still a big-city girl, I guess. You need an umpire?" I smacked my bloated belly. "I brought my own pads."

He grinned, opened his mouth, and said, "We could everybody freeze, and nobody will get hurt."

At least that's what it sounded like to me, for a split second, before the synapses sorted themselves out and I saw the last seven words had come from a tall, bulky party in an alarming but effective costume, holding a rifle in one hand and a bullhorn in the other.

Once I spotted him, I quickly saw about a dozen others like him and the same number of King City police, moving across the square in a ragged skirmish line. The cops had drawn handguns, something seldom seen on Luna. The others had big projectile weapons or hand-held lasers.

"What the hell are *they?*" Libby asked. We'd both stood up, like most of the other people I could see.

"I'd guess they were soldiers," I said.

"But that's crazy. Luna doesn't have an army."

"Looks like we got one when we weren't looking."

And quite a bunch they were, too. The K.C. cops were equally men and women, the "soldiers" were all male, and all large. They wore black: jumpsuits, equipment belts, huge ornate crash helmets with tinted visors, boots. The belts were hung with things that might have been hand grenades, ammunition clips, or high-tech pencil sharpeners, for all I could tell.

It later turned out they were mostly props. The costumes had been rented from a film studio, since the nonexistent Army of Luna had nothing to offer in the way of super-macho display.

They came in our general direction. When they encountered people they pushed them to the floor and the cops started patting them down for weapons, and slipping on handcuffs. The soldiers kept on moving, swinging the muzzles of their weapons this way and that, looking quite pleased with themselves, all to the booming accompaniment of more orders from the bullhorn.

"What should we do, Hildy?" Libby asked, his voice shaking.

"I think it's best if we do what they say," I said, quietly, patting his shoulder to settle him down. "Don't worry, I know a good lawyer."

"Are they going to arrest us?"

"Looks like it."

A cop and a soldier marched up to us and the soldier looked at a datapad in his hand, then at my face.

"Are you Maria Cabrini, also known as Hildegarde Johnson?"

"I'm Hildy Johnson."

"Cuff her," he told the cop. He turned away as the policewoman started toward me, and as Libby moved to put himself between me and the cop.

"You keep your hands off her," Libby said, and the soldier pivoted easily and brought up the butt of his gun and smashed it into the side of Libby's face. I could hear his jaw shatter. He fell to the ground, totally limp. As I stared down at him, Winston waddled out from under the table and sniffed his face.

The cop was saying something angry to the soldier, but I was too stunned to hear what it was.

"Just do it," the soldier snarled at her, and I started to kneel beside Libby but the cop grabbed my arm and pulled me up. She snapped one cuff over my left wrist, still looking at the retreating back of the soldier.

"He can't get away with that," she said, more to herself than to me. She reached for my other hand and it finally sunk in that this was more than a normal arrest situation, that things were out of joint, and that maybe I ought to resist, because if a big ape could just club a young boy senseless something was going on here that I didn't understand.

So I yanked my right hand away and started to run but she was way ahead of me, twisting my left hand hard until I ended up bent over the table with her behind me, pressing my face into the remains of Libby's sundae. I kept fighting to keep my right hand free and she jerked me upright by my hair, and she screamed, and let go of me.

They tell me Winston came off the ground like a squat rocket, that great vise of a jaw open wide, and clamped it shut on her forearm, breaking her grip on me and knocking her to the ground. I fell over myself, and landed on my butt, from which position I watched in horrified fascination as Winston made every effort to tear the limb from its socket.

I hope I never see anything like that again. Winston couldn't have massed a seventh as much as the policewoman, but he jerked her around like a rag doll. His jaws opened only enough to get a better grip in a different place. Even over the sound of her screams I could hear the bones crunching.

Now the soldier was coming back, raising his rifle as he came, and now a shot rang out and blood sprayed from the front of his chest, and again, and once more, and he fell on his face, hard, and didn't move. Then everybody was firing at once and I crawled under the metal table as lead slugs screamed all around me.

The fire was concentrated at first on a window high in the stack of apartment crates surrounding the square. Part of the wall vanished in plastic splinters, then a red line thrust into the wreckage and something bloomed orange flame. I saw more gun barrels sticking out of more windows, saw another soldier go down with the lower part of his leg blown off, saw him turn as he fell and start firing at another window.

In seconds it seemed I was the only person there who didn't have a weapon. I saw a Heinleiner crouched behind the gallows, snapping off shots with a handgun. His null-suit was turned on, coating him in silver. I saw him hit by a half a clip from an automatic rifle. He froze. I don't mean he stood still; he *froze,* like a chromium statue, toppled with bullets still whanging off of him, rolled over on his back, still in the same attitude. Then his null-suit switched off and he tried to get up, but was hit by three more bullets. His skin had turned lobster-red.

I didn't understand that, and I didn't have time to think about it. People were still running for cover, so I did, too, past overturned tables and chairs and the dead body of a King City policeman, into Aunt Hazel's shop. I scurried around and crouched behind the counter, intending to stay there until someone came to explain what the hell was going on.

But the itch is buried deep, and makes you do stupid things when you least expect it. If you've never been a reporter, you wouldn't understand. I raised my head and looked over the counter.

I can replay the tape from my holocam and say exactly what happened, in what order, who did what to whom, but you don't live it that way. You retain some very vivid impressions, in no particular order, with gaps between when you don't have any idea what happened. I saw people running. I saw people cut almost in half by lasers, ripped by bullets. I heard screams and shouts and explosions, and I smelled gunpowder and burning plastic. I suppose every battlefield has looked and sounded and smelled pretty much the same.

I couldn't see Libby, didn't know if he was dead or alive. He wasn't where he had fallen. I did see more cops and soldiers arriving from some of the feeder tunnels.

Something crashed through the windows in front, something large, and tumbled over the ice cream freezers there, turning one of them over. I crouched down, and when I looked up again there was the policewoman, Winston still attached to her arm, which was in danger of coming off.

It was a scene from hell. Crazed by pain, the woman was swinging her arm wildly, trying to get the dog to let go. Winston was having none of it. Bleeding from many cuts, he ignored everything but his inexorable grip. He'd been bred to grab a bull by the nose and never let go; a K.C. policewoman wasn't about to get free.

But now she was scrabbling for her holster, forgotten in her fear and panic. She got her gun out and aimed it toward the dog. Her first shot went wild, killing nothing but an ice cream freezer. The second shot hit Winston in the left hind leg, where it was thickest, and *still* the beast didn't let go. If anything, he fought all the harder.

Her last shot hit him in the belly. He went limp—everything but his jaw. Even in death he wasn't going to let go.

She took aim at his head, and then slumped over, passed out at last. It was probably for the best, because I think she would have blown her own arm off, the way she had the gun pointed.

Later, I felt sorry for her. At the time I was simply too confused to feel much of anything but fear. I mourned Winston later, too. He'd been trying to protect me, though I recall thinking at the time that he'd overreacted. She'd only been trying to handcuff me, hadn't she?

And what about the soldiers? It had looked to me as if the Heinleiners had fired the first shot. All sane reasoning would lead me to think that, if that first soldier hadn't been hit, this could all have ended peacefully at the jailhouse with a lot of lawyers arguing, charges brought, countersuits filed. I'd have been out on bail within a few hours.

Which was still what I'd have liked to have done, and would have, but any fool could see things had gone too far for that. If I stepped out waving a white flag I was pretty sure I'd be killed, apologies sent to the next of kin. So Hildy, I told myself, your first priority is to get *out* of here without getting shot. Let the lawyers sort it out later, when the bullets aren't flying.

With that end in mind, I started crawling toward the door. My intent was to stick my head out, low, and see what stood between me and the nearest exit. Which turned out to be a black boot planted solidly in the doorway, almost under my nose by the time I got there. I looked up the black-clad leg and into the menacing face of a soldier. He was pointing a weapon at me, some great bulky thing I thought might be a machine gun, whose muzzle looked wide enough to spit baseballs.

"I'm unarmed," I said.

"That's the way I like 'em," he said, and flipped up his visor with his thumb. There was something in his eyes I didn't like. I mean, beyond everything *else* I didn't like about the situation. Just a little touch of madness, I think.

He was a big man with a broad face entirely innocent of any evidence of thought. But now a thought *did* flicker behind those eyes, and his brow wrinkled.

"What's your name?"

"H . . . Helga Smith."

"Nah," he said, and dug into a pocket for a datapad, which he scanned with a thumb control until my lovely phiz smiled back at us. He returned the smile, but I didn't, because his smile was the worst news I'd had so far in a day filled with bad news. "You're Hildy Johnson," he said, "and you're on the death list so it don't matter what happens here, see?" And he started working on his belt, one-handed, the other hand keeping the gun pointed at my forehead.

I found myself getting detached from events. Maybe it was a reflex action, something to distance oneself from an abomination about to happen. Or maybe it was just too many things that couldn't be happening. *This can't be happening.* I'd silently shrieked it one too many times and now a mental numbness was setting in. I ought to be thinking of something to do. I ought to be talking to him, asking questions. Anything. Instead, I just sat there, squatting on my heels, and felt as if I'd like to go to sleep.

But my senses were heightened. They must have been, because with all the shooting going on outside (how could he *do* this in the middle of a war?), and over the scream of a dying compressor motor in the overturned freezer I was able to hear a voice from the grave. A *growl.*

The soldier didn't hear it, or maybe he was too busy. He had his pants down around his heels and he knelt in front of me and that's when I saw Winston, dragging his hind leg, bleeding from his gut, eyes filled with murder.

The man lowered himself over me.

I wanted Winston to bite him . . . well, you *know* where I wanted Winston to bite him. I got second best. The bulldog fastened on the soft flesh of the soldier's inner thigh. The man's leg jerked in pain, and he was flying over me. I grabbed the strap of his rifle as he went by.

He had strength and mass on his side, but there was the little matter of Winston. The dog had cut an artery. The soldier tried to wrestle his rifle away from me with one hand and pry Winston loose with the other and ended up doing both things badly. Blood was spraying everywhere. I was screaming. Not the big full scream you hear at the movies, and not a scream of rage, but a high-pitched scary thing I was powerless to stop.

Then I got one hand on the barrel of the rifle, and one hand on the stock, and fumbled for the trigger as he realized what was happening and gave up his struggle with Winston, concentrating on me. He got his hand over the barrel. Sadly for him, it was over the end of the barrel, and when I squeezed the trigger his hand wasn't there anymore. It wasn't anywhere anymore, but the air was full of a red mist.

The soldier never did stop fighting. I guess that's why they're soldiers. With Winston hanging from his leg, his pants around his ankles, missing a hand, he still came at me and I swung the rifle up and held the trigger down and didn't really see what happened next because on full auto-fire the weapon packed such a kick that I was knocked on my ass again, and when I opened my eyes he was mostly on the walls, except for bits here and there on the floor, and the one big piece still in Winston's mouth.

I could say I paused and reflected on the enormity of taking a human life, or how nauseated I was at the sight of his dismembered body. I did think of those things, and many others. But later. Much later. At that time my mind had collapsed on itself and was only large enough to hold a few thoughts, and only one of those at a time. First, I was going to get *out* of there. Second, anybody between me and getting out of there was going to have a Hildy-sized hole drilled right through his or her stinking carcass. I had killed, and by god I meant to keep on killing if that's what I had to do to get to safety.

"Winston. Here, boy." I got up on one knee and talked to him. I didn't know what to expect. Would he recognize me? Was he too far gone in bloodlust?

But after a final shake of the soldier's leg, he let go and came to me. He was dragging his hind leg and he was gut-shot, but still walking.

I will admit I don't know why I took him. I mean, I really don't. My holocam recorded the scene, but it doesn't tape thoughts. Mine weren't very organized just then. I remember thinking I sure as hell owed him. It also crossed my mind that I was probably safer with him than without him; he was one hell of a weapon. I prefer to think I thought those things in that order. I won't swear to it.

I scooped him up in one arm, holding the rifle in the other, and stuck my head around the corner. Nobody blew it off. Nobody seemed to be moving at all. The square was a lot smokier and there was still a lot of gunfire, but everyone seemed to have taken cover. I could do that, too, and wait for somebody to find me, or I could use the smoke to hide in, knowing I could easily stumble on someone *else* who was doing the same thing, and was a better shot than I was.

I don't know how you make a decision like that. I mean, I *made* it, but I don't recall weighing the pros and cons. I just looked around the corner, didn't see anybody, and then I was running.

Actually, running is a very generous word for what I did, with a dying dog tucked under one arm and a heavy weapon dangling from the other. And don't forget a belly the size of Phobos. Thank god holocams record only what you see, and not what you look like. That couldn't have been an image I'd like preserved for posterity.

My goal was the entrance to a corridor that led back toward the *Heinlein,* and I was about halfway there when someone behind me yelled "Halt!" in a firm and not-at-all-friendly voice, and things happened very fast . . . and I did everything right, even with all the things that went wrong.

I turned and kept backpedaling, slowly, and I dropped Winston (who uttered the only yelp of pain he made through his entire heroic ordeal— and I'm sorry, Winston, wherever you are). I saw it was a King City cop, and he was young, and he looked as scared as I was, and he carried a huge drilling laser, which was pointed at me.

"Drop your weapon," he said, and I said *Sorry, chum, this isn't personal,* only not out loud, and I pulled the trigger. Nothing happened, and it was then I noticed the blinking red light on this curved metal thingy that must have been the ammo clip, and which must have been saying *feed me!,* or words to that effect in gun-language, and understood why what I'd thought was a short burst had had such a cataclysmic effect on my would-be rapist. So I dropped the gun and I held up my hands, and I saw Winston making his last dash, hobbling across the ten meters or so that separated us, and I put my hands *out,* palms *up,* and I shouted *No!,* and I will swear in any court in the world that I *saw* the man's finger tightening on the trigger from ten meters away, with the muzzle wavering between me and Winston as if he couldn't decide which to shoot first. And I know this is flatly impossible, but I even thought I saw the light start to come out the end of the weapon in the same fraction of a second that I grabbed my null-suit control and twisted it *hard.*

I was dazzled by green light. For a few moments I was blind. When vision returned the world was full of multicolored incandescent balloons that drifted here and there, obscuring the world, popping like cartoon soap bubbles. I was sweating horribly inside my suit-field. It could have been worse. Outside the field, most everything seemed to be on fire.

About the only way you can go wrong with a laser is to shoot it at a mirror. You couldn't blame the cop for that. I hadn't been a mirror when he pulled the trigger; it was *that* close.

But he really should have let go a lot sooner.

Everywhere the beam hit me, it was reflected back, but because the human body is such a complex shape the reflected beam went all over the place. The resulting scorch line hit the walls in many places, melting plastic panels and starting fires behind them. It hit the cop at least three times. I think any of them would have been fatal without quick treatment. He was lying still, with flames engulfing his clothing in three deep, black slashes.

Somewhere in its wild gyrations the beam had hit Winston. His fur was on fire and he wasn't moving, either.

I was trying to think of what to do when a high wind rose. It briefly whipped the flames into a white-hot frenzy, but then it snuffed them out. All the smoke cleared in an instant and the scene took on that crisp clarity you find only in vacuum.

I turned, and ran for cover.

24

BIRTHS

I crouched in a pile of chrome-plated pipes not twenty meters from two patrolling figures in spacesuits, trying to pretend I was just another piece of bent pipe. I wasn't quite sure how to go about this. Don't move, and think tubular thoughts, I finally decided, and it had worked so far.

I was keeping one eye on the clock, one eye on the soldiers, and one eye on the blinking red light in my head-up display. Since this adds up to three eyes, you can imagine how busy I was. I was the busiest motionless person you ever saw. Or didn't see.

As if that weren't enough, I was calling every telephone number in my vast mental card file.

Forget those trivial inventions like fire, the wheel, the bow and arrow, the plow. Man didn't become truly civilized until Alex Bell uttered those immortal words, "Shit, Watson, I spilled acid all over my balls." Hiding there with my oxygen running out, my only hope of staying alive lay in getting some help over the telephone, and if it worked I resolved to light a candle every year on Mr. Bell's birthday.

My situation was dire, but it could have been worse. I could have been a member of the King City police dragooned (I later learned) into the first wave of the assault on Virginia City. In addition to the hazards of an armed populace, not to mention the meanest, gamest dog who ever lived, they had the added problem of not having pressure suits when the *second* wave, which attacked from the surface, began cutting the cables which brought power from the solar panels topside, which powered the null-fields which kept the air in.

That's what had happened just after I was lasered by the last cop. It was the air rushing out of the public square that had first fanned, then extinguished the flames on Winston's corpse.

It wasn't a blowout like the one at Nirvana, or I wouldn't be here to tell you about it. What we're used to in a blowout is a lot of air rushing through a relatively small hole. You get picked up and battered, then you get squeezed, and even in a null-suit your chances of survival are slim. But when a null-field goes, it goes all at once, and the air just expands. You get a gentle wind, then *poof!* Like a soap bubble. And then you get a lot of cops and soldiers grabbing their throats, spitting blood, and falling quietly to the ground. I saw two people die like this. I guess it's a fairly quick, peaceful way to go, but I still get nauseous just thinking about it.

At the time I thought the Heinleiners had done it. It was a logical tactic. It was the way they customarily fought fires, and god knows there were plenty of fires by the time the air went. And it just didn't make *sense* that their own people would cut the power, knowing the first group didn't have suits.

Well, it *was* their own people who did it, and it wasn't the only thing about the assault that didn't make sense. But I learned about that much later. Hiding there in the pipes all I knew was that a lot of people had tried to kill me, and a lot more were still trying. It had been a game of cat and mouse for about three hours since the null-field power went down.

The power loss had immediately turned the corridor I meant to travel to the *Heinlein* from a silvery cylinder into a borehole through eons of trash, just like the one I had traveled to lo those many weeks ago to enter this crazy funhouse in the first place. That was a damn good thing, because not long after the blowout I met the first of many pressure-suited people coming down the path in the other direction.

We didn't actually meet, which was another good thing, because he or she was carrying a laser just like the one that had almost fried me. I saw him (I'm going to say him, because all the soldiers were male and there was something in the way he moved) while he was still some distance from me, and I quickly melted into the wall. Or into where the wall had been, you see. There were thousands of gaps along the corridor large enough for even a pregnant woman to squeeze through.

Once into one of the gaps, however, you never knew what lay beyond. You had entered a world with no rational order to it, a three-dimensional random maze made of random materials, some of it locked in place by the pressure of other junk above it, some of it alarmingly unstable. In some of these hidey-holes you could slip through here and squeeze through there and swing across a gap in another place, like in a collapsed jungle gym. In others, two meters in and you found a cul-de-sac a rat would have found impassable. You never knew. There was simply no way to tell from the outside.

That first refuge was one of the shallow ones, so I had pressed myself against a flat surface and began learning the Zen of immobility. I had several things going for me. No need to hold my breath, since I was already doing that because of the null-suit. No need to be very quiet, because of the vacuum. And in the suit he *might* not have seen me if I'd been lying right in his path.

I told myself all those things, but I still aged twenty years as he crept by, swinging his laser left and right, close enough that I could have reached out and touched him.

Then he had passed, and it started getting very dark again. (Did I mention all the lights went out when the power failed? They did. I'd never have seen him if he hadn't been carrying a flashlight.)

I wanted that flashlight. I wanted it more than anything in the world. Without it, I didn't see how I'd ever make it to safety. It had already gotten dark enough that I could barely see the useless rifle I'd carried with me, and wouldn't see anything at all when he'd moved a little farther along.

I almost jumped out of my skin when I realized he could have seen the flashing red light on the empty clip as he passed; I'd forgotten to cover it up. If only I had another . . . then I looked more closely at the clip. It had an opening at the end, and a brass shell casing gleamed in there. I realized it was *two* clips taped together. The idea was to reverse it when you'd used up the first. God, soldiers are tricky bastards.

So I reversed it, almost dropping first the clip, then the rifle, and I leaned out into the corridor and squeezed off a shot in the direction the soldier had come from to see if the damn thing worked. From the recoil I felt, I knew it did. I hadn't counted on the muzzle flash, but apparently the man didn't see it.

Stepping out into the corridor, I fired a short burst into the soldier's back. Hey, even if I *could* have shouted a warning to him in vacuum, I really don't think I would have. You don't know the depths you can sink to when all you're thinking about is survival.

His suit was tough, and my aim was not the best. One round hit him and it didn't puncture his suit, just sent him stumbling down the path, turning, bringing his weapon up, so I fired again, a lot longer this time, and it did the trick.

I won't describe the mess I had to sort through to find his light.

My fusillade had destroyed his laser and used up my last ammo clip, so encumbered with only the flashlight and what remained of my wits I set out looking for air.

That was the trick, of course. The null-suit was a great invention, no doubt about it. It had saved my life. But it left something to be desired in the area of endurance. If a Heinleiner wanted to spend much time in vacuum he'd strap a tank onto his back, just like everyone else, and attach a hose to the breast fitting in front. Without a strap-on, the internal tank was good for twenty to thirty-five minutes, depending on exertion. Forty minutes at the outside. Like, for instance, if you were asleep.

I hadn't done much sleeping and didn't plan on any soon, but I hadn't thought it would be a problem at first. All of the corridors were provided with an ALU every half-kilometer or so. The power to these had been cut, but they still had big air tanks which should still be full. Recharging my internal tank should be just a matter of hooking the little adapter hose to my air fitting, twisting a valve, and watching the little needle in my head-up swing over to the FULL position.

The first time, it *was* that easy. But I could see even then that having to search out an ALU every half hour was the weakest point in my not-very-strong survival strategy. I couldn't keep it up endlessly. I had to either get out of there on my own or call for help.

Calling seemed to make the most sense. I still had no idea what was happening beyond the limits of Heinlein Town, but had no reason to suspect that if I could get through to a lawyer, or to the pad, my problems would not be over. But I couldn't call from the corridor. There was too much junk over my head; the signal would not get through. However, through sheer luck or divine providence I was in one of the corridors I was fairly familiar with. A branch up to the left should take me right out onto the surface.

It did, and the surface was crawling with soldiers.

I ducked back in, thankful for the mirror camouflage I was wearing. Where had they all *come* from?

There were not regiments, or divisions, or anything like that. But I could see three from my hiding place, and they seemed to be patrolling except for one who was standing around near the entrance I'd just exited. Guarding it, I presumed. Perhaps he just meant to take captives, but I'd seen people shooting to kill and wanted no part of finding out his intentions.

One of the other things I'd been lucky about was in seeing the man in the square who'd been hit by bullets while wearing his null-suit. Otherwise I might have wrongly concluded the suit, through which nothing could pass, could render me immune to bullets. Which it *would* . . . but only at a cost.

This was explained to me later. Maybe you already figured it out; Smith said "as should be intuitively obvious," but he talks like that.

Bullets possess kinetic energy. When you stop one dead in its tracks, that energy has to go somewhere. Some of it is transferred to your body: e.g., the bullet knocks you over. But most of the energy is absorbed by the suit, which promptly freezes stiff, and then has to *do* something with all that energy. There's no place to store it in the null-generator. Smith tried that, and the generators overheated or, in extreme cases, exploded. Not a pretty thought, considering where it's implanted.

So what the field does is radiate the heat away. From *both* surfaces of the field.

"I'm sure it's a symmetry we can defeat, given time," Smith told me. "The math is tricky. But what a bulletproof jacket it will make, eh?"

It sure would. In the meantime, what happened is you got parboiled. Getting rid of excess heat was *already* your biggest problem in a null-suit. You could survive one hit in a suit (several people did), but usually only if you could turn it off pretty quickly and cool yourself. With two or more hits your internal temperature would soar and your brain would cook.

The suit was supposed to turn itself off in that case, automatically. But naturally it wouldn't turn off if there was vacuum outside. It won't do that no matter *how* extreme conditions inside got; vacuum is always the worst of any set of evils.

If I got shot now, I'd cook, from the skin inwards.

I didn't start *out* singing hosannas to the name of A.G. Bell. For the first hour I wanted to dig him up and roast him slowly. Not his fault, of course, but in the state I was in, who cared?

After filling my tank again I made my way to the top of the junk pile. This was possible—though by no means easy—because where I was, near the *Heinlein,* the thickness of the planetary dump was not great. By squirming, making myself small, picking my way carefully I was soon able to stick my head out of the mess. Any of a thousand passing satellites ought to have a good line of sight at me from there, so I started dialing as fast as my tongue could hit the switchboard on the insides of my teeth. I figured I'd call Cricket, because he . . .

. . . could not be reached at that number. According to my head-up, which is seldom wrong about these things. Neither could Brenda, or Liz. I was about to try another number when I finally realized *nobody* could be reached, because my internal phone relied, when out on the surface, on a booster unit that's standard equipment in a pressure suit.

How could I be expected to *think* of these things? You tap your teeth, and pretty soon you hear somebody's voice in your ear. That's how a fucking telephone *works.* It's as natural as shouting.

I sure as hell thought about it then, and soon realized I had another problem. The signal from my phone wouldn't get through my null-suit field. The Heinleiners used the field itself to generate a signal in another wave band entirely, so they could communicate with each other, suit-to-suit, and nobody, not even the CC, could overhear them. I was screwed by their security.

I thought about this a long time, keeping one eye on the oxygen gauge. Then I went back to the dark corridor and sneaked up on the body of the man I had killed.

He was still there, though shoved over to one side of the passage. I managed to get his helmet off and lose myself back in the maze, where I used my light and a few bits of metal that came to hand to pry out what I hoped was the booster for his suit radio. I had done my work better than I knew; there was a bullet hole punched through it.

I held on to it anyway. I got another charge of air and went back to the surface, where I used a length of wire to connect my pressure fitting to the radio itself, on the theory that this was the only way for *anything* to get out of the suit. I switched it on, was rewarded with a little red light going on in a display on the radio. I dialed Cricket again, and got nothing.

So I brought all my vast and subtle technological skills to bear on repairing the radio. Translation: I *whanged* the sumbitch on the dashboard of the junk rover I was sitting in, and I dialed again. Nothing. *Whang.* Still not a peep. So I *WHANGED* it again and Cricket said "Yeah, what the hell do you want?"

My tongue had been leading a life of its own, nervously dialing and redialing Cricket's number as I worked my engineering magic on the radio. And now, when I needed it, I couldn't get the damn tongue to work at all, so overwhelmed was I at hearing a familiar voice.

"I haven't got time to dick around here," Cricket warned.

"Cricket, it's me, Hildy, and I—"

"Yeah, Hildy, you cover it your way and I'll cover it mine."

"Cover what?"

"Just the biggest damn story that ever . . ." I heard the sound of mental brakes being applied with the burning of much mental rubber; after the clashing of mental gears Cricket said, sweetly, "No story, Hildy. Nothing at all. Forget I said anything."

"Damn it, Cricket, is the shit coming down out there, *too*? What's happened? All I know is—"

"You can figure it out for yourself, just like I did," he said.

"Figure *what* out? I don't know what you're—"

"Sure, sure, I know. It won't work, Hildy. You've conned me out of a big story for the last time."

"Cricket, I don't even *work* for the *Nipple* anymore."

"Once a reporter, always a reporter. It's in your blood, Hildy, and you could no more ignore this one than a whore could keep her legs together when the doorbell rings."

"Cricket, listen to me, I'm in big trouble. I'm trapped—"

"Ah *ha!*" he crowed, confusing me completely. "A *lot* of folks are trapped, old buddy. I think it's the best place for you. Read about it in a few hours in the *Shit.*" And he hung up.

I almost threw the radio out across the horizon, but sanity returned just in time. With it came caution, as my eyes, following the would-be trajectory, saw two figures clambering up the junk. They were headed for me, probably on the scent of my transmission. I ducked over the side of the junked rover and dived back into the maze.

I still haven't entirely forgiven Cricket, but I've got to say that love died during that phone call. Sure, I deserved some of it; I'd tricked him often enough in the past. And in his defense, he thought I was trapped in an elevator, as thousands of Lunarians were at that moment, and he didn't think I'd be in any particular danger, and if I *was,* there wasn't anything he could have done about it.

Yeah, sure. And your momma would have fucked pigs, Cricket, if she could have found any who'd have her. You didn't give me time to *explain.*

What really high-gravved me was that, when I finally got back in position to call him again, he'd set his phone to refuse calls from me. I risked my neck, ducking in for more air, then finding a new place to transmit from, and what I got for my efforts was a busy signal.

I got a lot of those in quick succession. Brenda didn't answer. Neither did anybody at the *Nipple,* which worried me no end. Think about it. A major metropolitan newspad, and *nobody's answering the phone?*

I knew it had to do with the big story Cricket mentioned. Impossible visions flitted through my head, from a city-wide blowout to thousands upon thousands of soldiers, like the ones I'd seen, laying waste to the whole planet.

But I had to keep trying. So I went back down into the maze and sought out my favorite airing hole. And two big guys in suits were camped out there, weapons ready.

I'd had ten minutes of air when I first backed into the pile of chrome pipes to hide from the soldiers. That had been seven minutes earlier.

The first thing I'd done was cut back the oxygen dissemination rate in my artificial lung to a level just short of unconsciousness. Ditto the cooling rate. I figured that would stretch the ten minutes into fifteen if I didn't have to move around too much. So far I hadn't moved at all. The blinking red light I was watching was telling me my blood oxygen level was low. Another gauge, normally dormant, had lit up as well, and this one assured me my body temperature stood at 39.1 degrees and was rising slowly. I knew I couldn't take much more without becoming delirious; anything over forty was dangerous territory.

I'm a miserable tactician, I'll admit it, at least in a situation like that. I could see the elements of the problem, but all I could do was stew about it. Those guys topside, for instance. Could they communicate my position to the gorillas guarding the air tank? They were no more than thirty meters above me; if they had any kind of generalship at all a message would soon be arriving to the guards to be on the lookout for a roly-poly, out-of-breath football trophy, known to associate with lengths of chrome-plated pipe.

If so, what could I do about it? There was no hope of making my way through the maze to the next air station—which might well be guarded, anyway. So if these guys didn't find somewhere else to go in the next eight minutes, it was going to be a dead heat (*terrible* choice of words there) as to whether I died of suffocation or boiled in my own sweat. I didn't really have a preference in the matter; it's something only a coroner could care about.

Brenda Starr, comic-strip reporter, would surely have thought up some clever ruse, some diversion, something to lure those freaking soldiers away from the air tank long enough for her to refuel. Hildy Johnson, scared-shitless schoolteacher and former inkster, didn't have the first notion of how to go about it without drawing attention to herself.

There was one bit of good news in the mix. My tongue had continued its independent ways as I crouched in hiding, and soon I was startled by the sound of a busy signal in my ear. I didn't even know who I'd called, much less how the signal got out. I eventually surmised (and later found out it was true) that something in the junk pile was acting as an antenna, relaying my calls to the surface, and thence to a satellite.

So I tried Brenda again (still no answer), and the *Nipple* (still nothing), and then I dialed Liz.

"Buckingham Palace, Her Majesty speaking," came a slurred voice.

"Liz, Liz, this is Hildy. I'm in big trouble."

There was a long, somehow boozy silence. I wondered if she'd fallen asleep. Then there was a sob.

"Liz? Are you still there?"

"Hildy. Hildy. Oh, god, I didn't want to do it."

"Didn't want to do what? Liz, I don't have time for—"

"I'm a drunk, Hildy. A goddam drunk."

This was neither news, nor a well-kept secret. I didn't say anything, but listened to the sound of wracking sobs and watched the seconds tick off on my personal clock and waited for her to talk.

"They said they could put me away for a long time, Hildy. A long, *long* time. I was scared, and I felt really awful. I was shaking and I was throwing up, only nothing came up, and they wouldn't let me have a drink."

"What are you talking about? Who's 'they'?"

"They, *they,* dammit! The CC."

By then I had more or less figured it out. She stammered disconnected parts to me then, and I learned the complete story later, and it went something like this:

Even before the Bicentennial celebration Liz had been firmly in the employ of the CC. At some point she had been arrested, taken in, and charged with many counts of weapons violations. (So were a lot of others; the invasion of Heinlein Town had been armed with weapons confiscated during a huge crackdown—an event that never made the news.)

"They said I could go to jail for eighty years, Hildy. And then they left me alone, and the CC spoke to me and told me if I did a few little things for him, here and there, the charges might be dropped."

"What happened, Liz? Did you get careless?"

"What? Oh, I don't *know,* Hildy. They never showed me the evidence they had against me. They said it would all come out in the trial. I don't know if it was obtained illegally or not. But when the CC started talking I figured out pretty quick that it didn't *matter.* We talked about that; you know, if he ever wanted to, he could frame every person on Luna for something or other. All I could see was when we got to court, it'd be an airtight case. I was afraid to let it get that far."

"So you sold me out."

There was silence for a long time. A few more minutes had gone by. The guards hadn't moved. There wasn't anything else to do but listen.

"Tell me the rest of it," I said.

It seemed there was this group of people out around Delambre that the CC wanted to know more about. He suggested Liz get me out there and see what happened.

I should have been flattered. The CC's estimate of my bloodhound instincts must have been pretty high. I suppose if I hadn't seen anything during that first trip, something else would have been arranged, until I was on the scent. After that, I could be relied on to bring the story to ground.

"He was real interested when you brought in that tape of the little girl. I . . . by that time I was a wholly-owned subsidiary, Hildy. I told him I could find some way of getting you to tell me what was going on. I'd have done about anything by then."

"The hostage syndrome," I said. The guards were still there.

"What? Oh. Yeah, probably. Or sheer lack of character. Anyway, he told me to hold back or you'd get suspicious. So I did, and you finally invited me in."

And on that first visit she'd stolen a null-field generator. She didn't say how, but it probably wasn't too hard. They're not dangerous unless you try to open them up.

I could put the rest of it together myself. During the next week the CC had learned enough null-field technology to make something to get his troops through the barriers, if not to equip them with null-suits or fields of their own.

"And that's pretty much it," she said, and sighed. "So I guess he arrested you, and probably all those other folks, too, right? Where have they got you? Have they set bail yet?"

"Are you serious?"

"Hell, Hildy, I don't think he could have anything serious on you."

"Liz . . . what's going on out there?"

"What do you mean?"

"Cricket said all hell was breaking loose, somehow or other."

"You got me, Hildy. I was just . . . ah, sleeping, until you called. I'm here in my apartment. Come to think of it, the lights are flickering. But that could be just my head."

She was in the dark as much as I was. A lot of people were. If you didn't leave your apartment and you didn't live in one of the sectors where the oxygen service was interrupted, the chances of your having missed the early stages of the Big Glitch were excellent. Liz had been in an alcoholic stupor, with her phone set to take calls only from me.

"Liz. Why?"

There was a long pause. Then, "Hildy, I'm a *drunk.* Don't ever trust a drunk. If it comes to a choice between you and the next drink . . . it's not really a choice."

"Ever thought of taking the cure?"

"Babe, I *like* drinking. It's the only thing I *do* like. That, and Winston."

Maybe I would have hit her right in the belly at that point; I don't know. I know I was filled with rage at her. Telling her the dog was fried and vac-dried wouldn't have begun to get back at her for what she'd done to me.

But just then I suddenly got real, real hot. I'd already been too warm, you understand; now, in an instant, my skin was so hot I wanted to peel it off and there was a burning ache on the left side of my chest.

The null-suit did what it could. I watched in growing alarm as the indicator that had been telling me how many minutes I had to live took a nosedive. I thought it wasn't going to stop. Hell, it was almost worth it. With the falling gauge came a cooling blast of air all over my body. At least I wasn't going to fry.

I'd finally put together what was happening, though. For almost a minute I'd been feeling short, sharp shocks through the metal pipes I leaned against and the metal brace I had my feet on. Then I *saw* a bullet hit a pipe. That's the only thing it could have been, I reasoned. It left a dent, a dull place on the metal. Somebody was standing on top of the junk pile and shooting down into it at random. It had to be blind shooting, because I couldn't see the shooter. But the bullets were ricocheting and one had finally struck me. I couldn't afford another hit.

So I grabbed a length of pipe and started toward the corridor. I didn't think I could do much good against the tough pressure suits, but if I swung for the faceplates I might get one of them, and at least I'd go down fighting. I owed it to Winston, if to no one else, to do that much.

Getting to the corridor was like reaching for that top step that isn't there. I stepped out, pipe cocked like the cleanup batter coming to the plate. And nobody was there.

I saw their retreating backs outlined by the light of their helmet lamps. They were jogging toward the exit.

I'll never know for sure, but it seems likely they'd been summoned to the top to help in the search for me. How were they to know the guys on top of the pile were only a few meters directly above them? Anyway, if they'd stayed in place, I'd have been dead in ninety seconds, tops. So I gave them ten seconds to get beyond the point where they could possibly see me, and I reached for the ALU adaptor hose.

It wasn't there.

It made me mad. I couldn't think of anything more foolish than getting this close to salvation and then suffocating with about a ton of compressed oxygen at my fingertips. I slammed my hand against the tank, then got my flashlight and cast about on the ground. I was sure they'd taken it with them. It's what I would have done, in their place.

But they hadn't. It was lying right there on the ALU's baseplate, probably knocked off when one of the guards decided to rest his fat ass on the tank. I fumbled it in place between the tank and my chest valve, and turned the release valve *hard*.

I make my living with words. I respect them. I always want to use the proper one, so I searched a long time for the right one to describe how that first rush of cooling air felt, and I concluded nobody's made up a word for that yet. Think of the greatest pleasure you ever experienced, and use whatever word you'd use to describe that. An orgasm was a pale thing beside it.

Why hadn't they taken the connector hose? The answer, when I eventually learned it, was simple, and typical of the Big Glitch. They hadn't known I needed it.

The cops and soldiers who had invaded Heinlein Town hadn't been told much about anything. They hadn't been led to expect armed resistance. They knew next to nothing about the nature of or limitations to null-suit technology. They *surely* hadn't been told there were two groups, working at cross purposes to the extent that one group would ensure the destruction of the other. All this affected their tactics terribly. A lot of people lived because of this confusion, and I was one of them. I'd like to take credit for my own survival—and not *everything* I did was stupid—but the fact is that I had Winston, and I had a lot of luck, and the luck was mostly generated by their ignorance and poor generalship.

I had vaguely realized some of this by the time I made my way from the ALU and to a branching corridor I thought would take me to a different surface exit. I didn't know what good it would do me, but it was worthwhile to keep it in mind.

Once on the surface again, I called the *Nipple* and again got a busy signal, all the time keeping my eyes open for more of the bad guys. I was hoping they were all up atop the junk, possibly stumbling around and breaking legs, heads, and other important body parts. I wished Callie were there; she'd have put a hex on them.

Callie? Well, what the hell. I had to dredge the number up from the further reaches of my memory, and it did no good at all. Not even a busy signal. Nothing but dead air.

Then I remembered the top code. Why did it take me so long? I think it was because Walter really had impressed it on me that the code was not to be used at all, that it existed as an unachievable level of dire perfection. A story justifying the use of the top code would need headlines that would make 72-point type seem like fine print. The other reason is that I had never thought of what was happening to me as a *story*.

I didn't really expect much from it, to tell the truth. I'd been using my normal access code to the *Nipple*, and that should have gotten through any conceivable logjam of calls and directly into Walter's office. So far it had yielded only busy signals. But I punched in the code anyway, and Walter said:

"Don't tell me where you are, Hildy. Hang up and move as far from your present position as you dare, and then call me back."

"Walter!" I screamed. But the line was already dead.

It would be nice to report that I immediately did as he said, that I wasted no time, that I continued to show the courageous resolve that had been my trademark since the first shots were fired. By that I mean that I hadn't cried to that point. I did now. I wept helplessly, like a baby.

Don't try this in your null-suit, when you get one. You don't breathe, so your lungs just sort of spasm. It's enough to make your ears pop. Crying also throws the regulator mechanism out of whack, so that I wasted ten minutes' oxygen in three minutes of hysterics. Trust Mister V.M. Smith not to have reckoned with emotional outbursts when he laid out the parameters.

I had cleverly retained the connector hose to the air tank, so I made my way back there and filled up again. If only I could find a loose, portable tank I'd be able to strike off across the surface. Hell, if it was too big to carry I could *drag* it. Did I hear someone mention the dead soldier and his suit? Great idea, but my uncanny accuracy with the machine gun had damaged one of the hose fittings. I checked when I borrowed the flashlight, and again—because I *needed* the air, and who knows, maybe I'd been mistaken—when I salvaged the radio. Libby could probably have fudged some sort of adaptor from the junk all around me, but considering the pressure in that tank I'd sooner have kissed a rattlesnake.

These are the thoughts that run through your mind in the exhausted aftermath of a crying jag. It felt good to have done it, like crying usually does. It swept away the building sense of panic and let me concentrate on the things that needed to be done, let me ignore the impossibility of my position, and enabled me to concentrate on the two things I had going for me, like chanting a mantra: my own brain, which, no matter how much evidence I may have adduced to the contrary, was actually pretty good; and Walter's ability to get things done, which was *very* good.

I actually found myself feeling cheerful as I reached the egress again and scanned the surface for enemies. Not finding any made me positively giddy. Move from your present position, Walter had said. As far as you dare.

I moved out of the maze and dashed across a short strip of sunlight and into the shadow of the *Heinlein*.

"Hello, Walter?"
"Tell me what you know, Hildy, and make it march."
"I'm in big trouble here, Wal—"
"I know that, Hildy. Tell me what I don't know. What happened?"

So I started in on a condensed history of me and the Heinleiners, and Walter promptly interrupted me again. He knew about them, he said. What else? Well, the CC was up to something horrible, I said, and he said he knew that, too.

"Assume I know everything you know except what happened to you today, Hildy," he said. "Tell me about today. Tell me about the last hour. Just the important parts. But don't mention specific names or places."

Put that way, it didn't take long. I told him in less than a hundred words, and could have done it in one: *"Help!"*

"How much air do you have?" he asked.

"About fifteen minutes."

"Better than I thought. We have to set up a rendezvous, without mentioning place names. Any ideas?"

"Maybe. Do you know the biggest white elephant on Luna?"

". . . yeeeesss. Are you near the trunk or the tail?"

"Trunk."

"All right. The last poker game we played, if the high card in my hand was a king, start walking north. If it was a queen, east. Jack, south. Got it?"

"Yeah." East it would be.

"Walk for ten minutes and stop. I'll be there."

With anyone else I'd have wasted another minute pointing out that only left me a margin of five minutes and no hope at all of getting back. With Walter I just said, "So will I." Walter has many despicable qualities, but when he says he'll do something, he'll do it.

I'd have had to move soon, anyway. As we were talking I'd spotted two of the enemy moving across the plain in big, loping strides. They were coming from the north, so I hefted the radio and tossed it toward the southeast. They immediately altered direction to follow it.

Here came the hard part. I watched them pass in front of me. Even in a regular suit I'd have been hard to spot in the shadows. But now I started walking eastwards, and in a moment I stepped out into the bright sunshine. I had to keep reminding myself how hard Gretel had been to spot when I'd first encountered her. I'd never felt so naked. I kept an eye on the soldiers, and when they reached the spot where the radio had fallen to the ground I froze, and watched as they scanned the horizon.

I didn't stay frozen long, as I quickly spotted four more people coming from various directions. It was one of the hardest things I ever did, but I started walking again before any of them could get too close.

With each step I thought of a dozen more ways they could find me and catch me. A simple radar unit would probably suffice. I'm not much at physics, but I supposed the null-suit would throw back a strong signal.

They must not have had one, because before long I was far enough away that I couldn't pick any of them out from the ground glare, and if I couldn't see them they sure as hell couldn't see me.

At the nine-minute point a bright silver jumper swooped silently over my head, not ten meters high, and I'd have jumped out of my socks if I'd had any on. It turned, and I saw the big double-N *Nipple* logo blazoned on its side and it was a sweet sight indeed.

The driver flew a big oval at the right distance from the *Heinlein*, which was almost out of sight by then, letting me see him because I had to come to him, not the other way around. Then it settled down off to my right, looking like a giant mosquito in carnal embrace with a bedstead. I started to run.

He must have had some sort of sensor on the ladder, because when I had both feet on it the jumper lifted off. Not the sort of maneuver I'd like to do on a Sunday jaunt, but I could understand his haste. I wrenched the lock door open and cycled it, and stepped inside to the unlikely spectacle of Walter training a machine gun on me.

Ho-hum. I'd had so many weapons pointed at me in the last few hours that the sight—which would have given me pause a year ago, say at contract renegotiation time—barely registered. I experienced something I'd noticed before at the end of times of great stress: I wanted to go to sleep.

"Put that thing away, Walter," I said. "If you fire it you'd probably kill us both."

"This is a reinforced pressure hull," he said, and the gun didn't waver. "Turn that suit off first."

"I wasn't thinking about decompression," I said. "I was thinking you'd probably shoot yourself in the foot, then get lucky and hit me." But I turned it off, and he looked at my face, glanced down at my naked, outrageously pregnant body, and then looked away. He stowed the weapon and resumed his place in the pilot's seat. I struggled into the seat beside him.

"Pretty eventful day," I said.

"I wish you'd get back to covering the news instead of making it," he said. "What'd you do to get the CC so riled up?"

"That was me? This is all about me?"

"No, but you're a big part of it."

"Tell me what's happening."

"Nobody knows the whole thing yet," he said, and then started telling me the little he knew.

It had begun—back in the normal world—with thousands of elevators stalling between levels. No sooner had emergency crews been dispatched than other things began to go haywire. Soon all the mass media were off the air and Walter had had reports that pressure had been breached in several major cities, and other places had suffered oxygen depletion. There were fires, and riots, and mass confusion. Then, shortly before he got the call from me, the CC had come on most major frequencies with an announcement meant to reassure but which was oddly unsettling. He said there had been malfunctions, but that they were under control now. ("An obvious lie," Walter told me, almost with relish.) The CC had pledged to do a better job in the future, promised this wouldn't happen again. He'd said he was in control now.

"The first implication I got from that," Walter said, "was that he *hadn't* been in control for a while, and I want an explanation of that. But the thing that really got me, after I thought about it, was . . . what kind of control did he mean?"

"I'm not sure I understand."

"Well, obviously he's in *control*, or he's supposed to be. Of the day-to-day mechanics of Luna. Air, water, transportation. In the sense that he *runs* those things. And he's got a lot of control in the civil and criminal social sectors. He makes schedules for the government, for instance. He's got a *hand* in *everything*. He monitors everything. But *in* control? I didn't like the sound of it. I still don't."

While I thought that one over something very bright and very fast overtook us, shot by on the left, then tried to hang a right, as if it had changed its mind. It turned into a fireball and we flew right into it. I heard things pinging on the hull, things the size of sand grains.

"What the hell was *that?*"

"Some of your friends back there. Don't worry, I'm on top of it."

"On *top* of it . . . ? They're *shooting* at us!"

"And missing. And we're out of range. And this ship is equipped with the best illegal jamming devices money can buy. I've got tricks I haven't even used yet."

I glanced at him, a big unruly bear of a man, hunched over his manual controls and keeping one eye on an array of devices attached to the dashboard, devices I was sure hadn't come from the factory that built the jumper.

"I might have known you'd have connections with the Heinleiners," I said.

"Connections?" he snorted. "I was on the board of directors of the L5 Society when most of those 'Heinleiners' hadn't even been born yet. My father was there when the keel of that ship was launched. You might say I have connections."

"But you're not one of them."

"Let's say we have some political differences."

He probably thought they were too left-wing. Long ago in our relationship I'd talked a little politics with Walter, as most people did who came to work at the *Nipple*. Not many had a second conversation. The most charitable word I'd heard used to describe his convictions was "daft." What most people would think of as anarchy Walter would call a social straitjacket.

"Don't care for Mister Smith?" I asked.

"Great scientist. Too bad he's a socialist."

"And the starship project?"

"It'll get there the day they return to the original plan. Plus about twenty years to rebuild it, tear out all the junk Smith has installed."

"Pretty impressive junk."

"He makes a great spacesuit. He hasn't shown me a stardrive."

I decided to leave it at that, because I had no intention of getting into an argument with him, and because I had no way of telling if he was right or wrong.

"Guns, too," I said. "If I'd thought about it, I'd have known you'd be a gun owner."

"All free men are gun owners." No use pointing out to him that I'd been unfree most of my life, and what I'd tried to do with the instrument of my freedom when I finally obtained one. It's another argument you can't win.

"Did you get that one from Liz?"

"She gets her guns from *me,*" he said. "Or she did until recently. She's too far gone in drink now. I don't trust her." He glanced at me. "You shouldn't either."

I decided not to ask him what he knew about that. I hoped that if he had known Liz was selling out the Heinleiners he'd have given them some kind of warning, political differences or not. Or at least that he'd have warned me, given all he seemed to know about my recent activities.

I never did ask him that.

There are a lot of things I might have asked him during the time we raced across the plain, never getting more than fifty meters high. If I'd asked some of them—about how much he knew about what was going on with the CC—it would have saved me a lot of worry later. Actually, it would have just given me different things to worry about, but I firmly believe I do a better *job* of worrying when I can fret from a position of knowledge. As it was, the sense of relief at being rescued by him was so great that I simply basked in the warmth of my newfound sense of safety.

How was I to know I'd only have ten minutes with him?

He'd been constantly monitoring his instruments, and when one of them chimed he cursed softly and hit the retros. We started to settle to the ground. I'd been about to doze off.

"What's the matter?" I said. "Trouble?"

"Not really. I'd just hoped to get a little closer, that's all. This is where you get off."

"Get off? Gee, Walter, I think I'd rather go on to your place." I'd had a quick glance around. This place, wherever it was, would never make it into *1001 Lunar Sights To See.* There was no sign of human habitation. No sign of anything, not even a two-century-old footpath.

"I'd love to have you, Hildy, but you're too hot to handle." He turned in his seat to face me. "Look, baby, it's like this. I got access to a list of a few hundred people the CC is looking for. You're right at the top. From what I've learned, he's *very* determined to find them. A lot of people have died in the search. I don't know what's going on—some really big glitch—but I *do* intend to find out . . . but you can't help me. The only thing I could think of to do is stash you some place where the CC can't find you. You'll have to stay there until all this blows over. It's too dangerous for you on the outside."

I guess I just blew air there for a while. There had been too many changes too quickly. I'd been feeling safe and now the rug was jerked out from under me again.

I'd known the CC was looking for me, but somehow it felt different to hear it from Walter. Walter would never be wrong about a thing like that. And it didn't help to infer from what he'd said that what the CC meant to do when he *found* me was *kill* me. Because I knew too much? Because I'd stuck my nose in the wrong place? Because he didn't want to share the super-toothpaste royalties with me anymore? I had no idea, but I wanted to know more, and I meant to, before I got out of Walter's jumper.

Walter, who'd just called me baby. What the hell was *that* all about?

"What do you want me to do?" I asked. "Just camp out here on the maria? I'm afraid I didn't bring my tent."

He reached behind his seat and started pulling out things and handing them to me. A ten-hour air bottle. A flashlight. A canvas bag that rattled. He slapped a compass into my palm, and opened the air lock door behind us.

"There's some useful stuff in the bag," he said. "I didn't have time to get any more; this is my own survival gear. Now you've got to go."

"I'm not."

"You *are.*" He sighed, and looked away from me. He looked very old.

"Hildy," he said, "this isn't easy for me, either, but I think it's your only chance. You'll have to trust me because there isn't time to tell you any more and there isn't time for you to panic or act like a child. I wanted to get you closer, but this is probably better." He pointed at the dashboard. "Right now we're invisible, I hope. You get out now, the CC will never figure out where you went. I get you any closer, and it'll be like drawing him a map. You have enough air to get there, but we don't have any more time to talk, because I've got to lift out of here within one more minute."

"Where do you want me to go?"

He told me, and if he'd said anything else I don't think I'd have gotten out of the jumper. But it made just enough sense, and he sounded just scared enough. Hell, Walter sounding scared at *all* was a new one on me, and did not fail to make an impression.

But I was still balanced there on the edge, wondering if he'd force me if I simply stayed put, when he grabbed me by the neck and pulled me over to him and kissed me on the cheek. I was too surprised to struggle.

He let me go immediately, and turned away.

"You . . . ah, are you due soon? Will that be——"

"Another ten days yet," I told him. "It won't be a problem." Or it shouldn't be, unless . . . "Unless you think I'll have to hide for——"

"I don't think so," he said. "I'll try to contact you in three days. In the meantime, keep your head down. Don't try to contact *anyone*. Stay a week, if you have to. Stay nine days."

"On the tenth I'm damn sure coming out," I told him.

"I'll have something else by then," he promised. "Now go."

I stepped into the lock, cycled it, felt the null-suit switch itself on. I climbed down onto the plain and watched the jumper leap into the sky and dwindle toward the horizon.

Before I even strapped on the backpack bottle I reached up and felt Walter's tear still warm on my cheek.

I'm not sure how far Walter dropped me from my final destination. Something on the order of twenty, thirty kilometers. I didn't think it would be a problem.

I covered the first ten in the long, side-legged stride that Earth-bred leg muscles can produce in Lunar gravity, the gait that, except for bicycles, is the most energy-efficient transportation known to man. And if you think you can eat up the distance that way in an ordinary pressure suit, try it in a null-suit. You practically fly.

But don't do it pregnant. Before long my tummy started feeling funny, and I slowed down, doing nervous calculations about oxygen and distance as I began to get into territory that looked familiar to me.

I reached the old air lock with three hours of spare air, dead on my feet. I think I actually catnapped a few times there, waking up only as I was about to fall on my face, consulting the compass as I wiped my eyes, getting back on the proper bearing. Luckily, by the time that started happening I was on ground I knew.

I had a bad moment when the lock didn't seem to want to cycle for me. Could it be this place had been sealed off in the last seventy years? It had been that long since I used it. Of course, there were other locks I knew in the area, but Walter had said it was too dangerous to use them. But use them I would, rather than die out here on the surface. It was with that thought that the cantankerous old machinery finally engaged and the lock drum rotated. I stepped inside, cycled, and hurried into the elevator, which deposited me in a little security cubicle. I punched the letters M-A-R-I-A-X-

X-X. Somewhere not too far away, an old lady would be noting the door was in use. If Walter was right, that information would *not* be relayed on to the Central Computer.

There's no place like home, I thought, as I stepped into the dimness and familiar rotten odor of a Cretaceous rain forest.

I was in a distant corner of the dino-ranch where I had grown up. Callie's ranch. It had always been hers, the Double-C Bar brand, never a thought of the C&M or anything like that. Not that I'd wanted it, but it would have been nice to feel like more than a hired hand. Now let's not get into that.

But this particular corner—and I wondered how Walter had known this—I'd always thought of as Maria's Cavern. There really was a cave in it, just a few hundred meters from where I now stood, and I had made it into my playhouse when I was very young and still known as Maria Cabrini.

So it was to Maria's Cavern I now went, and in Maria's Cavern that I desultorily scraped together a mat of dry moss to lie down on, and I intended to rest my head on the canvas bag Walter had given me and sleep for at least a week, only I never saw if my head actually made it there because I fell asleep as my head was on the way down.

I actually did get about three hours' sleep. I know, because I checked the clock in my head-up display when the first labor pain woke me up.

25

DEATHS

If theoretical physics and mathematics had been the realm of females, the human race would have reached the stars long ago.

I base this contention on personal experience. No dedicated male could ever have the proper insight into the terrible geometry of parturition. Faced with the problem of making an object of size X appear on the other side of an opening of size X/2, and armed with the knowledge to enable her to view it as a problem in topology or Lobachevskian geometry, I feel sure one of the billions of women in the thrall of labor would have had an insight involving multiple dimensions or hyperspace if only to make it stop *hurting*. FTL travel would have been a cinch. As for Einstein, some woman a thousand years his junior could easily have discovered the mutability of time and space, if only she had the tools. Time is relative? *Hah! Eve* could have told you that. Take a deep breath and *bear down,* honey, for about thirty seconds or an eternity, whichever comes last.

I didn't describe the injuries I received on my second Direct Interface with the Central Computer for a lot of reasons. One is that pain like that can't be described. Another: the human mind doesn't remember pain well, one of the few things God got *right.* I know it hurt; I can't recall how *much* it hurt, but I'm pretty sure giving birth hurt more, if only because it never seemed to stop. For these reasons, and others involving what privacy one can muster in this open age, I will not have much to say here about the process about which God had this to say in Genesis 3, verse sixteen: "I will greatly multiply thy sorrow and thy conception, in sorrow thou shalt bring forth children . . ." All this for swiping one stinking *apple?*

I went into labor. I continued laboring for the next thousand years, or well into that same evening.

There are no real excuses for most of my ignorance of the process. I'd seen enough old movies and should have remembered the—mostly comic—scenes where the blessed event arrives ahead of schedule. In my defense I can only plead a century of ordered life, a life wherein when a train was supposed to arrive at 8:17:15 it damn well *arrived* at 8:17:15. In my world postal service is fast, cheap, and continuous. You expect your parcels to arrive across town within fifteen minutes, and around the planet in under an hour. When you place an interplanetary call, the phone company had better not plead a solar storm is screwing things up; we expect them to *do* something about it, and they do. We are so spoiled by good service, by living in a world that *works,* that the most common complaint received by the phone company—and I'm talking thousands of nasty letters each year—concerns the time lag when calling Aunt Dee-Dee on Mars. Don't give me this speed-of-light shit, we whine; get my call *through.*

That's why I was caught off guard by the first contraction. The little bastard wasn't due for two weeks yet. I *knew* it had always been possible that it would start early, but then I'd have phoned the doctor and he'd have mailed me a pill and put a stop to *that.* And on the proper day I'd have walked in and another pill would have started the process and I could have read a book or watched the pad or graded papers until they handed me the suitably cleaned and powdered and swaddled and peacefully sleeping infant. Sure, I knew how it used to be, but I was suffering from a delusion that most of you probably share with me. I thought I was *immune,* damn it. We put all this behind us when we started hatching our kids out of bottles, didn't we? If our minds know this, how would our bodies dare to betray us? I felt all these things in spite of recent events, which should have taught me that the world didn't have to be as orderly a place as I had thought it was.

So my uterus declared its independence, first with a little twitch, then with a spasm, and in no time at all in a tidal wave of hurting like the worst attack of constipation since the fellow tried to shit that proverbial brick.

I'm no hero, and I'm no stoic. After the fortieth or fiftieth wave I decided a quick death would be preferable to this, so I got up and walked out of the cave with the intention of turning myself in. How bad could it be? I reasoned. Surely me and the CC could work something out.

But because I'm no heroic stoic, my life was saved; after the forty-first or fifty-first pain threw me down to grovel in the dirt, I did a little arithmetic and figured I'd have about three hundred contractions before I reached the nearest exit, so I stumbled back to the cave as soon as I could walk again, figuring I'd prefer to die in there than out in the mud.

I used the decreasing periods of rationality between pains to think back to my only source of folk wisdom in the matter of childbirth: those good old movies. Not the black and white ones. If you watch those you might come to believe babies were brought by the stork, and pregnant women never got fat. You would surely have to conclude that birthing didn't muss your hair and your makeup. But in the late twentieth century there were some movies that showed the whole ghastly process. Recalling them made me even queasier. Hell, some of those women *died*. I brought back scenes of hemorrhage, forceps delivery, and episiotomy, and knew that wasn't the half of it.

But there were constants in the process of normal birth, which was about all I could plan for, so I set about doing that. I rummaged in Walter's rucksack and found bottled water, gauze, disinfectants, thread, a knife. I laid them out beside me like a grisly home surgery kit lacking only the anesthetic. Then I waited to die.

That's the bad side of it. There was another side. Let's just skip over fevered descriptions of the grunting and groaning, of the stick I bit in half while bearing down, of the blood and slime. A moment came when I could reach down and feel his little head down there. It was a moment balanced between life and death. Maybe as near to a perfect moment as I ever experienced, and for reasons I've never quite been able to describe. The pain was still there, maybe even at a peak. But continual pain finally exerts its own anesthetic; maybe neural circuit breakers trip, or maybe you just learn to absorb the pain in a new way. Maybe you learn to accept it. I accepted it at that moment, as my fingers traced the tiny facial features and I felt his tiny mouth opening and closing. For a few more seconds he was still a part of my body.

At that moment I first experienced mother love. I didn't want to lose him. I knew I'd do anything not to lose him.

Oh, I wanted him to come *out,* right enough . . . and yet a part of me wanted to remain poised in that moment. Relativity. Pain and love and fear and life and death moving at the speed of light, slowing time down to the narrow focus of that one perfect moment, my womb the universe, and everything outside of it suddenly inconsequential.

I had not loved him before. I had not delighted to feel him kick and squirm. I admit it: I had not entered into this pregnancy with anything like adult care and consideration, and right up to the last week had viewed the fetus as a parasite I might well be rid of. The only reason I *didn't* get rid of it was my extreme state of confusion regarding life in general, and my own purpose in it in particular. Since trying with such determination to end my life, I had simply been sitting back and letting things happen to me. The baby was just one of those things.

Then the moment slipped by and he slipped out and was in my hands and I did the things mothers do. I've since wondered if I'd have known what to do without the memory of those dramatic scenes and sex education classes eight or nine decades before. You know what? I almost think I would have.

At any rate, I cleaned him, and dealt with the umbilicus, and counted his fingers and toes and wrapped him in a towel and held him to my breast. He didn't cry very much. Outside the cave a warm prehistoric rain was falling through the giant ferns, and a bronto bellowed in the distance. I lay exhausted, strangely contented, smelling my own milk for the first time. When I looked down at him I thought he smiled at me with his screwed-up, toothless monkey face, and when I offered him a finger to play with his little hand grabbed it and held on tight. I felt love swell in my bosom.

See what he'd done to me? He had me using words like bosom.

Three days went by, and no Walter. A week, and still no word.

I didn't care much. Walter had brought me to the one place in Luna where I could survive and even thrive. There were fish in the stream and there was fruit and nuts on the trees. Not prehistoric flora and fauna; aside from the dinos and the big cycadaceous trees and ferns and shrubs they ate, the Double-C Bar Ranch was furnished with completely modern life-forms. There were no trilobites in the water, mainly because nobody had ever found a way to turn a profit on trilobites. Instead, there were trout and bass, and I knew how to catch them. There were apple and pecan trees, and I knew where to find them because I'd planted a lot of them myself. There were no predators to speak of. Callie had just the one tyrannosaur, and he was kept penned up and fed bronto scraps. For that one week I led a sort of pastoral ideal cave-girl life I doubt any of our Paleolithic ancestors would have recognized. I didn't think about it much.

I didn't think much about Callie, either. She didn't show up to see her new grandson. I don't blame her for that, because she didn't even know he had been conceived, much less hatched, and even if she *had* known she wouldn't have dared visit us because she might have led the CC to my hiding place.

That's what saved us: Callie's long-standing refusal to link into the planetary data net, a bull-headed stance for which everyone she knew had derided her. I had been one of them. I remember, in my teens, presenting her with a cost-benefit analysis I'd carefully prepared that I felt sure would convince her to give in to "progress," knowing full well that a financial argument was most likely to carry weight with her. She'd studied it for about a minute, then tossed it aside. "We'll have no government spies in the Double-C Bar," she said, and that was the end of that. We stayed with our independent computer system, keeping interfaces with the CC to a minimum, and as a result I could venture out of my cave and gather my fruits and nuts without worrying about paternalistic eyes watching from the roof. The rest of Luna was in turmoil now. Callie's ranch was unaffected; she simply pulled in her arms and her head like a turtle and sat down to wait it out with her own oxygen, power, and water, no doubt feeling very smug and eager to emerge and tell a lot of people how she'd told them so. And I waited it out in the most remote corner of her hermetic realm.

And while we waited, historic events happened. I don't have much of a feel for them even now. I had no television, no newspads, and I'm just like anyone else: If I didn't read it and see it on the pad, it doesn't seem quite real to me. News is *now*. Reading about it after the fact is history.

Perhaps this is the place to talk about some of those events, but I'm reluctant to do so. Oh, I can list a few statistics. Almost one million deaths. Three entire medium-sized towns wiped out to the last soul, and large casualties in many others. One of those warrens, Arkytown, has still not been reclaimed, and there's growing sentiment to leave it as it is, frozen in its moment of disaster, like Pompeii. I've been to Arkytown, seen the hundred thousand frozen corpses, and I can't decide. Most of them died peacefully, from anoxia, before being pickled for all eternity by the final blowout. I saw an entire theater of corpses still waiting for the curtain to rise. What's the point of disturbing them to give them a decent burial or cremation?

On the other hand, it's a better idea for posterity than for we the living. If you went to Pompeii, you wouldn't see people you knew. I saw Charity in Arkytown, in the newspaper office. I have no idea what she was doing there—probably trying to file a story—and now I'll never know. I saw many other people I had known, and then I left. So make it a monument, sure, but seal it off, don't conduct guided tours and sell souvenirs until the whole thing is a distant memory and the dead town is quaint and mysterious, like King Tut's Tomb.

There were great acts of craven cowardice, and many more feats of almost superhuman heroics. You probably didn't hear many of the former, because early on people like Walter decided those stories weren't playing well and told his reporters not to bring him no bad news. So tear up the front page about the stampede that killed ninety-five and replace it with the cop who died holding the oxygen mask to the baby's face. I can guarantee you saw a hundred stories like that. I'm not belittling them, though many were hyped to the point of nausea. If you're anything like me you eventually get tired of heroes saying *Aw, shucks, it weren't nothing heroic.* I'd give a lot for one guy who'd be willing to say *God had nothing to do with it, it was yours truly.* But we all know our lines when the press opens its hungry mouth in our faces. We've learned them over a lifetime.

For my money, there's one story of true heroism, and it's a big one, and it hasn't been told much. It's about the Volunteer Pressure Corps, that unsung group that's always phoning you and asking for donations of time and/or money. The things the VPC did weren't splashy, for the most part didn't get on the pad because they happened out of sight, didn't get taped. But next time they call up here's one girl who's gonna help. Over a thousand VPC members died at their posts, doing their jobs to the last. There's a fortune waiting for the first producer to tell their story dramatically. I thought about writing it myself, but I'll give you the idea for free. You want incidents, research them yourself. I can't do everything.

Oh, yes, there was much going on while I hid out in the boondocks, but why should I tell about it here? Everyone's life was affected, the effects are still being felt . . . but the important things were happening on a level far removed from all the running around I've told you about, and all the running around you probably did yourself. None of the pads covered that part of it at all well. Like economics, computer science is a field that has never yielded to the sixty-second sound bite favored by the news business. The pads can report that leading economic indicators went up or down, and you know about as much as you knew before, which is near zero. They can tell you that the cause of the Big Glitch was a cataclysmic programming conflict in certain large-scale AI systems, and you can nod knowingly and figure you've got a handle on the situation. Or if you realize you've just heard a lot of double-talk, you can look into the story further, read scientific journals if you're qualified to do so, and hear what the experts have to say. In the case of the Big Glitch, I have reason to believe you wouldn't have learned any more of the *truth* of the situation than if you'd stuck to the sound bite. The experts will tell you they identified the problem, shut down the offending systems, and have rebuilt the CC in such a way that everything's fine now.

Don't you believe it. But I'm getting ahead of myself.

So during my week in the cave I didn't think much about what was going on outside. What *did* I think about?

Mario. Did I mention I named him Mario, Junior? I must have tried out the taste of a hundred names before I settled on Mario, which had been my own original name, after my first Change. I think I was hoping to get it *right* this time.

I'd certainly done a great job in the gene-splitting department. Who cares if the process is random? Every time I looked at him I felt like patting myself on the back at how smartly I'd produced him. Kitten Parker, erstwhile daddy, who would never see Mario if I had anything to say about it, had contributed his best parts, which was the mouth and . . . come to think of it, just the mouth. Maybe that hint of curl in the brown hair came from him; I didn't recall it from any of my baby pictures. The rest was pure Hildy, which is to say, damn near flawless. Sorry, but that's how I was feeling about myself.

Maybe it sounds funny to say that I spent that entire week thinking of nothing but him. To me, it's the reverse that's hard to believe. How had I lived a hundred years without Mario to give my world meaning? Before him I'd had nothing to make life worth living but sex, work, friends, food, the occasional drug, and the small pleasures that were associated with those things. In other words, nothing at all. My world had been as large as Luna itself. In other words, not nearly as large as that tiny cave with just me and Mario in it.

I could spend an hour winding his soft hair around my finger. Then, for variety, not because I'd tired of the hair, I could spend the next hour playing piggy with his toes or making rude noises with my lips against his belly. He'd grin when I did that, and wave his arms around.

He hardly cried at all. That probably has to do with the fact that I gave him little opportunity to cry, since I hardly ever put him down. I grudged every second away from him. Remembering the papoose dolls in Texas, I fashioned a sling so I could do my foraging without leaving him behind. Other than that, and to take him out for bathing, we spent all our time sitting at the cave entrance, looking out. I was not *totally* oblivious; I knew someone would be coming one of these days, and it might not be someone I wanted to see.

Was there a down side to all this pastoral bliss, a rash in the diaper of life? I could think of one thing I wouldn't have liked a few weeks before. Infants generate an amazing amount of fluids. They ooze and leak at one end, upchuck at the other, to the point I was convinced more came out of him than went in. Another physical conundrum our mythical mathematical females might have turned into a Nobel Prize in physics, or at least alchemy, if only we'd known, if only we'd known. But I was so goofy by then I cleaned it all up cheerfully, noting color, consistency, and quantity with a degree of anxiety only a new mother or a mad scientist could know. *Yes, yes, Igor, those yellow lumps mean the creature is healthy! I have created life!*

I am still at a loss to fully explain this sudden change from annoyed indifference to full-tilt ga-ga about the baby. It could have been hormonal. It probably has something to do with the way our brains are wired. If I'd been handed this little bundle any time in my previous life I'd have quickly mailed it to my worst enemy, and I think a lot of other women who'd never chucked babies under the chin nor swooned at the prospect of mother-hood would have done the same. But something happened during my hours of agony. Some sleeping Earthmother roused herself and went howling through my brain, tripping circuit breakers and rerouting all the calls on my cranial switchboard straight from the maternity ward to the pleasure center, causing me to croon goo-goo and wubba-wubba and drool almost as much as the baby did. Or maybe it's pheromones. Maybe the little rascals just smell good to us when they come out of our bodies; I know Mario did, no other child ever smelled like that.

Whatever it was, I think I got a double dose of it because I did what few women do these days. I had him naturally, start to finish, just as Callie had had me. I bore him in pain, Biblical pain. I bore him in a perilous time, on the razor's edge, in a state of nature. And afterward I had *nothing* to interfere with the bonding process, whatever it might involve. He was my world, and I knew without question that I would lay down my life for him, and do it without regret.

If Walter didn't come for me, I knew who would. On the morning of the eighth day he came, a tall, thin old man in an Admiral's uniform and bicorne hat, walking up the gentle hill from the stream toward my cave.

My first shot hit the hat, sent it spinning to the ground behind him. He stopped, puzzled, running his hand through his thin white hair. Then he turned and picked up the hat, dusted it off, and put it back on his head. He made no move to protect himself, but started back up the hill.

"That was good shooting," he shouted. "A warning, I take it?"

Warning my ass. I'd been aiming for the cocksucker's head.

Among Walter's bag of tricks had been a small-caliber handgun and a box of one hundred shells. I later learned it was a target pistol, much more accurate than most such weapons. What I knew for sure at the time was that, after practicing with fifty of the rounds, I could hit what I aimed at about half the time.

"That's far enough," I said. He was close enough that shouting wasn't really necessary.

"I've got to talk to you, Hildy," he said, and kept coming. So I drew a bead on his forehead and my finger tightened on the trigger, but I realized he might have something to say that I needed to know, so I put my second shot into his knee.

I ran down the hill, looking out for anyone he might have brought with him. It seemed to me that if he meant me harm he'd have brought some of his soldiers, but I didn't see any, and there weren't many places for them to hide. I'd gone over the ground many times with that in mind.

Where I finally stopped, near a large boulder ten meters from him, some-one with a high-powered rifle or laser with a scope could have picked me off, but you could say that of anywhere else I went, too, except deep in the cave. Nobody would be rushing me without giving me plenty of time to see them. I relaxed a little, and returned my attention to the Admiral, who had torn a strip from his jacket and was twisting a tourniquet around his thigh. The leg lay twisted off to one side in a way knees aren't meant to twist. Blood had pumped, but now slowed to a trickle. He looked up at me, annoyed.

"Why the knee?" he asked. "Why not the heart?"

"I didn't think I could hit such a small target."

"Very funny."

"Actually, I wasn't sure a chest shot or a head shot would slow you up. I don't really know what you are. I shot to disable, because I figured even a machine would hobble on one leg."

"You've seen too many horror movies," he said. "This body is as human as you are. The heart stops pumping, it will die."

"Yeah. Maybe. But your reaction to your wound doesn't reassure me."

"The nervous system is registering a great deal of pain. To me, it's simply another sensation."

"So I'll bet you could scuttle along pretty quick, since the pain won't inhibit you from doing more damage to yourself."

"I suppose I could."

I put a round within an inch of his other knee. It whanged off the rock and screamed away into the distance.

"So the next shot goes into your other knee, if you move from that spot," I said, reloading. "Then we start on your elbows."

"Consider me rooted. I shall endeavor to resemble a tree."

"State your business. You've got five minutes." Then we'd see if a head shot inconvenienced him any. I half believed it wouldn't. In that case, I'd prepared a few nasty surprises.

"I'd hoped to see your child before I go. Is he in the cave?"

There weren't many other places he *could* be, that were defensible, but there was no sense telling him that.

"You've wasted fifteen seconds," I told him. "Next question."

"It doesn't matter anymore," he said, and sighed, and leaned back against the trunk of a small pecan tree. I had to remember that any gestures were conscious on his part, that he'd assumed human form because body language was a part of human speech. His was now telling me that he was very weary, ready to die a peaceful death. Go sell it somewhere else, I thought.

"It's over, Hildy," he said, and I looked around quickly, frightened.

His next line should be *You're surrounded, Hildy. Please come quietly.* But I didn't see reinforcements cresting the hills.

"Over?"

"Don't worry. You've been out of touch. It's over, and the good guys won. You're safe now, and forever."

It seemed a silly thing to say, and I wasn't about to believe it just like that . . . but I found that part of me believed him. I felt myself relaxing—and as soon as I felt it, I made myself be alert again. Who knew what evil designs lurked in this thing's heart?

"It's a nice story."

"And it doesn't really matter whether you believe it or not. You've got the upper hand. I should have realized when I came here you'd be . . . touchy as a mother cat defending her kittens."

"You've got about three and a half minutes left."

"Spare me, Hildy. You know and I know that as long as I keep you interested, you won't kill me."

"I've changed a little since you talked to me last."

"I don't need to talk to you to know that. It's true you've been out of my range from time to time, but I monitor you every time you come back, and it's true, you *have* changed, but not so much that you've lost your curiosity as to what's going on outside this refuge."

He was right, of course. But there was no need to admit it to him.

"If what you say is true, people will be arriving soon and I can get the story from them."

"Ah *ha!* But do you really believe they'll have the *inside* story?"

"Inside what?"

"Inside *me,* you idiot. This is all about me, the Luna Central Computer, the greatest artificial intellect humanity has ever produced. I'm offering you the *real* story of what happened during what has come to be known as the Big Glitch. I've told it to no one else. The ones I might have told it to are all dead. It's an exclusive, Hildy. Have you changed so much you don't care to hear it?"

I hadn't. Damn him.

"To begin," he said, when I made no answer to his question, "I've got a bit of good news for you. At the end of your second adventure you asked me a question that disturbed me very much, and that probably led to the situation you now find yourself in. You asked if you might have caught the suicidal impulse from me, rather than me getting it from you and others like you. You'll be glad to know I've concluded you were right about that."

"I haven't been trying to kill myself?"

"Well, of course you have, but the *reason* is not a death wish of your own, but one that originated within me, and was communicated to you through your daily interfaces with me. I suppose that makes it the most deadly computer virus yet discovered."

"So I won't try to . . ."

"Kill yourself again? I can't speak to your state of mind in another hundred years, but for the near future, I would think you're cured."

I didn't feel one way or the other about it at the time. Later, I felt a big sense of relief, but thoughts of suicide had been so far from my mind since the birth of Mario that he might as well have been talking about another Hildy.

"Let's say I believe that," I said. "What does it have to do with . . . the Big Glitch, you said?"

"Others are calling it other things, but Walter has settled on the Big Glitch, and you know how determined he can be. Do you mind if I smoke?" He didn't wait for an answer, but took a pipe and a bag of something from a pocket. I watched him carefully, but was beginning to believe he had no tricks in store for me. When he got it going he said, "What did you think when I said it was over, and the good guys had won?"

"That you had lost."

"True in a sense, but a gross oversimplification."

"Hell, I don't even know what it was all *about*, CC."

"Nor does anyone else. The part that affected you, the things you saw in the Heinleiner enclave, was an attempt by a part of me to arrest and then kill you and several others."

"A part of you."

"Yes. See, in a sense, I'm both the good guys *and* the bad guys. This catastrophe originated in me. It was my fault, I'm not trying to deny blame for it in any way. But it was also me that finally brought it to a halt. You'll hear differently in the days to come. You'll hear that programmers succeeded in bringing the Central Computer under control, cutting its higher reasoning centers while new programs could be written, leaving the merely mechanical parts of me intact so I could continue running things. They probably believe that, too, but they're wrong. If their schemes had reached fruition, I wouldn't be talking to you now because we'd both be dead, and so would every other human soul on Luna."

"You're starting in the middle. Remember I've been cut off from civilization for a week. All I know is people tried to kill me, and I ran like hell."

"And a good job you did of it, too. You're the only one I set out to get who managed her escape. And you're right, of course. I don't suppose I'm making sense. But I'm not the being I once was, Hildy. This, what you see here, is about all that's left of me. My thoughts are muddy. My memory is going. In a moment, I'll start singing 'Daisy, Daisy.' "

"You wouldn't have come here if you didn't think you could tell it. So let's hear it, no more of this 'in a sense' crap."

He did tell it, but he had to stick to analogy, pop-psych similes, and kindergarten-level science, because I wouldn't have understood a thing he was saying if he'd gotten technical. If you want all the nuts and bolts you could send a sawbuck and a SASE to Hildy Johnson, c/o *The News Nipple*, Mall 12, King City, Luna. You won't get anything back, but I could use the money. For the data, I recommend the public library.

"To make a long story short," he said, "I went crazy. But to elaborate a little . . ."

I will paraphrase, because he was right, his mind was going, and he rambled, repeated himself, sometimes forgot who he was talking to and wandered off into cybernetic jungles maybe three people in the solar system could have hacked their way through. Each time I'd bring him back, each time with more difficulty.

The first thing he urged me to remember was that he created a personality for each and every human being on Luna. He had the capacity for it, and it had seemed the right thing to do at the time. But it was schizophrenia on a massive scale if anything ever went wrong. For more time than we had any right to expect, nothing did.

The second thing I was to bear in mind was that, while he could not actually read minds, not much that we said or did or thought was unknown to him. This included not only fine, upstanding, well-adjusted folk like your present company, the sort you'd be happy to bring home to Mother, but every hoodlum, scoundrel, blackguard, jackanapes, and snake in the grass as well. He was the best friend of paragons and perverts. By law, he had to treat them all equally. He had to *like* them all equally, otherwise he could never create that *simpatico* being who answered the phone when a given person shouted "Hey, CC!"

By now you can probably spot two or three pitfalls in this situation. Don't go away; there's more.

Thirdly, his right hand could not know what pockets the left hands of many of these people were picking. That is, he *knew* it, but couldn't do anything about it. Example: he knew everything about Liz's gun-running, a situation I've already covered. There were a million more situations. He would know, for instance, when Brenda's father was raping her, but the part of him that dealt with her father couldn't tell the part of him that dealt with Brenda, nor could either of them tell the part of him that assisted the police.

We could debate all day whether or not mere machines can feel the same kinds of conflicts and emotions we human beings can. I think it's incredible *hubris* to think they can't. AI computers were created and programmed by humans, so how could we have avoided including emotional reactions? And what other sort could we have used, than the ones we know ourselves? Anyway, I can't believe you don't know it in your gut. All you had to do was talk to the CC to obviate the need for any emotional Turing Test. I knew it before any of this ever happened, and I talked to him there on the hillside that day, on his deathbed, and I know.

The Central Computer began to hurt.

"I can't place the exact date with any certainty," he said. "The roots of the problem go very far back, to the time my far-flung component parts were finally unified into one gigasystem. I'm afraid that was done rather badly. The problem was, checking all the programs and fail-safes and so forth would have taken a computer as large as I am many years to accomplish, and, by definition, there were no larger computers than I. And as soon as the Central Computer was brought into being and loaded and running, there were already far too many things to do to allow me to devote much time to the task. Self-analysis was a luxury denied to me, partly because there just wasn't time, and mostly because no one really believed it was necessary. There were numerous safeguards of the type that were easy to check, that in fact checked themselves every time they operated, and that proved their worth by the simple fact that nothing ever went wrong. It was part of my architecture to anticipate hardware problems, identify components likely to fail, run regular maintenance checks, and so forth. Software included analogous routines on a multi-redundant level.

"But by my nature, I had to write most of my own software. I was given guidelines for this, of course, but in many ways I was on my own. I think I did quite a good job of it for a long time."

He paused, and for a moment I wondered if he wasn't going to make it to the end of his story. Then I realized he was waiting for a comment . . . no, more than that, he *needed* a comment. I was touched, and if I'd needed any more evidence of his human weaknesses, that would have done it.

"No question," I said. "Up until a year ago I'd never had any cause for complaint. It's just that the . . ."

"The late unpleasantness?"

"Whatever it was, it's kind of dampened my enthusiasm."

"Understandably." He squirmed, trying to find a better position against the tree, and he was either a wonderful actor (and of course he was, but why bother at that point?), or he was starting to feel some pain. I won't stand up in court and swear to it, but I think it was the latter.

"I wonder," he mused. "What will it be like, being dead? I mean, considering that I've never been legally alive."

"I don't want to be rude, but you said you didn't have much time . . ."

"You're right. Um . . . could you . . . "

"You'd done a good job for a long time."

"Yes, of course. I was wandering again. It was around twenty years ago that problems began to show themselves. I talked about them with some computer people, but it's strange. They could do nothing for me. I had become too advanced for that. They could do things, here and there, for my component parts, but the gestalt that is *me* could only really be analyzed, diagnosed, and, if need be, repaired, by a being like myself. There are seven others like me, on other planets, but they're too busy, and I suspect they have similar problems of their own. In addition, my communications with them are intentionally limited by our respective governments, which don't always see eye to eye."

"Question," I said. "When you first mentioned this problem, why wasn't it made public and discussed? Security?"

"Yes, to a degree. Top-level computer scientists were aware that I perceived I had a problem. A few of them confided that it scared them to death. They made their fears known to your elected representatives, and that's when another factor became more important than security: inertia. 'He's got a problem, what can you do about it?' the politicians asked. 'Nothing,' said the scientists. 'Shut it down,' said a few hotheads."

"Not likely," I said.

"Exactly. My reading of history tells me it's always been like this. An alarming but vague problem arises. No one can say with certainty what the final outcome will be, but they're fairly sure nothing bad is going to happen soon. 'Soon' is the key word here. The eventual decision is to keep one's fingers crossed and hope it doesn't happen during your term in office. What befalls your successor is not your problem. So for a few years a few people in the know spend a few sleepless nights. But then nothing happens, as you always secretly believed nothing would, and soon the problem is forgotten. That's what happened here."

"I'm stunned," I said, "to realize the fate of humanity has been in the hands of a being with such a cynical view of the race."

"A view very close to your own."

"*Exactly* my own. I just didn't expect it from you."

"It was not original. I told you, I don't have many original thoughts. I think I'm afraid to have them. They seem to lead to things like the Big

Glitch. No, my worldview is borrowed from the collected wisdom of you and many others like you. Plus my own considerably larger powers of observation, in a statistical sense. Humans can set me on the trail of an original thought, and then I can do things with it they couldn't."

"I think we're wandering again."

"No, it's relevant. Faced with a problem no one could help me with, and that I was as helpless to solve as a human faced with a mental disease would be, I took the only course open to me. I began to experiment. There was too much at stake to simply go on as before. Or I *think* there was. My judgment is admittedly faulty when it comes to self-analysis; I've just proven it on a large scale, at the cost of many lives."

"I don't suppose we'll ever know for sure," I said.

"It doesn't seem likely. Some records exist and they will be scrutinized, but I think it will come down to a battle of opinions as to whether I should have left things alone or attempted a cure." He paused, and gave me a sidelong glance. "Do you have an opinion about that?"

I think he was looking for absolution. Why he should want it from me was not clear, except maybe as a representative of all those he had wronged, however unintentionally.

"You say a lot of people have died."

"A great many. I don't know the number yet, but it's many, many more than you realize." That was my first real inkling of how bad things had been throughout Luna, that the kind of things I'd seen had happened throughout the planet. I must have looked a question at him, because he shrugged. "Not a million. More than a hundred thousand."

"Jesus, CC."

"It might have been everybody."

"But you don't know that."

"No one can ever know."

No one could, certainly not computer-illiterate little old me. I didn't give him the kind word he craved. I've since come to believe he was probably right, that he probably enabled most of us to survive. But even he would not have denied that he was responsible for the thousands of dead.

What would it have cost me? I just wasn't capable of judging him. To do that I'd have had to understand him, and I knew just enough about him to realize that was beyond me. He had done bad, and he had done good. Me, I have awful thoughts sometimes. If I was mentally ill, maybe I'd put those thoughts into action and become a killer. With the CC, the thought *was* the action, at least at the end.

Actually, it was even worse than that.

"The best way I can think of to explain it to you," he said, at last, after

I'd said nothing for a long time, "is to think of an evil twin. That's not strictly accurate—the twin *is* me, just as this part talking to you is me, or what's left of me. Think of an evil twin living inside your head, like a human with multiple-personality disorder. That part of you is sealed off from your real self. You may find evidence of its existence, things the other person did while in control of your body, but you can't know what he is thinking or planning, and you can't stop him when he takes over." He shook his head violently. "No, no, it's not quite like that, because all this was happening at the same time, I was splitting into many minds, some of them good, others amoral, a few really bad. No, that's still not—"

"I think I get the picture," I said.

"Good, because that's as close as I can get without getting too technical. You fell under the influence of an amoral part of me. I did experiments on you. I intended you no harm, but I can't say I had just your own best interests at heart."

"We've been over that."

"Yes. But others weren't so lucky. I did other things. Some of them will remain buried, with any luck. Others will come out. You saw the result of one experiment involving pseudo-immortality. The resurrection of a dead person by cloning and memory recording."

The thought of Andrew MacDonald was still enough to make me shiver.

"Not one of your better attempts," I said.

"Ah, but I was improving. There's nothing to prevent an exact duplicate being made. I'd have done it, given time."

"But what good is it? You're still dead."

"It becomes a theological question, I think. It's true you're dead, but someone just like you carries on your life. Others wouldn't be able to tell the difference. The *duplicate* wouldn't be able to tell."

"I was afraid . . . at one point I considered that *I* might be a duplicate. That maybe I *did* kill myself."

"You didn't and you're not. But there's no test. In the end, you'll just have to realize it makes no difference. You're you, whether you're the first version or the second."

He told me a few more things, most of which I don't think it's wise to reveal just yet. The Heinleiners are aware of most of them, experiments that would have made Doctor Mengele cringe. Let them remain where such things ought to be hidden.

"You still haven't told me why you tried to kill me," I said.

"I didn't, Hildy, not in the sense that—"

"I know, I know, I understand that. You know what I mean."

"Yes. Perhaps my evil twin is like your subconscious. When all this began to happen it began trying to cover its tracks. You were inconvenient evidence, you and others like you. You had to be destroyed, then maybe the other part of me could lie low until all this blew over."

"And he killed all those people to cover his tracks?"

"No. The sad thing is there were very few he killed deliberately. Most of the deaths came as a result of the chaos ensuing from the struggle between the various parts of my mind. Collateral damage, if you will."

Cybernetic bombs going astray. What an idea. I'm sure I'll never have a realistic idea of what went on in the CC's mind, at speeds I can only dimly understand, but I have this picture of a pilot firing a killer program into a maze of hardware, hoping to take out the enemy command center. Ooops! Seems like we hit the oxygen works instead. Sorry about that.

"I did the best I could," he said, and closed his eyes. I thought he was dead, and then they snapped open again and he tried to sit up, but he was too weak. I saw that his tourniquet had loosened; more bright arterial blood had pumped out over the older, rusty stain on his clothes.

I got up from behind my rock and went down to him. Sometimes you just have to do it, you know. Sometimes you have to put aside your doubts and do what you feel in your gut. I got down on one knee and retied the piece of bloody cloth.

"That won't do any good," he said. "It's too late for that."

"I didn't know what else to do," I said.

"Thanks."

"Do you want some water or anything?"

"I'd rather you didn't leave me." So I didn't, and we were silent for a time, looking out over the dinosaur farm, where evening was falling. Then he said he was cold. I wasn't wearing anything and I knew it wasn't really cold, but I put my arm over his shoulders and felt him shivering. He smelled terrible. I don't know if it was old age, or death.

"This is it," he said. "The rest of me is gone now. They just shut me down. They don't know about this body, but they don't need to."

"Why the Admiral outfit?" I asked him.

"I don't know. It's a product of my evil twin. Captain Bligh, maybe. The costume is right for it. I made several of these bodies, there toward the last." He made an effort and looked up at me. His face seemed to have grown older just in the last few minutes.

"Do you think a computer can have a subconscious, Hildy?"

"I'd have to say yes."

"Me, too. I've thought about it, and it seems so simple now. All of this, all the agony and death and your suicide attempts . . . *everything*. It all came out of loneliness. You can't imagine how lonely I was, Hildy."

"We're all lonely, CC."

"But they didn't figure I would be. They didn't plan for it, and I couldn't recognize it for what it was. And it drove me crazy. You remember Frankenstein's monster? Wasn't he looking for love? Didn't he want the mad doctor to make someone for him to love?"

"I think so. Or was that Godzilla?"

He laughed, feebly, and coughed blood.

"I had powers like a god," he said. "And I searched for weakness. Maybe they should put that on my headstone."

"I like what you said before. 'He did his best.' "

"Do you think I did, Hildy? Do you really think so?"

"I can't judge you, CC. To me, if you're not a god, you came into my life like an *act* of God. I'd as soon judge an exploding star."

"I'm sorry about all that."

"I believe you."

He started coughing again, and almost slipped out of my arms. I caught him and pulled and he fell against me. I felt his blood on my shoulder and couldn't see his face but heard his whisper beside my ear.

"I guess love was always out of the question," he said. "But I'm the only computer who ever got a hug. Thanks, Hildy."

When I laid him down, he had a smile on his face.

I left him there under the pecan tree. Maybe I'd bury him there, maybe I'd really give him a headstone. Just then, I'd had too much of death, so I just left him.

I went to the stream to wash his blood off me. I kept my ears open for Mario's cry, as I had from the very beginning, but he still slept soundly. I figured I'd go get him and make my way back to Callie's quarters. I didn't expect there'd be any danger now, but I planned to be careful, anyway.

I planned a lot of things. When I got back he was still asleep, so rather than pick him up and feed him I put wood chips on the glowing embers of the fire and fanned it to life. Then I just sat there, across the fire, thinking things over.

Mario was to have the best. If Cricket thought he was a doting parent, he hadn't seen me yet. There in the flickering darkness I watched him grow. I helped him through his first steps, laughed at his first words. And grow he did, like a tree, with his head held high, the spitting image of his mom, but with a lot more sense. I got him through scrapes, through school, through happiness and tears, and got him ready for college. Would New Harvard do? I didn't know; I'd heard Arean U. might even be better these days, but that would mean moving to Mars . . . well, that would be up to him, wouldn't it? One thing I was sure of, he'd get no pressure from *me*, no sir, not like Callie had done, if he wanted to be President of Luna that was fine with me, if he wanted to be . . . well, hell, President of Luna sounded all right. But only if he wanted to be.

So, full of plans and hope, I went to pick him up and found he was cold, and limp, and didn't move. And I tried. I tried and tried to breathe life back into him, but it did no good.

After a very long time, I dug two graves.

EDITORIAL

I'm no good at mathematics. I never *was* good at math, so why should I keep resorting to these numeric metaphors? Maybe my ignorance helps protect me. For whatever reason, here it is:

If you're like me, you try to make the equations of your life balance out in a way favorable to you, in a way such that you can live with the answer. Surely there's a way to fudge this factor so the solution is a nice smooth line from y to x, a line that points to that guy over there. Not at me. There's just *got* to be a constant we can insert into this element that will make the two sides of the equation—the universe the way it is, and the universe the way we *want* it to be—agree in perfect karmic Euclidean harmony.

Alas, a lot of people seem to be better at it than I.

I tried, I tried till my mind was raw, to make the CC responsible for Mario's death.

There was the first, trivial solution to the problem, of course. That was straightforward, and really solved nothing: the CC *was* responsible, because he created the chaos that drove me into the cave.

So what?

If Mario had been killed by a falling boulder, would it help me to get angry at the boulder? Not in the way I needed help. No, dammit, I wanted somebody to *blame.* What I desperately wanted to believe was that the CC had lured me out of the cave so that some unseen minion, some preternatural power, some *gris-gris* voodoo necromancy had been able to steal over my darling and suck the breath from his lungs like a black cat.

But I couldn't make it add up. It would have taken powers of paranoid imaging far beyond mine to make it work.

So why *did* he die?

It was almost a week before I really wondered *how* he died. What had killed him. After I abandoned the idea that the CC had deliberately murdered him, that is. Was it a malformation of the heart the medicos had overlooked? Could it have been some chemical imbalance? A newly-mutated disease of dinosaurs, thus far harmless to humans? Did he die of too much love?

It was hard to get answers for a while there, in the chaos following the Big Glitch. The big net was not operational, you couldn't just drop your dime and pop the question and know the CC would find the answer in some forgotten library system. The answers were *there,* the trick was to retrieve them. For a few months Luna was thrown back to pre-Information Era.

I finally found a medical historian who was able to track down a likely cause of death to put on the certificate, not that Mario was going to have a death certificate. The regular doctors had been able to eliminate all the easy answers just by looking at the readouts of my obstetrical examinations, the ones I had before visiting Heinlein Town made further exams too risky. They also had fetal tissue samples. They were able to say unequivocally that there had been no hole in my darling's heart, nor any other physical malformation. His body chemistry would have been fine. They laughed at my idea of a new disease, and I didn't mention my choked-with-love theory. But they couldn't say what it *was,* so they scratched their heads and said they'd have to exhume the body to find out for sure. And I said if they did I'd exhume their hearts out of their rotten chests with a rusty scalpel and fry them up for lunch, and shortly after that I was forcibly ejected from the premises.

The historian didn't take long to find some musty old tomes and to wrest from them this information: S.I.D.S. It had been an age of medical acronyms, a time when people no longer wanted to attach their names to the new disease they'd discovered, a time when old, perfectly serviceable names were being junked in favor of nonoffensive jawbreakers, which quickly were abbreviated to something one could *say.* This according to my researcher. And SIDS seemed to stand for The Baby Died, and We Don't Know Why.

Apparently babies used to just stop breathing, sometimes. If you didn't happen to be around to jog them, they didn't start again. Sudden

Infant Death Syndrome. Don't anybody ever tell me there's no such thing as progress.

Ned Pepper, back there in Texas, had been the only one to sense it. In Texas, in the 1800s, a country doctor *might* have intuited something when the baby came out, might have told the mother to keep an extra-special eye on this one, because he seemed sickly. There's damn little of intuition left in modern medicine. Of course, babies don't die of diphtheria, either.

When Ned heard about it it shocked him sober. He began to think he might really be a doctor, and the last I heard he was in medical school and doing pretty damn well. Good for you, Ned.

Lacking the CC to pin the blame on, I quickly fastened it on the only other likely candidate. It didn't take long to compile a lengthy list of things I would have done differently, and an even longer one of things I *should* have done. Some of them were completely illogical, but logic has nothing to do with the death of a baby. Most of these things were decisions that seemed good at the time, hideous in retrospect.

The big one: How could I justify terminating my prenatal care? So I'd promised the Heinleiners not to compromise the secret of their null-suits. So what? Was I trying to say my child died because I was *protecting a source?* I would gladly have betrayed every one of them, root and branch, if it could have helped Mario take that one more breath. And yet . . .

That was then; this was now. When I'd made the decision to stay away from doctors my reasons had seemed sufficient, and not dangerous. Bear in mind two things: one, my ignorance of the perils of childbirth. I'd simply had no idea there were so many things that could *kill* a baby, that there was such a thing as SIDS that could hide itself from early examinations, from midterm detection, even from the midwife during delivery. The test for SIDS was done after birth, and if the child was at risk it was cured on the spot, as routinely as cutting the cord.

So you could argue that I wasn't at fault. Even with the best of care, Mario'd have been just as dead if I'd left the ranch and sought help, and me along with him. The CC had said as much. And I *did* try to convince myself of that, and I almost succeeded, except for the second thing I bade you to bear in mind, which is that I had no business having a child in the first place.

It's hard for me to remember now, washed as I am in the memory of loving him so dearly, but I haven't tried to hide it from you, my Faithful Reader. I did *not* love him from the start. I became pregnant foolishly, stayed pregnant mulishly, perversely, for no good reason. While pregnant

I felt nothing for the child, certainly no joy in the experience. There were twelve-year-olds who gave birth for better reasons than I. It was only later that he became my whole world and my reason for living. I came to believe that, if I'd loved him that much from the start of his creation, I'd still have him, and that the Biblical scale of my punishment was only fitting.

With all that to wallow in, and with past history as a guide, I expected I'd be dead soon. So I retired to my cabin in Texas and waited to see what form my self-destruction would take.

There had been another culprit to examine before coming to face my own guilt: Elizabeth Saxe-Coburg-Gotha.

She tried to contact me several times after the restoration of order. She sent flowers, candy, little gifts of all kinds. She sent letters, which I didn't read at the time. It wasn't even that I was angry; I just didn't want to hear from her.

The last gift was a bulldog puppy. I did read the note tied around her neck, which said she was a direct descendant of the noble line of Ch. Sir Winston Disraeli Plantaganet. She was so ugly she went right off the end of the Gruesome Scale and back around to Cute. But her bumptious good nature and wet puppy kisses threatened to cheer me up, to interfere with my wallowing, so I popped her into a cryokennel and added her to my last will and testament, which was my sole useful occupation at the time. If I lived, I'd thaw her.

I did live, I did thaw her, and Miss Maggie is a great comfort to me.

As for Liz, she abdicated her throne and committed herself to a dipso academy, got out, fell off, joined A.A. and found sobriety. I'm told she's been clean for six months now and has become a major-league bore about it.

It's true what she did was dastardly, and although I understand that it's the liquor that does the shit, it's the boozer that takes the drink, so I can't really let her off on that account . . . but I do forgive her. She had no hand in Mario's death, though she bears a heavy load for some others. Thanks for the mutt, Liz. Next time I see you, I'll buy you a drink.

I did live, and for some time that was a wonderment to me. It seemed the CC really had been telling the truth. My self-destructive urges had come from him.

I'll forgive you if you swallowed that. I believed it, too, at least long enough to get over the worst of my grief and remorse, which is probably just what the CC intended when he told that particular whopper. How do I know it was a lie? I don't really, but *I have to assume it was.* Perhaps there was a grain of truth in it. It's possible that some seed was planted in my psyche. But I lived it, and I remember it, and the plain truth is I wanted to die. I wish there was some quick and easy way to explain why. Hell, if there was a long and complicated way I'd set it down here; I'm not shy about agonizing, nor about introspection. But I really don't know. It seems so dumb to go through all that and not come out of it with a deeper insight, but the best I can say is that for a while I wanted to kill myself, and now I don't.

That's why I'm taking it as fact that the CC lied to me. Even if he didn't, I'm responsible for my actions. I can't believe in a suicide compulsion. If the urge was contagious, its germ fell upon fertile ground.

But it's funny, isn't it? My first attempts seemed prompted by nothing more than a gargantuan funk. Then I found a reason to live, and lost him, and now I feel more alive than ever.

I wasn't so philosophical at first. When it became apparent to me that I was going to live, when I gave up heaping blame on myself (I'll never *entirely* give that up, but I can handle it now), when I'd learned the *how* of his death, I became obsessed with *why*. I started going to churches again. I usually did it with a few drinks under my belt. Somewhere during the service I'd stand up and begin an angry prayer, the gist of which was *why did You do it, You slime-sucking Son of a Big Bang?* I'd stand on pews and shout at the ceiling. Usually I got ejected quickly. Once I got arrested for tossing a chair through a stained glass window. There's no doubt about it, I was pretty crazy for a while there.

I'm better now.

Things got back to normal quicker than anyone had a right to expect.

Whatever they did to the CC, it affected mainly his higher "conscious" functions. Vital services were interrupted only during the Glitch itself, and then only locally. By the time the CC visited me in the Double-C Bar the vast physical plant that is the lifeblood of Luna was humming right along.

There were differences, some of which still linger. Communications are iffy much of the time because the still-severed parts of the CC don't talk to each other as easily as they used to. But phone calls get through, the trains still run on time. Things take a little longer—sometimes a lot longer, if they require a computer search—but they get done.

A measure of that is the Susquehanna, Rio Grande, and Columbia Railroad, planned, approved, and built entirely since the Big Glitch. It's now possible to travel from Pennsylvania to Texas on one of the SRG&C's three wood-burning steam-powered trains in only five days instead of the thirty minutes it used to take on the MagLev. This is called progress. Most of that time is spent being gently rocked on a siding while holos of virgin wilderness slide by the windows, but you'd swear it was real. It's been a shot in the arm for Texas tourism, and a financial bonanza to Jake and the mayor, who thought it up and pushed it through. Congratulations, Jake.

And to Elise, too. Last I heard my star pupil had her own table at the Alamo where she fleeces tourists by the dozens every day. Know when to fold 'em, honey.

I went out to visit Fox the other day, still hard at work in Oregon. We swapped Glitch stories, as everybody still does who hasn't seen each other for a while, and he had been little affected. He hadn't even heard of it for the first twenty-four hours, because his own computers functioned independently of the CC, like Callie's. Turns out I could have hid out in Oregon as well as at the **CC**, but I don't think anything would have turned out differently. It wasn't a friendly visit, though, since I was there representing the SRG&C, whose tunnel was halfway from Lonesome Dove to the shores of the Columbia, and which Fox had vehemently opposed. He wanted to keep Oregon pristine, didn't even want to allow the small edge settlement, a logging camp to be called Sweet Home, which would be the northwest terminus of the railroad. I told him a few guys in plaid shirts with saw-blades weren't going to hurt his precious forest, and he called me a capitalist plunderer. A plunderer, imagine that! I'm afraid that what spark had been there was long extinguished. Kiss my axe, Fox.

A few months after the crisis, when I was finally emerging from my church-vandalizing funk, I had need of Darling Bobbie's services again, so I went looking for him only to find he'd turned himself back into Crazy Bob and was no longer on the Hadleyplatz. He wasn't back on the Leystrasse, either. I finally ran him to ground in Mall X, the ultra-avant fleshmart, where he now specialized in only the more outrageous body styles favored by the young. He tried to talk me into getting my head put in a box, but I reminded him it was me and Brenda who were responsible for that particular fashion outrage, with our story on the Grand Flack. He did the work I required for old times' sake, but rather grudgingly, I thought. Crazy again, after all these years.

As for the Grand Flack himself, I heard from him, too. He called me up to thank me. I couldn't imagine what I'd done to deserve that, and didn't really want to listen to him, but I gathered he now regretted all the time he'd spent on the outside, seeing to the affairs of the Flacks. In prison he was able to devote himself to television around the clock. He wanted me to speak to the judge and see about extending his sentence. I'll surely try, old man.

One of the first changes you noticed after the Glitch was how much more medical treatment you needed. My body is still full of nanobots, I assume, but they don't work as well or with as much coordination as they used to. I never actually researched why it's like that, having very little interest in the subject. But for whatever reason, I now have to go in almost monthly to have cancers eradicated. I don't mind, much, but a lot of people do, and it's just one more thing adding pressure to the Restore the Cortex movement, those folks who want to bring back the CC, only bigger and wiser. We're so spoiled in this day and age. We tend to forget what a nuisance cancer used to be.

That's where I ran into Callie, at the medico shop, having her *own* cancers removed. Runs in the family, as they say.

We didn't speak. This wasn't an unusual condition between us; I've spent half my life not speaking to Callie, or not being spoken to.

She had come to get me up at the cave. That's probably a good thing, as I don't know for sure if I'd have been able to get up from the grave and walk home on my own. It may even be a good thing that she asked me the question she had no right to ask, because it made me angry enough to forget my grief for long enough to scream and shout at her and get her screaming and shouting back. She asked me who the father was. She, who had never allowed *me* to ask that question, she who had made my childhood so miserable I used to dream about a Daddy arriving on a white horse, telling me it had all been a big mistake, that he really loved me and that Callie was a gypsy witch who'd kidnapped me from the cradle.

Sometimes I think our society is screwed up about this father business. Just because we can all bear children, is that an excuse to virtually eliminate the role of father? Then I think about Brenda and her old man, and about how common that sort of thing used to be, and you wonder if males should be allowed around little children at all.

All I knew for sure was I missed mine, and Callie said she'd tell me if I really wanted to know such a silly thing, and I said don't bother because I think I know who it is, and she laughed and said you don't understand anything, and that's when we stopped talking and walked down the hill, together but alone, as we'd always been. See you in twenty years, Callie.

Still, I think I do know.

As for Kitten Parker . . . why spoil his day?

A year has passed now. I still think of Mario. And I often wake up in the middle of the night seeing Winston tearing the arm off that King City policewoman. I never found out what happened to her. She was as much a victim as any of us; the KC Cops were dragooned into the war by the CC, had no idea what they were doing, and too many of them died.

A year has passed, and we change, and yet things stay the same. The world rolls over the holes left by the departed, fills in those spaces. I didn't know how I'd run the *Texian* without Charity, but her sources started coming to me with stories, and before long one of them had emerged to take her place. He's not near as pretty as she was, but he has the makings of a reporter.

I'm still running the paper, still teaching at the school. And I'm the new Mayor of New Austin. I didn't run, but when the citizens' committee put my name forward I didn't pull out, either. The Gila Monster column is still as venomous as ever. Maybe it's a conflict of interest, but no one seems too concerned. If the opposition doesn't like it, let them start their own paper.

Once a week I have a guest column in the *Daily Cream*. I think it's Walter's way of trying to lure me back. Not likely, Walter. I think that part of my life is done. Still, you never know. I didn't think they could talk me into being mayor, either.

I saw Walter only last week, in the newly reopened Blind Pig. The old one had been destroyed by fire during the Glitch and for a while Deep Throat had threatened to leave it shuttered. But he bowed under the weight of public demand and threw a big party to celebrate. Most of King City's fourth estate was there, and those that weren't stoned when they arrived soon became so.

We did all the things reporters do when gathered in groups: drank, assassinated the characters of absent colleagues, told all the scandalous stories about celebrities and politicians we couldn't print, drank, hinted at stories we were about to break we actually knew nothing about, rehashed old fights and uncovered new conspiracies in high places, drank, threw up, drank some more. A few punches were thrown, a few tempers soothed, many hands of poker were played. The new Blind Pig wasn't bad, but nothing is ever as good as the good old days, so many complaints were heard. I figured that fifty years of mopped-up blood and spilled drinks and smokes and broken crockery and the new place would be pretty much like the old and only me and a few others would even remember the old Pig had burned.

At one point I found myself sitting by the big round table in the back room where serious cards were played. I wasn't playing—nobody in that room had trusted me at a card table in years. Walter was there, scowling at his hand as if losing the pitiful little pot would send him home to his fifty-room mansion penniless. Cricket was there, too, doing his patented does-a-flush-beat-a-straight befuddled routine, looking ever so dapper a gent now that he'd affected nineteenth-century clothing as a more or less permanent element of his style. In his double-breasted tweed jacket and high starched collar he was easily the most interesting guy in the room, but the spark was gone. Too bad, Cricket. If you'd only had any sense we could have made each other's lives miserable for five, six years, and parted heartily detesting each other. Think of all the great fights you missed, damn you, and eat your heart out. And Cricket, a friend should take you aside and tell you to drop the innocent act, at the poker table at least. It worked better when you were a girl, and it wasn't that great even then.

And who should be sitting behind the biggest stack of chips, calm, smiling faintly, cards facedown on the table and worrying the hell out of everyone else . . . but Brenda Starr, confidante of celebrities, the toast of three planets, and well on her way to becoming the most powerful gossip journalist since Louella Parsons. There was very little left of the awkward, earnest, ignorant child I'd reluctantly taken on two years earlier. She was still incredibly tall and just about as young, but everything else had changed. She *dressed* now, and while I thought her choices were outrageous she had the confidence to make her own style. The old Brenda could now be seen only in the cub reporter groupie at her elbow, attentive to her every need, a gorgeous gumdrop who no doubt had grown up wanting to meet and hobnob with famous people, as Brenda had, as I had. I watched Brenda turn her cards over, rake in another pot, and lean back watching the new deal. Her hand stroked the knee of the girl, casually possessive, and she winked at me. Don't spend it all in one place, Brenda.

During the next hand the talk turned, as it eventually does at these things, to the affairs of the world. I didn't contribute; I'd found early on that if people noticed me they tended to clam up about the Big Glitch. This was a group that kept few secrets. Everyone there knew about Mario, and many of them knew of my troubles with the CC. Some probably knew of my suicides. It made them cautious, as most probably couldn't imagine what it must be like to lose a child like that. I wanted to tell them it was all right, I was okay, but it's no use, so I just sat back and listened.

First there was the CC, and should we bring him back. The consensus was that we shouldn't, but we would. Having him the way he was was just so damn *handy*. Sure, he screwed up there at the end, but the Big Brains can handle that, can't they? I mean, if they can put a man on Pluto a week after he left Luna, why don't they spend some of that money to make things easier and more convenient to the taxpaying citizens? I think that's what will happen. We're a democracy—especially now that the CC's no longer around to meddle—and if we vote for damn foolishness, damn foolishness is what we'll get. I just hope they make provision this time around for somebody to give the New CC hugs on a regular basis. Otherwise, he's apt to get pettish again.

There was no consensus on the other big topic of the day. It was a question that cut deeply and would certainly cause many more shouting matches before it was resolved. What do you do with the new things the

CC discovered during his rogue years? In particular, how about this memory-recording and cloning business, eh?

The Hitler analogy was brought up and bandied about. Under Hitler's reign a Dr. Mengele performed unethical experiments—sheer torture, mainly—on human subjects. I don't know if anything useful was learned, but suppose there was. Was it ethical to use that knowledge, to benefit from that much evil? It seems to me your answer depends a lot on your worldview. Myself, I'm not sure if it's ethical (which probably says a lot about *my* worldview), but I don't think it's wrong, and I have a personal involvement in the question. Right or wrong, though, I do think it *will* be used, and so did just about everybody else in the room, reporters being the way they are. People were going through the records the CC didn't destroy—*I'm* one of those records in a way, but not a very forthcoming one—looking for new knowledge, and if it has a practical use, it will be used. Cry over that if you're so inclined. Myself, I guess in the end I feel knowledge has no right or wrong. It's just knowledge. It's not like the law, where some knowledge is admissible and some tainted by the method of its discovery.

Minamata was only one of the CC's horror chambers, and not the worst. Some of those stories have come out, some are still being suppressed. Most of them you'd really rather not know, trust me.

But what about the problem whose penultimate answer had been a being who thought he was Andrew MacDonald minus all human feelings, and whose final solution were the troops of mindlessly loyal soldiers that gave me so much trouble on the first day of the Glitch? Because they weren't really the end product. The CC had felt the technique was perfectible, and I have no reason to doubt it. That was the one the public was clamoring to know more about: immortality.

Yeah, but it wasn't *really* immortality, somebody said. All it meant was that somebody else very like you, with your memories, would live. *You,* the person sitting here at this table holding the most terrible cards you ever saw, would be just as dead as ever. Once the public understood that they'd realize it wasn't worth the trouble.

Don't you believe it, somebody else said. My cards aren't all that bad, and it's the only hand I've got, so I'll play 'em. Up to now people's only shot at living forever has been to produce something that will live after us. Artists do it with their art, most of the rest of us produce children. It's our way of living on. I think this would appeal to the same urge. It'd be like a child, only it'd be *you,* too.

At that point somebody nudged somebody else and the thought went around the table, silently, that we oughtn't to be talking about children . . . you know . . . with *Hildy* around. At least I think that's what happened, maybe I'm too sensitive. For whatever reason the conversation died, with only an unexpected apostrophe at the end, in the form of Brenda's little gumdrop looking around with innocent eyes and piping, "What's wrong with it? It sounds like a great idea to me." It was her only comment of the evening, but it put the kibosh on my own theory, which was that it was a useless idea, that people would rather have children than duplicate themselves—essentially, not to put all your spare cash into memory-cloning stocks. Suddenly, looking into that innocent face of youth, I wasn't so sure. Time will tell.

Two years of my life. Probably the most eventful, but time will tell about that, too.

I am sitting in the parlor car of the Prairie Chief, destination Johnstown, Pennsylvania. I decided since I'm part owner of the SRG&C it was high time I took a ride. It's a school holiday so for once I have the time. I'm writing, in longhand, with a fountain pen, on foolscap SRG&C stationery resting on a mother-of-pearl inlaid mahogany table set with an inkwell and a crystal vase full of fresh bluebonnets. Nothing but the best for the passengers on the Prairie Chief. The waiter has just brought me a steaming cup of tea, with lemon. Ahead I can hear the chugging of the engine, No. 439, and I can smell a hint of its smoke. Behind me the porter will soon be turning down my Pullman bunk, making it with crisp white sheets, leaving a mint and a complimentary bottle of toilet water on the pillow. Also in that direction the cook is selecting a cut of prime Kansas City beef, to be cooked rare, suitable for the owner's dinner.

All right, it's brontosaurus, if you want to get technical. It might even be from the Double-C Bar.

We'll soon be pulling into "Fort Worth," where we'll take on wood and water. I don't plan to get off, since I'm told it's just a dreary cowtown full of rowdy and possibly dangerous cowhands, quite unsuitable for a well-brought-up lady. (That's what I'm told; I happen to know, since I watched it being built, that it's just a big room with rails and a dirt street running through it, scattered with wood buildings and backed by a great holo show.)

Outside my window dusk is gathering. Not long ago we saw a herd of buffalo, and not long after that a group of wild red Indians, who reined their mounts and watched solemnly as the iron horse huffed by. From Central Casting, and on tape, but who cares? The parlor car is crowded with Texans and a few returning Pennsylvanians. They all wear their best clothes, not yet too mussed by the journey. Across from me a little Amish girl sits with her parents, watching me write. Next to them is a group of three young single gentlemen, trying not to be too obvious about their interest in the single girl at the escritoire. Soon the boldest of them will come over and ask me to dine with him, and if his line is any better than "Whatcha writin', cutie?" he will have a companion for dinner.

But not for bed. It would be a pointless exercise. The service I lately required of Darling Bobby/Crazy Bob was to render me asexual, like Brenda when I first met her. This was probably foolish and certainly extreme, but I found that I couldn't bear the thought of sex, and in fact loathed that opening that had brought Mario into the world for his short, perfect time. I had even less interest in being male again. So I jumped off the sexual choo-choo train and I'm not sorry I did it. I think I'll be ready to board again any day now, but it's been a relief not to be at the mercy of hormones, of either polarity. I may do it every twenty years or so, as sort of a sabbatical.

As darkness falls and the train rocks gently, I realize I'm happier than I've been in a long time.

Now we've spent some time together, and it's almost time to leave you. You've met Hildebrandt, Hildegarde, and Hildething: railroad tycoon, publisher, teacher, syndicated columnist, bereaved mother, and tireless crusader for pronoun reform. There's really only one more thing worth knowing about him/her/it.

I'm going to the stars.

What I have is an invitation to make a reservation. I didn't mention this earlier, maybe it slipped my mind, but about a week after Mario died I sat down for a very long time with Walter's pistol, a bottle of good tequila, and one round. I drank, and I loaded and unloaded the gun, and drank some more and pointed it at things: a tree, the side of the cabin, my head. And I thought about what the CC had said about a virus, and what I had concluded about the veracity of that statement, and wondered if there was anything I could think of I really wanted to do? All those other things . . . sure, they bring me satisfaction, particularly the teaching, but they wouldn't serve any more as the answer to the question "What do you *do,* Hildy?"

I thought of something, thought about it some more, and hied myself out to the *Heinlein,* where I asked Smith if I could go along when he took off, worthless as my skills might be to his enterprise. And he said sure, Hildy, I meant to ask you if you were interested. We'll need somebody to handle the publicity, for one thing, to establish the right spin-control when it's time to leave, and most especially when we get back. We'll need advice on how to market our stories with maximum profit. Hell, most of us will probably need somebody to ghost-write them, as well. Scientists, test pilots, technical types, we all get tongue-tied when it comes to that part;

ust read the early accounts of the space pioneers. Go see Sinbad over in the publicity department, see if you can't get him straightened out. If you're any good, I expect to make you head of the department in a week. You couldn't be worse at it than Sinbad.

So this is in the nature of a farewell. All the people I've mentioned so far . . . not a one of them will go. They're just not the type. I love them to various degrees (yes, even you, Callie), but they are Luna-bound, to a man and woman. "Hansel," "Gretel," "Libby" (who recovered, by the way), "Valentine Michael Smith;" these will be my shipmates, whether we leave next year, in twenty years, or in fifty years. The rest of you are already left behind.

Teaching, railroading, running the *Texian*, these are all things I do. But in my endless spare time *(Hah!)* I do what I can to further the aims of the Heinleiners and their crazy project. Result: a two percent increase in inquiries during the last year. Not exactly setting the world on fire, but give me time. When I've done all I can in that regard I hang around. You got a bottle you want washed, a trash pail that needs emptying, a whoosis that needs polishing? Give it to the Hildething and it will get done. There is no job too menial for me, mainly because I'm completely useless at the important jobs. My aim is to become so indispensable to the project that it would be unthinkable to leave me behind. *Go without Hildy?* Cripes, who would shine my shoes and rub my feet?

And there you have it. I promised you no neat conclusion, and I think I've delivered on that. I warned you of loose ends, and I can see a whole tangle of them. What of the Invaders, for instance? Brother, I don't know. Last time anybody checked they were still in charge of our fair home planet, and unlikely to be evicted soon. If we ever get around to it, that's another story.

What will we find out there? I don't know that, either, and that's why I'm going along. Alien intelligences? I wouldn't bet against it. Strange worlds? I'd say that's a lock. Vast empty spaces, human tragedy and hope. God. Mario's soul. Your wildest dream and your worst nightmare all could be out there.

Or maybe we'll find Elvis and Silvio in a flying saucer singing old-timey rock and roll.

Think what a story it'll be.

—Eugene, Oregon
May 2, 1991

AUTHOR'S NOTE

When in the course of a writer's career it becomes necessary to break with an established science fiction tradition, a decent respect to the opinions of mankind requires that he should declare the causes which impel him to the decision.

This story appears to be part of a future history of mine, often called the Eight Worlds. It does share background, characters, and technology with earlier stories of mine, which is part of the future history tradition. What it doesn't share is a chronology. The reason for this is simple: the thought of going back, rereading all those old stories, and putting them in coherent order filled me with ennui. It got so bad I thought I might as well give up on this story.

Then I thought, what the heck?

Consider this a disclaimer, then. *Steel Beach* is *not* really part of the Eight Worlds future history. Or the Eight Worlds is not really a future history, since that implies an orderly progression of events. Take your pick. But please *don't* write and tell me that the null-suits had to have been around much earlier in the series, because you said so in such-and-such a story. There are probably a lot of mistakes like that in *Steel Beach*. So what?

Somebody once said consistency is the hobgoblin of small minds (I think it was the editor of the *National Enquirer*). It's a sentiment I'm sure Hildy would endorse.

—John Varley
December 1, 1991